# SHADOWS OVER THE WILDLANDS

## The Arath Saga Book 2

### Xander Rose

**Mythrunner Publishing**

This book is again dedicated to those who supported my wild ideas. To Heather for her review and edits. To Derek for allowing me to use you as a sounding board for ideas and plots, best of luck with your own book my friend. To my own real world Ella, you know who you are. And to all who read and enjoy the story that follows.

# CONTENTS

# CHAPTER ONE

*Fragments of the Fractured Soul*

~The Story So Far~

Alex's life was boring, and then he died. When he woke, he met with a goddess who offered him a chance at a new life in a wondrous world of magic and fantasy, complete with all the game mechanics and interfaces he had grown to love in his video games. In this new world he has taken a new name, Xavier Ardynvael, and he has found a companion in Ella Bree, an enigmatic woman who holds a mystery.

Xavier also founded a new settlement, Rynthavael, with around fifty villagers calling him Lord. The village is growing rapidly, and buildings are going up daily. His people embraced a fresh start of their own after the town of Bramblegate, their prior home, had been destroyed by raiders. Xavier went on to rescue one of the children and, in doing so, awakened two of the ley lines that made up the nexus beneath the settlement.

He has delved into dungeons and completed quests but in all honesty, was all just starting. That was until his latest adventure led to him being taken captive and carted off to the Animari settlement of Verdantspire Haven. There the elders charged him with a quest to assist in freeing some recently captured members of that community. Teamed up with the Beastmaster Lianna and her twin brother the Assassin Liosan they tracked down the raiders holding the captives and attacked. The fight was brutal and quick but unfortunately, for Xavier at least, it ended with a sword through his heart and darkness taking over his senses.

#

~Currently~

Xavier slowly opened his eyes. He was sitting face down on a hard wooden table. Groaning slightly, he sat up, his eyes squeezing closed again at the wave of dizziness that swept through him.

"What happened," he managed to croak out.

A voice cut through the silence like the soft hum of a thread being pulled taut, its sound resonated within him as much as it did in the space around him, feeling both impossibly ancient and unnervingly intimate. The words carried the weight of millennia, yet were spoken with the clarity of a whisper meant only for his ears. Each syllable reverberated through his chest, gentle yet commanding, as if the fabric of the universe shifted subtly with every word spoken. The tone held no malice or warmth, only the calm certainty of inevitability, making him acutely aware that every moment in the speakers' presence was a thread they had chosen to weave. It was also a voice that he knew well, it was the voice of Danu.

"You died," she said simply. "You died and discovered an aspect of my blessing that I did not think you would for a while. The fates weave an interesting and ever-changing pattern around you Alex."

Xavier opened his eyes in a panic. He was dead. Again? Already? Despair lit his features as he realized he had accomplished so little in his second chance at life. There was still so much to see in Arath, so much to do.

"Be at peace Alex," Danu's voice was soft and comforting. She placed a hand on his and as when he met her here before warmth and reassurance flooded through his body driving away the panic. "You bear my blessings remember, part of that is marking you as a Kael'Sharyn, a fractured echo." She laughed melodically as he winced at her words. "It is not as bad as it sounds. You will revive, in fact you will revive any time you die. However, the mortal mind was not meant to undergo such trauma. Each time you return from beyond the veil you run the risk of shattering your psyche. When that happens, you will be vulnerable to a final death."

Xavier stared across the table; the goddess was just as he remembered her. Her features were perfectly symmetrical giving her an otherworldly beauty. Smooth alabaster skin was framed by long flowing vermilion ringlets which only provided a greater contrast to her eyes. They seemed to change depending on her mood and now they were bottomless voids speckled with pinpoints of light. A soft smile lingered on her delicate lips as she finished speaking.

Xavier's breath caught in his chest once more at the sight. It was what distracted him so when he died on Earth, and it still had the same effect on him now. The beauty leaned forward across the table, her hand lifting from his to delicately touch his chest, right over where his heart lay. He could feel the beat of it surge to life once again and a warmth spread over his skin where her fingers lingered.

As Danu sat back in her seat, Xavier looked down and realized he was dressed as he had been when going to attack the raiders with the Animari twins. His leathers were cleanly cut through, however. The skin of his chest was exposed to the cool air of the cabin. Where her fingers had brushed was a new mark. It looked like a rock had struck a glass window. At its center was a jagged core, a focal point where the fatal strike occurred. The core appeared like a shimmering, opalescent well as if he were peering into a fragment of another realm. From the core, lines branched out in sharp, jagged patterns, like cracks on shattered glass only emphasizing the window similarity. These lines were asymmetrical, giving the appearance of something broken yet beautiful.

He looked back up to Danu, she smiled at him once more as the room faded from view.

#

The next thing Xavier felt was a full body ache with pain focused on his chest. Two female voices were shouting at one another adding to the discomfort of an already raging headache. He tried to sit up but found he was being held tightly. The voices stopped with gasps at his movement and groan.

Slowly he came to realize he was lying in someone's lap, his head and shoulders propped in their arms and clutched tightly to a soft chest. Opening his eyes and blinking at the harsh torchlight he looked to see who held him. A tear-streaked but joyous face looked back at him, Ella's face. She hugged him tightly once more. Beyond the familiar features of his companion, he saw the white and black furred faces of the Iskari, snow leopard Animari, twins Liosan and Lianna. After a moment he realized it had been Ella and Lianna arguing. That caused him to realize briefly that he had never actually heard Liosan speak.

Once more he tried to sit up, this time Ella relinquished her grip on him though she kept a hand on his back in case he should collapse. Pain flooded through his body and he noticed that the bar in his interface that showed his health was dangerously low and flashing. Ella handed him a handful of forest sage and he slowly chewed the earthy herb the pain fading over time as the plant took effect.

"How?" Lianna whispered. "You were dead, I saw the raider run you through and then the wound afterward. There is no way you could have survived that." Her voice trembled though Xavier wasn't sure if it was in awe or fear.

Xavier hesitated before answering, as he did so he looked around slowly realizing that they were still in the raider camp. He could hear the cries of the captives in the distance along with the crackle of the fire. The air was thick with the coppery tang of blood mixed with the stench of offal and viscera. The horrid stench that lingered after combat. Finally, he looked down at himself, his clothes and armor were soaked in blood. The rent in his cuirass and tunic matching what he had seen in the otherworldly cabin. On his skin, just as he had seen after Danu had touched him lingered the mark.

Everyone's gaze followed his and Ella gasped. "A Kael'Sharyn?"

"That is impossible," snapped Lianna, "they are myths. No one can come back from the dead. Even the highest of clerics cannot perform miracles like that." She glared at Ella again. "I do not know where you came from, but you speak falsely again."

Ella glared right back at the beastmaster. "As I told you before, I am his. My bond with him will always tell me where he is." She turned and lifted a hand to her hair, pulling it back to expose the tattoo like mark that sat behind her ear.

Xavier held up a hand to forestall the impending renewed yelling. He was thankful it was just the handful of them and not the captives as well.

"No," his voice was soft, intending to keep his words only to the ones present. He knew the captives were all Animari but didn't know if their hearing was as keen as their bestial counterparts. "I met with Danu; she called me the same thing. Said it was part of the blessing she had placed upon me." He looked to Ella, "I told you about her before."

Once more Lianna's mouth snapped shut, her eyes now held a mix of fear and wonder as she looked on the strange human. Part of her wanted to strike him down, humans could not be trusted. Another part of her wanted to learn more about this stranger who claimed to be god touched, had possibly befriended a Shadowmane, and spoke of a village where races mingled freely. She looked to Liosan, and her brother just shrugged before turning around and walking away, likely to go check on the prisoners.

Looking at the two women Xavier put voice to his thoughts. "What happened? How long was I..." he hesitated still not quite able to accept he had died again, "away? How did you get here?" The last question was focused on Ella.

Lianna was the first to respond. "Lio and I were able to kill the raider leader, the one who ran you through, shortly after he cut you down. The fight only ended a few minutes ago. When it did, I came to check on you fearing the worst was true and found her here holding your body. You were not breathing or moving, and she was crying over you." She pointed at Ella as she spoke. "She came out of nowhere."

"I told you I felt his need and came to him. I cannot explain it any clearer than that." Ella retorted.

Lianna looked like she was going to say something more, but Xavier intervened. "I know Ella, she has been with me for a while now. I saved her from an attack several weeks back."

Lianna looked between the two of them. "She was in Bramblegate? No, I remember now you said she was with you when you went to Bramblegate, and when you found the Shadowmane." She studied Ella a little closer, but the woman just seemed to be another human. "Alright, I still have questions on how you found us but if you are bonded it does give credence to your words." She sheathed the dagger that Xavier had only now realized she was still holding. "I am going to go search for the cage keys, that is if Lio has not already opened the lock." With those words she turned as her brother had and disappeared around the corner of the large tent.

Left alone with Ella, Xavier studied her quietly. "How did you get here? You were miles away when last I saw you. Still weak from what you did with the ley line."

She met Xavier's eyes and smiled her own emerald orbs near glowing with relief that he was alright. "We are bonded remember. As long as you carry my blade I will know where you are." A slightly impish smile touched her lips as she spoke the next words whispered softly so as to only reach his ears. "I am Vaeltheris"

That bombshell of a statement rendered Xavier speechless. His hand reaching for where the blade normally was sheathed at his side, he looked down at the empty scabbards before he remembered his swords had been in his hands during the fight. Ella picked the pair up from beside her and placed them in his lap. He picked up the named weapon and inspected it. The prompt hadn't changed again to confirm her statement but as he studied it he could feel a change to the blade. Her revealing that deep truth gave him a greater feel for the blade, and he could sense the connection to her.

"How is that possible? You said it saved you. I don't understand how it can..." He began and she cut him off by placing a finger to his lips.

"Secrets for now, the camp has ears, my master." She leaned closer to whisper into his ear. "When we are alone, I promise the full truth. You know the most important parts already."

Xavier nodded slowly, his world had been shattered and rebuilt by a second death, and now what he thought he knew about Ella was undergoing the same. What else did he not know about those closest to him? Was he going to find out his mastery of Rynthavael and the Syr'Vailen was a lie next? He looked to his forearm and the mark that signified him as the Ard'Maelor, the Sovereign of the Forge, the title Aelriva bestowed upon him when he claimed his domain slowly appeared on his skin. He let it fade once more and looked at the mark on his chest, oddly unlike his other mark it did not vanish.

With Ella's aid, he got to his feet and sheathed his two swords. Then he took a moment to really look at her. She had been unconscious and unwell when he last saw her. Now a part of him expected her appearance to change knowing what he did now about her connection to the sword. She still appeared to be a young human woman however and he knew he needed to hear her answers soon.

She had a striking appearance with an athletic build. Her complexion was fair with a warm undertone, and just a hint of freckles dusted across her cheeks. This still gave her a youthful, lively quality to her look. Her face retained the gentle, heart-shaped structure, with high cheekbones, a delicate nose, and full, softly defined lips he remembered from first seeing her. Her exquisite jade eyes flashed with a rare and vibrant radiant sparkle when she smiled back at him, which still felt earthy and enchanting. He noticed they somehow held an ancient presence though, that he attributed to her true nature. Her brunette hair, rich in dark brown tones with subtle highlights cascaded just past her shoulders. Once again, she was clad in rough cloth garb under soft supple leather armor.

"Come on then I suppose. Now that you're here we can see to finishing this quest I was given." He said as he turned to follow the path Lianna had taken. "I'm glad you're here though." He said glancing back over his shoulder at her. "Things just didn't quite feel right without you nearby."

She merely smiled back at him and moved to follow his lead. He moved quickly his mind racing as he considered the possibility that he was developing feelings for her. He didn't deny she was beautiful, and had she just been a normal woman he would have been thrilled to have her attention the way he did. Now though, he was torn, was it possible to love a sword? Was she actually the sword? Or was she something different? Gods that rabbit hole was deep when he started to head down it. He forcefully shut off that path of thought and refocused on the task at hand.

Joining Lianna, he and Ella both started to search the bodies of the dead. Xavier went straight to the corpse of the man who had killed him and after kicking it once in insolent anger he knelt and began to search through his pouches. Sighing as he did so he realized that yet again he had forgotten to use his insight during the fight. Granted he had not had even an option to with this asshole, but he could have with the rest of them.

While he was searching, he noticed that the icon on the right side of his UI was flashing indicating he had notifications. He consciously decided to review them later tonight while they were traveling or resting and keep his focus on setting the captives free.

It was a small pouch that hung around the neck of the raider leader where he found a key. Rising with a call to the others he ran over towards the cage wagons. Liosan was standing there with a pair of picks in hand about to test the lock when Xavier arrived. The assassin moved out of his way and he put the key in the hole of the lock and twisted it. A small snick sounded, and the lock fell away easily. Xavier grinned at Liosan and handed the key to Ella to unlock the other cages.

Soon a couple of dozen Animari gathered around the party, from what Xavier could see it was a blend of many different types. All of them were calling out their thanks and appreciation for saving them. As one of them, a small foxlike Vulpiri boy, forward from where he had been comforting a young Cervari girl with coloring like a fawn, to offer his thanks Xavier noticed the odd collar around his neck. Looking at the other captives he noticed that they all wore the metal band.

"Lianna? Can you tell me anything about these collars?" He called out, several moments later she was standing at his side and lifting the boy's chin.

"Ice and shadow damn them!" She cursed seeing the collar. "Suppression collars, at least they are not the full slave collars, they are nigh unto impossible to remove. Raiders and slavers use these to keep captives docile while they are transported to markets and pens. Search the tents the key rune must be here somewhere otherwise; they would not have been able to open the collars to place them."

One of the older captives, an Ursari from the looks, his large frame hunched with age but still bearing a dignified mien spoke up. "That one there," he pointed to where the mage lay dead from Liosan's attack, "She was the one who placed the collars on us."

Xavier nodded and quickly moved over to the corpse and began searching it as well. At the dead woman's waist, he found a small key. Pocketing it he continued searching but didn't find anything resembling a rune as Lianna had mentioned. He continued probing her body, though he had to pause noticing another more ornate collar wrapped around her throat. Taking a gamble, he rose and went to the large tent that he and the leader had come from.

Inside was dim, too dim to really see by and he scowled. Ducking back through the flap he called for someone to bring him some sort of light. Soon Ella strode up and passed him a warmly glowing torch. Ducking back inside he was able to make out three different cots, each one had a small table and other clutter around them. Under the second one, he found what he was looking for. A medium-sized chest with a small lock on it. The key fit into the lock and as he lifted the top he grimaced. Inside were dozens more collars. It was clear this group was ready to take as many captives as they could get their hands on. A small pouch was mixed in with the rings of metal, unlacing its top he poured a palm sized disk of dark stone into his hand. Both sides of the disk were etched with a single sigil that glowed with a faint light. Xavier focused on the mark expecting his skill in rune deciphering to trigger but nothing happened. Instead, he received a new prompt.

| **You have discovered:** Dark Stone Sigil Disk | **Item Class:** Rare **Item Quality:** Well Crafted **Weight:** 0.3 kg **Durability:** 60/100 **Description:** A palm-sized disk made of a smooth, black stone that absorbs light, giving it an eerie matte finish. An intricate glowing purple sigil is etched onto its surfaces. The disk |

emanates a faint hum of suppressed power, its magic specifically attuned to unlock suppression collars and similar magical bindings.

**Traits:**

- **Suppression Unlocker:** When activated, the disk emits a pulse of dark energy that disables suppression collars, breaking their magical seals.

- **Activation:** Requires a specific magical or spoken command to activate the sigil, ensuring only authorized users can utilize it.

- **Limited Uses:** Contains enough energy for up to 5 suppression collar deactivations before needing to be recharged.

"Of course, it couldn't be easy." Xavier groaned seeing the need for an activation command. "Why can't it ever just be a simple thing to rescue a bunch of captured people and make their lives easier." He pursed his lips. Well, he guessed that was an oddly specific complaint but still, it could be easier.

Heading back outside with the disk he rejoined the

gathering of semi-freed captives where they huddled around the rest of his party. He held up the disk. "I found the key, but it needs an activation to make it work."

The same Ursari elder as before spoke up once again. "Keltrak's Promise"

Xavier felt the stone in his fingers warm significantly, to the point he almost dropped it. Carefully he moved it closer to the young Cervari, and the ring about her neck parted as if bisected on an unseen hinge. It fell to the ground and snapped shut once more. The young girl started crying again in relief and darted back towards the duo who were obviously her parents. Xavier freed four more of the children repeating the same phrase as the Ursari had provided.

"That's all the charges it had. Unless you know a way to recharge it, I think we have to wait." Xavier handed the disk to Lianna. "You should hold it. We can give it to the elders when we get back to Verdantspire."

Lianna tucked the disk into one of her pouches. "Let us get everything loaded up into the wagons it can all be taken back to help give these people a fresh start." She pointed to the cage wagons "We should break those, however."

Soon everyone was stripping the dead of weapons, armor, and items. The raider's possessions, along with their tents and other supplies were quickly loaded into the waiting wagons. With all the hands they had to help it didn't take long for the work to be done. Xavier pointed out the collar on the mage's neck indicating to Lianna they should probably take it as well but noting he didn't have a way to unlock it. Her grimace spoke volumes to him about the item itself, but she didn't disagree with him. Liosan had found where the horses and mules had been hobbled for the night and soon the wagons were hitched. While they were destroying the cage wagons Lianna approached Xavier and held out the mage's collar. As he took it, he could still see where small smears of blood remained on the metal. He looked at the Iskari woman for a moment then decided he really didn't want to know how she had removed the item. He tucked it into his pouch to inspect later, and soon the much larger group was moving back out of the little valley and onto the dirt road that would ultimately lead them back to Verdantspire Haven.

# CHAPTER TWO

*Through the Eyes of the Wild*

The trip back to Verdantspire was mostly uneventful. The warden duo of Liosan and Lianna were able to guide the caravan down mostly unremarkable trails and paths deeper into the Silverwood unerringly towards the Animari settlement. Xavier road in one of the wagons with some of the captivity-weakened individuals. His body still recovering from the death and revival. None of those he had helped free begrudged him that position, nor his caretaker Ella in her spot beside him.

Though the animals and wagons helped make the trek faster it was still slower than the madcap dash that Xavier had achieved when it was just the smaller party of the Iskari twins, Frostclaw, and himself. He was fine with that however because he had a lot on his mind, between notifications, planning, and just coming to grips with the fact he had died again, let alone the world-altering revelation of Ella's true nature.

Xavier simply leaned against the back of the wagon bed, the others gave him room and Ella sat at his side, her hip almost casually pressed into the hilt of Vaeltheris. He decided to break things down into more manageable tasks. He would review his notifications first and then chew on his new status as a Kael'Sharyn. He glanced at Ella out of the corner of his eye. When they were alone, he would have her tell him the whole truth of what she was.

The first notification that came into view as he opened the icon was, unsurprisingly, dealing with the combat with the raider party.

---

**Your party has engaged and defeated an opposing party.**

- Raid Leader - Karthos Blackbane: 11,500
- Shadowmancer - Eryndra Duskwail: 8,400
- Beastmaster - Ralvik Thornclaw: 3,900
- Elite Guards (x4): 7,200 (1,800 each)
- Slavers (x4): 4,400 (1,100 each)
- Mounted Scouts (x4): 9,200 (2,300 each)
- Dire Wolves (x4): 4,400 (1,100 each)

**Total Experience Earned 49,000**

---

Xavier had to stop and reread that prompt several times, a single encounter with powerful individuals had netted him more than half of all the experience he had earned during his entire time in Arath. Closing that he moved to the next and frankly expected notification. A grin pulling up the corners of his lips as the radiant symphony of chimes reverberated through his head, accompanied by a booming voice reading the notification:

---

**"Hark and Hear! You have ascended in power. You have gained levels 8 - 12!**

The touch of the divine lingers upon you, granting **30 attribute points (6 per level)** to shape your destiny, an exceptional gift, elevated from the ordinary **4 points** per level by the **Blessings of the Gods (Danu)**. Choose wisely, for these points will define your path. You have 3 days to assign them, or they will fall to the whims of fate. Your growing prowess earns you a boon: **40% skill allocation** to distribute among your known skills. This is your

---

chance to sharpen the blade of a favored talent, forge new strength in an untapped domain, or balance your growth across disciplines. Let this moment be a cornerstone of your greatness.

**Rise, Seeker of Glory. The world awaits your will. Seek adventure, seek wisdom, seek love... and let your legend be forged in your choices. LIVE!"**

His level hadn't just increased it had leaped forward. Thirty attribute points was a huge boon to that fight, something told him that he was going to need every one of those and more, however as the words of Danu lingered in his mind. She had blessed him when she first brought him to this world, and though she hadn't given him a quest or anything it was implied that she had expectations of him.

"The goddess of fate," he murmured softly. "How much is her doing and how much is my own choices?"

"Did you say something master?" Ella inquired after his words.

"Nothing of note no. And don't call me master. That word has dark connotations where I am from." Xavier glanced to the side where the young woman sat.

She smirked at him. "I will try but you are my master, Xavier. You are bonded to my sword after all. Others will see my mark and expect a level of deference to someone. I may not wear a collar like others but am still a bound one." Her eyes sparkled slightly in the moonlight. "The morals and traditions of here are not the same as where you are from."

She was one of few that knew his origin, he was appreciative of her keeping the secret, but her subtle reminder made him purse his lips in thought. Was he right in trying to change something that seemed as fundamental to the world? Mulling that over made his eyes go distant as he pondered the ramifications of his potential actions. Sighing he shook his head finally; it was not something he could decide at the moment. His best course would be to help those he could for now and see what would come in the future. He turned his attention back to his notifications.

---

**Congratulations! You have learned a new skill:** Small Blades (Level 11)

Your continued work with daggers and small swords has evolved and merged these skills into a single-encompassing one. The Small Blades skill focuses on the use of light, fast, and precise weapons like daggers, knives, and short swords. Masters of this skill prioritize speed, precision, and agility over brute force, excelling at exploiting weak points and overwhelming opponents with rapid strikes. While small blades lack the raw damage of heavier weapons, they more than make up for it with versatility, finesse, and their ability to strike critical points with ease. "It's not the size of the blade, it's how many times I can stab you with it before you notice."

**+22% to damage with small blades. +22% to attack while wielding small blades.**

---

For achieving level 10 in Small Blades, you have improved from Novice to Apprentice. This has increased your precision and speed with these weapons. You also now gain a basic understanding of target weak points with these weapons.

**Chance to strike critical blows now +.5% per skill level. Total increased chance +5.5%.**

---

> You have earned 1000 xp for increasing your rank to
> Apprentice.

Xavier hadn't thought he had done much during the fight, he was already more than happy with the huge experience gain he had received from being in the same party as the much higher-level twins. He slowly replayed the combat in his mind, the fighting with the lower and lesser-geared slavers was still intense and he realized it had taken much more of his skill than he originally thought. He had no doubt that without the two Iskari, he would never have stood a chance beyond them but that was a whole other issue. With that realization, he continued through his notifications.

> **Congratulations! You have learned a new skill:** Light
> Armor (Level 8)
>
> The Light Armor skill represents expertise in wearing
> and utilizing light protective gear such as leather, padded,
> or chain shirts. This skill emphasizes mobility, agility,
> and precision defense over sheer durability. Masters
> of light armor turn their lack of heavy plating into an
> advantage, relying on speed, stealth, and clever movement
> to outmaneuver opponents and avoid damage. "Why take
> the hit when you can just not be there? Light armor isn't
> weakness—it's strategy."
>
> **+8% reduction in light armor movement penalty.**

He hadn't even realized his armor was slowing him down. He opened up his UI and examined his status. Switching over to the current effects tab he noticed an effect he hadn't paid very much attention to before.

> Armortoll – The reduction in speed, agility, and movement

due to worn armor.
Base Armortoll: -3% per piece of lightweight armor worn.
(Chest, Legs, Hands, Feet) Total: -12%.
Adjusted Armortoll: +8% reduction in total penalty.
Adjusted Armortoll: -11%

So even wearing the simple light leather armor he had been using still affected him. He wasn't overly surprised. That was a common issue in every game he had ever played. Still, the fact that aspects of this world so matched different game dynamics was just a little disturbing. He would have to look into what the penalties for other types of armor were. Not that he was overly keen on the idea of wearing something as cumbersome as plate armor, but it didn't hurt to know the options.

The next notifications were about individual relationship gains he had received from the now free Animari captives ranging from 50 to 100 points increase for each. He went through those with more of a glance to see the numbers but didn't focus overly much on them. He expected the people to return to their village or other Animari settlements.

Finally, he came to the one he was hoping for and an update to the quest that started him towards the raiders came up.

**Quest Update:** Break the Bonds.

Your audience with the elders of Verdantspire Haven, set you on a path of opportunity to prove yourself trustworthy. With the aid of the Verdantspire wardens Lianna and Liosan you have tracked down the raiding party responsible for taking the captives and slew them. You were able to free all of the captured Animari people and secured a way to remove their submission collars.

Return to the Verdantspire Enclave to receive your reward.

**Quest Objectives:** Assistance to Verdantspire Wardens in tracking and aiding in the destruction of raiding party along with the rescue of captured Animari individuals. Return to Verdantspire Enclave and speak with the elders.

**Potential rewards:**

- Trust and respect from the Animari of Verdantspire Haven.
- Potential settlement relationship between Rynthavael and Verdantspire Haven.
- +5000 Experience.

Xavier smiled in satisfaction, though he couldn't help but laugh slightly as a line from an old TV show played in his head. His smile broadened to a grin as he verbalized the words, "There's a plan in everything, kid, and I love it when a plan comes together." That drew a look from Ella and several others in the wagon. Xavier shrugged at the scrutiny and simply said. "A famous saying where I am from. Especially when everything works out."

As the wagons trundled on through the night Xavier wrapped up his new notifications and turned his attention to where to allocate his new points and skill percentage. The skill he wanted to update most currently was insight. He had a feeling that the stronger it became the better information it would provide. Several moments later he had made the change, and insight was now level 2. He scowled at how slow it seemed to level compared to his other skills. "Of course," he thought, "if I remembered to use it regularly that might not be an issue." He resolved to try and remember to use it on everyone and every creature he encountered.

With that task done, he looked to his attributes. Thirty points was a lot to play with. Having just come back from death he was sorely tempted to dump a large portion into his constitution to deepen his health point pool. That, however, seemed short-sighted. A long-term fix for a temporary problem. He did add four points to the stat however just to be safe bringing it to a respectable 18.

Now knowing the fact that his armor actively hampered his agility he decided to increase that as well. Being able to avoid getting hit and strike his foes better would indirectly reduce his chance of dying again and that was enough for him. That went for dexterity as well. He still hadn't quite figured out the difference between the two attributes, but both said they movement and speed in some way and fourteen more points were spent bringing them to 18 each as well.

That left him with twelve more points to allocate. Those were going to be more difficult as he was not sure of the correct path ahead of him. He thought back to the line about combat archetypes in his leveling prompt and another semi-translucent window opened in his view.

- **Warrior** – Masters of raw physical power, excelling in endurance and combat versatility. "When the enemy thinks I'm done, that's when I start hitting harder."
- **Rogue** – Stealthy and cunning, striking from the shadows with deadly precision. "If you saw me coming, I wouldn't be doing my job."
- **Cleric** – Divine warriors who heal, protect, and smite with the power of their gods. "When the light shines brightest, the shadows fall hardest."
- **Ranger** – Wilderness survivalists and marksmen, blending nature magic and precision strikes. "You'll never hear the arrow that ends you."
- **Sorcerer** – Natural-born wielders of untamed, raw magical power. "Magic flows through me,

whether I want it to or not."

- **Paladin** – Divine champions sworn to uphold sacred oaths and deliver justice or vengeance. "A blade in one hand, faith in the other. Together, they're unstoppable."
- **Monk** – Masters of martial arts and spiritual discipline, blending agility with supernatural power. "I am the storm in the stillness, the strike before you blink."
- **Barbarian** – Primal warriors fueled by rage, unleashing devastating physical attacks. "The louder I roar, the harder you fall."
- **Mage** – Arcane scholars who wield magic through study, knowledge, and discipline. "Knowledge is power, and I have studied everything."
- **Bard** – Performers of magic and music, inspiring allies and manipulating enemies through artistry. "One verse can turn the tide; one melody can end the war."

He had a good idea of what he wanted to do combat-wise. Though he felt it would be foolish to not at least examine all of the possibilities. Classes like the paladin or barbarian, though potentially powerful sounded either too onerous or reckless for his tastes. Mage could be interesting, but he had only learned or, for that matter, even seen a handful of spells in use and doubted he would be able to find more easily in the forests. Sorcerer, on the other hand, natural untamed magic? That was downright intriguing, and he wondered how that might play out. Ultimately it was Lianna's example that only served to reinforce his thoughts. Back when he was just playing games, be it table-top or video he always had a preference towards companion classes, summoners, Beastmasters, wardens, etc. The diversity of having another companion to take on more enemies or just balance out his shortcomings was just too useful to ignore. He looked closer at the ranger class and received updated information about it.

---

The Ranger - Skilled survivalists and marksmen, rangers are one with the wild, striking from afar or up close with the precision of a predator. "You'll never hear the arrow that ends you."

Specializations:

- Hunter: Experts at tracking and eliminating prey with deadly precision.
- Beastmaster: Fights alongside a loyal animal companion, a partner in battle.
- Feywarden: Uses mystical powers of nature to deceive and destroy.
- Stormstrider: Channels the forces of weather, striking with the fury of the storm.

---

There it was, Beastmaster, the subclass he had been hoping to see. His mind made up, he quickly selected Ranger as his archetype and a series of new prompts filled his view.

---

Congratulations Ranger! You don't just survive in the wild you own it! - Rangers are skilled survivalists, hunters, and marksmen who excel in traversing and thriving in the wilderness. Combining martial prowess, nature magic, and tracking expertise, Rangers are both guardians of the natural world and deadly hunters of their chosen prey.

Core Features of the Ranger

**Natural Explorer**

- Rangers are at home in the wilderness and gain unique bonuses in natural environments.

---

- Ignore difficult terrain and move faster while traveling in natural areas. At higher levels, this can be expanded to the ranger's party or group.
- Gain an advantage on survival checks for tracking, foraging, and navigation (+20% to skill checks).
- Spot hidden traps or ambushes more easily in outdoor settings (+20% to skill checks).

**Favored Enemy**

- Choose a specific type of creature (e.g., beasts, undead, dragons, or aberrations) as your favored enemy. As an initiate Ranger, you may select one favored enemy.
- Gain bonuses when tracking, fighting, or gaining knowledge about your chosen enemy type.
- Can identify weaknesses or behaviors unique to that enemy.
- Higher levels allow choosing additional favored enemies.

**Fighting Style** - Select a combat specialization to suit your preferred style:

- Archery: Bonus to ranged attack rolls.
- Two-Weapon Fighting: Enhanced ability to wield two melee weapons simultaneously.
- Defense: Improved armor class for survivability.

**Primeval Awareness**

- Rangers gain a supernatural sense of the natural world and their enemies.
- At higher levels rangers can detect the presence of certain creatures within a radius (e.g., undead, dragons, elementals).
- Higher levels allow the ability to commune with animals or plants for guidance.

> As an Initiate Ranger, you may now select your favored enemy and fighting style. Your favored enemy must be selected from beings you have fought in the past. These selections do not need to be made immediately.

Things were making more sense now about how they had been able to travel so quickly. Lianna had one of the class skills higher-ranked rangers received. Her Forest Running had been a huge help in catching up to the raiders. He shifted his view to focus on the new class archetype tab for Ranger and saw he had the skill now as well. However, it stated that it only affected him at his current level and only increased his speed by 50%. "Have to start somewhere," he thought to himself then continued reviewing his new abilities.

> - **Favored Enemy**: Unknown, you have yet to select a favored enemy.
> - **Fighting Style**: Unknown, you have yet to select a fighting style.
> - **Primeval Awareness**: Your ability to detect abnormalities, survive, and track creatures in the wild has been increased commensurate to your level of Ranger.

He was going to have to think long and hard about his favored enemy. To be honest, he had no idea what the complete scope of enemies there were, or which ones were immediate threats to his small settlement. That choice could wait for now. His fighting style, however, was an easy one. He was already working on improving his two-weapon fighting skill, having an automatic improvement in it due to his class was just icing on the sweetroll. Selecting that option gave an immediate skill boost to his style.

> **Congratulations! You have learned a new skill:** Two-

Weapon Fighting (Level 20)

The Two-Weapon Fighting skill allows you to effectively wield two weapons simultaneously, providing a unique blend of speed, versatility, and relentless aggression. Early on, the penalties for dual wielding can make it challenging, but as mastery grows you learn to unleash devastating combos, fluidly strike with both hands, and defend against attacks using either weapon. "Why settle for one blade when you can have two? Twice the steel, twice the chaos."

At your Apprentice (level 20) skill level you have the following penalties and abilities. -10% Main-Hand attack/damage, -20% Off-Hand attack/damage. Basic dual strikes, off-hand parry, simple dual weapon combos. You can currently wield a medium weapon in your main hand and a light weapon in your off-hand.

Yep, his new class was already amazing. Not only did it give a bunch of new abilities, but it also gave him a new skill, and not at level 1, he was starting the two-weapon fighting skill at level 20! It also explained why he was having such an issue with the two swords. He was just glad they counted as light weapons, and he could use them both still.

He turned to look where Lianna was walking and talking with one of the freed captives, as they had made their way towards Verdantspire she would occasionally stop and undo one of their collars as the key recharged. She had managed to remove a good number of them over the hours of their trek. Xavier hoped that he had managed to gain some respect in the skilled woman's eyes. He hadn't seen any prompt notifying him of a change in relationship with her, but his money was on that happening when he completed the initial quest. As a fledgling ranger, and hoping to follow her path of a beastmaster, he wanted to be on her good side and maybe get some advice and tutelage.

As those thoughts went through his mind a shout rose from the front of the caravan. Lights could be seen bobbing through the woods up ahead. Lianna made a distinct whistling sound, Xavier realized it mimicked one of the birds he had started to recognize in the woods. Well, it mimicked in sound but there was a precise pattern to the whistle. From the distance, off to the right of the group and away from the lights came a response. Lianna finally broke a smile and waved the group forward. They were almost back to the safety of the haven and were now being escorted by unseen wardens

# CHAPTER THREE
### *The Verdantspire Celebration*

It did not take long before the lights in the distance resolved into the Animari settlement of Verdantspire. A large gathering of armed guards, friends and family of the recently freed captives, and the elders were waiting for them. The cheers of the Animari fill the air, their joy and relief palpable as loved ones rush to embrace those thought lost forever. Tears of joy mingled with tears of pain and sorrow as they took solace in being reunited with those who had been missing.

Xavier, Ella, and the twins remained to the side until everyone had made it past then they moved forward to where the elders stood patiently. The Lynari elder was flanked by the others and she wore a small smile on her face, as Xavier came to stand before her.

There was a new warmth in the eyes of the diminutive feline woman as she spoke. "You have done as you said you would, and our people have been returned. Wounds can heal now for those who lost loved ones thanks to your deeds. Today, you have proven yourself not just a wanderer, but a protector of our kin."

As she spoke a prompt filled Xavier's vision.

**You have completed a quest:** Break the Bonds I.

By aiding the Verdantspire Wardens in destroying a raiding party and rescuing the Animari captives you have shown your trustworthiness to the elders of Verdantspire Haven. High Speaker Kaelith personally recognizes your efforts in aiding her warriors.

**Quest Rewards:** You have received +5000 personal relationship points with the Elders of Verdantspire, the Verdantspire Wardens and with each of the individuals you have assisted in returning.

Relationship has gone from +0, Indifferent – "Your existence doesn't affect me one way or the other. You're like a potted plant in the corner," to +5000, Close Friend – "They know a little too much about you, but somehow that's okay."

Increased settlement relationship between Rynthavael and Verdantspire Haven +1000, Mutual Respect – We recognize your worth my friend and will lend a hand in tough times".

+5000 Experience.

One more prompt followed the quest update informing him of additional personal changes in his relationship with the twins.

You have received +3000 relationship points with Lianna and Liosan Frostride.

The relationship points were not enough to elevate his standing with Kaelith or Lianna again, but they brought him more than halfway to the next level. It was progress, even if the system gave no fanfare.

Then Kaelith motioned for Xavier and the others to

follow. With a final glance back at the celebrations still unfolding behind them, she turned and walked steadily toward the heart of Verdantspire Haven.

The sound of drums and laughter faded as they passed deeper into the settlement. Elder Kaelith's voice dropped to a near whisper, low enough that only Xavier could hear her. "This victory has brought hope," she said softly, "but the Wildlands remain fraught with danger. If you are willing, there is more to be done."

Her tone was gentle, but her words bore weight layered with implication. This was not the end of their journey, but a turning point.

Xavier waited for the familiar chime of a system prompt. When none came, he blinked and looked over at the Lynari. "The people of Rynthavael are at your service, as am I, High Speaker. What can be done to assist you further?"

He tried to mask his mild frustration at the lack of a formal quest. The break in what had clearly been a chain unsettled him. Had he missed a condition?

Kaelith's response came with a dismissive wave, though not unkind. "That can be discussed later, Xavier. Tonight, we feast and celebrate those whose freedom you have restored. In the morning, we will hold a ceremony to solidify the bond between our settlements."

He nodded, falling into step beside her.

Their path wound through the inner rings of the settlement, and Xavier quickly realized an impromptu celebration was taking shape ahead. Tables were being arranged. Lanterns strung. Baskets of fruits, jugs of mead, and platters of spiced meats began to appear. The aroma of grilled root-vegetables, honeyed breads, and aromatic herbs already teased the air.

As they walked, their conversation drifted to lighter topics. Kaelith described various parts of the settlement with pride, points of interest, small stories of the stoneworkers and seedweavers who had built the place.

But one detail refused to leave Xavier's mind. Everywhere he looked, there were only Animari. Not a single elf, dwarf, or human.

After a while, his steps slowed. He turned to Kaelith and asked with a frown, "This whole time, I've only seen Animari. Is that normal... or am I missing something?"

The Lynari elder's pace faltered. She met his gaze with a silence that stretched several heartbeats. Her eyes held the weight of old sorrow.

"No, you are not mistaken," she said at last. "There was a time when we traded freely with all races. These streets once bustled with travelers, peddlers, and seekers. That time is gone."

She resumed walking, and Xavier matched her pace as she continued.

"The elves have become insular," she said, her tone laced with quiet disdain. "Their leaders now preach elven superiority, retreating deeper into the veilwood cities to the west. The dwarves of the mountains were never the most outgoing, but now? Their gates open less than ever, and even old alliances are crumbling. As for the northeast..."

Her expression darkened.

"The king who once united the nomadic tribes, he was once fair, once just. But something has changed. Now that kingdom has become a den of villainy and cruelty. Brutality cloaked in law."

"The clans and tribes of the Animari have pulled back," Kaelith finished. "Some vanish into hidden glades and shadowed valleys. Others, like those here, come to Verdantspire seeking sanctuary. This is what we shall speak of on the morrow."

They rounded a bend, and Xavier's breath caught.

#

Verdantspire's central plaza opened before them, a breathtaking blend of crafted artistry and natural wonder. A massive circle of pale flagstone, nearly a hundred feet across, formed the foundation of the settlement's heart. At its center stood a raised stone platform.

Floating above that platform was something truly wondrous.

A crystalline obelisk hovered five feet above the stone dais. It was elegant and alien, its shape smooth and multifaceted like an enormous cut gem. Beneath its transparent surface, intricate veins of emerald, gold-green, and silver shimmered and pulsed, flowing in delicate lattices like veins through living marble.

A soft hum resonated through the stone underfoot, subtle but ever-present. It ebbed and swelled in time with the pulsing strands of light that extended from the obelisk's base, threading outward through clear crystalline channels embedded in the flagstone. The energies moved like rivers beneath the skin of the earth.

Xavier stared, unable to tear his eyes away. Another nexus.

Kaelith watched him, her eyes gleaming. She extended her right arm, and with a shimmer, a mark appeared, bright and intricate. At its core swirled a vortex of motion, surrounded by curling, vine-like tendrils that formed glowing leaves in golden green. Around these were angular, shard-like shapes pulsing emerald, held in balance by feathered arcs in radiant silver. The whole mark shimmered with quiet motion, subtly shifting like a living tapestry of magic.

Behind Xavier, Ella gasped quietly, her hand flying to her mouth. The two nexus-bound leaders turned their gaze to her, but she only flushed and shook her head slightly in apology.

"I see you, Mark-bearer," Kaelith said softly. "Those who are bound to a nexus can sense another, if they know the signs. There is a resonance, a presence that reveals itself."

She lowered her sleeve and let the mark fade.

"This is why we protect Verdantspire so fiercely. This is the Lir'Valis—a nexus of Life, Air, and Earth. You need not show me your mark, Xavier, and I would advise you not to reveal it to any you do not trust."

He nodded taking her advice to heart.

"You have proven your resolve," she continued. "You have taken the first step toward earning the trust of my people. Tomorrow, that trust will be sealed. In time, perhaps we may be more than friends, true allies."

Xavier smiled. "I truly long for that day, High Speaker."

He turned his gaze outward, to the vibrant life around them.

The plaza was more than ceremonial. It was a living place. Buildings lined its edge, many half-grown, half-built in that same architectural style that defied easy classification. To the north stood a great hall, its smooth walls traced with glowing lines of emerald earth-aspected magic, grounding the building with a sense of weight and permanence.

Xavier imagined it as their seat of governance, and it gave him ideas for Rynthavael. Mental notes began forming, designs he'd share with his stonemason and carpenters back home.

To the left of the great hall, the first of three gardens nestled between buildings. This one held moss-covered stones, thick-rooted shrubs, and hardy plants thriving in rich, loamy beds, Earth-aligned, clearly.

To the west, an open-air market buzzed with life. Stalls and merchant pavilions stood side-by-side with stonework booths. Most of the vendors he could see appeared to be Vulpiri or Felvari, the fox- and felinekin Animari clearly comfortable in the role of merchants.

South of the market, another garden bloomed. This one was lush and radiant with vibrant flowers, humming insects, and quietly babbling fountains. Life magic saturated the space, and Xavier could feel it, even from here.

Past the Life garden lay a small grove of trees. Something about it felt sacred, though he couldn't place why. He resolved to visit it if he could.

The final garden, spanning between the grove and an open-air amphitheater, was a place of air and wind. Sparse trees rose amid wind-chimes and feathered ornaments that danced in the ever-present breeze. Pathways curved through the space, inviting contemplation.

The amphitheater itself was carved into the hill to the east, built with sweeping arcs and open acoustics. Xavier could feel the subtle threads of air ley magic twisting through its structure—he had no doubt it would carry any voice to the farthest seat with perfect clarity.

He shook his head slowly. It was all so much.

Like a tourist seeing one of the world wonders, he thought. But more than that... this was a natural wonder, fused with magic, history, and soul. The ley line nexus wasn't just powerful, it was alive.

He let himself breathe it in. The glyphs etched into the flagstones. The miniature crystals floating in lazy orbit around the obelisk. The way energies shifted in rhythm with the settlement itself.

This place wasn't just a home. It was the beating heart of a people.

#

As dusk deepened into night, Verdantspire truly came alive.

All around the plaza, tables and chairs were set out in graceful arcs. Lanterns swayed from woven arches and low-hanging branches, casting warm golden light across stone, bark, and fur alike. Dozens of Animari moved through the space with practiced efficiency, placing platters of food and drink in ever-growing abundance. Each table offered a feast, skewers of roasted meat glazed in honey and firepepper, braids of spiced bread still steaming, and fruit cut into petal-like slices that glistened with juice.

Mugs of brewed root-beer and berrywine passed from hand to hand. The air filled with the mingled scents of sweetleaf tobacco, toasted grain, roasted herbs, and citrus-laced oils. Every breath Xavier took seemed steeped in celebration.

Music rose from the dais at the heart of the plaza. A troupe of Animari players had gathered, their instruments a mix of drums stretched with scaled hide, carved bone flutes, and strummed stringed pieces shaped from twisted wood. The music they played was raw and powerful. It pulsed through the stone beneath Xavier's boots and stirred something ancient in his blood. The rhythm moved the crowd into motion, feet stamping, arms raised, tails swaying. The entire plaza had become a living thing, full of light and laughter.

From where he stood, Xavier could see the tide of the settlement converging. Animari of every shape and hue came from alleys and paths, drawn to the celebration. Young and old, sleek and shaggy, solemn and boisterous. The scale of the gathering was staggering. Hundreds, perhaps over a thousand, filled the plaza, and the crowd was still growing.

He was awed, humbled, and slightly alarmed. If these people had been enemies, Verdantspire would have crushed Rynthavael without effort. The realization made him even more determined to solidify the alliance Kaelith had hinted at.

The crowd surged, and he found himself at the center of a storm of gratitude.

A Cervari woman with soft brown eyes threw her arms around him, weeping gently. "You brought my son home," she whispered, then kissed his cheek before stepping away. Another Animari followed, and another. A trio of Felvari women approached, radiant with joy and drink. One kissed his temple. One pressed a flower into his hand. The last gave him a slow wink and a playful flick of her tail as she moved on.

Ella was suddenly beside him. She said nothing, but the slight tension in her jaw was unmistakable. She stood closer than before, and when another well-meaning Animari leaned in with a mug and a flirty grin, Ella's smile was calm and frosted.

"You alright?" Xavier asked quietly.

"I am observing," she replied, voice light but edged. "You are quite popular tonight."

He tried not to laugh. "Comes with saving the day, I guess."

A short distance away, Lianna stood flanked by a group of Vulpiri. One, a younger girl with an impressive amount of energy and very few personal boundaries, had taken to dragging Lianna toward the dance circle. Lianna allowed herself to be pulled, but the soft white fur of her cheeks had turned a rosy red. Xavier blinked. He hadn't known fur could blush.

She did not resist, nor did she seem comfortable. Her tail twitched in agitation, but she remained composed.

Liosan, by contrast, had vanished into the chaos and reappeared as a force of nature. He moved among dancers and tumblers with graceful abandon. He twirled with strangers, flipped through the air, sampled everything edible within reach, and left a wake of giggles, applause, and admiration behind him. He never uttered a single word. Not one. The boy danced, ate, drank, and laughed soundlessly. His joy radiated without voice.

Xavier watched him, curiosity growing. He had not once heard Liosan speak. Not even a whisper. A mystery for later.

A mug was pressed into Xavier's hand, filled with something light and floral. He drank cautiously. The brew was crisp, tinged with mint and honey. It warmed his throat and settled into his belly with a soothing calm. The world softened around the edges, and for the first time in a long while, he felt something close to peace.

Ella stood beside him once more. She placed a gentle hand on his forearm. "You have done well, Xavier," she said quietly. "They see you."

"I hope they see all of us," he answered. "This wasn't just me."

"They know. But it begins with you."

He let her words settle as he tilted his head back and gazed toward the stars. Lanterns swayed in the trees, casting their warm light like fireflies suspended on invisible threads. The obelisk in the plaza's center continued to pulse, its rhythm steady and serene. Crystalline streams of energy flowed outward like lifeblood through the stone.

He caught sight of elemental glyphs carved into the flagstones, each marking the flow of Earth, Air, and Life. Smaller crystals orbited the obelisk in slow, deliberate paths, shifting in harmony with the nexus.

The entire settlement felt alive. A place not merely built, but grown. Sustained by purpose. He closed his eyes and listened. Verdantspire was singing, and he was a part of it now.

#

A loud knocking shattered the pleasant dream he had been drifting in. Xavier groaned, cracking one eye open as the noise rattled through his skull like a drum.

"I'm up," he grumbled hoarsely. "Stop with the noise, it feels like you're banging directly on my head!"

Even his own voice was painful. The light filtering through the window felt like daggers, and the bitter taste in his mouth suggested he had imbibed far more than he remembered. He smacked his lips once, twice, and then watched as the door creaked open.

Ella stepped inside, radiant and composed. She looked like she had slept a full night and hadn't been at the same celebration as him.

"The High Speaker asked me to wake you. The ceremony is ready, and your presence is required," she said with a faint smirk, clearly enjoying his suffering. She held out a small glass vial.

"Drink this. It will help. I had a feeling you were overdoing it last night."

Xavier sat up slowly and took the vial with a dubious look. It wasn't that he distrusted Ella—far from it—but at the moment, he distrusted anything that wasn't plain water.

Still, he took a breath, braced himself, and tipped the vial back. A rush of ginger warmth spread across his tongue, then down his chest. In moments, the throbbing ache in his head faded. The tension in his shoulders melted. He blinked in astonishment.

"That was amazing," he said, holding the empty vial. "I would have given my right arm to have something like this back on Earth."

As soon as the words left his mouth, he stiffened. He looked around sharply, lowering his voice.

Ella gave a tired sigh and shook her head. "We are alone. And too high up for someone to be at the window. But you must be more careful, Master. We do not know who can be trusted with the truth that you are not of Arath."

Her tone was firm, but there was no harshness in it. She turned toward the door.

"Come now. Get dressed. It seems you have a busy day ahead of you. And the gods only know when we will be able to go home."

He waited until she had closed the door behind her before swinging his legs over the side of the bed. The motion was fluid now. No lingering ache or stiffness. That tonic truly was a miracle.

Crossing to the small basin of water that had been left

near the side table, he splashed his face and ran his fingers through his hair. It had grown longer since his arrival in Arath. It was starting to curl at the edges and fall into his eyes. He made a note to find someone to cut it before it became a problem.

A few minutes later, dressed and refreshed, Xavier stepped into the hall where Ella waited.

He offered a sheepish smile. "Lead the way. I have no idea where I'm going."

She smiled in return, softer this time. "That makes two of us. But we will figure it out."

Together, they descended into the heart of Verdantspire once more, this time not as guests at a celebration, but as representatives of a growing alliance. The new day had begun, and with it, the next step on the path.

# CHAPTER FOUR

*Shadows Over the Wildlands*

Ella guided Xavier out from the quiet building they had stayed in. Morning light filtered softly through the canopy above, casting dappled gold across the mossy stone. They were, he realized, only a couple of streets away from the nexus plaza. Yet she did not lead him to the prominent council hall he had noticed the night before. Instead, she veered down a narrow path that wound between that building and a sloped earthen garden lined with aromatic herbs.

As they walked, a voice drifted to him from ahead. It started as a vague murmur, but within moments he could clearly make out the rising tones of Lianna.

"No. I will not do it. How could you even ask that of me? You know what happened."

Her words carried a mix of outrage and pleading, raw and sharp. Xavier's steps slowed instinctively. He heard another voice respond though he couldn't make out the words, it was quieter and calmer, muffled by walls, High Speaker Kaelith.

They reached a small dome of smooth stone, barely noticeable from the street. Steam curled up from a narrow vent at the top, rising like a whisper into the air. Two Wardens stood outside the arched entrance, both feline-eyed and watchful. As Xavier approached, they nodded in recognition. One reached for the curved wooden handle and pulled open the door.

Inside the two women cut off speaking abruptly as they heard the sound of the door shifting. A wave of thick, heated air rolled over him, heavy with moisture and the sharp tang of unfamiliar herbs. Xavier recoiled slightly, blinking against the sudden fog. As he ducked through the low entrance, it felt as if he had been slapped in the face with a hot, wet towel. He grunted quietly, skin already starting to dampen.

The chamber inside was simple in structure, yet sacred in atmosphere. The floor was smooth stone, warm beneath his feet. A central brazier smoldered in a pit, surrounded by a ring of low benches cut directly into the rock. Steam hissed steadily from where water dripped over the heated stones. Through the haze, he made out several figures.

The elders were seated in a loose circle, their forms faintly visible through the shifting mist. Their clothes had been shed down to undergarments and light wrappings, their fur, feathers, and skin glistening with sweat. They sat in stillness, as though the heat alone could draw out truth.

Xavier glanced back. Ella was already slipping her tunic over her head, serene and unhurried, her expression utterly innocent as she met his gaze. She placed her folded clothes into a wicker basket by the wall and then took a seat in the circle without a word.

He narrowed his eyes at her, suspicion rising. "You knew," he murmured under his breath.

Her only reply was a faint smile, the kind that said yes, and perhaps next time you will not keep a lady waiting while you adjust your hair.

Resigned, Xavier sighed and began removing his own

garments, folding them neatly before placing them in the basket beside Ella's. He was just settling into a spot beside her when the door behind him creaked shut. The guard who had admitted them stepped out, taking the baskets with him, and left the chamber in sealed silence.

Steam curled thick around them. The air tasted of heated leaves and something faintly sweet, yet sharp beneath it. He glanced around the chamber, noting each of the elders in turn. Most appeared tranquil, their breathing slow, eyes half-closed. All but one.

Lianna.

The Iskari sat with her back against the curved stone wall, arms crossed tightly. Her soaked fur clung to her limbs, but it was her expression that struck him. Her muzzle was taut, ears pinned slightly back, and her narrowed eyes glinted with something fierce. Anger, maybe, or pain.

She did not look at him.

Xavier turned his gaze toward Kaelith, who was seated across from him in a posture of quiet dignity. Her silvery hair clung to her brow, but her golden eyes remained clear and sharp. He took a breath, tasting the heat again, and gave a small nod.

"I did not expect to meet with you in a room like this," he said, voice low but steady. "Though I am not about to complain. The heat feels good on muscles I did not know were still sore. I used to enjoy going to saunas back home."

He caught himself too late, lips still parted. His jaw clenched as he realized what he had let slip.

Kaelith's brow arched slightly. She turned toward one of the elders, the Vulpiri woman seated to her right. The elder raised one hand and traced a shape in the air, her fingers glowing faintly. Xavier felt a ripple pass through the space around them, like a soft shift in pressure. He could not tell exactly what had changed.

Kaelith faced him again.

"Elder Lyselle has just sealed the chamber," she said. "No sound shall pass beyond these walls until the rite concludes. But before we speak further, you must understand something... There is an herb in the water we use for this ceremony. As it steams, it becomes part of what we breathe. Its property is simple. While it lingers in your lungs, you cannot lie."

Xavier straightened. Ella did as well, suddenly alert. The words struck him like a stone. Xavier tensed, mouth dry despite the moisture in the air. His gaze darted toward Ella, who had gone very still beside him.

Kaelith lifted a hand, palm out in a calming gesture. "We mean you no harm, Xavier of Rynthavael. This is not a trap. We do not seek your secrets beyond your intent. But in these times, even trust must be measured. What is said here will never be repeated."

Around the circle, the other elders inclined their heads in solemn agreement. Only Lianna remained motionless, her jaw clenched tight. It took a pointed look from Kaelith before the Iskari gave the barest of nods.

While that didn't completely placate Xavier's mood at being tricked, yet again, by the smiling High Speaker, he did relax slightly and he breathed out slowly. He did not like being maneuvered, especially not like this. Still, the purpose was clear, and no one here had raised a weapon. He settled back slightly, though his mind remained cautious.

He huffed quietly. "Fine. I understand the need. Still, I am curious about this herb. Might be useful to have something like that back in Rynthavael."

The Cervari elder across from him smiled, her eyes gentle. "We would gladly provide you with cuttings. You have earned enough trust for trade to be considered. However, that is not why we gathered this morning."

Kaelith nodded once, the quiet air of command returning to her voice.

"No. This meeting is to determine the course between our settlements, and the future that ties us both to the wildlands beyond. The steam ensures that all words are true and honest for both our safety and your reassurance."

#

The steam swirled, thick and slow, cloaking the chamber in warmth and haze. Despite the closeness of the air, Xavier found his breathing had steadied. The tension of the truth-herb lingered in his chest, like the moment before a fall. But there was no turning back now.

"I can see the wisdom in your method," he said at last, meeting Kaelith's gaze across the room. "And I would see an alliance between our settlements. Rynthavael may be small, but I intend for it to grow. Not just to survive, but to stand again as the place it once was."

He had not meant to say quite so much. The words had tumbled out, drawn by the herb or perhaps by the truth of his intent. Either way, he did not try to pull them back.

Kaelith tilted her head slightly, studying him with a thoughtful gleam in her golden eyes. Then she gestured lightly toward Lianna, whose posture remained tense.

"That is as good a place to begin as any," the High Speaker said. "You recall what I told you last night. Our tensions with Arenvalis have worsened in recent years. But it was not always so. There were always raiders, yes, but they struck infrequently, and not with such focus on the

Animari."

She leaned forward slightly, her voice even.

"It was only in the last decade that this pattern shifted. And it began, or so rumor says, when sightings of King Rorik Ironthorn grew rare. We do not know if he is still in control, or if someone else pulls the strings. But we must find out."

She nodded again to Lianna. "We have asked her to accompany you. She is one of our few Wardens who knows the wildlands well."

Lianna's reaction was immediate. Her head snapped up, her eyes blazing.

"I will not go with the human to those lands," she said, voice raw. "You cannot possibly ask that of me. Why would you expect me to go back there?"

The words echoed in the stone chamber, and the silence that followed was heavy.

It was Elder Veyara who answered, her tone soft but unyielding.

"Niece. You are the best one to guide him, and you know it. We do not ask this of you lightly. Your history is not forgotten. But this must be done if we are to prepare for what is coming."

Xavier blinked. He now knew the relationship between the Elder and the twins he had noticed before. They were family just not as close as he had originally thought.

Lianna bared her teeth slightly, a snarl building in her throat, but her aunt's gaze kept her still. She folded her arms tightly across her chest and stared at the wall, rigid and silent.

Kaelith turned back to Xavier.

"We know you are an outsider, it is why we want to send someone familiar with the wildlands with you. They are more dangerous than ever before and someone unfamiliar with these lands could unknowingly end up in more trouble than expected. Even our Wardens speak of creatures behaving strangely, of signs twisted by strange hands."

Xavier's brow furrowed, concern rising in his chest. But before he could speak, Kaelith continued.

"And yes, we know you are not of Arath."

The words struck like a thunderclap. He suddenly felt like a very small animal in a room of hungry predators, though the Elders made no hostile gestures or even spoke harshly he felt trapped.

He stiffened, caught off guard. His mind raced. He had been careful. He had told no one. No one except Ella.

"How?" he asked, his voice low.

Kaelith's expression remained calm, her voice gentle.

"You did not have to say anything. Lianna told us of your blessings, but it was your actions that confirmed it. You do not speak like one of Eldoria. Nor do you act like one born here. We could have believed you came from distant lands, but your demeanor, your restraint, and your caution mark you as something else."

She shifted slightly, her tone softening.

"You said it yourself. Trust has not yet been fully earned., but I would like to believe it has begun. And I will swear this to you, Xavier of Rynthavael. What is shared in this place remains here. This I swear. This I swear. This I swear."

The final words settled over the room like a closing seal.

There was no magic in the air that he could feel, but a soft chime echoed in his vision.

> **High Speaker Kaelith Moonstride has sworn an Oath of Silence.**
> **All Animari beholden to Verdantspire Haven are bound by this vow.**
> **Any breach shall incur severe consequence.**

The prompt hovered for a moment before fading. Xavier felt the weight of it, more than just words. The world had acknowledged her oath. That was no small thing.

He looked to Ella.

She nodded slowly, her voice quiet. "They have sworn, Master. Oaths spoken in such fashion are heard. To break them would risk not only their lives but the honor and standing of all who serve them."

Xavier exhaled, long and steady. Then he nodded once and turned to face the circle of elders, and he began telling his story.

He spoke of waking up in a forest, of the strange interface and the mark on his body. He told them of the Nexus, of the ruins he had claimed, and of his intent to protect those who chose to live there. He did not mention Ella's true nature, nor the blade, but he told them the rest.

When he finished, silence returned.

Kaelith's expression remained calm, though something in her eyes had shifted. Perhaps understanding. Perhaps something older.

Lianna, by contrast, stared at him with stunned disbelief. Her mouth had parted slightly, the weight of his words still settling.

"You are right," Xavier said at last. "I am not from here, and without guidance, I would be lost. Ella has helped me where she could, but she does not know the wildlands. I would welcome Lianna's help, if she is willing."

Lianna closed her mouth, eyes clouding. She turned her gaze away.

"I cannot," she whispered. "Not to those lands. Please. Do not ask this of me."

She looked toward the elders now, no longer hiding her plea.

Sylara reached over and placed a gentle hand on her leg.

"Child. Do not let the past rule you. There is healing to be found, even in the ashes. Trust us. This is for the good of all, and for your own peace."

The younger woman's jaw trembled slightly. Her ears lowered. For a long moment, she did not move. Then, at last, she gave a small nod.

Sylara pulled her into a soft embrace and whispered something into her ear. When she let go, the elder returned to her seat, and Lianna sat quietly beside her, eyes on the floor.

> The Iskari Beastmaster Lianna Frostwhisper has offered to become your traveling companion.
> Do you accept? Yes or No

Xavier blinked as the prompt appeared before him, more vivid than most. He focused on the word "Yes," and the prompt dissolved into golden light.

He looked toward Lianna. Her face was unreadable now. Not angry, not defiant, only distant. As if she had stepped to the edge of something and could no longer see the way back.

He wondered what it would take to earn her trust. But at least, they had taken the first step.

#

The room was quieter now. The worst of the tension had eased, but the air still felt heavy. Steam clung to Xavier's skin like a second layer, wrapping him in warmth and gravity alike.

Kaelith waited until Lianna had resettled before she spoke again. Her voice was calm, but not gentle. It carried the weight of command.

"We ask this of you because the situation in Arenvalis has grown dangerous. Not just for us, but for all who live beyond its borders. You must go to Ironhaven, Xavier. Infiltrate the city if you can. Find the source of the change. Why has their aggression toward the Animari grown? What has twisted their king, or what force acts in his name?"

Her tone darkened slightly. "And if our people are still being sold within those walls, you are to free them."

Xavier's vision flared with light as a new prompt unfolded before him.

**You have been offered a quest:** Shadows Over the Wildlands

**Quest Type:** Major
**Issuing Faction:** Verdantspire Haven
**Quest Giver:** High Speaker Kaelith Moonstride

**Summary:**
Recent tensions between the Kingdom of Arenvalis and its neighbors have escalated beyond mere territorial disputes. Reports indicate a surge in hostilities toward

the Animari, as well as an increase in slave trade activity in Ironhaven. Verdantspire Haven cannot afford to ignore this growing threat.

Elder Kaelith has tasked you with infiltrating Arenvalis, uncovering the cause of its newfound aggression, and, if possible, dismantling any Animari trafficking operations within Ironhaven. However, the Kingdom of Arenvalis is no mere den of raiders; its laws are strict, its watchful eyes many, and its ruler, King Rorik Ironthorn, is not a man easily swayed. Proceed with caution, diplomacy may serve you better than steel, but you must be prepared for either.

## Objectives:

- Investigate the political shift within Arenvalis.
- Identify key figures behind the Animari slave trade.
- Liberate Animari captives without triggering open conflict.
- Determine whether King Rorik Ironthorn remains in power.
- Return with intelligence that can alter the course of war or peace.

## Challenges:

- Arenvalis is lawful, organized, and wary of outsiders.
- Ironhaven is heavily fortified; brute force will not succeed.
- Diplomacy, disguise, and infiltration are essential.
- Discovery may lead to permanent hostility from the kingdom.

## Consequences of Failure:

- Continued escalation of raids against the Animari.
- Potential severing of alliance with Verdantspire.
- Increased danger for Rynthavael.
- Risk of Xavier being marked as an enemy of the realm.

**Rewards:**

- Valuable political and strategic intelligence.
- Strengthened alliance between Rynthavael and Verdantspire Haven.
- Trust and honor among the Animari.
- 12,000 Experience Points

**Optional Rewards:**

- Unique relic or enchanted gear gifted by the freed.
- Additional settlement favor.
- Influence within Arenvalis, if diplomacy succeeds.

Do you accept? Yes or No

The quest text hovered longer than usual. Xavier read it once, then again. This was not some errand or dungeon crawl. This was a mission that could alter the path of nations. It took him several long minutes to read and then reread the details before finally focusing on yes and accepting the quest. It must be the next quest in the chain he was expecting to see last night. Now he understood why it didn't happen immediately. He needed the elders to better understand himself and to trust him more before something of this magnitude.

He focused on the word yes.

The golden glow of confirmation swept across his vision

and faded.

"I would be honored to help your people and mine with this quest High Speaker Kaelith. I would need to go back to Rynthavael and inform my people that I will be traveling and possibly away for a while due to this, however. They only expected me to be gone for a couple of days and this seems as if it would take much longer than that. If acceptable I will head home immediately and set out for Ironhaven within the week." Xavier bowed slightly as he spoke showing respect to the Elder and her companions.

Kaelith's voice softened as she saw the change in his expression. "We did not expect you to depart at once. You must speak to your people. Prepare. Ironhaven will not welcome you kindly."

She gestured toward the Ursari elder, seated with his heavy arms resting on his knees. Thror Ironpaw reached behind him and withdrew a small iron collar. Simple in design, its only feature was a locking sigil and a narrow groove worn smooth by use.

Xavier stared at it. His unease returned like a creeping tide.

Lianna's entire body tensed. Her eyes flinched away. Tears shimmered at the corners.

Kaelith spoke gently now, but every word struck like a hammer.

"This is part of why she resisted. If she enters the Wildlands freely, she risks being captured again. There are eyes and systems in place that treat all Animari without master as prey."

She nodded toward the collar.

"But if she wears this, she may be mistaken as already owned. It will mark her as a slave and protect her from worse fates. The key is yours. Place it upon her before you leave the woods, when prompted, you may choose to set restrictions or none. The illusion alone will suffice." Her gaze narrowed. "I am trusting you with one of ours. Do not betray that trust, Xavier."

He hesitated, then reached for the collar and the small rune-etched stone. It felt cold in his hand. Too cold for a thing that still carried the scent of bondage.

He turned to Lianna. Her face was unreadable now, expression shuttered, as though a door had slammed closed behind her eyes.

"You do not have to do this," he said quietly. "I can find another way. I would never ask this of you, not like…"

She cut him off with a short breath, sharp and ragged.

"The High Speaker is right. This is the best way."

She stood slowly, fur still damp, and turned to reveal her right hip. There, beneath the matted strands, the truth lay bare. A brand, faint but evident, shaped in an intricate sigil. The mark of ownership.

"That was mine," she said, her voice hollow. "Before my brother and I were freed. That is how I know the path you must walk."

Xavier felt the world tilt slightly. His mind reeled with the implications. Her rage. Her silence. Her scars. It was no wonder the woman hated humans so much. Also, why she had such aggression towards the raiders when they attacked the camp.

"I have no words," he whispered.

Lianna gave no reply. She walked from the room without a backward glance, steam trailing after her like smoke from a dying fire.

Xavier stared after her until the door shut behind her.

Then he looked back to the circle of elders.

"I will watch over her," he said. "As if she were one of my own. I swear to you now. She will wear this only when she must. No restrictions. No commands."

Kaelith gave a slow nod, accepting the vow.

It was Veyara who spoke next, her voice cold with meaning. "I will hold you to that. She and her brother are all I have left. If we did not believe in your worth, you would not be sitting here now."

Xavier inclined his head, her words landing with solemn clarity. Relationships in this world were more than political convenience. They were currency, shield, and weapon.

Kaelith rose slightly from her seat. "Go. Gather your things. Lianna will meet you at the southern gate. Your path begins there."

Xavier started to turn, then paused. "I have one request before I leave."

Kaelith looked at him, curious.

"My village is still small, and the wilds remain dangerous. While I am gone, would your Wardens watch over them? Just until I return."

Thror Ironpaw's low voice answered him. "We have asked much of you, human. More than most would give. We recognize the burden that places on your own. I will send Wardens to patrol around Rynthavael." He leaned forward slightly. "Who should they speak to, so they are not mistaken for threat?"

"Braegor," Xavier said. "He was once the alderman and still leads in my absence. He will know what to do."

Thror nodded. The matter was settled.

Xavier rose, the collar and key still clutched in his hand. Ella joined him silently, her expression calm, but her eyes studied him carefully.

They left the steam behind, and in the rising haze of the lodge, the elders exchanged quiet glances. Some were filled with worry. Others, with something far rarer in times such as these… Hope that this outsider human could be the change that prophecy had spoken of.

# CHAPTER FIVE

*A Felvari's Offer and Departing Verdantspire*

The steam-laced air of the sweat lodge still clung to Xavier's skin as he stepped into the cooler breeze beyond its wooden threshold. The heavy curtain of silence from the elder council was replaced by the subtle rustle of leaves and the low murmur of Verdantspire's life returning to rhythm. He blinked against the sunlight filtering through the canopy above, taking in the soft greens and golds of the forest around them.

To his surprise, a pair of baskets sat neatly outside the lodge entrance, one for him, one for Ella. Their gear had already been gathered and prepared. Polished blades, folded clothes, neatly bundled packs. Not just efficient, but anticipatory.

Ella reached down and retrieved her satchel, tightening the strap over her shoulder. "They expected us to leave immediately," she said softly, her voice low but not surprised.

Xavier nodded. "Feels like we were gently escorted to the edge of the current."

"Or carried by it," she replied.

They dressed quickly, speaking in low tones as they re-equipped. Neither voiced the weight still lingering from the elders' meeting, but it hung there in the quiet between buckles and clasps.

Xavier cinched the last strap across his chest. "Before we head out... think we could take a quick stop through the market?"

Ella glanced at him, tilting her head slightly. "Looking for something?"

"Not sure. Maybe just... not ready to leave without seeing more of this place."

She smiled faintly. "And you wish to give Lianna more time."

He chuckled. "That too."

No more needed to be said. Without another word, they turned down the worn trail that wound back toward the heart of Verdantspire, following the scent of spices and the distant clatter of coin.

The Verdantspire market bloomed like a living tapestry as they emerged into its winding paths, woven between ancient trees and moss-covered stalls. Sunlight filtered in slanted shafts, casting dancing patterns across colorful fabrics, carved trinkets, and baskets brimming with forest produce. The air buzzed with soft bartering, chittering laughter, and the sing-song calls of vendors enticing passersby.

Xavier took it in with a quiet smile. It felt more alive than any market he'd seen, less frantic than cities back on Earth, yet no less vibrant. Here, every merchant's wares seemed curated, personal, even proud.

As he had noticed before, the majority of stalls were run by Vulpiri and Felvari. The fox-kin and cat-kin Animari moved with practiced ease, their quick gestures and sharp eyes making clear who ruled the mercantile corners of this city.

"Khajiit has wares if you have coin," Xavier murmured to himself with a smirk.

Ella raised an eyebrow, catching the whisper. "What was that?"

"Just... an old memory." He didn't elaborate. She let it pass, her eyes already drifting across the wares.

"Your armor," she said after a moment, nodding toward his chest, "has seen better days."

Xavier looked down and grimaced. Scratches, loose stitching, and a growing rent near the waist made it obvious. It had served him since the earliest days in Rynthavael, but it was cobbled together, village-made and practical—not designed for the demands he now faced.

Ella gestured toward a nearby stall shaded beneath a wide canopy of woven leaves. "That one might suit you."

The Felvari merchant's stall was a medley of gleaming trinkets, tools, and leather goods. At the center, carefully arranged on a slanted display, rested a set of armor—sleek, dark, and unmistakably refined. Xavier stepped forward, drawn by the subtle luster of its treated hide and the faint scent of wild musk still lingering in the leather.

His fingers brushed the chestpiece, and the interface flared to life.

| You have discovered: | Item Class: Rare |
|---|---|
| Direwolf Hide Chestguard | Item Quality: Superb |
| | Weight: 4.5 kg |
| | Durability: 100/100 |
| | Description: A rugged yet flexible chestguard crafted from the thick |

| | hide of a direwolf, dyed dark gray to retain a natural, stealthy appearance. The reinforced layering enhances durability while keeping the wearer agile. **Traits:** - Wolf's Resilience: Provides moderate resistance to slashing and piercing attacks due to the thick hide. - Stealthwoven: The treated leather minimizes noise when moving, making it ideal for hunters and scouts. |
|---|---|

He picked up the next piece.

| **You have discovered:** Direwolf Hide Leg Guards | **Item Class:** Rare **Item Quality:** Superb **Weight:** 3.2 kg **Durability:** 100/100 **Description:** A set of reinforced leather leg guards offering both protection and freedom of movement. The flexible knee joints allow for fluid motion, while the thick hide shields against minor impacts and environmental |
|---|---|

| | hazards.<br>**Traits:**<br>- Enhanced Mobility: Designed to provide agility without restricting movement.<br>- Cold Resistant: Retains natural insulation, protecting the wearer from cold environments. |
|---|---|

The gloves followed.

| **You have discovered:** Direwolf Hide Gloves | **Item Class:** Rare<br>**Item Quality:** Superb<br>**Weight:** 0.9 kg<br>**Durability:** 100/100<br>**Description:** A pair of fitted gloves made from supple direwolf leather, ensuring a firm grip on weapons and tools. The fingers are reinforced with extra padding for hand protection without compromising dexterity.<br>**Traits:**<br>- Hunter's Grip: Increases grip strength, making it easier to handle weapons in wet or icy conditions.<br>- Clawguard Reinforcement: The fingertips are reinforced, reducing damage |

|  | from direct impacts or abrasions. |
|---|---|

Finally, he picked up the boots.

| **You have discovered:** Direwolf Hide Boots | **Item Class:** Rare<br>**Item Quality:** Superb<br>Weight: 2.5 kg<br>**Durability:** 100/100<br>**Description:** High-quality leather boots crafted from direwolf hide, offering silent footsteps and excellent traction on uneven terrain. The soles are reinforced with a thin but sturdy hide layer for added durability.<br>**Traits:**<br>- Silent Stride: Footsteps are nearly soundless, improving stealth movement.<br>- Firm Footing: Provides better balance and grip on unstable or slippery surfaces. |
|---|---|

The final piece examined revealed a new prompt.

| **You have discovered:** Direwolf Hide Armor Set | **Item Class:** Rare<br>**Item Quality:** Superb<br>**Weight:** 11.1 kg<br>**Durability:** 100/100<br>**Description:** A |
|---|---|

masterfully crafted leather armor set made from the resilient hide of a direwolf. This armor balances protection, mobility, and stealth, making it ideal for scouts, hunters, and light-armored warriors. The treated hide retains its natural cold resistance, while expert craftsmanship ensures superb durability and flexibility. The set includes a chestguard, leg guards, gloves, and boots, each designed to enhance the wearer's agility and endurance.

**Traits:**

- Wolf's Resilience: Provides moderate resistance to slashing and piercing attacks due to the thick hide.

- Silent Hunter: Footsteps and movements

are dampened, improving stealth.
- Predator's Adaptability: Increases reaction speed and agility in combat and tracking.
- Direwolf's Endurance: Reduces stamina drain from prolonged movement or combat.

Set Bonuses, Resistances, and Stats (When All Pieces Are Worn

| Attribute | Bonus | Description |
|---|---|---|
| Slashing Resistance | +10% | Thick direwolf hide provides moderate protection against cutting weapons. |
| Piercing Resistance | +5% | Natural padding absorbs some impact from arrows and thrusting attacks. |
| Cold Resistance | +15% | Retains insulation, preventing heat loss in cold environments. |
| Impact Resistance | +5% | Some shock absorption against blunt force attacks. |
| Mobility Bonus | +10% | Lightweight and flexible, allowing for quick movement and agility. |

| | | | |
|---|---|---|---|
| Stealth Bonus | +15% | Treated leather reduces noise, enhancing sneaking capabilities. |
| Grip Strength | +5% | Reinforced gloves improve handling of weapons and tools. |
| Balance Bonus | +10% | Enhanced traction from boots allows for improved footing on rough terrain. |
| Predator's Adaptabilit y | Active Bonus | Improves reaction time and movement speed when tracking or engaging in combat. |
| Silent Hunter | Passive Bonus | Footsteps are quieter, improving stealth-based actions. |
| Direwolf's Endurance | Passive Bonus | Reduces stamina drain by 8%, useful for prolonged battles or long-distance travel. |

Xavier stared at the display with growing awe. This was no ordinary set. The craftsmanship rivaled anything he'd worn in Earth's tactical gear or even seen in games. Not just well-made. It was designed with a purpose, every stitch tailored for survival and subtlety.

"Someone really knew what they were doing," he murmured. The fact that a designed set could carry so many bonuses inherent to its crafting was astonishing. It also reinforced the fact that Xavier still understood little about the world or its crafts, something he really needed to learn more about.

Ella glanced at him. "And someone needs to learn what that means."

He chuckled under his breath. "Yeah... I've got a lot to catch up on."

The sound of softly padded steps made him pause. Xavier turned, sensing her before she fully appeared, her approach a breath of air, a whisper of movement, deliberate and silent.

The Felvari merchant stepped into view, tail flicking once in idle amusement, eyes sharp and gleaming like polished emeralds.

The game was about to begin.

#

Xavier sensed her before he saw her. A shift in the air, the quiet hush of measured footsteps, too precise to be casual and too soft to be unintentional. She moved like a whisper through the crowd, deliberate yet unhurried, the kind of presence that drew attention without asking for it.

When she stepped into view, sunlight danced across her tawny fur-like hair, catching golden streaks that shimmered like coin. Her emerald-green, slitted eyes swept over him with a sharp, knowing glint, appraising not just in coin, but in character. A slow, amused smile tugged at the corner of her lips, as if she already knew how the conversation would end.

She was dressed in flowing robes of deep purple and midnight blue. Loose enough to suggest ease, fitted enough to promise agility. A finely worked leather belt rested low on her hips, lined with neat pouches that likely held more than trinkets. Secrets, ledgers, coin... maybe all three.

Her tail flicked once in idle rhythm, betraying a hint of

amusement as she stepped closer and spoke.

"Xavier, was it?" Her voice was smooth and warm, with a lilting cadence wrapped in familiarity and soft purrs. "Nyssara hears you are a man who appreciates quality. Perhaps we should discuss an arrangement, one that benefits us both, yes?"

Firelight danced in her eyes, though no flame was near. This was a woman who never left the table with less than she came for. And somehow, she knew his name.

He blinked, then remembered the celebration. She must have been there, listening, watching.

She gestured toward the armor pieces he held, her voice slipping into a practiced rhythm that made the words feel like silk brushing against coin.

"Ah, friend, this direwolf hide leather armor, so fine and superbly crafted, yes indeed! Nyssara sees that each stitch sings of skill and care, like soft whispers 'neath the moons. The hide is both strong and supple, protecting you as the direwolf's embrace would, ja. Wear it and feel the wild power of the lands themselves guide your every step, just as a gentle purr comforts the soul. Truly, this be a treasure worthy of a wanderer such as yourself."

Xavier had to bite back a grin. The voice, the cadence, it really did remind him of the feline traders from his favorite games. For a moment, nostalgia tugged at him, and he barely managed to stop himself from chuckling.

As he composed himself, he triggered insight.

| **Name:** Nyssara Shadowwhisper | **Race:** Felvari (Feline Animari) | **Disposition:** Welcoming |
|---|---|---|
| **Level:** Unknown | **Class:** Unknown | **Active Effects:** Unknown |

| Description |
| --- |
| The Felvari, or Catkin, are a race of nimble and cunning humanoids who embody the grace, agility, and predatory instincts of felines. Their feline features include pointed ears, sharp eyes, and long, expressive tails, while their fur-like hair comes in a variety of colors and patterns—ranging from sleek black and snowy white to golden tabby and spotted leopard-like designs. Their slit-pupil eyes, which shimmer in shades of green, amber, or icy blue, grant them superior night vision, while their lithe and flexible builds allow them to move with silent precision. Felvari are naturally inquisitive, clever, and independent, thriving on personal freedom and the thrill of the hunt. Though often playful and mischievous, they are also fiercely protective of their kin and highly adaptable to their surroundings. |

| Stats | | |
| --- | --- | --- |
| **Health:** 150/150 | **Stamina:** 140/140 | **Mana:** 140/140 |

"It is an amazing set of armor," Xavier said, giving the chestguard another look. "So well done that I fear I do not have the coin to purchase it."

Nyssara's ears twitched slightly.

"Ah, friend, you have a keen eye indeed, yes? I am Nyssara, keeper o' these prized wares, purr. Feast yer gaze upon this superb direwolf hide leather armor. Each stitch sings of wild grace and skill, a marvel truly wrought by the best hands in the lands, purr. The starting price is set at sixteen hundred gold coins, a fair sum for such quality, wouldn't you say? Now, perhaps we can parley like true kin and find a number that pleases us both, yes? Do consider, friend, and let the purr of satisfaction guide yer choice."

Xavier nearly dropped the piece of armor. The number echoed in his ears like the crack of a hammer. A small fortune, if it even qualified as small.

He glanced at Ella, who didn't seem particularly surprised.

He opened his inventory and inwardly groaned. Four platinum coins and seventy gold. Nowhere near enough.

Leaning in, he whispered, "How much is a platinum coin worth?"

"One platinum is worth a hundred gold," she whispered back, her brow arching slightly. "You have platinum?"

He nodded, trying not to wince.

Neither of them noticed the subtle twitch in Nyssara's ears. Her tail gave a slow, curling flick. She had definitely heard.

As Xavier scanned his satchel again, his eyes caught the small jewelry box tucked beneath the rations. He paused, then smiled.

He met the Felvari's gaze. "Do you have somewhere we could sit and discuss trade?"

Nyssara's smile widened.

"Ah, friend," she said, stepping aside with a graceful sweep of her arm, "come inside Nyssara's booth, purr. This little nook be our private haven, where we may parley freely without pryin' eyes. Step in, and let us discuss trade in peace, purr. There's much to show... and many secrets to share."

#

Nyssara led them through a pair of hanging silk veils into a small private alcove tucked behind her stall. The air here was scented faintly with spices and incense, calmer than the noise of the market beyond. Woven rugs and low cushions surrounded a small lacquered table. She moved with feline grace to her side of the space, curling onto a mound of pillows with practiced elegance.

She gestured for them to sit. "Come, friend, make yourself comfortable, yes? Let us speak of trade in comfort and quiet, purr."

Xavier and Ella eased down across from her. The cushions were soft, and the seclusion brought an odd sense of intimacy to the negotiation. He pulled his satchel into his lap and withdrew the small wooden box, careful not to reveal its contents too quickly.

He opened it slowly, shielding the inside with his palm as he and Ella both examined the jewelry nestled within. Most were fine pieces taken from the sealed chamber deep within Rynthavael's treasury. He wasn't ready to part with anything enchanted, but after a moment of quiet discussion and subtle hand gestures with Ella, they settled on one of the simpler rings.

Xavier withdrew it and placed it gently on the table.

| You have discovered: The Golden Laurel Band | Item Class: Common Item Quality: Superb Weight: 0.14 kg Durability: 80/100 Description: A thin golden circlet designed to resemble a laurel wreath, with fine leaf engravings. Traits: A symbol |
|---|---|

| | of refinement and status, reflecting light beautifully. |
|---|---|

Nyssara's eyes narrowed slightly. She said nothing at first, but one of her ears flicked sharply. Her tail stilled.

"Ah, friend, purr, what have we here?" Her voice dropped into a low, interested hum. "This ring, though fine in craft, is quite the unexpected treasure indeed. As a merchant who holds every glint of artistry in high regard, I must inspect it closer, purr."

She extended her hand, long fingers tipped with carefully groomed nails, and Xavier gestured permission.

Nyssara rolled the ring delicately between her fingers. "Let me have a proper look at its details. Each facet may whisper a tale of its own, yes? Now, do tell me its story while I admire its gleam, purr."

Xavier smiled faintly and leaned forward, weaving a story that bore some truth but veered carefully away from the ring's true origin. He spoke of finding it on a long-dead explorer buried in the mine he had recently unearthed, leaving out any mention of the ancient vault and Sylmyrian seals.

As he spoke, Nyssara brought a jeweler's loupe to her eye, humming softly with approval. A low, instinctual purr vibrated in her chest as she studied the fine leafwork and balance of the gold.

"Ah, my friend, purr, this ring be of fine quality indeed. There is a certain... tone to the metal, yes? The craft tempts one to fancy a Sylmyrian touch. Yet let us not leap after myths, purr. The Sylmyrian, enchanting as their legends be, are naught but whispers on the wind to most."

She set the ring back on the table, eyes still sharp with

calculation. "Still, the skill here is plain for all to see. A marvel in its own right, purr."

Xavier waited. She hadn't named a value yet, and that alone told him enough.

"Ah, friend," she continued after a long moment, "this ring ye offer is a wonder of craft, no doubt. Yet its worth falls a touch short of the grandeur of this direwolf hide leather armor, purr. There is a gap, yes, a difference in value that must be bridged if we are to strike a fair bargain."

She folded her hands. "Consider the ring a worthy credit toward the armor. The balance... we may speak of."

Xavier narrowed his eyes slightly. She had praised the piece, hinted at deeper worth, and still avoided giving any numbers. Classic. He closed the box and slipped it back into his satchel, leaning back into the cushion as he let the silence hang.

"I don't know if I can cover the difference," he said, slowly. "The armor is incredible, but we have long travels ahead. Jewelry like that might be more useful to trade elsewhere."

Nyssara's tail flicked once, the only break in her stillness. Her eyes remained steady, unreadable.

"Hold, friend. Wait before you scamper off with that fine ring. Let Nyssara offer you a deal as sweet as a moonlit purr."

She leaned in, elbows resting on her knees.

"Trade the ring along with a little extra. Say, one hundred gold coins, yes? And you will walk away adorned in the glorious direwolf hide leather armor, fit for a desert wanderer and as fine as the sands of Sunspire, purr. A deal so fair, it tickles the whiskers. What say you to this bargain, hmm?"

Beside him, Ella gave a faint nod. Xavier considered a moment longer, then pulled a single platinum coin from his pouch and set it on the table beside the ring.

Nyssara's eyes gleamed as both coin and ring disappeared into a concealed pouch with practiced efficiency. She rose smoothly and disappeared behind a curtain. A moment later, she returned with the armor pieces folded and bundled.

Xavier donned the new gear with Ella's help. It fit with uncanny precision, as if crafted for him. He ran a hand along the leather and caught his reflection in the polished buckle of the chestguard. He looked like someone who belonged here now.

And as he stepped out into the market again, a soft prompt blinked across his vision.

> **Congratulations! You have learned a new skill:** Barter (Level 5)
>
> The Barter skill represents a character's ability to negotiate better deals, manipulate prices, and maximize value when dealing with merchants, traders, and sometimes even black-market dealers. A skilled haggler can reduce costs, increase payouts, and even influence merchants into revealing hidden goods or giving exclusive deals. At higher levels, Barter turns every trade into a battle of wits, persuasion, and psychological warfare. "Why pay full price when you can make them think they got a good deal?"
>
> **+0.15% Discount on purchase prices**
> **+0.15% Increase on sales prices**

That confirmed that he had done enough for the world to recognize he had some skill in bartering. He still felt that he got the short end of the deal given he was certain that the Felvari was much more skilled than he was since she was a merchant.

#

Xavier stepped back into the sunlight, adjusting the strap across his chest as he rolled his shoulders in the new armor. The direwolf hide flexed easily with his movements, offering none of the stiffness he'd come to associate with heavier leathers. Every seam felt precise, fitted, right.

Ella glanced over at him, a faint smile tugging at the corner of her mouth. "It suits you."

He gave a half-shrug. "Feels like it was made for me."

She raised an eyebrow. "Perhaps it was."

They didn't linger long. The market buzzed around them, vibrant and shifting, but they moved with a quiet purpose now. Xavier picked up several useful items as they passed the stalls, field rations wrapped in leaf-bindings, a fresh water flask, a pouch of dried herbs that Ella approved with a single nod. Nothing extravagant, just what they needed to travel light and smart.

They kept their pace steady. Time mattered now. If Lianna had finished her own business quickly, they didn't want to leave her waiting at the gate.

By the time they reached the southern edge of Verdantspire, the din of the market had faded behind them. The trees thinned slightly into a small stone plaza where the path turned southward. There, waiting near the boundary stones, stood Lianna and Frostclaw.

Lianna's gear was the same as she had worn during the raid on the slaver camp. Close-fitting dark leather armor, a tall bow slung unstrung across her back beside a quiver of fletched arrows, and a short sword strapped at her hip.

Her small travel pack sat tight against the small of her back, while Frostclaw bore the rest, several bundles lashed together with crisscrossed leather cord over the snow cat's broad shoulders.

She looked up as they approached. Her expression was flat, tired. A shadowed thing had settled behind her eyes. This was not the fiery ranger Xavier had met at first. This was someone quieter. Someone carrying weight.

Frostclaw, as if sensing her mood, growled low as the two drew near, tail flicking sharply.

Lianna placed a hand on the big cat's head. "Enough," she murmured.

The snow cat quieted instantly.

Xavier slowed, and then noticed they weren't alone.

Standing off to the side, half-turned toward the forest path, was High Speaker Kaelith Moonstride.

She stood still, her presence quiet but impossible to ignore. Her golden eyes were half-lidded but unblinking, their sharp clarity making it impossible to read her mood. She watched them approach with a patience that felt ancient, a silence that carried weight without a word spoken.

There was a stillness in Kaelith that made Xavier feel as though he were being weighed, not judged but measured. It was the quiet tension of the wild, like standing at the edge of an ancient forest and wondering whether the trees would offer shelter or shadows. She watched them with the patience of a hunter and the insight of an elder, her gaze neither cold nor warm, but discerning. A flicker of amusement touched the corner of her lips, so brief it might have been imagined... a subtle, knowing smile that hinted at truths left unspoken. Her tufted lynx ears remained still, save for the occasional twitch, a gesture that might have meant curiosity, calculation, or quiet warning. As Xavier stepped closer, he felt as if he stood on a threshold, unsure whether she saw him as kin, as quarry, or as something not yet decided.

When he stepped into speaking distance, she lifted her hand and beckoned. He came forward and dropped to one knee without hesitation. It placed him at her level, eye to eye.

Kaelith rested a hand against his cheek. Her touch was light, but the gesture was not.

"You depart now with one of ours on an important mission, Xavier of Rynthavael," she said softly. "We trust her wellbeing to your care. Especially in regard to the collar within the Wildlands."

Her fingers lingered for a moment, almost maternal. "We do not forget what you have done for us. You have returned many already. Please see our daughter back to her family safely, human. Prove to us your worth."

She withdrew her hand. "May Lir's Embrace keep you, chosen of the gods."

Xavier recalled from the discussions the previous night that the Animari referred to Danu as Liranya and he quickly made the connection between the High Speaker's words and the deity. He met her gaze with calm resolve and replied in kind.

"May her embrace shelter you as well, High Speaker. I hope to return soon with news of what transpires in the kingdom, and with more of your kin, if I can."

Kaelith gave a faint, unreadable smile. She reached out once more and patted his cheek, then stepped back without another word.

Lianna turned and walked toward the forest without so much as a glance behind her.

Kaelith lingered a moment, eyes following them, then turned and disappeared into the deeper paths of the city.

Xavier and Ella exchanged a glance, then hurried to catch up.

Lianna moved quickly, her pace brisk as she slipped into the shadowed edge of the woods. She didn't speak or look back, and Xavier sensed that was deliberate. There was weight on her shoulders, and whatever conversation she'd had before meeting them had left its mark.

He and Ella exchanged a glance before following.

As they passed beyond the southern boundary stones, the city gave way to wild growth. Moss-covered trunks and towering branches arched overhead, their canopy casting the path in shifting layers of green light and shadow. The scent of damp earth and living wood filled the air. It was a different forest than the one they'd entered days before— not in shape or space, but in how it received them.

After several quiet strides, Lianna gave a subtle hand motion. A familiar prompt shimmered at the edge of Xavier's vision.

> You have been invited to join Lianna's Party.
> Accept? [Yes] [No]

He accepted. As the prompt vanished, icons for his party reappeared, each face familiar now. Beside them, a familiar status effect bloomed.

> **Forest Runner (Active – Party Buff)**
> Movement through forest terrain is increased by 15%.
> Noise from footfalls is reduced. Party coordination

improved in woodland environments.

The change was immediate. Their steps found rhythm again, smooth and instinctive. The brush parted more easily, the undergrowth seeming to yield to their passage. Frostclaw padded ahead, his heavy steps nearly silent despite the gear lashed to his back. Lianna led without pause, bow shifting lightly with her stride, her head forward and focused.

Xavier adjusted the strap of his new armor as he moved. The direwolf leather clung comfortably to his form, flexing easily with his movements. It felt like it belonged, like he belonged.

The city of Verdantspire Haven was behind them now. The Wildlands waited ahead, but first home. They ran south, the forest closing in around them. Not as strangers, not anymore. This time, they ran as a pack.

---

[Achievement Unlocked] – Trusted by the Wild
You have earned the blessing of Verdantspire's High Speaker and gained the trust of a Verdantspire Warden. Few outsiders still walk beneath these boughs with the goodwill of the Animari. Your path forward is no longer walked alone.

Rewards:

- Reputation Increased: Verdantspire Haven (Respected)
- Relationship Boost: Lianna (Trust Deepened)

---

# CHAPTER SIX

*Revelations in the Woods*

The forest blurred past in streaks of green and shadow, branches whipping by as the trio pressed south toward Rynthavael. For a time, silence reigned. Each of them kept to their thoughts, running with practiced ease across the uneven terrain. The air was cool, carrying scents of pine, loam, and the distant trickle of water. It should have been peaceful. But Xavier could feel the tension pulsing beneath every footfall.

After nearly an hour, the need to speak overcame him.

He quickened his stride, catching up to Lianna's side. "Lianna, if you do not mind... I have questions. You know where I come from now, or at least enough of it to understand I'm still figuring all of this out. And since you've been here far longer than I have, your insight might help."

The Iskari woman slowed her pace slightly. The nature of her talent drastically slowed the consumption of stamina along with increasing speed, so none of the trio were short of breath. However, it was difficult to maintain a long conversation with the treacherous terrain and trees whipping past at such speeds. She turned her gaze slightly, and he could finally see her face for the first time since they had departed. Her eyes were bloodshot and red-rimmed, a clear indication that she had been crying while they ran. Xavier winced, seeing the woman's features, and came to a complete halt, Ella almost bounced off his back as she nearly ran into him.

"What do you want to know, human?" Lianna asked. Her tone wasn't angry or mocking, just tired... heavy with sorrow. "We must not dally. The longer we take, the more risk from Arenvalis."

"It's not the slowing or danger that's making you cry, Lianna," Xavier said quietly. "You don't have to wear the collar. If you want to go back, we can find another way into Ironhaven."

"No." Her voice cracked on the word. "You think I have not thought of that already? You think I wanted this?" Her fingers curled tightly at her sides. "The elders believed this was the best way... and I could not argue. Gods know I do not want that cursed thing back on my neck. When I wore it before, I couldn't speak out... couldn't say no, couldn't even think clearly if my owner gave a command. I was a child. I never got to play, never got to be free."

Her voice hardened, rough with remembered pain. "At least my owner did not find Animari appealing. To him, we were just labor."

She spat the words out like poison.

"But if I go into Arenvalis without a collar, it will not matter what I want. My freedom will be taken by someone else. My people are not seen as people there. We are beasts, servants..." her voice dropped, edged by a guttural growl, "slaves."

The weight of her words struck both Xavier and Ella like a blow. Even Frostclaw responded, his deep-chested growl vibrating through the earth.

Xavier, suddenly aware of his body's tension, realized his hand had rested on the hilt of Vaeltheris. Lianna's eyes flicked toward the motion, narrowing dangerously. Frostclaw moved beside her, low and menacing.

Xavier pulled back immediately, both hands raised in a placating gesture. "I wasn't thinking... I'm sorry."

Ella stepped forward quickly, matching his posture, her voice soft. "Lianna, we are not going to hurt you. Xavier wants to help, not harm. You've heard of the Animari in our village... they are free. They live, work, and laugh with everyone else. That's what Xavier wants to create more of."

Lianna's posture stayed tense, but her breathing slowed. Her sharp eyes darted between them.

"He even dislikes when I call him master," Ella continued gently. "Though I am bound to him, he finds the title offensive."

"Then why do you say it?" Lianna snapped. "You say all the right things, but your behavior makes me trust him less. You're secretive about your bond. And how convenient that you just appeared at the raider camp? We left no trail. I know that. Forest runner conceals them."

That caught Xavier's attention. He glanced over his shoulder at the path behind them. No broken branches, no trampled grass, nothing out of place. It looked untouched, as if they had never been there at all.

Ella let out a long breath. "Secrets can be dangerous, I agree. But they are not mine to give anymore. I belong to Xavier, just as his blades do. One day, he may share the truth. Until then, know that I mean you no harm. Nor does he. Not to you, not to Verdantspire, not to any Animari."

Lianna's eyes lingered on them a moment longer. Then she turned and began walking again, slightly slower this time. She didn't speak, but she didn't push them away either. It was enough.

Xavier and Ella fell in step behind her, giving her a few paces of space.

After a moment, Xavier spoke again. "Lianna, what does it really mean to be traveling companions? I got a notification when you and Ella joined me. It felt... important. Like something more than just walking together."

"It means we have goals and wants that are in common," Lianna said. "You could have hired me to guide you south to the coastal cities of Drakkenport or Velanor, and I would have traveled with you as a guard or pathfinder. In that case, we would have been traveling companions... but not travel companions. The difference is subtle but important. We would share the road, but not the purpose. No alignment of will. No true connection."

She glanced briefly at Xavier, her voice calm but thoughtful.

"The world... sometimes it sees when people are moving toward the same purpose. It recognizes that unity and gives it a name. Travel companions. It is not common. We are both more and less than party members. It is not a formal bond. Not a contract. Just an echo of shared intent. I do not know much more than that. It is rare. But you say you and Ella are companions as well?"

Xavier shrugged slightly, then gave a small nod. "We became companions early on. Long before the bond." He hesitated. That question stirred his curiosity. He hadn't checked that particular screen in his interface since the bonding... not consciously, anyway.

His eyes drifted out of focus, just enough to pull up the familiar shimmer of the UI without tripping over the uneven trail ahead. He navigated to the appropriate tab: Companions.

Both Ella and Lianna were listed there, their names framed with faint silver borders. He could see some basic data... class designations, current levels, health and stamina bars, maybe a rough outline of general stats. No attributes, no skills. He assumed that was normal. Maybe even a limitation of whatever ranked access he had to their profiles.

"Yes," he confirmed aloud. "You're both on the list. So... even the interface sees you as more than just fellow travelers." He turned to glance at Ella and added, "See? You're more than just my bonded. You're still listed as my companion. At the very least."

Ella gave him a sidelong look and rolled her eyes slightly, though a faint smile tugged at the corners of her lips. She already knew that, of course. Xavier appeared on her list as well. But she had access to more details... deeper insights into the bond they shared due to Vaeltheris, things she wouldn't voice aloud with others nearby. Not yet.

Maybe, she mused, she would tell him more when they made camp. When the fire was lit, and Lianna had drifted off to sleep... when the shadows deepened and secrets could be spoken more freely. Their turn at watch might be the right time. She would know soon.

Xavier broached the next topic carefully. He already knew how volatile it could be, but he needed to ask. The more he understood now, the better he could plan their path forward.

"Is wearing that collar going to be an issue, Lianna?" he asked, voice low. "I don't want to force you into anything. It's obvious how much it bothers you."

The feline woman's shoulders slumped, her ears flicking

in discomfort. "I know you are an outsider," she said slowly, "but surely you had slavery where you came from."

She turned her head just enough to glance at him. Xavier nodded, sadness flashing in his eyes. She continued, her tone flat and subdued.

"It is not just a plain piece of metal. That thing is a bastardization of the old mage-control collars, the kind created after the Magewar Reckoning. It doesn't only mark you as a slave... it controls you. It binds your will. Whatever orders or limits are set when it's placed... the wearer has no choice but to obey them."

She paused, her voice catching slightly.

"That's why I had no freedom as a child. None. I have to trust that you will not place restraints on me again."

Her final words were whispered, barely audible, but heavy with the weight of old pain and fear.

Xavier remained silent for a moment, absorbing what she'd just said. Her words revealed more than she likely intended, and certainly more than he had known. The Magewar Reckoning? Collars for controlling mages? Were all mages enslaved at some point? Or still? The image of the raider mage flickered through his mind, the one with the metal ring around his neck.

Reaching into his satchel, Xavier pulled out the dark collar. "You got me this off that caster from the raiders," he said. "Does that mean this is a slave collar too?"

Lianna didn't recoil from the object the way she had when speaking of her own. Her eyes rested on it with recognition, not revulsion. Xavier noted the difference. It wasn't just the absence of personal trauma... there was something more.

"That is both true and untrue," she replied, her voice

more composed now. "A veyhn'shaar is a slave collar in the sense that it controls and limits mages. But if you place it on someone without magic, it is just a ring of metal. Nothing more. It does nothing to the bearer."

She looked at it again, a faint frown pulling at her lips.

"Most people don't even call them that anymore. Veyhn'shaar, I mean. The name is old. Now they're just called sealrings, or voidbands. Tools, nothing else. But drekh'tar, the true slave collars... those affect anyone. Mage or not. They don't suppress magic like the sealrings do, but in every other way, they're the same. Chains for the mind, not the body."

She shook her head slightly. "Why the sealrings only work on mages, I do not know. That's beyond my knowledge, and honestly... beyond what I care to understand."

They continued walking as she spoke, and her tone grew steadier with each step. The subject still sat heavy between them, but it no longer dragged like a weight behind her words.

Xavier wanted to keep her grounded in conversation, to keep her thoughts from circling back to the collar and its return. But more than that, he needed her to know, without question, that she had nothing to fear from him.

"I told the elders already, and I'll tell you again. If we go through with the disguise, I will place no restrictions on you. None. This is not about control, Lianna. It's about protecting you while we travel through hostile lands. That is all. I'm trusting you to walk beside me... and I hope you'll trust me in return."

Lianna said nothing for a moment. Her expression was unreadable, her pace steady.

"Time will tell, human," she replied at last. "Time will tell."

Without further word, she broke into a run once more, weaving between trees with the fluid grace of a predator born to the wilds. Frostclaw bounded alongside her, silent and sure-footed.

Xavier and Ella exchanged a glance, then pushed off the ground to follow. The forest swallowed their words, but not their resolve.

They ran together, for now. That was enough.

#

Night fell gently over the forest, shadows lengthening into a soft hush as the trees swayed in the growing breeze. The trio had traveled well past dusk before finding a small clearing, sheltered and dry, tucked between two moss-covered ridges. Frostclaw had guided them around several predators along the way, one a bear, the other a hulking green-skinned creature with arms long enough to scrape the forest floor. Whatever it was, they had no desire to confront it.

As Ella and Lianna gathered dry wood from the edges of the clearing, Xavier sat in the center, nearly giddy with anticipation. He had waited all day to try the rune he had discovered at the raider camp. His fingers tingled as he pulled up the interface and focused on the entry now listed in his interface.

---

**You have learned a new Rune**: Alarm

- **Level:** 1
- **Rank:** 1
- **School:** Air (Zephira) & Life (Vitalora)
- **Casting Time:** 1 minute

---

- **Range:** 30 feet
- **Duration:** 8 hours
- **Components:** V, S, M (a small silver thread or engraved rune stone)
- **Effect:** Inscribes a protective rune in a 20-foot radius, alerting the caster when an unauthorized entity enters the area.
- **Alert Options:**
  - **Audible Alarm:** A loud chime or ringing within the area.
  - **Mental Ping:** A silent alert to the caster (within 1 mile).
- **Rune Appearance:** Faint glowing glyphs, pulsing with soft sky-blue (Air) or golden-green (Life) energy.
- **Usage:** Commonly used for securing camps, doors, and hidden pathways against intruders.

Their camp was small, and the 20-foot radius would cover everything comfortably. It was no substitute for vigilance, but it added a layer of protection. He now understood why the raider mage had carried so many silver threads. At the time it had seemed odd... but now he knew they were material components.

So that mage had been a runecrafter too... or could all mages use runes? Was his crafting skill a parallel system, or something entirely separate?

He shook his head fiercely before going off down a rabbit hole he was unlikely to emerge from, especially since he knew next to nothing about runecrafting or magic. He had no answers. Not yet.

Drawing in a breath, he focused. A faint shimmer sparked on the ground before him, lines of golden-green light forming into a translucent glyph. The sight made his pulse quicken. It was the same rune he had seen back at the camp.

Instinctively, he reached for one of the silver threads and began tracing the pattern over the glowing sigil. As he worked, a string of words poured from his lips, foreign, untranslatable, and heavy with power. The final strand vanished into the mark, and the rune flared once, then settled into a dim, moss-toned glow that barely stood out from the forest floor.

He had done it. He had laid his first rune.

"May the world tremble," he said, eyes wide with exhilaration.

The rune shrieked. A loud clanging sound burst through the clearing, like metal struck against metal in furious rhythm. Xavier winced, clapping his hands over his ears just as Ella and Lianna emerged from the tree line, their arms full of firewood and their expressions thunderous.

"Sorry! Sorry!" he called out, dismissing the rune in a rush. The glyph flickered once, then vanished.

Both women gave him looks that could peel bark off trees.

"May the world tremble..." he muttered to himself again forlornly, and much more quietly this time, "...just not so loudly."

Reviewing the interface again, he noticed the alert options, something he had entirely missed in his eagerness. With a frustrated sigh, he reselected the rune and started the process again, this time adjusting for a mental ping rather than an audible one. He also marked it to exclude party members and their minions from triggering it.

The changes altered the glyph's lines slightly, the pattern shifting with more intricate curves. He traced it once more, his voice calmer, more confident this time. The rune settled with a muted, golden shimmer that vanished almost completely in the grass.

Satisfied at last, Xavier looked up as Ella and Lianna finished arranging the firewood. A quiet meal followed, crunchy travel bread, salted meat, and hard cheese. Simple, but filling.

As they ate, they planned out watches for the night. Xavier would take the first, Ella the second, and Lianna the final. Frostclaw, ever alert, would assist throughout the night without a formal shift.

Once the fire burned low, Lianna curled up near Frostclaw on the far side of the flames, drawing her cloak close and resting with practiced stillness. Her breathing slowed. She seemed asleep.

Xavier and Ella remained beside the fire, the warmth flickering across their faces as they shared quiet words about the journey so far. Xavier recounted what he had found in the mines beneath Rynthavael and his unfinished exploration of them. Eventually, his thoughts turned to something she had said days ago, something that still haunted him.

He leaned closer, speaking low. "All right. I think she's asleep. Now tell me... what do you mean you are Vaeltheris? That's kind of a big bombshell to drop on someone."

Ella blinked at him, tilting her head slightly. She still did not fully grasp all his euphemisms, but she understood the demand.

"It is... complicated," she said. "I am the sentience of the blade, but not only that. The blade holds the last memories and souls of the Sylmyrian people. That gives it a sort of awareness. I awoke one day holding it, about 20 or 30 years ago... quite frankly I lost count."

She paused, watching the firelight flicker in his eyes.

"Vaeltheris... the blade... it realized it was trapped. Alone, so eventually it gave birth to me. Not in a way you would call natural, but in the way of creation born from need. I am its echo, its daughter, perhaps its will given flesh. That is why I feel what it feels, and it feels what I do. We are linked. When you bonded to it, you bound me as well."

She looked down at her hands, flexing her fingers slowly.

"That is also why I cannot wield it. Except in its smallest form in self defense. I cannot carry it into battle. Wherever it goes, I may follow... and in moments of need, I can appear near it. Like I did when you died."

Xavier sat in stunned silence, staring at her.

Across the clearing, Lianna's breathing remained steady. But one of her ears had subtly turned backward, angled toward them.

At last, Xavier spoke. "I get why you kept it hidden. That's what you meant, isn't it? About the secrets not being yours anymore. Because now they're mine."

Ella gave a soft smile and nodded. "Yes, Master. Now that you have bound Vaeltheris, nothing can remain hidden from you."

She hesitated, then continued, her voice gentling. "Aelriva once spoke to me of a prophecy... before the fall of Sylmyria. We believe it speaks of the one who bears the mark of Syr'Vailen... the one who will carry Vaeltheris, and restore what was lost."

Her voice took on a rhythmic cadence, not quite song, not quite chant, as she recited:

"When the heavens burn and the earth does sigh,

A mark long forgotten shall pierce the sky.
From the ruins of ages buried deep,
A herald shall wake from an ancient sleep.

Bound by chains yet fated to free,
The weary, the lost, the enslaved, the plea.
With shadow and flame their path shall blaze,
Through trials of darkness and blinding haze.

Balance calls from the fractured core,
Where power slept in the times of yore.
The gods shall waver, their thrones shall shake,
As the chosen rises for justice's sake.

Beware the path of riddles and strife,
For truth lies tangled with death and life.
By will alone the course is set,
For the marked one holds the cosmos' debt.

An ancient bond, a world to mend,
The age-long cycles shall find their end.
Through trial and fire, the chains shall break,
And the gods' dominion the earth shall quake."

As her voice faded, the fire seemed quieter. Even the forest seemed to lean in around them.

Xavier stared at the embers. He said nothing at first. Then, finally, in a voice quiet with realization, he murmured, "So I'm not just some random pick after all. Danu's been playing the long game."

His fists clenched slightly. It felt too deliberate. Too guided. He thought back to what Danu had told him after his resurrection... about fate and freedom.

Fate is destined to happen. Who fulfills it is not known. If not you, someone else, days or even centuries from now, might be the one. You make your own choices. And if they fulfill what is to be... then you are the one.

At the time, it reminded him of something from a movie back home. Something about spoons not being real. But now it felt like a lifeline.

He would choose. He would act, and the world could deal with it.

The rest of Xavier's watch passed in silence. After their conversation, Ella lay down beside the fire, curling into her own blankets, and was soon breathing evenly, asleep. Frostclaw shifted only slightly on the far side of the clearing, lifting his head from time to time to glance at Xavier, then turning his attention outward toward the forest. Nothing stirred beyond the usual rustle of nocturnal life, bats flitting overhead, small animals scurrying through brush, the whisper of wind weaving through the trees. The wilds were calm tonight.

When his time came to rest, Xavier leaned over and gently shook Ella awake. She stirred, rubbing her eyes, and nodded as he stood, stepping away from the fire. Without a word, he settled into his own bedroll, the warmth of the embers still flickering against his back as sleep slowly took him.

#

Xavier stirred awake to the faint rustling of leaves and the low, steady rhythm of breathing. The fire had burned low, reduced to glowing coals that pulsed gently in the quiet morning. A chill clung to the clearing, heavy with dew and the scent of moss and damp bark.

He rubbed the crust of sleep from his eyes and pushed himself up to sit.

Lianna was watching him.

She sat across the fire, her arms resting loosely around her knees, her expression unreadable. Her sharp golden eyes met his for a moment, then shifted away without a word. Slowly, they drifted toward Ella, still bundled in her blankets nearby.

Xavier frowned slightly, pulling his pack closer as he moved to sit beside the fire. He didn't press her at first. He just started digging through his supplies, fingers brushing over the familiar textures of waxed cloth and dried food until he found what he was looking for.

"Something bothering you, Lianna?" he asked without looking up. "You seem tense this morning."

"I am fine," she replied, clipped and cold.

The words rang hollow.

He didn't argue. Whatever was brewing inside her, she wasn't ready to say it. He simply nodded to himself and pulled out enough food for the three of them, hard tack, a few pieces of dried fruit, and the last wedge of smoked meat.

Ella stirred as he leaned over and nudged her shoulder. She blinked once, then sat up slowly, brushing hair from her face. He handed her a portion of the food, then divided the rest between himself and Lianna.

Lianna took the meal without comment. She didn't thank him. She didn't meet his gaze. She chewed in silence, her movements precise and minimal, every motion controlled.

The rest of the camp was struck with equal quiet efficiency. Bedrolls packed. Ash scattered. No words spoken beyond what was necessary.

When they set off again, the silence remained unbroken.

Frostclaw took the lead, as always, his presence a comfort. Xavier focused on the rhythm of his steps, the steady beat of boots against earth, and the rustle of undergrowth as they wove through the trees. The morning passed uneventfully. No signs of danger, no beast, only forest sounds and filtered light above.

Then, just past midday, Lianna stopped. Without warning, she spun to face them, her hand resting on the hilt of her sword. "There is no way she is your sword," she hissed. "That is impossible. What else are you lying about? How did you fool the elders into trusting you?"

Xavier halted, stunned by the sudden outburst. He raised both hands instinctively, more confused than alarmed. "What are you talking about?" he asked. "Lianna... have you lost your mind? I know the thought of the collar scares you, but this is a new way to try and get out of it."

Ella came to a sharp stop beside him, her hand drifting to her bow. Her posture was defensive, not aggressive, but her eyes were wide with fear. Fear that the truth she had tried to hide was now a blade at Xavier's throat.

"I heard you two talking last night," Lianna snarled. Frostclaw stepped into place beside her, muscles tense, another low growl building in his throat. "I do not know what game you are playing, but I am not a fool. You must have tricked the elders... maybe even the truth steam. You lured me out here to what? Enslave me? Sell me to Ironhaven for favor?"

"For the gods' sake, Lianna," Xavier snapped, "can you not see that I don't want that? I told you, you could go back to Verdantspire if this was too much. Why would I offer you a way out if I planned to betray you?"

His hand went to his satchel, and he yanked out the collar, the same one she had worn in captivity. Without ceremony, he tossed it to the ground between them.

"Take the gods-be-damned thing and throw it away. It's

clear the plan of you going in disguise will not work. Ella and I will go to Ironhaven on our own. We'll figure it out without you."

While Xavier spoke, Ella stepped quietly to his side. Her eyes were calm now, her movements steady. Before either of them could react, she reached to his belt, drew Vaeltheris from its sheath, and held it flat across her palms. The metal gleamed in the scattered forest light.

"I do not expect you to trust me," Ella said, voice clear and unwavering. "There is no bond between us. But I am Xavier's companion, just as you are. And if you will not believe words... then I will show you, this is the only way I can think of to prove to you that he is not lying about me at least. I am Ella Bree Vael. In the tongue of a long dead people Vael meant blade. I was born of this blade just as you were born of your mother. I am the maiden of the blade."

She closed her eyes and light began to shimmer along her arms, moving from the blade into her hands. The glow traveled up her skin in golden filaments, pulsing with quiet rhythm. Her body began to lose cohesion, turning translucent, her form unraveling like mist drawn into the blade, and then, in silence, she vanished. Vaeltheris dropped to the forest floor with a soft clatter.

Both Xavier and Lianna stared.

He was the first to move, rushing forward to scoop up the blade, calling Ella's name in alarm. There was no response. No shimmer of magic. No voice. Just the cold weight of Vaeltheris in his hands.

Lianna could only stare, her mouth slightly parted. Her hand had left her sword. Frostclaw no longer growled.

They searched the clearing for a sign of her, calling her name, scouring the trees, but there was nothing. Ten minutes passed. Then, without warning, a soft golden glow appeared at Xavier's side.

Ella reformed slowly, the light coalescing into her shape like mist rising from dew. She looked tired, but her smile was gentle.

"It is not easy for me to do that," she said quietly. "It takes time to return. When I came to you from the village... I was drawn by the feeling of your death. That urgency gave me strength. Normally, I return to the blade, and it takes much longer to emerge again. I cannot die, not in the way others can. I will always return... so long as the blade exists, and so long as it is bound to your soul."

Lianna looked at her. Then at Xavier. Then back again. She had been so certain that the conversation she had overheard was just lies. All humans lied, even this one. She knew that to her core, but he had saved some of her people from the raiders. He had been respectful of her and her brother. He had died to save her people; she saw the mark of the Kael'Sharyn appear on his chest. He was god-touched. If she was wrong about Ella and Vaeltheris, could she be wrong about him as well. Her turmoil only grew as fear and loathing that had dominated her childhood and youth battled with what was right before.

Doubt warred with conviction inside her. Fear wrestled with fragile hope for him to be true. Everything she had known, everything she had believed about humans and their manipulations, shuddered under the weight of what she had just seen.

It was ultimately too much. Her body trembled, her knees buckled, and without a word, her eyes rolled back, and she collapsed into unconsciousness.

# CHAPTER SEVEN
*Decisions in Rynthavael*

As the Iskari collapsed towards the ground Xavier rushed forward and caught her guiding her down gently instead of letting her fall. Lianna's body was limp in Xavier's arms as he knelt guiding her gently to the forest floor. Her skin felt clammy beneath his touch; her breath shallow but steady. Frostclaw surged forward with a low, guttural growl that sent a ripple of tension through the trees, but the great cat halted when he saw Xavier was not harming her. His ears flicked, nostrils flaring as he scented the air, then let out a quiet chuff and padded close, settling protectively beside his fallen companion.

Ella crouched down beside them, her voice low and calm. "It is not injury or illness. This was something deeper. A wound of the spirit, not the body."

Xavier nodded quietly, brushing a strand of hair from Lianna's face. "I saw it in her eyes before she fell. Everything she believed... it cracked."

There was no need to say more. The two of them understood what had happened. Her hatred had been a shield for years, maybe her whole life. Seeing Xavier act against everything she expected of humans, risking his life for Animari, bearing a divine mark, traveling with someone like Ella, had torn a rift through the convictions she'd held onto like armor. Her body had simply followed the break in her mind.

They didn't speak much after that. Instead, they worked in quiet efficiency to make a resting spot. Xavier cleared a patch beneath the largest of the nearby trees while Ella unrolled a blanket and set a shallow stone bowl with fresh water near Lianna's side. The fire was kept low, just enough for warmth. They shared hardtack and cheese from their stores, chewing in companionable silence, both keeping one eye on the sleeping Iskari and the other on the dimming forest beyond.

When she stirred, it was gradual. A twitch of her ears. A flutter behind closed lids. Then her eyes blinked open, disoriented at first, catching sight of the canopy overhead before her gaze drifted down to find the two humans sitting nearby.

Ella offered a gentle smile. Xavier extended a hand with a piece of travel bread.

"You should eat," he said, voice even and without pressure. "We figured this was as good a place as any to rest. We can move on once you're ready."

Lianna sat up slowly. Her expression was guarded, but not hostile. She accepted the bread and nodded in thanks. Frostclaw remained close, his tail thumping once as she reached over to scratch the ruff beneath his chin.

Her silence lingered, but Xavier didn't press her for words. He could see the war still waging behind her eyes... old truths grappling with new revelations. The flicker of pain in her gaze was joined by something else now. Not trust, not yet, but something that could become it... Hope.

They rested a little longer, then began their journey toward Rynthavael once more. They traveled in silence for some time, the hush between them not uncomfortable, but reflective. The path was familiar, and with Lianna once again setting the pace, their progress was swift. Her movements were fluid, efficient, but there was something slightly more restrained about her now, less edge in her stride, more thought behind her glances toward Xavier and Ella.

Even Frostclaw seemed to sense the shift. He no longer kept himself between Lianna and the others, instead ranging a little ahead, ears alert and tail flicking with quiet confidence.

The hours passed beneath the whispering trees, the golden light of afternoon bleeding slowly into amber. Just as the sun dipped toward the treetops, Xavier caught the first whiff of smoke, and he slowed.

Ella did too, her gaze sharpening as they came around the final bend that opened onto the small rise overlooking Rynthavael. The forest parted ahead, revealing the village nestled in its sheltered valley.

There was far more smoke than he remembered.

Xavier's heart tightened. He leaned forward instinctively, scanning for flames, destruction, any sign of an attack. But as the view cleared, his breath caught for a different reason.

The village was intact. More than that it was alive.

Structures stood where before there had been only foundations. Scaffolding rose around new buildings, and dozens of figures moved through the central square, hauling materials, guiding animals, exchanging goods. Children darted between them, laughter echoing faintly across the trees.

"There were only fifty people when we left," he murmured.

Ella stepped beside him, her expression unreadable. "It was not like this before. The air feels heavier... more rooted. There is urgency here now. Purpose."

Xavier nodded, his thoughts racing. Growth was good. Growth meant progress. But it also meant exposure, and if Arenvalis truly stirred...

No. He shoved the thought aside. He would face it when he had to.

Together, the three of them descended the hill and began the walk toward the heart of the village.

#

As they walked, a flicker of pale green light burst to life beside Xavier's shoulder. Aelriva materialized in a pulse of ley-touched energy, her wings casting shimmering glints in the air.

"Tis good ye have returned, Ard'Maelor," she greeted him, voice lilting but solemn. "Yet I bear grim tidings. It seems the Kingdom of Arenvalis stirs from its slumber, growing ever more fierce toward its neighbors. Refugees have been pouring in, seeking the haven of Bramblegate and the river's bounty from their docks. But upon finding the village in ruins, they turned their steps deep into the forest. Thy modest band of hunters and scouts have discovered them and brought them hither. Many linger still, their hearts buoyed by tales of thy deeds in Bramblegate, hopeful that ye might grant them shelter and protection in these troubled times."

Xavier managed, just barely, not to startle at her sudden arrival. He kept walking, focusing instead on her words. Growth was necessary. He needed people to meet the requirements for leveling the settlement. However, he had hoped for something more deliberate, more planned.

Refugees could bring unrest and uncertainty. He'd seen enough stories back on Earth to know how fragile things could become when need outpaced resources.

Still, he couldn't turn them away.

Sighing quietly, he turned to the sprite. "How many new people do we have now, Aelriva?"

"Nearly a hundred souls have come to these lands," she answered, wings slowing as her tone shifted. "Some journeyed further down the river, seeking refuge in the south behind the protective embrace of forest and mountain. A desperate bid to escape the shadow of Arenvalis. Yet sixty-eight have chosen to remain, their numbers comprising thirty-two humans, twelve dwarves, ten halflings, six gnomes, six Animari, and two Gan Ceann. By fortune's grace, one among these carries the Vocation of Builder, whose skilled hands have swiftly advanced the work of crafting new homes for all who now call Rynthavael their sanctuary. Thus, our fledgling community grows ever stronger with each passing day."

Xavier caught the deliberate stress she placed on the word "vocation." Another new system to understand. He glanced toward her, frowning slightly.

"Okay. I know about gathering and crafting archetypes and subclasses. What's the importance of a vocation?"

Aelriva smiled, the change in her demeanor immediate. Her tone took on the familiar cadence of an instructor. "Listen well, Ard'Maelor. The path of a vocation is not akin to the simple art of gathering or crafting, which are but the common archetypes and subclasses of trade. A vocation is a higher calling, a mark of true mastery and dedication. To be recognized in such a way, ye must reach a personal level of fifteen so as to achieve thy subclass, and hone thy skills to at least that of a mid-journeyman, or level thirty in the requisite arts. Only then may ye stand before the great capitals and major cities to be certified in thy chosen vocation, unlocking talents and abilities far beyond the mundane. These specialized talents are what set thee apart, allowing thy craft to blossom into something extraordinary. So, take heed. If ye desire to wield true power in thy art, strive for the path of a vocation. For therein lies the promise of greatness."

Xavier nodded slowly. Another notch added to the ever-growing list of things to study and understand. "Right. So crafting archetypes and subclasses give skills and bonuses to individuals... like how my Rune Engraver subclass gave me the ability to decipher and channel runes. But didn't we already have a stonemason and carpenter building houses?"

He recalled their mention of limitations, basic structures, no blueprints, buildings without levels.

"Aye," Aelriva said, her wings sweeping in a slow arc. "Behold the fruits of their labor. Orrik and Rhett have been organizing and constructing homes and shops throughout the village. Yet it is Sorin Ravenna, the certified Builder, whose skilled oversight quickens our work as if touched by magic. The other carpenters and stoneworkers have taken her lead, transforming the old builder's hut into a proper workshop in but a short time. Now, cast thine eyes upon thy interface and see for thyself. Several grander buildings stand complete or near completion, gathered around the sturdy stone edifice of Hearthstead Hall, which shall one day serve as the town hall of our burgeoning village. Meanwhile, frameworks for smaller structures rise near the forge, heralding the promise of further growth. Truly, the difference under her guidance is as clear as day."

Xavier opened his interface with a thought. The village tab expanded across his vision, overlaying transparent information just above the path as they walked.

| Building Name | Quality | HP | Level | Material | Capacity |
|---|---|---|---|---|---|
| House 1–5 | Above Average | 300 | 1 | Stone & Wood | 1 Family each |
| House 6 | Superb | 400 | 1 | Stone & Wood | 1 Family |
| House 7 | Above Average | 300 | 1 | Stone & Wood | 1 Family |
| House 8 | Well Crafted | 350 | 1 | Stone & Wood | 1 Family |
| Lodge 1 | Well Crafted | 600 | 1 | Stone & Wood | Up to 30 Individuals |
| Lodge 2 | Superb | 700 | 1 | Stone & Wood | Up to 30 Individuals |
| Workshop | Above Average | 500 | 1 | Stone & Wood | N/A |
| Tradesman's Shops 1–5 | Varies | 450 – 600 | 1 | Stone & Wood | N/A (all incomplete) |
| Hearthstead Hall (Incomplet | Well Crafted | 1200 | 1 | Quarried Stone | N/A |

| e) | | | | | |
|---|---|---|---|---|---|
| Great Forge | Superb | 1500 | 1 | Quarried Stone | Up to 15 Individuals |

He blinked, letting the overlay fade. Just weeks ago, Rynthavael had been a ruin of moss-covered stone and forgotten pathways. Now... it was a living thing.

He turned to Aelriva, voice quiet but resolute. "Gather Braegor, Orrik, Rhett, this new Builder...Sorin, and Captain Coren. Also, anyone else you think might offer insight. Bring them to the Syr'Vailen. We need to discuss the threat from the north... and how to stand against it."

Aelriva bowed midair and vanished in a whisper of motes.

He had only just continued along the village path when a shape slipped from the brush, dark, sleek, and silent. Valkra emerged with quiet confidence, tail flicking as she approached.

Lianna halted mid-step. Her eyes widened, and a quiet gasp escaped her lips. "Is that...?"

Before Xavier could answer, she dropped to her knees in the dirt. "A shadowmane," she whispered, awe threading her voice. "You said you had rescued one, but I thought... I didn't think she'd still be so small."

Valkra padded closer, sniffing at Lianna's outstretched hand. The Iskari ranger remained still, letting the cub choose. After a moment, Valkra pressed her head into Lianna's palm with a soft rumble.

Lianna laughed, a sound filled with wonder rather than joy. "She's beautiful."

Frostclaw padded forward as well, his steps heavy but calm. He lowered his great head and touched noses with the cub. Valkra chirped, tails curling, then rolled onto her back, exposing her belly to the larger snow leopard in a clear display of affection and trust.

"She trusts him," Lianna said softly, fingers brushing Valkra's flank. "That is not something a shadowmane does lightly."

Xavier watched her, watched the way her shoulders softened, the wall behind her eyes thinning just a little more. It wasn't peace, not yet. But it was a start, and he would protect that, whatever it took.

#

The reunion with Valkra gave way to a quiet, steady rhythm as they made their way deeper into the heart of the village. The cub nestled contentedly in Lianna's arms, purring softly, her head resting against the Iskari's shoulder. Frostclaw padded beside her, occasionally glancing at the smaller cat with something almost paternal in his eyes.

They passed newly completed homes, framework for shops, and rising beams where walls were still being set. Villagers moved through the paths with purpose, many stopping to offer nods or a few quiet words as Xavier passed. Some were new—part of the refugee influx—but others he recognized from the earliest days of Rynthavael. He returned every greeting, watching the rhythms of a place growing into something more than just shelter.

Soon, they reached the central plaza, where the solid stone form of Hearthstead Hall rose from its foundation. Once the only usable structure among the ruins, it had served as their first refuge, a place of warmth and rest when everything else was wild. Now, its frame had been reinforced and expanded. Quarried stone strengthened its base, and scaffolding framed out additions that would one day make it the village's true heart.

Inside, the air shifted. Lanterns flickered in their sconces, casting soft light over newly laid beams and stonework. At the far end of the hall, behind where the hearth would soon be rebuilt, a stairwell led down beneath the structure, cut stone descending into the earth below.

They followed it down into the Warrens.

The temperature dropped as they descended. The passage led into a vast network of tunnels and chambers carved beneath Rynthavael. Though still partially under restoration, many paths had been stabilized and mapped. The walls bore signs of recent reinforcement, with timber supports and rune-marked guide stones indicating safer routes.

They passed storage alcoves, hollowed chambers prepared for future expansion, and narrow corridors that twisted into unknown darkness, but Xavier guided them with certainty. He knew where they were going.

Eventually, the main path widened and began to slope gently downward. Here, the air felt different, charged and purposeful. The tunnel opened into a vaulted chamber deep beneath the village. Stone pillars ringed the room, and at its center, embedded into the floor, was the mosaic.

Eightfold in design, it formed a circular emblem of interlocking leyline sigils. Two of the paths glowed softly, one with radiant golden-green light that pulsed like a heartbeat, the other with deep violet threaded in pale silver that shimmered like starlight on water.

The Life and Death ley lines. Awakened. Alive.

The six remaining paths remained inert, their forms

beautifully etched into the stone... Fire's jagged arcs, Earth's heavy rings, Air's spiraling runes, Water's flowing lines, and the subtle latticework of Light and Dark, but they held no glow, no motion. Not yet.

Lianna stepped into the chamber and froze.

Her eyes swept across the floor, breath catching as she turned slowly in place. "This is a nexus," she whispered, awestruck. "But not like Verdantspire. This feels deeper... older."

Xavier said nothing. He let her absorb it.

"No one ever spoke of this," she said. "Not in the halls. Not in the old tales. I never imagined something like this could be so close... and hidden."

"You weren't meant to know," Ella replied softly. "The knowledge was buried. Lost... or hidden for a reason."

Before Lianna could answer, the echo of footsteps drifted through the tunnel behind them. One by one, the others began to arrive.

Braegor appeared first, his head cradled beneath one arm, boots loud against the stone. Orrik and Rhett followed close behind, still marked with sawdust and grit. A tall human woman came next, expression sharp and eyes alert beneath the weight of her builder's harness... Sorin. Then came Captain Coren, his armor burnished and ready, and finally Amara, quiet as always, her bow slung and her expression already fixed on the Iskari newcomer.

A few others joined at the edge of the chamber... villagers who had heard whispers and followed them down, drawn by tension and curiosity.

They settled in a loose semicircle around the mosaic. The leyline hum beneath their feet lent the room a steady, grounding rhythm, one that seemed to hush voices before they could rise too high.

Xavier stepped forward, positioning himself at the mosaic's edge. Vaeltheris rested against his hip, silent. He did not draw it.

"You all know why I've called you here," he said. "You've seen the changes in the village. You've heard the rumors, and now, you've seen one of the reasons why."

He turned toward Lianna, who stepped forward at his gesture. Valkra remained curled in her arms, purring faintly. Frostclaw followed her like a silent warden.

"This is Lianna. A Warden of Verdantspire Haven. While I was away, I met her people. Their elders asked for help. Together, we freed some of their kin from the same kind of slavers that once raided Bramblegate."

The effect was immediate. A low rumble spread through the crowd. Shouts followed... anger, grief, raw fury as old wounds were pulled open. Voices rose sharply, echoing off the stone.

Xavier raised his hand and waited until the sound died.

"Arenvalis won't stop with Verdantspire," he said. "If refugees are already coming here, it means their reach is growing. We all know if they find us, they will come for them, and for all of us."

He paused, then continued. "I've agreed to the High Speaker's request to travel into the Wildlands and uncover what's changed. Why this aggression has spread. Why Animari are being targeted. Why the Kingdom grows bolder with each passing day."

His gaze swept across the group.

"We may be deep in the forest, but our only defense is that they don't know we exist. That won't last. We have to prepare. Before it is too late."

Silence settled briefly in the mosaic chamber, broken only by the soft hum of the leylines beneath their feet. Then Coren stepped forward.

The former soldier's voice was firm, low, and unshaken. "We need defenses, my lord. As you say, they do not know of us yet, but if they begin sweeping the woods, it is only a matter of time before they find us."

He gestured toward Sorin, who stood with arms crossed, listening intently. "With her help, we can build properly. Walls, trenches, towers. Enough to slow any force long enough for us to respond. I will also start formal training. We have enough able bodies now to form a standing guard."

He looked at Xavier. "Some of the refugees were guards before. Soldiers, too. By your leave, I will begin working with them immediately."

Xavier met his gaze and nodded. "See it done. Work with Braegor to get what you need."

He turned to the Gan Ceann smith, who stood nearby with arms folded holding his head on which one thick brow raised.

"I know you'd rather focus on your forge, but I still need you coordinating village needs for now. I haven't found someone else for the alderman's, or I suppose it would now be called the steward's, seat yet."

Braegor lifted his head, still tucked beneath his arm, and gave a deep, gravelly chuckle. "As you wish, Lord Vael. We have more smiths now, thanks to the refugees. Tools are being made. I can shift most of them toward outfitting Coren's new recruits. But we'll need more raw materials soon."

Xavier's reply came with a slight smile. "You're in luck. I found a mine, two days north. It's not fully mapped, and there's a stone bridge inside you should not cross. I was attacked by spiders past that point. But the mine before that seems safe. Send guards with the miners and keep them clear of the lower reaches."

Both men nodded in quiet agreement, and Xavier's attention shifted again.

Amara stepped forward from the edge of the crowd. Her voice, though calm, carried a sharp undercurrent. "Can we expect help from Verdantspire? We're still small, barely in the hundreds if you count our children and elders. If something comes while you're gone, I am not sure we could hold."

Xavier didn't hesitate. "Verdantspire has agreed to send rangers to patrol the woods around us. They'll help keep the beasts down and watch for intruders."

Lianna stepped beside him, speaking before anyone could ask. "Their scouts are already in motion. You can expect them within a day or two. The elders move quietly, but they do not delay when threats grow near."

Coren gave her a measured nod. "We will watch for them and make sure they are not mistaken for enemies."

Braegor grunted. "If they're anything like this Warden, I imagine they'll know how to move through a forest without being caught. Still, best we stay sharp."

Amara seemed reassured, though her eyes lingered on Lianna for a long moment, curiosity and respect evident in her expression.

Xavier turned back toward the gathered villagers and the leaders he had come to rely on. Their faces were worn but resolved. These were people who had been through fire and still stood. Not all were warriors. Not all were ready, but they believed in him.

Even the refugees at the edge of the chamber, uncertain and quiet, were listening now.

"So we begin," Xavier said. "We build. We train. We form alliances where we can." He let that settle. "Is there anything else we can do?"

It was Aelriva, now hovering near the center of the chamber, who answered.

"Aye. Wake the next ley line. The power of Earth doth bind and restore. It will strengthen Rynthavael's bones and defenses alike. Ye have grown enough now to descend deeper into the Deeps. Yet mark me well. Ye must first clear the first floor, for only then may ye press deeper, where the stone's hidden heart lies waiting."

As she spoke, a pulse of resonance rippled across the mosaic.

A translucent message appeared in Xavier's vision, unfolding in sharper detail than the previous simple quest prompts he was used to.

---

**Quest Accepted:** Drums in the Deeps I – The First Descent

The path below has long been shrouded in silence, yet silence does not mean stillness. Beneath the sanctuary of your nexus mosaic, the Deeps have slumbered, untouched and unguarded for untold centuries. What has stirred in the dark during your absence? What secrets lie buried beneath the stone?

**Objectives:**

- Explore and reclaim the first level of the Deeps beneath Rynthavael

---

- Confront whatever dangers have taken root in the darkness
- Secure the area to ensure future expansion and stability

**Rewards:**

- Access to lost resources hidden within the Deeps
- Access to the second floor of the Deeps
- Strengthened foundation for Rynthavael's future growth
- Other unknown benefits tied to your discoveries
- +5000 Experience

Tread with caution, but do not falter. What sleeps beneath does not always sleep forever.

Another prompt appeared almost immediately after.

**Quest Updated:** Sleeping Lines III – The Third Awakening

The veins of the Syr'Vailen slumber still, much of their power buried beneath the weight of ages. The nexus stirs, yet much remains untouched. Dormant lines wait to be woven once more into the fabric of the land.

**Objective:**

- Locate and restore another of the remaining dormant Ley Lines beneath Rynthavael
- Strengthen the ambient mana flow, unlocking new potential for the settlement
- Ensure stability during the reawakening process

**Conditions:**

- Reach Personal Level 15
- Retain mastery over the Syr'Vailen Nexus

**Rewards:**

- Increased ambient mana within Rynthavael's domain
- New settlement capabilities
- Enhanced wildlife presence and emergent quest opportunities
- +1500 Experience

The world's pulse is waiting to quicken once more. Will you be the one to awaken it?

Xavier studied the messages, then dismissed them with a thought. He looked around the chamber, expression calm but resolute.

"Thank you. All of you. Go and begin. Do what you must."

His eyes settled on Sorin. "I trust you can oversee construction. If you cannot handle the pressure, speak now."

The builder gave a short salute. "I will see it done, Lord Vael."

Without waiting for dismissal, she turned sharply and began calling out names, already organizing her teams as she walked back toward the tunnel.

In moments, the chamber began to empty, each of the villagers moving to their tasks with new purpose.

Only Ella, Aelriva, and Lianna remained beside Xavier, along with the two great cats, now resting near the outer edge of the mosaic.

He turned his gaze to Aelriva. "Why are they calling me

Lord Vael? And the quest says I need to be level fifteen to wake the next ley line. I'm not there yet. I'm only twelve."

She gave a soft laugh, the shimmer in her wings glowing faintly. "Aye, I may have told Braegor the meaning of the word Vael. As ye well know, it means blade. They now see ye as that very blade, Ard'Maelor."

She gestured toward the soft glow of Vaeltheris. "Twas he who first named ye so, and now it has taken root. Ye are a lord now, Xavier, whether ye accept it or not. And as for the ley line, ye shall be ready when the time comes. There is still much to do before the stone will yield and you can reach the Earthen Heart."

Xavier followed her motion, his eyes resting on the weapon at his side. When he looked up again, there was no hesitation. "Are we alone?"

Aelriva stilled. Her shifting eyes closed briefly, then opened again. "Aye."

"You knew about Ella," he said, voice quiet but certain. "About Vaeltheris. Even before she told me."

She hovered to eye level, then bowed, her wings keeping her aloft as she met his gaze again.

"Aye, I knew. She and the blade are the last spark of the Sylmyrian people. I have spoken with her often since her awakening. I guard the Syr'Vailen, and in doing so, I am bound to those who hold its legacy. That legacy now rests with ye."

She gestured toward Ella, then to the room itself.

"They will follow ye, Xavier. They already have. But more than that, ye must listen to them. Listen to her. For what ye carry is more than fate."

Xavier felt the weight of it all settle on his shoulders. He remembered what Danu had said about fate and destiny and knew it wasn't a completely forgone conclusion but there was too much that seemed to be lining up driving him towards some cosmic goal. He only hoped he was strong enough to survive the journey and protect those who had come to depend upon him. He did not speak right away, but when he did, there was no doubt in his voice.

"I will."

# CHAPTER EIGHT

*Beneath the Stone*

The decision to descend into the Deeps and attempt to restore the Earth Ley Line left little time for lingering in the village. If the trio hoped to reach Arenvalis without delay, every hour counted. Still, a brief detour felt warranted. Supplies were limited, and Xavier knew better than to ignore Aelriva's warnings. With danger lying ahead, healing tools were a necessity, not a luxury.

Xavier led Ella and Lianna through the winding corridors of the Warrens, making their way toward the healer's alcove near the vault. He half expected to find the space vacated, but a flicker of relief crossed his features when the familiar scent of crushed sage and bitterroot drifted to meet them.

Lila Fairbrook looked up from her workbench as they entered. Tanned from sunlight and firelight both, her hazel eyes gleamed with recognition beneath auburn braids. She smiled warmly.

"How can I help you, Lord Vael?"

Xavier resisted the urge to grimace. The title still sat awkwardly on his shoulders, a constant reminder of responsibilities he was only beginning to understand.

"We're heading into the Deeps, following Aelriva's

guidance," he said. "Anything you can spare for healing would be a blessing. I don't intend to get caught unprepared."

Lila nodded and led them to the back of the room where shallow wooden shelves held rows of small glass vials. The assortment was modest, but neatly arranged by potency and clarity. The upper rows contained simple crimson draughts. Further down, deeper reds shimmered with a golden tint. At the very bottom were just two vials, darker still and etched with faint warding runes.

Xavier stepped closer, his eyes widening. He had chewed forest sage leaves for minor scrapes and bruises, but these were something else entirely. He picked up a vial from each row, examining them with a sense of wonder.

| You have discovered: | Item Class: Common |
|---|---|
| Simple Healing Potion x 11 | **Item Quality:** Well Crafted |
| | **Weight:** 0.5 kg |
| | **Durability:** N/A (Consumable) |
| | **Description:** A small glass vial containing a crimson-red liquid with a faint herbal scent. The potion is a basic yet effective remedy, used by adventurers and healers alike to mend minor wounds and restore vitality. |
| | **Traits:** |
| | **- Gradual Restoration:** Restores 15-25 HP over 10 seconds after |

| | |
|---|---|
| | consumption. |
| **You have discovered:** Greater Healing Potion x 8 | **Item Class:** Uncommon **Item Quality:** Well Crafted **Weight:** 0.6 kg **Durability:** N/A (Consumable) **Description:** A deep crimson liquid with a faint golden shimmer, held in a reinforced glass vial. This potion provides stronger and quicker healing, making it a preferred choice for seasoned adventurers. **Traits:** - **Enhanced Restoration:** Restores 35-50 HP over 10 seconds after consumption. - **Wound Sealing:** Helps close minor wounds and slow moderate bleeding. |
| **You have discovered:** Superior Healing Potion x 2 | **Item Class:** Rare **Item Quality:** Exquisite **Weight:** 0.7 kg **Durability:** N/A (Consumable) **Description:** A rich ruby-red potion with golden veins swirling through the liquid. The vial is reinforced |

with protective runes, preventing magical decay. This potion provides rapid and powerful healing, allowing warriors to recover from near-fatal wounds.
**Traits:**
- **Advanced Regeneration:** Restores 75-100 HP over 10 seconds after consumption.
- **Deep Wound Sealing:** Closes moderate wounds, preventing excessive bleeding.
- **Minor Vitality Boost:** Slightly enhances stamina recovery for a short period.

"These are excellent," Xavier said, lifting one of the Superior vials gently. "Are they available, or are they needed for the villagers?"

"They're yours," Lila replied without hesitation. "I've already begun brewing more of the simple and greater ones. We've enough crystal powder for those. The superior two came from Bramblegate. I lack the ingredients to make more."

She hesitated, then added, "What we really need is more essence crystal. If you want potions like these to be sustainable, we'll need a steady supply."

A soft shimmer passed through Xavier's vision,

followed by a familiar prompt.

---

**Quest Offered:** Crystalline Dust

Magic requires more than will and words. Without the right materials, even the greatest artisans are left grasping at shadows. Essence crystals are the key. Seek them, and the path to greater craft shall unfold.

**Objective:**

- Locate a source of essence crystals or crystal dust
- Establish trade or gather/refine materials
- Deliver first supply to Rynthavael

**Rewards:**

- Access to advanced crafting and enchantment
- Strengthened magical infrastructure
- +1000 Experience

---

No sooner had the message appeared than another chimed in.

---

**Quest Completed:** Crystalline Dust

Through careful exploration, a Crystal Garden has been discovered, an extremely rare ley line phenomenon where all eight elemental aspects have crystallized into a physical form. A significant quantity of these essence crystals has been successfully harvested, opening new paths for magical advancement within Rynthavael.

**Completion Outcomes:**

- Large Stockpile of Elemental Essence Crystals – Sunfire (Light), Pyrric (Fire), Terrastone (Earth), Umbral (Dark),

---

Necrothite (Death), Aquaris (Water), Zephyrite (Air), and Vitalis (Life).

- Unlocks Enchantment & Infusion Potential – Enables essence-bound weaponry, ley line amplification, and artifact restoration.
- Increased Arcane Infrastructure – Strengthened settlement-wide magical stability due to the renewed connection to elemental ley lines.

**Rewards:**

- +2500 Experience. (Bonus experience due to going above and beyond basic requirements)
- Expanded crafting, alchemy, and enchantment capabilities within Rynthavael

He moved to an empty worktable off to the side and opened his satchel. As he began to unload the first crystal, pale with a soft green pulse, Lila turned... and froze.

More and more crystals followed. Reds tinged with flame, icy blues, pitch black, opalescent white streaked with gold. Each one resonated faintly with elemental power.

She nearly knocked over the alembic in her rush to reach the table. Her hands hovered above the gathered stones as her breath caught.

"I've added your access to the vault," Xavier said. "But I'm leaving these with you for now. Use what you need. I'll secure the rest once the village's defenses are in place. Additionally, once I finish clearing the first floor of the Deeps there is a large garden there that might help with your herbs and supplies."

He paused, fingers flicking through the interface as he opened the village management panel.

"You've already sworn your fealty. I have a request. Would you serve as Rynthavael's herbalist?"

It took several seconds before the question fully registered. When Lila turned from the crystals, her eyes were wide and wet. Without a word, she dropped to one knee.

"Yes, Lord Vael. I would be honored to serve in this role."

Xavier selected her name from the dropdown and confirmed her appointment. A soft pulse echoed through the air, subtle but certain, another piece of the settlement falling into place.

He reached out and took her hand, helping her to her feet. The glow in her expression had nothing to do with magic.

Around them, the other herbalists had gathered, whispering congratulations and clasping her shoulders. Pride warmed the room, mingled with renewed purpose.

Xavier stepped back from the celebration and checked the still-glowing edge of his interface. A blinking icon caught his attention, another minimized prompt. He tapped it open.

---

**Quest Completed:** Veins of the Earth
Upon discovering a viable mine and informing the village smith, you have ensured the flow of raw metal into Rynthavael. Crafting and defense potential have increased.

**Reward:**

- +1000 Experience

---

Xavier raised a brow. That one had triggered when he told Braegor about the old mine entrance. It had followed the same structure as Crystalline Dust, but it granted only the baseline reward.

Still, it had done the trick. Another chime rang in his ears, a soft resonance followed by glowing script across his mind's eye.

> **Hark and Hear! You have ascended in power. You are now Level 13!**
>
> The touch of the divine lingers upon you, granting **6 attribute points** to shape your destiny, an exceptional gift, elevated from the ordinary **4 points** by the **Blessings of the Gods (Danu)**. Choose wisely, for these points will define your path. You have **3 days** to assign them, or they will fall to the whims of fate.
>
> Your growing prowess earns you a boon: **20% skill allocation** to distribute among your known skills. This is your chance to sharpen the blade of a favored talent, forge new strength in an untapped domain, or balance your growth across disciplines.
>
> Let this moment be a cornerstone of your greatness.
>
> **Rise, Seeker of Glory. The world awaits your will. Seek adventure, seek wisdom, seek love and let your legend be forged in your choices. LIVE!**

Xavier dismissed the notification, pleased. Between potions, progress, and new potential, they were finally ready, and the Deeps awaited.

#

Using the distraction as a chance to leave the trio and pair of cats quickly made their way back to the mosaic chamber. The journey from the healer's chamber through the Warrens was quiet. The trio moved with solemn intent, their steps echoing softly through carved stone halls. Torchlight danced across the walls, casting flickering shadows ahead of them as they approached the chamber that lay at the heart of Rynthavael's underground soul.

They entered the wide sanctum housing the Syr'Vailen Mosaic, its surface stretching outward in an intricate ring of tile and stone. The pulse of awakened ley lines shimmered across two of the eight segments. The Life section glowed with soft golden warmth, steady and radiant. Death, its twin, throbbed in solemn pulses of deep black light.

The Earth tiles remained quiet. Dull brown and pale gray veins rested in stillness, unawakened, untouched by resonance.

Xavier stepped forward and knelt near it, letting his hand hover just above the dormant segment. He didn't need to touch it to feel the weight it carried. It was not asleep. It was waiting.

Ella moved beside him, her voice soft. "It will answer. When the time is right."

He gave a small nod but turned to Lianna instead, his expression steady. "I know the Elders told you to escort me to Arenvalis. But this... this is for my people. For this village. I can't walk away knowing I've left them exposed. Awakening the Earth Ley Line might give them the defense they need when I poke the beehive that kingdom has become."

He hesitated before continuing. "You don't have to come. I won't ask you to follow us into something that nearly killed Ella and almost shattered my mind. I know what it costs. And I wouldn't fault you for choosing to stay behind."

Lianna studied the humans standing before her. Her emerald eyes shifted back and forth, first to Xavier, the outsider who defied every expectation she had grown up with, then to the woman beside him, a sentient weapon in human form.

Even now, part of her wanted to cast off the responsibility given to her by the Elders. She could still walk away. Xavier had offered her that back in the forest, without condition, without pressure. She still carried the collar in her pack, her own one that she had picked up from where it lay discarded on the forest floor. The memory made her stomach churn, and she quickly pushed it from her mind.

The lordling intrigued her, more than she liked to admit. There was something about him, his choices, his words, his very presence, that called to her curiosity and to something deeper she couldn't name. He was not just strange. He was impossible. And she was drawn to him as surely as a moth to flame.

She didn't fully trust him. Not yet, but she couldn't walk away. Not until she understood who he truly was. Not until she saw how far that fire would burn.

She shook her head slowly, then met Xavier's gaze with her own. "We are traveling companions, Xavier. That means if I can, then I will follow you wherever you go."

Xavier let out a breath he hadn't realized he was holding. He nodded once in gratitude and turned toward the center of the mosaic.

Moving he pressed his palm to the keystone tile of the archway leading to the Deeps. A low hum answered the touch, not sharp but deep, like a buried heartbeat awakening in stone. Light rippled out across the ancient pattern as glowing script along the arch ahead shimmered to life.

The stone arch did not open into a void or elsewhere. It

revealed the top of a stairway carved directly into the rock, previously hidden by the enchantment's veil. This was not a portal in the traditional sense. It did not transport. It protected.

The threshold was a seal, a living ward set into the foundation of Rynthavael. It recognized those bound to the village and permitted only them to pass. No hostile creature from below could ascend through it. Not unless they too were granted passage.

Xavier stepped through the shimmering veil, which parted with no resistance at his approach. A faint ripple marked his passage. Ella followed, torch in hand, her bow slung across her shoulder. Frostclaw padded at her side, silent and alert. Valkra slipped after Xavier, almost invisible in the low light.

Lianna came last, her steps as quiet as the tension in the air. She kept her bow ready and her posture relaxed but watchful. Though she said nothing, her presence affirmed the choice she had made.

The stairwell descended into the dark. The walls changed from the shaped stone of the Warrens to rougher passages, natural and old. Dust hung in the air. The torches hissed softly as they flickered.

Above them, the seal of the mosaic faded from view, and the Deeps embraced them once more.

#

It was a short while before they exited the stairs into the entry hall that Xavier remembered from before. The two paths leading off to the crypt and the garden were just as they had last been, as was the large Ouroboros on the back wall. What had changed, however, was one of the archways near the Ouroboros. It was no longer solid stone. It was now open and revealed a new pathway. Taking that as an indication of which way they needed to go, Xavier led the way, both swords in hand.

Ella followed right behind him, her bow ready but with a torch in hand to illuminate the passages. Frostclaw and Valkra padded along side by side. The contrast between the large white snow leopard and the small ebon shadowmane panther cub would have been amusing in a different setting, but both carried an aura of danger as they prowled forward. Lianna brought up the rear, a bow in her hand as well, her eyes scanning everything. Her loyalty was still to Verdantspire, even if this young lordling and his village were potential allies.

Similar to their journey toward the Life Ley Line, the passage began as stonework but eventually gave way to rough stone caverns. As they moved through these tunnels, they began to feel slight tremors. The ground shook beneath their feet. Small rivulets of dust and gravel fell from the ceiling, clattering to the stone floor. The weight of tons of rock overhead wore on their nerves. Sweat slicked their clothing, and falling dust clung to their skin, leaving them feeling grimy and gritty. Even the two beasts began growling at each other in the narrow confines.

A collective breath of relief escaped the party when the passage walls abruptly disappeared, and a large cavern opened up before them. They stepped out and surveyed the terrain. It appeared partially collapsed. Rock formations littered the floor, intermixed with crystalline growths. Stalactites and stalagmites covered the ceiling and floor, though many had broken off, contributing to the piles of shattered stone. The torchlight didn't reach the far side, but they could make out a number of tunnel entrances at various heights and angles along the cavern walls.

Xavier sheathed his emberstone shortsword and lit

another torch from Ella's, adding more light and shadow to the chamber. With the added light, he stepped cautiously down the incline before them. The ground roughly evened out after a short descent. The party moved slowly into the chamber. Twenty feet in, the ground trembled ominously. Vibrations rippled beneath their boots, and crashing sounds echoed from deeper in the cavern as stalactites shattered and fell. They froze, spreading out to maintain balance and avoid colliding. As the tremors subsided, they looked to one another, then upward at the deadly daggers of stone above, their expressions grim.

They waited nearly a minute to ensure the tremors had passed. Then, Xavier stepped forward. He had only taken two steps when the ground to his left exploded. A geyser of stone and dirt erupted skyward. He yelled and threw his arms up to shield his face. Ella wasn't so lucky. A chunk of stone struck her in the shoulder, sending her sprawling. Her torch skidded across the floor and guttered out. Both cats darted clear of the debris. Lianna leapt back as her bow came up, an arrow nocked and pulled taut.

The dust settled. A screech of stone on stone echoed through the cavern. The ground beneath them rumbled as the creature within revealed itself. An enormous serpentine body emerged from the earth, its hide coated in jagged, rock-like scales streaked with veins of mineral. Four ember-like eyes locked onto them, filled with predatory hunger. Massive clawed forelimbs pulled the wyrm free from the ground. It reared up and coiled, ready to strike.

A guttural roar escaped its throat, sounding like stone grinding stone. The ceiling trembled again as stalactites swayed.

Xavier spent the mana and triggered *Insight*.

| **Name:** Stone Scaled Wyrm | **Disposition:** Ravenous |
| --- | --- |

The Stone-Scaled Wyrm is a titanic burrowing predator, its body covered in jagged, rock-like scales that grant it incredible durability. Reaching up to 30 feet in length, it moves through stone as effortlessly as a fish through water, using its clawed forelimbs and serpentine body to maneuver. Its four ember-like eyes glow with an eerie intensity, detecting vibrations deep within the earth. Its serrated maw is lined with crushing teeth capable of pulverizing even the sturdiest armor. When it moves, the very ground trembles, warning of its presence moments before it erupts from below to ambush prey.

| **Health:** 310/310 | **Stamina:** 200/200 | **Mana:** 0/0 |
| --- | --- | --- |

The thing was a horror.

A monstrous wyrm of stone and sinew, coiled in the darkness of the cavern like some ancient relic of the earth's fury. Its body glistened with obsidian-like scales, each the size of a shield and patterned with natural markings that shimmered faintly with dormant leyline energy. The scent of old dust, minerals, and something deeper, primordial, filled the air the moment it stirred.

His breath caught... then it lunged.

Its head snapped forward with a speed unnatural for something of its size. Teeth like jagged basalt jutted from its jaws, gleaming with a sheen of polished death. Xavier tried to backpedal, boots skidding on loose gravel, but the monster was faster.

Only luck, or divine intervention, kept those fangs from clamping down on his chest. He stumbled back, tripping over a shattered stone pillar, and went sprawling just as the maw snapped shut inches above him. The thunderclap of stone biting air rattled the walls.

He wasn't unscathed however.

A clawed forelimb lashed out in passing. The talons scraped down his side with brutal force, scoring his new leather armor and leaving three deep gouges in the hardened hide. Pain flared hot beneath the surface. The blow hadn't broken skin, but it left bruised muscle and battered pride.

The wyrm's roar shook the air like a subterranean storm.

That sudden burst of violence snapped the rest of the group into motion.

Ella moved first. She dove across the cavern floor, skidding over jagged stone, her fingers bloodying as they grasped her fallen bow. She spun, rose to a knee, and fired in one smooth motion. Three arrows flew, rapid-fire, the string a blur between her fingers.

They hit… but achieved nothing.

Each arrow shattered against the wyrm's armor-like hide. Scales deflected the shafts with a sound like breaking glass, leaving only superficial chips and faint scratches behind.

With twin snarls of fury, both Frostclaw and Valkra charged in. The great snow leopard bounded low, claws skittering for traction as he darted between the creature's legs. Valkra, smaller but faster, blurred into motion beside him, her black fur a shadow in the gloom. The wyrm's limbs lashed like scythes, but the pair moved with synchronized instinct, slipping narrowly through the chaos.

Frostclaw ducked beneath a sweeping tail that smashed into a column of stone, reducing it to rubble. Valkra darted forward, jaws snapping at exposed tendons between plated scales near a joint.

Their attacks barely registered.

Claws scraped stone. Teeth met resistance. But their assault drew the wyrm's attention at least, dragging it away from Xavier who was groaning and rolling to his feet. Blood slicked his ribs beneath the damaged armor, but he was breathing, and the jaws weren't currently trying to devour him.

Lianna, her eyes tracking every movement with a hunter's cold focus, had already realized what Ella's arrows had not accomplished. She lowered her bow—then abruptly aimed it skyward.

"What's she…" Xavier managed, but then her intention became clear.

She fired, not at the beast, but at one of the looming stalactites overhead.

The arrow struck true. A thunderous crack resounded from above, and a shard of the ceiling broke loose, a jagged stone spear the length of a man's arm. It plunged downward with an accelerating shriek and slammed into the wyrm's back.

The impact didn't pierce clean through the stone plates, but it cracked one, and the broken edges drove into the tender muscle beneath. The beast shrieked, this time in pain. A pulse of energy exploded outward from its body, a shockwave of tremor-magic that blasted through the room like a rolling earthquake.

A stun debuff hit them like a wall.

Xavier staggered, falling to one knee. The air hummed, ears ringing. The two cats were caught in the shockwave's radius, ten feet around the beast, and collapsed, stunned. Their bodies twitched as the magic sent their nerves screaming.

The cave groaned as more of the ceiling gave way. Several sharp protrusions overhead, already weakened by Lianna's gambit, cracked and sheared loose. They came tumbling down like deadly rain.

Lianna and Ella dove sideways as splinters of ancient stone plummeted past. One stalactite smashed into the ground where Ella had been standing moments before, spraying chips like shrapnel. Lianna tucked and rolled, coming up to her feet with another arrow nocked before she'd even regained full balance.

A second stalactite came crashing down and struck the snow leopard squarely across the shoulder. The stone gouged a deep furrow through fur and flesh, knocking the great cat to the floor with a ragged yowl.

The wyrm turned. Jaws opened wide, slammed shut around Frostclaw's torso.

The scream that tore from the great cat's throat was raw and terrible. Blood spilled onto the floor in a splatter of red and white fur. The wyrm lifted him slightly, shaking once, twice trying to crush him.

Then Frostclaw's instincts kicked in. His hind claws slashed upward in a furious rake. Talons found flesh. He gouged deep into the wyrm's side-eye cluster, blinding half the monster's field of vision.

The wyrm shrieked and dropped him.

Frostclaw hit the ground hard, blood trailing, but he limped away, still growling, still alive.

Lianna screamed, a series of words in rapid-fire Avara. Xavier's mind couldn't keep up, as it tried to make sense of the profanity coming from the Iskari Ranger, flickering with half translations: "[Unintelligible] stone-bastard!" "Vile spawn of mountain rot!" "Touch him again and I'll..."

Her bow fired again and again... each arrow aimed at the ceiling, trying to repeat her earlier success, but the wyrm had learned. It moved too erratically now. Each strike missed, and the falling stalactites merely added to the clutter and chaos of the battlefield.

Xavier's fingers twitched. The stun broke.

He surged to his feet, Vaeltheris glowing faintly in his grip. The blade pulsed with resonance, reacting to the elemental energy permeating the creature. As Xavier approached, he dropped into a low stance and slashed.

Vaeltheris met the wyrm's side, where the earlier crack still split its armor.

The enchanted edge sank deep, parting muscle and cartilage. Grey-blue blood sprayed out in a geyser, splashing Xavier's chest and arm. The wyrm recoiled violently, then whipped its tail.

Xavier saw it too late. The impact slammed into his ribs, lifting him off his feet and hurling him backward into a low pillar of stone. He crashed down in a crumpled heap, air driven from his lungs.

Ella gritted her teeth, helpless rage curling behind her eyes. Her arrows were worthless against the wyrm's scales, useless save for distraction. She cursed silently but refused to stop fighting. She scanned the beast again, searching for some kind of weakness, some vulnerable point.

And then she saw it... the broken scale on the wyrm's back from Lianna's first strike. Xavier's blow had widened the wound, exposing pulsing muscle beneath.

She drew a new arrow, tension singing through her shoulders.

The wyrm paused for a moment, breath ragged, trying to reorient after the last blow.

She released.

The arrow flew straight and true, and this time, it struck deep. The fletching disappeared into the soft tissue, and the beast screamed, truly screamed, as pain that it had likely not felt in decades surged through its body.

With a furious roar, the wyrm dove.

It didn't flee. It burrowed, vanishing beneath the cavern floor in an explosion of broken stone and dust. A grinding tremor rippled through the ground and then silence.

For several long heartbeats, no one moved.

Weapons held ready. Ears strained. The air was thick with dust and blood and the copper-salt tang of injury. Every footstep was hesitant. Even the animals held still, frozen by the predator's vanishing act.

Ella stepped forward, intending to check on Xavier.

That was her mistake.

The wyrm exploded upward directly beneath her.

Stone cracked and scattered in every direction. The blast launched Ella into the air like a doll, her bow spiraling away. She twisted mid-air, narrowly avoiding being impaled on the monster's waiting jaws, but its claws still caught her across the ribs.

She screamed as three long gashes opened along her side, blood soaking her tunic and spraying into the air. Landing hard she started to crawl away.

Xavier saw red.

As he roared and charged, Vaeltheris pulsed, vibrating in his grip. As he ran, the runes along the blade ignited with ghostlight. The weapon shimmered, its Ethereal Edge trait activating.

The blade phased, slipping partially out of the physical realm. A cool shimmer surrounded it. The lines between steel and spirit blurred. This was what the sword had been made for.

Xavier leapt, both hands on the hilt, teeth clenched. The wyrm's neck reared back to strike again, and he brought the blade down with all his strength.

Vaeltheris met the base of the skull, and sank in. Not through brute force, but through transcendence.

The blade bypassed the elemental layering of stone and Earth ley resonance, slipping past what no ordinary blade could touch. The wyrm's natural defenses meant nothing to the incorporeal strike.

It plunged to the hilt.

The beast convulsed, shrieking. Plates along its neck cracked outward as the ley-forged cohesion holding them together began to fail. Xavier clung to the hilt, his boots braced on the wyrm's neck, face coated in its blood.

He pulled and with a snarl, he ripped Vaeltheris free.

A gout of grey-blue ichor sprayed high, torn flesh and fractured scale spraying outward as the blade re-materialized mid-withdrawal. The wound opened like a canyon, and the elemental wyrm screamed.

Its death throes began. It thrashed and slammed into the cavern walls. Stone cracked and trembled. Entire sections of the ceiling threatened to collapse.

Xavier stayed atop it, riding the convulsions as the beast's body spasmed beneath him. The glow in the wyrm's ember-like eyes began to flicker, then dim.

Stone plates along its torso started to change, turning dull and brittle as the Earth-aspected essence unraveled.

Patches of its body began to revert into inert rock, flaking, cracking, falling away.

It slammed down in a final heave, quaking the entire floor. The low rumble that followed wasn't just breath it was an elemental collapse. A resonant groan rolled outward. The air thrummed. Dust fell like rain. The wyrm's chest gave one last shuddering rise, then fell flat. The last of its ley-anchored life energy dissipated in a fading flicker of dull ochre light.

A silence that followed was deep... Subterranean... Absolute.

Xavier stood atop the corpse, Vaeltheris still in his hand, panting. Sweat and blood mingled on his face. The silence dragged long enough to make every heart beat louder. Then, finally, nothing stirred. No tremors. No rise. No second phase. It was over.

He slid from the wyrm's corpse and dropped heavily to the stone beside Ella, who clutched her side with a pale face but a tight nod. Frostclaw limped to Lianna's side. Valkra prowled near Xavier, ears forward, body still tense.

#

Ella clutched her side, pale-faced but steady, her breath sharp through clenched teeth. Frostclaw limped to Lianna's side, his head low, thick white fur darkened with blood where the stalactite had struck. Valkra prowled near Xavier, twin stinger-tipped tails flicking anxiously, her lithe form still bristling with tension.

No one spoke. The stillness wasn't mere quiet—it was a hollow that echoed inside their chests. Only the sound of slow, ragged breaths and drifting dust accompanied the ringing quiet.

Xavier pulled a small vial from his belt, uncorking it

with one hand. "Just scratches, right?" he muttered, more to himself than anyone else.

Ella gave a shallow nod, still clutching her side. "Nothing vital."

He tilted the potion back, letting the thin blue liquid slide down his throat. It spread with a familiar warmth, dulling the ache in his ribs and numbing the burn of bruised muscle. Beside him, Ella accepted the vial he offered next, downing it without hesitation. She winced but stood a little straighter as the gashes across her ribs began to knit.

Across the chamber, Lianna crouched beside Frostclaw, murmuring soft reassurances in Avara as she examined the wound on his shoulder. The great cat whuffed once, low and annoyed, but didn't resist as she coaxed him to drink from another healing vial. The potion took effect quickly, and the worst of the bleeding slowed to a halt.

"He'll be fine," she said, glancing up. "Sore. Angry. But breathing."

Xavier gave her a nod of thanks.

Valkra circled once more before finally settling near Ella. Her twin tails stilled, and her ears rotated slowly, tracking every sound. Though unharmed, she remained keyed to every flicker of movement in the darkness.

"Status?" Xavier asked, his voice low as he scanned the group.

Ella rolled one shoulder. "Functional."

Lianna nodded. "Ready."

Frostclaw rumbled low in agreement, then slowly sat on his haunches.

> You have slain a level 15 Stone Scale Wyrm
> **+7200 Experience**

The experience surge washed over him, satisfying but not quite enough.

Experience to next level: 2735

Before they pressed onward, they took time to examine the corpse. It was an unpleasant task, made worse by the weight of silence and the cloying stink of ley-tainted blood, but necessary. Vaeltheris proved essential, its enchanted edge cutting through armored hide and chitin with patient precision. The process took time and no small amount of effort, but in the end, they were not disappointed:

| **You have discovered:** Stone-Scaled Plates x 9 | **Item Class:** Rare **Item Quality:** Superb **Weight:** 4.5 kg per plate **Durability:** 100/100 **Description:** Large, jagged plates of mineral-infused chitin, harder than steel and exceptionally resilient. These plates retain the wyrm's natural durability, making them ideal for forging high-quality armor and shields. **Uses:** - Armor Crafting: Can be used to forge heavy armor that grants resistance to |

| | bludgeoning and fire damage.<br>- Shield Reinforcement: A properly forged shield with these scales grants a +1 defense bonus and an earth-based reaction ability to absorb impact. |
|---|---|
| **You have discovered:** Tremor Core | **Item Class:** Very Rare<br>**Item Quality:** Exquisite<br>**Weight:** 2.3 kg<br>**Durability:** 95/100<br>**Description:** A dense, pulsating gemstone found at the wyrm's heart, brimming with seismic energy. It glows faintly with residual ley-line power and reacts to vibrations and movement.<br>**Uses:**<br>- Earth Enchantment: Can be embedded into weapons to add earthquake-like impact effects or seismic shockwaves.<br>- Alchemy & Spellcrafting: Used in the creation of earth-based spells, explosive runes, or shockwave grenades. |
| **You have discovered:** | **Item Class:** Rare |

| Wyrm's Fang x 2 | **Item Quality:** Superb<br>**Weight:** 1.8 kg per fang<br>**Durability:** 100/100<br>**Description:** Serrated, adamantine-like fangs capable of puncturing even enchanted armor. These fangs harden over time, increasing their natural piercing power.<br>**Uses:**<br>- Weapon Forging: Can be reforged into a greatsword, war pick, or polearm with armor-piercing properties.<br>- Alchemy: Ground into powder, it can be used to create potions that enhance physical resistance. |
|---|---|
| **You have discovered:**<br>Hardened Wyrm Hide x 3 | **Item Class:** Rare<br>**Item Quality:** Well Crafted<br>**Weight:** 2.5 kg per strip<br>**Durability:** 90/100<br>**Description:** The wyrm's inner hide, beneath its stone scales, is a dense, flexible material that resists heat and pressure. It retains trace seismic energy, making it ideal for specialized crafting. |

| | |
|---|---|
| | **Uses:**<br>- Lightweight Armor Crafting: Can be used to craft light or medium armor that grants tremor-sense within a short range.<br>- Alchemical Uses: When infused with magic, it can be used to create earth-resistant cloaks or belts that enhance physical fortitude. |
| **You have discovered:**<br>Echoing Heartstone | **Item Class:** Very Rare<br>**Item Quality:** Exquisite<br>**Weight:** 0.9 kg<br>**Durability:** 95/100<br>**Description:** A rare, mystical gem formed from the wyrm's lifeblood, solidifying into a core of residual sound and force magic. It radiates a low, harmonic hum, responding to vibrations and pressure.<br>**Uses:**<br>- Shockwave Enchantment: Can be mounted onto a shield or weapon, allowing it to emit shockwaves when struck.<br>- Tremor-Sense |

| | Attunement: If attuned, it grants the wielder a temporary tremor-sense effect when pressed to the ground. |
| --- | --- |

Xavier examined each item with care. Where once he would have needed Aelriva or interface prompts to understand what he was looking at, his recent studies in world lore, tomes on natural history, alchemical field guides, dwarven crafting scrolls, had given him a foundation. And as the items shimmered faintly in his vision, a new prompt appeared.

**New Skill Acquired:** Item Lore (Level 1 – Novice)
You can now identify rare and magical item properties with greater accuracy. Your understanding of crafting components, relic materials, and arcane residue allows for broader insight without the need for external appraisals.
**+2% success chance to identify unknown items.**
**+5% efficiency when salvaging or extracting usable components.**

A grin tugged at the corners of Xavier's mouth. Finally, something useful to show for the long nights of study.

Once the work was done, they rose from the grisly task of dismembering the corpse. All of them were stained with grey-blue gore and sweat, grimacing at each other in mutual disgust.

"Garden?" Ella asked, dryly.

"Garden," Xavier agreed.

The short trek back was silent but purposeful. At the pools near the awakened Life Core, they took the time to wash the worst of the blood and grime away. The water was cold, clean, and unexpectedly invigorating, a residual effect of the leyline's awakening. By the time they returned to the wyrm's chamber, they were cleaner, more alert, and ready to move forward.

They surveyed the cavern once more. Most of the tunnel mouths were broad and irregular, likely carved by the wyrm over time. But at the rear of the space, partially obscured by a bend, was a much larger tunnel descending at a shallow slope and veering to the left.

"Looks more deliberate," Lianna said, nodding toward it.

"Likely the path we need," Xavier replied.

He drew Vaeltheris and lit a torch in his off-hand, eyes narrowing. "We go as we did before. Slow. No surprises this time."

One by one, they moved into formation and stepped into the tunnel's shadow. The echo of the wyrm's death was already fading behind them but in the Deeps, the silence never lasted for long.

#

The tunnel floor sloped steadily downward, winding and curling upon itself like some stone serpent. As they descended, the direction of travel quickly became disorienting. There were no stars to guide them, no wind to whisper to the north or south, only the oppressive silence of stone and the uncertain path ahead.

What began as a single passage eventually fractured. A fork appeared. Then another. Soon there were offshoots to the left and right, some narrow, others wide, all leading into dim and echoing gloom. The Deeps were transforming into a labyrinth. It wasn't just a descent anymore, it was a maze of choices, most of which felt wrong.

To keep their bearings, they devised a method. At each new junction or turn they chose to follow, Xavier etched a sigil into the stone near the entrance, always the same mark, clean and deliberate, distinct enough to avoid mistaking it for a natural fissure or scrape. It was a blend of lines and angles drawn from Vaeltheris' edge, unmistakably their own.

The hours passed in agonizing silence, broken only by the crunch of boots, the flicker of torches, and the low, guttural grumbles of stone settling in unseen chambers. More than once, they found themselves looping back to old paths, forced to double back through collapsed corridors or impassable rubble. The stone seemed to twist of its own accord, an endless spiral into claustrophobic depth.

Xavier, glancing at his interface, saw that they had been exploring for the better part of eight hours. They were bone-tired, aching, and footsore by the time they entered a new chamber, larger than most they had seen so far. The air shifted as they crossed the threshold, the temperature dipping slightly, the scent turning stale and dry with old dust and a faint metallic tang.

The room was vast, a semicircular expanse shaped by forgotten hands. Once, it had been grand. Dwarven craftsmanship, unmistakably aged but not wholly ruined, greeted them in the shapes of pillars and archways, though many were shattered or leaning. Stone benches sat scattered near a cluster of thick support columns, some still whole, others broken like ribs. Crystalline sconces pulsed faintly on the walls, their fractured light casting long shadows that danced like phantoms on the far edges of the chamber.

Xavier stepped closer, eyes scanning the artistry carved into the walls... miners, smiths, stonemasons immortalized in relief. But time had not been kind. Deep gouges marred the carvings. Some were melted, others fractured by quake or claw. The damage was not all natural. Something corrosive had touched this place.

Pools of stagnant water glistened on the uneven floor, their surfaces shined with a sickly, iridescent film. Xavier stepped toward one but halted when a faint hiss rose beneath his boot. He jerked back instinctively. The pool sizzled where his toe had brushed the surface, acid.

They navigated carefully around the pools, keeping to dry stone where they could. Their destination became the bench cluster at the room's center, the most structurally sound portion of the space. It reminded Xavier of the miner rest-rooms from the old mine he had found in the Hollow Depths, places where workers would eat, drink, or sleep during long shifts underground.

They settled cautiously on the stone benches, leaning against the thick central pillars. Weapons remained close at hand. Their eyes scanned the gloom, but fatigue was winning. The torches flickered low and eventually guttered, leaving only the dim crystalline sconces to light the space. In truth, the softer glow helped their vision adjust, extending their field of sight beyond the narrow glare of flame.

They took turns on the watch, dozing in short shifts. The rest was shallow. Stone groaned and fell somewhere in the tunnels beyond. Faint echoes of distant collapse haunted the background, each sound a reminder that the Deeps did not sleep. Even the cats were tense, ears flicking at phantom noises.

It was during Lianna's watch that the silence changed.

It began as a scrap... barely audible at first. A faint dragging sound, metal on stone or perhaps chitin. She stiffened. Another scrape followed, louder this time, and from a different tunnel. Then came the clicks. Odd, uneven, almost like communication. One tunnel answered the next, then another.

Lianna rose slowly, her body tense, muscles coiled. She listened, the noise came from at least three passageways. She crouched low and gently shook Xavier and Ella awake. Both recoiled instinctively at the overwhelming scent that had begun to pour into the chamber.

It was a stench like no other… thick, stomach-turning rot mixed with bitter acid and foul minerals. It burned the nose and clung to the throat, metallic and fungal all at once. The air was suddenly foul, heavy, and nauseating. Even Frostclaw and Valkra growled low, twin signs of primal alarm. Their ears flattened, tails low.

The three stood, weapons at the ready. They formed a triangle, backs to one another, eyes to the tunnels.

Then the corrupted came. They did not skitter, they crashed. Twisted ankhegs burst from the tunnels, their forms grotesquely mutated. Where their carapaces should have been smooth, cracks split through, oozing bile that hissed and steamed as it touched stone. Their eyes glowed with a sickly green sheen that pulsed with flickers of spectral light.

Mandibles clicked and snapped in frenzied hunger. Their bodies twitched and shuddered with unnatural spasms. Every movement was wrong, too fast, too sudden, too jerky. Chitin plates ground together with brittle crunches. Acid drooled from their fangs.

Xavier's eyes flashed. Insight triggered. A pane shimmered before his gaze, and suddenly knew what the creatures were, and his stomach flipped in apprehension.

| **Name:** Corrupted Ankheg | **Disposition:** Frenzied |
| --- | --- |

The Corrupted Ankheg is a grotesque, twisted aberration, it's cracked chitin leaking glowing, acidic bile that sizzles against the ground. It's mandibles, jagged and malformed, drip with corrosive saliva, while its spectral, flickering eyes radiate an unnatural hunger. Moving in erratic, spasmodic bursts, it lurches forward with brittle, splintering movements, its warped body seemingly fighting against itself. The air around it is thick with the stench of decay and acid, a foul omen of its relentless, mindless aggression.

| **Health:** 180/180 | **Stamina:** 140/140 | **Mana:** 0/0 |

#

The ankhegs struck without warning.

Two erupted first. One burst from a tunnel beside Lianna, its gaping mandibles spreading wide as a pressurized hiss launched a stream of sizzling green fluid from its crown. Lianna twisted instinctively, the acid spray missing her by inches and steaming as it splashed onto stone.

A second shot forth near Xavier, its spray following a heartbeat later. He was not as quick. The corrosive fluid struck his shoulder and bare hand, flesh blistering instantly beneath the acid's bite. He cried out, scrambling back and shoving his burning arm against a nearby pillar, trying to scrape the fluid away before it ate deeper.

Ella moved to help him, but the stone beneath her gave way with a violent crack. A third ankheg exploded upward, its jagged mandibles clamping onto her ankle. She screamed, struggling as acid ate through her boot leather. Her hand, still gripping a drawn arrow, drove down repeatedly into the creature's head. It shrieked and flailed but held tight.

Frostclaw, already tensed for the attack, pounced as the

fourth erupted through the floor. The massive cat collided with it mid-surge, teeth clamping down on its exposed shoulder. Chitin cracked and crunched beneath his weight, acid hissing where it splashed across his fur. Still, the feline didn't let go, sinking his claws deep and tearing again.

Valkra moved like a living shadow. The shadowmane cub circled the creature assaulting Ella and launched herself forward. Her small but precise jaws found purchase at the base of its neck. Though her bite lacked Frostclaw's crushing power, her twin stinger-tipped tails lashed in unison, each tip piercing the cracked plating at the creature's joints. A pulse of paralytic venom surged through the strikes.

The ankheg spasmed. Then stopped, frozen in paralysis, its grip loosened, and Ella pulled free, dragging her leg clear with a gasp of pain.

The cavern erupted in chaos. Lianna drew her sword and circled the ankheg that had targeted her. The creature hissed and lunged again, forcing her back. Frostclaw continued to savage his target, the acid from its cracked shell eating into his fur, but the snow cat refused to yield. With each violent bite and rake of his claws, more corrosive fluid sprayed, yet he fought on with fierce resolve.

Xavier staggered to one knee, clutching his ruined hand as he fumbled for his second blade. His fingers burned, the pain dulling his coordination. Even so, he forced himself forward, slashing at the insectoid that loomed before him. The emberstone edge of his shortsword connected with brittle chitin, slicing through with sizzling force. He danced back from another spray of acid, gritting his teeth, pain narrowing his vision.

Ella and Valkra worked as a pair now. With her ankle freed, Ella regained her stance and stabbed forward, while Valkra circled for another strike. The ankheg twisted and snapped at both of them, but the two proved too agile. Though Ella's boot continued to hiss and melt, she fought through the discomfort, driving her attacks into weak points revealed by the cub's positioning.

Xavier's foe pressed harder. The pain in his hand slowed him, and the creature took advantage, snapping and lunging with mindless fury. Every movement tested his endurance. Each deflection, each cut felt heavier. But he refused to give ground.

With a final surge of effort, he dropped low, driving Vaeltheris into one of the creature's glowing eyes. It shrieked, limbs flailing wildly, but he didn't stop. His emberstone blade arced upward in the same motion, severing the neck just behind the jaw. The creature's body shuddered once. Then slumped. No final burst of acid came, the cauterized neck hissed quietly in the still air.

Breathing hard, Xavier turned to help the others. But it was over. Each of his companions stood bloodied but victorious. Frostclaw crouched beside Lianna, his sides heaving. Valkra had already moved back to Xavier's side, nuzzling into his legs with a soft chuff.

He collapsed to one knee, then to the floor entirely, legs giving out beneath him. Ella sank down across from him, breathing hard, while Lianna lowered herself beside Frostclaw, checking his wounds with a steady hand.

The air was thick with the stench of acid and blood. A soft chime sounded in Xavier's mind.

> Your party has slain 4 Corrupted Ankhegs
> **+6300 Experience.**

The accompanying prompt followed with its usual celebratory flourish.

**Hark and Hear! You have ascended in power. You are now Level 14!**

The touch of the divine lingers upon you, granting **6 attribute** points to shape your destiny, an exceptional gift, elevated from the ordinary **4 points** by the **Blessings of the Gods (Danu).**
**(Total: 12 unspent attribute points)**

Choose wisely, for these points will define your path. You have **3 days** to assign them, or they will fall to the whims of fate.

Your growing prowess earns you a boon: **20% skill allocation. (Total: 40% remaining)**

This is your chance to sharpen the blade of a favored talent, forge new strength in an untapped domain, or balance your growth across disciplines.

Let this moment be a cornerstone of your greatness.

**Rise, Seeker of Glory. The world awaits your will. Seek adventure, seek wisdom, seek love and let your legend be forged in your choices. LIVE!**

Xavier closed the message with a blink, then reached out and laid a hand on Frostclaw's flank. The big cat twitched under the contact but didn't pull away.

He whispered the words of the one life spell he knew, he needed to practice it more so it seemed right to do so now. His fingers moved in fluid motions, drawing light around them. Golden energy surged into the beast's wounds, knitting torn muscle and sealing scorched flesh. He repeated the spell until Frostclaw breathed easier and the worst of the burns had faded.

They drank potions in silence, letting the magic dull their pain and close raw wounds. No one moved far from one another.

"Do we try to rest again or push on?" Xavier finally asked, his voice low.

Lianna shook her head before he had finished. "We should not remain."

Ella nodded, her voice tight. "The longer we wait, the more likely more of those things find us. We should loot what we can and keep moving."

Xavier agreed with a grunt. Together, the three approached the carcasses, blades and tools in hand. Each piece was extracted with care, avoiding remaining acid that bubbled within the flesh.

| You have discovered: Corrupted Chitin x 18 | **Item Class:** Uncommon **Item Quality:** Above Average **Weight:** 3.5 kg per piece **Durability:** 80/100 **Description:** Dark, warped, and semi-melted, this chitin has absorbed the Ankheg's unnatural energy. The surface is twisted and uneven, giving off a faint acidic aura. Though its resilience is comparable to hardened leather, prolonged use may cause strange side effects. **Uses:** - Acid-Resistant Armor Crafting: Can be reforged into armor that grants |
|---|---|

| | acid resistance, though extended wear may lead to unpredictable mutations.<br>- Cursed Shield Forging: Infused by a skilled enchanter, it could be turned into a shield that absorbs damage at the cost of the wielder's vitality. |
| --- | --- |
| **You have discovered:**<br>Acid Gland x 4 | **Item Class:** Rare<br>**Item Quality:** Well Crafted<br>**Weight:** 1.2 kg per gland<br>**Durability:** N/A (Organic)<br>**Description:** A swollen, pulsing sac filled with highly corrosive bile. The gland writhes slightly, as if it still holds a lingering life force. The acid within is potent enough to melt metal, making it a highly valuable resource for alchemy and weapon enhancements.<br>**Uses:**<br>- Alchemy: Can be distilled into Acid Potions or weapon coatings, dealing 5-10 acid damage per hit for 1 |

| | hour.<br>- Traps & Warfare: Can be thrown as an acid bomb (30 ft. range, 15 - 18 acid damage in a 10 ft. radius). |
|---|---|
| **You have discovered:**<br>Warped Mandibles x 5 | **Item Class:** Uncommon<br>**Item Quality:** Well Crafted<br>**Weight:** 2.8 kg per mandible<br>**Durability:** 90/100<br>Description: Serrated, jagged, and partially melted, these mandibles still carry traces of mutagenic corruption. Despite their twisted appearance, they remain razor-sharp and can be reforged into deadly weapons.<br>**Uses:**<br>- Weapon Forging: Can be reforged into a blade or clawed weapon that deals bonus acid damage.<br>- Armor-Piercing Enhancement: Blacksmiths can use these mandibles to reinforce weapons, increasing their penetration against |

| | armored foes. |
| --- | --- |

Xavier added the harvested materials to his pack, sealing them away beside the wyrm remains. This time, the group was more meticulous. No acid spilled. No tools were lost. After a short deliberation they decided to move towards the most downward tunnel, knowing that their ultimate destination was a supposed stairway that would lead down to the next actual level of the Deeps.

# CHAPTER NINE
*The Hunger That Waits Below*

The tunnel leading away from the dwarven chamber sloped downward in a long, gradual curve, its walls lined with rough-hewn stone, worn smooth by the passage of time. Shadows flickered in the glow of their torches, stretching and shifting with every step.

The air grew heavier, thick with the scent of damp earth and mineral deposits. Each breath carried traces of something distant and unseen, while the occasional gust of stale air dragged with it a faint miasma of ammonia and rot. It was not foul in the sense of decay—it was older than that, somehow forgotten and preserved.

The attack by the insectoid ankheg had left its mark, not just in blood and broken stone, but in the lingering tension that now gripped the group like an unseen hand. Every faint sound in the darkness... a distant drip of water striking rock, the skittering of unseen vermin, or the soft crumble of loose stones, sent jolts of unease through the party. Shoulders tensed in preparation. Hands tightened around weapons. Eyes darted toward imagined threats that shifted just beyond reach.

Even those most accustomed to underground spaces found their nerves fraying under the weight of uncertainty. When a pebble dislodged and clattered down the sloping passage, someone started, inhaling sharply, only to exhale in relief as the noise echoed harmlessly into the dark. A nervous chuckle followed. Then another. The sound passed through the group like a shared confession of mutual anxiety. Laughter came quickly but it never lasted long. The silence swallowed it whole.

The descent stretched onward. Footfalls muffled against stone. Still, every step carried the unshakable awareness that something, or perhaps many things, might still be watching from the shadows ahead.

"These tunnels are horrible," Lianna muttered. Her hand rested lightly on the thick fur along Frostclaw's back. The great snow cat padded beside her in silence, sensing her discomfort and offering his steady presence.

Ella gave a quiet nod. She bent and scooped up Valkra with one arm. The little shadowmane cub was bristling slightly, ears flicking constantly, nose twitching. Ella's hold was gentle, but firm. It wasn't comfort she sought from the cub, it was a reassurance that they were still alive, still grounded.

"We've come too far to turn back without completing the floor," Xavier said over his shoulder. His voice was steady, though quieter than usual. "I think once it's cleared, we can rest easier before the descent to the next level and searching for the Earthen core."

He looked back at the two women. Concern shadowed his eyes, though his face remained resolute, his jaw set with determination.

They pressed forward. The tunnel grew steeper, and the air continued to thicken with the scent of damp stone and something far more ancient.

Xavier led, his fingers tightening on the hilt of Vaeltheris. His boots scraped over patches of loose gravel.

As they advanced, the tunnel shifted again. Some sections had grown strangely smooth... unnaturally so. In stark contrast, others bore jagged furrows gouged deep into the stone, as if something immense and clawed had raked through it without care.

The quiet grew heavier. Its weight pressed against them, broken only by the soft echo of water dripping or distant pebbles tumbling down unseen slopes.

Another chill gust of air snaked up the tunnel, heavier than the last, laced with a more distinct scent. It halted both Xavier and Lianna in their tracks.

It was not rot nor was it decay. It was something primal. Something aberrant.

The two exchanged looks.

Lianna's sharp gaze swept over the walls, searching for signs of fresh markings. Frostclaw growled low beside her. His ears flattened, the sound deep in his chest.

Valkra pressed tighter into Ella's arms, the little cub shivering once before her ears twitched as if hearing something just outside their range.

"There is something unnatural about this place," Lianna whispered. Her grip tightened on her bow. "It is not just deep tunnels. Something down there is waiting."

Xavier exhaled slowly. "Then I suppose we shouldn't keep it waiting for too much longer."

#

The tunnel widened without warning, opening onto the edge of a vast underground ravine. The path clung to the side of a sheer cliff, carved just wide enough for single-file passage. Far below, the void yawned, deep, silent, and seemingly endless.

Bioluminescent fungi clung to the far walls and the roots of distant stone pillars. Their pale blue and green glows pulsed faintly, casting shifting shadows that danced along the rock face with each flicker of light. The air held the stillness of a tomb.

Dust drifted lazily in the stagnant air. Then came the sound... pebbles rattling across the stone path. At first subtle, then again, and again, until it settled into a rhythm. Not random, it was a steady tremor. A heartbeat.

Xavier dropped to a crouch and pressed a gloved hand to the stone beneath his feet. The tremors were not part of the cavern's natural settling. Something enormous was stirring far below, and the slow, deliberate cadence of its breath shifted the very foundation of the chasm.

Lianna crouched beside him. Her fingers brushed across a groove carved deep into the stone wall beside the trail. "These are not caused by erosion," she said softly. "These are feeding marks."

Ella's voice trembled as she drew in a shallow breath. "We're walking into its nest?"

No one replied. The silence pressed down around them, more oppressive than any spoken confirmation. There was no alternate path. Only forward.

The group moved onward along the ravine's edge. The slope curved gradually downward, winding along the cliff wall like a scar. The light dimmed the farther they descended. Eventually, the path narrowed into a funnel leading to a wide stone archway. It looked natural at first glance, but the massive claw marks raking its sides told another story. Time had worn the shape... but something else had carved its edges.

Beyond the arch yawned a cavern, immense and

unnatural. Its ceiling vanished into an abyss above, swallowed by shadow. Even the faint bioluminescence from the fungi that clung to the ravine's walls seemed reluctant to reach this far. The glow dimmed, thinned, as if recoiling from whatever lay inside.

Their eyes slowly adjusted. What had at first seemed to be scattered debris revealed itself as something far worse. Bones lay across the cavern floor. Some were crumbling to dust with age, others splintered freshly, sharp and broken as though recently gnawed. Jagged fractures exposed marrow that had yet to dry. Rusted and broken weapons mixed with scraps of armor lay twisted among them, shattered hafts, bent blades, and scraps of cloth that hinted at long-forgotten battles.

A low growl rose from Frostclaw. His fur bristled along his shoulders and spine, and he lowered his head, ears flat.

Valkra had been set down once again as they descended. The cub immediately pressed herself against Xavier's leg, body trembling, twin tails lashing softly. Her ears twitched, listening to sounds the others could not yet hear.

Then it came... a wet, slithering sound, subtle but unmistakable. Not the scraping of motion, but something more internal. A body the size of a structure shifting in place. It wasn't traveling. It was waking.

Ella peered around the archway. Her knuckles whitened around the grip of her bow. "It's too quiet," she whispered.

Lianna narrowed her gaze and placed a steadying hand on Frostclaw's flank. Her feline eyes darted, following movement no one else could yet see. "No. It's not quiet. It's watching us."

Xavier's grip tightened. He let the torch fall from his hand, the flame guttering against stone, and drew the Emberstone blade with his off hand. "Then let's not be rude."

He stepped forward. A deep, bone-rattling tremor surged through the cavern. Pebbles danced and bounced across the uneven floor as the ground seemed to swell and contract beneath their feet. The bioluminescent glow from the fungi flickered erratically, pulsing in slow, uneven waves that mirrored the rhythm of something ancient and immense beginning to stir.

Then came the next tremor, and it was no longer subtle. The earth buckled and cracked, and the party staggered backward as the darkness ahead fractured open. From the shadows emerged a massive chitinous shape, its silhouette first defined by the long, jagged mandibles that scraped against the stone. The edges of the mandibles resembled the teeth of a rusted saw, curved and cruel.

Behind them followed a serpentine body, impossibly large, armored in thick plates of stone-hardened chitin. It moved with a disturbing fluidity, its many limbs flowing along the cavern walls with unnatural ease. It did not lurch… so much as it glided, coiling forward with eerie grace.

A low, grinding sound filled the chamber, but it was not a roar. It was the sound of a deep, deliberate inhale. Not in regular breath. Not in threat. It tasted as if  testing the air, sampling the scent of fresh prey.

The creature emerged in full, its many-limbed form unfurling along the rock like it had always belonged there. The cavern shook with its passage, a tremor in the bones of the world. Then it exhaled—a slow, shuddering breath that carried across the cavern like the sigh of some buried god.

It was obviously now watching them, and there was no doubt it knew they were there.

Xavier shifted his stance, blades raised in front of him

as he instinctively took a more defensive posture. "I think it knows we are here." His voice was low, tense. With that, he triggered Insight.

| **Name:** Nul'Zarak, the Maw of the Deeps (Apex Predator of the Deep Caverns) | **Disposition:** Ravenous Hunger | |
|---|---|---|
| A massive subterranean horror that has roamed the depths for centuries, Nul'Zarak is a fusion of wyrm and insectoid terror, its chitinous, stone-plated body perfectly adapted to the darkness. It relies on tremorsense rather than sight, lurking unseen before launching devastating ambushes. Its serrated mandibles can crush stone, while its gaping maw devours prey whole, trapping victims inside its crushing inner jaws. When cornered, it burrows through the cavern walls, using the environment as a weapon against its foes. Only those who understand the rhythm of the earth can hope to defeat this primeval beast. | | |
| **Health:** 650/650 | **Stamina:** 500/500 | **Mana:** 0/0 |

What he saw made his mouth go dry. The stonescale wyrm from before had been a brutal fight. This was something else entirely, a nightmare made flesh.

He raised a hand slowly, motioning for everyone to stay completely still as the abomination's massive head pivoted toward them. Its eyes burned like embers beneath its plated brow, mandibles flexing as if tasting their fear. They did not breathe. No one dared.

After an eternity compressed into a few strained heartbeats, the beast turned. Its titanic form slid back into the shadows, vanishing with unnatural grace between the columns of stone and fungus-lined walls. The tremors faded, but the weight of its presence lingered.

Xavier exhaled. "Back up the ramp. Slowly. We need

space to plan."

The group retreated several paces up the ravine path, just enough to gain higher ground without losing line of sight. Frostclaw moved with silent tension, ever vigilant. Lianna's sharp eyes tracked the cavern below, bow ready. Ella positioned herself near a crumbling column, keeping Valkra behind her, the cub low to the ground and trembling.

Xavier turned to them. "It saw us. It didn't strike. That means it's either cautious... or toying with us."

Ella's voice was quiet but steady. "It studied us. Like it was deciding whether we were worth the effort."

Lianna nodded. "It's not afraid. It's waiting. Letting us make the next mistake and walk into its trap."

Xavier frowned, still watching the archway. "Then we make none. We take the fight to it but on our terms."

He glanced between them. "This thing is worse than anything we've faced. When I used Insight, I saw more than just its nature. I learned it has a lot of characteristics of both the stonescale wyrm and the ankhegs, with something else making it much more malevolent but I couldn't identify what that was. It's not blind, but it hunts by tremor and scent."

Ella sighed, "great so my arrows will be less than useless again."

Lianna's voice sharpened with focus. "We do what we did before. Bring down the ceiling if we have to. Force it to rear up. We'll look for weak spots."

"Exactly," Xavier agreed. "I doubt we have much that can cut those scales." He inspected Vaeltheris' edge speculatively.

Lianna raised a finger, "Did you see how it moved? Its

underbelly looked decidedly different when it reared up to look at us."

"Yes, it seemed less armored there." Ella concurred, "if we can get it to rise up again, force that weak spot to be exposed then we could attack there."

"A good option," Xavier agreed, "we'll have to see if we can make it do that. Alright, so where do we fight it? Charge in, or try to lure it out here?"

"If we fight it here it is less likely to be able to burrow under us like the ankhegs and wyrm did." Ella stated as she gestured towards the ledge drop-off.

"It still might be able to collapse the ground though, and if it does…" Lianna frowned as she continued to stare over the edge. "I doubt any of us would survive that fall and it likely would remain half burrowed into the wall so as to not fall itself."

They all fell silent for a while chewing on different ideas before, one by one, they came to the same conclusion. They would have to enter the monster's lair and fight it there.

Ella nodded. "I still have oil flasks. If I can light a few fungal patches or stalactites…"

"Do it, the shadows are not our friend with this creature as it doesn't need to see us, but we need to see it." Xavier said. "Light and motion will be key. Lianna, back her up. Time your shots for distraction or to open a path."

He knelt beside Valkra, scratching gently behind her ears. "Stay close to Ella, little one. No heroics. Just survival."

Gear was checked. Arrows counted and oil-soaked cloths secured to arrowheads. Torches were relit and readied to be tossed. Frostclaw gave a low huff and padded forward, alert and ready the smaller ebony form of Valkra at his side.

As they walked Lianna took a deep breath, "We only get one shot at this. I doubt it will let us just run away."

"Then we need to make this count," Ella agreed. She rolled her shoulders slightly trying to relax some of the anxious tension building in them.

Xavier looked toward the cavern's mouth, where the darkness pulsed like a living thing. "We finish what we started. The core waits below. We clear this level, or we die trying."

With grim resolve, the party began their descent once more.

#

As the archway came into sight once again, Xavier and his group felt it, the oppressive weight of the presence lurking below. The air hung thick with the acrid stench of Nul'Zarak, mingling with the fetid rot of its past victims. Every instinct screamed at them to turn back, but they had already chosen their battleground.

Before they even reached the opening, Ella and Lianna acted first, moving with silent precision according to what they had planned. Each already carried a lit torch, the flames carefully shielded behind cupped hands and angled cloth to reduce their glow until the last possible moment. As one, they hurled the torches through the archway, sending them skidding across the stone floor. The flames spread flickering light over twisted bones and shattered remnants, breaking the darkness.

The moment the torches landed; their bows were drawn in near-perfect synchrony.

Their arrows streaked through the air, aimed not at the beast, but at the fungal clusters clinging to the walls and ceiling. The first burst apart in a spray of luminous spores, glowing green and pale blue. Then the second erupted, drifting downward and washing the stone in a spectral haze.

The creeping shadows recoiled. The darkness lost its grip as more of the cavern came into view. Portions of the battlefield emerged from the shadows beneath the drifting spores, revealing jagged bones, shattered weapons, and fractured stone. Much of the cavern remained cloaked in darkness, but enough was visible to glimpse the horror they faced.

Then came the answer.

A low, guttural tremor rolled beneath their feet, deep and resonant. Not merely movement. A warning. Dust trickled down from the ceiling as a massive force began to shift within the gloom.

The still-intact patches of fungus pulsed violently. They sensed it too.

Weapons raised, the group spread out, tension crackling in the air like drawn bowstrings. A thunderous crack of stone breaking split the silence.

Nul'Zarak emerged.

The great form slithered forward, chitinous limbs scraping across stone. Its segmented body dragged itself into the light, monstrous and terrible. It coiled around shattered pillars as it surveyed the room, tasting the air with a low rumbling breath. Mandibles dripped a noxious green fluid that hissed as it struck stone. It didn't charge, instead it watched, and calculated. Predatory intelligence shone behind burning red eyes.

It was without warning that it struck. With unnatural speed, Nul'Zarak lunged, mandibles clashing shut on the spot Xavier had stood a heartbeat before. The sound of the monster's impact echoed like stone shattering beneath a hammer. Xavier rolled aside, feeling the tremor surge through his bones.

"Keep it in the light! Keep moving, don't let it hit you!" Xavier barked, using a broken column to propel himself upright. But the others were already in motion.

Lianna and Ella split wide, circling the edge. Arrows flew, some clattering harmlessly off the stony armor of the great wyrm, others striking stone above. One arrow struck a stalactite with just enough force to dislodge it. The heavy spire crashed down, slamming into the creature's flank.

Nul'Zarak reared up, screaming in fury. The glow of the spores lit its exposed underbelly, where the segments were pale and vulnerable.

"There it is!" Lianna shouted. She loosed another arrow directly into the revealed flesh.

The beast howled. Mandibles snapped shut as it thrashed, crushing a pillar in its rage.

Moments later, It surged forward, snapping wildly as it chased Ella toward the cavern's edge. She dove behind a fallen boulder, short swords drawn while she discarded her bow in flight. As the creature twisted to track her, Ella darted forward again, blades flashing. One struck deep between its plates.

Suddenly, Nul'Zarak reversed direction, its tail slamming the ground near Frostclaw and Xavier. The cat leapt away in a blur of white fur and claws, while Xavier stumbled and caught himself on one knee.

Xavier recovered and retaliated, both blades now drawn. The Emberstone blade struck first, deflecting harmlessly off the creature's stony armor. Then Vaeltheris carved down along its flank. The ethereal edge sank partway into a joint, hissing as it met resistance, but didn't break through.

The creature burrowed and silence followed. The ground strained beneath their feet.

Then came the tremors.

Xavier tensed. He could feel the motion. "It's going to strike from beneath us, scatter!"

The floor exploded. Stone shattered outward as the creature erupted from the depths. The shockwave knocked Xavier backward. Boulders rained from above.

Lianna leapt to the side and fired a flaming arrow into a dense cluster of fungi on the ceiling. Spores erupted, coating the monster in a glowing cascade.

Ella's voice rang out, sharp and defiant. "Over here, buggy! You want me, come and get me!"

Nul'Zarak lunged toward her voice, rising high and exposing its underbelly once more.

"NOW!" Xavier roared.

Lianna's arrows flew. One after another struck deep.

Nul'Zarak screamed. Instead of retreating again, it retaliated. A quick twist of its body sent a spray of acidic bile arcing across the chamber. It hissed as it struck stone, melting a pillar's base and sending the top half crashing down. Xavier dove forward, dragging Ella clear just before it landed.

Smoke curled from the seared stone. Valkra growled, ears flattened, her body low and coiled. Frostclaw moved with her, the two cats flanking to the side as they tried to box the creature's motion.

The monster slammed one limb down toward Valkra, but the shadowmane cub darted under its mass, dragging her twin tails to distract it further. It snarled and tried to twist, but Frostclaw's weight crashed into its shoulder segment, claws tearing shallow furrows into its chitin.

"Good boy," Lianna breathed as she fired again. Her next arrow punched deep into the soft spot where limb met body.

Ella circled and charged again. Her short swords flashed, striking at a joint between leg and body. Sparks flew as one blade carved deep. The creature hissed and snapped its tail toward her, but she backflipped clear.

Xavier dove forward again, dual blades spinning. Emberstone scraped harmlessly. Vaeltheris hissed through the air, slashing just under a raised leg. A rivulet of blood trailed from the cut. Not deep, but it hurt.

Nul'Zarak reared up and slammed the cavern floor again, triggering another shockwave. This time it followed up by burrowing in place, vanishing in seconds.

"Eyes sharp!" Xavier called.

A moment later, the ground ruptured again. This time the beast came up beneath Ella and Lianna. The explosion of rock sent them tumbling apart. Ella rolled with the impact, one blade lost, but the other still clutched. Lianna rose with a snarl, bleeding from her temple.

Nul'Zarak lunged toward Lianna.

Frostclaw intercepted, leaping onto the creature's neck and biting hard into the small gaps between stone and chitin. Valkra followed, snapping at the base of its tail. The distraction gave Lianna time to retreat and fire again.

A quick succession of arrows left the ranger's bow, each one aiming for the vulnerable segments. Nul'Zarak screeched out in its pain, the massive abominable form writhing and twisting violently.

As the beast roiled in its suffering, Xavier, throwing

caution to the wind, lunged straight at the serpentine form of the monster. Though in pain, the creature was not without awareness, and it twisted, trying to crush the man in its massive mandibles.

Xavier was just able to twist Vaeltheris, wedging the blade's length between the overwhelming force of the pincer attack. The blade flared, its magical nature allowing it to resist the devastation of the attack.

Xavier wrenched the blade sideways, slowly forcing the maw open further and leaving a new exposure for the two archers.

Ella had retrieved her bow and both she and Lianna aimed shots, one flaming and the other plain, into the creature's throat.

The sharp projectiles pierced the delicate flesh. Each shot caused a new recoil from the abomination. Its massive coils thrashed against stone pillar fragments and sent cracks splintering across the ground. The newly spastic movements of the monster further destabilized the glow of the fungi. The pulsing lights flickered in chaotic patterns, adding to the jagged shadows thrown about the cavern.

Through the chaos, however, Xavier saw something else. Opportunity. As Nul'Zarak reared upwards to avoid the new searing pain within its mouth, the wounded length of its underbelly was exposed once again. Xavier charged toward the towering monstrosity, Vaeltheris flared in his grip as if reveling in the impending mortal strike.

Nul'Zarak had not become what it was through chance. It sensed the movement below and lunged down toward the assaulting human, its gaping jaws widening further in an effort to swallow the offending morsel whole. Air reverberated within the beast, a deep sucking force filled with the stench of death and decay roiled out of the abyssal throat.

Xavier didn't stop or hesitate. He leapt into the descending path.

Ella screamed in horror at what appeared to be a suicidal attack from the man she had become bound to. Lianna grimly bit her tongue, bidding the human a peaceful rest as she drew back yet another arrow.

Xavier had other plans than his own death. At the last second, he angled Vaeltheris sideways, jamming the enchanted blade between the awesome mandibles again, preventing them from slamming shut on his flesh. The Emberstone blade came upwards, leaving a scorching path through the inside of the creature's mouth.

The impact force of the monstrous bite sent tremors through Xavier's arms and shoulders, its pressure intense and even causing strain on the wondrous blade. Nul'Zarak screeched in fury and pain, determined to crush the offending obstacle. But Vaeltheris held, the enchanted blade flaring even brighter as it defied the weight of the beast's behemoth strength.

Xavier gritted his teeth, his muscles straining as he fought to twist the blade. Inch by excruciating inch the mandibles crept wider. Xavier could feel the raw primal power coiling beneath his digits, the visceral hunger that the beast embodied, ancient and endless, enough to claim countless lives and still be ravenous. But not today, Xavier thought to himself.

"Lianna, now!" Xavier cried out.

He had seen where Lianna had clambered atop a jagged rock formation, where she had already lined up her shot. The moment Xavier forced the maw open, she let her arrow fly. The shot streaked through the air, a trail of flame following behind it, piercing directly into the soft, exposed roof of Nul'Zarak's mouth.

It struck the roof of Nul'Zarak's mouth. The impact was instantaneous and devastating. A wet, sickening crack shook the beast moments before a violent, convulsing tremor started through it. Nul'Zarak's entire body seized, its mandibles shuddering as the arrow lodged deep inside, the burning tip searing flesh and nerve alike.

The scream that followed was apocalyptic.

The creature thrashed, slammed walls, and tore its own coils apart. Xavier barely freed himself and rolled clear. Rubble fell. Spores erupted in scattered bursts. And finally, the beast collapsed into a heap of twitching limbs and shattered chitin.

Silence fell.

Slowly, Xavier straightened, Vaeltheris still gripped tightly in his hands. It was over. The Maw of the Deeps had closed for the final time and would never open again.

# CHAPTER TEN
*Tremors of Fate*

The silence that followed was a heavy, oppressive thing, broken only by the ragged breathing of the group and the faint trickle of water through the distant stone. The Maw of the Deep lay in a collapsed heap, its grotesque form folded in on itself, a monstrosity finally stilled. Blood, ichor, and fragments of shattered carapace littered the stone underfoot.

Xavier didn't speak, every part of him ached, muscle, mind, and soul. He stood still, sword in hand, until the hum of his interface pulled his eyes from the corpse.

Notifications spilled forth in a shimmering cascade, some routine, some monumental. However, before he could read more than a few lines, a familiar sound rose behind him, a low, irritated growl.

Frostclaw padded into view, his snow-pale coat flecked with dust and fragments of rock. Between his teeth, he carried a writhing bundle by the scruff... Valkra. The shadowmane cub twisted and kicked in protest, high-pitched growls bubbling from her throat, but Frostclaw moved with unbothered patience. He carried her like an elder feline would carry a defiant kitten, and she was no match for his resolve.

Lianna, catching her breath as she hopped down

from her former perch, raised an eyebrow at the sight. Amusement flickered across her features, quickly giving way to something more thoughtful.

"You kept her out of the fight," she murmured to herself. There was no reprimand in her tone, only respect.

Frostclaw had made a deliberate decision. While the others fought the abomination, he had tucked Valkra away behind shattered stone, protecting her from a fate far too grim for one so young. Whether it was instinct or a growing bond, the great cat had ensured the cub would survive.

With a final huff, Frostclaw dropped Valkra unceremoniously onto the ground. She scrambled upright, shook herself off with a grumpy flick of her twin tails, and glared up at him with indignant golden eyes. He blinked slowly, impassive and regal. Something passed between them in silence.

I could have helped, you know.

It was there in the tail flick, in the exaggerated sniff, in the way she stalked to Xavier's side and pressed herself stubbornly against his leg.

"Looks like someone didn't appreciate the babysitting," Lianna quipped, brushing damp hair from her face.

Xavier chuckled tiredly, rubbing a hand across his forehead. "At least one of us had the sense to keep Valkra out of it. I thought she and Frostclaw would help like they did against the ankhegs, but that thing..." He trailed off, glancing toward the Maw's corpse. "No, Frostclaw made the right call."

Frostclaw didn't respond. He simply stood tall beside Lianna, the image of patient judgment. He had only done what was the best option for the little one. He would have rejoined the fray if Lianna had called or was in true danger.

While Lianna and Ella moved to praise the great cats, Xavier let himself sink to the stone floor, leaning against one of the monstrous fallen plates of the Maw's hide. He exhaled slowly, letting his focus blur just enough to bring the interface fully into view.

---

**Congratulations, Champions of Rynthavael!**

Through grit, steel, and unwavering resolve, you have conquered the First Level of the Deeps, securing it for the people of Rynthavael! What once lay in darkness, infested with corrupted ankhegs, stone-scaled wyrms, and the terrifying Maw of the Deep, is now cleansed by your courage and strength.

---

The fanfare that accompanied the message sounded like a celebration in full swing: trumpets, cheers, and the distant hum of voices. Xavier closed his eyes and let the victory sink in before reading the rest of the prompt.

---

**Achievements:**
Threats Eliminated – The dangers lurking below have been vanquished, ensuring the tunnels are no longer a death trap for the unwary.
Path Secured – Rynthavael's villagers can now begin expanding into this level of the Deeps, reclaiming lost knowledge and resources.
New Opportunities Unlocked! – With the first level cleared, the path forward to the Earth Core now lies open.

This is a momentous step in Rynthavael's growth, one that will be remembered for generations. But deeper mysteries and greater dangers still await. For now, bask in your triumph…you have carved safety from shadow,

---

strength from struggle, and victory from the abyss!

A momentous step. Xavier nodded slowly, reading each line as if committing them to memory.

**Quest Completed:** Drums in the Deeps I

The ancient stone trembles no more.

The first level of the Deeps beneath Rynthavael has been explored and secured. The unnatural echoes that once haunted the forgotten corridors have fallen silent, and with their passing, the halls now breathe once more with the promise of purpose.

Broken masonry has been cleared, collapsed passages mapped, and hostile forces purged. Rynthavael's people can now walk these reclaimed halls without fear—and for the first time in an age, the legacy buried beneath the mountain stirs toward renewal.

**Completion Outcomes:**

- Deeps Level 1 Secured – The area is now safe for structured expansion, storage, and mining.
- Hostile Entities Eliminated – All known threats within this level have been neutralized.
- New Resources Unlocked – Relics, rare stone veins, and materials hidden in the ruin are now accessible to your people.
- Future Questlines Unlocked – Lower levels of the Deeps can now be accessed for continued reclamation and story progression.

**Rewards:**

- Settlement Resource Gain – Materials recovered from ruins bolster Rynthavael's stockpiles.

> - Increased Infrastructure Stability –
>   Foundations reinforced; future construction
>   will benefit.
> - +5000 Experience
>
> "The echoes of the past fade, but the path ahead now
> hums with possibility. The Deep remembers. And soon,
> so shall you."

They had done it. The first level was theirs. A hollow ache gave way to something warmer: pride. Rynthavael would grow.

The next notification struck a different chord entirely.

> **Your name echoes beyond the depths!**
>
> By vanquishing the monstrous Nul'Zarak - Maw of
> the Deep, you have done more than claim victory, you
> have carved your legend into the world itself! Word of
> your triumph spreads like wildfire, carried by traders,
> scouts, and whispers in the dark. The depths trembled
> before you and your group's might, and now, all of
> Arath begins to take notice.
>
> +500 Reputation Gained
>
> Congratulations – Your reputation level has increased
> from Level 2 – "Who Are You Again? - Your name might
> be whispered in the winds, but most can't recall it. If
> you were a knight, you'd be the one who gets left out of
> the battle plan. People might nod at you in the market,
> but they're mostly confused." to Level 3 – "Somewhat
> Known, Still Forgettable - Ah, you've been spotted once
> or twice. Someone might remember you from a tavern
> brawl or for getting lost in the woods. But don't expect
> anyone to remember your name unless it's written on
> your cloak."

Xavier snorted. "Nice to know I'm still vaguely memorable. Maybe they'll spell my name right next time."

He wasn't sure how reputation worked in Arath. There was no one here to witness the fight, no herald, no scribe, and yet, the world knew. Somehow, it always knew. Sighing he chalked it up to another unique quirk of the world he still didn't fully understand. Dismissing that notification, he moved on to the next one.

> You have slain Nul'Zarak – Maw of the Deep!
> **+12,000 Experience**

The amount of experience made him sit up and reread the short prompt. He had thought the amount of experience gained from slaying the Stonescale Wyrm was immense, but this was another 50% on top of that. Twelve thousand for a single kill? It just went to show something he was learning quickly about Arath, danger and reward go hand in hand. The higher the danger the better the payout. Since he happened to survive this most recent encounter he was going to enjoy his proverbial meat.

> **Hark and Hear! You have ascended in power. You are now Level 15!**
>
> The touch of the divine lingers upon you, granting **6 attribute points** to shape your destiny, an exceptional gift, elevated from the ordinary **4 points** by the **Blessings of the Gods (Danu).**
> **(Total: 18 points remaining to distribute)**
>
> Choose wisely, for these points will define your path. You have **3 days** to assign them, or they will fall to the whims of fate.
>
> Your growing prowess earns you a boon: **20% skill**

**allocation.**
**(Total: 60% remaining)**

This is your chance to sharpen a favored talent, forge new strength, or balance your path.

**Rise, Seeker of Glory. The world awaits your will. Seek adventure, seek wisdom, seek love and let your legend be forged in your choices. LIVE!**

Xavier lowered the interface with a quiet exhale. Aelriva had been right, of course. She always was.

His eyes turned toward the darkened edges of the chamber. This level was cleared. The path further into the Deeps had only just begun.

#

Xavier remained seated against the broken carapace for several more minutes, mind buzzing not with the joy of victory, but the weight of what came next. Level 15. Exactly the level he needed to progress the chain tied to the Sleeping Lines. Aelriva had said as much, but of course, she hadn't said it directly.

He sighed. "You always know just enough, don't you?" he murmured aloud, though the sprite wasn't there to answer. She never was unless it served some higher design. That thought drew his gaze downward as his mind wandered to Danu.

It was becoming a pattern: beings with knowledge doling out truth only in curated fragments. Aelriva, the gods, even Ella to a degree. He trusted them... mostly, but the gaps in their answers, the purposeful vagueness, wore at him. Were they protecting him? Testing him? Or was it simply how power worked in this world: always behind veils, always one revelation away from collapse?

**New Quest Available:** Drums in the Deeps II

The first level of the Deeps has been secured, but the depths do not rest so easily. Faint tremors ripple through the stone, and distant sounds, scraping, shifting, something alive, reverberate from below. The deeper halls remain untouched, their secrets and dangers unknown. If Rynthavael is to claim the Deeps fully, the next descent must begin.

**Objectives:**

- Descend to the second level of the Deeps beneath Rynthavael.
- Identify and eliminate any remaining threats.
- Recover valuable resources, artifacts, or lost knowledge.

**Potential Challenges:**

- Stronger and more organized threats may lurk deeper.
- Structural instability, traps, and other unknown dangers.
- Unstable ley line anomalies could interfere with magic.

**Rewards:**

- Access to deeper resources within the Deeps.
- New crafting and construction materials.
- Potential discovery of ancient Sylmyrian relics.
- +6000 Experience.

"The silence of the first halls has been reclaimed, but below, the danger of the Deeps still lingers. Something waits in the dark. Will you be the one to unearth it?"

Xavier leaned his head back against the carapace, staring up at the glowing threads of fungus above.

"Of course it's a chain," he muttered. "Could be ten levels. Twenty. Who knows?"

He didn't dislike the idea. In another life, in another world, he would've welcomed an endless dungeon crawl, but this wasn't a game. They bled here. They died here. Furthermore, somewhere in the depths, the Earth Ley Line still called to him.

He pushed himself upright and turned toward the Maw's massive remains. As brutal as the fight had been, the real work was just beginning. Loot didn't appear magically. If he wanted anything useful, he had to carve it out of flesh and bone.

Not for the first time he lamented the fact they actually had to carve the corpse up and didn't just receive the dropped items by "looting" it like in some of the games he had played. Real life was just so much more, well messy than in games. Resigned to the dirty task, he hoped to find some source of water nearby instead of trekking all the way back to the Life Ley Garden.

With a resigned grunt, he resized Vaeltheris into a more utilitarian blade. The smell of blood and bile already turned his stomach, but he knelt and began to cut.

Within minutes, Ella and Lianna joined him. The Iskari ranger moved with practiced grace, unbothered by the gore. Xavier watched her for a moment, then finally asked, "How do you know where to cut?"

As they worked, Xavier took the time to press Lianna further, genuinely curious about her method and approach. To his surprise, the inquiry didn't draw a short answer but instead unlocked a flood of practical instruction. She explained how subtle shifts in coloration or thickness marked areas where connective tissue gave way to salvageable organs. She noted where glands stored venom, which muscles were fiber-rich and worth preserving, and how cartilage could be traced by feel alone beneath dense plates of armor.

It turned out she had attained adept rank in a rare skill called Bestial Lore. Not only did it deepen her understanding of animals, beasts, and monsters in general, but it also provided subskills that enhanced everything from combat tactics to harvesting. As she spoke, Xavier realized how much of her success in extracting valuable materials stemmed not just from instinct, but from layered knowledge.

He was just starting to wonder why he hadn't picked up the skill himself when suddenly...

**Congratulations! You have learned a new subskill:** Beast Harvesting (Level 1)

The Beast Harvesting subskill is a core part of Bestial Lore, focusing on the efficient extraction of valuable materials from creatures. Whether for crafting, alchemy, enchantment, or trade, a skilled harvester knows how to maximize the yield from a fallen beast. From mundane animal hides to the arcane essence of magical creatures, this subskill ensures nothing goes to waste.

Some see a monster. I see gold, potions, and high-quality armor waiting to happen."

**+0.3% Increased Yield.**
**+0.3% Reduced Risk of Material Damage.**
**+0.2% Increased Quality.**

**Congratulations! Since you have learned a subskill you have also gained the corresponding skill:** Bestial Lore (Level 1)

The Bestial Lore skill represents a deep understanding of animals, monsters, and magical beasts. It allows a character to analyze, dissect, and exploit the biological traits of various creatures, granting advantages in combat, survival, alchemy, and crafting. Hunters, beast tamers, and scholars alike benefit from understanding a creature's weaknesses, useful body parts, and behavioral instincts. The higher the skill level, the greater the insight, from recognizing a creature's mood to understanding how to harvest magical essences or counter beast-based curses.

"I don't just hunt monsters and beasts, I study them. That's why I'm still alive."

**+0.3% Increased Damage against creatures.**
**+0.3% Better Harvesting Yield.**
**+0.2% Better Beast Interaction.**

Lines of light etched themselves across Nul'Zarak's body, veins of knowledge he hadn't seen before. Tendons, bone joints, elemental cores, all subtly outlined as if the creature was revealing its secrets.

He grinned. "Now that's more like it."

For the next few hours, the trio worked tirelessly. Muscle was parted. Bone was cleaved. Ichor was carefully bottled and venom drained into Lianna's waiting vials. Each item as it was harvested was carefully identified and packed into Xavier's satchel.

Their rewards were considerable.

| You have discovered: | Item Class: Rare |
| --- | --- |

| Chitinous Mawplate x 2 | **Item Quality:** Well Crafted<br>**Weight:** 6.2 kg per plate<br>**Durability:** 100/100<br>**Description:** A massive fragment of Nul'Zarak's outer plating, hardened over centuries to a near-impenetrable density. The chitin is layered and mineral-infused, capable of withstanding tremendous force.<br>**Uses:**<br>- Armor Crafting: Can be reforged into heavy armor, a shield, or fortification plating. Properties:<br>- Natural Damage Resistance: Reduces non-magical slashing and piercing damage.<br>- Tremor Buffering: Dampens seismic tremors, providing stability against knockdowns.<br>- Potential Enchantment: If imbued with Earth Energy, it could grant resistance to underground hazards or seismic attacks. |
| **You have discovered:** | **Item Class:** Very Rare |

| Fanged Mandible of the Maw x 2 | **Item Quality:** Superb<br>Weight: 5.8 kg per mandible<br>**Durability:** 95/100<br>**Description:** One of Nul'Zarak's massive, serrated mandibles, still humming with residual power. The edges appear naturally jagged, honed by the creature's millennia of burrowing through bedrock.<br>**Uses:**<br>- Weapon Forging: Can be reforged into a scythe, glaive, or greatsword.<br>- Armor-Piercing Bolts/Arrows: The mandible's natural jagged edges make it ideal for high-penetration projectiles.<br>Properties:<br>- Jagged Edge: Wounds inflicted by this weapon do not close easily, making healing magic less effective.<br>- Burrowing Strike: On impact, the weapon delivers a concussive shock, fracturing armor and weakening enemy defenses.<br>- Earth-Touched: May |
|---|---|

| | react to the Earth Ley Line, gaining additional effects when used underground. |
|---|---|
| **You have discovered:** Eyes of the Maw x 2 | **Item Class:** Rare<br>**Item Quality:** Well Crafted<br>**Weight:** 0.9 kg per eye<br>**Durability:** 80/100<br>**Description:** The red, glowing eyes of Nul'Zarak, still faintly pulsing even after death. They seem to react to movement, as if still aware.<br>**Uses:**<br>- Alchemy & Augmentation: Can be distilled into potions or fused into weapons/ armor.<br>Properties:<br>- Darkvision Elixir: When refined, grants enhanced vision in absolute darkness.<br>- Tremorsense Augmentation: If embedded into gear, grants limited tremorsense, detecting enemies through vibrations.<br>- Elemental Resilience: |

| | Temporary resistance to blindness, illusions, or disorienting effects. |
|---|---|
| **You have discovered:** Mawborn Fangs x 17 | **Item Class:** Rare<br>**Item Quality:** Well Crafted<br>**Weight:** 0.7 kg per fang<br>**Durability:** 90/100<br>**Description:** Several smaller fangs from Nul'Zarak's inner maw, razor-sharp and laced with residual venom. These natural blades remain lethal even after extraction.<br>**Uses:**<br>- Weapon Crafting: Can be shaped into daggers, claws, or armor-piercing arrows.<br>- Alchemy & Poisons: The venom can be distilled into a paralytic agent.<br>Properties:<br>- Armor-Piercing: Weapons crafted with Mawborn Fangs ignore natural armor resistance.<br>- Paralyzing Toxin: When refined, the venom can be applied to arrows or melee |

| | |
|---|---|
| | weapons, causing temporary paralysis on targets.<br>- Unstable Corruption: If mishandled, the venom can cause hallucinations and erratic movement. |
| **You have discovered:** Chitin & Shell Fragments x 23 | **Item Class:** Uncommon<br>**Item Quality:** Above Average<br>**Weight:** 2.0 kg per fragment<br>**Durability:** 80/100<br>**Description:** Shattered remnants of Nul'Zarak's outer plating. While not as resilient as the Chitinous Mawplate, these pieces retain some of their natural density and can be repurposed into lighter armor or reinforced plating.<br>**Uses:**<br>- Armor & Shield Crafting: Can be reforged into durable light or medium armor.<br>- Fortification Material: Can be layered onto structures, making them more resistant to seismic shockwaves. |
| **You have discovered:** | **Item Class:** Rare |

| Residual Acidic Ichor x 4 | **Item Quality:** Well Crafted<br>**Weight:** 0.5 kg per vial<br>**Durability:** N/A (Liquid)<br>**Description:** A thick, dark-green fluid extracted from Nul'Zarak's stomach lining, retaining highly corrosive properties. This ichor bubbles and shifts as if it still carries a remnant of its monstrous origins.<br>**Uses:**<br>- Alchemy: Can be distilled into Acid Potions or weapon coatings, adding 5-10 acid damage per strike for 1 hour.<br>- Siege Warfare: When boiled down and concentrated, it can melt through stone and metal, making it an effective material for acid-based traps or siege weapons. |
| --- | --- |
| **You have discovered:**<br>Burrowing Tendon x 4 | **Item Class:** Rare<br>**Item Quality:** Exquisite<br>**Weight:** 1.5 kg per strand<br>**Durability:** 90/100<br>**Description:** A long, |

sinewy tendon harvested from Nul'Zarak's burrowing muscles. This material retains a natural elasticity and high-tension strength, making it a prized resource for crafting enchanted rope, high-tension bows, and flexible armor joints.

**Uses:**

- Enchanted Rope Crafting: Can be woven into unbreakable cords, climbing ropes, or grappling hooks.

- Bowstring & Whip Reinforcement: Blacksmiths can reinforce bowstrings, whips, and tethers, increasing weapon durability and tensile strength.

- High-Tension Gears & Traps: Artificers can use these tendons in complex mechanisms requiring flexibility and durability.

Lianna, as it turned out, was proving worth her weight in gold, quite literally. Not only could she locate the most valuable parts of the beast, but she had also come prepared with empty vials, reinforced containers, and preservation wraps. Every detail was efficient, deliberate, and refined through experience.

Xavier continued to marvel at the dimensional fold of his satchel. Watching something the size of a wagon axle vanish into the mouth of a leather bag never got old. Still, the enchantment didn't wholly eliminate mass, it only mitigated volume. With every item added, the weight pressed heavier across his shoulder. Soon enough, it would begin to slow him down.

He hoped they'd find the Earth Ley Line soon, not just to fulfill the divine nudge tugging at his soul, but because if they descended any deeper with this much weight, his fighting ability would be compromised.

Even with the trove of materials, most of the items, while wondrous, didn't strike him as markedly different from other unique drops they'd recovered from earlier monsters. All except one.

Something buried deeper within the beast called to him. A magnetic pull, like a siren's whisper threading through the marrow of the earth.

He carved his way inward, pausing often to take the specimens passed to him by Ella and Lianna. Each part had its value, but nothing matched the pull of what lay ahead. Finally, his hand pressed into something different, dense and heavy, humming with unnatural stillness.

Two things happened the moment he touched it: a new prompt appeared, framed in a brilliant crimson glow, and the cavern around them rumbled faintly, a tremor passing through the stone like a breath exhaled from the world itself.

Xavier could feel the resonance pulsing in time with his heartbeat. Something old. Something deep. Something alive.

| You have discovered: Nul'Zarak's Ley-Infused Heart | **Item Class:** Legendary<br>**Item Quality:** Masterwork<br>**Weight:** 8.5 kg<br>**Durability:** 100/100<br>**Description:** A massive, petrified core of residual ley energy, buried deep within Nul'Zarak's remains. It throbs faintly, as if linked to something deeper beneath the surface.<br>**Uses:**<br>- Ley Enchantment & Artifact Creation: Can be attuned to the Earth Ley Line.<br>Properties:<br>- Earth's Pulse: Grants an enhanced connection to the Earth Ley Line, allowing the wielder to sense ley fluctuations underground.<br>- Stonebound Fortitude: Increases physical resilience and resistance to knockback effects.<br>- Burrower's Insight: Grants temporary perfect navigation in underground tunnels, preventing the user from |
|---|---|

getting lost.

"This isn't just a part of that creature," Xavier stated as he lifted the throbbing stone piece free from the tender flesh, its weight much more than its size would indicate.

"No," Lianna agreed as she looked around them watching dust and sand settle from the tremor. "It caused the whole earth to move. Considering what it came from I am almost afraid to think what it is signaling"

Ella grimaced slightly thinking about the implications, "whatever it is, it just rang a very large bell"

Xavier hefted the piece of stonelike material thoughtfully, something about it still called to him. Something similar to what he felt pulling him further down into the Deeps. "I don't think whatever it is truthfully means us any harm. I feel a more calming and calling presence from it. I think its associated with the Ley Lines. We need to go deeper and find the Earth Ley Line to be certain though."

#

Finished with the corpse of the Maw, they collectively decided to explore its den. Hopefully they could find some water to wash the putrid innards of the beast from their armor and bodies before they continued the search for the passage to the next level. Ella and Lianna retrieved their torches from near the entry archway, and Xavier lit another from the one Ella was holding. Between the torchlight and the bioluminescence of the fungi that crept along the walls, the darkness of the cavern was pushed back, revealing a sight that was both tragic and awe-inspiring.

In the center of the cavern stood a large stone archway, nearly twice the size of the one that had led them into the chamber. Its upper half had collapsed, strewn as rubble across the floor, but what remained was still carved with remnants of intricate designs and faded frescoes. From what the trio could make out, they appeared to depict some kind of trade occurring beneath the arch. Caravans passing through, goods changing hands, figures of various races bartering and gathering.

This impression was reinforced by the many broken columns and foundations scattered throughout the chamber. Closer inspection revealed traces of worked stone laid in deliberate patterns, distinct pathways that hinted at roads winding through what had once been a thriving outpost. The cavern had not always been a monster's den. From its layout and remnants, it had clearly once served as a market, a trade station, or perhaps a bastion of subterranean civilization.

Passing through the fractured archway, the group followed the remains of the roadway. It was wide, more boulevard than trail, and still bore signs of its original grandeur beneath the grit and ruin. Several hundred yards deeper, half-shrouded by the lingering gloom, they came upon a shattered obelisk. Its once-proud shape had been marred by deep gouges and jagged claw marks. Nul'Zarak had used it as a scratching post. A monument desecrated.

Xavier moved close, brushing his fingers against its gouged surface. Along the surviving base, faint sigils remained, small inscriptions in various scripts. His Linguist trait activated, flooding him with recognition. Sylmyrian was the most prominent, but also present were Khazridan of the ancient dwarves, a swath of archaic Avara for the Animari, and fragments of Sylvaerion, Velkrithian, Nimbrahan, and Brindallan—prime elvish, early Zar'kannan, old gnomish, and ancient halfling, respectively. Each time his mind identified a new language, a prompt whispered confirmation: New Language

Acquired.

His list was growing enormous. And he had only been in Arath for a few weeks.

The ruin held more than lost language. Among the rubble lay signs of a terrible conflict. Broken shields. Shattered weapons. Skeletal remains wearing what was left of armor, tattered, pitted, stained with age. One crushed skeleton leaned against a fractured pillar; a snapped staff clutched in its hands. Nearby, a long-decayed scrap of fabric fluttered, the last remnants of a banner now colorless and rotted to near transparency.

Xavier moved slowly among the dead. Many were human. Others were clearly gnomes, dwarves, halflings, and some Animari. A few bore strange anatomical marks he could not place until Lianna identified them.

"Zar'kannan," she said quietly. "The Marked Ones."

"They fought a battle here," Xavier murmured, taking it all in. "But not against each other. There are no formations. No barricades."

"Odd that we haven't found any elven bodies among them," Lianna added, gesturing toward another pile of bones. "I saw some of their sigils back there."

Xavier nodded, pointing toward a shadowed portion of the cavern. "Every major race is represented here. Except the elves."

Ella knelt near a fallen slab. "Not quite," she said. "Look at this."

They gathered around a broken stone tablet. Dust obscured the carved symbols, but Xavier wiped them clean and knelt. The letters glowed faintly beneath his touch. Sylvaerion.

Beware the Maw... beyond the gate... only hunger

remains.

Beyond the tablet lay a grim tableau, dozens of corpses, elegantly armored in what must have once been shining plate and supple leathers. Time and decay had stolen their beauty, but not their meaning.

"The elves were here," Ella confirmed. "They just fell deeper in. It was not a random attack. Everyone was fighting against something. From the looks of it something massive."

Lianna tossed aside the piece of broken weaponry she had been inspected. "Fighting something and they lost. Given the devastation I would guess this was either when the Maw first arrived or when they tried to take the cavern back from it."

Xavier could only nod in agreement. "At least they were avenged, even if it took far longer than it should have."

Looking around Xavier frowned, his mind was working. Something nagged at the back of his mind. A phrase, a passage, a map...

A small bit of information was drug to the surface. A brief passage in one of the lore books he had been reading mentioned grand underground highways and trade posts. Remnants of old empires and powerful dwarven crafting... what they were called though he couldn't quite...

"Could this have been part of a Grey Road?" he asked aloud.

Ella and Lianna exchanged a glance. Ella stepped forward slowly. "It might have been. But the Grey Roads are ancient... thousands of years old. These corpses are... maybe a century? Less?"

"The cold down here preserved them better," Xavier said. "But yeah, I don't think they died when the place first fell into disrepair and ruin, not when the Maw first took it. I think these corpses were part of an army sent to try and retake it. That means the Deeps under Rynthavael could likely connect to other places and a far larger subterranean system than I had even guessed at."

Lianna's brow furrowed. "We have tales... my people, I mean. Stories of deep folk, traders, and lost tribes. There has always been rumors and stories about creatures and monsters who would come out of the deep dark caves and caverns to steal unruly children and unwary travelers. Ghosts under the mountains. But I thought they were just stories to frighten children."

Xavier offered a grim smile. "Every myth has a grain of truth. At least back where I'm from. Turns out a lot of those myths were just echoes of Arath."

Despite the macabre surroundings, their banter lightened the mood. Shared weariness, shared understanding. They moved deeper into the chamber.

Eventually, they reached the nest.

Set far from the chasm that had granted them entry, the deepest part of the cavern held a gruesome domain. A massive circular depression marked its heart, the stone worn unnaturally smooth from the constant coiling of Nul'Zarak's enormous, armored form. Jagged rock encircled the pit like broken teeth, and from its rim rose towers, not of stone, but of bone.

They weren't mere heaps of discarded remains. These were spires, deliberately constructed. Each one arranged with grotesque precision, crowned with shattered weapons and rusting bits of armor like morbid trophies. A throne room of death. Proof that Nul'Zarak's mind, while bestial, was not without cruel intent.

Blackened fungi pulsed and shimmered around the

nest, far thicker here than elsewhere in the cavern. The closer they drew to the lair, the more vivid and erratic the pulsing became, like the slow beat of a festering wound. They had seen small patches of it before, clinging to walls or blooming from cracks in the stone, but here it coated the ground in dangerous density.

Xavier paused to inspect it. His herbalism skill triggered briefly—but returned nothing. No classification. No warnings. Just... silence. That, more than anything, made his skin crawl.

"I don't like the look of that," he muttered.

"Neither do I," Ella added. "Let's avoid it."

No one argued. The trio skirted wide around the worst patches, instincts trumping curiosity.

Among the bones here and there, among the remains, were much larger and older skeletons. Far too large to be human or any of the other races they had found so far. It clearly marked the Maw of the Deep as the area's apex predator. He had held this location from great and powerful beasts and seeming armies in the past. Xavier looked to the two women who accompanied him and offered a silent prayer of thanks to Danu and any other gods who might be listening that they had not met the same fate as so many before.

Ella nudged one such skull with her foot and shivered. "This isn't just a feeding ground. It's a graveyard."

"No," Lianna corrected. "It's a lair. Clearly that creature had been here for decades if not centuries. It may have been what drove out the original inhabitants. Its size alone along with the marks and damage we had found just leading here show that it kept the number of other creatures in the area under control." She looked to Xavier, "Your people will have to patrol and watch over this level to keep it from becoming infested again. You need more villagers."

Xavier nodded solemnly. "You're right. If we can hold this space, it could be a fallback point. Aelriva said the Syr'Vailen protects from things coming up. I wonder if it protects from above, too." He made a mental note to discuss it with the sprite before he left for the wildlands.

They moved past the nest, deeper into the gloom. And there, at the far edge of the cavern, they found it... The gate.

It rose from the stone like a monolith, twice the height of any man, sealed and weathered by time and violence. Deep gouges scarred its face, claw marks, fractures, splintered symbols. Something, perhaps Nul'Zarak, had tried to tear through it and failed. An impressive feat considering how the monster had burrowed through the stone of the cavern floors and walls with relative ease.

Sigils glimmered across its surface, too worn to decipher yet pulsing with quiet resonance.

Lianna stepped close, running her fingers delicately along one of the symbols. Her hand paused at a particularly deep gouge.

"It looks like it was designed to contain something," she murmured. "Or to defend against it. The real question is, was it the monster we just killed? Or something worse beyond?"

At the gate's center, a jagged, human-sized hole yawned wide where the stone had shattered inward to reveal a narrow path into blackness. The light from their torches did not penetrate far. The darkness within was absolute, absorbing illumination as if defying their presence.

A strange pressure radiated from the breach, coiling through the air like a weight on their shoulders. The air was colder here. Older. The ley energy hummed faintly, resonating with Xavier's bones.

He stepped forward, eyes fixed on the gap. "I know we need to go that way," he said softly. "The ley line is calling me. I've felt it before... when I woke the first two. It's like they're speaking to me."

He glanced at Lianna. "I didn't say anything before, but I felt it in Verdantspire too. Not as strong as here, but... still there. Friendly, even."

Lianna raised an eyebrow at him but said nothing. She didn't fully understand him yet, but each step they took together, she grew closer.

Ella tilted her head toward the gate. "Well. Standing here staring at it isn't getting us anywhere."

Without warning, she strode forward and vanished through the opening. Her torchlight disappeared at once, swallowed by the dark.

A beat of silence passed.

Then Valkra followed, the panther cub slipping through with a flick of her stinger-tipped tails. She paused just inside, turning back toward Xavier with a slow, deliberate blink.

Xavier sighed. "Of course."

Lianna crossed her arms, arching a brow. "That was definitely a challenge."

He chuckled, loosening his blades. "Let's not keep them waiting."

He stepped through the breach and the dark swallowed him whole.

Lianna followed immediately, torch in one hand and bow in the other, arrow nocked and ready. Frostclaw brought up the rear, the great cat's eyes gleaming in the faint light.

Beyond the threshold, the air grew heavier still. Damp stone, old blood, and something ancient clung to the walls and ceiling like breath. The pulse beneath their feet throbbed faintly, as if the earth itself had acknowledged their arrival.

Whatever lay ahead, the Deeps were far from finished with them.

# CHAPTER ELEVEN

*The Path of Stone*

Xavier stepped cautiously through the doorway and into the vast, silent expanse beyond. The moment his foot crossed the threshold, he felt it—the change. The air around him shifted with a sudden weight, pressing down against his chest and shoulders as though the stone itself had drawn breath and was now holding it.

Just ahead, Ella and Valkra stood still and alert, their silhouettes lit by the golden flicker of torchlight. The little shadowmane's twin tails were arched high, stingers flicking with restless tension. Lianna emerged behind him moments later, her bow half-lowered, and Frostclaw padded forward with a low chuff, flanks brushing lightly against the narrowing corridor.

It was quiet. Too quiet Xavier thought.

The dripping water that had haunted every chamber of the Deeps thus far, the ambient breath of the place, was gone. No clatter of falling droplets. No scurry of stone lizards or squeak of deepmice. Only the crackle of their torches and the muffled rhythm of their boots against ancient stone filled the space.

Xavier raised his torch and cast its shifting glow across the corridor. The effect was immediate. Where once rough-hewn cavern walls clawed outward from natural faultlines, now the stone was impossibly smooth, almost polished in places. Walls curved with deliberate symmetry. The floor bore no grooves or clefts but instead formed a clean, slightly concave path that guided the eye deeper into the dark.

Above them, the ceiling arched gently, unnaturally uniform in both height and contour. Every surface here spoke of design, not erosion. Craft, not collapse.

"The caverns are gone," Xavier murmured, voice hushed by the reverent hush of the corridor. "This is... different."

He swept his torch again, catching faint seams in the floor and wall, construction marks, just visible beneath layers of dust and age.

"This must be a Grey Road," he said, more firmly now. "I don't know what else could explain worked stone like this, buried this deep."

Ella stepped beside him, lifting her own torch to examine the stone. Her expression was calm, but her eyes scanned with purpose, sharp as ever. "It certainly does not feel like natural caverns anymore. This was made by hands, or something close to it."

Lianna moved to the nearest wall, letting her gloved fingers brush along its surface. She closed her eyes for a breath, her expression shifting into thoughtful concern. "No tool marks... but this was placed, carved, and fitted." She paused. "And... there's something more. Do you feel that?"

Xavier stepped closer, placing his hand beside hers. The moment his palm pressed against the stone, a subtle pulse surged up through his arm, soft, rhythmic, steady. A deep resonance not unlike a heartbeat, but slower, heavier. It thrummed with the essence of the earth itself.

He exhaled quietly, sensing the truth of it. "It's alive," he whispered. "Just like the others. We're close to the Earth Ley Line. I can feel it."

He looked to the others, his tone shifting. "Stay sharp. If we're this near, there's no telling what might be guarding it."

With that, he drew Vaeltheris from its sheath. The blade shimmered faintly in the torchlight, its edge catching subtle emerald highlights that hadn't been there before. It pulsed in time with the hum of the corridor.

They moved forward slowly, cautious steps echoing outward into the depths.

As they delved deeper, the structure around them grew stranger, less like a tunnel and more like the remnants of a sunken highway. Massive waystones lined the flanks of the passage, their tops barely visible above mounds of rubble and time-thick dust. Some stood straight and defiant; others leaned at dangerous angles, cracked and half-buried. Their faces were etched with symbols long since worn down to ghosts. Inscriptions that had once told stories, marked paths, or given names to places no longer known.

They passed beneath shattered archways that spanned the corridor at intervals, their keystones fractured and sagging, the weight of untold years pulling them slowly apart. One had collapsed entirely, forcing them to climb through a narrow break in the rubble before the road continued.

"These were waystations," Xavier said quietly. "Rest points, maybe... places for caravans to regroup, or traders to meet."

"Now they are graves," Lianna replied, her voice cool. "No one comes here anymore."

Farther in, the passage widened slightly, and the walls bloomed with artistry. Mural carvings, worn and battered, emerged from the shadows, scenes etched deep into the rock by practiced hands. Though fractured and incomplete, the imagery still told a story: caravans laden with goods; beasts of burden with wide shoulders and multiple legs; merchants dressed in strange, heavy robes; guards with blades at their hips and strange runes carved into their shields.

The murals carried on for dozens of feet, curving with the passage. Some chambers they passed through showed large, open markets frozen in stone, while others hinted at subterranean gatherings, rituals or festivals now lost beneath the mountain.

"They weren't just building a road," Xavier said softly, reverently. "This was a civilization… under the earth."

Ella didn't speak, but her eyes followed the carvings with quiet awe. Valkra stayed close to her legs, tail twitching with unease.

It wasn't just the imagery that disturbed Xavier. The further they walked, the more wrong the path beneath them began to feel. The stone shifted.

At first, it was subtle, just a slight tilt, as though the floor had settled unevenly. But then, without warning, one section dipped sharply downward, forcing them to scramble for balance. A few moments later, another portion lifted abruptly beneath their feet, as if something massive had heaved from beneath the surface.

"These changes…" Xavier muttered. "They're not erosion. They're… warping."

"Magic?" Ella asked.

"Or worse," Lianna answered, eyes narrowing. "This is

not just the passage of time. Something altered this road. Something powerful."

Xavier felt it too. The rhythm of the Earth Ley Line was stronger here, but not stable. As if something had twisted it, pulled it, bent it out of its natural shape. The thrum in the stone no longer felt entirely benign. It was still familiar... but agitated. Like a creature stirring in its sleep.

"What happened here?" he whispered. "And what's still down there, waiting?"

They pressed forward in silence, their path now carved through the buried bones of legend and ruin alike.

#

They had been walking for nearly an hour, the rhythm of their steps long absorbed into the silence around them. The twisting, unnatural shifts of the road beneath their feet had become strangely familiar, dip and rise, pitch and roll, like walking across the ribs of some great buried beast. The very stone groaned at intervals, not loudly, but enough to unsettle. Like it remembered being something else.

Xavier had started to feel the Earth Ley Line more keenly as they progressed. A subtle pressure deep in his bones. A thrum, a pull, it came in waves now, stronger the deeper they went. It was not what first stopped him however.

It was the bones.

In the center of the road, scattered across the smoothed stone like discarded kindling, lay a small pile of pale, clean remains. They were not ancient. Not yellowed by time or weathered by dust. They were recent, no more than a few days old.

Xavier raised his hand and dropped into a crouch, signaling the others to halt.

Ella shifted to a covering position with smooth precision, arrow already knocked. Her stance was rigid, eyes sweeping the shadows with practiced tension. Valkra crouched beside her, shoulders hunched, twin stingers twitching, ears angled toward the deeper dark ahead.

Lianna stepped forward and knelt beside Xavier, her gloved hand already reaching for one of the longer bones, a femur or thick forelimb, cracked open along the center. She turned it, eyes narrowing.

"These are fresh," she murmured. "Not just scavenged. Look at the break, split at the joint, the marrow drawn out. Something fed recently."

Xavier frowned, leaning in. The cracked bone wasn't shattered randomly. The break was deliberate, clean, and forceful. Something had known exactly where to bite and how to get what it wanted.

"That's not time or pressure. That's predation," Lianna added. Her tone was quiet but edged. "Too clean to be age. Too purposeful to be accident."

Xavier's gaze shifted across the corridor. The torchlight caught more fragments now, other bones, partially hidden in alcoves and under slumped debris. Some were full skeletons, others no more than a few ribs scattered like teeth from a shattered jaw.

"We're not alone," he said softly.

He rose and moved a few steps forward, scanning the nearby walls. His eyes caught it then... long, deep furrows carved into the stone. At first, he thought them old cart-grooves or tool marks. But the angle was wrong. The shape was too violent.

He crouched again, tracing one with a fingertip.

"Claw marks," he muttered. "Not unlike the ankhegs...

but still different. Shallower, more vertical. Not from digging. Maybe from climbing."

He looked to Lianna. "Ideas?"

She shook her head slowly. "Nothing that lives in the upper tunnels. These... this feels older, deeper."

Ella stepped beside them, arrow still drawn, her voice low. "Whatever it is, it knows this ground better than we do." She tilted her head slightly, listening. "We're in its territory now."

The group pressed on with grim caution.

The corridor began to narrow. At first it was subtle, just enough to force them into a tighter formation, but soon the walls drew inward like a throat preparing to swallow. No longer could they walk side by side. They were down to two abreast, shoulder brushing shoulder. The walls felt closer than they were.

Beneath their feet, the stone began to grind again. Subtle to begin with. Then with a low, rattling groan, the floor shifted. Their steps grew uneven, unstable. One moment their boots touched stone and found no resistance, weightless, as if walking across a dream. The next, gravity slammed into them, doubling their burden with each movement. It hit like a storm front: dizzying, disorienting.

Frostclaw's claws scraped the ground more than once to steady himself. Valkra skidded with a low growl, her limbs tensing as she adjusted to the fluctuations. The group pressed forward through the choking air, muscles strained, balance uncertain.

Xavier staggered once, catching himself on the wall. The hum of the ley line had grown louder.

Only now it wasn't just the earth that was whispering.

They heard something else.

At first, it was nearly imperceptible, a soft faint clicking, like fingernails on stone. Rapid and sporadic. Then it came again, stronger. A second source joined it. Then a third.

All around them. The noises were not footsteps. They were not breathing.

It sounded more like skittering. A thin, rapid staccato of motion, above, behind, ahead. Like the stone itself had started crawling.

Xavier froze, every hair on his arms rising.

Lianna turned in place, her posture going rigid. "Did you hear that?"

"I hear too much," Ella whispered. Her bow remained drawn. "They're around us."

Valkra crouched low, her body tense. Frostclaw's ears laid flat, lips peeled back in a low snarl.

Xavier lifted Vaeltheris. The glow from the blade pushed against the dark, but it didn't reach far. The torchlight now seemed dimmer, as if the very shadows were resisting illumination.

The skittering grew louder, closer. It was in the walls. In the ceiling.

Then, without warning, the darkness moved.

Carapace-clad, elongated, inhuman things emerged from the dark. Their limbs were segmented, curved like hooked scythes. Their torsos were lean and wrong, moving with a boneless grace. Mandibles clicked softly, rhythmically, but no sound escaped their mouths.

No breath, no roar, just movement.

From the shadows above, a shape dropped, no sound of

descent, only the scrape of claw on stone and the sudden blur of movement. A second shape followed, then a third clung to the side wall, limbs coiled tight, lashing out in a sudden blur of motion.

The two of them that had dropped, landed in the center of the group, limbs flashing, hooked arms striking for anything in reach. The third, still attached to the wall, lashed downward with a vicious overhead strike that sent the group scattering.

The fourth remained above them, unmoving. Waiting.

Its lidless, glowing eyes locked on Xavier.

It was studying him, and it was hungry.

#

The first of the two creatures that had dropped into the group lunged straight for Xavier. Its long, segmented limbs moved with sickening fluidity, and its mandibles snapped shut just inches from his face with a sharp clacking sound. The hooked claws on its forearms slashed outward in a brutal cross, the arc of one swing passing dangerously close to his throat.

Xavier threw himself back, barely avoiding the decapitating strike. As his boots skidded across the stone, he triggered Insight, his mind narrowing into focus as the familiar glow pulsed behind his eyes. Text unfolded across his vision instantly, clean and sharp.

| **Name:** Flesh-Feeder | **Disposition:** Feral Aggression |
|---|---|
| The Flesh-Feeders are opportunistic subterranean predators, drawn to areas of death, ley energy fluctuations, and weakened prey. Though they lack higher intelligence, they hunt with eerie coordination, | |

using their natural camouflage, burrowing tactics, and fast, brutal attacks to overwhelm their victims.

| **Health:** 95/95 | **Stamina:** 80/80 | **Mana:** 30/30 |
|---|---|---|

Grimacing, Xavier surged forward as the creature raised its claws again. Vaeltheris came up in time to intercept the attack. The silvery blade flared with a soft blue-white glow as it caught the center of the monster's forelimb. The impact was solid, and for a moment the feeder resisted... then the enchanted edge cut through with precision, shearing bone and chitin alike.

The severed claw struck the ground behind him with a wet crunch.

The creature reeled back, its mandibles clicking in a frenzied rhythm. The wound leaked black ichor in thick, pulsing gouts, but it did not retreat. Instead, it lunged again, jaws snapping toward Xavier's face with wild desperation.

To his right, the second Flesh-Feeder surged toward Lianna, but it never reached her.

Frostclaw, moving with a blur of white fur and silent fury, leapt between them. The snow leopard collided with the feeder mid-pounce, throwing it off course. His massive jaws clamped down on the back of the creature's head, crushing the chitin with a crack that echoed through the corridor.

The creature writhed, legs flailing, but the damage was already done. It was trapped beneath the cat's weight, its head locked in Frostclaw's jaws. Lianna fired a quick pair of arrows into the gaps along its thorax. The shafts buried deep, piercing joints and vital tissue.

The monster twitched once. Then it went limp.

On the wall, the third feeder had not stopped moving.

It clung to the stone just above the group, its long limbs coiled like a spider. As Ella shifted position, it lashed out with a sudden, vicious swipe. The hooked appendage struck hard against the stone as she deflected it with the reinforced spine of her bow.

Using the opening, Ella loosed an arrow upward in a tight shot. The shaft buried into one of the monster's lidless eyes with a soft wet pop, sending a burst of dark ichor splashing across the rock—and down onto her.

The creature shrieked in silence, its body spasming. It clawed at the embedded arrow with frantic strength, tearing the shaft free and spraying more of the sickly black fluid across the stone.

It lunged again.

Ella ducked low, the hook passing just over her head as she rose behind it. Her next shot struck the weak point between the creature's shoulder and torso. The arrowhead drove deep.

The feeder's limbs jerked wide, mandibles parting in a silent howl.

All around them, Valkra darted between the chaos, her sleek black form weaving through the combat. Her claws and teeth harried the remaining feeders on the ground, but her attention never lingered long in one place.

A sharp growl escaped her throat. She circled quickly around Frostclaw and turned toward the one still grappling with Xavier.

One of her twin tails lashed forward, the stinger driving into a soft spot behind the feeder's leg.

The effect was immediate.

The creature froze mid-attack. Its limbs stiffened. The venom coursed through its body like fire. Whatever animus had driven it to madness was halted in place.

Xavier didn't notice. Not at first.

His world was narrowed to the feeder's gaping maw and the single remaining claw. When the creature suddenly stopped, caught in some invisible grip, he wasted no time.

He dropped his torch. Both hands closed around Vaeltheris's hilt.

The first strike removed the remaining arm.

The second swept horizontally across its neck. The chitin parted with a clean slice, and the monster's head soared through the air in a slow, spiraling arc.

The third strike came down hard, splitting the carapace from collarbone to sternum. The silvery glow of Vaeltheris flared as the blade drove deeper, cleaving through the core. The two halves of the Flesh-Feeder slid apart and hit the ground on either side of Xavier with wet thuds.

He stood over the ruin, panting, his body still locked in the rhythm of combat.

In the time it had taken Xavier to dispatch his opponent, Ella had not let up.

Every time the wall-clinging feeder lashed down, she turned or dodged. And every time it overextended, she answered with another arrow. Each shaft found its mark. The creature slowed with every hit, the blood loss and pain dragging at its movements.

Finally, its grip on the wall gave out.

The feeder collapsed to the ground in a loose sprawl of limbs and twitching joints. A final shot zipped through the air with a quiet tzzt and buried itself in the gap between its ruined and remaining eye.

It shuddered violently, then stopped.

High above, the fourth Flesh-Feeder remained where it had been, clinging to the wall well beyond reach. Its mandibles clicked rapidly in consternation. It shifted its weight back and forth, uncertain. The deaths of its kin, the smell of blood, and the rising call of hunger pushed it closer to frenzy.

Then the ground beneath them trembled. It was not the tremor of battle. Not the impact of claws or blades. The earth itself responded.

Xavier felt the surge of power, deep and ancient, rolling through the stone like a pulse. The ley line beneath them roared to life. Gravity shifted violently around them, dragging and lifting in a chaotic flux.

The feeder lost its grip and It fell from the wall like a stone dropped in water.

It struck the ground hard enough to fracture its carapace. Limbs flailed, trying to rise, but they were too slow.

Vaeltheris pierced its side in one smooth motion.

Two arrows, one from Ella, one from Lianna, found openings in the broken plating. The creature convulsed. For a moment, its legs scrabbled weakly across the floor. The shafts of the arrows taking the few remaining hit points that it had.

Then it died.

A silence settled over the corridor.

Then a soft tone echoed through Xavier's mind.

> You have killed Flesh-Feeders x4

> **+4000 experience**
> **(Bonus: +250 – flawless teamwork and environmental adaptation)**
> **Total Earned: +4250 experience**

The prompt lingered for a moment before Xavier dismissed it. He stood breathing heavily, Vaeltheris still in his hands, the faint light along its edge dimming once more.

He glanced to Ella first, then to Lianna. Both were winded but unhurt. Frostclaw bore a shallow cut along his foreleg, already being tended to. Valkra paced slowly among the corpses, twin tails flicking.

Xavier exhaled a long, tired breath and finally sheathed Vaeltheris. "That was too close," he said.

Lianna nodded once, wiping blood from her fingers. "And getting closer every time. These ambushes... they are learning."

"I am less worried about the feeders," she added. "The stone is worse. The gravity—those shifts are unnatural. I have only heard of such things in the Blasted Lands. And those were left in ruin by spells meant to rewrite reality."

Ella looked at the trembling stone beneath her boots. "The Earth Ley Line?" she asked.

"I think so," Xavier replied quietly. "And it knows we are close."

He paused, gaze fixed ahead where the corridor dipped once more into shadow.

"I just do not know yet if it's trying to help us..." He drew a breath. "...or drag us under."

#

The ground pulsed again beneath their feet, but this

time the resonance changed.

It centered on Xavier. His words were almost prophetic.

He felt it before it struck, an invisible force rising from beneath the stone, wrapping around his legs, his spine, his core. A sudden surge of power yanked him forward without warning. The pressure seized his body and dragged him down the corridor toward the deeper dark.

He stumbled once, nearly falling as the world tilted. Every instinct screamed to resist. Muscles strained as he threw his weight backward, boots skidding on the stone, one hand clawing for purchase along the wall. The pull grew stronger, the ley line's call shifting from subtle whisper to violent demand.

Xavier roared against it.

He slammed one foot down hard and dropped to a knee, forcing his weight into the earth. The magic relented only a heartbeat later, vanishing as quickly as it had come. The sudden absence of pressure left him breathless.

He knelt in the passage, gasping.

The others were already running.

Ella reached him first, her expression tight with alarm. She dropped beside him and grasped his arm, steadying him without a word. Her hand was firm, grounding.

Xavier nodded slowly, a breath still caught in his chest. "I'm alright," he managed.

Lianna followed just behind, placing a hand on his shoulder. Her touch lingered longer, her fingers tensing slightly as if testing for injury.

Xavier gave a tired pat to her hand in return. "Sore," he admitted. "But nothing broken."

He rose slowly, muscles tight, a few scrapes along his

side where his armor had ground against the floor during the pull. His breathing slowed. The ley line had wanted something, but it had not taken him. Not yet.

There was a moment's quiet between them before they moved on, choosing not to return for the corpses of the fallen feeders. The cost of remaining in this corridor any longer was not worth the risk.

They continued downward.

The passage narrowed again, twisting left, then right, then dipping sharply into a low run where the ceiling pressed close. Their footsteps echoed differently now, dulled by the depth. The air grew cooler, thick with ancient weight, and then the path opened.

They emerged into a vast, domed chamber that stretched far beyond the reach of their torches. The vaulted stone above was lost in shadow, but the acoustics of the place spoke of enormous space. The air here felt ancient. Pressed. Watching.

At the far end stood a towering archway, unlike any they had seen before.

It was pristine.

Where other structures had crumbled beneath time's weight, this gate remained untouched. The stone shimmered faintly, as if resisting decay by sheer will. Etchings in intricate spirals adorned its surface, curving inwards toward three recessed circular indentations spaced evenly across the face of the door.

From within those carved lines, veins of emerald light pulsed with life. The magic was not wild or erratic. It was controlled. Contained. It breathed in rhythm with the earth beneath them.

Xavier stepped forward slowly.

The moment his boot touched the stone before the archway a second time, the entire structure flared with golden light. The three circles pulsed in unison, rising in brilliance until they glowed like molten coins against the emerald.

A tremor rippled through the cavern. Stone groaned in response, and then it spoke.

The voice came not from the gate but from everywhere. A deep, sonorous rumble filled the space, the sound of boulders grinding beneath mountains, of buried weight pressing down through the ages.

"The weight of the earth is eternal. Do you seek its strength, or will you crumble beneath it? The trials of the Earth Ley Line have begun."

The echo lingered for a full breath after the words faded.

Ella winced, her bow already halfway raised. "Why is it always trials?" she muttered. "Just once I would like one of these ley lines to greet us kindly. Maybe say it's glad we came and just let you awaken it without trying to kill us." She turned her glare toward Xavier. "You are the one they want, after all."

Xavier gave her a tired glance, then faced the gate again. "Power isn't given," he said quietly. "It's earned."

He stepped forward, closing the remaining distance between himself and the gate.

His hand rose slowly and came to rest on the carved stone. It was warm. Not from heat, but from pressure. It pulsed beneath his palm with steady strength. Magic stirred, rising in resonance, testing him. He could feel it crawl into his skin, weighing his intentions, measuring his will.

Then, just as suddenly, it stopped.

The power withdrew like a held breath released.

The massive stone parted at its center without a sound. Dust rose in fine curtains as the two halves of the archway slid aside, revealing another passage beyond.

A deeper road. A darker depth.

The ley line had opened the path.

Xavier sighed softly. He already knew there would be nothing easy beyond that threshold. The Earth Ley Line did not give anything freely.

Still, he stepped forward, crossing beneath the gate and into the blackness ahead, with the others close behind.

The trial had begun.

# CHAPTER TWELVE

*The Weight, The Rhythem, and The Watcher*

Once past the gateway, the darkness that had obscured the room slowly vanished. As if awakened by something treading a long-unused pathway, a dormant presence stirred. Clumps of moss and lichen clinging to the walls and ceiling began to gently glow, their bioluminescent shapes bathing the chamber in a soft, green-gold light. The glow pulsed in time with an unseen rhythm, ancient and slow, like the deep breathing of the earth far beneath the valley above.

Xavier and the others carefully made their way across the smooth stone floor to the center of the chamber. Ahead stood another archway, closed and sealed against passage. It loomed like a sentinel, its surface unmarked save for a faint shimmer that hinted at powerful wards. Between them and that sealed door rose the only other feature of note: a small stone plinth protruding from the floor, waist high, and unadorned save for a shallow depression at its top in the shape of a handprint.

The three companions exchanged glances, then circled the plinth. It bore no traps that any of them could detect, no sigils or glyphs that suggested an overtly harmful enchantment. Xavier in particular spent several long minutes meticulously examining every exposed inch of the stone and surrounding floor. Only when he was satisfied did he speak, his voice cutting through the charged silence.

"This is clearly the way forward. I have no doubt that the doorway will not open without this being triggered." He set his torch down, the light of the moss more than enough to illuminate the surrounding area.

Ella caught his arm before he could place his hand on the plinth. Her grip was not forceful, but it carried weight, nonetheless.

"Wait," she said, voice low but tense. "One of us should do it. Not you. You are too important to lose again."

Her fingers trembled slightly where they held him. Xavier looked down at her hand, then up into her eyes, those bright jade-green eyes that always seemed to shimmer with more than just life and light. Now they shimmered with fear.

Xavier gently removed her hand from his arm, voice steady. "The quest to wake the lines is mine. I should be the one to activate them. It might not react to anyone else. Besides, you're both here to make sure I'm safe."

Ella's jaw tightened, and she looked away. "Safe?" she whispered, more to herself than to him. Her eyes didn't meet his again. Instead, she turned her back to the group, body rigid. She shifted her stance so she could face outward, watching the room, guarding, but it was a feint.

Her real purpose was to hide the shimmer of tears that clung to her lashes, unshed and unspoken. The bond between them, the soul-deep connection forged through Vaeltheris, thrummed with her worry. She could feel the echo of Xavier's heartbeat through it, steady and calm, and it only deepened her fear. What if that heartbeat stopped?

Lianna had watched the exchange silently. When Ella looked to her for support, the Iskari only shook her head.

She did not speak, but the look she gave said enough: Xavier was right. If any of them were to do this, it had to be him.

Xavier took a long, slow breath, then stepped forward. He lifted his hand and placed it into the depression so that his whole palm aligned with the vague imprint in the stone. As soon as his hand fully covered the mark, the room changed.

A deep vibrational thrum resonated through the plinth, rising up Xavier's arm and into his body. It surged through him like liquid stone, grounding into his feet before radiating outward. The wave passed through the room, and the entire chamber reverberated in response.

A weight slammed down upon everyone. It wasn't merely gravity. It felt as if the entire valley floor and the layers of bedrock above had awakened and were bearing down upon their frames, pressing them toward the stone. Xavier collapsed to one knee beneath the pressure. Lianna hunched, her Animari resilience the only thing allowing her to remain partially upright. Ella's bow dug into the floor as she used its length to brace herself, trembling with effort. Frostclaw and Valkra were both driven to the ground, low yowls of distress escaping before even those sounds were crushed beneath the weight.

To the others, the experience was singular: suffocating pressure, bone-deep and unrelenting. It felt like the world itself was attempting to erase them from existence. Time lost all meaning beneath the unyielding weight.

But Xavier's awareness fractured... separated. The chamber fell away from his senses, his vision darkening at the edges as he was pulled inward, downward. He could no longer see his companions or the two felines. Everything narrowed to the feel of the stone beneath him and the echoing thrum that now pulsed inside his bones.

The vibration had changed. It no longer roared, it whispered. Faint and resonant, it trembled in the marrow of his limbs. The sensation reminded him of distant rockfalls, like the hush before stone shears away into the depths.

Desperate for anything other than the crushing weight, he latched onto the resonance. Slowly, the vibration became a guide, a thread through the darkness of pressure. As he surrendered to it, he felt... watched. Not in a predatory way but observed by something vast and ancient. The whisper held no words, only impressions: age, patience, stillness... a presence that had endured for eons.

He tried to rise, and the whispers became jagged, rough, grinding against his senses like stone on stone. Pain lanced through him. Blood trickled from his ears, his nose, the corners of his eyes. The weight threatened to shatter not just his body, but his mind.

He froze, gasping. Then slowly, with trembling resolve, he stopped struggling. He let go. The more he yielded, the gentler the presence became.

"The river does not fear the stone, nor does it break against it."

With those thoughts came release. Light bloomed beneath him, faint emerald pulses that rippled through ancient runes etched invisibly into the stone floor. They pulsed in time with the rhythm in his bones.

He wasn't seeing so much as he was sensing, feeling. The runes weren't magic. They were memory. Stone's memory. Weight and time given form.

His consciousness stretched outward. He felt the rise and fall of landmasses, the patient growth of roots, the crumbling of lost cities. He became not separated from the world but part of it, nestled within its unshaken foundation. For a moment, Xavier was the earth.

From the walls, figures emerged, shaped of rock and crystal. They did not attack. They watched. They had seen others undergo this trial, many crushed, few enduring. One stepped forward and offered a hand.

Xavier, eyes closed, accepted.

As their fingers met, the pressure vanished. The presence whispered one last time, no longer testing, but affirming.

"You have stepped into the flow. Now, you are part of it."

The chamber dissolved around him, giving way to a boundless horizon of stone and sky. His awareness swelled, attuned to the heartbeat of Arath itself. Then, gently, the vision faded. He was himself again, but not unchanged.

The stone figures melted back into the walls, silent witnesses to a bond formed in silence and stillness.

Back in the waking world, the pressure lifted. Ella staggered upright, nearly overbalancing as the sudden freedom made her light-headed. Her voice was a ragged gasp.

"What happened? Gods, that was horrible."

Lianna regained her posture more gracefully but narrowed her eyes. She studied Xavier carefully, he stood tall now, steady and unmoved.

"You did something," she said quietly. "Did you not?"

Frostclaw and Valkra stirred, whining softly but rising. The weight was gone, but the memory of it lingered.

Xavier looked at his hand, then at the stone beneath his feet. His voice, when he spoke, carried the depth of something newly understood.

"The earth does not fight. It does not yield. It simply is. To stand with it is to be upheld. To fight it is to be buried." He glanced toward the still-sealed archway. "The weight was never really there. It was our perception of it. Or… mine. Now that I have accepted it, the Earth Ley Line has accepted me. This part of the trial is passed."

A deep chime echoed through the chamber. The stone doors began to grind open, revealing the path beyond.

"The earth yields to no will," Xavier said softly as he stepped forward, "but welcomes those who yield to it."

Ella followed without hesitation, brushing a lone tear from her cheek before her posture firmed with quiet resolve. Lianna trailed after, thoughtful and silent, her expression unreadable.

Behind them, the two great cats moved as one, Valkra's keen gaze lingering on Xavier with new curiosity.

#

The archway gave way to another chamber that unfurled before them, vast and shadowed in solemn grandeur. Stone surrounded them on all sides, but it was not lifeless. It hummed. The very air thrummed with a presence older than kingdoms, older than memory. The silence gave way to deep, rhythmic vibrations that coursed through the ground. It was not quite sound, not quite motion, but something felt in the marrow.

It was the breathing of the world.

Beneath their feet, they realized, the floor was a vast mechanism of concentric stone rings. Each was carved with glowing runes that pulsed in a pattern both measured and disrupted, like a slumbering heart trying to find its rhythm again. The pulses beat against their boots, subtle but steady, a low-frequency resonance that tugged at their instincts.

Along the perimeter, towering monoliths of black basalt loomed like ancient sentinels. Their surfaces were streaked with veins of emerald leyline energy, which flickered like lightning caught in stone. But they were not still. Each one tilted, rotated, or shifted at intervals, deliberate yet fractured in their cadence, as though each were a note trying to return to the song it had forgotten.

The vibrations beneath the party's feet made the floor seem alive. Xavier closed his eyes briefly and could feel the pulse trying to pull him downward again. This time it was not in danger, but in invitation. This was no chaos. It was harmony lost and waiting to be restored.

At the very center of the room stood a solitary pedestal carved from primal stone, unmoved by time or disruption. As Xavier approached, its surface shuddered, and from nothingness, an inscription carved itself into being. The words shimmered in quiet emerald light, subtle, confident, ancient.

"To move the earth, one must know its rhythm. Align the song, or be buried in silence."

As the last word etched itself, the chamber trembled. The monoliths became agitated, their movements more erratic. The cadence of their shifting lost what little symmetry it had. Their glow fluctuated like an orchestra falling out of sync with itself.

Lianna winced, her ears flattening back. "The stones… sing, but out of key and out of sync. It is uncomfortable to listen to. Not quite painful, but… wrong."

She wasn't exaggerating. Even Frostclaw and Valkra seemed unsettled, the great cats pacing warily, growling low in their throats. Their tails flicked with unease.

Ella pulled an arrow from her quiver, holding it lightly by the shaft. The fletching trembled in time with the air currents. "The stones are not moving on their own. They're reacting to something. And whatever it is... it's out of balance. If we make the wrong move here, I don't think the chamber would collapse... it would correct itself violently."

Xavier didn't answer at first. He stood still and let the leyline's rhythm seep into him. The heartbeat of the earth was no longer foreign, it was familiar, like an echo he now recognized as his own. The leyline didn't merely resonate through stone, it sang, and he was now attuned to its melody.

With his eyes closed, the world narrowed to sensation. Each monolith resonated with a different tone. Together, they formed a broken chord. He could feel them straining to harmonize, each shift of basalt a beat in a song seeking order. The rings in the floor were not simply mechanisms, they were the time signature. The whole space was a great stone symphony, and it had forgotten how to play itself.

He moved toward the central pedestal and laid a hand upon its surface. He didn't press down. He didn't impose his will. He listened.

The song of the leyline was there. Low, ancient, and not meant for ears. It moved through the soil and the bone, through time and memory. It was the patience of sediment, the cycle of erosion and renewal. It was slow and relentless. Perfect in its steadiness.

His fingers shifted slightly across the pedestal. He pointed to one ring in particular. He could tell it was slightly misaligned from the rest. "There," he said softly.

Ella crouched and adjusted the segment he indicated. As it clicked into place, the monoliths' tempo changed. Some slowed. Others tilted differently. Still others began to pulse in softer, more consistent beats.

Lianna's sharp eyes widened. "The noise... it lessens." She moved opposite Ella and knelt beside another ring, ready for direction.

The process became meditative. Minutes slipped into long stretches. Time lost definition. The song demanded patience. The vibrations deepened, the space between each pulse becoming easier to track. They were no longer random; they were measures. Phrases in a buried composition.

Xavier guided them silently, his words few. He did not so much command, he conducted. Every movement was deliberate, every correction an act of coaxing harmony back from discord.

Subtle signs of fatigue crept into them all. Ella's shoulders sagged slightly, her breath quiet but uneven from the repetition of crouching and rising. Lianna's brows knit tighter with each correction, sweat beginning to bead near her temples. Even the cats had grown still, watching but no longer pacing, their ears twitching to the shifting rhythms. Only Xavier remained still, centered at the pedestal, the earth's resonance flowing through him like a second pulse.

The monoliths slowed, their rotations drawing into graceful arcs. Their runes shimmered in harmony, soft emerald matching the leyline beneath the floor. The rings stopped shuddering. The pulses aligned. Finally, the song of the earth, deep, resonant, and unshakable filled the chamber.

It could not be heard with mortal ears. It was not a melody. It was truth. The truth of stone.

It was the song of pressure. Of growth through time. Of silence, broken not by noise, but by meaning.

Xavier opened his eyes, and the world was still. Everyone present could feel it... that something eternal had settled. That they had been accepted.

A notification shimmered into view, hovering faintly just before their eyes.

---

**Trial Passed – Earth Ley Line Harmonized**
+4 Constitution, +4 Endurance permanently granted to: Xavier, Ella, Lianna.
Earth Ley Line Core revealed. Quest "Sleeping Lines III" updated.

---

Each of them drew in a breath that came easier than the one before it. Their fatigue eased, replaced by new strength, a steadier heartbeat, lungs fuller. The leyline's song had not just touched them... it had changed them.

A deep, resounding tone filled the chamber, however, it was a soundless sound, one that vibrated in the bones rather than struck the ears. The pedestal before Xavier slowly sank into the ground. The monoliths stilled, and though they did not move again, the group felt their silent observation watchful, and waiting.

Above the place where the pedestal had been, script shimmered in the air. None of them knew the language, but its meaning imprinted directly onto the soul.

"He who walks with the earth need not move mountains. He need only know where they will stand."

The deep resonance of the ley line pulsed through the chamber, steady and unshaken, as the final monolith locked into place. The once-chaotic sequence of floating stone slabs now stood in perfect harmony, their ley-infused glyphs aligned in an ancient, forgotten pattern. A low hum of power swelled, filling the cavern with an unspoken acknowledgment. The trial was not over, but it had shifted.

As the echoes of the last movement faded, the far end of the chamber, previously obscured by the ever-shifting monoliths, began to stir. The ley pulse deepened, rolling through the ground like the weight of a mountain settling into place. A fracture split the stone, not with the violence of collapse, but with the precision of something shifting and awakening. Stone peeled away, not crumbling but moving with purpose, layers sliding aside as though the cavern itself were making way for something greater.

#

From the newly revealed recess in the far wall, a colossal figure emerged, its massive form composed of living stone, glowing ley-veins, and ancient vines that wrapped around its limbs like the memory of roots. Its body was not jagged but shaped, molded by the slow will of the earth, as though it had grown rather than been built.

Xavier stepped forward instinctively, opening his awareness as he triggered Insight. The leyline's rhythm surged through him. Insight bloomed in his thoughts, and he immediately understood what stood before them. His scowl deepened as the information settled into his mind.

| **Name:** Verkhaz, the Earthbound Watcher | **Disposition:** Impassive |
|---|---|

| A colossal being of living stone, molten ley veins, and deep-rooted vines, Verkhaz is an ancient sentinel of the Earth Ley Line. His four massive arms, each carved from unyielding rock, rest in deliberate stillness, not in idleness, but as a silent test for those who stand before him. His helm-like head, etched with constantly shifting runes, does not see in the mortal sense but perceives through the ley itself, attuned to the balance of the world. |
|---|

| Health: ???/??? | Stamina: ???/??? | Mana: ???/??? |

With each step, tremors rippled outward in slow waves, not shaking the ground but settling into it, pressing down as if the world itself were acknowledging the arrival of something sacred. is helm, shaped like an ancient warrior's crown and carved with faintly shifting runes, tilted slightly, as if studying them, not just with perception, but with purpose. He did not advance, did not brandish weapon or magic. He simply stood, four arms hanging, as motionless as carved pillars at his sides. It was not an idle stance. It was a question. An invitation. A silent judgment awaiting an answer.

Xavier's eyes narrowed. A flicker of pale light crossed Vaeltheris as it hummed faintly against his back. The blade seemed to resonate with the thing before them, not in alarm but in recognition. He opened himself to the leyline and felt the guardian's presence ripple through it like a boulder dropped into deep water. The being did not see through eyes. It felt through the earth.

A voice emerged from the stone, not spoken but felt. It vibrated in their bones, heavy and steady.

"You have walked the remnants of a Grey Road, endured the earth's weight, and moved with its rhythm. But to wield its power, you must stand against its might."

Ella's hand flexed around the curve of her bow. "You always take me to the most interesting places," she said, voice dry. "You do know I didn't have to fight titanic stone guardians before I met you, right?"

Xavier stepped forward, eyes never leaving the towering figure. "Could be worse," he muttered. "I could have invited you to dinner with wyverns instead."

Lianna's tail flicked once as she moved to his opposite

flank. "No. This is absolutely you. If this is what waits beneath Rynthavael, I shudder to imagine the Wildlands. Likely a kingdom of dragons."

Xavier gave a soft grunt. "Let's survive this before we worry about what's next."

The guardian did not react to their banter. It waited, still, and observing.

Then Xavier moved.

He surged forward, Vaeltheris flashing in a quick arc aimed at the creature's midsection. The strikes were precise, timed to hit at the joints, the seams, the carved indentations between the plates of stone. His blade rang out with sharp clarity, each impact like a hammer against an anvil. But nothing gave. The guardian did not block, did not dodge, did not even shift. It simply endured.

Frustration surged. Xavier struck higher, then lower. He feinted and followed through with a reverse cut to the shoulder. Still nothing. The construct stood unbothered, as though his attacks were nothing more than leaves brushing against the surface of a cliff.

Then it was its turn to move.

One of its massive arms swept across the space with the weight of inevitability. Not fast, but final. Xavier tried to raise his blade, but there was no time. The strike caught him full-on and hurled him across the chamber.

Pain erupted through him. He crashed against the floor and skidded to a stop near Ella and Lianna. His vision blurred. Dust filled his mouth. His ribs burned with every breath.

Ella dropped beside him, her hand already reaching to stabilize his shoulder. "Xavier?"

"I'm fine," he groaned, forcing himself to sit upright.

Blood smeared the corner of his mouth. His head throbbed, but clarity returned with each breath. A quick check affirmed what he was afraid of. "Half my health gone in one hit. That... figures."

As he struggled to rise, the others charged.

Ella's arrows flew with lethal speed, each one aimed with precision honed by countless battles. They struck, but splintered harmlessly against Verkhaz's stone hide. Not even a crack formed.

Lianna and Frostclaw surged forward. The Iskari moved with grace and power, her blades arcing in flawless cuts. Frostclaw mirrored her, weaving around the guardian's legs. They struck from multiple angles, perfectly timed, coordinated without words. Yet the stone denied them. Their blades and claws left no mark.

Even Valkra leapt, lashing with both tails. She landed with force, but the guardian did not even seem to notice. She bounced back, low to the ground, bristling.

Verkhaz shifted once, sending out a wave of force that disrupted their footing. The message was clear. This was not a battle of speed or fury. It was a test.

Xavier pushed himself fully upright. He looked at the others, all breathing hard, all skilled, and all ineffective. Then he turned back to the guardian and remembered the beat of the leyline. The slow, steady rhythm beneath the stone. It was not violent. It was not rage. It was presence. Endurance. Truth.

To move the earth, one must know its rhythm.
He who walks with the earth need not move mountains...

Xavier exhaled slowly. The frustration drained from his limbs. He stepped forward once more.

"Get back," he said, his voice steady now. "It can't be hurt like that. I think I understand what this is."

Ella didn't hesitate. She stepped back, her eyes fixed on him. Not questioning, but trusting. Lianna held her position a moment longer, then nodded and moved beside her. Frostclaw fell in at her heel. Valkra circled wide and sat, watching Xavier with eerie focus.

He closed his eyes.

The pulse was there, just beneath the floor. A heartbeat too deep for ears. It guided his breath, his stance, his intention. He didn't fight it. He let it carry him.

Verkhaz moved again. The construct stepped forward. One massive arm rose.

Xavier moved in turn, not against the blow, but with it. He angled his body, guided the force past him, let it slide down the edge of Vaeltheris and continue its course. His footing shifted. His weight followed the rhythm. He did not resist. He yielded to it.

Another blow. This one came faster.

Xavier spun aside, trailing the flow of energy, letting it graze past. His movements were not evasive. They were in tune. He did not impose himself on the fight. He joined it.

To Ella and Lianna, it was unlike anything they had seen. Xavier danced with the titanic earth construct. Their movements seemingly choreographed now.

He and the guardian moved as one. A harmony of breath and force, of will and stone. Vaeltheris was no longer a weapon. It was a conductor's baton, guiding the rhythm of a symphony older than kingdoms or even mountains.

Step, pivot, redirect. Strike not to harm, but to complete the movement.

The pulse of the leyline grew louder in their bones. Not

sound, but pressure, meaning.

Then, at the peak of the rhythm, Xavier stepped into the final beat. Vaeltheris extended, and its tip tapped the center of Verkhaz's chest.

There was no violence. No flare of magic. Only silence.

Verkhaz stilled.

Then, slowly, the guardian knelt.

The pulse settled, deep and steady. The air became still. The construct rose again with careful purpose and began to descend into the floor. The runes across its form dimmed one by one. It did not vanish in defeat, but in completion.

As it sank, its voice returned.

"You have felt the weight of the earth and moved with its song.
The path ahead will test more than your strength. It will test your foundation.
Do not forget the patience of stone, nor the wisdom of roots.
Go forward, knowing the earth will always remember."

Then it was gone, melded back into the very earth and stone that had borne its creation.

Ella lowered her bow with a tired sigh and leaned against the stone wall. "Why does it feel like we just got lectured by a mountain?"

Lianna crouched beside Frostclaw and began checking his limbs. "If all stone thinks like that, I may start apologizing before I step on pebbles."

Xavier chuckled quietly, still standing where the guardian had been. He let the others speak. Their voices grounded him. Their presence brought him back from the weight of the moment.

He said nothing more, but in his silence, the stone beneath his feet felt steadier than ever.

#

At the center of the chamber where Verkhaz had vanished, the earth groaned and parted. The movement was not violent, but deliberate, like ancient breath slowly exhaled from the bones of the world. From within the opening, a massive crystal rose, its surface faceted and alive with pulsing veins of emerald ley energy. It beat like a heart, slow, steady, and deep.

The stone pillar beneath it resembled those that had held the cores of Life and Death. Yet this felt different. Somehow heavier and more grounded. The Earth Ley Line did not flare or burn or whisper. Instead, it stood, it endured.

Xavier stepped forward alone. The others remained quiet behind him. Their wounds were fading, their breathing steadier, yet the moment held a weight that silence did not dare disturb.

He reached out and placed his hand against the smooth crystal surface.

A surge of power flowed through him, not sharp like lightning, nor fierce like flame, but dense and steady. It poured into him like soil settling over roots. Not overwhelming but encompassing.

It did not speak. It simply acknowledged. He felt the shift ripple through his soul.

> **Quest updated:** Sleeping Lines III
>
> You have gained the understanding of Earth. It is not a power to bend or control, but one to embrace and guide.

Return to the Syr'Vailen to complete the quest
and finalize the awakening of the Ley Line below
Rynthavael.

The pressure faded from the air. The tremors stilled. The
chamber, once filled with movement and struggle, now felt
still and sacred, as though the land itself were holding its
breath in contemplation.

Behind him, Ella exhaled and rolled her shoulders. "Why
does it feel like even the floor is wiser than us now?"

Lianna snorted softly and crouched to check Frostclaw's
side. "Because it probably is. Earth remembers everything. I
imagine it's holding ages worth of judgment for all who've
come before."

"It wasn't as hard as it looked," Ella said with a faint grin,
brushing dust from her leathers.

Lianna glanced over her shoulder. "You collapsed during
the first trial."

"And I recovered magnificently. That's what matters."
Ella rejoined.

Xavier turned back to them with a tired smile. Their
banter eased the lingering pressure in his chest. He could
feel their bond more deeply now, not just the emotional
weight of shared danger, but something subtler. Trust
earned, and deepened.

They had come through it together.

He looked back to the newly opened passage in the
far wall, the one that had appeared behind Verkhaz. With
the guardian gone, its scale was finally clear. The hallway
beyond sloped deeper into the earth, its entrance framed
by worn stone reliefs half-buried by ancient sediment and
glowing root tendrils.

Not all had been revealed or completed on this floor, but this was not the time to continue forward.

They had achieved what they came for.

Xavier turned from the path ahead and looked back once more at the crystal, its glow casting long shadows across the floor. The heartbeat of the leyline continued, now joined with his own. The earth did not speak of what lay ahead. It offered no visions, no warnings.

It simply endured, and now, so would he.

He nodded once to the silent crystal, then stepped back to rejoin his companions.

It was time to return to the surface. Time to finish what they had started in Rynthavael.

Time to prepare for the Wildlands.

# CHAPTER THIRTEEN

*Rynthavael Awakens*

The return to the surface passed without incident. They had not ventured too deeply into the second level, and whatever had been drawn by the stirrings of the Earth Ley Line had not lingered long enough to notice their retreat. The thick pressure that once choked the Deeps began to loosen, dispersing with each step upward.

Even so, the weight of the place still clung to them. The Deeps had grown quieter, but not empty. Somewhere far behind them, deep beneath stone and time, the leyline still pulsed, its power sinking into the bones of the ancient halls.

Xavier paused near the edge of the broken roadway, casting a last look toward the massive carcass of the wyrm. Its ruined form lay crumpled and still, the pale sheen of its broken plating dulled by stone dust. It no longer loomed. Now it simply lay forgotten, a relic of danger already fading into myth. Without the oppressive weight of the leyline's defense pressing against their senses, the tunnels had softened. Crumbled pillars, collapsed archways, and hollow echoes filled the vast spaces, but no longer with menace. The ruins had grown still.

Even so, Xavier's attention lingered on the worn stonework as they crossed the old road. The jagged cracks in the tiles, the branching paths and shadowed alcoves... they whispered of possibility. This place, for all its silence, could serve them again. A fallback. A last redoubt if the surface ever came under siege. He made a mental note to bring the idea to Sorin. The village's new builder had an eye for load-bearing walls and subtle instability, and Xavier trusted his judgment when it came to restoration. There were places here that could be reinforced quickly. Others, he suspected, should never be touched.

But those conversations could wait. For now, the only direction was up.

As they climbed, Xavier's senses began to shift again. His awareness of the stone had deepened since waking the Earth Ley Line, and now it sang faintly beneath his feet, quiet pulses like the echo of distant drums traveling through the stone. Every shift in weight, every scrape of boot against tile, carried deeper resonance. The ground beneath them was no longer passive. It breathed, slow and deep, like a slumbering giant beneath their steps.

He paused for a moment, eyes narrowing, and tilted his head.

"What is it?" Lianna asked softly, glancing over her shoulder.

"Something moved," Xavier murmured. He closed his eyes and reached outward. "Far above us. Off to the right. Small, quick... I think it's a rodent burrowing through the dirt."

Lianna raised a brow. "That's impressive. And... distracting?"

"Very," he muttered, rubbing the bridge of his nose. "I'm hoping this becomes background noise eventually."

Beside him, Ella chuckled gently. "It will. The ley does

not shout forever. In time, it becomes a heartbeat. You will learn to listen past it."

Xavier let out a slow breath, letting her words ground him. Together, they stepped into the wide rotunda that marked the entrance to the lower Deeps. All three slowed, the chamber had changed.

At first glance, it was the same space, the broad floor of smooth tile, the thick fluted columns, the curve of the ceiling high above. But something in the air had shifted, it was warmer... denser. The faint scent of damp earth and clean stone replaced the dry mustiness of before. Where cracks had once splintered across the tiles, many had sealed. The floor was smoother. The wear along the walls lessened. The space felt less forgotten.

Xavier stepped forward, then stopped. A low groan echoed faintly through the chamber. Not from behind them, but from beneath. A long, slow exhale of pressure rising from the stone, as though the land itself stirred in recognition of their presence.

Ella knelt and placed a palm to the floor. "The pulse has risen. It's climbing toward the mosaic... preparing."

Lianna tilted her head, eyes narrowing as she sniffed the air. "It smells like the forest after rain. Like wet stone and root."

Xavier nodded slowly. The beat beneath his feet had steadied. It no longer felt like echoes. It felt like there was a purpose. The leyline was awake now, and it was moving upward, stretching toward the surface like something long buried finally remembering the sky.

Without a word, the trio ascended the steps leading toward the mosaic chamber. As they rose, the air changed again, now with tension and breath, a sense of coiled strength that had not been there before.

The earth was ready, and something was waiting to meet them.

#

The steps opened into the wide circular chamber that housed the Syr'Vailen mosaic, and as Xavier emerged from the archway, the low murmur of gathered voices greeted him.

The chamber had become a natural gathering place over the past weeks. With construction ongoing aboveground, it offered a sheltered meeting space for planners, builders, and those still learning the rhythms of their new home. Today was no different. Nearly two dozen figures dotted the edges of the room, speaking in low tones over tables and benches hastily assembled from salvaged beams. A few turned as the trio entered, their conversation faltering. Then more followed, until the chamber began to quiet.

The moment Xavier's boots touched the edge of the mosaic, everything shifted.

A deep vibration rippled outward, faint but undeniable, like the breath of something vast beneath the forest floor disturbed by his presence. The ground groaned underfoot, not violently, but as if stretching, awakening, remembering. The resonance flowed upward through the soles of his boots, into his calves, into his spine, anchoring him in place.

A hum spread across the air, low and pulsing. The scent of moss and fresh loam thickened with every heartbeat.

Ella's breath caught. "It's responding. It knows you."

The Earth section of the mosaic, once dull and colorless, a muted patch of tiles barely distinguishable from the rest, began to stir.

It started with a single flicker. A soft shimmer rolled

over the brown and green hues, like sunlight catching damp stone. Then, slowly, the colors deepened, darkening into rich emeralds and earthen umbers. Lines once etched but lifeless began to glow faintly, forming veins of luminous green that traced through the stone like buried roots waking to spring.

The very tiles began to shift. They moved subtly, realigning along seams invisible before, turning and clicking into new positions as if solving a puzzle left half-finished for ages. With each shift, new patterns emerged, fractals of branches, tendrils of stone and vine, arcs of root that threaded beneath the images already carved into the floor.

A new tremor rippled through the chamber. Cracks, long dormant and dry, spread outward from the Earth section. Yet instead of breaking, they bloomed. From the seams rose soft moss, tendrils of pale gold lichen, and the smallest of saplings, their leaves faintly aglow. The forest itself was pushing upward through the mosaic, answering the call.

Lianna stepped back, eyes wide, her voice hushed. "It's not just awakening. It's growing."

From deep below, a low rumble echoed again. It built slowly, like thunder rolling through layered stone, the deep voice of the land drawing breath. The very walls pulsed with resonance that made the air feel dense, thick with energy. Every surface in the room seemed to respond, not with threat, but with presence. With purpose.

The symbol at the heart of the Earth section, a stylized tree with thick roots and a broad, unfurling canopy, flared to life. Its emerald glow surged through the chamber, threads of power lacing outward, connecting with the walls, the floor, and the people within.

Xavier stood motionless as the vibrations coursed

through him. The leyline was no longer dormant. Its power coiled through his body like water flowing through buried channels, grounding him and threading into his bones. He could feel its pull... not just toward the mosaic, but downward, deep into the loam and stone beneath the valley. The leyline wanted to reach farther, deeper, as if the forest floor itself beckoned him toward its ancient heart.

A child among the villagers gasped. "Mama... the floor is breathing," she whispered, tugging on her mother's sleeve.

"It's not just the floor," another voice said, one of the refugees, a former miner from Bramblegate. He stepped forward slowly, hands trembling at his sides. "I can feel it in my chest. Like the whole valley's waking up."

The hum began to fade, and the shaking stilled, though the room was not as it had been. The Earth section of the mosaic now glowed with quiet vitality, its colors vivid and alive. The contrast to the still-dormant sections around it was stark. Where once the whole mosaic had seemed aged and silent, now a third of it pulsed with power.

A shimmer of light gathered near the edge of the chamber, and Aelriva appeared, her small frame floating just above the tiles. Her wings glimmered with earthy light, the veins within them patterned like moss-laced crystal. She regarded the newly awakened section in silence, her presence threaded with the pulse of the leyline.

Her voice carried across the chamber in a soft, melodic rhythm. "Aye... the stone remembers what it once was. And through yer hand, the Syr'Vailen stirs anew. It breathes now, and the earth listens once more."

She remained near the mosaic, ever-watchful, bound to the confluence she served.

All around Xavier, murmurs rose. Not in panic or confusion, but in awe. Villagers spoke in hushed tones about what they had felt, what they had seen. One woman wiped tears from her eyes and whispered a prayer of thanks. A young man pressed his palm to the tiles and laughed, claiming he could feel the difference in his skin.

Xavier turned slowly in place. The Earth had awakened... and the Syr'Vailen Nexus had answered. Its threads of power were no longer buried and forgotten. They had stirred beneath the valley, reached upward through root and stone, and answered his presence.

The glow of the mosaic dimmed, settling into a gentle pulse. The air no longer trembled, and the deep resonance faded into a steady, quiet rhythm beneath their feet. One by one, the villagers resumed their movements, though most cast occasional glances toward the now-living Earth section, still shining in deep greens and bronze-kissed browns.

Xavier let out a slow breath. His heartbeat, which had matched the surging rhythm of the leyline only moments ago, gradually returned to normal. Around him, conversation resumed in hushed tones, curious, reverent, but no longer stunned.

Several of the newer villagers from Bramblegate hovered near the edge of the mosaic, their faces reflecting the light, eyes wide with something between awe and disbelief. One young woman crouched, brushing her fingers across the warm tilework. She whispered something too low to catch, but the way her expression softened said enough.

"They've never seen anything like this," Ella murmured beside him.

Xavier nodded, his voice low. "Neither have I."

A grizzled man in a leather apron stood just off to one side, his hands stained with dust and pigment from stonework. He stared at the floor, brow furrowed, then looked toward the vaulted ceiling with a slow shake of his head.

"The stone... it hears us now," he said quietly. "It's not dead like it was. I swear, it's listening."

Xavier didn't speak. He was still watching the mosaic, still feeling the echo of the leyline settling into place. It was hard to describe, like standing in the presence of a forest that had taken root overnight, all its strength coiled just beneath the surface.

A soft chiming sound echoed in his ear, followed by a familiar flicker of light at the edge of his vision. The notification icon blinked, reduced to a faint shimmer during the awakening, but now gently insistent.

He opened it with a thought.

---

**Quest Completed:** Waking the Earth – The Foundation of Power

The Earth Ley Line has awakened. Its power, once buried beneath ruin and neglect, now flows freely once more, reinforcing the foundations of Rynthavael. The land responds, its strength renewed. The echoes of the past linger, but the path forward has been reclaimed.

**Completion Outcomes:**

- Earth Ley Line Restored: Strengthens Rynthavael's ley network, stabilizing magic throughout the settlement
- Reinforced Settlement Defenses: Earth-aligned energy bolsters natural fortifications
- Resource Gain: Access to enchanted stone, ley-infused minerals, and earthen essence for crafting and construction
- New Settlement Spell: Living Forest

---

Labyrinth
- Future Questlines Unlocked: Further expansion into the Deeps and mastery of elemental ley energy

**Rewards:**

- Increased ambient mana in Rynthavael's lands
- Enhanced crafting and ley-based construction capabilities
- +7500 Experience

"The foundation is set. The earth endures, and now, so shall you."

He smiled faintly. Before he could close the window, another opened.

**Quest Completed:** Sleeping Lines III

Another of the slumbering ley lines beneath Rynthavael has been restored, their energy now pulsing through the land once more. The flow of magic has strengthened, resonating with the settlement and its surroundings. As the nexus grows in power, so too does the world around it.

**Completion Outcomes:**

- Increased Ambient Mana: The land of Rynthavael now thrums with ley energy
- Expanded Wildlife Presence: The renewal of the ley lines attracts greater natural harmony
- Enhanced Quest Opportunities: The ley's restoration opens new paths, unlocking hidden locations and magical anomalies
- Nexus Stability Reinforced: Strengthened connection between Rynthavael and its ley

network

**Rewards:**

- Settlement-wide magical enhancement
- Potential emergence of rare magical flora and fauna
- +1500 Experience

"The lines no longer sleep. The nexus awakens, and with it, new possibilities unfold."

Another window shimmered to life.

**Quest Accepted:** Sleeping Lines IV – The Weave Deepens

Though several ley lines have been restored, the nexus beneath Rynthavael remains incomplete. More lines slumber, their energy buried beneath layers of stone and time. As the weave of magic strengthens, so too does the complexity of its restoration. The path ahead grows more demanding, but the rewards will shape the future of the settlement.

**Conditions:**

- Personal Level of 20
- Retain Mastery of the Syr'Vailen

**Objective:**

- Continue the descent into the Deeps and locate the next dormant ley line
- Overcome the challenges guarding their flow
- Restore the ley lines to further increase the ambient mana and unlock new potential within Rynthavael

**Challenges:**

- Ley Line Instability: The deeper the nexus awakens, the more volatile the magic becomes
- Elemental Reactions: As multiple ley lines are restored, their interactions may create unforeseen magical anomalies
- Deeper Cavern Hazards: The uncharted depths bring new threats - creatures and forces drawn to the ley's awakening

**Potential Rewards:**

- Increased Mana Flow in Rynthavael
- New Environmental Effects
- +2000 Experience

The weave of the world is vast, its threads entwined in forgotten depths. More remain to be found, more to be restored, will you see the pattern through?"

Xavier closed the quest list. Before he could take another step, the world around him shimmered again.

**"Hark and Hear! You have ascended in power. You are now Level 16!"**

The touch of the divine lingers upon you, granting **6 attribute points** to shape your destiny, an exceptional gift, elevated from the ordinary **4 points** by the **Blessings of the Gods (Danu).**
**(Total of 24 points remaining to distribute)**

Choose wisely, for these points will define your path. You have **3 days** to assign them, or they will fall to the whims of fate.

Your growing prowess earns you a boon: **20% skill allocation (Total of 80% remaining)** to distribute among your known skills.

This is your chance to sharpen the blade of a favored talent, forge new strength in an untapped domain, or balance your growth across disciplines. Let this moment be a cornerstone of your greatness.

**Rise, Seeker of Glory. The world awaits your will. Seek adventure, seek wisdom, seek love... and let your legend be forged in your choices. LIVE!"**

The brilliance faded. Xavier exhaled. His gaze lingered on the newly awakened section of the mosaic for a moment longer, then he turned toward the stair leading up.

"Let's eat," he said, voice quiet but warm.

Ella smiled. "Agreed."

Lianna tilted her head. "I think Frostclaw and Valkra are already hunting."

"They deserve it." He chuckled softly. "So do we."

Together, the trio moved toward the surface, leaving the quiet hum of the Earth Ley Line behind them, for now.

#

They ate on the wide stone terrace just outside Hearthstead Hall, the midday sun stretching across the tables where food had been set out for the day's laborers and scouts. Plates had been piled high with roasted greens, herb-smoked fish, and dense seedcakes sweetened with honeyroot, comforting, nourishing fare that the village's cooks had taken pride in preparing.

Xavier sat with his companions, eyes half-lidded as warmth crept through his limbs and the ache of recent battle faded. He felt no soreness, only a satisfying heaviness, as if the earth itself had embraced him. Their quiet was companionable. Even Frostclaw, stretched across the shaded edge of the stone flooring, rumbled contentedly.

When Xavier turned his attention back to his food, he was surprised to find his plate empty. He felt full and sated but couldn't remember the taste of the meal. That irked him more than he expected. The meals he'd enjoyed before in the village were always a small treat, something to look forward to amid stone and ruin.

He pressed his lips together, resolving to pay more attention next time.

With a stretch, he pulled open the settlement interface. The new spell still called to him, the reward granted by the Earth Ley Line. It was the first new settlement spell he had gained since receiving the Kael'Sharyn mark, and he was eager to see it in full.

The spell tab opened with a subtle shimmer.

The familiar entry for Summon Forest Golems glowed faintly, unchanged. But beneath it, one of the previously greyed-out spells had become readable and clear. Living Forest Labyrinth.

The name conjured dramatic images, towering hedgerows, twisted paths guarded by axe-wielding beasts. But what he read was subtler, more elegant, and far more dangerous.

---

**Settlement Spell:** Living Forest Labyrinth

- **Spell Type:** Defensive Barrier – Natural & Ley-Bound
- **Mana Cost:** Initial Cost: 1,000 Mana, Upkeep: 250 Mana/day
- **School of Magic:** Earth (Terramara) & Life (Vitalora)
- **Range:** Encircles Rynthavael's Outer Borders
- **Duration:** Persistent (as long as upkeep is

---

maintained)

**Effect:** The Living Forest Labyrinth manifests as a sentient, ever-shifting woodland, designed to obscure, mislead, and repel intruders. Paths twist and change at will, preventing unwanted entry while guiding allies safely through.

**Key Features:**

- **Shifting Terrain:** Trails change unpredictably, ensuring no intruder can map or memorize the landscape.
- **Natural Misdirection:** An unseen force compels trespassers to wander in circles, subtly nudging them away from Rynthavael's heart.
- **Selective Passage:** Only those recognized or welcomed by the settlement can find safe routes through the labyrinth.
- **Ancient Resonance:** The spell is woven directly into the ley lines, drawing upon Earth's strength to fuel its continuous evolution.

**Defensive Strength:**

- **Prevents Large-Scale Invasions:** Forces enemies to split up and get lost rather than march in formation.
- **Repels Lesser Threats Automatically:** Sapient individuals with weak wills are instinctively deterred.
- **No Physical Barrier Needed:** Unlike walls, the labyrinth is alive and reacts organically to threats.

**Weaknesses:**

- **Ley Disruption:** If the ley line is disturbed, the labyrinth may weaken or temporarily lose its

effect.
- **High Mana Upkeep:** Requires daily investment to maintain its adaptive properties.
- **Not Impassable:** A skilled druid, Animari tracker, or leywalker may find a way through with effort. It also does not affect naturally occurring beasts or creatures.

**Additional Notes:** This is Rynthavael's first true defense, a gift from the Earth Ley Line. It ensures the settlement remains hidden and protected, allowing only those deemed worthy to pass.

Xavier leaned back slightly, impressed.

The spell didn't conjure walls or summon protectors. Instead, it awakened the land itself, twisting paths and guiding roots, shaping the forest into a living, breathing ward. Not built but grown.He scanned the permissions interface and began assigning immunity.

The villagers, every name, even the newly arrived refugees, were added. Then the Verdantspire Wardens. They would be patrolling, after all. It would be foolish to confuse allies. With a few mental gestures, he granted administrator status to Ella, Braegor, and Coren. After a moment's thought, he added Lianna. She was more than just his ally. She was his contact with Verdantspire, and she had proven herself beyond question.

The final approval hovered. He selected it.

A pulse of warmth surged through his chest. Magic stirred from beneath Hearthstead, the leyline answered. The moment passed.

He stood and turned toward the others, a grin forming. "Want to see what this new spell can do?"

Ella raised an eyebrow, rising beside him. "Should we be

concerned?"

"No. Just curious." He replied.

Lianna was already walking. "Come on. Top floor's got the best view."

They made their way to the upper balcony of Hearthstead Hall. The climb was easy, the structure more solid now, its beams humming with low strength as if it was more resonant and alive.

At the railing, Xavier pulled up the interface one last time. Activate Spell?

He confirmed it.

The pulse that answered came not from within, but from beneath, from the Syr'Vailen itself. It radiated outward in silence, a wave of intention racing through the stone and soil.

Nothing changed.

Seconds passed. Then... The canopy stirred.

Far below, the forest began to shift. Leaves rustled without wind. Trees stretched skyward, thickening, leaning. Branches curved and twined, pathways narrowing. A single trail near the edge twisted slightly, then again, looping on itself before straightening once more.

Lianna blinked, then laughed softly. "It moved."

"I thought the spell was subtle," Xavier muttered.

Ella pointed to the northeast. "Look."

One of the hunting paths bent away from its original direction, redirecting a group of returning villagers in a slow arc. The moment they passed, the trees shifted again, closing the route behind them. No crunch of branches. No forced growth. Just gentle, unyielding movement.

Below, a voice called out in quiet awe. "That wall wasn't this solid yesterday," a mason remarked quietly, knocking twice on the stone. "It's like the earth decided to brace with us."

Xavier's breath caught. He looked down, hands resting on the railing. Even the banister felt different. Firmer, as if it had always meant to be there.

He brought up the construction interface.

Sure enough, across every building in the village, durability ratings had increased by nearly fifteen percent. The Earth Ley Line's touch lingered not just below, but above, infusing every wall, every path.

Ella stepped close beside him, watching the forest ripple and adjust. "Even the woods know who they shelter now."

He nodded slowly.

Rynthavael lived, and for those who did not belong, the road to its heart had just become a great deal harder to find.

# CHAPTER FOURTEEN

*Wardens, Beasts and Bonds*

The next several days passed with relative stability, yet the air in Rynthavael carried a weight it had never held before. Momentum.

Where once there had been hesitation, caution bred from too many close calls, there was now purpose. The undercurrent of uncertainty that had kept the people wary had begun to shift. In its place, confidence had taken root.

Word of the Living Forest Labyrinth had spread quickly. The enchantment now wove through the trees like a watchful sentinel, turning the woods into a defense as alive as the people it sheltered. Paths bent around strangers. Trails vanished behind intruders. The Silverwood itself had become an ally. No longer was Rynthavael a fragile foothold in contested land. It had become something more.

New structures rose daily. Walls thickened, towers climbed higher, and homes took on a permanence once thought reckless. No longer did settlers build with the caution of temporary survival. They were building for legacy.

Xavier stood near the edge of the new training grounds, where several warriors sparred beneath the

SHADOWS OVER THE WILDLANDS

eye of Captain Coren Halewood. The sound of wooden weapons striking shields and bark-wrapped poles filled the clearing, punctuated by sharp commands and the grunts of exertion. Coren moved along the line, barking corrections with the efficiency of a man who had drilled soldiers longer than most had been alive. He had taken well to his role here, more commander than guard now, and his presence lent the settlement a grounded edge.

Nearby, a team of craftsmen placed the final beams atop Hearthstead Hall. The structure that had once served as makeshift shelter was becoming the heart of the village. Meeting chambers were already being framed beside it, their beams rising like ribs from the earth. Decisions were no longer just about staying alive. They were about what came after.

He turned toward the edge of the forest. A faint rustle of branches was followed by the low murmur of returning voices. Several hunters emerged from the treeline, accompanied by figures who moved too smoothly to be ordinary men.

They came clothed in armor that shimmered with the shifting hues of the canopy, woven leathers and bark-threaded plates that seemed to vanish between the flickers of light. There was no mistaking them. Verdantspire had answered the call and their promise.

Xavier made his way toward the northeastern gate, newly completed and still bearing the fresh scent of worked timber and rune-burnt sigils. The figures moved with fluid grace, each step measured and deliberate. They did not disturb the forest; they moved as part of it.

At their head walked a lone Duskhari. He paused just beyond the threshold, golden eyes scanning the village. The survey took only seconds, yet Xavier felt the man had absorbed everything. His gaze settled on the young lord with a weight that demanded acknowledgment.

A single gesture halted the others. The Wardens eased into stillness. Only the lead figure stepped forward.

He was tall, at least a head taller than Xavier, his sleek black fur patterned with faded scars where it showed beneath his armor. Bark-inlaid plates wrapped across his shoulders and chest, bound by leather and sinew. His long tail moved in steady rhythm behind him.

There was something in his presence, a stillness that did not feel passive. It felt like coiled potential.

"Kaelar Thornclaw," one of the returning hunters said as they drew near. "Captain of the Wardens."

Kaelar nodded once. His voice, when it came, was low and deep, like a storm rumbling just beyond the trees.

"Rynthavael... she stands on a ley convergence, yeah? An' the land... she feelin' it stir. Ain't just yer people wakin' up. The forest, she rememberin' too."

His gaze drifted toward the woods again, as if they whispered something only he could hear.

"She shiftin'. Pullin' old things from their sleep. Beasts gone from memory, drawn back by the hum o' mana thick in the roots. Ain't natural... not like this. Not since before even the oldest tales were spoken. You've done somethin', lordlin'. Not just for yer folk, but for the world. The land... it listens. And now it's answerin'."

Xavier opened his mouth to speak, but Kaelar lifted a hand.

"Don't take it as scoldin'," he said, voice calm but sure. "It ain't. This comes from High Speaker Moonstride herself. She say ye need to know... wakin' a nexus ain't like lightin' a hearth. It don't burn clean. It burns deep. It calls to what's buried in the marrow o' the land. Not just spirits and mana... but things forgotten for good reason."

His words fell like stones into still water. Even the wind seemed to hold still.

"Some be predators, aye, mean an' quick. But others? De be older. Born when the world still bled raw magic. Ain't beasts in the way ye know 'em. They don't care for gods or borders. They hear the call o' a nexus, and they come walkin'. That's why I brought Wardens, not messengers. We ain't here for talk. We're here to keep what stirs out where it belongs."

The silence that followed was thick, but not hostile. It was the pause of truths acknowledged.

Xavier stepped forward and placed his right fist into his left palm, bowing low.

"Rynthavael welcomes you, Wardens of Verdantspire." He straightened and gestured toward the older man now approaching from the training field. "This is Captain Coren Halewood, commander of our village guard. He'll be the one to coordinate with you on patrols and defense."

Captain Coren arrived then, as if summoned by name alone. He and Kaelar regarded one another in silence. No words passed, but after a long moment they clasped forearms. Recognition passed between them, born not from shared culture, but from the mutual weight of leadership.

Kaelar gave a single gesture, and the other Wardens moved with disciplined ease. They fanned out toward the forest's edge, never fully letting go of the wild that clung to them. They did not ask for shelter. They did not need it as they were accustomed to life in the wilds of the woods.

"They'll camp at the edges," Kaelar said, walking beside Xavier. "Trees speak clearer out there. We'll keep watch from both sides."

As they moved through the village toward the training grounds, Xavier accessed the labyrinth's permissions and added the new arrivals. Kaelar received elevated access, equal to Coren's. It would allow him to guide others in and out, should the need arise.

The last light of day stretched across Rynthavael, casting long golden streaks through the clearing. The forest no longer felt still. It felt like it was waiting.

#

The sun hung low by the time Xavier, Coren, and Kaelar returned to the training grounds. The drills had ended, and the field now held only the echo of bootsteps and the fading scent of sweat and churned earth.

They walked together in measured silence, a rhythm forming between them that required no effort. Xavier found himself glancing toward Kaelar more than once. The man moved like a predator at ease, always alert, but never tense. His steps made no sound in the grass.

Discussion turned toward patrol routes, defense patterns, and the integration of Warden tactics into the village's routines. Coren, ever pragmatic, nodded through most of it, occasionally offering a sharp observation or quiet agreement. Kaelar spoke with slow certainty, not to command but to inform.

Eventually, the Duskhari turned toward Xavier.

"I'll have my Wardens take yer hunters out in pairs," he said. "We'll sharpen their ears and teach 'em how to listen proper. Forest tells ye more than any track if ye know what to ask."

Xavier nodded. "And the scouts?"

"Aye, them too. We'll run 'em through the outlying

paths. They'll learn to move quiet, see with more than their eyes. Forest's changed... they'll need to change with it."

Before Xavier could answer, Lianna approached. She moved quickly across the grounds, her expression caught somewhere between surprise and wariness. Her left fist rose to her chest in a crisp salute as she stopped before Kaelar.

"Captain Thornclaw," she said, voice steadier than her eyes. "It is good to see you."

Kaelar returned the salute without hesitation. His voice softened, though it still carried the gravel of his kind.

"Ahh, greetin's to ye, sister Warden. Yer brother sends his thoughts. Says he's been watchin' the wind for news of yer hunt. An' I see now why."

Lianna allowed a brief smile to break through. She stepped forward and embraced him, a quick gesture of kinship. "I'm sure he is. And I'm sure he's trying to guess whether I've gotten myself eaten yet."

Kaelar chuckled, a low rumble in his chest. "That'd be a poor bet. I see it in yer stance. Ye've grown. The wild sits easier 'round ye now. That don' come without walkin' places no one else has tread. Tell me, how fares Frostclaw? That beast still prowlin' at yer side?"

Lianna's tension melted into a short laugh. She stepped in and embraced him. "He is. Out hunting, actually. With a new friend."

"A new friend?" Kaelar's brow rose.

Xavier stepped forward, catching Kaelar's curious glance. "Her name is Valkra," he said. "A Shadowmane cub."

Kaelar's amber eyes locked onto him, narrowing as if trying to see beneath skin and thought. His tail gave a single sharp flick.

"A Shadowmane," he said, almost to himself. "Far from their lands. That one chose ye, did it?"

Xavier gave a slow nod.

Kaelar studied him a long moment more. "Rare, that is. Real rare. Ain't just beasts, those ones. They carry spirit. Instinct older than language. They don't bond easy. Don't bow to command. For one to walk with ye... that speaks to somethin' deep in yer soul."

Xavier said nothing. He held the Duskhari's gaze, but his fingers curled slightly at his sides. Kaelar seemed to see it, and he gave a slight grunt of approval.

"Ye'll have to tell me that tale sometime."

There was a pause, but only a brief one. Then Kaelar's eyes turned distant.

"We saw signs on the way in. Claw marks on stone, deep as axe cuts. Bark torn from trees older than memory."

He paused, as if measuring his next words.

"At first, we thought it was a bear. But the scent... wrong. Heavy. Markin' territory, not wanderin'. Deliberate."

Xavier frowned. "What kind of creature marks stone like that?"

Kaelar looked toward the forest, his eyes distant.

"A Gloomclaw Mauler," he said.

The name hung in the air, unfamiliar to Xavier, but not to Lianna. Her breath caught.

"That's... I thought those were legend."

"Aye," Kaelar said. "And maybe they were. But I've seen signs before, long ago, when I was young. Even then they were rare. Not mindless, not reckless. They think. Watch. Wait. Then strike when it matters."

Xavier's brow furrowed. He shifted his stance, eyes scanning the darkening edge of the trees.

"They're drawn to power?"

"They're drawn to change," Kaelar answered. "To places where the land stirs. The Mauler didn't come by accident. It came because this place speaks now. Because somethin' old and deep has started breathin' again."

Xavier's hand drifted to Vaeltheris, not quite gripping the hilt, just resting there. His jaw tightened. A slow breath slipped through his nose.

"I didn't mean to call it."

"Course ye didn't," Kaelar said. "But the land she don' care what ye meant. When a nexus breathes after an age of silence, the world hears it. Not just people. The wild hears too."

Lianna folded her arms, her voice quiet. "Do you think it's watching us now?"

Kaelar didn't answer at once. He just looked toward the forest, as though trying to see what waited behind the silence.

"Aye," he said at last. "Not close. Not yet. But it's near enough. Testin'. Decidin'."

He turned back to Xavier. "It'll come when it's ready, and when it does, it'll choose who walks away."

#

The last sliver of sun vanished behind the trees, and the glow of day faded into gloom. Rynthavael settled into its evening rhythm. Hearthstead Hall flickered with lamplight, the last merchants folded cloth over their stalls, and returning hunters slipped in through the gates with their final catches.

A breeze rolled through the village, carrying the damp scent of moss, soil, and pine. Xavier walked the inner edge of the palisade, watching torches hiss and sputter against the rising dusk.

It started with a feeling. A breath held.

The hairs along his arms lifted. The air seemed to still, thickening into something too quiet, too expectant. He paused, one hand brushing the wooden support of a watchtower.

The forest had gone silent. No birds. No insects. No crackling of small branches beneath paw or claw. Just the faint creak of the palisade and the breath of the village itself, unaware.

Then came the horn.

Its sound split the silence like a blade through glass. High and sharp, it echoed from the western flank of the wall.

Xavier ran.

Boots struck dirt and gravel as he moved. Another shout rose, panicked and clear.

"Something's moving! Big, fast, coming straight through!"

He rounded a corner, passing startled villagers and wide-eyed guards. The torches atop the wall flickered violently, their flames dancing against a sudden gust of wind. The air had changed. It carried a musk now, pungent and sharp, wet stone and old fur, tinged with rot and challenge.

Xavier vaulted the last stairs to the top of the walkway, his eyes scanning the treeline. Kaelar was already there, and Lianna appeared moments later, her bow in hand.

Then he saw it. A shape detached itself from the shadows beyond the torchlight. It moved slowly, deliberately. Massive. Its silhouette was like that of a warhorse, but broader, lower, heavier. Shoulders thick as boulders rolled with each step, and its coat, if it could be called that, was fur woven with shadow, too dark to catch full light. Its eyes glowed with a steady amber, unblinking, too far apart to be natural.

Xavier triggered Insight.

| **Name:** Gloomclaw Mauler | **Disposition:** Calculated Domination | |
|---|---|---|
| A towering force of muscle and primal instinct, the Gloomclaw Mauler is more than just a beast, it is a ruler of the untamed wilds, an apex predator that has honed its craft over generations. It does not attack recklessly, nor does it hunt for sport. Instead, it watches, learns, and strikes with overwhelming power only when it deems its prey worthy of the effort. Its massive ursine frame is covered in coarse, shadow-woven fur, blending seamlessly with the Silverwood's darkness. Its claws, the length of daggers, are reinforced by natural keratin as strong as obsidian, capable of tearing through reinforced wood and stone. It does not rely on brute strength alone, however, this is a predator of precision. | | |
| **Health:** 720/720 | **Stamina:** 550/550 | **Mana:** 0/0 |

The creature did not charge.

It stalked forward with the patience of something that had never lost a hunt. Its movements were quiet for its size, a soft thump of padded weight against earth, then stillness. It stayed just outside the torchlight, a shape glimpsed in pieces, shoulder, snout, one gleaming eye.

Then came the sound. The sudden cacophony of wood

splintered.

The beast raked a single claw across one of the palisade's outer support beams. The timbers groaned beneath the gouge, deep and jagged. Guards on the walkway flinched. One nearly lost his footing, catching himself against the edge. Another loosed an arrow reflexively. It vanished into the dark with a faint snap of wood.

Kaelar's tail lashed. His eyes were narrowed, sharp with understanding. "It ain't just huntin'," he said. "It's makin' a point."

Xavier's grip tightened on Vaeltheris. The sword hummed faintly, but he didn't draw it yet. He could feel the pull of the ley beneath his boots. The Earth stirred, alert and watching.

The Mauler moved again. Not fast, nor slow, just enough to keep attention on it. A shifting shadow between trees.

Its lunge was sudden and volent. With the sound of a landslide, the beast crashed into the wall.

Claws dug deep. Wood screamed and split apart as the Mauler tore a section of the palisade free. One of the guards dove aside just in time, his spear clattering into the dark below.

The Mauler was inside.

The torn wall groaned behind it, shredded like paper under the weight of its entrance. Torches snapped in their brackets, casting flickering shadows over the monster's bulk. The ground seemed to brace itself beneath the beast's steps.

Lianna's bow sang. Three arrows flew in rapid succession. One clattered against the Mauler's hide without leaving a mark. The second buried shallowly into its shoulder, too thin to stop its advance. The third, aimed low, found the soft join beneath its front leg. The beast jerked and grunted, not in pain but in recognition. It turned, eyes narrowing.

Kaelar barked a sharp command, and the Wardens moved in. They didn't try to surround it, no, they understood better. Their formation shifted, drawing the Mauler's gaze away from the heart of the village, giving it no clear path forward. Spears angled low, feet spread wide.

Ella climbed the nearest tower like smoke rising from a lantern. She reached the platform and drew her bow, but held her shot. Her breathing slowed. She watched the scene playing out below awaiting her moment for the perfect shot.

The Mauler watched too. It didn't lash out at the closest target. Instead, it shifted its weight and stepped sideways. Muscles bunched beneath its fur. Its head swayed low, eyes scanning, anticipating.

It moved like a fighter. One who had learned from countless battles.

Then its gaze locked on Xavier. He felt the world tilt, not just threat. Recognition.

The Mauler had not come for blood. It had come for him.

It charged. Xavier met it halfway.

Vaeltheris lit in his grip, cold light flashing across steel. The impact rocked the ground. Claws tore furrows in the dirt. Xavier's boots skidded, but he held firm. The blow should have broken him.

It didn't. The Earth held him.

Not stone, not soil… something deeper. Beneath his feet, the ground thrummed. Like a second heartbeat, slow and ancient. He could feel the tension in the roots beneath the village. The memory of mountains. The weight of time.

The Mauler's claws scraped across Vaeltheris with a shriek of friction, and sparks flew. The muscles in Xavier's arms screamed, but he didn't fall.

The earth lent him weight, balance, silence. Not just strength, but something older. A stillness that resisted all force.

This is what it means to awaken a line, he thought. Not just power... but being seen. Challenged.

Kaelar struck next. The Duskhari moved with sudden precision, sliding in behind the Mauler's right flank. His spear flashed, burying deep in the creature's ribs.

The Mauler roared. It wasn't in pain, but anger.

It spun, its massive forelimb sweeping wide. Kaelar was ready. He dropped low and rolled, letting the strike mostly pass over him. He came up crouched, blood trailing from his temple where the edge of a claw had caught him.

"Hold its front!" Kaelar snapped. "Don't let it pin you down!"

Xavier shifted right, keeping the Mauler's focus. He slashed low with Vaeltheris, striking for a foreleg. The blade met resistance, hide like layered bark, but cut through. The Mauler hissed and jerked back a step.

It learns, Xavier thought. Every moment, it learns.

Then Frostclaw hit from the side. The snow leopard burst from behind a half-collapsed structure, a blur of pale fur and fury. He slammed into the Mauler's hind leg, claws raking deep. The beast stumbled, weight thrown off for just a breath.

Valkra followed, a shadow leaping from above.

She struck the Mauler's back, claws gripping thick fur, twin stingers driving into flesh. She snarled as the beast bucked, twisting and trying to throw her loose.

Xavier pressed in. Vaeltheris swung again, slicing toward the Mauler's neck. The blow landed, shallow but decisive. The Mauler recoiled, backing away from the press of blades and beasts.

It adjusted. Its stance widened. It circled, not retreating, but reassessing.

It's not wild, Xavier realized. It's not afraid. It's testing us. Testing me.

Then he understood. The Mauler hadn't come to kill indiscriminately. It had come to judge.

As it threw Valkra off and staggered back, its amber gaze returned to Xavier. The amber orbs were not filled with hate, not hunger. Instead, he could see the weighing there, the calculation... the measure.

From the tower above, Ella exhaled. Her arrow loosed, flying straight and silent. It struck beneath the Mauler's jaw, embedding in soft flesh where no armor of fur could protect.

The Mauler reared back. It did not scream. It stepped back, deliberate, and controlled.

Blood dripped from its neck, slow and thick.

Then it turned.

It walked, heavy steps shaking the earth. At the edge of the forest, it paused beside a tall standing stone. With one claw, it carved a single, deep mark into its surface. It added another beside it. Then another.

No one spoke.

The Mauler vanished into the dark, and the silence that followed was not relief. It was the kind that comes when a predator departs... but remembers the scent.

#

The defense of the village redoubled in the wake of the Mauler's retreat. Even with night draped across the land, the carpenters were already at work, hauling timber and binding supports beneath the light of torches. They moved with urgency, driven not by fear but necessity. The palisade had to be whole again before dawn.

Those who had fought lay scattered near the training grounds or beneath the shade of still-standing towers, some seated, others sprawled where the adrenaline had finally let go. Their breaths came slow. Their eyes were heavy. They had survived something ancient, and all of them knew it.

Xavier sat with his back against a broken section of railing, a half-empty tincture bottle clutched in one hand. Kaelar crouched beside him, one arm wrapped in cloth where claws had torn through leather. The healer's work had been quick, but the bruises would last until morning.

They had been lucky. Luckier than anyone had a right to be.

The village held its breath long into the night, waiting for the sound of movement, for a second assault that never came. Eventually, one by one, the guards rotated out. The watch doubled, but the tension faded. The silence held.

By the time the moon cleared the trees, Hearthstead Hall flickered with firelight again. Long shadows danced along its walls, stretching over crates and packs arranged in quiet preparation. The supplies for their journey were ready.

Xavier remained, kneeling near the last of their gear. He tightened the strap of a waterskin, then checked the seal on a satchel of dried meat. His hands moved with precision, but his mind was elsewhere. He was focused, not anxious.

The way one prepares before a fall.

Ella's approach was soundless. Just the faint shift of her weight on stone. She didn't speak at first. She stood beside him, her presence familiar now in a way that needed no announcement. Steady and unshaken.

After a moment, she reached into her satchel.

Xavier glanced up as the movement caught his eye. What she held made him freeze.

A collar. Dull metal, unmarred by decoration, simple and cold. In another life, it would have meant nothing. But here, in Arath, and especially in Arenvalis, it was a symbol he couldn't ignore. A memory, a wound and a truth he hated.

Ella turned it in her fingers. Her face gave nothing away. "I will wear it," she said.

Xavier stared at her, then stood. His jaw clenched. "You don't have to."

She tilted her head, eyes searching his. "You said the same about Lianna. But she will, because she must. We need her to guide us through Arenvalis. They will not suffer the afront to see her without it."

His hands curled slightly at his sides. "You shouldn't have to bear that weight just to make things easier."

"Maybe not," she said, voice quiet but sure. She rolled the collar once more between her fingers, then met his gaze. "But you're looking at it wrong."

She stepped closer, holding it up between them.

"Lianna wears hers, and it reminds her of chains that once held her. You see it, and it reminds you of what you hate. But me?" She shrugged. A faint smile touched her lips. "It's just a piece of metal."

Xavier didn't answer. He studied her, eyes tracing her face, the calm in her expression. She wasn't untouched by what it meant, but she had power in how she faced it. She always had.

"It's not about what it means to me," she continued, softer now. "It's about what it means to her. If I wear it, she won't be alone in it. She'll know she's not the only one bearing the stain. That matters."

He breathed out slowly. The tension left his shoulders. "And what does it mean to you?" he asked.

She grinned, tossing the collar once in her hand, then triggered the rune that released its binding lock. The sigil glowed briefly before dimming, and she tossed the rune key to Xavier. With a snap, the collar settled around her neck, loose but intentional.

"It means I get to piss off some slavers and make them underestimate me." She winked. "And that, I'm perfectly fine with."

Xavier shook his head, lips twitching into a reluctant smile. "You're impossible, you know that?"

"That's why you like me."

She gave him a quick, light punch on the arm and stepped back, arms crossing over her chest. Her tone softened again.

"If we're going to play our parts, we do it right. Ironhaven doesn't get to set the rules. We do."

He looked at her for a long moment, something unreadable in his eyes. She wasn't just a companion. Not just a part of Vaeltheris. She stood apart from the blade now, real and breathing, and entirely her own.

She turned and walked toward the door, her steps

SHADOWS OVER THE WILDLANDS

unhurried.

The faint echo of her footfalls against the stone floor lingered, fading into the quiet like a ripple across still water.

For a moment, Xavier stood in the hush that followed, and it felt like the world had taken another breath, just like before the Mauler arrived. But this time, it didn't feel like a warning. It felt like a promise.

He looked down at the rune key in his hand, then toward the door she had passed through.

She wasn't just the sentience of his blade.

She was flesh and blood and... radiant. Fierce in a way that didn't burn, but illuminated.

The realization hit him, quietly, without defense.

The reason he hated the idea of her in a collar wasn't because of what it meant.

It was because it would mark something he had already started to feel.

He was falling for her, and that made all the difference.

# CHAPTER FIFTEEN
*Into the Wildlands*

The night was cool and quiet, the heady aroma of the Silverwood drifting on the gentle evening breeze. Moonlight filtered through the canopy, painting silver dapples across the mossy ground. Faint chirps and the rustle of distant branches echoed softly, reminders that the forest never truly slept. Kaelar stood at the edge of the settlement, his golden eyes locked on the young Shadowmane cub that sat just beyond the treeline. Valkra held an unnatural stillness. It was not the stillness of a frightened cub, but that of a predator who had learned patience, one who had learned to wait. Her sleek, dark fur melted into the night, nearly camouflaging her from view. Only her piercing golden eyes reflected the glow of the distant torchlight. Her twin tails, long and supple like a cat's, ended in wicked, stinger-tipped barbs that flicked faintly with tension, each holding the threat of paralytic venom.

Kaelar exhaled through his nose. The Duskhari and Shadowmanes had long shared a bond, an unspoken understanding between Animari hunters and the panthers who moved like ghosts through the wilds. Their ancestors had fought beside one another, passed down stories of kinship, of hunts shared, of losses mourned. But this cub had chosen Xavier, and Kaelar needed to understand why.

He stepped forward, each movement deliberate and respectful. Valkra's ears flicked, but she did not turn. She had known he was coming. He hadn't masked his approach —that would have been an insult.

"Tell me somethin', little huntress," Kaelar said, his voice low and even. "How is it ya came ta de Silverwood?"

Valkra's tails curled slightly, but she offered no sound. Kaelar crouched, resting his forearm on his knee. His tail swayed slow and thoughtful behind him.

"Shadowmanes don' belong here," he continued. "Not in dese woods. Yet here ya are."

Her gaze shifted, not toward him, but toward the thick trees beyond. The path she had taken to reach this place.

Kaelar understood. A Duskhari didn't need words to speak with a Shadowmane. He could read the tilt of her ears, the tension in her tails. His voice softened.

"Yer mama."

Valkra did not move, but one tail flicked, sharp and deliberate.

Kaelar's jaw tightened. "Who took her?"

The cub's ears flattened, and her tails lashed. A quiet breath escaped her, half-snarl, half-sorrow. He exhaled slowly.

"Shardfangs."

Valkra's golden eyes burned with confirmation. Kaelar had faced those beasts before—larger, more cunning than wolves, armored in jagged scales, driven not by hunger but by bloodlust. His eyes drifted to the faint scars along Valkra's flank.

"She fought 'em."

A flick of the ear. Barely a nod.

"'Course she did. Das what a mama do."

Kaelar pictured the scene. The pack closing in, glowing eyes in the dark. A wounded but unyielding panther, fangs bared, holding the line so her cub could flee. A final roar. A sacrifice.

His voice dropped lower. "She gave ya time ta run, didn't she?"

A slow blink. A pause.

Kaelar nodded. "She knew what she was doin'. Knew ya was worth savin'."

His gaze followed hers as it shifted back toward the settlement, toward Xavier's quarters.

"But ya didn' just run, did ya?"

Valkra's eyes met his.

Kaelar gave a knowing snort. "Non, little shadow. Dey found ya. Dey came when the night was thick with blood an' fangs, when yer mama made her stand. Dey fought beside ya. Not as hunters, but as kin."

Xavier and Ella. The ones who had found her, stood with her, and finished what she couldn't.

He nodded slowly. "Ya walk with 'em now. But make no mistake. It weren' just their choice. It was yers."

Valkra's twin tails curled slowly. Deliberately. Kaelar stood, arms crossing over his chest.

"Aight, listen up, little huntress. Since ya made yer choice, I'm givin' ya a charge."

Valkra's ears twitched.

"He don' got the instincts ya got. Don' see the world the

same. But he's walkin' a path that needs him ta be more'n he is now. You've been watchin' him. Now, watch over him."

A long pause. Then Valkra nodded.

Kaelar gave a satisfied snort. "Good. We got an understandin'. Keep him safe, little huntress."

He turned away and disappeared into the dark, the sound of his steps swallowed by the whispering trees and distant hoots of nocturnal birds.

But his night was not done. The shadows welcomed him as he moved through the forest until he reached another familiar figure.

Frostclaw lay stretched across the stone floor outside the chamber Lianna had claimed. Moonlight gleamed along his silvery-white coat, the massive cat appearing carved from snow and shadow. As Kaelar approached, Frostclaw raised his head, golden eyes narrowing in lazy recognition.

Kaelar knelt, laying a hand gently against the cat's muzzle. The response was immediate: a deep, resonant purr vibrated through Frostclaw's chest.

"Been a long road, eh, old friend?"

Frostclaw blinked slowly. The years hadn't dulled the sharpness in his gaze. Kaelar remembered the first time they met: a snowstorm, a blood trail, two terrified Iskari cubs clinging to the back of this fierce beast. The memory rose unbidden, thick with the scent of pine and frost, the cries of the dying, the oath he had sworn in silence.

"Found 'em once, ya did," Kaelar murmured. "Found 'em when no one else would."

Frostclaw leaned forward and pressed his broad forehead to Kaelar's brow. The gesture was powerful and sacred.

I will guard them still.

Kaelar's voice dropped to a whisper. "Bring her back, ya hear? Her and de others. Ain't no shadow deep enough ta take 'em from me."

The big cat gave a slow, deliberate blink and returned his head to his paws. Kaelar stood, the silent weight of trust settled between them.

Without another word, he turned and slipped once more into the night, swallowed by the forest and the songs of the leaves.

#

The morning air carried the scent of damp earth and the lingering crispness of night. Above Rynthavael, the sky blushed in muted hues of violet and deep amber as dawn stretched its fingers across the valley. Though the village had settled into a rhythm, the battle the night before had broken its cadence, leaving behind a quiet energy as its people rose early.

They gathered in hushed clusters along the main path, not to stop the departing trio, but to witness. Eyes held respect, not fear. All knew what this journey meant, not just for Xavier, Ella, and Lianna, but for Rynthavael itself.

The Wildlands were stirring. Arenvalis was pushing southward. The future of this place, this fragile hope they had built, now depended on what lay beyond the safety of its wards.

Kaelar waited at the village gates, arms crossed, golden eyes unreadable. He had insisted on walking with them as far as the edge of the settlement.

"Won't have ya slippin' off like ghosts," he had muttered the night before. None had argued.

They walked together, past standing stones that shimmered faintly with ley-infused sigils, through paths shaped by foot and time. They moved deeper into the forest line where Rynthavael ended and the Living Labyrinth began.

This part of the Silverwood had been reshaped by awakened magic. The Earth Ley Line pulsed here, ancient and deep. The trees grew taller, broader, their roots entwined in deliberate, rune-marked spirals beneath the soil. The air shimmered faintly with ley resonance, cradling those who belonged and confusing those who did not.

For three days, they traveled beneath that enchanted canopy. The forest welcomed them. The wind was gentle. Paths opened without command. Food was easier to find. It felt like home, but slowly, subtly, that welcome faded.

At first it was hard to notice. The moss grew thinner, the root patterns less distinct. The temperature shifted. The whispers of the ley line, once constant beneath Xavier's awareness, grew fainter until they vanished entirely. Then came the message. His interface dimmed and greyed, flashing a warning.

You have stepped beyond the bounds of Rynthavael's influence. Settlement benefits are no longer active.

Xavier lowered his hand from the rune-script interface, a weight settling in his chest. Around them, the trees were still beautiful, but no longer protective. The air carried no subtle warmth, only a creeping chill.

The others felt it too. Ella stiffened. Lianna slowed, ears twitching.

Even Valkra's twin stinger-tipped tails flicked with agitation. She crouched lower, scanning the underbrush.

Frostclaw moved closer to Lianna, his breath a low rumble.

What had once felt alive and cradling now felt... watchful. The Silverwood beyond the ley's embrace stood silent and still, not in rest but in warning. The trees were taller still, but brittle. Their branches twisted skyward like claws, and no birds sang from their limbs.

Ella rolled her shoulders. The collar at her neck shifted with the motion, the faint click of metal startling in the silence. "Yeah," she muttered, voice tight. "Definitely not home anymore, is it?"

No one replied. They didn't need to.

Kaelar stopped at the next bend in the trail, one hand resting against the bark of an old tree. He turned to face them.

"Ain't too late ta turn back, y'know," he said quietly, though they all knew it wasn't a real offer.

Ella managed a grin. "Wouldn't be fun if we did."

Kaelar snorted but didn't smile. He turned his gaze to Xavier.

"Wildlands ain't what dey used ta be. Land's restless. People too. Ain't just soldiers out dere. Somethin' else stirrin'. Somethin' foul."

Xavier nodded. He had felt it since the leyline's voice had gone quiet. That silence wasn't emptiness. It was dread.

Kaelar crouched down to Valkra's level. Her ears twitched, eyes alert.

"Ya remember what I told ya, little huntress?"

Valkra gave a slow nod, her tails stilled but tense.

"Good."

Kaelar stood and stepped back. "Ain't gon' hold ya up.

But don' forget, y'all got somethin' ta come back to."

Xavier met his gaze and bowed, cupping his right fist into his left palm.

Kaelar nodded once, then turned, fading into the underbrush. In seconds, he was gone. The trees whispered as he passed, then stilled.

The road ahead was silent, and it had only just begun.

#

With Kaelar gone and the woods growing more oppressive, the trio paused just beyond the boundary of Rynthavael's reach. The stillness pressed in, heavy and unwelcoming. They gathered beneath a twisted ash tree, its bark pale and cracked like old bone. No birds called. No insects hummed. Even the wind seemed to hold its breath.

Lianna's eyes kept flicking to the collar at Ella's throat. She had been watching her more closely the past few days, curious, conflicted, and quietly horrified at the ease with which Ella wore the hated band. However now, standing here on the edge of enemy territory, she understood why.

Xavier broke the silence. "I still say you don't need to do this, Lianna. We can find another way."

She reached into her pack, fingers closing around the cold metal. Slowly, she withdrew her own collar and stared at it. Her ears pinned back.

"Thank you, Xavier." Her voice was little more than a whisper. "But you know as well as I do, this is the best way forward. Even if it feels like a knife in my own skin."

Without waiting, she activated the rune stone and tossed it to him. Then, with practiced precision, she closed the collar around her neck. It snapped shut with a sickening finality. Black runes pulsed across the band.

A new prompt flickered before Xavier:

The Drekh'tar has been placed and recognizes your authority. You may now configure restrictions for the Iskari slave Lianna. To finalize restrictions, speak the command: "By my will, you are bound."

Options populated instantly, speech restrictions, obedience controls, pain induction protocols. Each was more grotesque than the last. He felt his stomach churn as rage surged beneath his skin.

How could anyone look at these tools and think this system was just? This wasn't governance. It was enslavement masquerading as order.

His jaw clenched. Hands trembling, he ignored every command. He looked at Lianna, then whispered, "By my will, you are bound... until I can safely free you."

The runes flashed, then dimmed to a steady glow. Lianna swayed slightly.

Ella stepped in without a word, one arm sliding around her. The two women stood close, foreheads nearly touching.

"I have you, chain-sister," Ella whispered.

Lianna let out a slow breath and nodded, her hand briefly grasping Ella's. It wasn't just support. It was solidarity.

Moments later, she pulled a folded packet from her cloak, forged slave documents. Xavier unfolded them, noting how thorough they were. Ella handed him a second set without being asked.

He looked between them. They had planned this together. He didn't need to ask who had led. It didn't matter.

He tucked the papers away and looked toward the trees ahead. There was no turning back now.

#

The road grew harder beneath their boots. As the trees thinned and gave way to rolling scrub and bramble-choked hills, signs of Arenvalis' presence became impossible to ignore. Tracks littered the road—boot prints, wagon grooves, even the deep scarring of iron-spiked wheels. The scent of oil and iron tinged the air.

They passed no other travelers, but the atmosphere changed. The ground felt compacted by too many feet, too often. Patrols had been here, and recently.

Frostclaw and Valkra moved to flank Xavier instinctively. Lianna had warned that slaves wouldn't normally be allowed bonded animals, so they would need to maintain the illusion. The great cats peeled off silently before the road crested. They would rejoin later.

Ella and Lianna fell in behind Xavier, heads lowered just enough to convey submissiveness without groveling. It was calculated, practiced.

Xavier adjusted the angle of his shoulders, recalling the posture and gait of the mercenaries he had fought. Confidence with a hint of menace. Authority, but not arrogance.

As they approached a wooden barricade stretched across the road, two guards stepped into view. Armor gleamed under the noon sun, and their tabards bore the rising flame crest of Arenvalis.

One raised his hand, palm outward. The other rested a gauntleted fist on the pommel of his sword.

"Halt. State your business."

Xavier didn't flinch. "Mercenary work. Bound for Ironhaven."

The reply brought a mounted officer out from the shade of a nearby awning. He guided his horse forward at a slow trot, scrutinizing Xavier first, then letting his gaze drift to the women. He studied them long enough to make Xavier's skin crawl.

"The slaves?" the officer asked, tone flat.

"Mine."

"Papers."

Xavier retrieved the forged documents and handed them over. The officer leafed through them slowly, then motioned to Lianna.

"Step forward."

She obeyed with no hesitation, though Xavier caught the tension in her shoulders.

"Name?"

"Lia," she said quietly, eyes downcast.

The officer leaned forward over his saddle, watching her. "Obedient. How long have you owned her?"

Xavier forced his voice to remain level. "Long enough."

The man smirked. It made Xavier want to reach for his blade.

He turned his gaze to Ella. "And this one?"

Ella tilted her head, eyes briefly flicking to the officer's knee before answering, "Same."

Xavier nearly groaned.

The officer's expression didn't change. He simply nodded. "They'll do."

He handed the papers to a waiting soldier, who returned them to Xavier. "Welcome to Arenvalis, mercenary. Behave yourself. The Wildlands are being tamed. You won't get away with what passed for lawlessness in the past."

He turned his horse and retreated into the shade.

As they passed through the checkpoint, Xavier felt a brush against his cloak. A folded scrap of parchment was pressed into his palm. He made no move to look back.

The cluster of buildings thinned quickly, and within the hour, Frostclaw and Valkra rejoined them, emerging from the grasslands with practiced subtlety. They continued in silence until the sun dipped low, painting the horizon in burnt orange.

That night, they set camp beneath the twisted remains of an old pine, its upper branches scorched and broken. The fire they built was small, shielded from the road.

Xavier sat apart for a moment, fingers closing around the folded parchment that had been slipped into his palm. He pulled it free and unfolded it.

The handwriting was rough, hurried, but the message in Avara was clear:

Watch the ruins. The fire still burns.

He stared at the words, letting them settle in his chest. It wasn't just the message, it was the fact that someone had risked slipping it to him. Someone had seen past the disguise. Someone believed he was worth the risk.

For the first time in days, hope stirred, but it was cautious, edged with the weight of what they were walking into. Xavier didn't trust easily anymore, but this was something he yearned to believe.

He handed the note to Lianna.

She read it silently, then looked up at him. Her expression was harder to read than usual, but he saw the flicker of emotion there, relief, tempered by resolve.

"We're not alone," she said. Her voice was soft but steady. "Not completely."

Xavier nodded. "No. But we'll have to be careful. Whoever left this, they're playing a dangerous game. Just like we are."

They sat together in the firelight, quiet for a time. Ella had wandered to the edge of the camp with Valkra, giving them space.

Lianna shifted slightly, pulling her cloak tighter.

"You ever think about what we're giving up to do this?" she asked.

Xavier met her eyes. "Every step. But if it means tearing down what they've built, it's worth it. Even if we don't get to see the end."

She nodded again, slower this time. "As long as someone does."

The fire cracked between them. In its glow, the collar at her throat cast a faint reflection, echoing Ella's not far off. Symbols of submission, but also of strategy, of rebellion hidden beneath a lie.

The fire still burned. In ruins, in people, in hope disguised as chains.

Xavier watched the flames flicker and whispered, "Let it burn bright enough to guide them home." And then he said nothing more.

# CHAPTER SIXTEEN

*Tithe of Blood*

That night, Xavier took the first watch.

The others had already bedded down, the fire little more than a smoldering ember-ring beneath the stars. He sat quietly on a rock, the plains stretching in all directions, open and quiet in a way that unsettled him. The sky above was vast and unfamiliar, the wind carrying whispers he couldn't quite place. With a slow breath, he opened his interface.

The inventory tab came first.

Most of what they had salvaged from the Deeps now rested back in Rynthavael's armory. Poisons, spare weapons, extra armor, all catalogued and accessible to the guards and crafters. A clean decision. In battle, he often forgot half the things tucked into his satchel, and it made more sense for that gear to serve the village than rot at the bottom of his pack. Besides, Rynthavael needed every edge it could get.

Satisfied, he moved on.

The skills tab opened smoothly, the list longer than he remembered. Notifications had been disabled by default, an earlier choice to cut down distractions, and he was surprised by how much progress had been made without him noticing. What had once been a scattered handful of basics was now a growing web of layered training and potential.

He let his eyes move over each category, scanning for trends and gaps. Martial skills had improved across the board, small blades especially, nearly ready to level again. It made sense. He had been fighting constantly since the day he arrived. Spear and club proficiency were lagging, but he hadn't used them much since Bramblegate. His dual-wielding techniques were developing well, and light armor was becoming second nature.

Crafting and gathering skills had come along more slowly, though woodworking and herbalism were clearly benefiting from recent foraging trips. Survival sat at fifteen now, bolstered by countless campfires, shelters, and meal preps. Even cooking had nudged upward. He smirked slightly at that one.

His attention lingered on the two magic entries.

**Life Magic – Level 1**
**Death Magic – Level 1**

Both were barely touched. He'd nearly forgotten they were there.

It wasn't that he lacked interest. He simply hadn't had the space to focus on anything beyond survival... avoiding death, protecting the group, learning how to fight. Vaeltheris had demanded his full attention, and rightly so. But it struck him now that he was wasting potential. If magic was part of what this world had given him, ignoring it would eventually get him killed.

His attention moved to the small blades skill again, hovering over the near-complete progress bar. With a short nod, he dumped the 80% skill growth he'd been sitting on from his last level into it. That bladework had saved his life more than once. Might as well let it keep doing so.

Then he reorganized the entire layout.

Instead of one long, cluttered list, he sorted them into four categories: Martial, Crafting, Magic, and General. Much better. Each section could now be scanned quickly and cleanly, the structure clear and accessible. He took a quiet breath and closed the tab.

Next came attributes. Nothing new to assign, he'd remembered to apply his points last time. Still, he let himself take in the numbers again. Level sixteen, only a few weeks into living in Arath and already his stats had grown far beyond what he'd ever expected. His body showed it too, broad shoulders, lean muscle, faster reflexes, sharper instincts. He caught his reflection faintly in the interface window and raised an eyebrow.

"I suppose fighting to stay alive every other day has its benefits," he murmured.

He gave the city management tab a glance out of habit. Predictably, the red alert hovered at the top of the screen.

**Outside of Sphere of Influence – Remote Access Denied.**

No surprises there. He closed it with a quick tap and let the interface fade.

The night air was cool against his skin. Lianna had set a low, smokeless fire earlier, just enough warmth to heat water and soften rations. He'd watched her do it with practiced care, each motion deliberate. He was confident he could replicate it now if needed. Another minor skill gain. He leaned back against the stone, listening.

The plains were quieter than the forest. Too quiet in Xavier's estimation. There was no underbrush to rustle, no owl calls overhead, no distant chirps from the dark. Only the steady whisper of dry wind through grass, and the occasional flick of Valkra's twin tails as she prowled near the camp's edge.

He narrowed his eyes toward the horizon, senses stretching. Even with the Ley Line of Earth humming faintly beneath his awareness, he couldn't shake the feeling that something was out there, watching, and waiting.

That was when he heard Lianna stirring.

#

Lianna rose from her bedroll with a fluid grace that barely disturbed the silence. The firelight caught in the pale fur of her ears as she made her way over to where Xavier sat. He turned toward her before she spoke, already aware of her approach. The Earth Ley Line resonated softly beneath the surface of the ground, and he felt its subtle vibration shift as Lianna neared, her footsteps registering like ripples across stone.

"Quiet night?" she asked, voice low.

"It has been so far," he replied, matching her tone. "Different sort of quiet... but still quiet. I can't quite shake the feeling that something's building out there."

She nodded slowly. Her eyes moved across the darkness, but her body remained tense. The fur along her arms and the back of her neck hadn't settled. Her hand drifted toward the collar at her throat, brushing it once, then again. Not absentmindedly. There was purpose in the motion, like a habit born of long discomfort. When her fingers found the metal, her expression tightened into something close to a scowl, but heavier, worn in.

"I have it for now," she said, lowering herself beside him. "Go get some rest. The gods know we'll need it if things go badly."

Xavier didn't move. His eyes tracked the way her hand lingered near the collar, how her posture never quite relaxed.

"I will," he said, "but I've got a couple of questions first."

Her gaze shifted to him again, curious. "Questions for me?"

He gave a faint, tired smile. "I know I usually ask Ella. But I respect your insight too... and she's admitted she hasn't traveled much beyond Rynthavael. You have."

Lianna's ears twitched slightly at the compliment, and after a short pause, she nodded. "Alright. Ask."

"Magic," he said, the word landing heavier than he expected. "Aside from that slaver back at the foothills, I haven't seen much of it. I know it's real, but I expected more. More visibility, more presence. It's like it's hiding or being hidden."

"Because it is," she said softly, her eyes fixed on the plains. "You have not traveled far yet, but what you've seen is no accident. Magic is real, and it is powerful, but in most places... it is suppressed. Constrained. Feared."

She paused, fingers curling slightly against the edge of her thigh.

"An age or two ago, there was a war. The magi rose up. They challenged kings and councils, tried to carve empires out of nations. Declared themselves rightful rulers through power alone. They nearly succeeded."

She glanced at him, serious now. "I'm no historian. You should ask the Elders or read more of those old books. But what came after... that is remembered. The world turned on them. Some were hunted, others captured. Bound. Collared. Magic was stripped from their hands, their will broken."

She tapped the collar around her throat. This time, the motion had more force behind it.

"This wasn't meant for people like me. It was originally for them."

"Zor'kaan," Xavier murmured, the word surfacing in his thoughts without effort.

She blinked, mildly surprised. "Yes. That's the old name."

He frowned. "So now, what... all mages are bound like that?"

"In most nations, yes," she said. "They're required to register. Tracked. Watched. Most can only cast small things... cantrips, trinkets, and such. Anything serious, anything dangerous, is outlawed. All of it is for the same reason. 'The safety of the people.'"

The bitterness in her voice was sharp, but familiar. Too familiar.

Xavier's eyes dropped to the collar again, its dull metal catching the last glow of the firelight. He had seen it for days now, seen it on her and Ella, but he hadn't really thought about it, not like this. The weight of it, the history, and the branding. His chest tightened, and a quiet guilt settled in. Not the explosive kind, not outrage. This was something quieter, a more insidious guilt. A realization that he had seen chains without thinking about who they were built for or what they actually meant.

"What about divine magic?" he asked, voice lower than before. "Clerics, priests... are they shackled too?"

"Not with collars," she answered. "They're bound in other ways. By doctrine. Oaths. Their magic comes from gods, and so they are watched by temples and churches, not governments. In some places, those temples rule outright.

But even there, divine casters are seen as vessels, not threats. Not like the magi."

He exhaled slowly. "So when we reach Ironhaven... or Thandor's Reach... I probably shouldn't ask around about spells or grimoires."

"Not unless you want one of your own," she said dryly. A faint smile touched her lips. "Besides, it's clear the collars Ella and I wear are not Zor'kaan, but Drekh'tar."

The words sparked instinctively in Xavier's mind, the ancient tongue unwinding itself with sudden clarity.

**Zor'kaan:** Sealed Power.
**Drekh'tar:** Submission Binding.

He stared at her collar, the implications sitting heavy in his chest. "I hate everything about that," he muttered.

Lianna's silence lingered, not the empty silence usual at the end of conversation, but pregnant with the weight of the topic. The firelight caught the edge of her collar as she turned her gaze back to the plains, the meaning clear in the stillness between them.

He stood slowly and nodded. "Thank you. That gives me a lot to think about. I just... I should've studied that slaver's collar more carefully. Before we handed it off."

"You may get another chance," she said, not looking at him.

He passed the watch to her and returned to his bedroll. The fire crackled faintly behind him as he lay down, but the silence in his mind was louder than anything outside. He closed his eyes, but he didn't sleep right away.

It would take time before the weight of that conversation settled into rest.

#

Morning brought a brittle light across the plains. Pale clouds drifted low, veiling the sun as if the sky itself wanted to remain unseen. The trio rose in silence, dressed, and shared a cold meal from their dwindling rations. No birdsong greeted them. No insect hum. Only the dry whisper of grass and the quiet clink of gear being packed away.

There had been no game the day before. Not even old signs of it. Hunting had been sparse, and they'd chosen not to press the issue, letting Valkra and Frostclaw seek what they could. Even the great cats had eaten little.

As they returned to the road, what little remained of it, Xavier found his eyes drawn again and again to the horizon. What should have been a thoroughfare was now cracked and narrow, overgrown in places, its edges crumbling beneath dry grasses and encroaching roots. Stone markers leaned or lay half-buried, worn smooth by time. There was no maintenance here. No travelers. No care.

He walked in silence, letting his boots fall in time with his breath, eyes scanning the ground. He searched for anything that might stand out, disturbed soil, bent stalks, and shallow impressions. The tracking skill wasn't instinct yet, but the repetition was building familiarity. Patterns were beginning to form in his mind, like the first pieces of a language he didn't yet know how to speak.

However, this road remained silent. No footprints. No wagon grooves. Not even the padded marks of passing animals. The grass was dry enough to crunch beneath his boots, but it gave no clues. The land didn't feel empty, it felt abandoned.

"Lianna," he said quietly. "Are you seeing what I'm seeing?"

She moved up beside him, sharp eyes already scanning the terrain. "I am," she said after a moment. "There is something wrong here. Even the land knows it."

She gestured out to the open plains. "Frostclaw and Valkra struggled yesterday. They barely found enough to feed themselves, and I'm worried it will be worse today. We may need to buy meat from a merchant the next time we find one... if we find one."

As if summoned by their names, both cats emerged from the tall grass at the road's edge. They moved more cautiously than usual, keeping close to the group. Frostclaw's ears twitched with each shift of air. Valkra's stinger-tipped tails swayed low and tight, her muscles coiled with unease.

Xavier slowed to a stop. He turned slowly in place, listening. Looking. The land around them was too still. No insects buzzed. No birds circled above. Even the wind had gone quiet.

He activated his Perception skill.

The world sharpened, detail by detail. The grass leaned not with the breeze, but away from something unseen. The soil bore no insect tunnels, no hidden trails. Even decay felt muted. It wasn't just that life had gone missing.

It had fled.

Everything natural had been pushed outward, driven away not by chance, but by presence. The stillness wasn't emptiness. It was avoidance.

His stomach tightened.

Ahead of them, a low ridge rose from the plains. Xavier increased his pace without a word, the others following behind. Grass crunched beneath their boots; each step too loud in the hush around them. At the top, the land spread wide and flat… and dead.

No herds moved. No smoke rose. No paths crisscrossed the open field. It was still. Hollow.

Then he saw it, or rather, Ella did. She pointed with a quiet word, and his eyes followed her gesture to a collapsed structure half-buried near the base of the ridge. It had once been a waystation, clearly, though now only blackened beams and scattered stone remained. The ruin looked like it had been abandoned for years, yet something about it didn't sit right. The destruction didn't seem old enough. The damage was too purposeful.

They descended in silence. It took half an hour to descend to the site. The air grew denser as they neared, the temperature dropping just enough to be felt. The scent of old ash clung faintly to the still air, dry and sharp. The burn wasn't fresh, but it hadn't aged fully either. Xavier picked his way through the rubble while Lianna moved ahead.

She called him a few minutes later, her voice clipped and tense. "Xavier. Over here."

He crossed to her quickly. She crouched low, fingers brushing the soil. Broken blades of grass. Drag lines. Shallow prints. A splash of dried blood darkened the pale dust.

"Multiple sets coming in," she said. "Only one set leaving. Someone was taken… or many."

A thin smear of blood followed the trail heading out. It was still fresh enough to draw flies.

"Raiders?" he asked.

"Or slavers. Not that there is any real difference now," she snorted. "It looks like they took prisoners. Alive."

A sharper voice broke across the ruin.

"Here!" Ella called, the urgency in her voice cutting clean through the air.

Xavier and Lianna moved quickly to where she stood. Ella was at the edge of the structure, beside a partially buried marker post scorched unevenly by fire. She didn't look at them, only raised her hand toward what was carved into the wood.

A crude brand. Fresh. Burned with force and intention. The mark of Ironhaven.

Xavier's breath caught in his throat. The firelight from memory danced behind his eyes, of the checkpoint, the false pleasantries, the silence that followed. This wasn't a coincidence. He stared at the symbol. It was not a warning for survivors, nor was it a trophy. It was a message.

"They wanted this seen," he said. "This wasn't just an ambush. It was staged."

Lianna's ears flicked as she returned to the tracks. "They were dragging something. Someone. They're not far ahead. Slowing down in places... the weight of captives."

Ella joined them again, voice lower now. "There was no one left inside. No signs of a fight beyond the attack. They were near the checkpoint, and still no response. That tells me everything."

Lianna nodded slowly. "Which means the slavers, or whatever they call themselves, are operating without fear. Maybe even support. I've never heard of them working this deep into the Wildlands. Before, they stayed to going out beyond the edges."

Ella's gaze met Xavier's. "What do we do?"

He didn't answer immediately. His fury wasn't loud. It didn't burn at the surface. It sat deep, cold and certain. The brand in the post. The silence of the land. The fear etched into every absence. This wasn't a single act. It was a pattern. A design.

"I want to tear them apart," he said. "But we can't risk blowing our cover. Not yet."

Lianna's tone was steady. "Then we follow. Our disguises held at the checkpoint. If we keep our distance, we'll learn where they're going... and who's backing them."

Xavier looked again at the mark, then down the trail. The blood trail glistened faintly, catching the dull light. The weight of it settled in his chest.

"If Ironhaven's working openly not just beyond the borders but within the kingdom itself... if Arenvalis is letting this happen... then this isn't just random slaving. It's a system, a web."

Both women nodded.

They turned toward the trail, their steps careful now. Measured. Deliberate. Frostclaw and Valkra moved ahead their forms fading into the tall grass, , bodies low, senses sharp.

This wasn't a chance encounter. It was the edge of something larger, and they had just stepped into its shadow.

# CHAPTER SEVENTEEN

*Chains in the Dust*

The midmorning sun cast long shadows across the rugged terrain as they followed the caravan's trail. Xavier, Ella, and Lianna moved in near silence, their pace steady but cautious. Frostclaw and Valkra lingered at the edge of their vision, close enough to help if needed, far enough to avoid drawing attention. Tension gripped the group more tightly with every step away from the ruined waystation.

Signs of slaver activity were everywhere. These men moved with impunity across the Wildlands. That knowledge pressed heavily on Lianna. Her hand rose more than once to brush the collar at her neck, her fingers curling briefly before she dropped them.

Still, she led without hesitation. Her instincts as a tracker overrode everything else. The shifting earth and broken rock posed no obstacle to her practiced eye. She moved with certainty, guiding the group as they shadowed the path toward Ironhaven.

Every so often, she crouched low, fingers brushing the ground. Xavier knelt beside her each time, listening as she quietly explained the trail's secrets.

"These grooves?" she murmured, pointing to the packed

indentations in the dirt. "Wagon wheels. Heavy load. The soil's sunk too deep."

She cast a glance toward him, voice tight. "Either supplies... or bodies."

Farther along, she indicated clusters of bootprints and hoofmarks.

"Guard formations," she said. "Disciplined spacing, rotating positions. They're not a disorganized pack. These are professionals."

Xavier studied the layout. The prints moved with purpose. The rhythm of it reminded him of drilled soldiers. Not the wild chaos he might have expected. They were organized, efficient, dangerous.

Just ahead, Lianna halted. The soil changed. The indentations here were smaller, barefoot, uneven. Exhaustion clung to every step.

"Slaves," she said. Her voice had lost its edge. What remained was cold, brittle certainty.

Frostclaw stopped behind her. His ears flattened as he crouched low in the grass, pale eyes watching. Valkra crept closer to Xavier's side, the fur along her spine bristling. She didn't understand slavery, but she recognized fear in the scent of disturbed ground.

Time dragged. The sun crept higher. It was nearing late morning when Lianna stopped again. She dropped to one knee, motioning them over.

"Here," she said, fingers tracing where a second path split off from the caravan's track. "This one ran."

Xavier followed her gaze. The prints veered away, sharper, deeper at the toes. Every step screamed panic.

She moved along the path a few paces, then pointed

again. "They stumbled here. Scraped up, kept moving."

Her hand hovered over a faint groove between steps. "Shackled. Ankles bound."

Ella joined them, a hint of hope in her voice. "At least they tried, right? Maybe they got away."

Lianna didn't answer. She had already turned back toward the main trail, scanning ahead.

Another set of prints waited just beyond, a second path, calm and deliberate. Measured steps and large boots.

"I have my doubts," she said quietly.

Xavier crouched again, studying the alignment. The two sets moved side by side now. Not in chase, but in convergence.

"A slaver," Lianna muttered. "They noticed."

They followed the signs through tall grass, each footstep dragging them closer to what they didn't want to see. The wind stirred dry stalks, but the air felt still, watching the drama as it played out.

At the place where the paths joined, the earth bore the truth.

Scrapes in the soil and torn grass. Deep gouges from thrashing limbs. A body had fought here, hard. Fought to stay free.

Then blood. Not a pool, not fatal. Just enough to hurt. Enough to punish.

From that point on, the tracks continued together. One set strong and straight. The other faltered, unsteady, and slowed.

"They didn't make it," Lianna said. Her tail flicked once, then stilled. "They were caught. Dragged back."

Silence settled.

Ella's fists clenched at her sides. "Damn it... I hoped at least one of them made it."

Xavier said nothing. His gaze had already turned forward, fixed on the road ahead.

The caravan was still moving. Still dragging lives toward Ironhaven, and they followed.

#

The trail wound steadily onward, the deep grooves of the caravan's passage pressed into hardened earth. Eventually, it merged with a broader road, smoother, flatter, shaped by years of relentless travel. Though easier to walk, the path offered little cover.

They clung to the edges, slipping between patches of tall grass and scattered stone. Every movement had to be calculated. Every step carried risk. The wind, once wild, now felt sharp and deliberate, brushing across their backs like the breath of something unseen.

By midafternoon, the sun began its descent, painting the plains in golden hues. The light was beautiful, but the moment felt hollow. Nothing about this land welcomed them anymore. The Wildlands bore no peace, only silence.

Ahead of them, the caravan continued to crawl toward its destination. Glints of armor caught the sunlight. Chains clinked faintly. Shadows slumped under the burden of bondage.

They could see the caravan clearly now, the shape of it. The cruel intent of its cargo. No one spoke.

Ella's fingers hovered near her bowstring. Her sharp gaze followed the caravan's motion with disciplined intensity. Every staggered footstep and shift in formation drew her attention. She measured, calculated, then let it go. There was no clean opening.

She remembered Bramblegate. The chaos of that first skirmish. The smoke, the shouting, the way everything teetered on a blade's edge. That ambush had been a surge of instinct, of opportunity. This wasn't the same. This needed patience. Every piece had to fall exactly right.

Lianna's tail lashed behind her, a quiet reflection of the storm gathering beneath her stillness. Her shoulders were drawn tight and her expression locked. This was the world she had fled. The rhythm of the march, the metallic scent of control, all of it threatened to pull her backward in time.

Frostclaw moved in silence beside her, his head low, muscles tense. His presence anchored her. He had smelled this rot before. He had helped her escape it once, and he felt its shadow growing again.

Behind them, Xavier kept his breathing steady. Beneath his ribs, something burned.

The temptation clawed at him. He could strike now. At dusk, they'd have the cover. He could slip between the wagons, bring the blade down without a word. They could be gone before the slavers ever knew.

His hands twitched, but he didn't reach for his weapons. It would be easy. However, it would be wrong.

Every link in the chain they broke here would reforge itself unless they shattered the forge. He could feel that truth like heat against his skin. If they acted now, the system would swallow the loss and replace it. Nothing would change.

He let the thought pass. Let the image dissolve. Then he exhaled and stepped forward.

"We keep trailing them," he said. His voice was calm, but

it carried weight. "If we move too soon, we lose our chance to see what's really happening."

Ella's hand eased away from her bow. Her shoulders sagged just slightly.

Lianna turned her head toward him. Her lips parted as if to argue, but she stopped herself. The truth had already settled in her gut. Her fists clenched at her sides. She gave a tight nod, not agreement, but in understanding.

One caravan, even one filled with suffering, could not be the focus. Not yet.

There were deeper chains, roots they hadn't seen. The raids, the silence from the city, the growing hunger for captives, it all pointed to something greater. They needed to know why.

That truth did not ease the weight of the choice.

Valkra drifted close to Xavier's side. Her movements were slow, uncertain. She made a low, warbling sound and flicked her tails against his leg. Her eyes remained fixed on the caravan, her body tense. She didn't understand slavery, not fully, but she understood danger. She could feel the predator's presence. She could smell the fear in the wind.

They continued forward, their path narrowing, the wild grasses thinning. The sun bled lower across the horizon, its light stretching long and cold.

Each step brought them closer to the heart of something they would one day break. It was not time for it now, not yet.

\#

As the day wore on, the landscape began to change. Wild grasses gave way to trampled earth, packed flat by heavy boots and wagon wheels. The road lost its natural rhythm and took on the marks of control. Each mile felt more rigid than the last.

The air shifted. Once crisp with the scent of open plains, it now carried the stink of ash, smoke, and metal. A bitter tang clung to their tongues. It tasted like old blood.

Wind whispered through chains strung along the roadside, setting them clinking against rusted stakes. Some swayed loose, others held weight.

They passed the first figure just beyond a crooked bend. He was slumped, still breathing. His arms hung limp inside his bindings. His body bore the marks of long hours exposed to sun and pain. Farther along, more followed. Not all moved.

Xavier's jaw tightened. He kept walking.

Beside him, Valkra slowed, her nostrils flaring. Her paws hesitated on the packed trail. A low noise rumbled deep in her throat, not aggression, not fear. Something older and more primal. She turned her head slightly, ears twitching toward the hanging bodies.

The fur along her spine rose as she passed a twisted iron stake, the metal streaked with dried brown. Her gaze lingered too long on one figure, barely conscious, a wet rasp the only sound from their throat. She remembered this.

It wasn't the same place, but the feeling was familiar. When the shardfang wolves had circled her dying mother, the air had smelled the same, copper tang, dust, and the slow stink of helplessness. Something inside her recoiled. She padded closer to Xavier without a sound.

Frostclaw's posture mirrored hers. The great snow leopard walked close to Lianna's side, his pale eyes narrowed, ears tucked slightly back. He didn't snarl or growl. He didn't need to. Everything about his movements warned of what he saw.

Closer to the gates, the road became worse. Spiked iron rods jutted from the ground at uneven intervals, some sharp and clean, others twisted and rusted, stained by old memories. Chains dangled between them. A few remained empty. Most did not.

Figures were bound in cruel displays, some alive, some long past suffering. One woman whimpered as they passed, her voice raw and broken. The wind pulled her words away before they could form anything more than sound.

Ella stopped for half a step before forcing herself onward. Her eyes didn't leave the woman.

Wooden stockades and auction platforms rose just beyond the path's edge. They stood in various states of disrepair, abandoned remnants of past sales. Captives had once been displayed there like livestock beneath the sun, priced and prodded for the highest bidder.

Their splintered beams held the ghosts of countless transactions, stained with sweat, dirt, and the memory of shackled wrists. Weathered banners still hung overhead, swaying from crude poles, once-proud merchant guilds now overwritten by the heraldry of Arenvalis' noble houses. A grim reminder that even misery had its patrons.

They reached a rise in the trail, and Ironhaven unfolded before them. The city swelled with movement beyond the stockades. Shadows shifted at the gate. Wagons rolled forward. Slavers barked orders. The walls loomed taller with each step.

Jagged walls of stone and blackened steel rose high against the fading sky, uneven in construction, reinforced over decades with whatever material was at hand. Towers leaned slightly in places, patched by timber, scrap metal, and rubble. Smoke curled from dozens of chimneys, coiling into a permanent haze that smothered the sky above the city.

Torches burned high along the wall, casting flickering halos in the growing dusk. Behind them, the clang of hammer against steel echoed faintly, constant and unrelenting.

Xavier caught the rhythm. Two beats, a pause, then one final strike. Over and over again.

The scent of burnt wood and smelted iron clung to his skin. It sank into his hair, into his clothes. He could feel it on his tongue.

Above, the sky had begun to shift. Three moons now hung visible overhead... Pyrrastra, Umbraeth, and Zephira. The crimson flare of Pyrrastra bled against the haze. Umbraeth hovered behind it like a bruise in the stars. Zephira shone cold and distant.

Their light cut through the smoke just enough to silhouette the city in cruel glory. Ironhaven looked more beast than place, its towers like jagged teeth, its breath reeking of ash and oil.

They slowed and silence filled the air between the members of the group.

#

Slavers and armored guards funneled new arrivals toward the gates ahead. Captives moved in tight, controlled formations. Their wrists and ankles were shackled in lines, posture bent by fatigue and hopeless repetition.

Caravans creaked forward on groaning axles, weighed down by cargo and bodies alike. Mercenary companies clustered near the road, some laughing, some quiet, others cleaning their weapons with mechanical ease.

None of them intervened. To them, it was just another day.

Xavier's group slowed. Just ahead, the very caravan they had tracked approached the checkpoint. The lead wagon stopped near the open gate, the slaver captain barely glancing up from his seat.

A brief exchange followed. Papers were handed over, and coin passed between hands. No questions were asked. No names confirmed.

The gates yawned open. The slavers gave a signal.

One by one, the captives were prodded through.

The city took them without protest. Swallowed them whole.

Near the back of the column, a young Leopari slave staggered.

She was chained directly to the rear axle of the last wagon, her posture lower than the others, spine curled in a way that spoke of pain rather than submission. Her fur was short, sun-dulled, and dust-caked, patterned in faint rosettes across her limbs and shoulders. A mottled trail of blood streaked down her leg where the iron shackle had broken the skin.

Xavier was close enough to pick out details of the woman. Lean and wiry, she moved with sharp, instinctive tension, all coiled energy and resistance. One of her eyes was swollen nearly shut, but the other burned... focused, alert, unwilling to fall. Her arms were bound behind her back, forcing her forward at an angle that kept every step painful.

She limped. Each time her pace faltered, the chain yanked her forward again.

No one spared her a glance.

Xavier's gaze lingered on her. That was the one. The one

who had made a break for it. The escapee.

She had paid for it in bruises and blood, but she still walked on her own feet. Still refused to collapse. That, more than anything, told him her will hadn't broken.

Ella followed his line of sight. Her mouth pressed into a grim line. She said nothing.

Lianna's ears lowered slightly. Her tail gave a flick, subtle and sharp.

Ella moved a little closer. Her voice barely rose above the sound of the chains ahead. "I hate this place already."

Xavier's grip on Vaeltheris tightened, the leather creaking beneath his fingers. "We'll tear it apart one day."

He didn't raise his voice, but the promise in it didn't need volume. It only needed truth.

They reached the final rise in the road.

Ironhaven stretched before them.

The towers flanking the gate leaned inward at jagged angles, forming a warped arch above the entry, crooked and toothlike, a broken mouth left wide open.

Torchlight flared along the walls; their flickering orange halos positioned like eyes peering down from either side. The gate itself remained open, a black iron divide between one world and the next.

From deep inside the city, forge hammers struck in rhythm. Two beats. A pause. Another strike. The sound repeated itself again and again. Almost machine like in its rhythm to Xavier's ears.

Smoke bled upward in slow spirals. The air grew heavier with every step. The stench of sweat, soot, and scorched metal pressed against their skin.

Xavier exhaled once, then straightened.

His stance shifted as he stepped forward into the part he would play. A mercenary captain, measured, aloof, unbothered by cruelty.

Ella lowered her head, mimicking the posture she had seen too many others forced to adopt. Her steps slowed, measured, careful not to draw attention. She moved with quiet control, but her fists clenched briefly before she tucked them out of sight.

Lianna's eyes narrowed. Her expression turned distant, unreadable. The way her shoulders dropped, the way her arms hung slack, it wasn't performance. It was memory. The shape of obedience etched into her as a child, returning now like a scar pressed too hard.

They said nothing. They did not look back. Together, they passed the outer perimeter.

The gate rose around them, ringed in iron and stone, the opening jagged with rusted teeth.

Ironhaven stood waiting, and it welcomed them with open jaws.

# CHAPTER EIGHTEEN

*City of Chains*

The gates of Ironhaven loomed ahead, towering constructs of iron-bound wood reinforced with darkened beams and ancient rivets. Though worn by age, they remained defiant, a brutal promise of the order enforced beyond. The road leading toward the portal was grooved not by travelers seeking fortune, but by the weight of chained feet and the boots of those who traded in misery.

As they neared the entrance, Xavier subtly adjusted his stance. He had already taken on the role of a slaver-mercenary days ago, but here, under the scrutiny of the city's watchmen and stone-faced bureaucracy, he refined it further. His stride grew heavier, self-assured, matching the swagger of the others funneling into the city. His face held a flat, impassive set, as if the suffering around him were as unremarkable as stone.

Ella and Lianna followed close behind, heads bowed in well-practiced submission. They wore the armor of fighting slaves valuable, dangerous, and owned. Each step was controlled, their hands kept well clear of weapons. Their stillness wasn't meekness. It was studied restraint.

Behind them, Frostclaw and Valkra walked in loose unison, their presence deliberate. The two great cats... shadow and snow, trailed the group with quiet menace, their pacing aligned like silent sentinels. Together, the party moved as one, giving the appearance of a slaver with highly trained, potentially volatile assets.

Two guards waited at the final checkpoint before the gate. Both bore the sigil of Arenvalis, clad in layered leather and steel. One was older, hard-eyed and broad-shouldered, his hooked nose casting a hawkish silhouette across the papers laid before him. He barely looked up as slavers passed, his gaze fixed on the stack of coin growing at his elbow. The lives behind the chains did not interest him. Only the toll and bribes growing in number.

The second guard, younger and leaner, noticed Xavier's group approaching. His gaze passed from Xavier to the two women, then fixed with hungry interest on Lianna.

"Papers," the older one demanded without glancing up.

Xavier stepped forward and offered the forged documents with calm efficiency. The guard took them with a grunt, flipping through with bored indifference. When Xavier dropped a few coins on the table, the pages were suddenly deemed acceptable.

The younger guard was not so easily distracted. "Not often you see one of these properly collared," he said, smirking as he tilted his head toward Lianna. "Snow leopards usually bite harder than they're worth. Did this one give you trouble?"

Xavier turned and gripped the collar at Lianna's throat, drawing her closer with a slow, deliberate motion. His fingers curled against the cold metal, brushing the runes as if to remind her and the guard of its weight.

"Not yet," he replied, voice clipped. "She took some work to break, but she knows what happens if she forgets her place."

Lianna's posture never wavered. Her ears flicked once, the only visible crack in her otherwise stony control.

The younger guard chuckled, eyes gleaming with approval. "That kind needs reminding. Pity to waste good stock because someone went soft."

Xavier gave no response. His jaw ached from holding back the bile rising in his throat. He kept his expression blank. Inwardly, he hated every word.

Beside him, Ella stood rigid, her face still and unreadable. But Xavier could feel the tension rolling off her like pressure before a storm. They had known such interactions were inevitable. That didn't make them easier to endure.

The older guard finished with the papers and gestured them through with a dismissive wave. "They're clear. Move along."

The moment passed. The gaze lifted. And with practiced calm, Xavier stepped forward, leading them through inner gate of Ironhaven's open maw. Like a hungry beast the city swallowed them whole.

#

Inside the city, the world changed again. Ironhaven's streets were a crooked mess of uneven stones and smoke-streaked buildings, their edges hunched like scowling faces under the moons' veiled glow. The air choked with a noxious blend of oil, sweat, sewage, burnt wood, forge-smoke, and desperation. Above, haze from countless fires turned moonlight into a sickly wash of reddish purple, bleeding across rooftops like a bruise.

They kept to the main thoroughfare. All around them, life moved with grim purpose. Slavers barked orders. Mercenaries jostled through crowds, heavy with steel and swagger. Merchants hawked goods while cages lined the outer walls of the market square, each one filled with the broken, the bound, or the silent.

In one cage, a gaunt boy stared at the ground. In another, two young girls huddled together beneath a dirty blanket, eyes too tired to cry. Some captives wept, others screamed, and a few simply watched the crowd pass them by, faces blank with defeat.

Xavier clenched his jaw as they passed, his fists curling at his sides. He said nothing. He could not save them now, not yet. But he saw every face and it deepened the cold rage already building within him.

Near the heart of the square, a raised platform dominated the space, stained wood, steel reinforcements, and a set of wide stairs leading to a place no one wanted to climb. The auction had already begun.

Lianna kept her eyes low, tail stiff as a rod. Though she said nothing, Xavier could sense the way she seethed beside him. Frostclaw padded behind her, silent as ever, but his ears were flat, and his gaze stayed fixed on his bonded partner's distress. They didn't walk as a pair, not here, not openly as a slave wouldn't have a bonded beast. However, the bond between them was tangible to those who knew.

Valkra moved closer to Xavier's side, brushing his leg now and again. She didn't understand the purpose of chains or auctions, but she knew predators when she saw them. Her hackles lifted as she passed a slaver who reeked of blood and spice.

From beside him, Ella murmured low enough for only him to hear. "What is our first move... Master?"

Xavier inhaled slowly through his nose. The title twisted something in his gut.

"We get our bearings," he answered. "This city isn't just slavers. It's mercenaries, politics, contracts. There's a network here. Somewhere in it, there's a way to pull the thread loose." He nodded toward the auction block. "And we see who's being sold next. The ones from the caravan will end up here eventually."

They wove through the edge of the crowd, careful to stay close and keep an unobstructed view of the platform. The auctioneer was already calling out offers.

He was not theatrical, not in the way one might expect. Not loud or grand. His voice was oily and steady, the practiced cadence of a man who had sold more flesh than food. He didn't shout, he didn't need to, the square carried his voice naturally.

"Animari stock from the northern woods," he said, as though describing lumber. "Healthy backs, minimal scarring. Two trained for labor, one for sport. Opening bid begins at thirty."

There was no pause for drama, no showmanship. Just efficiency. Names were not used, slaves didn't have names. The merchandise was paraded, turned, assessed. Bidding happened with curt nods and raised fingers.

Xavier watched. He memorized faces, skin tones, tail movements, and… injuries. One boy had a burn along his shoulder. Another Animari woman had a limp. Some came from the Wildlands, others from caravan raids near the Silverwood or Ironpeak. He kept count.

The line dwindled, and then… A figure was dragged up the stairs.

Xavier's eyes narrowed. He recognized her. The runaway from the caravan they had tracked. The one who had almost escaped.

She was taller than most women here, built with compact power. Her clothes had been traveling leathers once, but now they hung in torn strips. Her furred legs were scraped, bruised. A long purple welt ran down her right cheek, puffed around the eye. One ear bore a small nick. A fresh lash mark peeked beneath her sleeve. But she stood tall.

Her back was straight. Shoulders square. Her ears, long and rabbit-like, remained high and alert. Her amber eyes were sharp with tension, not fear. A fighter's stare. Someone who had been cornered before and survived.

The auctioneer twisted her arm, forcing a stagger. She hissed between her teeth but didn't cry out. Didn't lower her gaze.

The crowd murmured, but the interest was lukewarm. Wounded runaways weren't prized purchases. She was bruised, defiant, unbroken. Not worth the hassle, most thought.

Which made the bidding brief.

Xavier lifted his hand.

Lianna stiffened beside him, a quiet intake of breath. Her look snapped toward him, eyes narrowing with a flare of betrayal... until understanding began to dawn.

Ella, silent, gave a slight nod, then shifted her weight to subtly block Sihri from view.

The auctioneer's head turned. He acknowledged the bid. Another slaver countered, barely.

The man who countered glanced Xavier's way, lips thinning as he weighed his chances. His eyes moved from Xavier to the two women behind him, taking in Ella's composed stillness, not the stillness of submission, but of quiet readiness, like a drawn bow held steady. Lianna remained motionless as well, yet there was something tense in the set of her shoulders, something feral in the subtle twitch of her tail that betrayed no fear, only restrained contempt.

Then he noticed the cats.

Frostclaw's pale eyes tracked him with unsettling focus, while Valkra stood angled beside Xavier, her sleek muscles taut beneath her shadowed fur, twin tails slowly sweeping in mirrored arcs. The entire group radiated an unspoken threat, not loud or theatrical, but unmistakable, a quiet smoldering promise of violence.

Whatever interest the bidder had cooled in an instant. He hesitated... then lowered his gaze and hand. No more bids followed.

Xavier raised his hand again becoming the final bid.

Moments later, he stepped to the side table, presenting forged credentials and a small stack of golden coins. The paperwork was processed with routine efficiency. The collar's rune crystal, marked with Sihri's ownership signature, was handed to him.

The Leporini was shoved down the stairs, stumbling forward. Lianna caught her, steadying her with a hand to the arm. The rabbitkin jerked at the contact, then froze when Ella stepped in, whispering something too quiet to hear. Whatever she said made Sihri bristle.

She scowled, but didn't pull away.

The crowd had already turned. The last of the merchandise was processed. The day's auction concluded with the clink of coin and the closing of ledgers. People dispersed, returning to their alleys, their vices, their cages.

Something fundamental had shifted. For the first time since entering the Wildlands, Xavier's group had not just observed, they had intervened. Quietly and precisely they had taken action. A single chain had been purchased, but its collar now rested in the hands of one who despised what it stood for.

Without fanfare, they turned from the square and slipped into the city, the newest "slave" walking at their side, posture guarded, but upright.

#

The streets of Ironhaven were dim and oppressive by the time they slipped away from the auction square. The echoes of haggling voices, the clink of coin, and the low moans of defeated slaves still lingered in the air like ash after a fire. Xavier and his group didn't stop. They kept to the shadows, moving with practiced caution until they came upon a narrower lane, tucked between squat stone buildings where the stench of the market began to fade.

There, half-hidden beneath ivy and soot, hung the sign of a small inn. It swayed gently in the breeze, hinges creaking beneath rust and time.

The carving was faded but intact. The Emberdrift Hearth. A lone fox curled beneath the roots of a gnarled tree, embers glowing faintly within its hollow trunk. Some parts of the sign were singed at the edges, charred as though by real flame. Beneath the image, an inscription had been carefully etched: Sanctuary to those who seek it. Shelter to those who keep it.

Lianna tilted her head, studying the carving. "It is meant to be subtle. If you do not know what you are looking at, you simply see an old inn."

Ella gave a quiet, approving hum. "And it's just far enough from the main streets. Less scrutiny and less chance of being overheard."

Xavier didn't hesitate. "Then it'll do."

Inside, the inn's warmth settled around them like a blanket. The air carried the faint scent of lavender smoke and beeswax polish, comforting and clean. Low-burning hearths cast flickering light across the room, and lanterns swayed gently from overhead beams worn smooth with age. The innkeeper behind the counter gave Xavier a brief nod and asked no questions. The right coin, as always, bought more than shelter. It bought silence.

They secured a modest room on the second floor, tucked into the corner of the building where the walls were thick and the window faced a narrow alley behind. The floor groaned underfoot as they stepped inside. The space was tight, but secure, just enough room for rest and caution.

While Xavier and the others began to settle in, Ella quietly excused herself and returned downstairs. She came back several minutes later carrying a wooden tray balanced in both hands. Upon it rested five plates with earthenware bowls, four filled with steaming broth beside seasoned flatbread, and a fifth with strips of raw meat wrapped in a linen cloth. The scent of marrow, thyme, and mint clung to the warmth of the tray, blending comfort and practicality in equal measure. Without a word, she set it on the narrow dresser near the wall. She set the bowl of raw meat on the ground near where Frostclaw and Valkra waited.

Then she picked up one of the cups and crossed to Sihri.

The rabbitkin woman sat stiffly on the edge of the bed, her small tail curled tightly against her back. Her ears flicked often, each twitch betraying tension even as she fought to keep her expression still. Since leaving the square, she hadn't spoken, though her eyes were sharp, assessing.

She scanned each of them in turn. Ella first quiet,

watchful, and composed while going about her tasks. Then Lianna, arms crossed near the door, her weight settled in that familiar posture of someone always ready to move. Sihri's gaze dropped lower, settling on the two beasts resting near the hearth.

Frostclaw held her gaze briefly, then yawned and closed his eyes. The snow leopard was familiar. Sure he was larger than a normal one, but he was still natural.

Valkra, however, watched her closely.

The shadowmane's green eyes remained fixed, unblinking, her twin tails moving with a slow, deliberate rhythm. There was something unnerving in her stillness, a quiet awareness that felt too focused, too intentional to be mistaken for mere animal instinct. Sihri's gaze lingered, narrowing as she studied the shadowmane more closely. This creature wasn't just intelligent, she was fully present, watchful in a way that suggested calculation rather than curiosity.

She wasn't a pet, and she certainly wasn't just a beast. Whatever she was, Sihri could feel the difference.

Xavier crouched beside the bed, resting his forearms on his knees to meet her gaze without looming. "You're not a slave here," he said simply.

Her ears twitched. Her gaze narrowed, though she didn't flinch. "It did not look that way in the auction."

Ella offered the broth to her, her voice quiet. "That was a cover. We needed to blend in to get this far."

A quiet pause followed. Lianna's eyes remained fixed on Sihri. There was no suspicion in her gaze, only recognition. This one hadn't broken. Even with chains around her neck and bruises down her arms, she carried herself like someone still ready to fight.

The sight stirred something old and unsettled. Arms folding tighter across her chest, Lianna shifted her weight against the doorframe. It was too familiar the collar, the glare, the defiance. Sihri burned with a fire she remembered well, though her own had long since faded to embers. That anger hadn't cooled in the rabbitkin. At least, not yet.

The rest of the room held only the basics: a narrow bed, a cracked dresser, and the furred shapes of the two large cats resting near the hearth. Sihri's gaze returned to Xavier.

"We're not slavers," he said again. "We've already freed others." He hesitated, then added, "And when we leave this place, once we're beyond Arenvalis' reach, I'll remove that collar myself. For now... I'd rather not call you 'slave.' What is your name?"

She stared into the cup for a moment. Steam curled toward her face as she answered. "Sihri. Sihri Swiftclaw."

Her voice was low and calm but guarded. She didn't look away. "So, what am I now?"

"Free in all but name."

A long pause followed. She studied him carefully, like she expected a catch hidden somewhere behind his words. Something too good to believe.

Xavier lifted the rune-bound crystal he had received from the auction. He hadn't set its commands earlier. The moment had not required it and to do what he was about to in public would have drawn attention he was not ready for. Now he pressed his thumb to its edge. A subtle shimmer danced across the metal band around her neck, barely more than a flicker.

"By my will, you are bound to my command alone," he said quietly. "No other restriction is placed on you. Until I can safely free you again."

Sihri's breath caught. She didn't speak, but her fingers lifted and brushed the collar lightly, tracing the rune. There was no lock to undo, no key to remove, yet something in its weight felt changed. Not gone, but lighter.

Her posture shifted, just enough to notice. She leaned forward, no longer bracing to run.

"Fine," she muttered. "I'll follow, but I will keep my eyes open."

Lianna allowed a faint smirk to tug at her lips. "Good," she murmured. "You would be a fool not to."

The tension in the room eased. Not gone, but thinner. Trust had not been earned, yet the possibility had been acknowledged. For now, that was enough.

Beyond the thick walls of the Emberdrift Hearth, Ironhaven groaned with the weight of chains and smoke. Inside, the firelight flickered gently as silence settled in.

Tomorrow, they would begin picking at the roots.

# CHAPTER NINETEEN

*Quiet Bonds, Quiet Resolve*

The soot-filled sky of Ironhaven cast the early morning light in a dim, rusty hue as it filtered through the inn room's warped glass panes. The upper floor of the Emberdrift Hearth groaned faintly with the shift of bodies stirring awake. Though the beds were bug-free and the rooms private, a lingering unease clung to the air, heavy and unspoken. It mirrored the haze outside, thick with smoke and iron dust. The city breathed with a slow, sullen rhythm, as if reluctant to wake.

Xavier sat at the edge of his bed, elbows on knees, rolling his shoulders one at a time. A pulse seemed to echo through the room, quiet and steady like a second heartbeat. He couldn't shake the sense that Ironhaven itself was alive, that the walls around them listened, pulsing with tension. Every breath he drew carried grit and weight, like the city pressed in from all sides.

He stood, adjusting the twin scabbards over his shoulders. Vaeltheris settled into its place with a whispering metallic sigh, and he shifted the Emberstone short sword until it rested just right along his back. The weight was familiar, but in this place it also felt like armor against the unseen.

Near the window, Lianna stood motionless, a dark

silhouette against the ruddy light. Her gaze was fixed on the alley below, posture stiff with barely masked tension. She wore the travel shawl they had picked up the day before, the soft folds pulled up to conceal her collar. Still, the line of her shoulders betrayed her mood. Even in silence, the strain showed for anyone who knew her. Her tail flicked once, sharply.

In the far corner of the room, Sihri sat on the folded bedding she had chosen instead of the offered cot. She had spoken little since joining them, even after they left the market. But her silence was not vacant. Her eyes flicked from face to face, tracking movements, cataloging details. Behind the guarded expression was a quick mind, sharp and calculating.

Xavier caught her gaze briefly. He dipped his chin in a slight nod. It wasn't a command or even a greeting. Just an acknowledgment. You are still safe with us.

She didn't return the gesture, but she didn't look away either.

Valkra shifted from her curled position near Ella's cot, letting out a quiet, breathy rumble. The little shadowmane had stayed close to Ella through the night, curled tight as if the tension outside had crept into her sleep. The bristled edges of her fur twitched, ears flicking at sounds that didn't reach human ears.

Ella rose with practiced ease, brushing dust from her trousers and stretching briefly. She gave Xavier a small smile before slipping out the door without a word.

A short while later she returned, pushing the door open with her hip, a large wooden tray balanced on her hands. The smell of spiced fried potatoes, browned sausage links, and soft eggs filled the room with unexpected warmth. Despite the undercurrent of tension, the scent tugged at something more primal, hunger, comfort, the echo of something resembling normalcy.

Ella set the tray on the center table without fanfare. "Eat. We may not get another good meal today."

The group gathered around the table. Spoons and fingers claimed portions in quiet coordination. Frostclaw padded forward from the shaded corner where she had been resting, settling at Lianna's feet and earning a quiet scratch behind the ears. Even Sihri shifted closer, though she didn't speak. She picked through her portion with care, eyes still scanning.

They ate in silence, each lost in thought. The taste of food couldn't completely dull the weight of the day ahead.

Then came the knock.

#

The knock at the door was firm, not hurried, but official in its rhythm.

Xavier set his cup down, eyes narrowing slightly. Ella moved first, brushing her fingers on her tunic as she stepped across the room and opened the door.

A middle-aged man stood in the hallway, wearing the brown-stitched vest and bronze collar clasp of an innkeeper's staff. His eyes didn't quite meet hers.

"Message just came through," he said, voice clipped and tight. "Every inn was given a copy."

He handed over a folded parchment, then turned and walked away without waiting for acknowledgment.

Ella unfolded the paper and read quickly. Her expression tightened. "Routine inspection. All unregistered slaves must report to the Registrar's Hall by end of day for verification and classification."

Xavier stood and stepped closer. "What's the catch?"

"They're sweeping the entire district. Anyone not on the books gets confiscated." She glanced toward Sihri. "You're exempt. You were bought here, and your record's handled by the market."

Sihri gave a single sharp nod, her expression unreadable.

Ella continued, voice softer now. "Lianna and I are 'foreign property.' We need to be officially registered under Kingdom records."

The silence that followed was heavy.

Lianna's claws clicked softly against the ceramic bowl she held. She set it down and stood, tail flicking once in irritation. "They are tightening the leash." Her voice was low and cold. "Testing for weakness."

Xavier didn't flinch. "Then we register."

Lianna turned sharply toward him. "We are playing into their hands."

"We're buying time," Xavier replied. "It's the only way to keep you both safe right now. If we resist this, the whole cover collapses. One wrong step and they drag you away in chains."

She didn't respond, not with words. Her jaw clenched and her shoulders tensed, but she said nothing more.

Xavier moved to the chest near his cot and unlatched it. Inside were folded satchels, a hidden compartment of documents, and the carefully forged registration papers—one for him as master, two for Lianna and Ella as bonded slaves, and Sihri's actual certificate. He checked each one, inspecting the wax seals and hidden marks before tucking them into a leather roll and sliding it into his belt pouch.

He met Ella's gaze, then Lianna's. "We walk in, do what we must, and walk out. That's all."

Lianna gave a curt nod. Ella simply stepped forward and lifted her shawl, tucking it to better hide the collar again.

Once everything was in place, Xavier stepped out onto the balcony for a moment, surveying the street below. The city was fully awake now. Ironhaven's rhythm was a grinding one… workers, merchants, guards, and slaves alike moving in tired procession.

Behind him, the others gathered what they needed. When they rejoined him at the doorway, he gave a final nod, then led them down the stairs.

Outside, the day had already grown thick with heat and smoke. Frostclaw and Valkra were secured in the caged wagon they had purchased the day before. The guards hadn't said anything at the time, but their stares had lingered too long. Better to avoid drawing more attention.

Then they began the march to the Registrar's Hall.

#

The streets of Ironhaven were already alive with motion, though nothing about the city's pace felt natural. It was the trudging rhythm of survival, shackled movement, sharp-eyed patrols, and the ever-present scrape of metal on stone. Even the breeze tasted of smoke and rust.

The Registrar's Hall was only a handful of streets away from the Emberdrift Hearth, but each step felt longer than the last. The walk might have been short, yet it stretched beneath the weight of too many watching eyes.

Xavier walked at the front, posture even, expression unreadable. His presence projected quiet authority, but beneath it, he was alert to every shift around them. The back of his neck prickled with awareness. Every patrol they passed seemed like they lingered a moment too long. Every citizen gave them a glance, then looked quickly away.

Sihri followed directly behind him. She kept her head lowered, as expected of a slave, but her long ears twitched with every sound. Her movements were precise, her silence deliberate. Anyone watching would have seen a well-trained servant. However, Xavier saw something else... the tension in her hands, the alertness coiled in her spine.

Lianna walked behind Sihri, her jaw set, eyes fixed forward. She said nothing. Her hands remained clenched at her sides, claws just short of breaking the skin of her palms. The shawl hid her collar, but not the fury simmering beneath her stillness.

Ella walked beside her, a half-step back. Their movements were in sync. Whether by intention or instinct, they mirrored one another, the rhythm of their steps aligned. Ella said nothing, but her presence steadied the line between Lianna's anger and control. Every so often, her gaze shifted sideways, not to check on Lianna, but to share the moment.

They rounded a corner, and the Registrar's Hall came into view.

It rose from the street like a monument to control, tall and thick-walled, its facade carved with symbols of authority that gleamed with a dull polish. Brass-ringed lanterns lined the entrance path, casting weak light over smoke-stained stone. Twin statues of chained figures flanked the heavy doors, their faces bowed beneath the weight of iron circlets.

At a glance, the building was meant to impress, but not with beauty. It was built to dominate.

The caged wagon holding Frostclaw and Valkra was led up to a tether post beside the entrance, just beyond the wide central steps. Xavier secured the reins himself, tightening the hitch and brushing his fingers briefly across the bars. Valkra watched him with unblinking eyes, her posture low but quiet. Frostclaw gave a low chuff and turned in a slow circle before settling down again.

Satisfied, Xavier cast a glance over the cart, then turned his attention to the hall ahead.

The doors were thick ironwood banded in blackened steel. Two guards stood on either side, halberds held vertically in precise formation. They didn't stop the group. One gave a slight nod as Xavier approached, recognizing the document case tucked under his arm.

Inside, the air shifted. Cooler than the outside, but no less oppressive. The scent of old ink and scorched parchment hung beneath a layer of cloying incense that couldn't quite mask the hints of blood and metal beneath it.

The floor stretched out in black-veined marble, polished to a dull sheen by years of foot traffic. Gilded chains hung between support pillars, some in decorative loops, others ending in real cuffs. A few were occupied. Slaves knelt near the base of columns, heads bowed, wrists bound to the chains with heavy clasps. None spoke.

At the far end stood a long counter staffed by a row of scribes, each clad in charcoal robes threaded with iron stitching. They moved in practiced rhythm, taking scrolls, stamping forms, calling names without inflection or warmth.

One of them looked up and gestured for them to approach.

"Slaves for verification, step forward," the man said flatly.

Ella, Lianna, and Sihri moved without hesitation. As

one, they stepped from behind Xavier and approached the counter, quiet and composed. The room didn't react. The chains creaked. A page shuffled parchment. Somewhere deeper in the building, a voice shouted an order no one in the hall acknowledged.

Only the silence of procedure remained.

#

The streets of Ironhaven were already alive with motion, though nothing about the city's pace felt natural. It was the trudging rhythm of survival, shackled movement, sharp-eyed patrols, and the ever-present scrape of metal on stone. Even the breeze tasted of smoke and rust.

The Registrar's Hall was only a handful of streets away from the Emberdrift Hearth, but each step felt longer than the last. The walk might have been short, yet it stretched beneath the weight of too many watching eyes.

Xavier walked at the front, posture even, expression unreadable. His presence projected quiet authority, but beneath it, he was alert to every shift around them. The back of his neck prickled with awareness. Every patrol they passed seemed like they lingered a moment too long. Every citizen gave them a glance, then looked quickly away.

Sihri followed directly behind him. She kept her head lowered, as expected of a slave, but her long ears twitched with every sound. Her movements were precise, her silence deliberate. Anyone watching would have seen a well-trained servant. However, Xavier saw something else... the tension in her hands, the alertness coiled in her spine.

Lianna walked behind Sihri, her jaw set, eyes fixed forward. She said nothing. Her hands remained clenched at her sides, claws just short of breaking the skin of her palms. The shawl hid her collar, but not the fury simmering beneath her stillness.

Ella walked beside her, a half-step back. Their movements were in sync. Whether by intention or instinct, they mirrored one another, the rhythm of their steps aligned. Ella said nothing, but her presence steadied the line between Lianna's anger and control. Every so often, her gaze shifted sideways, not to check on Lianna, but to share the moment.

They rounded a corner, and the Registrar's Hall came into view.

It rose from the street like a monument to control, tall and thick-walled, its facade carved with symbols of authority that gleamed with a dull polish. Brass-ringed lanterns lined the entrance path, casting weak light over smoke-stained stone. Twin statues of chained figures flanked the heavy doors, their faces bowed beneath the weight of iron circlets.

At a glance, the building was meant to impress, but not with beauty. It was built to dominate.

The caged wagon holding Frostclaw and Valkra was led up to a tether post beside the entrance, just beyond the wide central steps. Xavier secured the reins himself, tightening the hitch and brushing his fingers briefly across the bars. Valkra watched him with unblinking eyes, her posture low but quiet. Frostclaw gave a low chuff and turned in a slow circle before settling down again.

Satisfied, Xavier cast a glance over the cart, then turned his attention to the hall ahead.

The doors were thick ironwood banded in blackened steel. Two guards stood on either side, halberds held vertically in precise formation. They didn't stop the group. One gave a slight nod as Xavier approached, recognizing the document case tucked under his arm.

Inside, the air shifted. Cooler than the outside, but no less oppressive. The scent of old ink and scorched parchment hung beneath a layer of cloying incense that couldn't quite mask the hints of blood and metal beneath it.

The floor stretched out in black-veined marble, polished to a dull sheen by years of foot traffic. Gilded chains hung between support pillars, some in decorative loops, others ending in real cuffs. A few were occupied. Slaves knelt near the base of columns, heads bowed, wrists bound to the chains with heavy clasps. None spoke.

At the far end stood a long counter staffed by a row of scribes, each clad in charcoal robes threaded with iron stitching. They moved in practiced rhythm, taking scrolls, stamping forms, calling names without inflection or warmth.

One of them looked up and gestured for them to approach.

"Slaves for verification, step forward," the man said flatly.

Ella, Lianna, and Sihri moved without hesitation. As one, they stepped from behind Xavier and approached the counter, quiet and composed. The room didn't react. The chains creaked. A page shuffled parchment. Somewhere deeper in the building, a voice shouted an order no one in the hall acknowledged.

Only the silence of procedure remained.

The scribe moved from behind the counter with a slow, practiced gait. His robes whispered across the stone, the iron-thread stitching catching what little light filtered in from the high windows. He opened the small gate in the side partition and stepped toward the women, extending one hand expectantly.

Xavier passed him the documents. Three scrolls, neatly prepared. Two forged, one authentic.

The scribe unrolled them without comment. His eyes flicked between names, classifications, and identifying marks. He handed Sihri's papers back almost immediately. The city's official stamp and auction seal were already in place.

"A local purchase," he muttered, more to himself than anyone else. "The others?"

He stepped closer to Ella and Lianna. His gaze was clinical, like one might use for livestock. At a gesture, another figure approached... a collared mage, younger, hooded, eyes downcast. His hands were pale and ink-stained, but they moved with fluid precision as he began a soft incantation under his breath.

Sigils formed between his fingers. The spell was subtle but invasive.

The runes on each collar, Ella's, then Lianna's, flared to life. A muted light pulsed along the metal bands, then faded back into stillness as the mage's hands lowered.

Lianna flinched as the spell brought back memories. It was slight, but enough. Xavier saw the way her pupils contracted, the tension that spiked through her shoulders. Her hand twitched at her side. The mage noticed, too, and hesitated a heartbeat before stepping back. The spell had done its work. He said nothing.

Xavier kept his expression still, his jaw locked, but his focus never wavered from Lianna. Her breathing was shallow. The glow of the collar had dredged something from below the surface. Something raw and unwelcome.

The scribe made no comment on the reaction. He moved to the counter again and retrieved a wide stamp from a tray of ink. With deliberate slowness, he pressed it to the remaining two documents, then returned them to Xavier without looking him in the eye.

"The papers are passably in order," he said. "Next."

Xavier nodded once and turned away. He said nothing as the group gathered behind him, their movement swift and silent. The sound of chains brushing stone followed them as they left.

Outside, the heat and smoke rushed back over them like a wet cloth wrung from ash. The guards at the door gave them no notice. The street had grown more crowded in their absence, but no one looked their way. Not directly.

They descended the steps without speaking. Not until they reached the cart did Xavier glance back toward the building, its chained columns catching the light like old scars.

Frostclaw stirred and whined softly. Valkra shifted her weight, her eyes locked on Lianna as she approached.

Xavier placed a steadying hand on the cart rail and exhaled.

#

They returned to the inn in silence.

Though the registration was behind them, it had left its mark. Not in words or wounds, but in the heaviness that clung to every step. The room on the second floor felt smaller than before, as though the city's gaze had followed them inside.

Lianna stood alone on the narrow balcony. Her hands rested on the iron railing, claws tapping a slow rhythm against the weathered surface. Her tail lashed once, then again. The sky beyond was still rust-colored, but now the clouds carried the dull orange glow of the forges below.

Xavier stepped into the doorway behind her and paused. He didn't announce himself. His presence was quiet, steady, unpressing. After a moment, he joined her, placing one hand on the railing beside hers.

"Are you alright?" he asked gently.

Lianna didn't turn. Her voice, when it came, was low and strained. "They looked at us like we were not people. We were only property to them."

"You know that isn't true," Xavier replied softly. "It's only a disguise. One we wear to protect the truth."

"I know," she whispered. Her voice cracked, just slightly. "But knowing doesn't change how it feels. Wearing this again... going through that all over again. It digs in, it rots."

Xavier didn't answer right away. His silence wasn't empty, just respectful. Beside them, the haze over Ironhaven churned slowly, indifferent.

Sihri's voice drifted from near the hearth, quiet but clear. "You walked beside him on the way back. That means something. You know it does."

Lianna turned slightly, surprised by the interruption. She hadn't heard Sihri rise.

The Leporini stood now, posture still guarded but no longer distant. Her arms were crossed tightly across her chest, and her ears angled back, but her eyes were steady.

"They did not break you," Sihri continued. "I saw that today."

The silence that followed was different than before. It wasn't empty. It was full of something just beginning to form... understanding, recognition. The space between them had shifted.

Lianna studied her for a long moment, then looked

away. Not in dismissal, but in thought.

Ella stepped onto the balcony without a word. She moved to Xavier's other side, her hand brushing his. He reached out instinctively and laced his fingers with hers.

The four of them stood there, not speaking. The air carried the sounds of Ironhaven, sounds of metal striking metal, distant shouting, the low hiss of steam. But on the balcony, it was quiet.

Something new had taken root. It was not trust, not yet, but perhaps the beginning of it.

\#

The rest of the day passed under a watchful sun veiled by smoke and cinders. The city never slept, not truly. It pulsed with iron rhythms, its veins carrying chains and coin in equal measure.

Xavier remained in the room with Lianna and Sihri. Though the inspection had been passed, neither woman wished to test Ironhaven's tolerance for foreign Animari walking freely, especially not after what they had just endured. The collars might fool the scribes and guards, but they didn't protect against scrutiny, and the city was thick with eyes.

Ella, however, moved freely.

She slipped through the streets as a bonded servant running errands for her master. No one questioned her. She carried bags, nodded when addressed, and kept her posture low. But her eyes never stopped moving. Every alley she passed, every wall scrawl, every merchant's mark, she watched for signs.

Lianna had described the symbology to her earlier. Markings used by sympathizers or those working within the resistance. Chalk slashes behind water barrels. Broken chain links etched into the side of crates. A triangle with a line drawn through the center, faded almost to nothing on the side of a laundry post.

Most people would pass them without thought. Ella did not.

She found two such signs that day. One behind a blacksmith's delivery stall, half-scratched away, and another beneath a slat of wood in a shuttered alley. It was not enough to call it contact, but it was something. A trail, faint and cautious.

When she returned to the inn, dusk had begun to settle over the rooftops. The haze outside glowed with the fire of furnaces, and the air had grown thick again with heat and ash. She stepped into the room quietly, setting her purchases aside as Xavier looked up.

"I found something," she said.

Lianna straightened.

They sat around the small table near the window, the heavy curtains drawn partway to soften the glow from outside. Ella pulled a rough map from her belt pouch, one she had sketched on the fly, marking two locations with a faint coal line.

"This one," she said, pointing near the edge of a smithing quarter, "is recent. The mark was smudged, but intact. The other's older, it might be abandoned, might not."

Lianna studied the map, her eyes narrowing. "That alley used to be a passage for market runners. If it's still clear, we might be able to use it as a staging point."

Ella nodded. "It could also be a drop point. I didn't linger."

Xavier leaned in. "Do we move on it tonight?"

"Too soon," Lianna replied. "We watch first. Let it settle. If we show interest too quickly, they'll vanish."

"Then we wait," Xavier said. "But not idly."

They began to talk in low tones, discussing routes, fallback paths, and signs to watch for. It wasn't full strategy yet, but it was the beginning. The tension in the room hadn't vanished, but it had shifted. No longer the silence of helplessness, but the quiet of planning.

Outside, Ironhaven continued its endless churn. Inside, something else stirred... intent, purpose, and the first glimmer of resistance.

#

The sun dipped lower behind the blackened skyline, though little of its light reached the streets of Ironhaven. What remained was scattered and sickly, filtered through the forge-smoke and drifting ash that stained the sky in hues of bruised red.

Inside the room, Ella and Lianna huddled close over the map. Quiet conversation continued at the table, deliberate and focused. Sihri had drifted from the hearth to the open balcony doorway, standing just inside the frame, arms crossed tightly against her chest.

She didn't move when Xavier stepped beside her. The air outside was thick with heat, and the scent of coal hung in every breath. One of her hands braced lightly against the stone wall, steadying herself.

"I'm fine," she muttered, not opening her eyes.

"I didn't say anything," Xavier replied.

"You were about to."

He didn't deny it. His intent was clear in his actions.

They stood in silence for a few moments more, the sounds of the city rising faintly beneath them, shouts from vendors, the crack of hammers, chains being dragged across stone.

Sihri opened her eyes but kept them focused on nothing in particular. Her voice, when it came, was quiet and flat. "You didn't have to bring me with you today. I know the way these cities work. I could have stayed behind."

"I did," Xavier said simply.

He didn't look at her when he said it, but his voice held a quiet conviction. "Because they needed to see you. That you were real. That you mattered."

Sihri didn't reply right away. Her posture didn't chang, but something in her shoulders eased, just a little. A tension she hadn't realized she'd been holding slipped loose.

When he stepped beside her fully, she didn't flinch.

When she turned to glance at him, her expression held neither distrust nor surrender. Only awareness. Recognition, perhaps, of something she hadn't expected to find.

She didn't thank him; the words were not there yet. However, she didn't walk away from his company either.

#

Ironhaven wore the dark like armor.

The lamplight below was dull, filtered through layers of soot and smoke, and the glow of distant forges cast flickering halos over the rooftops. The streets pulsed with movement even at this hour—buyers and sellers, shackled workers, and wandering guards all weaving through the alleys like blood forced through tired veins.

On the narrow balcony outside the second-floor room, Lianna leaned against the railing. Her eyes swept the haze-cloaked skyline, but her focus wasn't on anything beyond the edge of the city. The metal collar at her throat felt heavier than it had that morning. It lacked any real restrictions or limitations, but it carried weight all the same.

She didn't speak when Ella joined her.

The younger woman stood close without intruding, shoulder brushing lightly against Lianna's. They remained like that for a while, both gazing into the middle distance, listening to the city breathe.

"You carried yourself well today," Ella said at last. Her voice was soft, a thread rather than a rope. "Even when they tried to strip that from you."

Lianna let out a low sound, half breath and half chuff. Not quite a laugh. "They didn't need to try. The world's already doing a fine job of that."

She paused, then added, "I hate pretending. I hate wearing this collar again. I hate this whole situation."

"I know," Ella said gently. "But survival sometimes means wearing the mask until you can take it off yourself. On your own terms."

Lianna turned her head slightly. "You wear it too well."

Ella's smile was distant. "Only because I used to be something else. The collar doesn't dig as deep into me as it does for you. Or for Sihri."

Footsteps padded behind them, light but not hesitant. Sihri stepped out into the night air, arms crossed, her posture guarded. She didn't look at them. Her gaze was fixed beyond the railing, out into the haze.

"It is always like this, is it not?" she asked quietly. "The silence, the waiting. Knowing they see you as nothing but a tool. Something to be used."

Lianna turned to her fully, her eyes softer now. "Yes. And no."

Sihri looked up, her ears half-tilted, unsure.

"The silence, yes," Lianna continued. "But the waiting? That ends when you decide it should."

There was no challenge in her tone. No command. Only the simple offering of a truth.

Sihri met her eyes. "How long did it take you?"

Lianna looked back toward the city, her jaw working. "Still deciding."

Ella gave a quiet laugh under her breath. "Aren't we all."

The three stood there for a while, saying nothing more. The balcony was small, but it held them. The collar didn't vanish. The weight didn't lift. But they weren't alone beneath it anymore.

Sihri broke the silence again, her voice small but steady. "He could have left me on that stage. Sold me to someone else."

Lianna nodded slowly. "He didn't."

"And we won't," Ella added. "You're with us now. For better or worse."

Sihri's ears twitched. Her arms remained crossed, but something shifted in her face. Not a smile, not yet... but something close to the start of one.

Inside the room, behind the partially drawn curtain, Xavier sat in one of the plain wooden chairs. His eyes were closed, his body still, but he wasn't asleep. He listened without leaning forward, without breaking the moment. He didn't move, but he understood.

Whatever bonds were forming out there in the dim glow of Ironhaven, they were real. Not built from strategy or necessity, but from something far older and far harder to name.

#

The balcony outside drifted to silence and remained quiet. The three women still standing at the wooden railing but each with their own thoughts now.

Beyond the curtain, only faint murmurs of the city crept through the cracked window panes. The scent of forge-smoke still lingered, curling around the frame and settling into the grain of the wood. Inside, however, the weight within the room had shifted.

Xavier sat alone by the cold hearth, Vaeltheris leaning against the wall beside him. The light was dim, little more than the fading glow from the city outside. He didn't speak. He hadn't moved in several minutes.

He had heard every word spoken by the trio.

Not out of intent, but because the silence of that moment had drawn him to stillness. The kind of silence that asked to be respected. That told him this wasn't the time for strategy or action.

It was the time to listen.

He didn't pretend to understand what burdens they carried wearing those collars. He coud not understand it, not fully, but he could feel the shape of it in the air. The way Lianna's voice had cracked without breaking. The rare openness in Sihri's tone. The steady thread of strength Ella continued to offer without asking for anything in return.

It wasn't fully trust yet. Not all the way, but it was a

beginning in that direction.

He let his eyes close, just for a moment, and drew in a breath through his nose. Even here, the scent of ash clung to everything. The city was still a blade and still a cage. However, somewhere between the walls of the Emberdrift Hearth, something different was starting to form.

That bond he could sense between the women, that was important. That was something Xavier felt was worth defending.

# CHAPTER TWENTY

*Ashes in the Smoke*

The Emberdrift Hearth was unusually quiet as it woke. Outside, a dense haze clung to the windows of Ironhaven, not just fog, but the bite of smelted ore and soot drifting from the nearby forges. Inside their upper room, the silence held, not from tension, but from purpose. Each of them worked, alert and focused, as the city murmured beyond the walls.

Xavier sat at the narrow table in the corner that doubled as a desk. Scattered across it were hand-sketched maps, crude diagrams of Ironhaven's districts, and a growing list of notes compiled from whispered conversations and street-level observation. Patrol patterns, noble movements, market rotations, everything pointed to two names. A noble by the name of Ivarik Tharn and something known as the Shadow Court.

Every red-marked ink line on the map intersected at these threads. There was no solid evidence yet, only trails half-buried in slaver gossip and whispers beneath alley eaves, but even faint hope was enough. Somewhere in these lines were the keys to the captives still trapped.

He rubbed his eyes, then leaned back opening his UI. He had actually earned several new skills and ranks in them throughout the work. Espionage and persuasion were both at rank 4 now in his skill tab.

| Skill | Progress to Next Level | Description | Bonuses |
|---|---|---|---|
| Espionage | 23% | Espionage is the skill of stealthy infiltration, covert operations, intelligence gathering, and subtle sabotage. Masters of espionage move unseen, listen unnoticed, and gather vital secrets without raising alarms. This skill is perfect for rogues, spies, scouts, and shadow operatives who prefer brains over | +1.6% Success Chance on Infiltration & Theft Tasks. +1.2% Chance to Avoid Detection. +0.8% Bonus to Social Deception (Synergizes with Persuasion). |

| | | brawn and know that the best kill is the one nobody saw. | |
|---|---|---|---|
| Persuasio n | 42% | Persuasion skill is all about getting others to see things your way. Whether that means convincing, manipulatin g, deceiving, charming, or commandin g. It governs your ability to influence others in dialogue, leadership, negotiations , or tense social encounters. It's the favored tool of diplomats, con artists, | +1.2% Success Chance on Persuasion/ Deception Checks. +0.8% Influence Bonus when interacting with strangers. +0.8% Increased Profit/Discount from Social Haggling (synergizes with Barter). |

| | | charismatic leaders, and silver-tongued bards. | |
|---|---|---|---|

Across the room, Lianna crouched by her weapons, slowly sharpening her curved blades. Her gaze rarely lifted, but her ears twitched now and then, keenly attuned to the others. Frostclaw rested beside her, his sleek body relaxed but ready, tail flicking in lazy rhythm as his golden eyes swept across the room. His mistress had not spoken much since sunrise, but the tension in her shoulders said enough.

Ella moved with quiet purpose, tending to small rituals of care. She passed from gear to gear, cleaning and sorting, checking water flasks, adjusting the cinches on traveling packs. From time to time, she paused to crouch beside Sihri and gently rebind the fading lash wounds with fresh ointment. The Leporini woman bore the treatments in silence, her expression unreadable, eyes drifting always toward the window where she listened more than spoke.

Sihri, for her part, still had not spoken much other than to relay snippets of conversation she would overhear when she sat near the window. Her silence was not fear, Xavier realized, but calculation. She was watching. Absorbing. Testing this strange new shape her life had taken.

Valkra had claimed her new favorite place, beneath the window bench, curled against the stone. She dozed lightly, opening one eye whenever someone moved too fast or spoke too sharply.

Xavier exhaled and set both palms on the desk.

"We need more," he said at last, voice low and certain. "These names... Ivarik, the Shadow Court, they're just ghosts unless we find something real to tie them to. A trail we can follow."

He looked to Ella. "You're sure about this contact? The Whisperbroker?"

Ella nodded once. "The name came up more than once. Always with care. Always behind lowered voices. If it is a trap, it's a very carefully laid one."

Xavier gave a small grunt of acceptance and turned to a cloth bag tucked beneath the table. "Then we go in force. No splitting up. Everyone stays sharp."

He drew out a pair of dark leather gloves from the bag he had purchased the night before, thick, worn, iron-studded across the knuckles. He turned them over, inspecting the battle scarring with a faint smile.

| | |
|---|---|
| **You have discovered:** Pit Fighter's Gloves | **Item Class:** Uncommon<br>**Item Quality:** Well Crafted<br>**Weight:** 0.8 kg<br>**Durability:** 38/40<br>**Description:** A pair of thick, reinforced leather gloves with iron studs sewn into the knuckles. Scarred from repeated combat, the gloves are padded to protect the wearer's hands during unarmed strikes while delivering greater force to each blow. Once worn by underground pit fighters and slave-gladiators, these gloves are as brutal as they are |

effective.
**Traits:**
- Reinforced Knuckles: Adds +2 to unarmed strike damage (bludgeoning).
- Hand Protection: Prevents hand injury from repeated strikes or blocking attacks.
- Grip Support: Slightly improves grapple checks and weapon retention.

He tossed them toward Sihri with a casual flick.

"Your registration said you were a pit fighter. You might need these today."

She blinked at the gloves where they landed on the edge of her bedding. For a moment, she didn't move. Her ears twitched once, uncertain.

The gloves bore the scars of another life, creases along the knuckles, frayed stitching at the wrist, the faint scent of leather oiled but not cleaned. The weight of the past, of her previous slavery and escape, to her new capture and Xavier purchasing her hadn't lifted, but something else had settled beside it.

Slowly, Sihri reached out. Her fingers hesitated just above the surface, trembling ever so slightly. Then she touched them.

Her breath caught.

"These... these are not shackles," she whispered.

"No," Xavier said. "They're yours. Use them when you're ready."

She pulled the gloves close, her hands wrapping around them as though expecting them to vanish. For several long heartbeats, she said nothing. Then her chin lifted, and the tremble in her arms was gone.

"I'll earn them," she said. Her voice was soft, but beneath it ran steel.

Ella, from where she crouched nearby, caught Xavier's eye and gave a quiet smile. Lianna said nothing, but her gaze lingered on Sihri with a flicker of something softer behind the usual sharpness.

For the first time since her chains had been cut, Sihri sat just a little straighter.

#

They left the Emberdrift Hearth shortly after midday, slipping into the grim cadence of Ironhaven's streets. Above, the city center bore a cold order, soldiers in iron-etched cloaks patrolled beneath the black banners of Arenvalis, and merchants called wares from behind barred carts. The air here still held the acrid sting of coal smoke, but it was filtered through stone arches and an illusion of civility.

That illusion vanished block by block as they descended toward the lower district.

Here, the cobblestone fractured into slag-veined patches, half-melted from decades of forge runoff. The walls wept rust from iron bolts hammered too deep. Smoke clung to everything roof tiles, window glass, the folds of clothing. Voices sharpened, then vanished altogether. People moved differently here. No shouts, no swagger. Only glances held too long or not at all.

Even Frostclaw, who rarely blinked at the world, lowered his head and walked closer to Lianna's side.

Ella guided them forward. She had spent the day prior gathering what whispers she could without drawing too much attention. The name had surfaced more than once, often spoken with caution or traced onto tables with nervous fingers.

Their destination was a small shop known as The Hollow Root. Tucked in a narrow bend between two leaning forges, it looked like nothing. Just another apothecary built into a sunken wall of blackened stone. Its wooden sign hung crooked, half-rotted, depicting a faded sprig of something herbal. Two men in soot-covered aprons drank outside one of the nearby workshops and made a show of not looking at the group as they passed.

Lianna's ears flicked as she stepped closer to the doorway. She raised her hand, then pointed without a word. Above the lintel, nearly hidden beneath layers of grime and charcoal dust, was a faint symbol: a black flame curled in the grasp of a gnarled vine.

"No coin," she murmured. "Only favors."

Xavier gave a single nod. The mark confirmed what they'd suspected. This wasn't just an alchemist's shop.

Inside, the air was thick with bitter smoke coiled in from slow-burning incense bowls, their fumes laced with dried moss and something acrid that clung to the sinuses. Rows of glass bottles lined the shelves, some filled with tinctures or colored fluid, others holding things better left undescribed. A humming buzz came from a darkened vent above, faint and rhythmic like a whetstone across bone.

Green light pulsed dimly through stained glass lanterns, flickering against the uneven walls and creating shadows that shifted in unnatural ways.

From behind a sagging curtain of black velvet stepped

the shopkeeper.

He was tall, skeletal, with parchment skin stretched tight over bones like a sculpture carved too thin. His robes hung in layers, stained by sap, ink, and decades of breathless secrets. One eye was cataract-clouded, milky and unmoving. The other burned, literally, with a dull orange glow, like the last coal in a dying forge.

He said nothing at first. Just stared.

When he did speak, the sound was rasp and smoke, worn raw from too many deals.

"Three shadows... and a bound bunny girl," he said, his eye fixing on Sihri. "Curious coin for this side of the city."

No one corrected him. It would've been pointless as his words summed the group perfectly.

He stepped forward only a pace. His breath, when it came, was visible. A faint mist curled outward, tinted green at the edges before vanishing.

"What do you seek?"

Xavier moved carefully, drawing no weapons, showing no fear. He had been warned that money would get him nothing here. He hoped that his offering, a small vial of shimmering essence infused crystal, a rare fragment he kept back from the harvest in the crystal garden would suffice and mark his knowledge about such items. It was not meant to be a full trade, but a sign of authenticity.

He did not hold it out like an offering. Instead, he let the Whisperbroker see it, then gestured toward a nearby shelf.

"I'm not here to buy," Xavier said. "This is proof. I know what's beneath the surface. And I want names."

The Whisperbroker's gaze did not leave him.

The silence that followed wasn't passive, it was

measuring. That one burning eye roved not across Xavier's face, but into it, as though searching behind his skin. The air grew heavier.

Then, with no discernible movement, the broker gestured toward the curtain he had emerged from.

"Come."

Ella, Lianna, and Sihri tensed, but Xavier motioned them to wait. He followed the figure into the back without another word.

The back room was worse than the front.

The smoke here was denser, thinner lines curling from tiny braziers built into the walls. The heat wasn't oppressive, it was misleading, dry and calm, masking something deeper. Vials and jars were scattered across long counters, but none of them were labeled.

At the center sat a low wooden table carved with strange markings, covered in a spiderweb of residue stains from a hundred exchanges. Xavier set the essence vial carefully upon the edge.

The Whisperbroker seated himself across from him. His hands, long and bone-thin, folded beneath his chin. Ink and burn scars laced his fingertips, the marks of someone who had transcribed more than he had spoken.

He didn't blink. Not once but sat staring at Xavier.

When Xavier began to speak, it was carefully, his tone even and deliberate.

"I've heard the rumors. A noble named Ivarik. A power called the Shadow Court. Animari vanishing without trace, and whispers of something older... beneath all this."

The old man offered no interruption. No scoff.

Only silence. But it was not indifferent, it was attention.

So, Xavier pressed further. He spoke of ley lines, not in detail, but in suggestion. He mentioned imbalance and elemental unrest. The glimmer of Animari rebellion, scattered but growing

The broker still said nothing, but he was listening. That much was certain.

When he finally spoke, it was slow, like breath through ash.

"You did not come for names," he said. "You already know the key ones."

He leaned forward slightly. "But I will give you three truths. You'll know what to do with them."

His voice sharpened, not growing louder, but more exact.

"First. There is one more name you should know. Tavrek Halestorm. One of the Court's fists. Brutal. Methodical. Loyal to the fire behind the throne."

Xavier's jaw tightened. The name was unfamiliar, but the tone said enough.

"Second. There is an auction. Three days from now. Private. Underground. They will sell an Animari with blood not seen in generations. The kind the old orders used to covet."

He paused long enough for the words to bite.

"And third... if the Court is fire, Tavrek is smoke. Be careful smoke suffocates long before the flames catch."

He leaned back. The interview was over.

Xavier rose without asking for more.

He retrieved the vial, but the Whisperbroker did not stop him. The man had not moved since delivering the last word. He simply watched, that burning coal eye unblinking, like it saw something already written.

Xavier stepped back into the front of the shop, mind racing. There wasn't much to go on, but it was enough to be dangerous.

The others waited in silence. The green-glass lamps still flickered. The shop felt colder now, as if the flames beneath the Hollow Root had sunk deeper, withdrawn.

Xavier did not speak until they had exited the apothecary and moved several streets away, the noise of Ironhaven slowly swallowing the weight of what he had learned.

#

They returned to the Emberdrift Hearth just before dusk. The low sun caught the forge soot in the air and turned it into bloodstained haze. Inside the inn, the common room throbbed with noise, mercenaries roaring over dice rolls, slavers trading coin behind curtained booths, and somewhere beneath it all, the clink of chains echoing from memory rather than stone.

Upstairs, the group gathered in silence.

The warmth of their private quarters did little to cut the weight pressing into the space between them.

Sihri sat near the hearth, legs drawn up, arms wrapped loosely around her knees. Her ears twitched with every voice raised below, but she no longer flinched. Instead, her gaze kept sliding toward Xavier. She didn't ask what he had learned. Not aloud, but the question was there... in the tilt of her head, in the way her shoulders tensed each time he shifted.

Lianna stood near the window, half in shadow. Her arms were crossed tight across her chest, and her tail lashed in restless arcs behind her. She shifted to lean against the far wall, arms crossed, tail twitching erratically.

When Xavier finally spoke, it was low and grim. "There's going to be an auction. Three days from now. One of the prizes... is a rareblood Animari. Old lineage. Valuable to the wrong kind of people."

Lianna didn't move at first. She had heard the phrase "rare Animari" before when she was a slave in truth herself. It was something she had always heard before someone was broken.

Then her claws flexed slightly at her biceps, digging into her sleeves. "They'll flaunt her," she said. "Like meat on a festival spit. They always do. Dress her in gold to contrast her collar." Her voice cracked at the end, not with tears but with fury so deep it had forgotten how to burn.

Xavier met her gaze when she finally turned.

"We'll stop it," he said. No flourish. Just the shape of intent, sharp-edged and worn from use.

Lianna gave the faintest nod, but her jaw stayed tight, as if the promise was too heavy to rest on words alone.

Ella moved toward Sihri then and knelt beside her. She held a fresh cloth damp with salve, but didn't lift it. She waited first.

Sihri did not recoil. Instead, she extended her arm without being asked, letting Ella check the healing lash marks. Her posture had shifted since this morning, less guarded, less caged. The tremble was gone from her hands. She no longer hunched to vanish.

Valkra padded across the room and settled beside the Leporini girl, resting her head in Sihri's lap. The low rumble of the cub's purring vibrated against Sihri's legs, and this time, Sihri reached down and ran her fingers gently through the panther's soft fur.

The moment lingered for several minutes.

"You think he's lying?" Sihri asked suddenly, eyes still on the fire. Her voice was quiet but no longer hollow. "About stopping it?"

Ella looked toward Xavier, who was once again seated at his desk, pen scratching across a folded map.

"No," she answered softly. "He's been through what you have. Not the same chains, but chains all the same."

Sihri frowned, one ear flicking toward Ella. "But he's human."

Ella tilted her head slightly, thoughtful. "He is, but now... he is something else. Not because of what he is, but because of what he chose to carry. He is bound to a path as surely as that collar would have bound you to one."

Sihri finally turned to look at her, brow furrowed. "And that's enough?"

"No," Ella said. "But for my master... it's a beginning."

The word landed, heavier than expected. Sihri studied her. "Why do you call him that... Master? It is clear he does not like slavery. You have stated yourself how the collar does not actually affect you."

Ella looked away from the hearth and back to Xavier.

"It doesn't," she replied. "Not like yours did. But I am bound to him. By soul, not law. I chose to do so and bound my very being to him. He is worthy of being called such even if he does not accept it."

Sihri's grip on Valkra's fur tightened slightly. "But it's still binding."

"It is," Ella said. "But a chosen bond can give strength. A

forced one only steals."

Sihri stared into the flames, lips pressed into a line. The silence that followed was not uncertain. It was contemplative.

#

That night, Ella, Lianna, and Sihri found themselves outside on the Emberdrift's narrow balcony. Below them, Ironhaven's streets glowed orange with torchlight and forge fire, the light rising in waves that made the city seem to flicker, alive, but not breathing. The air above the inn was warmer than it should have been, touched by heat rising from stone and steel, but the balcony itself felt removed from the chaos. Quiet. Still.

Lianna leaned over the railing, her elbows resting on the iron bar, ears twitching at every scream or shouted curse that drifted up from below. Her tail flicked once, then settled.

"It is a sickness," she muttered. "This whole city."

Ella didn't disagree. She sat nearby on the ledge, arms folded over her knees, her gaze focused more on Lianna than on the street. The flickering light from below played across Lianna's fur, casting narrow bands of gold and shadow across her shoulders.

"You held yourself together at the registration," Ella said softly, returning to a thread of conversation left unfinished. "That wasn't easy."

Lianna's jaw tightened at the memory. Her shoulders rose slightly, tense, but she nodded. "I did not do it for me," she admitted. "Did it so he would not have to see me break."

Her voice was quiet, but clear. There was no shame in it, only a lingering uncertainty about how much that choice still weighed on her.

Sihri stepped forward then, silent at first. She came to stand beside them, arms crossed, not guarded but thoughtful.

"He didn't flinch when he paid for me," she said. "Didn't leer. Didn't look at me like they did."

Her voice carried no disbelief now, only a kind of dawning comprehension. She wasn't trying to convince herself anymore, she was stating a fact. In that simple truth, something changed.

The three women stood together, shoulder to shoulder. The noise from Ironhaven's underbelly rose in uneven pulses, but up here, it seemed a world away. The glow of the forges didn't reach their faces. Only the moonlight did.

"The collar doesn't define you," Ella said, voice barely above a whisper.

Lianna turned to her, then looked at Sihri. Her gaze lingered, and for a moment, the only sound was the wind brushing against the iron rail.

"No," Lianna said. "But I wear it in these lands until the law breaks. It is how I can help with his mission here."

The words carried weight, but they didn't burden her. They gave shape to her choice. She stood taller after saying them.

They remained there a while longer, the silence between them losing all the tension it once held. In that quiet, something unspoken passed between them an understanding forged not just from shared pain, but from decisions made in its wake.

Below, Ironhaven burned, but above it, the three of them stood together, unbound in all the ways that mattered.

# CHAPTER TWENTY-ONE

*Ash Beneath the Iron*

The group had kept their room at the Emberdrift Hearth, though the inn had changed around them in ways more felt than seen. What once held a flicker of comfort clinging to its wood-paneled walls had dulled into something strained and brittle. Laughter no longer drifted from the common room below, only the low thrum of voices muttering through smoke and tension. The hearth still burned, but its warmth no longer reached far.

The inn had become a reflection of Ironhaven itself. The city was rotting from within.

Downstairs, mercenaries hunched around heavy tables, their armor streaked with soot, dried blood, and darker things. The scent of scorched leather and hot iron hung in the air, cut through with the copper tang of spilled blood. Slavers mingled in small, hooded knots, hunched over mugs of thick, tar-like ale. Couriers slipped between them like shadows, parchment tucked into belts and pockets, many bearing broken, clumsily resealed sigils from Arenvalis noble houses.

Upstairs, it was quieter, but no less heavy. Xavier leaned against the windowsill, his eyes scanning the alley below.

Mist curled through the narrow street, blurring the form of a wagon as it rattled by. Iron bars ran along its sides, half-covered by thick canvas that did nothing to hide the clinking of chains or the low, muffled cries from within.

He watched it vanish into the haze and felt a knot form in his chest. The lack of inspectors, of coin exchanges, of even a token gesture of legality, none of it surprised him anymore. However, the silence was worse. The silence was complicity. This was not oversight. It was orchestration.

Behind him, the door opened and shut with a soft click. Ella's footsteps padded across the stone, and a moment later a sealed scrap of parchment landed on the table beside him. She pulled her damp hood back, strands of dark hair clinging to her cheek as she stepped beside him.

"It's another Animari caravan," she said softly. Her voice stayed low, even here in the privacy of their room. "No paperwork. No inspection. No coin exchanged. They passed through the lower eastern gate just before dawn. Just waved through."

In the corner, Lianna sat on her cot, methodically oiling one of her curved daggers. She didn't look up.

"That matches the last two," she murmured. "They are operating outside the bounds of the law. It has to be the Shadow Court. No one else wields enough influence to suppress the city guard this completely."

Ella nodded. "They're accelerating. That auction... it's not just trade. It's a convergence. Every major power is being drawn to this city."

By the far wall, Sihri remained quiet, seated cross-legged on her low bed. Valkra was curled at her feet, breathing in rhythm with the Leporini's steady pulse. The shadowmane cub's twin tails flicked slowly in sleep. Then one eye opened and turned not toward Sihri, but Xavier.

She blinked once, then shifted, resting more fully against the floor with a soft sigh.

"She's getting attached to you," Lianna said, her voice softer now, but still focused. She finally looked up, eyes flicking from Valkra to Xavier. "Valkra. She's choosing you."

Xavier glanced at the cub and felt something stir within him, low and steady. It wasn't just affection. It was recognition. A thread pulled taut between them, unseen and undeniable.

"I know," he said quietly. "Once we're away from here, I want to speak with you. About the bond you share with Frostclaw."

Lianna gave a simple nod, as if she had been expecting the request. "We will speak when the moment is right."

Silence followed, heavier this time. Not awkward, but laden with mutual understanding. Eventually Xavier spoke again.

"The collars... they're working. No one questions the ones marked as property."

Ella crossed her arms. "So long as they're worn openly, it keeps most people from interfering. The guards see the papers and move on."

Xavier nodded. "Then we split. Ella, Valkra, and I will keep tracing the Whisperbroker's trail, names, symbols, sources of power. You and Sihri move among the auction lanes. Take Frostclaw. Pose as scouts for your supposed master. Find out who's buying and where the slaves are being moved."

Lianna's expression remained unreadable, but she gave her assent. "Understood. I will note rotation patterns and house affiliations. We will avoid direct contact unless necessary."

"Good," Xavier said, straightening. "Let's move before the city stirs too much."

As they left the room and stepped out into the Emberdrift's hall, the silence behind them lingered. Around them, Ironhaven pulsed like a festering wound. The tension had grown beyond whispers now. Something deep beneath the stone was shifting. Something that had been buried too long... was starting to burn.

#

The city choked on its own breath.

Xavier's group moved through the eastern alleys of Ironhaven with practiced ease, shadows folding around them like a second skin. The streets here were quieter, the people thinner, but the air was heavier, laden with smoke, sweat, and something older. Something wrong.

The Ironmaw Barracks loomed ahead, jagged and dark, its outer walls fused from scorched black stone and riveted steel. The building sat hunched in the center of a cleared plaza like a predator at rest, its presence radiating heat that shimmered faintly even in the cool morning air. The reek of burnt oil, blood-drenched leather, and sulfurous ash clung to the surrounding stones. Beneath it all, Xavier caught the faint scent of brimstone, sharp and stinging, a foul promise carried on the wind.

They slipped behind the collapsed edge of an old forge, peering through gaps in rusted metal and shattered stone. From their vantage, the yard spread below like a wounded battlefield, ringed by flickering braziers that pulsed dim red against the gloom. Crimson-clad soldiers moved in timed patrols, their boots echoing against the ground in relentless cadence. Their armor was etched and scorched, dyed in shades of blood and iron. Every movement was measured. Mechanical. Too precise.

Then the air changed. It grew heavier, thicker. Like the moments before a lightning strike, when the world held its breath.

He emerged from the northern arch of the barracks, his gait slow and unchallenged. Tavrek Halestorm.

He moved with the inevitability of an avalanche crashing down a mountains side, every step punctuated by the groan of his infernal plate. Matte black armor encased him from neck to heel, each plate lined with thin, glowing runes that pulsed like coals stirred from slumber. They didn't just glow, it seemed that they breathed, inhaling and exhaling faint threads of red light, as if the metal itself was alive and aware.

Around him, soldiers snapped to rigid attention without being told. Mercenaries stepped aside in silence, eyes fixed downward. Even two passing nobles bowed their heads, robes swishing as they moved quickly out of his path.

"Tavrek Halestorm," Xavier whispered. "That's no officer. That's... something else."

Ella didn't speak at first. Her breath came slow, shallow, her posture coiled with restrained fury. "He is the blade in Ivarik's hand. The threat behind the voice. He doesn't command. He enforces."

Below, Tavrek halted near the central brazier. His voice rang out like hammered steel, clear and cold.

"Purge the forgeries."

His tone was not loud, but every head turned toward him.

"Any Animari registry that does not survive the flame... burn the bearer as well."

A murmur ran through the yard. A junior officer flinched, hesitating before saluting and turning away. Another, an older man with a stained command sash, exchanged a brief, worried glance with a subordinate.

Tavrek did not react. He simply turned, inspecting the formation as if reading their souls.

From further down the line, another voice drifted upward.

"They're placing Reavers along the outer walls," one soldier muttered to another. "Whole units. Taking over gate control and tower posts."

"A siege net," Ella whispered grimly. "They're ringing the city in Redmaws. It's not just intimidation... they're setting the jaws of a trap."

Xavier's expression darkened. "Halestorm is baiting it. We're running out of time."

Ella nodded. They didn't speak again. Not as they slipped away from the ruined forge, not as the sulfur sting faded behind them. The heat lingered longer than it should have, and the weight of what they had seen stayed heavier still.

#

The slave lanes stank of rot.

Lianna and Sihri moved silently through the crumbling alleys that bordered the auction yards, weaving between sagging walls and twisted iron pens. The air was foul with sweat and excrement, clinging to the skin like grease. Rusted chains dragged over flagstones. Iron collars clicked and strained with every motion from the crowded wagons. The scent of urine and old blood hung thick above it all.

Everywhere they looked, there was squalor. Not the

kind born from poverty, but from disregard. From the belief that those in cages were less.

Lianna wore a simple grey shift, the fabric coarse and stained. It left her collar exposed, the sigil etched into the metal glinting faintly in the morning haze. Beside her, Sihri looked just as unremarkable. Two slaves, walking without fear because they were expected to be invisible.

They had spent nearly an hour like this, walking the lanes and studying rotation patterns, when Lianna stopped cold.

Her breath caught in her throat. Her body locked.

He stood across the yard, framed by a low-burning brazier and a row of caged children. Mekal.

The slaver's frame had thickened with age. His hair, once black, had dulled to iron-gray and retreated from his temples. However, his voice still carried that same wheezing gravel, and he laughed with the same thunderous cruelty that had once haunted her nightmares.

More than that though, it was the scar that confirmed him. A long, ropey thing running from his shoulder to his elbow. A jagged, gleaming line of ruin that had not faded.

He raised one hand and shoved a young otterkin boy, barely past his tenth winter, into a cramped cage. The child stumbled, falling hard against the bars. Mekal barked a laugh, then turned, still grinning, to speak to a handler nearby.

Lianna's claws flexed. Rage flooded her chest like ice water laced with oil, and her heart began to pound in her ears. Frostclaw shifted behind her, the great cat's fur bristling, his eyes glowing faintly with the same fury etched in her bones, but he held position, waiting.

"Do you know him?" Sihri asked, stepping close, her

voice barely above a whisper.

Lianna gave one sharp nod.

"He does not recognize you like this," Sihri said, eyes still forward. Her voice stayed calm, smooth as velvet but edged with tempered steel. "And that is a gift. One you must not waste."

Lianna didn't answer. Her throat had gone dry.

Sihri pressed gently, her tone soft but anchored. "If you act now, we lose everything. This city will swallow you whole, and we will never reach those who built this rot."

Lianna trembled where she stood, shoulders tight with fury, teeth clenched hard enough to hurt. Her breath came in quick, shallow bursts. "He is the one who marked me," she said at last. "He's the one who killed Frostclaw's mother. I was just a child."

Sihri reached out and touched her wrist. Her grip was light but unwavering.

"You are not that child anymore," she said. "And you are not alone."

It took every scrap of discipline Lianna had to turn away. Her body shook with the effort. She could still hear Mekal's voice behind her, laughing, giving orders, joking about the worth of souls in chains.

"I will remember," she whispered. "I will end him. If not today... then soon. I know his face. I know where to find him now."

Frostclaw pressed his flank against her leg, silent and steady. Together, they walked on.

#

Nightfall crept through the warped windowpanes of the Emberdrift Hearth, casting long shadows across the uneven floor. The room had grown colder with the sinking sun, and the fire in the hearth hissed against the damp that had begun to seep in through the stones.

Ella spread a parchment across the table, her fingers smoothing it flat with practiced ease. The rough-edged page was marked with overlapping ink lines, auction routes, patrol rotations, estate entrances. All scrawled in the same hurried hand.

At the center of it all, two names repeated again and again. Every trail they'd followed led back to them.

"Tavrek Halestorm," Ella said, her voice quiet. "And Lythara Veyne."

Xavier's head lifted. The name hit something deep in him, like a memory he didn't know he had. He whispered it back, slower this time. "Lythara... Veyne."

He sat back, the name echoing in his thoughts, dragging fragments of whispered stories behind it, half-heard rumors in dark corners, muttered prayers from frightened merchants, and the occasional terrified silence when the name alone was mentioned.

"I've heard that name before," he said. "Spoken like a legend. A succubus no one truly believed existed."

Ella didn't look up from the parchment. "She exists, and she's here. She leads the Redmaw Reavers."

Lianna, seated near the hearth, blinked. Her voice was controlled but touched with unease. "She is not a slave?"

"No." Ella met her gaze. "The information I gathered says she is a guest. She's been invited to the private auction."

Lianna frowned slightly, her arms crossing. "What kind of succubus commands a company known for razing cities, disappears for years... and resurfaces now, in Arenvalis, among nobles?"

Xavier answered, almost absently. "One with a purpose."

Ella pointed to a cluster of inked runes on the page. "The Marked Ones, her soldiers, are everywhere. In Halestorm's command structure, in auction security, in the personal guard of noble houses. They are not hiding. They are integrated."

"They're using them," Sihri said, her voice low. "Not as monsters. As tools. Soldiers."

Xavier ran a hand through his hair. "Not just tools. Symbols... it's transformation. These people weren't all forced into this. Some of them chose it."

Ella's expression darkened. "They're reshaping the kingdom. From within. One soul at a time."

Lianna looked to the parchment again. "How many?"

Ella's answer came without hesitation. "Dozens. Maybe hundreds."

A silence followed heavy and bitter. The kind of silence that came when truth stopped whispering and began to scream.

#

Night enveloped the city, and beneath it Ironhaven smoldered beneath the red-streaked sky.

On the balcony, Lianna and Sihri stood side by side, arms folded as they watched the smoke rise from the auction yard below. The glow wasn't bright, but it was steady, low fires, unseen but unfailing, winding like veins through the stone heart of the city. The air shimmered faintly with heat. Ash drifted on the breeze like restless thoughts.

Frostclaw lounged just behind them, stretched across the threshold, head resting on his massive paws. Nearby, Valkra nestled beside the doorframe. The shadowmane cub stirred, lifting her head as her gaze flicked toward the window where Xavier sat in silhouette, outlined by firelight.

"She feels him," Sihri said softly, watching the cub.

Lianna's voice came distant, quiet. "She chose him."

Inside, Xavier sat cross-legged on the floor. Vaeltheris rested across his knees, humming with a low, pulsing resonance that only he seemed to hear. He traced the runes on its hilt absently, his mind clouded with a thousand broken threads, each pulling in a different direction but all leading to the same knot.

"Lythara. Tavrek. The Reavers," he murmured.

Ella stood behind him, her hand resting gently on his shoulder. She didn't squeeze or speak right away. Her touch was enough.

"You're thinking of the Court," she said quietly.

"I'm thinking about the noose around this city's... hells, this kingdom's... neck." He looked up briefly, then down again, returning to the blade. "It's tightening."

Ella didn't speak at first. When she did, her voice was quiet, firm. "Then cut it."

Xavier's fingers stilled. "If we're wrong..."

"Then we burn it all," she said. "From the inside out."

Valkra rose from where she had been lying and padded silently across the floor. Her eyes glowed faintly in the flickering firelight. She paused at Xavier's side, then lay down beside him, her flank brushing his leg.

He reached out and rested a hand on her fur, fingers splayed gently against the rise and fall of her breath.

He was not alone. Not anymore. He had found friends and companions in this world, more than he had ever known on Earth. And in their presence, he had found something else, purpose.

Outside, the city's breath trembled, and in the distance, the Shadow Court moved.

# CHAPTER
# TWENTY-TWO
*A Fateful Meeting*

They were running out of time. With only a couple of days remaining before the so-called private auction, every waking moment was spent reinforcing their false identities. This morning found them cloistered in the cramped loft above a merchant's shop, where the Whisperbroker's contact, a known forger, waited.

Xavier stood still in the stifling room, his back close to a wall lined with faded tapestries and stacked scroll chests. The ceiling angled sharply, pressing low like a weighted hand, and the single narrow window admitted only a sliver of morning light. The air was thick with the pungent scent of aged parchment, oiled leather, lamp smoke, and fresh ink, clinging to his tongue with every breath. His tunic clung to the sweat on his lower back, and even Valkra had curled uneasily near the stairwell, disliking the closeness.

Lianna paced by the window, her silhouette tense against the wan light as she watched the street below. Her tail flicked once, twice, betraying her restlessness. She scanned for guards or worse, Redmaw Reavers. The name alone stirred a kind of dread few admitted aloud. Ella stood near the pair of scribes, silent and focused, her jade eyes tracking the quills scratching over parchment with mechanical speed. The rapid movements of the scribes filled the silence with a rhythm that sounded more like ritual than labor.

Xavier's breath came slow, measured. He could feel the weight of every risk they'd taken pressing on his shoulders like the ceiling above him. It wasn't fear, exactly, but a tightening sense of inevitability.

One of the scribes finally sat back, stretching knotted fingers. Murell was thin, with wisps of silver hair clinging to his skull and a pair of thick spectacles that magnified watery eyes. Ink stained his fingertips and sleeves. He tapped a stack of documents lightly with the back of a crooked nail.

"These will endure scrutiny," he rasped, voice dry as the parchment he crafted. Then his eyes met Xavier's through the lens-glare. "But linger not under Halestorm's gaze, nor his hounds. The Redmaw have... ways of peeling truth from lies."

A slight tremor slipped into Murell's voice on that last phrase. Xavier noticed. So did Ella.

Xavier stepped forward and placed a small pouch of gold beside the documents. Murell's eyes flicked toward it. For a heartbeat, his hand hovered above the table, fingers twitching. Then he swept it into a hidden sleeve-pocket with the swift efficiency of a man who knew not to look too long at what might curse him.

"You were never visited. You forged nothing," Xavier said softly, his tone cool but edged. "If anyone asks, Sihri was purchased from the pits of Zhyrdan. She fights on my behalf. That tale is your truth."

"Zhyrdan," Murell murmured, nodding faintly. "The southern desert... very difficult to verify. Smart.

Understood Master Vesh. You will not find anyone who can provide a better match to official paperwork. These records will withstand scrutiny as long as you can match the proper demeanor."

He paused, as if weighing the next words against some internal measure. Then: "You did not hear it from me, but the last man who tried forging slave writs for the Devorath estate vanished after his third sale. The Redmaw do not forget."

Ella stepped in, lifting the first sheet and scanning its markings. Glancing over them briefly she noted that they resembled the ones for her and Lianna. Handing the majority of the stack to Xavier, her expression remained unreadable, as she handed the parchment designated for Sihri over with a quiet, "Ready, Master?"

Xavier accepted the rest, thumbing briefly through them before adding them to the set for Ella and Lianna. All in order. He looked up, catching each of their eyes in turn, Ella's steady calm, Lianna's simmering defiance, Sihri's raw quiet strength.

His throat tightened slightly. They were not property. Not acquisitions. Every moment of this deception felt like rot beneath the skin, but it was the only path forward.

He turned, voice quiet. "We are. Let's go speak with the merchant."

#

The Broken Banner tavern reeked of old ale, stale sweat, and wood smoke. Low ceilings and poorly vented hearths trapped the heat like a bad temper, and the light was a sickly amber smear across greasy tables and flickering shadows.

Xavier sat in the dim corner booth, body coiled beneath

his stillness. Every creak of a stool or muttered laugh seemed to sharpen his awareness. Across from him, Ella and Lianna wore simple garments that left their collars visible. They moved with deliberate restraint, radiating controlled submission. Sihri stood to the side, arms crossed and jaw set, the flick of torchlight catching on the dull metal studs of her wraps.

He hated this. Hated the way eyes crawled over the women like they were nothing more than acquisitions. The mask he wore itched at his soul.

They'd cultivated their story with care. Xavier, as Xanthus Vesh, a desert-born trader of rare combat-trained slaves, here to present wares to Ironhaven's elite. The ruse had held so far. But now the stakes had risen.

"Relax," Ella murmured, lips barely moving.

"Easier said than done," Xavier replied, voice low. "We're betting everything on this."

"Orick will deliver," Lianna said with disdainful sarcasm. "At least, until he decides to sell us out."

Xavier managed a grim half-smile at the Iskari woman. "Hopefully, we've paid him enough to keep his loyalty for tonight."

As Xavier finished his retort, a shift in the tavern's mood silenced them.

It started with the barkeep straightening and the nearby patrons going suddenly quiet. Conversations trailed off. Chairs scraped as some subtly moved aside.

Orick, the merchant they'd bribed handsomely with multiple valuable gems, arrived first, quick-footed, sweating, and sharp-eyed. He leaned in close, voice tight.

"You're fortunate, friend," Orick whispered, leaning in close. "The right ears have heard. An envoy will meet you shortly. But he'll want to inspect your... stock personally."

Xavier bristled his stress about the forged documents welling in his gut. "Inspect how exactly?"

"A simple evaluation, nothing dangerous," Orick reassured quickly. "They prefer authenticity and exclusivity. Just maintain your facade. Villa Devorath demands only the best."

He disappeared into the crowd just as a cloaked figure entered.

The man moved with surgical confidence, boots silent on warped floorboards. His cloak parted slightly, revealing tailored velvet and a silver clasp worked into a stylized flame. Every patron he passed drew back.

The envoy came to a stop before their table.

"You are the slaver Xanthus Vesh?"

Hearing the title made Xavier want to spit. Slaver, it tasted like ash in his mouth.

"I am," he answered, cool and even. "You've come to inspect the wares?"

The envoy nodded, his tone clipped. "Stand them."

Ella rose first, eyes level, posture graceful but resolute. The envoy circled her slowly. His gaze lingered a beat too long, searching for weakness, for signs of spirit or brokenness.

"Defiant," he murmured.

Xavier offered no reply.

Next came Lianna. She stood fluidly, but her jaw tightened. Her tail coiled close, her ears flicking once in restrained distaste. The envoy walked behind her, slow and deliberate. He said nothing, but his smirk deepened.

Finally, it was Sihri's turn. She stepped forward, chin high, stance firm. Her hands hung relaxed, but tension rippled beneath the surface.

The envoy circled her twice. He studied the way her legs braced naturally, her balance impeccable, her gaze locked forward and unflinching.

"This one is a fighter?"

"A champion from Zhyrdan," Xavier said, his voice carrying a note of practiced pride. "She won twenty-seven bouts before I claimed her."

"Impressive," the envoy admitted, eyes glittering greedily. "And these?" He gestured at Ella and Lianna.

"Exotics, strong-willed. Perfect for buyers who relish a challenge." Came the flat response from Xavier.

The envoy exhaled sharply, half amusement, half approval. He produced a scroll case from his coat and extended it.

"Your invitation to Villa Devorath. Be discreet. The guests appreciate subtlety."

Without waiting for a response, he turned and strode out, parting the silence in his wake like a blade.

The tavern slowly exhaled.

Lianna leaned closer, voice low and acid. "Discreet. Easy when you trade in lives."

Xavier closed his hand around the scroll. "Tonight, we step into the fire."

#

The carriage moved like a shadow through Ironhaven's noble quarter. Gaslight lanterns hung from arched gateways and ivy-strewn walls, casting warm halos over polished stone. However, inside the covered compartment, silence reigned.

Xavier stared through the narrow slit in the carriage door as the streets gave way to open lawns and manicured hedges. The villa loomed ahead, tall walls crowned with wrought iron, the great gate flanked by torches burning blue-white with alchemical flame. Villa Devorath, lair of the powerful, playground of the cruel.

As they passed beneath the archway, Xavier felt it: the weight of gilded eyes, the scent of perfume trying to smother corruption.

Guards stopped them. Polished helms, enameled breastplates, emotionless faces. One took their invitation and examined it with careful disdain. Xavier held his breath, but the scroll was returned with a sharp nod.

Inside, the villa revealed itself in layers. Floors of marble veined with gold. Hallways lined with statues of mythical beasts frozen mid-prowl. Murals too pristine to be real. It was opulence made weapon.

They crossed a grand foyer where nobles mingled like predators in velvet. Voices carried... measured laughter, whispers behind fans, wine poured like blood into crystal.

Xavier's gaze scanned the ballroom. Ella walked beside him, Lianna and Sihri behind. They were quiet, expressions unreadable. He knew what they must feel. Knew what he felt: disgust hidden behind a smile.

The extravagant ballroom was filled with Ironhaven's, and to a lesser extent Arevalis', nobility, each eager to conceal their darker appetites beneath a veneer of sophistication. Xavier scanned the crowd carefully, noting each potential ally or adversary, his pulse steady despite the inherent danger of their position.

Xavier spotted a familiar face, a minor nobleman he'd previously charmed with tales of conquest and slave acquisition. Lord Estivar approached, a goblet in hand, his expression curious and slightly amused.

"Master Xanthus," he drawled. Dressed in forest-green finery, the man moved like a snake in high grass. His smile was polished to perfection, but his eyes gleamed too brightly. "Your presence tonight is an unexpected pleasure."

Xavier inclined his head with a calm he did not feel. "Lord Estivar. I had not expected recognition."

Estivar's gaze lingered, first on Xavier, then unapologetically on the women behind him. "Your name has risen swiftly. Swiftclaw, is it? The champion?"

Xavier gave a thin smile. "A worthy acquisition."

"More than worthy," Estivar murmured, eyes narrowing. "Coin is one thing, but prowess... that speaks louder. You've made waves, Master Vesh."

Xavier offered a polite chuckle. "Let us hope they do not become ripples that draw sharks."

Estivar raised his goblet slightly. "Spoken like a man who knows his depths. Enjoy the evening."

The noble turned and vanished into the throng, leaving behind the faint scent of cloves and something sour.

Xavier let his breath slip out slowly. "The masks are thin here," he murmured.

Ella gave a faint nod. "And the fangs are close beneath."

He adjusted his collar and turned back toward the ballroom.

#

A hush rippled through the ballroom like a drawn breath.

It began with the herald's voice, sharp and crystalline as he stepped forward from beneath the grand arch. "Presenting the Lady Lythara Veyne, Commander of the Redmaw Reavers."

The double doors opened, and silence thickened. Nobles froze mid-sentence, eyes pivoting toward the entrance. Even laughter died, replaced by subtle adjustments, goblets lowered, fans stilled.

She entered as if the hall belonged to her.

Lythara moved with a predator's ease, each step unhurried yet utterly deliberate. Her tall, lithe form was framed by the archway like a portrait brought to life. The moonlight behind her caught faint crimson glints in her obsidian-black hair, which fell in shimmering waves over shoulders armored in lacquered leather and etched steel. Her armor, tight-fitting and dark, bore faintly glowing crimson runes that pulsed like a heartbeat beneath the surface.

The runes drew the eye, but it was her presence that held it.

Dusky skin shimmered subtly under the chandeliers, laced with faint undertones of deep red. Her face was striking, all high cheekbones, sharp lines, and crimson, slitted eyes that glowed faintly beneath heavy lashes. When those eyes swept across the crowd, people stepped back without knowing why.

Polished black horns curved elegantly from her brow, curling like obsidian crowns streaked with glowing red veins. A subtle heat followed in her wake, as though the fire of her legend walked beside her.

Xavier felt his Kael'Sharyn mark stir. Not pain, not quite... but a recognition. A ripple in his soul.

Then her gaze locked on him.

There was no mistaking it. Across the sea of silks and secrets, her eyes found his with uncanny precision. Her nostrils flared, and her steps slowed. Her expression shifted, just slightly, into something too knowing, too intent.

A whisper, soft and layered with restrained power, brushed against his mind. "You wear many masks, but only one burns."

His breath caught.

She knew.

And yet, she said nothing. Her gaze lingered a heartbeat longer, then slipped away as she descended into the gathered nobility, drawing a tide of admirers in her wake.

Xavier stood frozen, a goblet in hand, his heart echoing the truth beneath her words.

Lianna leaned close. "What just happened?"

Xavier's voice was low. "She saw through everything."

Ella's hand brushed his lightly. "But she's not exposing us."

"Not yet," he said.

Lythara glanced over her shoulder once more, her crimson eyes unreadable.

"She's watching," Xavier murmured. "And waiting."

Ella nodded. "Then so do we."

Lord Estivar noticed Xavier's distraction. "Fascinating, isn't she? And it seems you have already caught her attention."

"Indeed," Xavier murmured carefully. "Perhaps my reputation precedes me more than I realized."

Estivar chuckled quietly, though his laughter lacked genuine warmth. "I'd advise caution, Master Xanthus. Lady Veyne's attentions are as perilous as they are flattering."

Xavier smiled faintly, lifting his goblet slightly in acknowledgment. "Advice noted, my lord."

And the masquerade continued around them, oblivious to the game that had just begun.

#

As the evening progressed, Xavier carefully maneuvered himself toward a secluded balcony overlooking the villa's expansive gardens, leaving the women with other slaves in the group. The air outside was cooler, touched with the floral sweetness of nightbloom and the faint echo of distant strings drifting through open windows. He had scarcely leaned against the marble balustrade when he felt it... an almost imperceptible rise in heat, followed by the scent of charred wood, scorched cinnamon, and something older, like stone warmed by ancient flame.

Lythara materialized beside him, silent as a falling shadow.

The atmosphere around her shimmered faintly, as though the night itself bent to accommodate her presence. The faint red runes on her armor pulsed beneath the lacquered black, casting subtle flickers of light against the marble railing. Her crimson eyes reflected the glow of the ballroom's firelight, but deeper within them stirred something more ancient, smoldering embers banked beneath layers of silence and wrath.

"You wear your deception remarkably well," she

murmured, her voice hushed, resonant, edged with an elemental undertone that seemed to vibrate in the bones. "But illusions fray under divine scrutiny. Especially those not born of this world."

Xavier turned to face her, keeping his hands resting on the railing. "Clearly, and I suppose introductions are unnecessary," he said evenly. "Though I'm surprised you didn't simply expose me."

Lythara's gaze didn't waver. "Exposure gains me nothing. Not yet, and what you carry... the Kael'Sharyn mark is not so easily hidden. Its fracture pulses beneath your flesh like a dying star. Even layered in false names and borrowed silk, you burn."

He stiffened. "How do you..."

"I've walked through pacts that thread through the bones of nations," she said quietly. "Your resonance stirs echoes in me I thought long buried. That wound of yours, Xavier... it howls."

Her voice dipped lower, almost reverent. "Ivarik's grip is more than chains of law or dogma. It is the slow drowning of will beneath divine decree. He binds Arenvalis not with power, but with belief, siphoned and twisted until even rebellion fuels his sanctity."

Xavier's breath caught. Her words felt too close to truths Ella had hinted at but never fully spoken. "Then what do you want, Lady Veyne?"

She turned fully to him now. The space between them warmed tangibly. "Freedom. Not just for myself, but from the whole damned tapestry of control. My contract is infernal, yes... but its threads are laced with divine spite. If I pull wrongly, I vanish, but if undone with care... perhaps I become more than a weapon shaped in someone else's fire."

He looked back toward the ballroom. Ella, Lianna, Sihri, silent among strangers, their strength muted by roles they had been forced to wear.

"Then you are like them," he said. "Trapped. Branded."

"Different cage," she replied, her smile sharp. "Same architect."

She stepped closer. The scent of her deepened, smoke curling off cedar, something faintly metallic. "You are fracture and flame. I am ash and memory. Allies, Xavier?"

He hesitated, feeling the weight of that offer. "If trust grows amidst shadows."

"Then we risk together," she said. "But should you falter... know that flame purifies as much as it destroys."

A noble stepped onto the balcony, his gait relaxed but his interest predatory. "A new companion, Lady Veyne?"

She turned toward him, voice cold and precise. "Curb your curiosity. Some secrets are barbed, and bite when grasped."

The noble bowed stiffly and withdrew. Tension lingered in his wake like the stench of snuffed tallow.

Lythara faced Xavier once more. "Our enemies are not merely powerful. They are old. Their victories are carved in doctrine, their sins sung as scripture. Cracks form, however, slowly and surely."

"Tonight," Xavier said softly, "I trust you."

She nodded. "Then let our gamble begin."

She extended a sealed parchment toward him. Her fingers brushed his as he accepted it, and the heat of that contact lingered, flickering across his skin long after she turned and vanished through the door.

He stood alone, the distant hum of music behind him, the pulse of his mark steady beneath the collar of borrowed finery.

The garden stretched before him, but it was the fire at his back he felt most clearly. His heart thudded with quiet if not desperate hope. The delicate threads of trust woven tonight could either save him and those he sought along with this intriguing new player, or it would doom them all forever.

# CHAPTER TWENTY-THREE

*The Auction of Flesh*

The next day stretched endlessly, every moment drawn thin with anticipation. No one spoke more than necessary as they kept a low profile, avoiding any risk that might shatter the fragile veil of their disguise before the auction began.

In the quiet of Xavier's chamber, the four of them circled around his desk. Maps, scribbled notes, and folded parchment cluttered the surface, each page a piece of the puzzle they had assembled during their time in Ironhaven. Names had been gathered. Descriptions matched. Shadow Court figures had emerged from the mist of rumor into something that could be tracked. The Redmaw Reavers were no longer a distant threat but a looming one, and Lythara Veyne had shifted from whispered possibility into a tenuous thread of potential alliance.

Each of them reaffirmed their roles. The plan had to be perfect, or at least convincing. Xavier spoke with measured calm as he outlined the order of things, then deferred to the others to speak freely.

Ella and Lianna did not hide their discomfort. It rippled quietly beneath their expressions as they listened, both women visibly straining against the idea of being inspected as commodities. Lianna's fingers curled tightly around the edge of the table, her knuckles pale. Ella's tone remained steady, but her eyes betrayed a quiet flicker of tension that she couldn't quite suppress.

Sihri said nothing at first. She looked down at the forged gladiator documents in one hand, then brought her other hand to her side where the studded gloves were tucked into her belt. Her fingers brushed against the leather, resting there for a breath before curling tightly around one of the wraps. When she looked up, her gaze was calm and direct.

"I will pass whatever scrutiny they give me," she said simply. "Let them look. I've lived it."

The silence that followed was not one of doubt, but shared acknowledgment. She had lived it. Not in stories or theory, but in chains and blood and sand. Her posture was straight, but not rigid. Her confidence came not from bluster, but from experience.

Lianna gave her a small nod, the gesture slow and respectful. Ella reached over and gently squeezed Sihri's forearm, then met her gaze with a quiet look of support.

In a nearby corner, a faint rustle drew Xavier's eye. Valkra had stirred from her curled position, her dark coat almost invisible in the shadows. Frostclaw remained at her side, silent and watchful. Both had sensed the shift in mood. Xavier crossed the room and knelt, resting a hand gently on the young shadowmane's head.

"You two stay here tonight," he said softly. "This place we're going... they wouldn't welcome your kind."

Valkra blinked slowly, then nestled against his leg. Frostclaw gave a low chuff, as if in agreement.

"They'll be safe," Lianna murmured behind him, her

voice quiet but certain. "The innkeeper knows to leave them be."

Xavier watched the pair for a moment longer, then stood and turned back to his companions.

There was no way to soften what they were walking into. No clean victory waiting at the end of the night. But every one of them had chosen this path with open eyes.

He reached out and closed the last folder on the desk.

"Tonight, we survive," he said, his voice low. "Tomorrow, we strike."

#

Evening had fallen hard over Ironhaven, cloaking the city's upper district in shadows that clung to every stone facade and wrought iron fence. Xavier moved with practiced calm, though the weight in his chest grew heavier with each step toward the structure named in the invitation. From the outside, it appeared unremarkable, tucked discreetly between two noble villas. It might have been a storage hall or service building for the upper class, were it not for the pair of guards who flanked the entrance.

They were Redmaw Reavers.

They stood still as statues, clad in dark crimson armor traced with faintly glowing runes. The markings pulsed with restrained violence, radiating menace like heat from a forge. Their presence was a quiet declaration that this was no ordinary gathering, and any misstep here would be fatal.

Xavier forced his breathing into rhythm as he drew the invitation from his satchel. The parchment bore no embellishment beyond a subtle embossed seal, but it was genuine. Lythara had handed it to him personally at the Devorath estate, its simplicity masking the authority it carried. He held it up, his fingers tightening slightly despite his composed expression.

One of the Reavers stepped forward, silent and deliberate. His eyes, cold and unreadable, studied Xavier before taking the parchment. The silence stretched as the guard examined the document, his gaze flicking back and forth with slow precision. The moment dragged, each heartbeat growing louder in Xavier's ears.

At last, the mercenary gave a curt nod and stepped aside.

Xavier reclaimed the invitation with careful control, then walked between the armored figures without hesitation, his expression composed in the cool detachment required of Xanthus Vesh.

Inside, a narrow chamber awaited. Stone walls, bare but for a single unlit sconce, framed the entryway. Xavier stepped aside just enough to let the others enter behind him. Ella, Lianna, and Sihri moved quickly to his side, each of them alert, each playing their part. He met their eyes one by one, reading the tension, the readiness, the quiet resolve.

Ella's calm mask had returned. She stood just behind him, her gaze clear and steady, a subtle flicker of reassurance passing between them. Lianna held herself taut, her movements smooth but clipped, her control just thin enough for Xavier to see the tension behind it. She didn't like this. Neither did he. But she would hold her part.

Sihri, in contrast, stood tall and alert, her leather-wrapped fists hanging loosely at her sides. The metal studs in her gloves gleamed faintly in the lantern light. She glanced once around the room, eyes sharp, posture firm, a guardian waiting for the first sign of trouble.

Xavier gave a slight nod, then turned toward the stairwell descending into the earth.

There was only one path forward.

The stairs were hewn from rough stone, spiraling downward, lit by scattered lanterns that flickered from recessed alcoves. As they descended, the sounds began to rise—a low hum of conversation, distorted by distance, punctuated by the haunting strains of stringed instruments playing some muted, melancholic melody.

Somewhere behind him, Lianna's voice broke the silence with a whisper. "If I start to lose it, elbow me."

"I'll grip your wrist instead," Ella murmured back. "Less obvious."

The quiet exchange grounded Xavier more than he expected. They were each holding the line in their own way.

From just behind, Sihri exhaled slowly through her nose. "Feels like walking into the pit again," she said under her breath. "Crowd waiting to see if I bleed or break."

No one responded aloud, but Xavier gave a subtle nod she would see. They understood. This was no arena, but the danger, the scrutiny, and the stakes were no less real.

The stair opened suddenly into a vast subterranean hall.

Torchlight flickered along polished pillars and vaulted arches. Banners hung between columns, rich with thread-of-gold embroidery, each one depicting scenes of conquest, ceremony, or empire. The floor beneath their feet gleamed faintly, swept clean and slick like dark marble. From afar, it might have passed for a grand ballroom.

Yet the glamour of wealth could not mask what it truly was.

Along the walls stood cages, each one reinforced with blackened steel and guarded by armed watchers. Within them were Animari captives, displayed like trophies. Some stood with shoulders back and jaws clenched, eyes burning with quiet rage. Others knelt or slumped, their stares hollow. Chains hung from their necks, wrists, or ankles, gleaming in the low light like accents on a cruel exhibit. Most wore little beyond their collars, their forms presented with calculated intention to showcase "stock."

The murmurs of the crowd washed over it all. Laughter, low conversation, idle appraisal. Buyers circled the cages like patrons at a gallery, discussing the captives' traits and origins with chilling detachment.

Xavier paused near the bottom step, his eyes sweeping across the chamber. The bile in his throat threatened to rise, but he forced it down. This was worse than the open markets. There, cruelty had at least been openly visible. Here, it had been dressed in silks and candlelight, perfumed and made palatable for those who fancied themselves above it.

He stepped forward, guiding Ella, Lianna, and Sihri deeper into the room.

They walked in formation, Ella and Lianna close at his sides, heads lowered in the submissive posture expected of high-priced acquisitions. Sihri moved just behind and to the right, her shoulders squared, the proud bodyguard of a man with wealth to flaunt. Xavier led them, each movement precise, every step measured to project control.

His gaze cut through the veil of civility with sharpened clarity. Nobles cloaked in elegance moved like dancers between the cages. Merchants lingered near the auction floor, whispering into the ears of masked handlers. Woven among them were others, far more dangerous figures in fine robes marked by subtle signs: horns hidden beneath hoods, eyes that glowed faintly, tails that twitched with quiet sentience.

Zar'kaan. Marked Ones.

They hovered near the most powerful clients, silent and watchful. Lianna had warned him of their presence, and now Xavier saw them clearly. One stepped from the shadows nearby, his presence unsettling even before Xavier called upon his skills.

He focused, pushing his awareness outward with quiet intent. The world softened for a heartbeat, and knowledge stirred behind his eyes as he triggered *Insight*:

| **Name:** Malakar Voidborne | **Disposition:** Insatiable Ambition |
|---|---|
| Born under an abyssal bloodline, Malakar Voidborne embodies the chaotic ferocity of his heritage. Standing tall with a lithe yet muscular frame, Malakar's ashen skin is marked with molten cracks radiating fiery heat. Jagged obsidian horns erupt from his brow, and his burning eyes shift colors in moments of intense passion or fury, hinting at his tumultuous inner nature. His claws, as sharp as tempered steel, are capable of tearing through armor, and his presence alone instills unease, amplified by his innate ability to manipulate darkness and fire. Driven by an insatiable ambition, Malakar seeks power to rise above the suspicion and prejudice of his mortal kin, torn between embracing the chaos within or harnessing it to shape his destiny. ||

| **Health:** 325/325 | **Stamina:** 300/300 | **Mana:** 200/200 |
|---|---|---|

The insight faded, sinking into his mind. Xavier dismissed the prompt for now. There would be time to act on it later. For the moment, what mattered was control and awareness.

Even so, a flicker of satisfaction took root behind his focus.

He was stronger than before, and he would need that

strength tonight.

#

With practiced ease honed during their days in Ironhaven, Xavier guided his "property" through the crowd. Every movement was measured, every pause deliberate. He navigated the press of finely dressed attendees with subtle calculation, positioning their group in a vantage point that offered a clear view of the auction floor while drawing minimal attention. Their survival hinged on that illusion, his control, their roles, the masks they wore.

Each step pressed heavier against his chest.

The chamber's grandeur could not disguise its truth. Every silk-draped table, every flickering lantern and embroidered banner served to soften the cruelty, to cloak brutality in finery. It was working too well. Conversations flowed with calm detachment, as nobles, merchants, and masked agents murmured over prices and lineage as though discussing wine vintages or prized falcons.

It ground against his soul.

His Unyielding Liberator trait surged within him, aching to act, to tear apart the illusion and expose what this place truly was. But impulse would doom them all. He forced his jaw to loosen, steadying his breath. This was no gallery of suffering, but a system, deeply entrenched, expansive, and carefully orchestrated behind veils of wealth.

He closed his eyes briefly to resist the urge. Toppling the entire hierarchy of this horror felt like a dream. Unreal. Yet clarity formed in the weight of that despair. He would not, could not, save everyone tonight. But he could strike a real blow. He could end the compulsory enslavement of the Animari people. That focused, attainable goal anchored him.

A quiet system prompt surfaced behind his eyes:

| **Trait Update:** Tempered Liberator | **Effect:** |
|---|---|
| Witnessing firsthand the entrenched structure of slavery within Arenvalis, and the systematic cruelty enacted in Ironhaven, tested your resolve profoundly. This caused your Trait: Unyielding Liberator to evolve into Trait: Tempered Liberator. Seeing beyond the casual brutality of surface markets into the targeted and ruthless oppression of the Animari, you experienced a moment of weary introspection. The scale of slavery's evil seemed overwhelming, even insurmountable. Yet, you found clarity in pragmatism, narrowing your goal to decisively ending the compulsory enslavement of the Animari peoples. This focused commitment steadied your nerves, | • Steeled Pragmatism: Xavier gains enhanced bonuses to morale and mental resilience when strategically working toward realistic, clearly defined goals against slavery and oppression.<br>• Focused Justice: While retaining swift decisiveness, Xavier now better discerns when immediate force or longer-term strategies serve the greater purpose of dismantling systemic oppression.<br>• Dreaded Purpose: Xavier's unwavering clarity and determination instill greater fear and uncertainty in opponents, especially those who directly participate in organized oppression. |

SHADOWS OVER THE WILDLANDS

| sharpened your resolve, and transformed your purpose into a practical, achievable mission. | • Symbol of Hope: Xavier's pragmatic yet compassionate leadership inspires deeper loyalty and cooperation from oppressed communities and potential allies, making him an influential figurehead in targeted movements for liberation. |
|---|---|

He dismissed the prompt without reacting. Resolve returned in its place.

His eyes swept across the room again and landed on Lord Estivar.

The noble moved with calculated grace, drifting between clusters of guests with the ease of long familiarity. Each conversation was measured, each gesture purposeful. He leaned toward one figure in ceremonial crimson, then exchanged whispers with another whose smile was too still. Estivar was no mere guest. He was involved. A player. Perhaps a controller.

His gaze flicked toward Xavier and lingered a moment too long. Recognition blended with curiosity. Then his eyes held just a trace of suspicion.

Xavier kept his expression neutral. He let his eyes drift past as though the man wasn't worth notice.

Lianna stiffened slightly beside him. He didn't need to glance to feel the change in her posture. He brushed two fingers gently against her wrist in reassurance. She gave a faint nod.

Ella shifted closer without hesitation, a small but deliberate adjustment. Her stance read as both protective and subservient, consistent with her role.

Behind them, Sihri kept a firm, quiet vigil. Her wrapped fists remained lowered but ready. The subtle creak of her leather gloves marked the rhythm of her breath. She did not fixate on any single face. Her gaze swept constantly, catching angles, exits, and tension.

The crowd began to shift. Conversation softened to a hush.

From a shadowed corner of the hall, a slender figure stepped into view.

His dark robes were trimmed in silver, but he wore no visible mark of station. No weapon. No sigil. Yet the crowd parted for him. No one needed to be told who he was. Authority moved with him like an unseen wind.

He approached with a measured pace. When he stopped before Xavier, he extended one hand.

"Documentation, Master Vesh."

The words were soft. They left no room for refusal.

Xavier produced the sheaf of papers and handed them over without hesitation. His bearing shifted slightly, adopting the poise of someone accustomed to privilege and power.

The man took his time. Each page received a careful read. His eyes lingered longer on certain details than others. Nothing escaped his scrutiny.

Eventually, his gaze lifted to Sihri.

"Your gladiator appears impressive," he said, tone neutral.

"She was undefeated in twenty-seven bouts in the pits of Zhyrdan," Xavier replied. "The investment was considerable. Worth every coin."

The official stepped closer to Sihri, appraising her silently. Then his voice dropped, faint and demeaning.

"Demonstrate, bunny."

The words were simple, but the meaning behind them was not. It was a command meant to reduce her, to remind her that in this place, even strength must kneel.

Sihri's gaze flicked once to Xavier.

He offered a slow nod. Permission, nothing more.

With a breath, Sihri shifted, her stance widened, weight balanced. She flowed into a short, brutal kata, a fighter's demonstration, not for beauty but for effect. A sharp jab, a spinning low elbow, a heel hook pivot into a grounded shoulder feint. She transitioned between each motion with surgical control, ending in a coiled, silent crouch.

A ripple passed through the nearby onlookers. A few murmured under their breath. Some watched with cautious interest. One or two stepped subtly back.

Before the official could speak again, another voice entered the exchange.

"Surely, Overseer, such demonstrations are unnecessary tonight."

Lythara's voice slipped through the air with velvet smoothness. Its warmth was honeyed, but underneath it flowed a thin current of iron.

She stepped into view, graceful as ever, her presence shifting the attention of everyone nearby. Tonight, she wore a dark, high-split gown, its subtle shimmer catching the torchlight with each step. It was a stark contrast to the armored presence she had displayed at Devorath's estate, a reminder that her strength lay not only in battle but in command of perception. She offered no introduction, only a slight tilt of her head toward the official.

"Master Vesh's reputation is becoming rather well known," she continued, offering a faint smile.

The Overseer hesitated. Whatever weight her presence carried, it surpassed his.

"As you say, Lady Veyne." He returned the papers to Xavier and offered a polite incline of his head. "Enjoy the auction."

Lythara held Xavier's gaze a heartbeat longer, then slipped silently into the crowd once more.

Xavier exhaled. The group had passed another test, he was keenly aware of how narrowly they'd avoided deeper scrutiny. At the same time he was quietly appreciating the delicate balance of the new alliance with the succubus and her place of power within the city.

He also didn't miss the glance Estivar gave in their direction. Nor did he miss the subtle shift in the Zar'kaan.

They were not focused on merchandise. Their gaze had never lingered long on any Animari slave.

Instead, they watched the crowd. Their placement formed no consistent pattern, but their spacing ensured no influential figure moved without one nearby. One of the Marked stood just behind a merchant who spoke too loudly. Another tilted his head at a noble whose gaze lingered too long on an off-limits cage.

They weren't just present. They were directing attention without speaking a word.

Reavers kept the structure. Zar'kaan controlled the silence. Even Lythara, with all her sway, had earned only a ripple of their regard.

If anything broke tonight, the Zar'kaan would respond, and there would be no room for mercy.

#

The murmurs faded as a sharp crack split the air.

A gavel struck wood at the far end of the hall, drawing every eye toward the raised dais. The auctioneer stepped forward, a lean, hawkish man draped in embroidered silks of indigo and brass. His thin lips curled into a smile that held no warmth, only performance.

"Esteemed guests," he began, his voice smooth and chilling, "we begin tonight's proceedings with a rare prize, captured from the remote hills bordering the Blasted Lands and the Ironspire Peaks."

From a dark corridor beside the stage, two Redmaw Reavers emerged, dragging a bound captive between them. The heavy clink of chains echoed as they hauled her into the light.

Gasps rippled through the crowd.

The young Lynari woman stumbled but did not fall. Her tawny fur, dulled with grime, clung to her slender frame. Long hair fell in tangled mats past her shoulders. Her wrists bore the weight of iron manacles, chafing the fur and skin beneath. When she lifted her head, her golden eyes blazed with defiance despite the dull sheen of fatigue behind them.

Xavier's jaw tightened. He said nothing.

The auctioneer raised a hand, gesturing toward her with a theatrical flair. "Of noble Animari blood. Lynari, untouched, spirited, and fiercely agile. Such specimens are increasingly difficult to obtain, especially those not yet broken. Ideal for the discerning collector or ambitious trainer."

Lianna had not moved, but Xavier felt the tension rising in her body beside him. Her breath came in shallow, uneven bursts. She stared at the captive, expression rigid, her hands clenched in her sleeves. The fury in her eyes needed no words.

The first bid came from a noblewoman across the chamber, her hand raised with lazy detachment. The auctioneer seized on it, his voice rising with eager rhythm. Numbers escalated quickly. More nobles joined in, drawn by the performance, by the perceived rarity of the prize. Each offered sum rolled from the auctioneer's lips with practiced ease, feeding the hunger in the room.

Xavier felt Lianna lean ever so slightly closer. He reached across the space and touched her forearm, just once. His fingers rested there with gentle pressure, a silent message of shared pain and purpose.

She did not look at him, but her jaw shifted, and some of the tremble in her frame eased.

On the dais, the auctioneer proclaimed the final bid. A tall aristocrat in crimson velvet gave a subtle nod, his eyes gleaming with cruel satisfaction. The Lynari woman was pulled away, her head high despite the force dragging her into the shadows. Whispers of approval followed her disappearance. The bar had been set.

Beside him, Lianna whispered, barely audible. "How can we stand by and watch this?"

Xavier's response came quietly, but every word carried weight.

"Because tonight, watching is how we learn that we are not enough. Tomorrow, with this knowledge, we'll act."

Lianna's gaze shifted toward him at that, a flicker

of acknowledgment in her expression. Her silence said everything. She understood. They all did.

The auctioneer cleared his throat with a flourish. Another name. Another captive. The ritual continued.

Xavier watched it unfold, each sale etching the truth deeper into his resolve. This place would not be dismantled by rage alone. But it could be undone. What had been exposed tonight could no longer be ignored.

Tonight, he watched. Tomorrow, he would begin to unmake it.

#

The auction wore on.

Captives came and went, each new entry sparking brief flurries of excitement that quickly settled back into the room's languid cruelty. Xavier held position near the outer column of the hall, the illusion of casual interest cloaking the storm coiling behind his eyes. Every sale cut deeper, every bid another confirmation of the rot nestled within Ironhaven's nobility.

Ella leaned subtly against his shoulder, her posture the picture of obedience, but the contact between them carried weight. She could feel it too, revulsion in his silence, fury honed into stillness.

Sihri shifted her stance nearby, hands folded over her midsection. The studded leather of her gloves creaked faintly as her fists clenched and eased. "Feels like the pits," she murmured again. "Crowd waiting for weakness. For blood."

Lianna gave a quiet nod of agreement, eyes sharp as they swept across the room. Her silence since the Lynari auction was not withdrawal, but restraint.

His gaze returned to the crowd. His attention

sharpened.

Earlier, he had noticed the Zar'kaan lingering at the periphery, silent, powerful, unmistakable. Now he studied them in motion. They moved not like soldiers, but sentinels of influence. They did not posture or display. They simply existed, woven seamlessly into the fabric of the event.

Three drew his particular notice.

The first was a statuesque woman marked with pale, spectral sigils that shimmered when she moved. The second, a gaunt male figure with elongated fingers, stood in precise silence beside an elder noble whose ring bore the insignia of the Chain Concord. The last, smallest of the trio, wore flowing crimson silks and a delicate porcelain mask. Behind the mask, faint violet eyes burned not with hunger, but judgment.

None of them interacted with one another. None seemed surprised by anything they saw. They weren't here to witness. They were here to ensure.

Xavier cataloged their faces, their movements, and their patterns. This auction was not merely a marketplace. It was a performance for hidden powers, and the Zar'kaan were the instruments of unseen control.

As the evening crawled on, Xavier found the auction hall increasingly stifling. He left the trio of women behind, trusting them to observe who purchased which captives, and stepped away from the main crowd. He slipped toward a quiet alcove near a towering pillar, far enough from the floor to avoid attention but close enough to observe. The shadows there offered a temporary reprieve.

He had only been there a few moments when he sensed a presence approaching. The air shifted, warmer, charged with a familiar tension.

"You're handling yourself remarkably well, Xavier," came Lythara's voice, soft and smooth beside his ear. The casual intimacy in her tone was a calculated veil over something more dangerous.

He turned slightly to face her. Her crimson eyes met his with clarity, their faint glow catching in the torchlight. Beneath her poise, he saw purpose.

"Thanks to your timely intervention," Xavier murmured. "Why did you deign to risk yourself like that?"

She stepped closer, one arm sliding around his in a display that appeared flirtatious to any onlookers. Her tone, however, sharpened. "Because our interests align more closely than you may realize. I see what you wish to accomplish... and what you cannot."

Xavier studied her closely. Her phrasing held weight.

"That's not all," he said quietly.

A pause followed. Lythara's gaze flicked over the room, checking for listeners despite the natural insulation of her presence.

"There is a place beneath Ironhaven Citadel," she said, her voice dropping lower. "It's called the Vault of Chains. Ivarik uses it to store secrets... records of bloodlines, infernal contracts, everything used to enforce slavery. Not just for the Animari, but anyone bound by oath or sigil."

Xavier's jaw tensed, thoughts racing. "Your contract among them?" he asked.

Her answer came with a flicker of something raw, quickly hidden behind her usual mask. "Yes. Mine... and something more critical. The binding sigil of King Rorik."

His breath caught, the magnitude of it slamming into place. "That's how Ivarik controls him."

"It's the key," Lythara confirmed. "Break the binding, and you shatter his hold on the throne. Possibly even the Shadow Court's influence over Arenvalis itself."

Xavier stepped back slightly, taking her full measure. "Why are you telling me this now and what else do I need to know?"

"Because tonight is an opportunity," she said, her expression deadly serious. "The vault is heavily guarded, trapped by infernal machinations and wards. But it is vulnerable, especially now, with so many resources and new individuals committed here. The chaos of the auction pulls resources away. If there is a time to act... it is soon."

"What do you want in return?" he asked, though he suspected he already knew.

"Freedom," she said, simply. "Destroy my contract. Break my chains. You will have more than my gratitude. You will have me as your ally, in full."

Their eyes held for a moment. Something unspoken passed between them, not desire, but conviction. A mutual understanding, solidifying the fragile trust between them.

"Then we move quickly," Xavier said at last. "Tonight, we plan. As I told Lianna... tomorrow, we act."

Lythara smiled, slow and faint, then let it vanish behind her mask. "Be ready, Xavier. The hardest part is yet to come."

She melted back into the crowd, leaving him with the pounding of his pulse and the weight of a plan solidifying in his mind.

#

The hours of the night grew long, and the auction neared its bitter conclusion. What had begun in solemn

SHADOWS OVER THE WILDLANDS

anticipation had curdled into a feverish mix of hunger and cruelty. The hall, once subdued, now buzzed with eager tension. Every Animari brought forth seemed more exotic, more desirable to the twisted nobility of Ironhaven.

Xavier gave a slight gesture, guiding Ella, Lianna, and Sihri from their observation post along the columned wall. They slipped away from the main throng, toward a shadowed alcove near the exit, distant enough to avoid the attention of lingering guards or watchful eyes seated in power.

Lianna's expression had hardened to stone. Her eyes shimmered with restrained fury, her jaw tight, her hands clenched so fiercely that her claws had drawn small lines of blood along her palms. "Watching this... knowing we could not do anything," she whispered, voice choked with emotion, "it was unbearable."

Xavier rested a firm hand on her shoulder. His voice held steady, though inside, his own restraint frayed at the edges. "We did what we had to tonight. Knowledge is power. We gained more than they know." He glanced to each of them, then continued. "Lythara's information changes everything. If the Vault of Chains holds what she claims, we can strike at the roots. Destroy the documents and shackles binding Animari bloodlines... and Rorik."

Ella nodded slowly. Her jade eyes reflected solemn approval, quiet resolve settling into her expression. "It is a risk," she said softly, "but a worthy one."

Xavier's gaze shifted to Sihri. The Leporini stood alert and rigid, still cloaked in the guise of a prized fighter, but something softened in her when he looked her way. She gave a slight nod.

"I am ready, Master," she said simply. "Whatever must be done."

The words carried no irony, no submission. They were a vow. One earned, not forced.

Xavier inclined his head in return. The fire behind his eyes was clearer now, focused. "Then tomorrow, we act. We break into the vault. We destroy the sigil holding Rorik, and we free Lythara from her bondage. With that leverage, we begin unraveling the system that enforces compulsory enslavement."

Lianna exhaled slowly, the fury in her gaze tempered now by purpose. "Then let us waste no time," she said. "We have work to do."

They stood in silence for a moment, letting the weight of their choices settle between them. Xavier turned once more to glance across the hall. The grand auction floor was littered with the remnants of a night soaked in greed, cruelty, and twisted pageantry. The images seared themselves into memory, cages, chains, hollow eyes dulled by hopelessness. All of it etched deep into the resolve now anchoring their hearts.

He turned sharply, leading the others down the dimly lit corridor. Their steps fell silent across the polished stone, swallowed by the fading hum of a dispersing crowd.

As they emerged into the night, Ironhaven's chill wind rushed to meet them. The air was crisp, cutting away the stifling heat of torchlight and whispered depravity. The streets beyond lay quiet, cast in moon-shadow beneath the fractured glow of Pyrrastra. The crimson sliver of the moon broke through cloud cover, painting the city rooftops in pale red.

Xavier paused and lifted his gaze. The night no longer seemed still. It carried weight, pressing down with purpose.

"We are stepping into dangerous territory," he said at last, his voice low. "After tonight, we will have fewer shadows to hide in."

Lianna met his gaze without hesitation. "We have seen the worst they can do," she replied. "Now it is time they saw what we can do."

Ella stepped closer beside him, her presence grounding. "What we witnessed tonight can't be forgotten. It can be changed. We begin that tomorrow."

Xavier turned to Sihri, who had relaxed only slightly. Her jaw remained set, but the flicker of battle-readiness lit her eyes.

"I trust each of you," he said. "Tomorrow, we strike the Vault. We free who we can. We remind Ironhaven that its chains are not eternal. Tonight however, we have another task."

Lianna's voice was iron. "It is time to turn the tables."

He nodded once, then led them into the deeper alleys and corridors of the city. No words passed between them as they moved. None were needed as they had seen the cost. They had gathered the names, the paths, the truths hidden behind masks of luxury.

Their steps carried them farther from the auction's gilded cruelty and closer to the firestorm that waited just ahead.

# CHAPTER
# TWENTY-FOUR
*The First Act of Rebellion*

The mood was heavy as the group made their way back to the Emberdrift Hearth. Though their resolve had hardened, a quiet impotence gnawed at each of them, the sheer breadth of the system they faced stretching out like a stormfront too vast to contain. When the door to their quarters clicked shut behind them, the noise of Ironhaven faded to a dull echo. Silence settled in its place, thick and bitter with the weight of what they had witnessed.

Lianna stood near the window, her arms crossed tightly over her chest. Her claws dug into the fabric of her sleeves with a tension that did not ease. Pyrrastra had set and now Vitalora had risen high, the golden-green moonlight spilling through the panes and painting her in soft hues that belied the storm coiled in her shoulders. Frostclaw lay near her feet, his tail twitching in agitation as he mirrored her unrest.

The others moved in grim efficiency, each aware that stillness would bring only more reflection. Part of their time in the city had been spent gathering names, nobles, merchants, mercenary bands. Who purchased the most, who traded in rare Animari, who trafficked in silence beneath banners of legitimacy. They had traced routes, memorized sigils, mapped holdings and passageways. The details formed the skeleton of something greater, a reckoning yet to come.

Ella was the first to break the silence. She moved to the scarred wooden table and unrolled a fresh map, her voice low but edged. "The noble who bought her. I saw the signet. House Venmire. Most likely Halvaric Venmire himself. His estate is in Blackspire Hollow, along the southern ridges of the Ironspire foothills."

Xavier stepped beside her, his jaw tight. "Venmire..." The name stirred something foul in his memory, gathered from whispers in alleys and wary glances in taverns. He did not finish the thought. He didn't need to.

Sihri sat nearby, methodically tightening the wraps on her hands. She didn't look up. "A slaver noble. Known for collecting trophies. Rare Animari, mostly. Rumors say he favors them docile. Or broken." Her voice did not falter. "Protected by court law. Slaves are property. And nobles tend their possessions however they like."

Lianna's reply was a growl low in her throat. "That Lynari girl will vanish behind those walls. If we delay, she is lost." Her words were edged with a helpless fury that trembled just beneath the surface.

Xavier gave a sharp nod. "Then we do not delay." He leaned over the map, his finger tracing a winding trade road that twisted from Ironhaven through the foothills and eastward. "He won't hide, not here. He'll ride openly, well-guarded, but confident. The auction is sanctioned. The laws shield him. If he left just after the bidding, he would have taken this route, past the trade slope and toward his estate. His guards will be complacent this close to the city."

Ella's eyes narrowed as she studied the terrain. Lianna

joined her, still seething, and shook her head. "If he's already on the road, we will not catch him by the main route. We have no mounts. Frostclaw could carry one, maybe two, but that is all."

A knock echoed on the door, sharp and coded... three raps, a pause, then two more.

All of them turned.

Xavier moved swiftly, his hand resting on the hilt of his blade as he cracked the door open. The corridor beyond was dim, shadowed. A figure stood in silhouette, the sigil of the Redmaw Reavers emblazoned on his cloak.

A soft voice issued from beneath the hood. "Message from Lythara. She anticipated your needs."

Xavier's eyes narrowed. He opened the door wider, but his fingers did not leave the hilt. The figure stepped through with quiet confidence and pulled down his hood.

The infernal blood was plain to see, dusky skin traced with ember-glow veins, and horns curling back from his temples like polished obsidian. The sigil of the Redmaws adorned his chest, but it had been inverted.

He held out a scrap of parchment, worn with age but intact. "There's a smugglers' path beneath the east wall. It starts in an abandoned wine cellar and leads through forgotten tunnels. You'll surface outside the patrol rings, near an old quarry." He gave a quick flash of sharp teeth in a grin. "She said you would want to come and go without the guard's eyes upon you."

Ella took the parchment, studying it quickly before laying it beside the map. She began matching points with practiced ease. "Here, and here... yes. It works. Look here, Lianna, this ridge, the treefall, the bend near the dry streambed..."

Lianna's eyes gleamed. "We can intercept them. Strike before they reach the bridge. Get in, free the girl, and disappear."

Xavier moved to her side. His voice was calm but firm. "Not just her. Any Animari in that caravan. Any slave, no matter the mark on their wrist."

Behind them, the Zar'kaan dipped his head once. "Then may your hands be swift, and your blades silent." Without another word, he stepped into the hall and vanished, his presence fading like mist beneath moonlight.

Xavier looked across the room. "Gear up. We move in five."

Ella buckled her quiver and tested the tension of her bowstring with deft fingers. Sihri cracked her neck, then slammed her fists together with a low breath. Frostclaw brushed against Lianna's side as she checked her gear, grounding her rage with silent reassurance. Valkra had already taken her place beside Xavier, tail low, muscles coiled.

No one spoke as their minds were on their own thoughts.

They left through the rear stairwell of the Emberdrift Hearth, shadows wrapping around them like cloaks. Their path took them through quiet alleys, past shuttered stalls, and finally to a crumbled building where the stone gave way to old cellar steps. The air grew colder as they descended, the tunnel ahead yawning open like a wound in the bones of the city.

Each step carried the weight of purpose.

This was no rescue alone. This was retribution. Justice, measured not in coin or courts, but in blood.

#

They moved through the forgotten passage like shades through a tomb, silent, driven, and grim. The smugglers' tunnel was narrow, damp, and cloying with mold. Cracked stone pressed in on all sides, reinforced only by decaying timber supports that groaned under the weight of time. Where water had not claimed the walls, dust choked the air. It clung to their clothes, to their throats, mingling with the sour reek of rot that clung to every surface.

They allowed nothing to slow their stride. Only one path remained, forward, toward the chains that still held the innocent.

Hours passed in darkness, with only memory and the crude parchment map from Lythara's contact to guide them. Yet they did not falter. Sihri led the way through the tunnels with uncanny instinct, her Rabbitkin senses keen in the press of earth and stone. When at last they emerged, the air turned crisp and clean, and they found themselves at the bottom of an abandoned quarry nestled against a jagged cliff. The map had not lied.

Above them, the stars gleamed cold and unblinking. All the moons had sunk beyond the horizon, save one. Necroth loomed alone in the sky, a black disk blotting out the stars —a silent herald of what was to come. They were beyond Ironhaven's walls now, deep in the Wildlands, where justice was not dictated by courts but by will and blade.

They moved quickly to the spot they had identified as a possible ambush location. From the ridge overlooking the valley below, torchlight flickered in the distance. A small camp lay nestled in a clearing beside a dry creekbed. Two wagons rested beside a firepit, surrounded by six guards with mismatched armor and lax stances. A line of slaves, shackled and weary, sat bound to the rear of the second cart.

Xavier's eyes narrowed. Among them was the Lynari girl. Even in the dim firelight, her silhouette was unmistakable. Despite her fur being matted with grime, she retained her proud posture, her golden eyes sharp. She had not yielded. Not yet.

Without a word, he unsheathed his weapons. In his right hand, Vaeltheris shimmered faintly, its etched runes pulsing with latent resonance. In his left, the Emberstone shortsword flickered with a molten glow, casting flickering reflections on the rock around him. Heat radiated from the blade, a silent promise in the night.

He looked to the others. Ella gave a single nod, already drawing her bow. Lianna's gaze was fixed on the camp, storm-bound and still. Sihri cracked her knuckles. No words were needed.

The first arrow flew from Ella's bow and struck true. It buried itself in the throat of a perimeter guard with a whisper of breath and the soft thud of a falling corpse. A heartbeat later, chaos erupted.

Xavier descended like judgment made flesh. Vaeltheris tore through chainmail with ease, the enchanted edge cleaving clean through a guard's shoulder with a shimmer of silver light. The Emberstone blade followed, biting deep into another's ribs. Flame blossomed from the wound, searing flesh and cloth alike. The man screamed, clutching his side before crumpling, smoke rising from his charred leathers.

Sihri tore past Xavier, a blur of motion and fury. Her fists struck with terrifying force. One guard crumpled under a brutal elbow, while another stumbled back, clutching a jaw shattered by her backhand.

From the trees to the west, Valkra leapt. Both her tails struck like whips, venomous stingers piercing a fleeing sentry in the neck and thigh. He convulsed violently before collapsing, paralyzed and wide-eyed.

The confusion was all the opening Lianna needed.

She and Frostclaw slipped between the trees, silent as falling snow. She reached the slave line swiftly, her curved daggers flashing as she broke locks with practiced precision. Frostclaw stalked nearby, his snarls keeping threats at bay.

She had just finished the penultimate shackle when a voice froze her blood.

"Well, well. Looks like the little kitten grew claws."

Lianna spun, face pale.

From the shadows stepped a man she had haunting her memories and occupying her nightmares, his visage as twisted and cruel as ever before. Mekal, older now, but no less vicious. A jagged scar split one temple, pulling his sneer into something inhuman. His presence soured the air around her.

"You," Lianna hissed, her grip tightening on her blades.

Mekal laughed, slow and cruel. "I remember that face. The little Iskari runt. Shame about your mother. She screamed so sweetly. Almost made her last."

The world went red.

Lianna charged, twin daggers flashing. Their blades clashed with snarls and sparks, Mekal's style savage and taunting. He struck with elbows, knees, dirty tricks meant to humiliate, not kill. But Lianna had trained for this. Every parry, every counter came honed from years of rage. She was no longer prey.

Frostclaw lunged to protect the slaves as another guard closed in. His claws tore through leather and mail, casting the attacker aside in a heap of blood and bone.

Steel clashed in a blaze of sparks. Lianna darted inward, too fast for Mekal's guard to recover. One dagger swept low and carved across his ribs, drawing a gout of blood that sprayed hot across her forearm.

He reeled, coughing, crimson bubbling at the corner of his mouth. "You're nothing without your pack," he spat, voice ragged, blood misting the words.

Her eyes burned with fury. "I am my pack."

With a snarl, she slammed her knee into his thigh and drove her blade up beneath his ribs, burying it deep. His body lurched forward with a strangled choke. The breath fled his lungs in a rattling gasp, and his sword slipped from numb fingers, clattering to the earth like a fallen verdict.

Their eyes met, his wide with shock, hers locked in iron resolve.

She stepped in close, their faces inches apart, her voice a blade all its own. "For my mother."

The second dagger pierced his chest in a brutal thrust, the point driving through muscle and bone until it found the hollow beat of his heart. He convulsed once, gurgled... then crumpled at her feet, blood soaking the ground beneath him.

Across the clearing, Xavier cleaved through the last remaining guard. Vaeltheris turned aside a wild swing, and the Emberstone blade replied with a searing cut across the man's chest. Flames danced along the wound, and the soldier fell screaming.

Then Xavier saw him... standing at the far edge of the firelight.

The Overseer. The same one from the auction. Their eyes met across the camp, and for one long second neither moved. Then the man turned and vanished into the trees.

Xavier cursed. Chasing him now would risk everything.

He turned to Ella. "Get them moving. Quietly. We've been seen."

Sihri helped guide the slaves to their feet. Some wept. Others simply stared, dazed.

The Lynari woman rose slowly. Her voice was hoarse, but unshaken. "You were at the auction. You came for us."

Xavier nodded. "We do not leave our people in chains."

She looked past him to Lianna, still standing over Mekal's body. "I remember you. You are no slave."

Lianna didn't answer. She only nodded once, her expression unreadable, then turned back toward the freed.

They moved quickly. Supplies were taken from the wagons, the campfire extinguished to prevent a wider blaze. The Wildlands held their breath, the wind whispering through the trees like a benediction.

Freedom had been won, paid for in blood beneath the gaze of the death moon.

---

As they guided the former captives into the shelter of the forest, Xavier paused a moment to examine the prompt following the battle.Your party has engaged and defeated an opposing force.

- Caravan Commander – Mekal: 6,800 XP
- Overseer (Escaped – No XP awarded)
- Veteran Caravan Guards (x3): 5,400 XP (1,800 each)
- Regular Guards (x3): 3,600 XP (1,200 each)
- Taskmaster Slaver: 2,000 XP
- Bound Warhounds (x2): 1,600 XP (800 each)

---

He hadn't known about the taskmaster nor the hounds but vaguely remembered hearing howls through the din of combat.

The next notification came with the almost Pavlovian endorphin rush as a radiant symphony of chimes reverberated through his head, accompanied by a booming voice reading the notification:

---

**"Hark and Hear! You have ascended in power. You are now Level 17!**

The touch of the divine lingers upon you, granting **6 (12 total remain) attribute points** to shape your destiny, an exceptional gift, elevated from the ordinary **4 points** by the **Blessings of the Gods (Danu).**

Choose wisely, for these points will define your path. You have **3 days** to assign them, or they will fall to the whims of fate.

Your growing prowess earns you a boon: **20% (40% total unallocated) skill allocation** to distribute among your known skills.

This is your chance to sharpen the blade of a favored talent, forge new strength in an untapped domain, or balance your growth across disciplines. Let this moment be a cornerstone of your greatness.

**Rise, Seeker of Glory. The world awaits your will. Seek adventure, seek wisdom, seek love and let your legend be forged in your choices. LIVE!"**

---

#

They traveled under cover of darkness, weaving through forgotten deer trails and dry creekbeds beneath the hush of the Wildlands. Lianna led the way, eyes sharp as frost, while Valkra scouted ahead without a sound. The stars wheeled above them, cold and watchful. Necroth remained fixed in the heavens like a black sentinel, casting no light, only its oppressive presence.

As they walked, Xavier considered the path ahead... and the choices he had just made.

He had allocated his points carefully. Four had gone to Charisma, a belated admission that presence and persuasion mattered as much as steel in cities like Ironhaven. Two more he'd poured into Dexterity and Agility, the cornerstones of his fighting style. Each brought him to a solid thirty, and he could already feel the sharpened edge of his movement. The final four he cast into the esoteric realm of Luck, driven by a hunch more than reason. Everything had fallen into place during the rescue... too perfectly. He suspected he was burning through more fortune than he had any right to, and whatever came next would demand every drop he could muster.

The cold deepened as they entered the lower foothills. When they finally reached the rendezvous point, it was a lonely shrine half-buried in moss and time. A single lantern flickered at its base, barely holding back the dark.

Three figures stepped from the trees, resistance agents clad in forest-worn cloaks, their only mark the faint green-threaded sigils embroidered into the cuffs of their sleeves. The leader, a broad-shouldered Vulpiri with rust-red fur and shrewd eyes, offered a faint grin.

"You're early," he said. "Good. Time is a luxury we don't carry. We got the message less than an hour ago."

Xavier met him halfway and gave a curt nod. "They need to be in Verdantspire within two days. No delays."

The Vulpiri's gaze swept over the rescued Animari. Some leaned on each other. Others limped, their eyes still dazed and hollow. His eyes settled at last on the Lynari woman. She met his stare with calm defiance, unflinching.

"She'll make it," the agent said, voice turning grave. "They all will."

Ella moved quietly among the freed, offering waterskins and cloaks with gentle words. Her touch was light, but the comfort it gave was real. Lianna stood apart, still cloaked in shadow, her expression unreadable. Frostclaw stayed pressed to her side, silent, unmoving.

When the group was nearly ready to move, Lianna stepped forward and pulled a sealed scroll from her belt. She handed it to the Vulpiri without ceremony. "Give this to Elder Kaelith," she said softly. "She'll know what to do."

The agent accepted the scroll with both hands and nodded. "It'll reach her. Word for word."

At his signal, two more figures emerged from the trees. One was a Zar'Kaan with ashen skin and ember-bright eyes. The other, a Lupari woman whose curved blade hung like a statement at her hip, wore a silver chain around her throat like a badge. The transfer was swift. They moved with practiced precision, veterans of many such handoffs.

As the final freed Animari passed by, the Lynari woman paused beside Xavier.

"Thank you," she said, her voice quiet, but steady.

He nodded once. "Live free. That's all the thanks we need."

Without another word, she turned and followed the others. The resistance faded into the trees like smoke, swallowed by the wind and dark. No footprints marked their passing.

Xavier turned back to the remnants of his party. The fire of action had burned away, and in its place was something colder, something heavier.

Necroth still loomed overhead.

Now, they had to descend once more into Ironhaven. Into the dark.

#

The Emberdrift Hearth lay still when they returned. Silence held the space like a breath not yet released. The oil in the lamps had burned low, casting faint shadows along the worn wooden floor. Above, the occasional creak betrayed someone stirring in the upper rooms, but the hearth below had long gone to ember.

They moved upstairs in silence, the kind not born of fear but of gravity, each step steeped in the weight of what they had done. The cost. The truths. The blood spilled that did not always wash away the ache it left behind.

Lianna bore the heaviest burden.

She sat on the floor, still in her leathers, her back resting against the foot of her cot. Her twin daggers lay across her lap, the dried blood still flaking from the grooves in the metal. Frostclaw curled beside her, his body a silent guardian even in sleep. His tail flicked now and then, as if responding to dreams… or to her unrest.

She had not spoken since handing the sealed letter to the resistance runner. Not a word on the march back. Not even a whisper.

Xavier sat nearby, methodically cleaning Vaeltheris until its edge gleamed once more. The Emberstone shortsword rested untouched beside him, its fire-forged nature needing no care. His hands worked with quiet focus, but his eyes never left Lianna. Concern pooled in their depths.

"The Lynari woman mattered to you more," he said quietly. It was not a question. The truth already sat between them.

Lianna didn't look up. Her grip on one of the daggers tightened, the tendons in her hand pulled taut. "She reminded me of my sister," she said, voice tight and raw.

Xavier said nothing. He knew when words were a balm and when silence was its own kind of comfort.

From the windowsill, Ella gazed into the storm-churned night. Necroth still loomed overhead, but now its black silhouette was veiled by thick, roiling clouds spilling in from the east.

"You saved her," she said softly. "You gave her a chance at something better."

But Lianna remained still. Her silence stretched into the room until it felt brittle.

"I thought killing him would... do something," she whispered at last. "Bring peace. Closure. A release from what he did to us. But now... it's only absence. Empty. And somehow... that is worse."

Ella stood, moving to her side and kneeling quietly. Her tone was gentle but anchored. "You feel what you need to feel, Lianna. Rage, sorrow, grief, it all matters. What's important is that he cannot hurt anyone again."

Lianna's head bowed. A single tear slipped down her cheek, catching in the dried blood on her blade. "He murdered my mother. Tortured Frostclaw's dam to death. Branded Lio and me. Sold us like chattel. I've dreamed of ending him for so long... I thought it would set me free. But it didn't. I feel nothing but the cold."

"You ended him," Xavier said. He knelt a respectful distance away, voice steady. "Sometimes justice doesn't bring peace. It just stops the bleeding. I once saw a man executed who killed a child… it didn't bring healing. Just a silence that didn't scream anymore."

His mind drifted back to that trial and execution. The image of the little slain girl… He blinked once, brushing at the corner of his eye. Ella noticed but said nothing.

Frostclaw stirred beside Lianna, lifting his head with a soft chuff. Sensing the shift in her breathing, he pressed into her arm. She finally released her daggers and buried her fingers in his fur, her breath catching in her throat.

Then came the knock.

Sharp. Measured. Coded.

Sihri was on her feet instantly. She unlatched the bolt and stepped aside. A lean Animari slipped inside, his fur streaked with ash and his slave collar still clasped around his neck. The scent of the city clung to him, filth, soot, and haste.

"They're moving," he gasped. "Halestorm's activated the city guard. He's pulled in Redmaw mercs and every Arenvalis soldier still in the city. They're sweeping the upper tiers. Word is already out."

He swallowed. "They're hunting you, the rogue mercenary from the south. They're searching for your 'property.'"

Xavier stood slowly, his breath leaving in a slow exhale. "The Overseer."

Ella looked up, her eyes sharpening. "He made it back. That's what you meant… when you said we were seen."

"They're locking the gates," the messenger added. "They'll search the city block by block. If they find you here, everyone tied to this safehouse will burn with you."

Lianna rose, her grief falling away like shed skin. Her voice was steel. "We can't stay. If we linger, we doom everyone who's ever used this place."

Xavier nodded. "Then we move. Now."

He turned to the others. "Gear up. We go below."

Lightning split the sky outside. Thunder followed like a war drum, and rain began to fall in sheets.

"To the Vault?" Ella asked, already buckling her quiver.

"Yes," Xavier answered. "That's the rot beneath Ironhaven. Lythara said there's something inside that can break the chains binding the kingdom. If we wait, we lose our only chance."

The Vulpiri messenger pulled a folded scrap of parchment from his tunic and handed it over. "She marked a sewer entrance. It'll get you into the catacombs. No patrols, too unstable, but it leads close."

Xavier took the map. His eyes hardened. "Then it's time we end this."

They moved without further words. Frostclaw rose with Lianna. Valkra waited at the door, her tails twitching like coiled whips. Sihri cracked her knuckles with the sound of distant thunder. Ella checked her bowstrings and blades. Xavier slid the Emberstone shortsword into its sheath, the flicker of its molten edge dancing briefly across his face.

Behind them, the Emberdrift Hearth fell back into silence.

Above them, Necroth watched through storm-choked skies.

Ahead, darkness waited, and beneath the city, the chains would rattle… and break.

# CHAPTER
# TWENTY-FIVE

*Secrets in the Dark*

True to the messenger's word, the sewer entrance lay just beyond the Emberdrift Hearth, hidden behind a cluster of stacked crates and discarded barrels. One by one, they descended the rusted ladder. Valkra and Frostclaw leapt the short distance to the tunnel floor with practiced ease. The grate was slid back into place behind them before any passerby stirred from slumber or shelter.

Rain roared above, washing the alleys clean, but beneath the streets, only the soft trickle of runoff filled the silence. The storm's fury was reduced to muffled groans through the layers of stone and wood. The air hung thick with mildew, rot, and the sour tang of wet iron. Walls pressed close around them, the narrowness adding a claustrophobic weight to every breath.

At the front of the group, Xavier paused to light a single lantern. He held it low, allowing its glow to spill across the slick floor and wet stone. The light cast narrow shadows across the walls, and every movement of water sent them skittering like fleeing spirits. The glint of rusted pipework and the glisten of damp brick blurred the edges of everything, lending the tunnel a dreamlike disquiet.

He said nothing as he advanced, his boots splashing through shallow water. Words would have broken the concentration they all relied upon. Every step had weight. Every breath was wrapped in silence.

Ella walked close behind him, her movement fluid and sure. She moved like shadow given purpose, eyes constantly shifting across the gloom. Her hands hovered near her weapons, drifting from her bow to her twin blades in subtle rhythm. Though she made no sound, her presence brought steadiness. She anchored the space behind Xavier, an unseen ward against what might stir in the dark.

Lianna came next, several paces behind Ella. Her expression was unreadable, her features carved into an emotionless mask. Water dripped from the ceiling, soaking the fur lining of her cloak, but she gave no sign she noticed. Since slaying Mekal, she had grown more reserved, withdrawn behind a silence that felt newly constructed and tightly sealed. Frostclaw walked beside her with the grace of falling snow. His large paws moved without sound, even as the water rippled around him. He remained vigilant, casting frequent glances at Lianna, his tail brushing lightly against her leg as if to remind her she was not alone.

Sihri brought up the rear. Her Leporini frame moved lightly along the uneven stone, ears flicking at each creak or splash that echoed through the tunnels. Her hands twitched every so often, either readying to strike or bracing to flee, depending on what instinct deemed necessary. Tension coiled through her like a spring wound tight. Her eyes never stopped moving.

Valkra darted between them, a small phantom with twin tails flicking side to side. She sniffed at the air and touched each of them in passing, her silent way of counting the whole. Her nose lifted often as if she could smell danger before it formed.

Xavier studied the map Lythara had given them. It had led them deep into long-abandoned stretches of the city's old runoff system. The scent of rot and runoff clung to every surface, but beneath it, something else lingered. There was an undercurrent of scorched dust and dried blood, not fresh, but ancient. The stone held the memory of suffering. The further they traveled, the stronger it became. Something had died here long ago, and the walls had never forgotten.

They turned down a broader passage. Two broken supports jutted from the wall like snapped tusks, their shapes unmistakable. Xavier raised his lantern slightly and nodded toward the beams.

"We're getting close to the cistern," he said quietly. "According to the map, it should be just ahead."

"It's quiet," Sihri murmured. "Too quiet, even for a sewer."

Ella nodded but did not speak. Behind them, a faint splash echoed. It was distant, but sharp enough to draw the party's attention. Lianna stiffened, one hand drifting toward a dagger's hilt.

Sihri's ears angled toward the sound. After a pause, she whispered, "Not pursuit. Just runoff. The storm's working in our favor, masking our passage. Harder for anyone to follow."

Lianna's tension remained. She was not reacting to the idea of pursuit, and the others understood that without needing words. Her fear lay deeper, beneath the surface. Frostclaw nudged her gently with his shoulder, a quiet reassurance that tethered her to the present.

Xavier slowed, letting Ella move past him briefly so he

could match pace with Lianna. He kept his voice low. "You alright?"

Lianna gave a curt nod, her voice rough. "Just... remembering."

He accepted the answer without pressing her further. A glance over his shoulder found Sihri, who nodded back, silently agreeing to keep close to Lianna as the group moved forward.

The tunnel narrowed again, the walls slick with damp. Eventually, the passage opened beneath a wide, moss-covered archway. A faint glow flickered beyond it.

Xavier raised a hand to halt the others. His voice remained low. "A lantern. Marked here, center of the cistern. I didn't expect it to be lit."

Ella retrieved her bow and nocked an arrow. She held it low and undrawn, not in threat but in readiness. Beside Lianna, Frostclaw issued a soft growl. The sound was low and warning. Valkra pressed into Xavier's leg, her eyes fixed on the shadows ahead.

They advanced slowly as one, the echo of their footsteps lost beneath the thunder that rolled above. The storm was distant now, its voice hollow through the layers of stone.

The cistern came into view. Rounded walls rose high, ringed with crumbling shelves and corroded metal. Broken pipes protruded like skeletal arms. At the center of the chamber, resting atop a collapsed stone pillar, stood a single lantern. Its pale flame flickered without wind, casting faint light into an otherwise empty room.

Xavier lowered his lantern and scanned the recesses of the chamber. Shadows clung to every corner. The cistern felt like a forgotten wound left to fester beneath the city's skin.

Above them, thunder rumbled again. The pressure was growing. It pulsed through the stone around them in time with the storm outside.

Something was waiting. Whether memory or threat, none could say.

Not yet.

#

The party lingered in the stillness of the cistern, breathing in air heavy with damp moss and rust. Lantern light continued to flicker across the rounded walls, casting long, broken shadows over the water-slick floor. Faint reflections danced in the puddles pooled between worn flagstones. A hint of rot and iron clung to the air, enough to wrinkle their noses with each deeper breath.

Xavier crouched low at the front of the group, one hand brushing the stone floor as his eyes moved methodically across the chamber. He studied the wall angles, searched for signs of passage or ambush, and watched the alcoves that might hide a threat. The instincts carved from weeks of combat had taken root. Terrain came first. Emotion could wait.

The others moved into place behind him. Ella slipped to his left, positioning herself to cover the widest arc of approach. Her bow was strung and an arrow already nocked, held low and steady, prepared for anything but not yet drawn. Her posture was calm, balanced, ready to shift fluidly between silence and action.

Lianna mirrored her on the right, less tense than before but still pulled inward. She remained alert though, her eyes tracking motion. Frostclaw moved with deliberate caution, placing himself between Lianna and the center of the chamber. His movements were graceful, each step measured, as if he felt something stirring beyond their senses.

Valkra stayed close to Xavier, her twin tails twitching with growing tension. Her ears angled sharply as her nose lifted to taste the air. She darted short distances through the group, then returned, circling his leg in silent warning.

At the rear, Sihri hovered near the archway. Her long ears pivoted between directions, her body half-turned to cover both retreat and reinforcement. Her fingers twitched occasionally, caught between striking and fleeing, whichever came first.

Xavier raised a hand. The group froze. Something wasn't right. The lit lantern was strange enough, but there was another presence layered beneath the stillness. A kind of hush that didn't feel natural.

A voice emerged from the dark, soft and unmistakable.

"I did not think you would actually come."

Lythara stepped forward from the shadows at the far end of the chamber. Her cloak clung to her, still damp from the sewers. She wore no illusion and no mask. Her crimson eyes shimmered faintly, not with infernal heat, but something quieter. She looked tired.

"You left us an invitation," Xavier replied, lifting the crude map her contact had provided. "I assumed you meant us to follow it."

Lythara's gaze swept over the group. Ella now stood beside Xavier, bow in hand but lowered. Lianna remained farther back, arms loosely at her sides, face unreadable but aware. Sihri stayed by the archway, crouched and still, waiting for the first sign of betrayal. Frostclaw and Valkra kept to their companions, heads low, watching the succubus with silent warning.

"I did," Lythara said. "But things have changed. Halestorm has put the city into full motion. Redmaw mercenaries and the Arenvalis guard are combing Ironhaven from the upper tiers to the gutters. They are searching by the block."

Xavier didn't move. He had felt the noose tightening the moment they returned to the inn. "We took the path you recommended. The sewer entrance was no more than twenty paces from the rear door."

Lythara gave a slight nod. She reached into her cloak and produced a second, thicker map. She held it out without stepping closer.

"This one is accurate. The previous path was a test to see if you were being followed. What you hold now is the real way forward."

Xavier stepped forward and took the parchment from her hands. He unrolled it slowly, scanning the inkwork. This map was different. Depth markers, elevation levels, collapsed corridors, outdated patrol routes, and fallback channels filled its surface. It was the kind of map drawn by someone who had walked the paths beneath Ironhaven more than once.

Ella leaned in over his shoulder. "It matches with the older sewer schematics we found. This one's real."

Lythara's voice remained steady. "The Vault lies beneath the southern foundation, below the slave markets. The direct tunnels were sealed long ago or buried in traps. The slave tunnels are the only surviving route. Most were destroyed after the uprisings. What remains will be unstable and unpleasant, but they lead close."

She stopped. The weight of the words reached the others before they responded.

Sihri's voice was quiet but sharp. "So what are we walking into?"

Lythara met her gaze. "Pain. Forgotten corridors. Secrets sealed to ensure no one ever found them again."

Lianna shifted slightly, her jaw clenched. She didn't speak, but her silence rang with knowledge of the stories whispered beneath the Animari chains.

Xavier stepped in again, redirecting the conversation before it spiraled. "You said you can guide us."

"I can lead you to the threshold," Lythara answered. "My contract prevents more than that. The closer I get to the Vault, the stronger the binding reacts. I cannot pass through its wards without Ivarik."

Lianna's arms crossed. Her voice was cool and flat. "And we're supposed to trust you not to vanish the moment we turn our backs?"

Lythara didn't flinch. Her tone stayed level. "I'm not asking for your trust. I'm asking for your will to go further than I can. Because if none of you do... I remain like this. Bound to serve without a voice. Without a choice."

Her voice didn't falter. She didn't raise it either. The exhaustion in her words carried far more than volume ever could.

Lianna faltered for a breath. She began to respond but caught herself, the reply dying on her tongue.

Xavier regarded Lythara closely. Not with suspicion, but with quiet judgment. He saw no deceit in her expression. Only desperation. It was not the panic of someone afraid of death, but the hollow kind worn by someone who had lived too long inside a cage.

"You've endured longer than most," he said. "And now

you want out."

"Yes." Her reply was quiet but certain. Her eyes did not waver as they met his.

Valkra gave a low growl. The tension in the room had shifted. Xavier raised his hand, not just to her, but to the others. His palm hovered for a breath in a silent request for patience.

Lythara saw the motion and stepped back. Her hands rose slightly, empty, open.

"I'm not your enemy," she said. "I just want to be free."

Xavier's response came without hesitation. "So do we."

The words hit harder than expected. Lianna looked at Lythara again. Her gaze didn't soften, but the set of her shoulders eased. It wasn't trust, not yet, but a grudging understanding. A recognition of something similar.

Xavier folded the map and handed it to Ella. She tucked it away with careful efficiency. He had committed the path to memory already. Remaining here any longer would only increase the risk.

"We move now," he said. "The storm won't shield us forever."

#

Xavier had expected Lythara to lead them out of the cistern and into the tunnels beyond. Instead, the lanterns hissed softly in the silence, their flames casting long, reaching shadows against the damp stone walls. The air grew heavier with each passing breath. The chamber no longer felt like shelter. It felt like it was watching them.

No one moved.

Xavier said nothing. There was no need to press yet. He simply watched her. Lythara remained at the edge of the lantern's glow, her posture rigid, not with defiance or fear, but with something else entirely. She looked caught in place, like someone bracing against a pain they could not escape.

He began to see it in the small things... fingers that twitched at odd intervals, the slight catch in her breath. She wasn't preparing a strike. She wasn't hiding something. She was holding something back. A burden. Something pressing hard enough to be felt through the very act of standing still.

Ella broke the silence.

"You mentioned before that your name is stored in the Vault," she said. "What exactly did you mean?"

Lythara's response came after a long exhale. Her voice was softer now, and lacked its usual certainty.

"My contract," she said. "It's not metaphorical. It exists, etched into infernal parchment, bound in blood and sealed by magic. Ivarik himself signed it, and it's kept in the Vault below."

Xavier lifted his lantern and took a step closer. The movement wasn't aggressive, but it was intentional. He let the light wash over Lythara's features, watching her closely.

His *Espionage* skill was still undeveloped, barely past the threshold of competence, but it had begun to sharpen his instincts. He noticed the small shifts others might miss— the angle of her gaze, the tightness at the corners of her mouth, the measured rhythm of her breath. She wasn't evading. She wasn't hiding. Everything in her posture said she believed what she was saying.

He lowered the lantern.

"What's in the contract?" he asked, voice quiet.

Lythara met his gaze. There was no flinch, only the steady weight of resignation.

"Obedience, silence... pain, whenever I resist."

She paused before continuing, her words more careful now.

"There's one clause I've never been able to understand. A single line near the end, written differently from the rest. It reads, 'Only one truly unbound can sever this pact.' That part is unlike any other I've seen in similar bindings."

Xavier held still, but his thoughts surged. He didn't outwardly react, though his fingers twitched ever so slightly. Ella, standing nearby, noticed the motion.

He inhaled, slow and steady, and brought one hand to his chest. Beneath cloth and leather, the mark of the Kael'Sharyn rested dormant. It did not glow, but he felt its awareness stir. There was no pull, no searing burn, only a sensation, like a key recognizing the shape of a lock.

Lythara took a single step forward.

"I know you carry the Kael'Sharyn," she said. "I can feel the fracture in your soul. It resonates with the pain I've carried for lifetimes."

Xavier didn't speak yet. His mind raced, not only with the implications of Lythara's words but with something deeper... the meaning behind it all. It couldn't be a coincidence that he was the one standing here, that he alone bore the mark tied to her only hope of freedom. This moment felt too precise, too intentional. Another thread in a web he hadn't meant to walk into but had followed nonetheless.

There was a pattern forming, one he still could not fully see. Each step on this journey, each revelation and burden, kept circling back to the same truth: someone or something had placed him on this path for reasons still hidden from him.

He thought of Danu. Her voice echoed in memory, that careful dance between offering truth and cloaking it in riddles. Choice, she had said, was sacred. But choice meant little if the roads were already laid out, each one curving back toward some divine expectation. His doubts stirred again, quiet but growing. These moments were happening too often, lining up too perfectly. It felt less like fate and more like design. Even now, with no visible hand guiding him, he could feel the pull, the pressure of something unseen shaping the path beneath his feet.

Not for the first time, he wondered just how much of his will was truly his own.

When he finally spoke, the uncertainty in his voice gave shape to his thoughts.

"I have a trait, something tied to the mark. It's called *Unbound Possibilities*. The description says I follow the rules of this world, but I'm not constrained by them."

Lythara's eyes brightened, just slightly. Her gaze moved from him to the rest of the group, then back again. She nodded slowly.

"Maybe that's what the clause means. Maybe it's not about what you are, but what you're capable of doing."

Lianna shifted behind him, her voice edged with doubt. "Why would a devil leave an escape clause in a contract? They don't make allowances for mercy."

"Because it was never supposed to be fulfilled," Lythara said. Her tone no longer held the sharp confidence of a manipulator. There was only bitter truth. "Infernal laws thrive on absolutes. Ivarik must have believed that no such being existed. That clause was meant to mock me. To dangle hope like a blade too far to reach."

Her gaze returned to Xavier. "Until now."

Xavier took another slow step forward. "Even if I am the one that can do it, I don't know how."

"But you might find out," she said. Her voice dropped to a whisper, as if a noise too loud would chase away the small flicker of hope. "And that's more than I've had in longer than I can remember."

The cistern held quiet. The only sounds came from a distant pipe and the muted rumble of thunder through the city's bones.

Xavier gave a single nod. It wasn't a promise. It wasn't certainty. It was an acknowledgment that the path was open.

"I'll try."

Something subtle released in Lythara. Her stance loosened, the tension in her shoulders faded. She didn't smile, but the change was real.

Her eyes moved to Lianna.

"I know what I have been. I know what I've done. I'm not asking for forgiveness. I don't expect it. I only want to move forward."

Lianna didn't answer at first. Her arms stayed crossed. Her expression didn't soften, but it cracked, just a little. A moment later she gave the faintest of nods, reserved but not dismissive to the succubus' admission. It was not an outright rejection but recognition of the situation.

Xavier turned to the group, his gaze lingering on each of them in turn. He wasn't just checking for readiness. He was measuring resolve.

Weapons could be drawn and armor worn, but amongst

allies trust, vulnerability and shared intent had to be carried.

"We need to move soon," he said. "We stay quiet. Move quickly."

His eyes returned to Lythara.

"Get us to the Vault. We'll handle the rest."

She inclined her head, and for once... she didn't speak, she didn't need to. They all understood what needed to be done.

#

The corridor narrowed further as the group descended deeper beneath the streets of Ironhaven. The stone walls were slick with ages of moisture and grime. Each step they took sent faint echoes spiraling into the darkness ahead. Xavier led the way, lantern held low in one hand, his other resting on the hilt of Vaeltheris. The flame cast a wavering glow across crumbling mortar and rusted pipework, revealing just enough to guide them forward without announcing their presence.

He paused often, not from fear, but to read the space around them. His hand would drift from his weapon to the nearest wall or support, his fingertips grazing worn stone or lingering on the edge of a fractured beam. The instinct came unbidden. His connection to the Earth Ley Line whispered subtle truths to him. He felt collapse patterns, traced the movement of drafts, noted the density of moisture in the air. He did not need to speak the details. His senses were mapping the path as surely as any drawn parchment.

"There's a shift in airflow," he murmured. "A larger chamber is ahead."

Lythara nodded, she had been following slightly behind

him. "That would be the eastern pens."

Sihri's nose twitched, and her voice raised enough to be heard from her position at the back of the group once again. "Pens?"

Lythara's voice was tight as she admitted her knowledge of the place. "It was where they kept Animari captives before they decided what to do with them."

The group continued walking and rounded a final corner that emerged into a chamber more ruin than intact structure. One side had nearly completely collapsed, the ceiling sagging almost to the ground where its support beams had failed. Along the walls chains hung from rusted hooks giving credence to what Lythara had stated about the place. Most disturbingly however was the floor that bore long-dried bloodstains and the faded, overlapping etchings of countless captives into the stones of the walls.

Xavier paused at the edge of the chamber. His eyes swept through the space once again noting high corners, alcove shadows, and possible ambush angles. Nothing living moved. But that did not preclude the memories from doing so.

When Lianna reached the chamber, she stepped forward and froze. There were no words that came from her, she didn't have any. Her expression said enough though as the memories and horror fought beneath the mask she struggled to keep in place. At her side Frostclaw growled softly, sensing her distress he leaned into the Iskari woman's leg causing her to instinctively stroke his head with a free hand.

As Xavier had noticed, scratched into the walls, between the chains and cracks, were claw marks and symbols, crude spirals, crescent slashes, sigils of resistance.

"I know this mark," Lianna finally whispered as she

stepped closer to a distinctive three-spike triangle etched beside a set of rusted shackles. "We carved these... when we were taken. When we didn't want to be forgotten."

Sihri swallowed nodding as she moved to look as well, her ears folding back exposing her own emotional response. "I've seen ones like that. In the pit walls. They never explained."

"They weren't meant to," Lianna said bitterly. "We were not people to them, we had no meaning, and they wanted us erased, not remembered."

Xavier knelt by one of the markings and ran his gloved fingers over it. He didn't speak. He let the moment settle, let the others take in the truth laid bare in this room. His silence was deliberate a tactic he'd learned long ago back on earth. Words had weight, but stillness could make them heavier.

Lythara stepped into the chamber carefully, hesitantly. She didn't touch the chains though her gaze lingered on them. When she spoke her voice was quiet, almost reverent. "I walked through here once. A long time ago. Escorting a Cervari boy to the scribe pit. I doubt he could have been more than eight winters."

Lianna turned sharply. "You..."

"I didn't lay hands on him," Lythara said cutting the Iskari off before, raising a hand before letting it fall. "But I didn't stop it either." She didn't cry, but her voice cracked slightly heavy with the memory. "I was, am bound. That doesn't stop me from still remembering the look in his eyes when I let the door close behind him."

Ella shifted her weight, her jaw tight. Sihri looked down, silent.

Lianna opened her mouth to speak, then stopped and

after a moment, she said, "You remember more than you admit."

Xavier stood slowly and stepped toward the far wall. His hand brushed faint indentations near a collapsed passage once again led by his connection with the earth. "This route was sealed intentionally," he said, inspecting the stonework. "They didn't want anyone getting in... or out."

Lythara followed his gaze. "The archive chamber lies beyond that. Bloodline records. Animari families traced across generations."

Lianna stiffened at the implications. "So they could decide who to breed... and who to break."

"Yes," came Lythara's whispered response.

Xavier walked the room again, he was now mapping its perimeter, not just the space, but the memories that lingered. He noted where the walls bowed, where the floor dipped, places where pain had pooled and curdled into history. To him they were places that mattered. He ultimately came to stop beside Lianna, her hand lightly grazing one of the chains.

"We should burn this," she muttered.

Xavier looked at her. Not with judgment but with a quiet certainty.

"No," he said. "We remember it first. Then we bury it like they tried to but this time on our terms."

Lianna nodded. "No more erasing the truth."

Lythara, watching them all, whispered something too soft to catch. But the look on her face wasn't the mask she wore in Ironhaven. It was gratitude, gratitude and guilt.

Xavier signaled the group onward. "Let's get going the vault's close now according to the map." His tone was calm, steady, but to those who knew him there was something behind it now. He held deeper resolve, etched not just in duty and his mission, but in justice for what had been done.

#

The silence that followed their departure from the slave pens was not born of fear but of reflection. Each of them carried the weight of what they had seen, processing the memories in solitude. Xavier took the lead once more, his lantern casting a soft, flickering glow. Iron and mortar gradually gave way to smoother, more ancient stone. The corridor's construction changed. Where once it had been laid with precision, it now bore the signs of having been shaped rather than built. The path ahead seemed less crafted by mortal hands and more carved by time and power.

The air thickened as they progressed. It grew heavier, more humid. There was no breeze to stir it, only a stillness that seemed unnatural. Each step forward added to the sense of pressure, as if the stone around them was holding its breath.

Xavier paused and placed a hand against the wall. He leaned in, his voice low. "Old ley bleed. This place is different. It wasn't constructed like the pens. It was shaped."

Ella ran her fingers across the stone beside him. "It feels older."

They continued, descending at a gradual slope. The temperature dropped slowly, until their breath began to mist in the air.

"We're close," Lythara said.

Xavier glanced back. "To the vault?"

Lythara gave a single nod.

Without warning, the tunnel opened into a wide, perfectly round chamber. Its floor was smooth in places, polished like glass. The only two exits were the tunnel they had come from and another directly across. In the center of the chamber, a dry basin sat recessed into the floor. Spiral carvings stretched from its edge and radiated outward, crawling up the walls like vines. The patterns pulsed faintly in the lantern light.

Ella came to Xavier's side. Her eyes narrowed. "I don't hear anything."

He listened, the realization crawling down his spine. "Exactly. No echoes. No wind. No life."

Lythara's voice dropped to a whisper. "Not the vault. The memory ward. It traps you in yourself."

They crossed the threshold.

The world shifted.

---

### Xavier's Vision

Xavier blinked. The stone was gone. White walls surrounded him. He stood in a hospital hallway beneath flickering fluorescent lights. The scent of antiseptic hit hard. He knew where he was.

The nurse appeared ahead of him, her expression heavy with grief. She didn't need to speak. He already knew what she would say. He looked past her, toward the familiar door.

His hand reached for the handle.

Inside, his brother lay still beneath a sheet. Tears blurred Xavier's vision. He remembered the crash. The guilt. The voice in his head returned.

You weren't there.

The scene shifted, and the hospital dissolved. Blood soaked his hands, it was not his brother's. It was his own. Blood from battles in Arath. Bramblegate, Rynthavael, slave caravans, all the deaths he couldn't prevent. He was surrounded by the corpses of the innocent that he had tried to save.

You fail everyone.

As the guilt and doubt grew and threatened to overwhelm him, he felt the Kael'Sharyn mark under his shirt throb once. Further cracks grew in its design, but it saved his sanity

Xavier clenched his jaw. "Not now." He muttered to himself as he pressed a hand to his chest and pulled himself free of the visions. The chamber snapped back to the circular room and he saw everyone else standing slack and glassy-eyed.

---

### Ella's Vision

Ash fell like snow and Ella stood in a twilight realm of ruin. It was an endless plain of shattered stone and broken spires. Beneath her feet the ground was scattered with the spectral remnants of armor, glass-like weaponry, and silver banners tattered by time.

And the ghosts, the ghosts were everywhere. Faint, flickering presences drifting through the haze, men, women, children. She knew they were the Sylmyrian people. Their faces carried both grace and sorrow, their voices a chorus of whispers without words. They moved around her like wind in a dead forest. None met her eyes. None acknowledged her.

She called out, her voice laced with yearning. "Do you not know me?"

Nothing. No one responded to her. They continued to drift, lost in their own patterns, remembering a world long gone. She reached for one of them, a child with silver-white eyes who paused... but did not see her. He passed through her hand as though she were the ghost. She held her hands out and looking down at them, she saw nothing. She had no body, no shadow, no reflection in the black-glass pools at her feet.

I am Vaeltheris, she remembered the mantra repeating in her mind over and over. I am the blade... and the soul inside it.

Yet even here, in this graveyard of memory, in the resting place of her own people, she was utterly alone. They did not recognize her. They did not answer. She was their guardian, their voice, their will. But here, she was forgotten.

Memory shifted and she remembered when she had first awakened, there had been nothing with her in the darkness. No voices, no faces, no presences. Only silence, the blade laying at her feet and the knowledge that she still existed when everything else was gone. That solitude had become her cage and within it she wept a single word escaping her lips. "Alone..."

Until a sound arose. It was not from the ghosts, not from the blade. It came from the world beyond the vision. From him.

Xavier's hand took hers and it was warm, real, present. She felt her form coalesce, her shape return, and once more her limbs were solid as her breath returned to her chest.

His voice, quiet, steady, real, "you're not alone anymore."

In her mind the ghosts faded, not gone, but distant

once again watching and waiting. She closed her eyes and remembered who she was as she leaned into Xavier's arms.

---

### Lianna's Vision

Fire devoured the trees and houses. Screams echoed in the dark. Her mother's arms wrapped around her and Liosan, voice hoarse as she begged them to run. They had no chance. Slavers swept through the village like wolves.

Liosan signed at her, "Don't leave me!" His tiny fists flailed, trying to hold onto her. It was no good however, she was dragged away.

Lianna screamed for him. For her mother. For anyone.

Then the searing pain of the branding iron blossomed on her hip once again. The cold metal closed around her throat.

She stood in chains, a broken child weeping as she was watching it happen again. Completely powerless, helpless, broken.

But then, she felt something unseen, Frostclaw brushed against her leg and a voice cut through the fire.

Xavier. His voice sounded through the ruins and calamity that reigned around her, and it was calm, strong, supportive. "You're not there anymore."

She gasped and dropped to her knees, the vision broken and she could see the stone chamber once again. Slowly she rose to her feet, steadier than ever before.

---

### Sihri's Vision

Sihri stood in the arena. She felt the hot sand on her feet. She felt and smelled her bloodied fur. Across the sands from her stood another Animari fighter, a Cervari boy, barely a teenager. She didn't want to kill him.

The crowd screamed. Her overseer's voice rang out. "Finish it."

She remembered hesitating before. The pain of the punishment, the hunger of withheld food. The sound of his body collapsing when she finally obeyed, and the haunting image of a fallen opponent, their eyes wide with betrayal and pain. The memory was visceral, a searing reminder of the price of her survival. She hadn't cried then she couldn't and survive that did not stop her from crying now though.

Then she felt it, a forehead pressed against her. Hands holding her and others resting on her shoulder. When she opened her eyes Ella knelt in front of her, pressing their foreheads together. Xavier and Lianna both stood next to her, their hands on her shoulders giving her support as well.

"You're not in that place anymore." Ella whispered softly. "You are with us now."

Sihri nodded, just once, and breathed.

---

## Lythara's Vision

Wings of beautiful white flashed in a sky of gold. She remembered flying, her soul unburdened, free, whole. She felt overjoyed and whole, something she couldn't quite place or remember fully, until she wasn't anymore.

Suddenly she plummeted through shadow, her wings torn apart. Infernal chains laced her limbs. A contract scorched itself into her soul. Her voice was stolen. Her identity erased. Through it all Ivarik's laughter followed her down.

"You will obey." His voice echoed in the darkness.

She saw herself signing the pact before her, not with ink, but with blood and screaming. Pain exploded behind her eyes as the bindings etched themselves in her very being.

Then nothing. No not nothing, a hand on hers. She opened her eyes, bloody tears streaking from their crimson orbs as she lifted them to see a human hand laying on the back of hers. Xavier, his hand around hers. His voice, low but steady. His eyes were not condemning her for what she was, nor were they pitying. They were filled with concern.

"You're safe with us now Lythara." He said softly. "Welcome back."

And something broke inside of her. It was not pain, not sorrow, but the illusion of permanence. He could help her, she knew it to her core, the small spark of hope grew and started to take a deeper hold on her.

---

**Present**

The chamber pulsed, like a heartbeat that struggled forward, with a final wave of pressure. The air seemed to hold its breath as it clung to the last vestiges of magic. In the smooth stone room each of them stood, alone in mind, but scattered across memories too heavy to bear. Slowly something shifted.

Xavier moved first. He pressed his hand firmly over the Kael'Sharyn mark on his chest, grounding himself as the last echoes of blood and guilt faded from his mind. He blinked slowly, and the chamber returned. He could once again see the smooth stone underfoot, a basin at its heart, his team scattered and stricken. They weren't moving, not truly, not yet.

He stepped toward Ella. Her breath caught as he reached for her, fingers brushing hers. She gasped as sensation rushed back into her limbs. His hand closed around hers, and she felt it, warm, real, present. In her mind her body formed again, her voice returned. She leaned into him, reveling in his warmth and presence as she felt tears slipping down her cheek.

"You're not alone anymore," he said quietly, and the last whisper of ash receded from her soul.

Lianna was next. Her knees hit the stone, but Frostclaw was there leaning into her along with Xavier. He knelt beside her, one hand steadying her shoulder. She looked up, lost and dazed, her breath ragged.

"You're not there anymore," he told her, his voice low but certain.

Frostclaw pressed close, and Lianna let out a long, shuddering breath. Her eyes slowly cleared, and she stood cautiously, but with new strength.

Nearby Sihri's shoulders shook, her breath hitching as the memories of the arena clawed at her. Until she felt the hands touched her from all sides. Ella's forehead pressed gently to hers. Xavier's palm rested on one shoulder. Lianna's touch anchored the other.

"You're not in that place anymore," Ella whispered. "You're with us now."

Sihri opened her eyes. Saw them, felt them, and she nodded once, and the vision shattered around her like glass.

Nearby, Lythara whimpered as she curled forward, bloody tears streaked down her face, and her fingers trembled over the floor. Slowly she felt Xavier knelling in front of her as he took her hand firm, and steady in his own. Her crimson eyes opened, meeting his.

"You're safe with us now, Lythara," he said gently.

"Welcome back."

Her lips parted, but no words came, only a trembling breath as the weight lifted from her shoulders. The ward's grip broke in full, and something inside her, the flicker of hope something she'd thought lost, sparked to life.

The basin at the center of the room stopped pulsing. The runes dimmed. The silence settled fully over the room once again, but it was no longer suffocating. All around the chamber, they moved. Coming to each other, it was not fear of the past that pulled them together, it was a renewed connection they felt.

Lianna reached for Sihri's hand. Sihri took it, fingers still shaking. Frostclaw shifted to stand between the two as they leaned against him in support.

Ella stood shoulder to shoulder with Xavier, her fingers laced with his once again, grip still firm, her spirit reignited.

Valkra padded over and leaned into Xavier's leg, her twin tails curling low, her eyes blinking clear.

And Lythara, for the first time in centuries, stood not as a commander, not as a chained thing, but as part of something real and that embraced and supported her.

They looked to one another, the memories had bruised and battered each of them but hadn't broken them. The Echo Ward's magic, once sustained by isolation and pain, unraveled. It hadn't lost or failed in its power. They had simply moved beyond its visions.

Xavier's voice was quiet, but every syllable carried. "We survived the past; it cannot control us anymore. We're not alone anymore and won't be going forward."

No one needed to respond, the experience had built a deeper connection between them and as a collective they moved into passageway towards their goal.

# CHAPTER TWENTY-SIX

*The Vault of Chains*

They had walked for a short while after leaving the Mirror Ward. The corridor ahead gradually narrowed until it only allowed them to move in pairs. The carved stone walls seemed to swallow every sound, muting even their footsteps. The flickering sigils of the Mirror Ward had long since faded behind them, leaving only the cold quiet broken occasionally by the crunch of boots on scattered gravel.

After another ten minutes, the air changed. A subtle hum rose through the stone, faint but steady, pulsing like a heartbeat hidden deep beneath the earth.

The corridor opened into a circular chamber. Faded reliefs clung to its walls, ancient depictions of bindings and decrees etched in forgotten tongues. Some belonged to dead languages, others to non-mortal speech. Xavier, despite his gift for language, could not decipher them. Whatever meaning they held remained locked away.

At the back of the chamber stood the Vault of Chains.

A single stone arch framed its entrance. Seamless and unadorned, it gave no sign of magic. There were no glyphs or shimmering wards, only the silent weight of dormant menace that hung heavy in the air. Xavier reached out with his senses, attuning to the earth beneath. Nothing stirred, but the ground felt watchful, cautious.

Lythara moved past the group and approached the vault. Her steps slowed as she neared the threshold, her crimson eyes narrowing in concentration. A slight furrow appeared in her brow. She drew a steady breath and stepped forward.

The pain struck immediately.

She stumbled back, gasping, as though an invisible force had clutched her chest and squeezed. Her claws scraped furrows in the stone as she caught herself, and her tail whipped behind her with violent agitation.

Xavier stepped quickly to her side and extended his hand. "Lythara?"

She met his gaze with effort, her voice strained. "I told you. The contract forbids it. He made it so I cannot enter without him."

She tried to speak through the pressure. "The clause was written carefully. I cannot pass into any place where the pact is kept unless Ivarik is present. His presence unlocks the way for me. It is another of his games, a leash tied not to my body, but to my soul."

There was no barrier to see, no magical veil or sigil. Only that crushing pressure, internal and unyielding.

Ella joined them, placing a hand gently on Lythara's arm. "Are you alright?"

Lythara stepped back from the vault's edge. With distance, the pressure faded, and her breathing steadied. She straightened with effort, the composure returning to her voice. "The pain vanishes when I move away. It does not wound me, only enforces the terms. I cannot cross. If I try, it will kill me... or worse."

The group stood in silence.

Xavier turned back to the arch. His voice held quiet resolve. "You said your freedom is inside. We'll bring it back to you."

Lythara remained silent, her gaze lingering on him. When he finally looked back, their eyes met, and a silent understanding passed between them.

Ella gave Lythara's arm a final squeeze before moving forward. "We won't fail."

Behind the succubus Lianna checked her bow then gave Xavier a silent nod. Sihri adjusted the bindings of her fighting wraps, her ears twitching warily as she moved towards the Vault. Valkra and Frostclaw were the last two to follow, not because of hesitation just the limitations of the corridors leading the chamber had held them in rear guard.

Without further words, they crossed the threshold one at a time. No magic flared. No curse triggered. They simply vanished into the vault's darkness.

Lythara remained behind.

She stood alone in the lantern's glow, her eyes fixed on the place where they had disappeared. She did not turn away. The force that held her back was not made of stone or spellwork. It was a command written in infernal ink, etched into the core of her being, and it bound her more tightly than any visible chain ever could.

#

Crossing the threshold into the vault brought a palpable change to the very air around them. As they followed the downward spiral of the corridor, the atmosphere grew heavier and more oppressive. The weight of the earth settled around them like lungs closing in, each breath denser than the last. Sound diminished into a muffled hush, even their footsteps and breathing seemed dulled by the weight of ancient stone.

The walls along the corridor bore faint sigils, most long faded into near invisibility. But some pulsed dimly, their glow sluggish and weak, like the failing heartbeat of something vast and dying. The presence of such arcane marks confirmed what they had already begun to feel—this vault was older than memory.

Xavier halted as the path forked ahead. Placing a hand against the wall, he closed his eyes and reached out, not with sight or sound, but with the sense granted to him by the Earth Ley Line. He listened to the tension in the stone, the pressure beneath the surface, the silent stories carried by the earth. One path held something unstable, fractured —an old collapse or a trap meant to deceive.

He opened his eyes and gestured toward the left passage. "This way," he said quietly.

Ella followed without question. Lianna came next, eyes sharp and movements taut, scanning every edge of the corridor. Frostclaw stalked beside her, his muscles coiled beneath his fur, breath measured, hackles barely raised. Sihri moved behind them with ghostlike grace, ears swiveling constantly. Valkra brought up the rear, her footfalls soundless, her body low and tense, twin tails flicking as her eyes scanned every shadow. Even the youngest of them could sense they were not alone.

As they pressed deeper, Xavier began to notice strange flickers of movement at the edge of his vision. At first he dismissed them as tricks of the light, but then a thin seam in the stone ahead pulsed faintly with red.

He raised a hand, signaling a stop. Moving ahead, he crouched near the seam, careful not to touch it. He studied it from several angles until a notification appeared in his mind:

Keen Eye and Trap Awareness have identified a hidden trap.

Nothing more. Xavier sighed. Leaning close, he gently blew away a layer of dust. A dull crimson glyph shimmered faintly beneath the grime. It had been etched into a slightly discolored stone tile, subtle enough that even his trained eye had almost missed it.

Ella knelt beside him. "Containment rune," she said quietly. "It collapses the ceiling onto whoever triggers it. Cruel and brutal."

Xavier nodded, but his eyes remained fixed on the glyph. Though the lines were unfamiliar, there was something about the structure that felt almost... logical. He studied the layering of curves, the sharp tapers, the sequence of bends. It was like staring at a lock, and slowly recognizing the shape of its key.

"Let me try something," he murmured. He began tracing the rune in the air, not copying it precisely, but following the rhythm of its flow. The image sharpened in his mind, each stroke feeding an intuitive understanding. Finally, he completed the last flourish.

The rune pulsed once, then dimmed and faded.

Ella blinked. "You just disarmed a containment trap you've never studied."

"I didn't study it," Xavier replied. "I understood it. Like I already knew the pieces... and just had to see how they fit."

Ella offered a brief smile. "Then that rune is yours now."

Another notification confirmed it:

| You have learned a new | Level: 2 |
| --- | --- |

**rune:**

**Rune Name:** Containment Glyph – Crushing Seal

**Rank:** 2

**School:** Earth (Terramara) & Structure (Sub-discipline of Binding Runes)

**Activation Type:** Touch or Proximity

**Effect:** Upon activation, the rune compresses the surrounding structural supports in a sudden surge of force. This creates a cave-in, targeting the area directly above the triggering individual, crushing them beneath falling stone and debris.

**Purpose:** Designed for lethal containment, this glyph prevents trespassing or tampering by punishing unauthorized access with structural collapse. Often used in vaults, tombs, and ancient ruins where preservation of secrecy outweighs preservation of the structure.

**Mechanics:**

- Trigger Zone: Touch or 5–10 feet radius depending on the rune's design.
- Delay: 1-second delay after trigger to allow

SHADOWS OVER THE WILDLANDS

| |
|---|
| activation of compression spell.<br>- Collapse Radius: Up to 15 feet in diameter, depending on structural size and rune strength.<br>**Appearance:** The glyph appears as a spiraling, angular rune pattern, etched into stone with jagged geometric edges. It pulses with a dull amber glow when dormant, brightening rapidly when triggered. Faint vibrations may be felt nearby by those attuned to Earth magic. |

They resumed their path. With each step, Xavier's Keen Eye lit faint glows across the corridor, red for dormant traps, soft white flickers for hidden secrets tucked into crevices or seams. He made a mental note to return for the secrets if time allowed.

Suddenly, Frostclaw growled low. His ears twitched sharply toward the ceiling. Behind the group, Valkra mirrored the reaction, her posture tense, tails whipping with unease.

Lianna placed a steadying hand on Frostclaw's back, her voice low. "Something's moving. Above us, maybe behind."

They halted, weapons ready. But the silence held, and nothing came.

"We're running out of time," Xavier said. "Let's move."

They continued with brisker steps, eyes sharp for traps.

The corridor bent one final time before it opened into a triangular chamber. On the far wall stood three immense stone doors. Each bore a glowing emblem carved into its surface, the only parts untouched by the thick layers of dust.

Xavier approached the symbols, and his talent for languages activated. Ancient Ignithari... the language of the Phoenix Empire, long forgotten rival of the Sylmyrian Dominion.

He read them aloud: "Containment. Records. Sigils."

He turned to the group. Ella gave a slight nod.

"We find the Animari records and Lythara's contract first," Xavier said. "Then we look for the binding sigil on King Rorik. Let's move."

#

As they began moving towards the doors a faint white glow caught Xavier's attention. He paused and looked towards it more directly and noticed it originated from a spot nestled low along the base of the left-hand wall where the stone wall met the floor. It was tucked back into a shallow recess that was nearly swallowed by shadows which is why it had caught his attention. As he looked closer it pulsed once then held a steady glow, gentle and nonthreatening. Stepping away from the others he knelt to look closer.

Lianna followed him, "Trap?" She asked, her expression was cautious.

"No," he replied as he brushed away a fine layer of dust. "Traps glow red to my skill; this one is white. I noticed some earlier as well, but we bypassed them for time. I think this is a hidden secret or passage."

His fingers probed around the edge of the glow until

he found a faint seam, it was barely perceptible but to his eyes, augmented by his earth sense, it was unmistakable. He pulled out Vaeltheris and resized the blade to a small dagger. Carefully he slipped the blade into the groove and gave a firm but cautious twist. A soft click sounded behind the wall and a recessed panel slid open revealing the hidden cavity.

As the light fell upon the small space he saw a tightly bound bundle wrapped in oilcloth, resting atop the bundle was a circular stone disc that was about the size of his palm. The disc was dark and highly polished, shimmering faintly under the torchlight he could see its surface was inscribed with incredibly fin rings of concentric runes.

Carefully he picked it up, keenly aware of its ancient nature. As his hand closed on it he noticed it felt unnaturally cold to the touch. As soon as it was lifted more to the light and he could see the etchings his talent triggered again and he understood the writings and their meanings.

"Ignithari," he murmured. "Ancient Phoenix Empire…"

There was a slight intake of air from Ella as she moved to his side. "Are you sure?"

"Absolutely." He rotated the disc slightly and pointed. "See these are not words, they are coordinates. Multiple ones. My guess would be locations."

"Locations for what?" Lianna asked.

He shifted the disc so she could see them as well. "Vaults maybe? Other significant places. The symbols on the door are Ignithari as well."

Ella scowled slightly. "So they built more of these?"

Xavier nodded. "I assume these are all over where their empire was or had embassies."

On a hunch he changed his map interface, zooming it out until he could see the entire continent. A couple thoughts later he had added the various coordinates to the map as well and they glowed faintly in his vision. His assumption was right and the majority of them were in the Shattered Expanse.

"Most of them are in the Shattered Expanse," he murmured.

There was a long silence before Ella spoke again. "The Shattered Expanse was where the heart of the Phoenix Empire was prior to the Skyfire Cataclysm. If this one survived maybe some of the others survived there."

She didn't voice the rest of her thoughts though everyone had come to the same conclusion. That region had long been scorched into silence. Its unstable ley lines made it highly dangerous as they triggered arcane storms and mutated the flora and fauna found there. The nomadic tribes that lived along its boarders rarely ventured far or long into its interior. Its surviving secrets, if any remained, were sealed under ash and blood. But if something there still stirred, it might hold truths even older than the Vault they stood in now.

Xavier looked back at the bundle, still unopened. "We'll deal with the rest later. But this," he said, sliding the disc and bundle into his satchel trusting its space folding nature to protect them from damage, "this matters."

Whatever the Phoenix Empire meant to hide... it had just started to whisper again.

#

They stepped out of the alcove and started to move down the corridor leading to the central door. As they moved the corridor narrowed as the pressure in the air thickened, along the walls frost started to show but it wasn't from cold, the temperature stayed neutral. The frost increased as the dormant magic drew inward like a held breath until the shimmer appeared.

A translucent veil rippled across the passageway blocking further progress. It was nearly invisible unless they shifted to view it at an angle. Under Xavier's eyes it pulsed faintly with layered glyphwork, resembling concentric circles nestled inside each other, their outermost edges anchored to the walls with carved sigils. Xavier stopped the party once again and Ella peered over his shoulder.

"It's a live ward across the whole corridor," she stated.

Behind them everyone else stopped immediately and Ella moved to stand beside Xavier to get a better look. Her eyes narrowing as she stepped closer and studied the structure.

"It is not passive," she said. "It looks like a containment field. If triggered incorrectly it will not just lock us in it could obliterate everything within its reach."

Lianna growled from behind them, "Lovely." She then shifted to a low stance and turned to eye the ceiling and passageway behind them.

Sihri kept herself closer to the wall, her own stance low and still as well. Nearby even Valkra and Frostclaw were wary, both of their feline forms alert but unmoving as they could sense the threat from the ward as well now.

Xavier crouched near the base of the wall. His Rune Deciphering skill stirred as the sigils swam into mental alignment. They weren't Ignithari like the other markings they had found, but the containment logic was clean even elegant, in a brutal sort of way.

"Look here, they're using mirrored glyph anchors," he said, fingertips hovering just above a junction point. "It creates a pulse loop. If we break just one side, the whole thing detonates."

Ella looked at what he pointed out before she scanned the upper glyphs. "Here. That sequence there, it's a resonance echo. If we mirror it from the base junction and fold it through the center loop, it'll collapse the lattice safely."

Xavier closed his eyes briefly picturing what he had seen and what Ella had pointed out. The runes arranged themselves in his mind and he could see sequence, purpose, pattern. He felt the rhythm of the glyphs more than saw it. As though the stone itself was whispering how it wanted to be unraveled.

"I can do this," he said, and reached out carefully. He traced the mirrored rune sequence in reverse, carefully following Ella's directions. As his finger completed the final arc, a low hum vibrated through the stone. The veil pulsed once, twice, and then silently vanished. The air stilled.

Lianna exhaled slowly. "Subtle enough."

"No sparks or explosion is a win," Sihri added under her breath.

Ella gave Xavier a faint smile. "You're picking this up faster than I expected."

Xavier smirked at her before he straightened, his gaze falling on the massive door now fully revealed ahead. Its sigil was unmistakable, etched deep into the center in angular Ignithari script that matched what they'd seen before was a single word. Records.

Xavier stepped forward, resting a hand briefly on the stone. "This is it. The archive."

The Vault door stood before them, waiting.

Placing hands on the door Xavier pushed, it swung inwards with minimal effort, the craftsmanship such that it still was almost perfectly balanced. Inside the chamber was vast and still, its ceiling was vaulted and soared into the darkness above their heads, its details lost in the inky blackness. No light illuminated the chamber, the sole source of light being the torches that the group held aloft. For Xavier though, there were other faint white illuminations. His Keen Eye was triggering and revealing secret locations hidden away throughout the chamber.

Xavier stepped inside and scanned the walls slowly. He let his focus shift across the soft indistinct white glows. Most of them were dull, likely archival caches tucked behind stone panels or false shelves. All of them but one that is, it shimmered just a little brighter than the others, its shape larger and more distinct. It came from the back of the chamber, hidden beneath a sagging shelf that had old Animari knotwork carved into patterns across its edges.

Already moving towards the area Xavier spoke, "There is something here."

Behind him the other fanned out and he crouched down near the base of the shelf. A seam in the floor, it didn't match the rest of the floor, and he felt the distinct difference as he traced his fingers over the edge. As the dust was cleared the seam glowed brighter to Xavier's eyes.

"Help me clear this away," he told the others.

Sihri and Ella helped him clear several old crates and bundles of dry-rotted cloth off the shelf and move it out of the way. Beneath everything Xavier identified a pressure plate, it was not etched with any glyphs as had been found in the hallway leading here. Gingerly Xavier triggered the plate, and the floor groaned before a large panel slid out of the way with the low rumble of stone on stone. As the dimly lit opening widened, they could perceive a new stairway leading down.

Xavier sighed and rolled his eyes, the cliche of numerous games coming back to him. "Of course there is a hidden floor," he muttered.

Behind him Lianna groaned as well. The tension of the excursion into the vault wearing on the Iskari who much preferred the out of doors.

Ella tilted her head, listening. "No wards. No alerts. It was meant to be used, just not found easily."

Xavier led the way down. The hidden chamber below was small but meticulously preserved. Dozens of scroll cases lay organized by kin-type, each bearing the old Animari sigils: Cervari, Ursari, Vulpiri, and many more. Their wax seals remained intact. There was no dust here, no decay, this place had been preserved by intentional magic, not to protect the world from its contents, but to protect the contents from the world, and ravages of time. Xavier's hand hovered over one scroll case marked with a silver leaf: Lynari. He didn't touch it, yet.

"There's more," Ella said, moving toward a secondary alcove at the chamber's edge. "Look here."

A thick, black-bound case lay atop a pedestal, surrounded by faintly glowing runes of suppression, not defense. Again they were runes of storage careful, delicate magic.

These runes were unfamiliar now. His trait did not translate them unlike the others. Turning to Ella he raised an eyebrow to explain them.

Scowling slightly, she studied them for a long moment. "Infernal, these are not wards nor defenses.

Just preservation." She surmised, pulling from the ageless knowledge within the souls inside Vaeltheris

"It's a contract," Xavier guessed.

Ella nodded in agreement. "An infernal one."

His gaze sharpened as he knew of only one contract likely to be down here. "Lythara's."

He took a slow breath and reached for the case. As his fingers brushed it the white glow from his Keen Eye pulsed briefly... then faded, as if satisfied. No ward triggered. No alarm sounded. He lifted the contract case and turned to the others.

"We've got what we came for." But as he glanced back toward the shelves, toward the thousands of years of Animari bloodlines sealed here, hidden from the world he knew they'd uncovered far more than a mission objective. They'd uncovered a truth someone had gone to great lengths to bury.

#

Some time later they emerged from the hidden archive and left the hall of records. Making their way back towards the other sealed corridors they turned towards the one marked 'Sigils.' Xavier's enchanted satchel hung heavy, even with its weight reducing capabilities, it carried the bundled Animari records and Lythara's contract nestled inside its magical space. He could feel their weight pressing down on him more than just physically, they bore on his every step.

Frostclaw lead the way this time, tail low and steady as he prowled looking for danger. Valkra remained closer to Xavier now, her ears twitching and eyes darting from shadow to shadow alert to every possible change within the vault.

The right most chamber stood at the far end of its own stone hall, much like the records one had. Its massive door was cut from the same dark stone, likely granite, as the others but here the glyph seemed to be cut deeper, sharper even into the stone backing. Xavier shuddered slightly as it felt like a wound to the stone more than simple carving. As they moved closer the details of the sigil came more into focus it was not just 'Sigils' as previously noted, it actually read 'Sigils of Binding.'

Xavier started to move towards it but after the first step his senses recoiled at the assault on them. The magic in this hallway was denser than any previously experienced. It didn't compose of a warding barrier like with the hall leading to the records. It was focused on the door explicitly and it was woven with exquisite complexity not just brute force. Studying each rune that surrounded the doorway, Xavier could instinctively tell that they interlocked, like overlapping chains. They were not passive, nor were they reactive, they were binding a vastly intricate lock meant to do nothing more than keep the door sealed and deny passage to any but the one who laid them.

"That has to be it," Ella hissed as she studied the sigils as well. "Lythara said King Rorik's binding sigil was here. This must be the chamber that holds it."

Xavier couldn't disagree with her, but it seemed to obvious, the markings on the door were newer than the others but still done in the same script just with a different energy to his feelings. Almost as if an obvious trap were being laid for someone.

Xavier approached the door carefully, running his hand just above the surface. He didn't need to touch it to feel the resistance. The runes didn't flare or spark at all, in fact they didn't challenge him in any way. They simply existed, sealed in layers upon layers, forming a cipher of magical energy. He tried to parse the structure of the runes. His skill in rune deciphering enough to let him see that the lines coiled back into themselves, the arcs overlapped, repeating symbols nested three deep like recursive logic loops he had coded back on Earth. Every rune referenced another the whole thing was a self-protecting script.

"It's locked beyond anything I've seen," he murmured. "A living seal."

Ella stepped closer, one hand resting on the wall near the door as she focused once more drawing on the knowledge held within Vaeltheris. Her expression hardened as it came to her.

"They wove the wards with redundancy," she said. "If one link is tampered with, the others reset the entire structure. It is meant to outlive any tampering attempts."

"Can we break it?" Lianna asked, watching the corridor behind them with practiced tension.

"Not now," Xavier said, stepping back. "Not without unraveling the full structure. It'd take hours... or a key."

Ella's eyes flicked to him. "You think the Ignithari disc could be part of it?"

Xavier didn't answer immediately. His thought it might be possible, but this magic didn't feel like it was Ignithari. He had noticed the difference between the older magics they had unraveled and this one. It was Arenvalan. Likely cast or reinforced by Ivarik himself.

"It might be, but we'll need something more," he said at last. "And time we don't have."

Sihri shifted her weight. "Then we move before the Vault decides we've overstayed our welcome. We have already been here longer than we should have."

They turned as one, backing away from the door

that rebuffed them so completely. Xavier looked over his shoulder one last time, the faintest ripple stirred across the binding glyph. There was no sound no change in glow, but the door had noticed him; and something behind it had felt that recognition.

They hadn't made it far from the 'Sigils of Binding' door when a pulse of pressure swept through the Vault. It was not an explosion, it was not even a noise, but a ripple. The kind that shivered through the bones rather than the skin. The kind that meant they had been noticed by something. Xavier stopped mid-step. Valkra froze beside him, her hackles raised, body low and trembling in silence her tails lashing anxiously once again.

Then they heard the sound. Slow, purposeful bootsteps. It was not stone shifting, not magical mechanisms or even magical wards exploding in alarm. It was a person.

"Contact," Lianna whispered, already moving into a flanking position. Frostclaw mirrored her instinctively, lips peeled back in warning.

From the corridor behind them, just beyond the now unsealed Records door they had explored first, a shape emerged. It was tall and shrouded in a cloak of gray-black silk that moved like smoke. No features could be seen beneath the veil of the hood, only the outline of a humanoid figure, and a glint of something metallic beneath the folds: bracers, breastplate perhaps, or armor too finely crafted to make noise. It didn't speak. It had no reason to it was just there to deal with the intruders. And its presence was wrong, not infernal, abyssal, not elemental. Just... cold, controlled and surgical.

Ella stepped forward her twin swords held at the ready, her voice steady. "Ward construct?"

"No," Xavier said, instinct cold and certain in his gut.

"It's not part of the Vault."

Lianna's arrow was already notched and aimed towards the figure. Sihri moved to take slight cover in one of the alcoves her fists held at the ready.

The Enforcer didn't slow. It advanced with fluid steps, raising one hand as if to summon something but there was no spell cast, no chant rose from the folds of the hood. Only the feel of pressure sharpening in the air. Then the first blow came fast.

In the space of a blink, it was on them. Its strikes coming with precision rather than brutality. Xavier blocked the swing with Vaeltheris, back in his preferred short sword form, barely redirecting the force, but it was like trying to stop a moving wall so massive was the strength of the unknown being. He tried to trigger Insight but the skill was rebuffed as well only giving him a single piece of information. The things title "Enforcer." The thing didn't breathe, it didn't flinch, and it didn't miss.

Lianna fired. The arrow glanced off a shimmer of force just beneath the cloak. Not magical shielding, ward-forged armor. It was much finer than even what they had seen on the Redmaws or Lythara.

"A Shadow Court agent," Ella breathed. "It has to be."

"We have no proof," Xavier said grimly, dodging a sweep that cracked the stone beside him. "And it wants to keep it that way."

Sihri flanked it from behind, her metal reinforced wraps clanging against the armor beneath the cloak, but the thing twisted away before she could land a solid strike. It lashed out catching her with the back of a gauntleted fist. She rolled with the blow, cursing in pain but alive.

"We're not winning this fight," Ella said, own attacks

landing grazing blows that barely staggered the thing. "Grab the records. Get out."

Xavier slashed in a controlled arc the Emberstone sword following behind Vaeltheris' lead, covering Sihri's retreat. "Lianna, try and cover our escape."

"Gladly," the Iskari woman replied.

The team disengaged in a controlled rhythm, leapfrogging as they backed toward the path leading to the Vault's exit. Xavier felt the scrolls and contract thudding within the satchel against his hip. The mission was complete. They had what they needed, but the Vault would not let them go quietly. The Enforcer didn't pursue with rage. It didn't shout. It simply followed, methodically, without urgency, like a butcher preparing a table.

"Let's move!" Xavier barked, leading the retreat as Sihri pulled down a shelf behind them, hoping to slow the pursuit for precious seconds.

They didn't win the battle. That was not the goal. They didn't need to. They just had to escape with the truth of what they had found. They ran.

The halls of the vault sped past them as they ran up the winding corridor. Sigils, statues, traps and hidden compartments, empty chambers and silent wards all flashed by as they fled. The atmosphere had taken on an even heavier presence, as if the very structure of the subterranean location resented the fact that they were within.

However, no alarms sounded, no traps triggered, and no spells flashed into being to harm them. No, the only thing that hounded their steps was the soft echo of the deliberate footsteps following close behind them

As they rounded the corner and could see the archway

that marked the entrance to the vault Xavier hazarded a glance behind. The Enforcer had stopped, it now stood at the edge of the most recent corridor they had exited, its veiled hood turned specifically towards him. It was watching from the distance, and it made no further move to pursue them. It threw no parting attack, it didn't even make a sound, retaining its eerie silence.

As Xavier struggled to understand the difference the being lifted a hand. It reached out, pointing two extended fingers together towards Xavier and made a gesture so subtle it could have easily been missed.

Xavier, however, felt it. A prickling raised on his skin, faint, cold and worrisome. Somehow, he knew the Enforcer had marked him, not with a wound or a glow but something had been placed. He didn't know how he knew but he knew that a memory, or a trace, or some type of link lingered between him and the Enforcer, something that would have to be delt with in time.

Then the shadows swallowed the figure, and it was gone.

#

They emerged through the archway into the cold stone of the chamber that held the entrance of the Vault. A short distance from where they paused Lythara stood waiting with anxious patience for them.

The calm stillness of the air outside the archway was a balm to their nerves and almost felt surreal after the tension inside the vault. They still cast about furtively searching for the figure that had pursued them but vanished into the shadows before they escaped.

Sihri collapsed against one of the walls, her breathing still coming hard and fast from the flight. "Well... that sucked," she wheezed.

Lianna still held an arrow to string and turned to aim it back in the archway, she didn't let it lower until she was certain nothing was still pursuing them. "Yes, it did but we made it out."

Frostclaw and Valkra both circled the group several times before settling nearby their companions. Both of the felines still had raised hackles but they were otherwise unharmed by the foray into the Vault.

Ella stepped to Xavier's side, her hand briefly touching his arm as she glanced to the satchel. "You still have it all in there correct?"

"All of the Animari records... and Lythara's contract," he responded with a nod, his voice low and tense still.

Ella sighed in relief. "Then we did it, we still need to address the King's binding but we did the majority of what we came for."

Xavier didn't respond, his gaze lingered on the gloom beyond the archway. "No... we didn't just take information," he murmured eventually. "We took notice as well."

Lianna glanced at him ready to draw the bow again hearing his words. "Do you think it will follow us then?"

Xavier considered her question a moment then shook his head. "No, not for now. I don't think it needs to now. I think it knows me now."

Ella looked at him sharply. "You felt it?"

Sighing Xavier nodded. "Yeah, when it pointed at me and made the gesture."

The small party moved to gather around Lythara. The succubus was still unable to go closer to the Vault, so they compromised.

She stood tense, restrained by the clause in the contract that kept her away from the vault and eyeing them anxiously. Her reaction was visible when Xavier pulled the infernal scroll case from his satchel. Her breath caught and she surged forward a single step before the bindings of the contract stopped her once again.

Holding the case up Xavier spoke to her. "It's here, we got it as promised." He held the case out so she could clearly see it. Though it was still sealed, bound, and held her as firmly as before, Lythara's shoulders straightened and her eyes glimmered brighter with that tinge of hope from before.

# CHAPTER TWENTY-SEVEN

*A Devil's Bargan*

Their ascent through the catacombs beneath the city was arduous but unhindered by any further traps or enemies. As they emerged to the roads in silence, breathless and worn, they struggled to shake off the echoes of their experience in the Vault.

The storm that had provided cover and help to shield their infiltration had broken sometime during their ascent, its howling winds and crashing thunder now reduced to a light scattered drizzle.

The black night sky had lightened significantly, giving way to a pale bruised horizon. Dawn approached now, cold and unwelcoming harsh light. The streets of Ironhaven were beginning to stir with its usual early movements: patrols were regrouping, watchtowers changing rotations as the new shift blinked to life.

Guided by Lythara through the crumbling alleys and forgotten passageways, the small group slipped deeper into the city's underbelly, heading into shadows where even the guards feared to tread. It was in these depths where old smugglers refuges were found. One in particular of interest to Lythara.

In Ironhaven's lowest tier, behind a half-collapsed wall was where she found the hidden entrance she sought. It was an old smuggler's tunnel that had not seen use in decades, until she had found it during one of her late-night walks. Dust caked the stone floor, and the stagnant air was heavy with the scent of mildew.

Lythara pressed in ahead of the group, she was silent and focused, her hand tracing over the wall searching for something only she knew about. Finally, she found what she was looking for and her fingers traced out the outline of a concealed latch mechanism, rusted but still intact and working. With a sharp twist of her hand the latch turned, and the wall creaked open. As it shifted it revealed a narrow passage that wound downward into the rock of the city. Behind her the group groaned slightly at the thought of going underground once more.

"This way," the succubus said softly, and quickly stepped down the passage not bothering to wait for confirmation from the others.

Resolute, they followed behind her in silence, their footsteps muffled on the old stone of the floor. The tunnel walls were bereft of attached decoration or adornment and were damp to the touch. The ceiling of the passage was supported by old beams that sagged under the weight of time.

There was no light source within the tunnel, only the dim flicker of the torch that Ella had lit at the rear of the group. Shadows twisted back and forth across the corridor, dancing their macabre movements over long forgotten carvings and grime encrusted crates that were stacked in corners where the smugglers that used this tunnel hid their goods.

After several twists and turns, they emerged into a

small chamber carved directly out of the stone. It bore the marks of rushed crafting, reinforced beams, makeshift benches carved of stone, rusted chains bolted into the walls. Along one side a semi-collapsed fireplace squatted; it still bore the stench of long burned coal. The room had once sheltered fugitives and now it would shelter their group.

Central to the chamber was something out of place, a raised slab of dark obsidian, cracked but still intact. Its polished surface swallowed the flicker of torchlight that landed upon it, black as the void of Necroth. It wasn't a part of Ironhaven's foundation, it didn't even come from this region. It had been brought here, likely by Lythara, and set in this room for a purpose, waiting for what was about to take place.

The surface of the slab was barren, silently daring Xavier to move to it. Xavier could feel the weight of the infernal scroll, nestled in the special folds of his satchel, press into his side. It had not changed since they left the Vault, but his awareness of it, its very presence had grown heavier with burden.

Just inside the entrance of the chamber Lythara loitered, her gaze swept across the room with a haunted familiarity. Her eyes did not go to the others in the group, instead they settled on the slab. Her gaze pulled to it as if it were a gravestone bearing her name.

"This place once provided shelter for those who were fleeing gods, before the smugglers used and forgot it," she murmured, her tone was quiet and distant. "I thought it seemed fitting to be a place to break the contract, doesn't it?"

Again, she didn't expect an answer. Her arms clutched around her middle as though she was trying to keep something from breaking loose inside her body.

Xavier slowly crossed to the slab, unslinging his satchel with deliberate motions. The leather of the bag creaked softly the sound loud in the otherwise silence of the room. Reaching in he withdrew the scroll, sealed in red thread and etched with infernal glyphs that throbbed with faint power. He delicately placed it on the stone slab and a low breath escaped his lips as he stepped back. The scroll didn't move, but the air around it changed as if recoiling from the obscene object.

Ella moved closer to Xavier's side; her torch held higher as it cast long shadows over the uneven stone. Taking a knee near the slab but deliberately avoiding touching it or the scroll she studied it. Her brow furrowed in concentration as she examined the threads, the symbols and the heat sucking aura that surrounded the parchment.

"It is clearly infernal," she whispered. "But there is more than that here, there is divine magics as well. Something ancient, patient. Something that watches and waits behind locked doors." She scowled. "They are not opposing forces, they are complicit. Like a slave's collar sealed with a priest's blessing. The magics working together to ensure the binding."

Lythara did not respond. However, the furious twitch of her tail along with her pained inhale of breath through her nose spoke volumes. Her eyes were locked onto the scroll laying on the slab, as if seeing something that had haunted her nightmares for lifetimes in the flesh once again.

The rest of the room was silent and attentive. Lianna remained where she stood by the tunnel entrance, her bow held carefully in one hand as her gaze shifted between Xavier and the slab of obsidian. Frostclaw paced around the circumference of the chamber slowly, his body low and ears pinned back though no growl slipped from his chest. Valkra had moved to stand beside Xavier's leg, her small body was tense, her fur standing on end with her anxiety, twin tails lashing furiously behind her as if she was just waiting for something to strike.

Sihri, on the other hand, leaned against one of the crumbling pillars. The metal-studded wraps on her hands catching the torchlight and glinting like small stars. She had not spoken since they entered the room, but her posture was that of the ever-wary fighter she was. One foot bounced slowly on the ground, reminiscent of the way brawlers kept loose before a fight. However, even she ever composed, kept glancing furtive glances at the stone slab and one could see the tension she held in her jawline.

No one moved closer. Even Vaeltheris, from its spot on Xavier's hip, had gone silent. No hum, pulse or anything coming from the blade. Xavier studied the scroll for a long time. Moments drug out as he kept his breath steady and tried to figure out what he needed to do next.

As he did, the mark of the Kael'Sharyn slowly began to warm on his chest. Its faint light began to grow beneath his shirt. It was a soft steady glow, not bright in the slightest, nor with any urgency but as if it knew what was coming.

As the mark awoke, something inside Xavier stirred. It was not fear, or even confusion. Instead, he gained a quiet certainty. Though he did not know what he was supposed to do, he knew beyond a doubt that it was time for him to do it.

#

The silence in the chamber deepened, it pressed in from the stone walls like a second skin to those standing within. The scroll continued to rest on the obsidian slab, still and waiting, like a tether stretched almost too tight its very presence hummed against the edge of everyone's awareness. No one dared move, no one even dared breath too loud for fear of shattering the stillness and drawing some unforeseen foe forth.

No one that is, until Xavier stepped up to the edge of the slab. He did not bother to speak to the others, to tell them what he was doing or even ask them for permission to try something. In his core he knew what the answer would be, and he knew it was in his hands alone now.

Reverently he stretched his hand out over the scroll. His fingers did not close to grip it, they didn't try to crush it or break the multitude of seals on it. They just lightly touched it. The mark on his chest continued to pulse softly beneath his shirt, each thrum of power synchronized with a growing warmth in his palm and fingertips. He did not trace out any glowing runes of power, there were no whispers of incantations that escaped his lips. He only had the quiet resolution of knowing he stood precisely where he was destined to be.

With that knowing he closed his eyes and began to speak. The words forming in his mind drawn upon knowledge he did not realize he had access to, as if something was speaking through him instead of to him. He spoke not with power but with pure intent.

"I reject the chains forged in lies. I refuse the law written in cruelty. I sever what was never meant to bind. In this balance, I unmake this oath and contract."

As the words left his lips they reverberated, not aloud nor even with magical power. They reverberated in the very bones of the stone walls of the chamber itself. On the slab, something began to change. The scroll twitched, then began to tremble beneath Xavier's fingertips. A soft crackle filled the silence left by the reverberating words. It sounded like someone stepping on frost coated grass.

One by one, the seals on the scroll began to unravel.

They did not snap or even explode violently. They came apart as if deliberately picked to pieces. Red threads unraveled and curled away like ash escaping into a gentle breeze. Infernal glyphs glowed as if heated to white hot metal then vanished into oblivion.

The final seal, that which Ella had identified as the divine marking branded into the parchment itself, flickered as if resisting the unbinding then it too broke and faded. The parchment of the scroll curled inwards, its edges blackening as if burning to an unseen flame and in a final whisper and gasp of dust it was gone as if it never existed.

As the dust vanished, Lythara collapsed to her knees. A choked gasp escaping her lips as her aura exploded out from her form. Involuntarily she unleashed a flare of shadow and heat, the essence laced through with silver threads like bursts of lightning. Lythara clasped her hands to her chest and curled forward trembling faintly. Her breathing came in shallow uneven gasps. For a moment the room flooded with intense desire, brimstone, and pain and then it too was gone as quickly as it had come. Its passage left the succubus pale, shivering... and free.

Ella moved quickly to her side, keeling and placing one hand on the woman's back as she murmured quiet reassurances to her. She provided the shocked woman grounding and stability as she grappled with the sudden change in her fortune. No one else in the chamber moved, still thrown off balance from the pulse from the succubus as her contract broke.

Where Xavier stood, he had not moved his hand at all. It was still extended, the residual warmth of the powers and the scroll slowly fading from his fingertips. His heart thudded resoundingly, not from strain but from the very weight of what he had just driven from the world.

His mind grasped at what had just happened, he hadn't

channeled magic. He hadn't even invoked some divine name. He had just known what to say. Behind him, Ella's torch flickered once and the Kael'Sharyn mark pulsed with it before going dormant once more. Something intrinsic had shifted. A path chosen as surely as if he picked a fork in the road.

#

Scant moments passed when a shiver passed through the chamber. Again, it was not wind, not magic, no it was something colder, something aware. Xavier looked up in fear fully expecting the Enforcer to be standing beyond the slab.

A sigh of relief had just started to leave his lips seeing the space vacant when the shadows behind the slab started to move and stir. It tore at the mind because they did not move with motion but with a presence. Ella's torchlight flickered and faltered. Frostclaw froze mid-step and flattened his ears, teeth pulled back in a silent snarl. Valkra let out a low resonant growl as she pressed into Xavier's leg, her hackles even more on end than before.

As Xavier watched, the air behind the slab seemed to fold into itself like a silken curtain drawn through unseen hands and a figure emerged from the disturbance.

Xavier had never seen him before but the moment he appeared Xavier knew who it was. Not from sight, but from instinct. The wrongness that bled from the form and filled the room like a sickness was telling. The man who emerged into the light of the torch was tall and his features were sharply defined. He held a chancellor's poise with the weight and bearing of a warlord.

His frame was wrapped in a long overcoat of fine dark material, though its cut was austere and military in structure it still was fine enough for a noble. Beneath the coat, fitted armor of blackened mail and burnished leather gave a faint gleam, the visible surfaces were etched with fine infernal sigils that seemed to waver if one stared at them for too long of a time. It was the attire of one who felt at home both in the courtly halls of nobility and the councils of war on the battlefield.

When Xavier's eyes fell on the newcomer's face, he beheld features that were composed and bordered on handsome, clean refined angles, but they were expressionless in a way that unnerved any who beheld them.

"Well," the figure spoke, the voice coming out like steel wrapped in soft velvet. "That was... inconvenient."

No one in the group moved. Lythara kept her head down, she did not need to look up to know who was there. Instead, she spoke softly, "Ivarik Tharn..."

The others stared openly at the man. One they had only heard of in whispers and rumors. The one who was supposedly behind the changes to the slave laws, the foundation of the Shadow Court, the impetus behind the coming potential war.

Near the wall, Sihri tensed, her eyes narrow and focused. Lianna's grip tightened to a white-knuckle grip on her bow as her breath froze in her throat. Frostclaw shifted slightly to place himself between the obvious threat and his mistress, his muscles pulled taught beneath his fur as he prepared to defend her with his life. Ella remained frozen next to Lythara, her fingers still lingered on the succubus's back, but her eyes were on the stranger, hard and calculating.

Xavier, however, stepped forward to the stone slab, placing himself between his companions and the hellish presence that now filled the room like smoke from the fires of the abyss.

In turn Ivarik's gaze shifted to him and his mouth curled up at the edges, it was not in joy, or even mockery. The cruel smile was something even darker, recognition.

"You do not recognize me," he said calmly. "Not fully yet, but you have heard my name." He took a slow deliberate step forward, and though the floor did not crack under his booted foot it felt as if it should have. "I am Ivarik Tharn, Chancellor of the Kingdom of Arenvalis." His smile grew wider at his next words. "Architect of the slave accords and Lord of the Shadow Court." He was not even bothering to hide his machinations from the group. Even so his next words were the most shocking. "Devil of Nekros."

The last words hung like a brand burned into the very air of the chamber. Xavier did not speak, the others didn't even breath such was the weight of the admission.

"You have a choice Kael'Sharyn," Ivarik continued as if nothing were amiss. "You can decide to become the gods' enemy. Danu's last desperate gamble, one shrouded in defiance as it pretends to offer freedom."

His eyes flicked to the huddled form of Lythara then back to Xavier. The cruel smile on his lips shifting to one more calculating "Or you could have everything, protection, power, dominion. A place at my side in ruling. I will even leave your companions untouched and give you further lands and a title here in the kingdom. Imagine adding those to your paltry little village in the woods."

He gestured to dismissively to the slab and then motioned to Lythara. "All I ask is submission, obedience... and her return."

The offer hung in the air, heavy with a weight of its own. Xavier stood still and quiet. Once more the mark of the Kael'Sharyn pulsed on his chest suffusing his body with warmth and certainty. He did not respond with rage, righteousness, or fear. He simply spoke the truth of his being.

"No."

His response landed with a weight heavier that that of the offer. The weight of finality. He felt his mark flare in response to the word, not in light or heat but resonating with his choice, a silent refusal that echoed through the stone walls.

Almost imperceptibly, Ivarik recoiled at the word. His mask slipped for the barest fraction of a moment, just enough to be noticed. A tightening at the corner of his mouth, a flash of something feral in his eyes, the slip of his form showing the true shape of the devil it masked. The breaking of the contract had wounded him more than he cared to admit.

"You've made your choice then," the calm certainty of his voice was gone, now laced with venom and hatred. "And the gods do not forget defiance."

Around his form the shadows rose and wrapped, their shape like curtains rippling in a violent wind. The torchlight flashed to darkness for a single heartbeat and when it returned, he was gone. The silence lingering in the air in his absence was not that of peace and security, it was an unspoken warning.

#

The silence was ever-present filling the chamber like an oncoming tide. The torch did not crackle in it. Wind did not stir within it. Only the ragged sound of breaths, inhaled, held and released unevenly filled the absence.

Lythara remained kneeling on the stone floor, her shoulders curled into a hunched form as her hair cascaded around her face loosely. Her hands shook where they grasped the hem of her cloak. She could not quite grasp that her chains were well and truly gone. She was free to follow her own path for the first time in her memory. She did not sob; she could not sob. Her body instead shook with the weight of something far to expansive for simple tears.

Ella remained kneeling beside the succubus. She did not speak but simply stayed there with one hand gently on Lythara's back, resting between her shoulder blades. Her presence an anchor for the emotionally ravaged woman and letting her know that she wasn't alone in this moment. That this pain, this collapse, didn't have to be done in isolation.

It was Sihri turned away first, pacing along the far wall, her jaw tight, her breath hissing through her teeth. It was not fear that knotted her stomach, not doubt either. It was an overwhelming ache of helplessness knowing that even now, even after all they'd done, he could still find them, still reach them.

Lianna lowered her bow, slowly. Her eyes hadn't left Xavier. She didn't speak, didn't ask what he had done or how. Something in her gaze had changed. It was like she was seeing him clearly for the first time. He was not just the one who helped slaves escape. Not just the one who carried a strange sword and stranger allies. He was the one who had stood before a devil and said no. The growing admiration she had for him before felt a pale comparison to the new feelings that stirred within her now. Frostclaw moved and returned to her side, brushing up against her leg. Unthinking she rested a hand on his head and considered the future.

Valkra crept back to Xavier, silent, ears still low. She pressed her small body against his shin, protective and uncertain. He crouched for a moment and placed a hand gently atop back. The motion steadied them both. When he stood once again, he remained near the slab, unmoving. His hand hovered over his chest, where the Kael'Sharyn mark had begun to fade once again back to its dormant state, its glow dimming, its warmth retreating.

His mind rolled what had happened back and forth as he struggled to comprehend it all. Breaking the contract, he hadn't spoken a spell. He also hadn't drawn on Ella's knowledge or Vaeltheris's memory. It was something he'd simply... known. The words had come like breath. The action like instinct. And now, in the stillness that followed, he didn't feel triumphant. After the appearance of Ivarik, he felt... hollow. Like something had been given, and something taken.

He looked at his hand. Then slowly at the others. No one spoke. No one asked what had happened. They all felt it as keenly as he had. Something had shifted. In the soul of the freed, in the silence of the marked, in the heart of a watching world something had shifted.

And far away, in the blessed realm of Elunara, a place unseen by mortal eyes, Danu watched, silent, unseen, and unblinking.

# CHAPTER TWENTY-EIGHT

*The Flight from Ironhaven*

As the moments passed from Ivarik's departure the silence shifted from weighty to an overwhelming hollowness. The vacuum left in his wake was like that of a vast predator passing though the forest, close enough to threaten but just far enough for it to not take notice. The scent of his presence, smoke and brimstone, still clung to the walls like a shadow, however. No one shifted at first. It was not due to fear, they knew he had left, but instead due to bone-numbing fatigue. The exhaustion that was born not from exertion but from true survival harboring too much truth of the situation.

Xavier was the first to move, he blinked slowly as his eyes became readjusted to the flickering light of the torch in Ella's hand. On his chest he could still feel the Kael'Sharyn mark, it had ebbed back to its usual dormant state however the echo of its last surging pulse reverberated in his bones as if to tell him, "Your path has been chosen now."

Behind him, Ella and Lythara rose, their motions slow and deliberate. On her feet the succubus staggered but did not fall. She was weak, her limbs unsteady and her breath shallow and ragged. Despite this she now had a strength, a tension, in her spine that was previously lacking. The fire of survival and new freedom had reinvigorated her will. When she lifted her eyes to meet Ella's she nodded to the woman, a small silent nod of thanks and appreciation.

Sihri pushed off the wall she had been against. Her face hardened like stone with her inward focus. "That... he... he walked in like he had been here all along," she said through clenched teeth, her voice soft and low. "We had come in here like ghosts in a tomb and yet he still found us like we had paraded in."

Xavier turned to look at her, his voice just as soft. "He didn't find us." His gaze shifted towards Lythara. "He had found her." There was no anger or accusation in his voice, just the simple statement of fact. "And now he knows she's gone"

Lythara didn't flinch at his words. The edges of her eyes tightened slightly but she realized he was not holding her at fault.

The small group stood there staring at one another weighing options until Lianna moved. She secured her bow and crossed the room soundlessly. Stepping past Xavier without looking at him her shoulder brushed lightly against his. Not dismissive, or even aggressive, more as if ensuring herself of his presence, an anchor in the moment. "Then we flee," she stated simply. "We flee before he sends something far less courteous and accepting."

Nodding slowly Ella spoke. "Agreed," she murmured and doused her torch. The darkness surrounded them though faint light from bioluminescent mosses kept it from complete darkness. "No fires, no speaking unless necessary, we flee until we are clear."

Xavier turned to retrieve his satchel from next to the

stone slab. His eyes lingered on the large piece of obsidian. It was cool once again, inert and dark. That did not shake the sensation he had that it had been observing everything, the scroll, the unbinding, the devil's offer. It had been observing, remembering and judging, all of the events clinging to its smooth surface like a scar left by a wound.

Stepping to his side Ella gently took his hand. "Leave it," she said softly and pulled him towards the exit. "It is done." He glanced at her and nodded once before they both turned as he shouldered his gear.

Frostclaw moved to flank Lianna again. Valkra circled near the exit and let out a soft growl. The cub impatient, alert and anxious to depart.

Behind them, Lythara stretched out a single hand and ran it over the smooth glassy surface of the stone slab, not in reverence or thanksgiving but simple farewell, a closure of an age of suffering in her life. She then turned as well, her voice soft but resolute in its tone. "I remember the way out, follow me."

With that they moved quickly, back into the dark once again, shadows folding around them like a lovers embrace while they fled the chamber.

#

The worn tunnel ran before them, narrow, slickened with moisture and wear, its walls narrowing enough to brush shoulders in places and in others the stone of the ceiling sagging under the weight that collapsed supports that were no longer up to the task of bearing their burden. Time and the damp had worn the old smugglers' passages into jagged arteries beneath Ironhaven, veined with black mold that streaked the stone walls and ceilings. Through it all the group ran, Lythara in the lead.

The succubus' steps were certain, her body hunched

slightly forward as if she was sensing the way as much as seeing it. Her eyes, long adapted to the dark due to her biology more than familiarity, caught faint light from the bioluminescent mosses and compared it to her memories. Her traversal of the tunnels was more the return of someone instead of one exploring them. Every turn, every sloped decent and ascent, every jutting beam was familiar to her in a way that transcended simple sight.

"Step to the right here," her voice drifted back to the trailing group when she paused at the edge of a narrow cleft. "There is a crack in the tunnel on the left that will cause a collapse under weight."

Trusting her guidance, the group followed without question. Directly behind her Xavier followed with Valkra at his side, tight enough against his leg to aid his movements in the dark but not hinder him. The cub's ears flicked in constant vigilance, her eyes scanning the darkness for threats as her twin tails lashed in anticipation.

Behind them came Lianna and Frostclaw, the ranger carrying her bow low with an arrow on the string but undrawn. Ella came next near the rear and ready to aid Sihri if needed. The Leopari gladiator brought up the rear, her kinship with rabbits making her more comfortable in the underground tunnels than the rest but her fingers still twitched and clenched making her leather fighting wraps creak.

As they continued the air became thicker with age and mildew. The silence broken by the rhythmic droplets of water trickling through the walls. As times the moss that lit the tunnel thinned and they passed through stretches of complete blackness. Despite this, Lythara did not slow. Her fingers brushed against the stone of the wall every now and then, tracing over faint etchings from ages past, contraband sigils, smugglers codes and memory anchors.

"How many times did you walk these tunnels?" Xavier asked softly, his voice barely discernible in the darkness.

Glancing back briefly Lythara replied. "Enough to learn where the city forgets," her tone was steady and even. "Even shadows need to have their own roads sometimes."

In time they passed the remains of an old cart, its form long since rotted and its contents indiscernible except for the barest glint of a rusted blade peeking through age worn cloth. Nearby another sagging beam groaned softly overhead the weight of decades settling further. Xavier placed a hand on the stone wall, his fledgling earth sense flaring in warning of fractures overhead, old but on the verge of collapse.

"Keep low here," he murmured softly. "The roof is weak, don't speak"

The group passed beneath the groaning wood one at a time in silence, their breathing shallow and stressed until they reached an area beyond where the tunnel widened once again. Soon they came to an old junction. Here the moss thickened briefly, its glow illuminating a small expanse of carved stone. A worn and faded smuggler's sigil, three knives bound in a circle, was etched into the wall.

"Last turn," Lythara said. "Exit's ahead, behind a root-choked wall. We'll have to slip through single file."

As they rounded the final bend, the tunnel widened briefly, then narrowed into a slanted corridor choked with dangling roots and debris. Lythara moved without hesitation, her hands skimming along the wall until she found a faint ridge, a wooden frame set into the stone, half-swallowed by decay and time. She pressed inward and something creaked. After a few moments a hidden panel gave way with a low groan, revealing a narrow crawlspace angled sharply upward. Faint air filtered through, cooler, sharper, tinged with soot and distant torch smoke. The scent of wet stone gave way to the acrid mix of woodsmoke, tanner's ash, and the iron tang of city watch patrols.

We're beneath the old tanner's quarter," Lythara whispered. "Just beyond this slope is the eastern trade ward. If we time it right, we can reach the wall before the upper districts realize we're gone."

Xavier drew in a breath, tasting the shift in pressure, the subtle drop in tension beneath the city's weight. "Still inside the walls," he muttered.

"For now," Lythara said. "But not for long."

Lianna's expression was grim. "It'll be crawling with patrols soon. We need to move the moment we surface."

"There's a collapsed outer watch post just past the first alley," Lythara added, already slipping into the incline. "That's our way out."

Behind them, Valkra growled softly still showing her impatience. Sihri's muscles tensed, ready to run or fight as required. Frostclaw loomed like a silent shadow beside Lianna, nostrils flaring at the change in air.

Ella extinguished the last glimmer of moss-light with a brush of her fingers as the group ascended and at last, as they reached the top of the crawlspace and emerged behind a half-crushed brick wall in a refuse-strewn alley, the veil of the undercity fell away. Beyond the broken arch, the outer districts of Ironhaven stirred beneath the first light of dawn. Chimneys smoked. Streets bustled faintly with the earliest merchants and tattered banners fluttered in the windless morning. They had escaped the depths, but Ironhaven still loomed around them, and the walls had not yet been breached.

#

The outskirts of the city heaved breaths of smoke and silence in uneven bursts, as if the very buildings were exhaling something foul from its depths. They had emerged into the graybelt, the crumbling ruined district in the furthest southwest corner of the city. Here the streets were broken and cramped with ruin, the buildings abandoned, collapsed or half burned, the refuse of forgotten industry and commerce piled into damp corners. However, even through the ruins, the weight of Ironhaven's control still thrummed.

All around them were reminders that Ironhaven wasn't just a fortress city. It was a market of flesh and bodies, Arenvalis' primary slave hub and a place where coins flowed like blood and chains were a currency of their own. In the distance they could see the upper tiers of the city that gleamed with polished stone and gold trimmed banners a gilded front to the trade, but down here in the lower districts the truth was visible in every open space.

The open-air stalls, their cheap canvas providing bare cover in the rising sun, stood in rows not far from the alley where the group rushed through. Even at this early hour they could hear the slavers setting up their auctions, preparing to display racks of collars, shackles and custom brands being laid out beside the wooden blocks that had been worn smooth and glossy by scores of bare feet. From one of the pens, they could hear the sounds of hoarse coughing rising from those who hadn't been sold the day before.

Keeping to the shadows in the alleys Lythara moved with purpose, holding her cloak tight about her form her steps sharp and precise as she wove the path for the others to follow. She had walked these roads before, collared by her contract. Now she led the group, moving ahead of them to guide them through the forgotten cracks in Ironhaven's façade with a hunter's focus.

"Just ahead, there," she said as she pointed between two collapsed storage silos. "There is a spot in the southern bulwark, the storms split it a couple weeks ago, it is unwatched." A slight smirk touched her lips, "I made sure of that."

Xavier followed her gesture he could see where the wall slumped like a weary sentinel. The edifice supported a ruined scaffold near the breach, its boards blackened by fire, and its supports cracked. It was a perfect exit that no one expected anyone to use due to the danger of its collapse.

"They won't guard what they think no one dares," Lianna murmured.

But the city had other thoughts, and they heard a voice ring out from behind them.

"Stop! Stop right there!"

A shout echoed across the rubble, followed by the rapid clatter of boots. Two slave wardens emerged from the ruin's edge, one raising a crossbow, the other drawing a hooked glaive etched with the marks of the Ironhaven guard on its blade. Their red-and-gold sashes gleamed in the gray morning light, marking them as enforcers of Ironhaven's markets.

"You didn't just breach the Vault; you violated the heart of the Exchange. Halestorm has every city guard, Arenvalis conscript, and Redmaw blade not loyal to your whore commander sweeping the streets. You've made a wound that bleeds through every ledger in Ironhaven... and we intend to close it, slowly, and with your corpses as the suture."

Xavier moved to intercept; however, it was Lythara who

stepped ahead of him she raised her hand and traced four sigils through the air, each one glowing red-hot, sharp and controlled. They sank into the foundation stone beneath the scaffold. A symbol flared, Xavier's skill for runes identified it as the Mark of Collapse moments before it sank deep into the wall's marrow.

"Collapse," she said softly. "And remember who broke you."

The world seemed to pause on bated breath before the glyph detonated. The scaffold shrieked and crumpled. The wall shuddered. A gout of flame and pulverized mortar blasted outward, swallowing the wardens' shouts. The stone cracked with thunderous noise and the breach yawned wide.

"Move!" Xavier barked, he had already scooped up Valkra and ran forward through the rising smoke.

The others sprinted, through fire, through falling dust, over splintered boards and broken stone. The city's wall gaped around them as they fled into the grasslands beyond the city, one by one, they cleared the breach. Frostclaw leapt the last fallen beam, his fur streaked with ash. Sihri rolled through the dust and came up on her feet. Ella climbed out last, cloak tattered at the hem, her breath ragged. Suddenly they were free.

The hills beyond the wall stretched outward in pale morning gray, rocky scrubland, thorned ridges, and long trails barely visible through the shifting mist. The Silverwood was not nearby. Its shadowy green line was a distant smudge on the eastern horizon, at least four or five days' hard journey away. They had escaped the city but the wilds ahead would not shelter them easily.

Xavier looked back over his shoulder once. Smoke still curled from the shattered bulwark, glowing faintly red where Lythara's sigil had burned the foundation. Somewhere within the city, nobles were waking to the scent of fire, and Tavrek Halestorm's hunt would already be tightening.

"We've bought hours," Lianna said, falling in beside him. "Not days."

"Then we run," Xavier replied, "until the Silverwood swallows us whole."

And without another word, they fled into the wildlands, no longer just escaped fugitives, but carriers of the wound Ironhaven would bleed from for the rest of the burgeoning war.

#

As Xavier's party ran into the early morning fog concealing the wildlands, behind them Ironhaven was awake. It was not with the bustle of trade or the rhythms of a market city rising for another day of coin and cruelty, instead it was with the sharp, spiraling panic of a system realizing it had been wounded.

In the heart of the Exchange District, the first auction stalls were still being unfurled, their canvas flapping loosely in the wind. A few unsold Animari slaves knelt beneath iron arches. Their eyes were half-lidded, unaware that the ledgers, their very commodification, were gone. However, the merchants knew, and the wardens knew, and deep in the armory, beneath the banners of the Slave Exchange and the sigils of the Crown, Tavrek Halestorm stood overlooking a map of the city, its sectors etched in blood-colored chalk.

The reports were still coming in. "They hit the Vault of Chains just before the fourth bell," said a courier, her voice tight with controlled fear, the commander was known for lashing out at those who displeased him. "Broke through the outer catacomb, used old smuggler routes where we found a ritual slab. One of the infernal contracts was destroyed."

"Which one?" Tavrek asked without looking up.

"Veyne's," came the soft voice quivering in further fear.

The chalk snapped in his hand, but Tavrek didn't flinch. He simply turned to the massive war-table and placed the jagged half back in its slot. His eyes, icy gray and framed by age lines earned in the southern campaigns, settled on the scattered icons representing guard companies, conscripted Arenvalis troops, and Redmaw squads.

"Deploy the Halberd line to the granary quarter. Reinforce the Exchange tier with First Pike. I want snare circles at every known breach point, magical or mundane."

"Sir, if they've already cleared the wall, the trails..."

"The scrub will not hide them," Tavrek said flatly. "They have days before they reach the Silverwood. That's three hundred hours of open land. We have twelve hundred boots in the city, a hundred Reavers not loyal to Veyne, and the eastern pikes already sweeping the lower terraces. We will outpace them. And when we do..."

He looked to the forgebrand officer at his right, a former Reaver lieutenant with half his face burned and eyes like scorched coin.

"No prisoners. Not this time." He stated coldly.

The officer nodded once. "Understood."

Outside, bells began to toll, not in alarm, but in coordination and command. The slave houses, for the first time in decades, had closed their ledgers mid-morning, buyers were turned away, coins returned and auctions delayed. No trade was to take place until the breach was resolved. Ironhaven did not mourn the dead guards. No it mourned the loss of control.

In the Noble Quarter, cloaked men whispered in drawing rooms lit by everburning lanterns. The Shadow Court had not spoken publicly, but their silence spoke volumes. Within the deepest depths of the city the Vault of Chains was quietly being sealed and moved. One contract destroyed meant the others were vulnerable.

Tavrek Halestorm stood alone in the guards keep as the last pieces were set into motion. He stared out the high window overlooking the cracked eastern bulwark, smoke still trailing in thin streams from the ruin.

"They've drawn blood," he murmured. "But they've forgotten what it means to bleed Ironhaven." He turned, cloak snapping behind him, and gave his final order. "Seal the city, and light the beacons. I want runners sent to Thandor's Reach."

# CHAPTER
# TWENTY-NINE

*River, Flame and Faith*

The sky above the Wildlands slowly turned bruised grey in color, and on the horizon, they could see the faintest stain of smoke rising from the eastern quarter of Ironhaven. Even at this distance, across miles of dry ridges and the thorn-raked scrub of the lands the wound they had opened in the flank of the city still smoldered on in accusation of their actions.

They had not stopped running since escaping through that wound, opting to run through the day and most of the night. The brutal pace took them southeast before veering sharply westward to avoid any roads, ruins, checkpoints and waystations. Lianna's pathfinding skills had been ruthlessly pushed to find them a way through gullies, dry creek beds and broken hills that left the party exhausted, bent legged and scraped of palm.

Now, however, the first light of morning fell upon them as they crouched in a natural hollow that was tucked into a wind scoured bluff. It was not so much a shelter as much as an obscure location that provided them with a spot where they would be overlooked by searchers unless they knew precisely where to look.

Xavier leaned back against the hard stone wall, his breathing shallow and every movement caused aches and pain. In the satchel at his side, he felt the weight of the ledgers, not physical weight but the burden of knowledge. They were more than simple parchment and ink, they were the collective of proof, thousands of names, dates, sales, brands and ancestry. The anatomy of a trade that minimizes lives to no more than simple numbers, commodities. His fingers moved to hover over the flap of his satchel though he did not give in to opening the bag, for now.

At the end of the small hollow, Lythara crouched at the edge of the shadow, her eyes fixed on the thin plume of smoke in the distance. "They will be sweeping this quadrant already," she all but whispered. "Halestorm will not assume we went to the east. He knows how fugitives think and will predict we ran for cover instead of confrontation with his forces."

"He will be right," Sihri muttered as she brushed dust off her clothing and wraps. "We really are not ready for large confrontations."

"It does not matter," came Lianna's voice from overhead. Her face popped into view as she peeked over the edge. "There are riders on the high ridge, four maybe five, but they are sweeping wide. I am guessing they are scouts."

"Colors?" Ella asked. She did not look up from where she was tending to one of Valkra's paws, the cub had scraped it raw during one of their descents and it was causing her trouble.

"I did not see any house banners. They were black on red though," Lianna responded.

Lythara sighed. "That means they are Redmaw, likely the ones that stuck with Ivarik."

Tensing at the news Xavier asked, "Are they tracking us?"

"It does not seem like they have found our trail yet," came Lianna's response. "But they will."

Lythara's voice was flat when she finally spoke again. "Tavrek Halestorm won't rely on city guards, not for something like this. He will have the Redmaw Reaver remnants out in force, those who were not loyal to me, anyway. He will also use the soldiers and the conscripts from Arenvalis' Army... they'll be obedient, but slow. It's the Reavers we need to worry about."

Ella finished with Valkra's paw, giving the cub a soft pat. "Then we keep moving before they catch our scent."

Xavier glanced again at the satchel. "They're not chasing slaves," he said quietly. "They're chasing what we took from their vault."

Lythara's crimson eyes met his. There was no fear in them, no anger, only clarity. "You did not just take documents," she said. "You wounded them. You carved through their illusion of control. You made the system bleed."

A dry wind kicked dust off the bluff's edge, scattering it into the air like old ash. It caught the sun just beginning to rise, turning every particle gold for the span of a breath before they vanished again.

"And Ironhaven," she added, "doesn't forgive those who make it bleed. Now they want to prove it was just a fluke."

They moved in silence after that, slipping into the ravine beyond the bluff's edge, as they departed they left no trace but a broken heel print and a trace of shadowmane blood. Behind them, the wind carried the last curls of smoke from the eastern bulwark, a whisper of rebellion, already fading into legend.

#

The wildlands stretched out around them like a sun-bleached wound, rolling hills of brittle grass, shale-cracked ridges, and long-forgotten trails half-swallowed by time and weather. The sparse trees that remained were stunted and dry, their roots clutched at dust of the land instead of rich fertile soil.

The wind graced them with its presence often and it always had grit on its breath. They traveled in silence, no fires lit their nights, no songs filled the air, no easy words passed between them. Only desperate rush and anxious looks for any sign of being trailed.

The days passed in sun and stone, each hour measured in blisters, breath, and raw endurance. Their path arced south-westward to avoid the ruins of Bramblegate, then angled south again. They always kept the distant shadow of the Silverwood just over the horizon, like a promise they weren't yet allowed to reach but ever drawing them onwards.

Lianna led most often, her sharp eyes scanned the terrain with instinctual and skillful caution. Frostclaw padded beside her, his movements were silent as breath, and he occasionally stopped to sniff the wind. Where roads once crossed these hills, nature had long since reclaimed them with thorns and dry washouts.

Sihri marched near the center of the group, muttering under her breath, the words were from her homeland, sharp-edged and rhythmic. Her movements were steady, coiled, the gait of a fighter conserving every ounce of strength. Her cutting humor was gone now, replaced by a narrowed focus.

Xavier walked second behind Lianna, his satchel grew

heavier by the day. The ledgers seemed to press against his hip with the weight of history. Each time he adjusted the straps, he could feel the pressure of names against his body, children, families, brands, prices.

Ella had taken to moving beside him often, never asking if he was alright. She only kept pace, her presence a quiet tether of strength and support. When the terrain grew rough, she would catch his arm without comment. When they passed old cart tracks or scorched earth, she'd murmur about their likely age and origin.

Lythara trailed behind most of the day, always watching their flanks. She didn't speak often, but she noticed every shift in the wind, every bird that stopped singing. The farther they traveled from Ironhaven, the more her expression shifted, going from numb, to haunted, to something distant. Freeing her had removed her chains, but not the scars.

"They will stop sweeping behind us by now," she said late on the third day. "If we were not caught by now, Halestorm will likely assume we are running deep."

"Isn't that exactly what we're doing?" Xavier asked.

"No," she said. "Running would mean we're trying to vanish. We are not, not really anyways. You are heading toward something, not away."

He didn't respond, because she was right. He just hadn't named it yet and he was slightly disturbed at how she had figured that out.

On the fourth evening, they crested a rise and saw it, a thin line of green cutting across the world to the south. Not Silverwood proper, not yet, but its outer thickets. Trees that had grown tall and defiant despite the thinning soil and Arenvalis' distant reach. They didn't celebrate. They knew they were not safe from those they had injured yet.

They set camp beneath a cluster of leaning stones that once served as a watch platform for trade caravans. Now, it was shelter if just barely.

Xavier knelt beside a crumbling foundation and pressed his hand to the earth. He closed his eyes. Through his connection to the ley, he felt the memory of passage, not Arenvalis guards or soldiers, not Reavers. He felt something older, quiet. Something that had moved through the stone decades ago and still lingered in the bones of the earth.

"We're close," he said quietly.

Lianna nodded, her eyes already turned south. "Tomorrow, we reach the first bend of the river."

#

They had a collective sigh of relief when the river finally came into view just as the sun began to dip behind the treetops, its glow cast the Silver Reach in radiant hues of gold and rust. The banks were soft with moss and worn stone, the current strong but not violent, a living ribbon drawn through the woodlands eastern hem.

They reached the banks wordlessly. It had been nearly six whole days of constant frenetic movement. Rushing along half-hidden paths, ghosting through Reaver patrols and ghosting away from any sign of life to get this far. Now the water, real flowing water, not the water they had that trickled from a cracked spring or seeped through ruined stone, lay just before them a reward for survival that no one had dared ask for during their flight.

Camp was the first priority though. They moved out of habit now, rolling out cloaks and bedding, checking their packs, unstringing bows. They still did not dare light fires, nor pitch tents. The camp was just open air next to the gentle babble of the river.

Xavier didn't speak, as the others settled into their evening routines, he shouldered his satchel and slipped away upriver. He followed the curve of the bank until the sounds of the group faded behind him, not far, but just far enough to be alone.

It was there that he was able to find a small tide pool tucked between some stone outcroppings, the water had carved out softer earth leaving behind a natural large stone tub against a shallow embankment. A place the world had forgotten that was shielded by moss covered rocks and sheltered beneath willow boughs.

He undressed slowly, the silence welcome, but the solitude more so. Setting the satchel atop his piled clothing he moved to the water of the pool. A sharp inhale was the only noise he made, the water was frigid, but clean. As he stepped in, the cold wrapped around his calves, thighs, chest, each inch a baptism and cleansing of what had come before. He didn't gasp besides the initial one, instead he simply let it take him. The current whispered over stone, pulling the weight from his muscles, the dust from his skin, the pressure from his thoughts and, for the first time since Ironhaven, he let himself go still.

Back at camp, the others moved without hurry until they noticed his absence.

Sihri stretched her arms overhead and cast a look upriver. "He wandered off. Probably found a place to sulk, or bathe, likely both."

"He deserves a minute," Lianna muttered, as she checked Frostclaw's pads for burrs or small twigs from the scrub of the Wildlands.

Ella glanced in the direction Xavier had gone and smiled faintly. Then she set her gear aside, rose, and walked without a word.

It was Sihri who moved next. She stripped off her bracers and overshirt casually with practiced motions before she wandered off, tossing a grin over her shoulder. "If he drowns, I call dibs on his pack."

"Leave the cloak," Lianna called dryly. A few moments passed before she followed them, quietly, not rushed. She didn't explain herself to anyone as she did so.

Lythara lingered the longest, she was watching the water with her usual detached amusement. Then she exhaled through her nose, slow and deliberate, and made her way upstream as well.

Xavier was waist-deep in the tide pool when he heard the first splash. He turned and saw Sihri, grinning, already up to her neck.

"You didn't think we would let you have the river to yourself, did you?"

He blinked, more surprised by her nudity than her joining him. "I was hoping."

She laughed and dove under the water.

Ella appeared next, slipping into the water without comment, calm and serene. Her presence didn't disturb the peace, instead she simply joined it. Her eyes met his once, and she smiled softly before drifting toward his side settling next to him her fingers just brushing his under the water.

Lianna stepped into the pool a moment later, hands behind her back, her expression neutral. "I will be over here," she said simply. "No commentary."

"Wouldn't dream of it," he muttered.

Finally, Lythara waded in gracefully, unhurried, letting the water rise around her like it was part of her. "For fugitives," she mused, "you all take bathing very seriously."

"We're hiding in plain scent," Sihri replied, splashing water toward her.

It earned a ripple of laughter. Even Lianna smirked at the comment.

Frostclaw padded along the edge, dipped a paw in, then flopped dramatically into a shallower part of the pool. Valkra, after sniffing the cold surface and sneezing, retreated indignantly to a patch of moss with a huff.

For the first time in what felt like an eternity, they laughed, not because they had won, or because they were safe, but because they had survived long enough to feel like people again. The water carried the sound downstream. The wind didn't betray them. As the stars began to rise, for that brief moment, the world let them rest.

#

After the bath, the river's chill still clung to their damp skin as they returned to their camp. Overhead the last of the day's light filtered through the thick canopy like rays and fragments of timeworn gold. No one spoke but collectively they all moved slower now, it was less from fatigue and more from the release of the tension they had been carrying since breaching the city wall. The river had taken something from each of them as it flowed past their bodies, it washed away the weight of smoke and fear that had still clung tenaciously to them. In its wake it left them quieter, sharper, and refreshed.

As they settled back in around the campsite, Ella gathered together a small ring of stones.

"A small fire here should be fine," she said softly running her fingers over the moss-lined creation. "Here, the trees should break the wind, and any smoke will be dissipated by the canopy."

Lianna nodded from nearby where she was helping brush and dry Frostclaw's fur. "Arenvalis was not running patrols this deep into the woods yet. The canopy should also help spread and mask the scent as well."

Xavier caught Ella's eye for a short period then gave a small nod. "Alright but just enough to keep warm."

As a group they gathered dry twigs, bark and small fallen branches, guided by Lianna's survival skill. Something that increased Xavier's own skill by a point much to his pleasure. When the Ranger sparked the fire to life with practiced ease, it was low, small and nearly smokeless, just a faint glow instead of a burning beacon. To the group, however, even the small flame felt like defiance to what they had fled from. They were nearly safely back to their lands now.

As the darkness gathered they formed a loose circle around the fire, cloaked and quiet in the dusk's gloom, none of the worlds moons had risen yet just the faint light of the fire and stars that broke through the canopy lit the world around them.

They remained quiet, not out of the tension of their flight but instead out of reflection of what had happened. The fire's warmth slowly leeched chill from skin and replaced it with its own sensation. Sirhi stretched her long digitigrade legs out. Valkra curled up near Xavier's bedding, her fur still sticking up in patches from the damp that clung to it. Lythara sat with her knees drawn up close, her crimson eyes flickered with the flamelight, ever unreadable.

Xavier leaned against a tree root, staring down into the firelight as if it held answers the stars overhead refused to give. "Why do the gods keep interfering?" he asked at last.

"I keep reading of their interactions with mortals in the legends of this world, and what are they really like?"

There was no hesitation. Lythara sat forward, her voice calm. "There are three pantheons," she said. "And none of them stay idle."

She proceeded to tell of the Radiant Pantheon. They were supposedly the champions of good, yes, but also enforcers of order. She told how they were led by Solara, and their ranks were full of Lawful Good, Neutral Good, and Chaotic Good deities who wielded light and right like a hammer.

She then described the Veiled Pantheon, led by Danu. The gods of balance, endings, and the turning of the great cycle. Lawful, True, and Chaotic Neutral in nature. They were seen to intervene only when the balance is at stake. And even then... rarely with mercy coming down on everyone equally and brutally normally.

And finally, she told of the Boundless Pantheon. Led by Nekros, they seek transformation through ambition and collapse. Lawful Evil, Neutral Evil, Chaotic Evil deities, their gifts always come with a price. And they never forget or forgive a debt they see as owed.

"They all shape the world in their image," Lythara concluded. "Some with chains, others with silence, but always with consequence."

Sihri tossed a twig into the flame and watched it catch fire before she asked, "So mortals are what? Footnotes in divine arguments?"

"Footnotes that bleed," Xavier murmured.

Ella looked over to Xavier, her eyes steady. "And maybe, eventually, one that writes back."

The fire crackled softly between them. The wind had

died. Even the river's voice seemed as if it had grown hushed, as if it too, was listening.

They didn't speak again for a while. But the silence no longer felt uncertain, instead it felt like the moment before a question finds its answer.

#

The fire had settled into a quiet rhythm just embers now, low, slow, warm. It was the kind of fire built by those who knew how to hide and still needed light.

Lianna hadn't spoken during the conversation about the gods, but as the silence stretched and the fire flickered lower, she finally leaned forward, her arms resting across her knees. When it came her voice, was thoughtful, not bitter, but measured.

"I don't know everything. No one really does. But there's a story I've heard more than once."

The others turned to face her as they listened.

"It's said that in Year 12898, it is currently the Year 13097," she clarified for Xavier, "the gods enacted something called the Divine Edict of Order. Not all of them mind you, just the ones who follow law aspects. It was gods from the Radiant, Veiled, and even some from the Boundless Pantheons."

She looked toward the fire, as if she could see the tale reflected in its glow.

"They didn't send down heralds or divine signs, there was no thunder from the sky. It was just a... change, a shift in how the world moved. What was once questioned became unquestionable and what was debated became law."

As she spoke, she drew a line in the dirt beside the fire. "After that, things changed in Arenvalis. The slave codes got sharper. More permanent. Noble houses stopped claiming divine favor, they started invoking it. Then there are the rumors about the Shadow Court..." she paused. "They didn't appear overnight, but they grew stronger as the years went by, like something unseen had opened doors for them, they were the quiet ones, the hidden ones, the ones ruling the Kingdom in the shadows."

She looked up. "As to how the Edict was decided, no one speaks of it openly, no one confirms it. But I've heard the stories, travelers, Animari elders, even some temple initiates who spoke too freely after wine and that is how I have put this together. They said the Edict was a vote, one that Danu opposed. The rumor is that she stood against it but was outvoted. And after that... she stopped speaking altogether with the other Pantheons."

Ella frowned, her gaze distant. "If it's true, it explains a lot."

"Truth or not," Lianna said, "the world changed after that year, and none of it changed in our favor."

Sihri tossed a pebble into the fire circle, her expression unreadable. "So the gods handed down balance... and called it justice."

"They handed down structure," Lianna corrected. "And left us to call it whatever helped us survive it."

The fire crackled softly. Xavier stared into the coals, his jaw clenched tight. "If it was real... if they really did that... what happens if someone breaks that law?"

No one answered for a long moment. Then Lythara, voice like velvet soaked in smoke, "then they're not just breaking the law. They're breaking the illusion of control., and the gods, even more than Ironhaven," she added, "hate losing control."

The fire dimmed to embers. No one spoke again, but at that moment something had shifted, not in fear, but in clarity.

#

The evening passed and each turned introspective. Over time they shifted and made themselves comfortable to rest. The fire had long since burned down to mere glowing coals, no longer bright enough to even cast shadows but their heat radiating out to warm those nearby and hold the group close to the small pit.

Most of the group had since gone still and quiet. Sihri dozed lightly, her back resting against her pack and her cloak draped over her legs. Valkra lay curled up beside Ella, her body rising and falling with each of her slow deep breaths. Lianna reclined opposite the fire from Xavier. She was leaning against a moss covered rock and through hooded eyes was watching Frostclaw's ears twitch as the great snow leopard dreamed his dreams.

Xavier also remained awake. He was seated near the fire's edge, his arms draped over his indrawn knees loosely. The night was in its depth now, thick with the light of stars and several moons that gave an odd glow to the mist rising from the river. Xavier smirked slightly thinking how it seemed that the world was in pause between major events, then he snorted slightly, having a feeling of portent.

Unclasping his wrists, one hand moved to his chest. It came to rest over where he knew the Kael'Sharyn mark sat. It didn't burn per say but it tingled, a subtle hum. It wasn't the urgent sense of warning, just enough to let him know it was there, waiting and perhaps listening. He had listened while the others spoke of gods as rulers, of this Edict as a chain that bound the world to a specific path.

While he could see that as a possibility, he had broken

a devil's contract with barely a touch. He had been able to sever something that should have been beyond mortal, and if Lythara was right, beyond immortal ken. He, a man from Earth, had been able to shatter it without spell, without prayer, just his will.

That is what troubled his thoughts now, and he wasn't sure what it meant in the grand scheme of things. "Maybe this mark isn't just Danu's blessing," he murmured to himself. "Maybe it is her crack in the proverbial wall, her way of breaking this Edict."

Beside him he heard someone stir, a soft rustle, Ella. She sat down quietly at his side. As she did so she pulled her cloak tighter about her shoulders warding away the chill night air. The soft glow from the embers touched her face gently and brought softness to her solemn expression.

"You think it is meant to break something?" She asked softly.

He hesitated then nodded. "Maybe," he responded. "Or maybe its Danu's way of reminding the gods that they are not untouchable either."

Ella didn't speak in response, instead she leaned into him resting her head on his shoulder while he mulled the possibilities.

"The gods bind the world with their laws, the system enforces them," Xavier finally continued his thoughts aloud. "But everything, even laws, have beginning and endings."

From her spot across the fire, Lianna stirred. She still hadn't fallen asleep. She shifted slightly now watching the pair subtly. Watching Xavier subtly, something unreadable in her hooded eyes. It was not distrust anymore, but it was uncertain and growing.

Lythara was the only one who sat apart from the small group around the fire, her legs were drawn to her chest, and she rested her chin on one knee. When Xavier glanced her way, their eyes met for a heartbeat in length. Her gaze was sharp, curious, and hungry in a way that had nothing to do with the usual appetites of her kin.

So softly that no one heard it the succubus whispered. "You do not even realize it yet. You have already begun to unmake the designs of the gods."

A popping from the fire drew Xavier's attention back to it as a coal broke and collapsed upon itself sending a brief puff of ash and cinders skyward into the night. He reached out and nudged a charred stick deeper into the embers.

"They rule from above," he said quietly, "but its us who bleed. Maybe its time that mortals write something of our own."

The fire flared briefly as the stick caught flame once again. It cast soft light across the faces of the watchful and the sleeping alike while overhead the stars and the moons continued their relentless trek across the night sky.

# CHAPTER THIRTY

*The Dream and the Chain*

The soft soothing sounds of the river didn't so much fade into silence as they lulled Xavier into peaceful slumber. At first it was the deep dreamless sleep of the soul exhausted, he was aware of nothing around him besides the vast expansive darkness that oft times followed days of exhaustion and exertion. That did not last however, the darkness started to thin, faint light resolving into the world around him.

He did not open his eyes to the trees and sounds of the Silverwood and the Silver Reach River next to their camp, instead he found himself standing in a vast and boundless field. The grass lit silver by the faint light while overhead the sky had taken on the tint of deep twilight. Disturbingly there were no stars in that expanse, no heavenly bodies whatsoever, instead he beheld undulating constellations, their cold light formed from seemingly living sigils that wrote and rewrote themselves on the inky canvas of the night sky.

And he was not alone.

Ahead of him, the mist slowly parted to reveal a woman veiled in soft silver, her long luminous hair of sanguine sheen flowed like silk strands disturbed by a unseen and unfelt breeze. There was no boisterous or loud fanfare to her presence, it was a soft, deliberate and inevitable presence, like the slow turning of seasons and the grinding passage of time. Her eyes were fathomless, the dark orbs reflecting not himself standing before her but seeming the whole of creation.

She, Xavier knew without introduction. He had seen her before even if not in this form… Danu.

Before he could react, she opened her mouth to speak and the voice that issued forth was like a stream cascading over ancient stones. It was ageless, calm and yet it carried the weight of everything that had come to pass, existed and was yet to be.

"The world stirs, child of earth and echo. Beneath the mountains you have not yet climbed something sleeps, a nexus of lines older than the gods' decree"

The sound of her words reverberated through the very ground he stood upon, a tremor that shook as deep as bedrock itself. Overhead the sigils shifted from constellations to form the outline of a vast mountain, at its roots was wrapped a radiant core that pulsed, then pulsed a second time, then faded to silent presence.

"It sleeps not by nature but bound by chains wrought in fear. Fear of what you might yet revive and awaken."

A thousand questions thundered through Xavier's mind, a hundred thousand fought in the darkest recesses of his conscious thoughts straining to be brought forth. He opened his mouth to speak but only silence issued forth. No words came, the dream held him perfectly in a silent audience. And Danu stepped closer. He could smell the subtle scent of rain on dry soil, that clean smell of nitrogen as the drops first started to strike clung to her robes.

"Another chain binds closer still though."

Overhead the sky changed once again. The mountain vanished and was instead replaced by a crown, a shattered crown, a jagged line sundered its middle and it was suspended over twisted and gnarled tree roots. The whole image was bound with sigils of divine nature that burned gold and white in color. The roots of the tree twitched but their movements were weak bound as they were by the glowing chains.

From right in front of him Danu whispered, "the king yet lives."

Xavier's eyes were drawn back to hers and her gaze was piercing.

"His throne stolen, his will caged. It was not mortals who could seal him thus but the will of those who would call themselves stewards of order."

Above, the fractured crown slowly spun, a faint and soft silver light bleeding from its cracked edges.

"He cannot rise while the chain holds, and without him neither can the land be restored."

Danu's body began to shimmer. Its wavering form dissolved into drifting motes of light that the unseen wind scattered across the twilight lit fields, but even as she vanished her final words filled the air and hung there as gentle as falling ashes.

"To wake that which was silenced, you must first seek to free what was shackled. Trust yourself to find the way."

As the last echoes of the goddess' voice faded the dream and the very field that he stood in began to unravel as well. The silver grasses melted into hazy mist and the sigils that stood for stars folded in upon themselves.

Xavier fell.

And he kept falling, deeper into the darkness, until his eyes opened to the cold breath of dawn's light.

#

Dawn's breath lay cold on his skin as he returned to consciousness. It was laced with the damp scent of the nearby river and heavy with the faint loamy musk of the dew crusted earth. For a long time, Xavier just lay still, caught between the ghostly remains of the fading dream and the crisp reality of the waking world. The memory of silver fields, burning sigils, and Danu's voice clung to his mind like mist and refused to relinquish their hold easily. However, the soft murmur of the Silverflow and the gentle rustle of the leaves in the trees grounded him back in the waking world and he opened his eyes to the quiet camp wrapped in the grey gentle mist of early morning.

Exhaling slowly, he felt the weight of what he had seen settle in his breast like a stone lodged too deep into a shoe to easily be shifted. Nearby the embers of the fire from last night gave the faintest of glows as the breeze fanned them lightly, a fragile heartbeat against the early morning chill. Beyond them, Ella sat, watching him closely. Her gaze was sharp and steady but wholly unreadable in the pale gloomy light.

"You saw her again did you not?" She finally whispered, so as to not disturb the others in the camp.

Xavier nodded slowly once, then shifted to a sitting position. His muscles were sore from sleeping on the ground and the hard journey they had taken to get here from Ironhaven. It was not that which caused him the heaviest burden though, that came from the knowing that Danu had provided. He remained silent for a few heartbeats, trying to align the fragments of the dream into a coherent thought he could put to words.

"She didn't come with a warning this time," he stated eventually, his words certain as he spoke them. "She came with a truth and a choice."

Ella rose and shifted to kneel beside him, she was close but not crowding him, her presence providing a steady weight to anchor himself to in the tumultuous thoughts of the morning.

"Tell me?" She prompted him.

Xavier drug fingers through his hair, the cold dampness of the air clinging to each strand and his skin only lending to the leaching of his body's heat.

"There is another nexus, this one buried beneath the Ironspire mountains. It's ancient but suppressed. Forced to slumber by the gods in ages past. However, that was not the most critical point she made, nor is it what matters most at the moment." His hands clenched into fists against his knees. "King Rorik is still alive, he's alive and imprisoned. He's not the one ruling. He's bound beneath Thandor's Reach by divine sigils. Shackled by those who claim to be the very stewards of order."

That proclamation caused Ella to intake a sharp breath, one she didn't even bother to hide. The sound caused Lianna to stir from across the clearing, her ears twitching as she heard the low voices. By her side Frostclaw lifted his head and blinked into the mist. A few moments later, even Lythara prowled over, her tail flicking lazily behind her and her sharp crimson eyes taking in everything.

"Did you say the King is imprisoned?" Lianna asked quietly, her voice rough with disbelief. "The rumors were he was severely injured and possibly killed leading a charge against rebels.

"Lies," Lythara mused. "Convenient ones, a bound king

rallies rebellions whereas a dead or injured heroic one drums up the morale and support for the power behind the throne, suppressing that of the rebels." She crouched beside a fallen branch and began toying with one of the broken branches in idle thought. "Who better to write such lies than the gods themselves?" Her voice was low and cutting, like a sharp blade. "Fear dressed up as stability. Order bought with broken crowns."

Xavier bobbed his head in agreement then turned his gaze to the northeast where maps said Thandor's Reach, its magnificent towers unseen, were supposed to lie beyond the forest's edge somewhere in the rolling hills and plains of the Wildlands.

Speaking more to himself than those around him he murmured. "We're not here to start a war. We don't need to burn Arenvalis to the ground so we won't need an army." Pushing himself to his feet the mist swirled around him like the whispers of old buried things. "We need to break just one chain."

Ella rose beside him. She did not speak but her posture and presence spoke volumes. She was bound to him not just through Vaeltheris, but she had tied her very essence to his soul and would follow him into the abyss and back if he needed it. Her eyes shifted towards the capital as well.

Lianna rose next, her hand resting on Frostclaw's head as her eyes narrowed. "If it will help my people, you need but show me the way and I will walk it with you."

Lythara's smile was lazy as she leaned back on her heels more. The broken branch rolling between her fingers. Her posture was casual but her gaze, those crimson orbs were sharp as a razor. "Breaking chains always makes noises," she said softly. "We should plan how we slip away afterwards before the gods send more than whispers and dreams to dog our trail."

Like Ella, Sihri didn't speak. Her actions were more than words. She simply adjusted the leather wraps on her fists and flexed her fingers as her ears twitched towards where Xavier looked.

Looking at those gathered around him, Xavier's chest swelled even as his stomach knotted. The weight of their agreements wrapped around his shoulders like a mantle. Then he felt it again, the faint hum beneath the soles of his boots, the slow, inexorable stir of the earth, and deeper still, almost out of reach, the soft pulse of life, and a colder shiver of death brushing faintly against his awareness. The Syr'Vailen's bond to him was strengthening, the leylines were listening and the world was beginning to waken once again.

"And soon," Xavier thought to himself. "So too would the sleeping king."

#

While they moved through the forest the mist continued to thicken around their calves, curling in low coiling tendrils over the woodland floor. The light seemed to struggle to pierce through the dense ancient canopy of the Silverwood trees resulting in the world being cast in muted hues of gray and green. No one spoke; they were all lost in thought. The weight of Xavier's dream, the truth of it, hung heavy on their minds a silent thread that tied their thoughts and themselves to a single way forward.

Xavier led the way, his boots moving over the damp earth with barely a whisper, he was not as skilled as Lianna in this, but he was getting better. As he took each step, he started to notice a subtle vibration reverberating through him, a tremor he might have ignored but he was paying closer attention to the slight changes about him. It was why when he felt them now, he noticed.

As he walked, his mind on the new sensation beneath his feet he casually brushed his fingertips over the bark of a nearby tree. Through that ancient oak he felt another sensation that gave him pause and for but a heartbeat he felt the world shift. A deep slow pulse moving through the soil and stone beneath his feet similar to when he could feel caverns with his nascent earth sense. He could swear he felt Arath's patient breath and heartbeat, while he focused for an additional fleeting moment, he felt other sensations brush his mind, He felt the sap of the tree surge with life, and off in the distance he 'knew' a small squirrel like corpse lay decaying. Those sensations were not as sure as the earth sense and as he pressed his palm flat to the tree he sought them again. Only this time they faded away like the mist surrounding them slipping through his grasp. They faded, resisted, vanished. Only the earth remained, a slow faint steady hum beneath his feet deep below the soil.

Ella moved to his side, her presence silent and steady, quite for several moments before she asked, "You felt it, did you not?" Her voice was cast low but clear to his ears.

He let his hand fall from the rough bark of the tree and nodded. "For a moment, though its not constant or consistent."

Ella studied him thoughtfully, her head slightly canted to the side. "No, it likely would not be. Not yet," she said gently, "the bond you made... it is like catching a thread in the storm. Sometimes it is strong and easy to grasp and other times it slips away."

"The earth sense lingers though," he murmured. "It's the others that are harder to hold onto."

Ella's smile was small, a knowing smile if not a certainly understanding one.

"Earth is patient," she said, "it waits. The others...

maybe they will come easier the longer you grow with them. They may have been first, but they are not as solid as earth even if they are just as immutable."

Xavier looked at her quietly. It was slightly disturbing how she could almost know what he was thinking or feeling. He chalked it up to her being bonded to his soul as he had no other explanation for it.

She opened her mouth to speak again, pausing briefly as if she was carefully considering her words. "If you truly want to understand the sensations you are feeling, you should speak with Aelriva when we get back to Rynthavael. She knows the old ways better than I recall, she knows the Ley better and will likely have answers that I do not."

The suggestion hung between them like a quiet offer. A quiet promise of knowledge. He slowly nodded in agreement as a ripple of both anticipation and unease flowed through him. He would seek out the knowledgeable little sprite, but for now he had to walk in ignorance, blind faith in the earth beneath his feet and what sensations it offered him.

Ahead of the small group the path forked into the mist. Lianna moved past the two quickly and held up a hand signaling without a word for everyone to wait. A crisp birds whistle left her lips before she moved again and, interestingly to Xavier's mind, Sihri, Valkra and Frostclaw all reacted. Sihri darted to one side vanishing silently into the fog like a living shadow. Following her came the small dark form of Valkra, her tails low and poised as her paws carried her silently over the ground. Down the other path Frostclaw ghosted forward following the direction that Lianna had taken, his great form melding into the mist like a ghost.

Xavier watched them scatter into the trees ahead, scouting the path for any sign of danger. As they vanished from sight he slowed his breath, steadying himself. As he did so the sensation of connection, he had felt faded further, leaving only the quiet constant murmur of the earth underfoot, the old deep song of roots and stone, the heartbeat of the world itself.

A few breaths later he heard Lianna's voice float back to them.

"The trail is clear. Valkra has caught the scent of a deer but there are no patrols."

Xavier sighed in relief as Lythara drifted up beside him. Her voice a low purr when she spoke.

"Careful, Lord Stonewalker. Listen too long to the heartbeat of the world and you might forget your own."

Xavier shot her a glance out of the corner of his eye. The teasing title brought a faint smile to the corner of his lips.

"I think I will risk it... demoness."

The succubus flashed a sharp and amused smile in return.

"Good, dull men are such terrible company after all."

They pressed deeper into the trees, the mist thickening, the old game and hunting paths twisting between gnarled roots and ancient stones. Xavier closed his eyes briefly, reaching for the sensation again. Only the Earth sense remained. The brighter currents, those of Life and Death, had retreated. He knew he would have to seek them again another day. Another day when he had more patience and guidance to do so.

Ahead, Sihri and Valkra flickered back into view, then slipped once more into the shadows. Frostclaw circled back to Lianna's side before vanishing among the trees.

#

Deep beneath the polished stone floors of Thandor's Reach, hidden from the gilded banners and bustling marketplaces above, the air grew still and heavy. There were no windows here, no light or fresh air. The sounds of the waking city were unable to pierce this deep into the stone underbelly. Only the cold flicker of candlelight, burning with a faint, sickly gold lit the room. A figure knelt at the center of the chamber, draped in ceremonial robes of white and gold, the sigil of Solara stitched proudly across her back.

To any who saw her walking the palace halls, she would seem a priestess of the Divine Light, and a devout servant of the Edict of Order, however, here away from watchful eyes, she shed the mask. She rose slowly, drawing the golden veil free to expose beneath it, her true face was hidden by a stark, bone-white mask. It was a skull crowned by a sunburst, the unmistakable mark of Nekros, the god of death and endings masked beneath the Edict's bright facade.

The priestess of Nekros moved toward the heart of the chamber, where a glyph shimmered and twisted in the air, sigil of divine make. A binding seal. At its center floated a fragile image: a fractured crown, caught in a web of gold and white light. The seal was anchored in the very Edict of Order itself, pulsing faintly with each slow heartbeat of the spell.

She extended one pale hand toward the glyph, and she felt it. A tremor, not within the stone beneath her sandals, but inside the magic itself. It was a flicker of instability where there should have been only absolute stillness.

"The chain weakens..." she whispered, voice soft as falling ash. "The will stirs."

Footsteps echoed lightly across the stone. The priestess

turned as another figure entered. This one was cloaked in gray and black, their face hidden behind a smooth obsidian mask. An agent of the Shadow Court.

It was the masked agent who spoke first, their voice low and measured but unidentifiable as male or female. "You felt it too."

The priestess inclined her head slightly. "The king strains against his bindings. Someone... or something... touches the weave beyond what should be possible."

The agent folded gloved hands behind their back. "The human. The one the Animari shelter. He stirs lines we were told and thought long buried."

The priestess turned back to the glyph, watching the fractured crown as it trembled, ever so faintly. "It was inevitable. No chain, however blessed by law, remains unstrained forever." She paused, her voice cooling even further. "He cannot be allowed to come to the Reach unchallenged. Nor may the slumbering heart beneath the Ironspires be disturbed."

The agent bowed slightly. "The Chainsworn are already in motion. They will harry him in the wilds. Delay him. Cut away his strength and ultimately kill him."

A thin smile curled behind the priestess's mask, it was a brittle thing, untouched by warmth. "Let them. One fracture invites another. If he reaches the king, if he loosens the chain even slightly..."

She reached out, tracing the trembling glyph with two fingers, whispering a prayer in the old tongue of Nekros' followers of ages past. The fracture steadied, but the damage was done, the glyph's pulse was no longer perfect. The crack had been seeded, and chains, once cracked, rarely hold forever.

Somewhere beyond these gilded walls, a ripple extended in the deep wilds and the waking bones of the earth, a mortal had begun to shake the heavens themselves without even knowing it.

# CHAPTER
# THIRTY-ONE
*A Call to Verdantspire*

It took several more days, even with Lianna's Forest Runner buff, for the small group to draw close to Verdantspire Haven. The mist still lay heavy on the forest floor the morning when Xavier and his companions finally emerged on one of the paths from the dense woodlands. Verdantspire stretched out beyond, a settlement born of living root, stone, and vine. Grown from and of the forest instead of imposed upon it.

Above the majority of the buildings Xavier could feel as much as see the Lir'Valis, Verdantspire's nexus of Ley lines. Its crystalline obelisk veined with the colors of the lines it was composed of, life, earth and air.

The settlement breathed with quiet life even from a distance. Low curving buildings, some grown, others built, lay half sunk into the earth, bridges woven from vine and branch connecting upper floors to one another.

The three distinct gardens that Xavier remembered from his first visit circled the center of the city in their intentional patterns. Lanterns of polished crystal illuminated the mists with a soft light breaking the last of the pre-dawn's dim light, giving sure sight of the pathways without disturbing the spirit of the Silverwood. At Xavier's side he could feel the tension drain out of Lianna when she beheld her home once again.

Besides Lianna, Xavier could feel the tension lessening in the whole group. Ella brushed damp strands of hair from her face. Lythara's crimson gaze swept over the settlement carefully. Even Sihri's quick restless energy softened beneath her calm exterior. Frostclaw and Valkra were the only two seemingly unaffected. They moved with a casual predatory calm beside their chosen companions still watching the woods.

It was only a few moments after they spotted Verdantspire before a birdcall broke the hush of the surroundings. It was too distinct to Xavier, too sharp. A signal. Mere seconds after its sound figures emerged from the trees and undergrowth like wraiths, Verdantspire Wardens silent and focused in their moss-cloaked forms. They were a cross-section of Verdantspire's bloodlines: Lupari with their lean, wolfish grace; Falconi with sharp, alert eyes; and Duskhari moving like shades across the forest floor. The lead Warden, a Falconi whose cloak was streaked with silver threads, stepped forward, his spear in hand but angled harmlessly downward.

An eyebrow raised slightly as he glanced to Xavier, Lianna and Ella. They were known and the fact that Lianna and Ella both wore a slave collar still gave him a momentary pause. Then his eyes shifted towards Sihri and Lythara. Narrowing his eyes slightly, he studied them. After a while he moved on from Sihri, she was clearly Animari and still wore a slave collar though he could feel the inherent danger in her she was not a threat.

Lythara, however, he knew there was something much more dangerous about her than anyone else standing before him. His gaze hardened as his grip tightened on his spear until he forced himself to relax. She was traveling with known individuals, she was not threatening them, and they had accepted her. For now he would trust Xavier and his party. He relaxed his grip and spoke softly."You are expected," he said simply, voice low and steady. "Come."

Though his eyes flashed briefly to Lianna his attention remained on Xavier. There were no elaborate greetings, nor declarations. Verdantspire was a place of quiet actions, not empty ceremony. The Wardens fell into a loose escort around them, guiding the group deeper into the Haven's living heart.

As they moved, villagers began to gather along the edges of the paths they remembered those amongst this group who had returned captured friends and family. They had remembered the celebration and the quiet sendoff. Now they witnessed their return weeks later and were wary of the news they brought. Things had worsened during their absence and talk of war and raids were heard amidst them. Rumors traveled faster than feet and the throngs gathered to hear what news was brought.

Xavier didn't stop to meet the eyes of any of the Animari gathering around the procession. His mission wasn't done yet and the satchel with the records felt like it carried the weight of the world in it on his shoulder.

They passed down the same streets Xavier remembered leaving and through the central plaza where the Lyr'Valis hung moving towards a cluster of low, woven birch structures, it was where the council's traditional meeting place stood, the sweat lodge.

Built from living wood and layered hides, it sat low to the ground, smoke spiraling from a small vent at the top. The scent of cedar, burning sage, and fresh earth hung heavy in the damp air. Xavier knew it was a place of decision, of testing, of truth, and the Wardens brought them to its entrance, then stepped aside.

Standing in front of the doors, flanked by the traditional guards, stood a diminutive figure that Xavier recognized. Kaelith Moonstride, the High Speaker. She was small, even for a Lynari, her silver-flecked hair braided tightly against her head, her lynx-tufted ears flicking subtly with each shift of the mist. Though she barely came up to Xavier's chest, she carried herself with the assurance of someone who had seen storms far greater than any mortal army. Her golden eyes were sharp and clear, measuring Xavier and his companions without warmth, but also without immediate condemnation.

"You were sent into the wildlands and darkness," Kaelith said quietly, her voice carrying through the morning air. "Have you returned with light, or only more shadows?"

Xavier unslung his satchel anxious to be relieved of the weight of so many ledgers and documents of the Animari slaves that were carried within. "We have news and so much more."

Kaelith's gaze remained on him for a heartbeat before she gestured to the entrance of the lodge. "Then come," she said. "Let the council hear what you have brought."

With that she disappeared into the entrance of the lodge without waiting for a response from Xavier. The guards caught the flaps of the entrance and held them open for Xavier. As he stepped inside, the air shifted. It was hotter, thicker and tinged with burning herbs much like the last time he was there. Within, the Elders awaited, seated around a shallow pit of glowing stones, the heat and steam rising to curl between them.

Here, judgement of what was brought would be passed, and the next steps forward would be decided.

#

As Xavier took a seat in the spot opposite the Elders, the air pressed heavy to his skin. It was thick with herb-laden steam rising from the glowing bed of stones in the center. Cedar, sage, and other unknown herbs filled every breath and seeped into his clothing and skin alike. The Elder Council of Verdantspire sat silent and waiting for his report, their faces half-shrouded by the swirling steam.

After he sat Xavier pulled his satchel forward to his lap, he could feel the magic that empowered its spatial bending properties. Likewise, he could feel beyond his own items and sundries the parchment and documents it carried. The centuries of broken oaths, stolen truths and bloodline descriptions.

Carefully he withdrew several precisely chosen documents, a ledger bearing the names of various higher profile Animari captured and sold at auctions like the one he attended. A blood-sealed edict formalizing the laws targeting the Animari in general. And, finally, a coded letter hinting at the unseen powers that ruled Arenvalis from within.

These exact documents he laid with reverence before the council. The rest, along with their weight of countless lives recorded in the ink and blood of their incarceration remained within the confines of his satchel. He then straightened and met the steady gaze of Kaelith before turning to lock eyes with each of the rest of the council nodding briefly in recognition of their authority in this domain.

"These are but a sliver," he spoke softly. "I carry a full archive of information that there is not room to divest here but will give to you once we finish and your judgement is made."

Kaelith listened then nodded in assent. "Continue."

Xavier drew in a deep breath; he remembered the last time there were truth telling herbs mixed into the steam. He did not need them then nor did he need them now. The truth was something he wanted to tell them but knew they needed the reassurance. When he spoke it was with the conviction of his Tempered Liberator trait.

"Slavery has long been legal not only in Arenvalis but Arath as a whole," he began. "However, recently the blade of this system has been sharpened in the Wildlands and Arenvalis. The Animari are not mere victims of chance and place like other potential slaves, they have been targeted as prey by legal decree. Your kin are hunted, captured, sold as chattel all with the King's seal branding each transaction as righteous and legitimate."

A low dangerous growl erupted from the Ursari Elder, Thror Ironpaw. The Cervari Elder, Sylara Dawnshade lowered her head in prayer a series of beads, well worn with use, played through her fingers as she did so.

"Ironhaven stands at the crux of Arenvalis' slave trade," Xavier continued. "It uses these weaponized laws. Entire bloodlines have been cataloged, broken, and sold to the highest bidder with bureaucratic efficiency." His hand rested on the ledger he had presented.

He then went into details about what they had found in Ironhaven. He recounted the hidden paths they had walked, the spies they shadowed, the contacts they had made, and the guarded knowledge they had spirited away. Finally, he spoke of the Animari they had been able to quietly save during their time in the depths of the city. After it all he pressed forward, his voice hardened with his resolve.

"King Rorik is still alive and normatively on the throne, but he does not rule freely from there. Ivarik Tharn and his hidden collective move within and behind the court. Their unseen hands are guiding Arenvalis into deeper darkness than ever."

It had not seemed possible, but the air of the lodge grew thicker as steam coiled and pressed down like a living thing gorged on the weight of his story.

"We freed those that we could," Xavier grimly admitted. "But the network is vaster than we could have anticipated. A single strike at its heart would have doomed us all to slaughter. We chose to bring back truth to you instead of ashes."

Kaelith leaned forward, one arm reached over the hot stones and with a single claw she drew the blood edict closer to her and into the center. She let the heat blacken the edges of the document, the steam rising caused the markings to run and ruin. The action was simple, unmistakable. She accepted the truth he brought and was determined to bring about its ruin.

Looking up from what she had done Kaelith's eyes met Xaviers. Her voice filled the lodge with clear tones like iron striking stone. "You have honored your word Lordling."

With that simple statement a new prompt filled Xavier's vision.

---

**Quest Completed:** Shadows Over the Wildlands
**Status:** Complete (Partial Success)

You pierced the veil of deception that cloaked Arenvalis, exposing the dark currents driving its cruelty. Though unable to shatter every chain, you returned with the truths needed to rally Verdantspire and kindle the hope of freedom yet to come.

**Rewards:**

---

- • +12,000 Experience
- • Verdantspire Haven Relationship: Increased to Ally Status
- • Animari Trust: Morale +10% (Settlement-wide)
- • Safe Passage Routes Established between Verdantspire Haven and Rynthavael
- • Access Unlocked: Verdantspire Warden scouting support in addition to Verdantspire Warden ongoing protection for Rynthavael
- • Optional Rewards Available: Future favors from freed Animari captives
- • New Quest Chain Unlocked

Dismissing the prompt after he quickly read it Xavier was left with only the dense herb-sweetened steam and the steady gaze of those arrayed before him.

Kaelith sat back, once more flanked by the rest of the council, her voice was steady but laden with portent.

"This part of your journey has ended," she said. "But the root of the issue remains. So long as King Rorik is bound by unseen chains, the suffering and enslavement of the Animari will endure."

The Falconi Elder, Arven Flamefeather's voice cut through the thick air. It was low and grim as he spoke. "If Rorik's crown is bound to another, Arenvalis is already lost."

Veyara Frostwhisper, the Iskari Elder, spoke next, her voice colder than Arven's. "If he can not be set free, then the kingdom must be brought down, before it drags us all into ruin."

Kaelith lifted her hand motioning the others to silence. The steam swirled round her catching the dull red glow of the stones and painting her fur in shifting hues highlighting its natural silver color.

"There may still be a chance of hope. If King Rorik can be freed from Tharn's grip we may yet see our kin freed without the cost of war." Her golden eyed gaze centered on Xavier once more. "We have a harder road, a new charge to offer you."

There was a hiss of steam as Sylara added another ladle full of herb-infused water to the bed of rocks. Another wave of scented water vapor filled the already heavy air.

Kaelith continued, "Will you walk deeper into the shadows over the wildlands?"

---

**You have been offered a quest:** Breaking the Chains of the Throne

The heart of Arenvalis lies poisoned by unseen hands. To free the Animari—and to save the Wildlands from conquest—you must either redeem the King or break the kingdom's chains by force. The choice will forge the future.

**Objectives:**

- Infiltrate Thandor's Reach, the capital.
- Unmask the forces twisting the court.
- Free King Rorik—or prepare Arenvalis for collapse from within.
- Dismantle the legal foundations of Animari enslavement.

**Challenges:**

- Entrenched enemies shield the King from truth.
- Discovery risks igniting civil war.
- Treachery lurks behind every smile.

---

**Penalties for Failure:**

- The Animari's extinction as a free people.
- Threats to Verdantspire Haven and Rynthavael.
- Exile, betrayal, or death under Arenvalis' hand.

**Rewards:**

- The potential abolition of Animari slavery.
- Political realignments empowering Verdantspire and Animari freedom.
- Relics, alliances, influence—and a place in the shaping of a new future.
- **+25,000 Experience** (base), with bonuses for diplomacy, infiltration, or decisive victories.

Xavier took several long moments reading and rereading the prompt before him. The steam in the lodge thickened, golden tendrils of light filtered in adding to the ambiance of waiting. The stones red core glowed brighter. The council waited, seemingly holding their breath along with the world itself. Xavier knelt near the center of the lodge; the weight of the choice loomed heavy on his shoulders... but he knew there was no real choice for him in this instance. He thought about Ironhaven, those broken and bound there. He thought of all that might be lost, families broken, innocence taken. He also thought about all that could potentially be saved.

His voice, when he spoke finally, was low and unwavering. "If we stop now, everything we have fought for will be nothing but ash. If we turn away those still bound are left to suffer."

The steam seemed to take on a life of its own wrapping around him like a shroud of righteous fury. "I will take this path and walk it wherever it demands."

A ripple passed through the council, slow bobs of their head in acceptance. Kaelith deliberately inclined her head to him.

"Then Verdantspire Haven stands with you Xavier of Rynthavael."

One by one, the Elders assented. Ironpaw gave a low grunt of approval. Dawnshade whispered a blessing. Even Frostwhisper gave a terse nod, blade sharp, of approval.

Kaelith spoke once more after the councils' actions. "By the will of Verdantspire and the ley lines of old, let it be witnessed that there is an alliance between our people and those of Rynthavael."

The stones hissed anew as fresh water struck them. Outside a new heavy wind began to stir in the ancient woods. No longer a whispering breeze but rising to a true wind, ominous portent of the next chapter of Xavier's journey, into the shadow, into a future yet unwritten. Fate was twisting around him and not even the gods could see what was to come.

# CHAPTER THIRTY-TWO

*Roots and Bonds*

The air outside the sweat lodge was crisp and cool on Xavier's skin as he emerged from the heavy steam-soaked air within hours later. It was tinged with the scent of rain-soaked soil and distant wildflowers adding a delicate fragrance. Above, the canopy of Verdantspire Haven filtered the light into soft green hues, as if the very forest breathed with them.

Xavier moved quietly alongside his companions, Ella, Lianna, Sihri, Lythara, and their feline friends Valkra and Frostclaw, as they were guided through the winding forest paths by a pair of Verdantspire Wardens. Their guides were silent but steady, carrying staves crowned with woven herbs and small talismans that faintly shimmered with energy.

The path soon opened into a quieter part of the settlement, where the guest dwellings were sculpted and coaxed into shape within the massive trees. The structures here were seamless blends of life and craft, smooth walls of living wood curved into gentle arcs, doorways framed in vines heavy with blooms, and roofs layered in moss and flowering ivy. Every part of Verdantspire Haven lived and breathed around them.

Inside the quarters were much like Xavier remembered, though these ones might be a little more comfortable than the last ones due to their change in status with the Animari people. Though still simple they were deeply comforting. Fresh reed mats covered the floor, still warm from being in the day's sun. Along the walls were carved niches that held bowls of herb-laden water, natural aromatics filling the air with scents of cedar, sage and lavender. In the center of the rooms were low tables that held not only fresh fruit but nut breads and simple clay cups of steaming spiced tea.

It was not the luxury of the higher sections of Ironhaven, but it offered a much more welcoming gift, peace. A gift freely offered by people who knew and valued its worth.

Xavier crossed the room and sat his satchel down beside one of the mats, he methodically began to unbuckle his weapons and remove his travel gear. He had a deep ache in his muscles, not from injury but from that weariness of carrying a unseen burden of overwhelming proportions.

The rest of the group took up their own positions around the room to relax and wait. Ella moved to one side of the room, sitting cross-legged with a quiet sigh, her bow and shortswords stacked neatly beside her. Lianna lingered near a shallow bowl of water, trailing her fingers along the surface as if grounding herself through the motions. Sihri, true to form, sprawled across one of the mats and pulled a light woven reed blanket over herself with a soft, contented sigh. Lythara stood near a window carved through the living wood, her crimson eyes half-lidded as she gazed outward toward the faint, pulsing glow of the Lir'Valis Nexus. For a long while, no one spoke.

The herbal steam rising from the water bowls wrapped them in warmth and subtle fragrance, easing the tension that had clung to their bodies like second skins. Outside, the faint sounds of Verdantspire Haven drifted in. They could faintly hear the measured cadence of Warden scouts moving along patrol paths, the soft clatter of stones being laid along ritual trails, and the gentle, musical notes of woven chimes stirred by the evening wind. Beyond those sounds, however, they could hear another building commotion, something was being prepared. Xavier could feel it humming beneath the surface, the gathering of community, the stirrings of another ceremony.

This would not be a grand feast, not a victory parade, no this was something older. Something rooted in tradition. They had not simply succeeded in their quest, they had earned a place in Verdantspire, through blood, fire, and truth.

Xavier leaned back against the curved wall, the living wood warm against his shoulders, and closed his eyes for a moment, the scent of herbs filled his lungs and for the first time in a long while he was able to just relax and be relatively at peace. He took the time to review the minimized prompt he knew would be there from the quest completion.

"Hark and Hear! You have ascended in power. You are now Level 20!

The touch of the divine lingers upon you, **granting 12 attribute points (6 per level)** to shape your destiny, an exceptional gift, elevated from the ordinary **4 points** per level by the **Blessings of the Gods (Danu).**

Choose wisely, for these points will define your path. You have **3 days** to assign them, or they will fall to the whims of fate.

Your growing prowess earns you a boon: **40% skill**

**allocation** to distribute among your known skills. This is your chance to sharpen the blade of a favored talent, forge new strength in an untapped domain, or balance your growth across disciplines. Let this moment be a cornerstone of your greatness.

**Rise, Seeker of Glory. The world awaits your will. Seek adventure, seek wisdom, seek love... and let your legend be forged in your choices. LIVE!"**

Having learned the hard way in the past, he examined his attributes. He noticed he had received an additional 2 points in Endurance and checking the log he confirmed it was due to the long-extended flight from Ironhaven. He took the time and assigned his points, increasing Strength by 4, Constitution by 4, and having a weird feeling he put the final points into Luck. This brought his scores to:

| | |
|---|---|
| Strength: | 20 |
| Constitution: | 30 |
| Intelligence: | 14 |
| Agility: | 30 |
| Endurance: | 22 |
| Wisdom: | 16 |
| Dexterity: | 30 |
| Charisma: | 20 |
| Luck: | 28 |

Satisfied he closed the tabs out and simply relaxed for a while.

#

They came for him not long after sunset, when the light of the Lir'Valis Nexus had begun to arc across the distant canopy. The door to the guest quarters opened without a knock, and a Warden stepped through with a slow, deliberate bow. No words were spoken, but the intent was evident in the actions.

Xavier rose fluidly and began quietly re-strapping his belt before checking Vaeltheris once over then moved to follow. Ella moved to stand with him but paused as the Warden held up a hand it was not in warning, but ritual.

"This part is for you alone," Lianna translated softly from behind him, her voice low. "Tradition."

He hesitated, glancing to her in askance. She gave a single nod, then reached out and placed two fingers over her heart. Ella did the same, silent but watching. Sihri waved lazily from the mat. Lythara met his eyes and inclined her head the barest inch. Bracing himself he stepped outside.

The path to the plaza had changed. Not in direction, but in presence. The forest was alive not loud, but more aware it seemed, each step was accompanied by the subtle stir of branches, the low pulse of air through leaf and vine. The trail was marked by wreaths of silverthread grass and ribboned bundles of root and bloom tied to guiding posts. Lightstones flickered above the trail like stars that had taken residence among the trees.

As the Warden led him through, the trees began to thin and the hum of the ley lines intensified, rising not in volume but clarity. By the time they reached the edge of the Nexus Plaza, Xavier could feel it pulsing beneath his boots, a rhythm that mirrored breath, heart, earth.

The Lir'Valis Nexus hovered at the center of the stone platform, its crystalline form awash in pale light that shifted between green, gold, and soft silver. Glyphs inlaid in the flagstones pulsed faintly in harmony. Small crystals orbited lazily around the obelisk, catching and refracting light like droplets caught in slow motion.

Around the plaza, dozens,perhaps hundreds,of Animari

stood in respectful silence. Ursari, Cervari, Vulpiri, Falconi, Duskhari, Iskari and many others he didn't know the names for. Some wore ceremonial leathers marked with carved totems, others wore simple traveling cloaks dusted from the road. Some had flowers or woven bands in their fur or hair. Most held nothing in their hands, simply there to witness. The thing that caught Xavier's attention was that none were armed.

High Speaker Kaelith stood upon the steps before the obelisk, dressed in a mantle of pale root-threaded cloth and leaves stitched with silver. Thror Ironpaw flanked her on one side, arms crossed, unmoving. Sylara Dawnshade stood to the other, her antlered brow bent slightly in calm focus. The rest of the council were arrayed along the circle's perimeter present, watching, but silent.

Kaelith gestured once, and the Warden escorting him stepped aside and Xavier took the final steps forward on his own, stopping at the center where the veins of light converged. The Nexus pulsed overhead behind Kaelith, brighter now.

"Long have we guarded this place," Kaelith said, her voice carrying with no need for effort. "The breath of the ley, the whisper of the old roots. We held fast while the world grew hard and cold beyond our trees." Her golden eyes held Xavier's without blinking. "You walked into fire when we asked it of you. You returned not with blades, but with truth. Hard truth, truth that binds, truth that severs."

She stepped forward, holding out a small object woven from pale root fibers, threaded with strands of deep green and a single crimson bead. It smelled faintly of fresh-cut earth. "You brought Rynthavael to our attention, a small fledgling village barely enough to really be called that," she said. "But now it stands on its own, and not as a shadow of the old, but as the beginning of something new."

She placed the woven talisman into Xavier's open hand. "Verdantspire does not offer allegiance lightly. But tonight, we offer it fully to you Lord Vael and to Rynthavael." The Lir'Valis brightened in response, a soft rising breath of wind curling outward from the platform as the crystals around the obelisk flared with light.

#

As the last of the light from the Lir'Valis dimmed into its gentle pulse and the Animari of Verdantspire dispersed into small clusters, Xavier descended the platform and wove through the quieting plaza. The warmth of the ley still hummed beneath his boots, but the ceremony was over. He realized that what came next would not be witnessed in stone circles and sacred flame, it would be decided in halls of power and shadowed streets. He also realized that there wouldn't be a celebration of their return, the threat of Arenvalis still lingered. No, tonight was just a ceremony to recognize the fledgling alliance.

He caught sight of Lianna beneath one of the broad-limbed trees at the edge of the plaza. She was standing with her arms crossed and her weight leaning slightly into one hip. Her gaze was distant, but the tilt of her ears flicked slightly at his approach. Beside her lounged a second figure, same height, same white and black colored fur, same lean frame, but where Lianna stood with alert stillness, the man who Xavier now recognized as her brother Liosan exuded a casual defiance of formality.

Liosan leaned back against the curved trunk of the tree, arms draped over one of the low branches like a jungle cat at rest. His right leg bent lazily at the knee, toe tapping the stone in a rhythm only he could hear. His long fingers spun a strip of leather between them with idle precision, though his pale eyes watched Xavier with a flicker of amusement. And he was barefoot. Of course he was.

When Xavier drew near, Liosan grinned and gave an exaggerated wave with both hands, then flicked his fingers into rapid-fire signs that ended with a dramatic flourish.

Lianna didn't bother translating the first part. She just rolled her eyes. "He says it's about time you showed up. He was worried the Lir'Valis swallowed you."

Xavier didn't bother to tell her that he understood the sign language used by Liosan. The fact that Liosan had made a crude joke didn't really need to be acknowledged if she wasn't going to.

Liosan signed again, more gestures than sentence, and cocked his head like he expected a round of applause.

Lianna went on, "...and that since you have already adopted his sister, it is only fair you deal with the rest of the family."

Xavier raised a brow. "Is this his way of asking to join us?"

Liosan's grin widened. He slid from the branch in one smooth motion and strode forward with a loose, easy gait, signing as he walked.

"He says," Lianna translated, "he is already coming. He is just letting you pretend it is your decision."

That earned a short huff of breath from Xavier and a half smirk. He was more amused, not annoyed.

Liosan stopped a few paces away and tossed the strip of leather into Xavier's hands. It was blackened and soft with use, carved with the Animari glyph for oath in sharp, deliberate strokes. The edges were frayed, but it had clearly been carried a long time, likely prepared well before this moment. Xavier slowly came to realize that it was likely when they first left with Lianna.

He tapped his own chest twice, then pointed at Xavier, then signed something slower. His posture never lost its looseness, but his eyes, just for a moment, held something quieter, more somber, beneath the humor.

Lianna's voice dropped slightly as she spoke his words, "He says he follows his sister's path, and now yours. Until you no longer walk it."

Xavier closed his fingers around the strip and gave a nod. "Then he's welcome," he said. "And his timing is..."

Before he could finish, Liosan was already behind him, slipping into position with exaggerated silence, shadowing Xavier's stride like a stage mimic.

"...horrifyingly punctual," Xavier muttered.

Lianna choked back a laugh. Liosan beamed. No ritual bound him. No proclamation marked his place. He simply moved forward, hands behind his head, tail flicking slightly as he fell into step beside Xavier as if he'd always been there.

The ley pulse continued beneath the plaza, steady as breath. From the trees beyond, a warden's horn called low and long, once for nightfall, and twice more to mark the shift of the patrols.

#

The next morning came softly, with light threading through the high canopy like gold-stained silk. Verdantspire Haven stirred early, not with noise, but with motion, Warden patrols shifting routes, merchants folding away night covers, scouts returning with fresh-tied bundles of moss, root, and dried leaf and the general population going about with daily life.

Xavier stood near the guest dwelling's arched doorway, securing the last of his items and pouches to his belt.

Liosan lounged nearby atop a root that had grown into a natural bench, chewing a stem of sweetgrass. It was clear that he had a blatant disinterest in the concept of punctuality. He offered no help, only a sideways glance and a one-handed wave when Xavier looked his way.

Ella emerged from within, her movements precise. Her bow was slung across her back, the short spear bound to the side of her pack and her twin swords sheathed at her belt similar to Xavier. She said nothing, but the slight nod she gave was enough. Lianna followed moments later, checking the new trail maps provided by the scouts. Her hair was pulled into a tight braid. Her eyes, though calm, watched everything.

Lythara strode up to the group, her gait swaying with the preternatural grace of her race. Her crimson eyes roved over everyone already present and she nodded slowly. She was clad in her dark leathers once again and appeared much more rested and ready to travel once again.

Sihri arrived last, arms stretched high in a long, lazy arc. She wore a short cloak now, fastened with a smooth obsidian pin, and the curve of a smile ghosted her lips.

"I dreamed of too much wine and a terrible idea involving that Duskhari scout from last night," she announced, brushing a leaf from her ear with a flick of her hand. "You all rise far too early for people who pretend to value wisdom."

Xavier tugged the last strap tight. "Seems we're ready."

A rustle of movement behind them signaled Kaelith's approach. She moved lightly, her fur brushed smooth, and she was dressed not in her ceremonial mantle but in the simpler layers of a Warden's traveler, light leathers, woven root-thread cords, her walking staff in hand. The golden eyes that met Xavier's held none of the ritual distance of their previous conversations.

"There is little I can give that will shield you where you now go," she said. "But these will aid you, in the ways that matter."

She passed him a folded bundle wrapped in herb-lined cloth. Inside were several small pouches: a set of Animari healing powders, a sealed flask of concentrated bloodroot elixir, and a rolled scroll written in Verdantspire script.

"Directions to the hidden passes near Thandor's Reach," she explained and pointed to the scroll. "Paths long forgotten by the kingdom, watched by none but wind and time but our scouts remember."

Xavier accepted the bundle with a nod, slipping it into his pack with care.

"Others will come," Kaelith said, her gaze sweeping over the group. "You have planted something that has begun to grow. Even in silence, roots spread."

Liosan tilted his head, signing something sharp and sly.

Kaelith looked at him, unamused. "You may be clever now. But I expect you to return."

Liosan grinned and offered her a bow that bordered on mockery, but the look he gave her afterward was not a jest and once again bore his odd contrasting somberness.

Kaelith reached into her sleeve and withdrew one last item, a thin strand of white-vined root, still faintly pulsing with life. She wound it into a loop and placed it in Xavier's hand.

"When you are far from trees and can no longer feel the breath of the ley beneath your feet, hold this. And remember that you do not walk alone."

She stepped back then guided them to the small

plaza where they had departed for Rynthavael previously. Warden scouts were already gathering at the eastern edge of the plaza, where the shadow paths began to thread their way into the deeper wilds. None of them would go far, just far enough to ensure they passed beyond Verdantspire's reach unseen.

Xavier turned once to look back at the Lir'Valis Nexus, its glow now calm, like the quiet surface of a deep spring. He took a calming breath. "Let's go."

The group began to move. Sihri fell into step beside him, one brow lifting as she cast a glance back over her shoulder.

"Ah, farewell to green things and still mornings," she murmured, brushing fingers across a vine as they passed. "I shall miss the hospitality. I shall not miss the scent of wet leaves stuck in fur. I miss the arid sands of home." She then clicked her tongue and grinned. "Now, let us go where the lies wear crowns."

The forest whispered softly around them, and the road ahead waited without judgment.

#

The path they followed curved southward through the deep-folding woods, winding its way back toward Rynthavael. The atmosphere of the forest had softened since their departure, there was less tension in the roots, fewer watchful eyes from the canopy above. Here, the air smelled of moss and loam, of river stone and fresh bark. The Verdantspire Wardens who had guided them to the first ridge were gone now, having vanished into the trees without farewell. Their part was done, what remained was the return home to prepare for the next leg. It was not in triumph, not yet at least, simply necessary.

Xavier led the way, the woven talisman Kaelith had given him resting beneath his cloak. Each step closer to home and the Syr'Vailen brought the subtle hum of ley resonance stronger beneath his boots, the deep pulse of the earth ley line that fed Rynthavael and the lands under his purview, growing louder the closer they came. Not in sound, but in sensation, a presence beneath the soil that welcomed them in quiet recognition.

Ella moved just behind him, her gaze sharp and steady, watching for more than threats. Lianna was ahead and to the side, occasionally pausing to check the path—more out of instinct than concern. The forest was familiar now, the Living Labyrinth protection bent it for them showing known paths back home.

Sihri wandered a few steps off the trail, hands clasped behind her head as she hummed low and tuneless. "Verdantspire had beauty," she said aloud, not looking at anyone. "But this land... this land listens."

Liosan trailed behind the group, arms relaxed and gait casual, a thin twig between his teeth, signing brief quips to no one in particular. Occasionally he glanced back over his shoulder, as if expecting the trees themselves to follow.

They passed the fork near the Blackroot spring, the first spring Xavier had found in the settlement, by midday, where the stream curved in a crescent around the hill and joined a hidden pool at its base. The markers they had carved before leaving remained intact, freshly tended, even. Someone had kept the path clean in their absence.

By the time the treeline broke and the hills of Rynthavael came into view, the scent of fresh cut wood, soil, and hearth fire reached them on the wind. Homes had been raised. Trails had been widened. There were more people now, visible even from this distance. A few figures stood atop the central ridge, already turning toward them, next to them stood several Wardens, their outfits distinct from those of the Rynthavael guards.

Xavier paused near a sun-warmed stone, resting a hand briefly against its surface. The air here was different, charged, awake. He did not speak but simply admired the growth and change of his fledgling village.

Ella stepped up beside him and gave a single nod. Lianna did not stop walking. She was already moving downhill. Sihri stretched her arms toward the sun, toes curling in the moss. Liosan signed something quick and sharp.

Lianna glanced back over her shoulder, translating with a smirk. "He says the prodigal menace comes, and expects a meal, possibly applause."

Xavier exhaled once through his nose and started walking. The valley welcomed them home without a word.

# CHAPTER THIRTY-THREE

*Rynthavael Reborn*

The forest path sloped gently into the small valley, its length winding through mist-laced trees that felt older than they had weeks before. The air smelled of sap and soil, of growth, not wild growth but claimed and cultivated. A hush lingered in the underbrush, not born of fear, but of attention. Xavier led the way in silence.

This time, he was not just returning, he was seeing. As he walked, he realized most of his previous time in the village had been distracted or focused tightly on individual tasks. This time his eyes lingered on the changes, the way the trail had widened through steady footfall, the subtle curve of cleared garden plots between tree roots, the woven charms hung from arching limbs. These weren't the signs of a camp or a temporary refuge. This was a home. His home.

Ella walked beside him, calm and quiet, her bow secured, eyes reading the land as if testing its pulse. Lianna followed, moving with practiced grace. Her Iskari fur caught dapples of light beneath the canopy, her armor marked in the forest-toned layers of a Verdantspire Warden. Frostclaw stalked beside her, as usual he was silent and alert.

Sihri moved a pace behind, ears twitching at each birdcall. "So, this is the village you spoke of?" Her voice was warm and dry, steeped in the cadence of desert halls and old wind. "Quieter than I expected. Smells like roots and moss and... uncertainty."

Behind her, Liosan walked backward, his pale-furred tail flicking lazily. He spun a branch between his fingers, rosetted fur blending with the shadows as if he belonged here already. Valkra padded close to Xavier, her shoulder nearly brushing his boot as her twin tails flicked casually.

Lythara trailed behind, her crimson gaze flicking between tree, path, and canopy. She remained wordless, watching the subtle shift from wild wood to claimed land.

The trail curved around a final bend and the valley opened before them. Rynthavael blossomed in it center. What had once been a hopeful clearing now spiraled with deliberate structure. Homes of timber and stone rested snugly into earth-sculpted paths. Simple bridges linked raised walkways between the larger trees. Vegetable gardens bloomed along spiraled terraces. Smoke curled from stone chimneys, and colorful banners stirred gently in the morning breeze.

There were no shimmering wards, no glowing glyphs. That briefly made Xavier wonder, he had seen runes for protection and alarm. He had learned one from the slaver encampment when he first traveled with Lianna and Liosan. Why wouldn't the village have some? Instead, Rynthavael's protection came from the land itself, the Living Forest Labyrinth, the watchful eyes of Verdantspire's Wardens, and the fledgling force that had been trained in its defense. It was not polished, but it was alive and growing stronger each day.

More importantly it was Xavier's. His and his peoples. No horns greeted them. No sentries called out, but they were seen, and word quickly spread. A girl dropping berries into a woven basket paused. A young human tending to stones near a stream stepped back and touched a hand to his chest. A pair of guards stood quietly near a growing post, not raising alarm, only recognition.

Xavier stepped forward onto the threshold stone of the village proper, where a new sigil had been carved. He recognized it, it was of Sylmyrian design, balance. As his foot came down, the leylines pulsed beneath his feet.

A warm surge of mana rose from the valley floor, coiling through his chest, not a warning, instead it was a welcome. The Syr'Vailen recognized the return of its master. Then came light.

A spiral of glowing motes twisted into the air before him, hovering, gathering, and unfolding into delicate wings of ley-thread and shimmer. A tiny figure emerged, her skin pale like polished quartz, her hair braided in ivy and starlight. Her green eyes shone with deep, ancient knowing. It was Aelriva. She floated in the air before him, arms crossed, a smirk tugging at her lips.

"Aye, so ye return at last, Ard'Maelor," she said, her voice lilting with the melody of forest wind and stone-song. "The land's been holdin' its breath waitin' on ye. Now it exhales."

The leylines beneath them responded again, slower this time. Grounded, Xavier's growing attunement giving him a greater feel for the elemental powers of the land.

Sihri tilted her head as she peered at the sprite. "She glows."

Liosan signed quickly. Lianna translated without emotion. "He says she's already running the place."

Aelriva gave a knowing look toward Liosan. "Aye, sharp one. Best keep up." Her gaze returned to Xavier. "Ye've stirred the deep root, Ard'Maelor. But not all what wakes answers to yer call. Some roots drink too deep, twistin' their reach 'til they strangle what oughta grow. And some things that answer... were never meant to."

She spun midair once, wings flicking a trail of leylight. "Still. Ye returned. That means somethin'. Come. Let the land show ye what's grown while ye wandered." And with that she darted off toward the village's heart, trailing shimmering motes in her wake. Xavier's gaze followed her.

Behind him, Lythara tilted her head ever so slightly, watching the sprite's trail with narrowed, crimson eyes. Her voice was low, almost to herself. "She is not fae. Not wholly. And not bound in the way spirits usually are." Her fingers flexed once by her side, the faintest ripple of heat rising from her skin. "She watches with old eyes. Feels... tethered. But not leashed."

Lianna gave her a sidelong glance. "You think she's dangerous?"

Lythara didn't look away. "I think she is power wrapped in memory. And power, even when friendly, demands respect." She blinked once, then turned to follow.

From the shaded path ahead, a broad shadow emerged, black-furred, towering, tail swaying with quiet rhythm. The faint scrape of bark-leather and soft footfall matched the movement of someone who had spent more time in the woods than out of them. The Warden Commander, Kaelar Thornclaw.

He stopped just inside the path, amber eyes sharp beneath the hood of his armor. His gaze swept over the group once before landing squarely on Xavier. "Well now," he said, voice low and rolling like distant thunder. "If'n she be de first ta greet ye, then I reckon my job just got easier."

Xavier smiled and clasped forearms with the stoic Warden. "You held the line? Kept my people safe?"

Kaelar's mouth twitched, it was not quite a smile. "Aye. Held it. Watched it shift, yeah? But listen here, lordlin', the forest, she don't sit quiet no more. Mana's stirrin' thicker than ever, and there's things out there what ain't just wanderin'. Some sniffin' round like shard wolves at the edge. Others... older. Hungrier."

He gestured toward the village's heart with a flick of his hand. "That's why I brought more Wardens. We ain't just here for words, non. Verdantspire honors the pact. We'll keep yer folk safe. What wakes with the ley, we'll handle it, as we always have." He paused a beat. "Best be ready, though. What comes next ain't just roots an' good growin'."

Then he stepped aside, and a second figure came forward, a Cervari woman, steady and composed. Her armor was marked by travel, green-threaded and dust-worn. A scroll tube hung at her side.

"I am Vaerin Mossvale," she said, voice clear. "Kaelith sent me with writ and seal to serve in your absence. I have not tried to rule in your absence, only kept the rhythm alive."

Kaelar nodded once. "She's done more'n that, lordlin'. She kept it breathin'. Kept it goin'."

Xavier broke the seal and read Kaelith's message. It was simple and to the point. Much like the Lynari woman's speech. Trusting in his new ally he looked up and met Vaerin's gaze. "Then let's see what you've held together."

She inclined her head and turned. "Come, Lord of Rynthavael. There is much to see." And beneath them, the Syr'Vailen listened.

#

The path through Rynthavael curved inward like a spiral of breath drawn to its source. Homes tucked against root and stone that stood quiet but occupied, their doors flanked by tools, baskets, drying herbs, and children's toys. A pair of children raced barefoot across one of the bridges spanning the inner garden basin. A passing hunter waved to Lianna briefly, then ducked into a low-braided thicket.

Xavier slowed as they walked down the pathway. He saw it now, truly saw it. Not the burden of leadership, not the cost and strain, but instead he saw the result. The people here no longer looked like they were surviving, they were living, thriving, and appeared happy.

The group passed under a high arch of curved timber and entered the central circle ahead stood Hearthstead Hall, the town's heart and gathering place. The wide structure stood nestled between three great trees that he did not remember but had a feeling that the powers of the earth and life ley lines were manifest in them. The building's doors were new and carved from old-growth oak, painted with stylized leaves in green, gold, and blue.

As they crossed the threshold into its shadow, Xavier felt the nexus as it stirred. Aelriva appeared in a flicker of woven light above the entrance, arms folded, wings spread wide in the filtered sun. She twirled once midair, her voice light and lilting.

"Ah. There it is."

Xavier felt it before he saw it, an impression behind the eyes, a pulse of meaning too sharp to ignore and a new prompt formed in his vision.

**Settlement Updated:** Rynthavael

Level Increased → 2

- Mana Cap increased to 3,000
- Radius expanded to 20 miles
- Population Threshold for next level: 100 → 200. Current population: 143.
- Structures Required for next level: 15 → 45. Current number of structures: 26.
- Settlement Quests Completed: 5 → 10. Current number of settlement quests completed: 6.
- Tier 2 civic and production roles unlocked

**Current Active Roles:**

- Steward/Mayor
- Healer/Herbalist – Lila Fairbrook
- Carpenter/Woodwright
- Builder/Mason
- Captain of the Guard – Coren Halewood
- Blacksmith/Armorer
- Farmer/Grower
- Hunter/Tracker
- Guards/Sentinels
- Cook/Baker
- Fisherman/Angler
- Scout/Pathfinder

This was quickly followed by another pair of prompts, one detailing a finished quest and the second illustrating the next quest in that particular chain.

**Quest Completed:** Reforge the Past II

Rynthavael has reached Settlement Level 2.

Once known as Cael'Anthir, the ancient Sylmyrian stronghold has shed the final weight of its past. Reclaimed and renamed under your guidance, Rynthavael now rises not as a ruin, but as a living symbol of rebirth. The ley lines stir in response, and the people gather with purpose. The bones of the old world have become the foundation of something new.

**Completion Outcomes:**

- Settlement Level Increased to 2.
- New Name Confirmed: Cael'Anthir is now Rynthavael.
- Expanded Building Capacity, Role Access, and Mana Cap.
- Increased Radius of Influence and Defensive Potential.
- +5000 Experience.

"The past is honored, but it no longer binds you. From the ashes of Cael'Anthir, Rynthavael rises newborn and unbroken."

---

**Quest Accepted:** Reforge the Past III – A Beacon Rekindled

With Rynthavael stabilized and renamed, the time has come to move beyond survival and into resurgence. A symbol of purpose must rise from within its heart, a Legendary Building that anchors the settlement's identity and rekindles the memory of what once was. But to support such a structure, the settlement itself must grow.

This is a settlement improvement quest for a settlement bound to you. You cannot refuse.

**Quest Objectives:**

- Increase **Rynthavael to Settlement Level 3.**
- See the **Settlement Interface** for population, building, and quest requirements needed to advance.
- **Construct or restore one Legendary Building**

within the settlement (e.g., Mael'Anthir, the Great Forge).

• Ensure the Legendary Building is completed and integrated into the settlement.

**Penalties for Failure:**

• **Stagnation of growth.**
• Delayed access to higher-tier infrastructure, magic systems, and leadership roles.
• Missed opportunity to solidify Rynthavael's place as a rising power.

**Potential Rewards:**

• A **Level 3 Settlement**, unlocking broader capabilities and expansion potential.
• A **Legendary Building**, granting unique bonuses and systems tied to its purpose.
• Expanded building limits, population capacity, and mana flow.
• **+7500 Experience.**

"You have reforged the past, now shape what stands above it. Raise the beacon, expand the walls, and let Rynthavael rise beyond memory into legacy."

Xavier blinked as the prompt faded. "Five settlement quests?" he murmured aloud. "I don't remember completing that many."

Aelriva arched a brow as she descended slowly to hover at eye level. "Aye, ye wouldn't. But ye told me t'keep the village breathin' while ye were away, and so I did. The dangers came, as they always do. Wolves with cracked bones, a hornback boar gone twisted with death-mana, a pair o' raiders drawn by silence. I brought word to Kaelar and to yer steward."

Vaerin, standing near the central hearth circle, nodded once. "We dealt with each. Quietly."

Kaelar's arms crossed. "Weren't fancy. But we don' let danger linger in our wood, non."

Ella glanced at Xavier. "You delegated. It worked."

Sihri traced a slow arc in the dust with her toe. "Feels like the land's remembering what it's like to be settled."

Lianna looked toward the treetops. "Wardens watch from the ridges now. The paths are cleaner. The trails are more defined. The patrols are real and effective."

Lythara's eyes narrowed. "And so are the threats."

Aelriva's expression didn't soften. "Balance, Ard'Maelor. It be not just about holdin' peace. It be about knowin' what moves when ye place a stone in the river." She turned slightly, her gaze distant for a moment, as if listening beneath the earth. "The ley hums steadier now. Hearthstead holds firm, but the Syr'Vailen still breathes below, an' it remembers more than most."

Xavier said nothing for a long while, then he looked across the open floor of the hall, where a worn set of stairs led down into the warrens, the path to the Syr'Vailen Nexus, where the Earth, Life, and Death threads had already awakened. The hall creaked softly as the wind brushed through its eaves. The village was growing, now it was time to plan and to shape what came next.

#

The air in Hearthstead Hall had grown quiet and still. Thick not with tension but with potential. Outside, the winds rustled branches overhead, but inside the great stone and timber hall of Rynthavael, it felt as if the forest itself held its breath.

Xavier rested one hand on the scroll Vaerin had presented and turned slowly to face the circle of companions gathered before him. "You've all done more than hold the line," he said quietly. "Rynthavael grew... even while I wasn't watching."

Vaerin bowed her head slightly. "We did as was needed, my lord."

Kaelar gave a slow shrug of one shoulder. "Ain't build this place for titles. Built it so it'd hold." His golden eyes settled on Xavier, steady as stone. "An' it's holdin' stronger now."

A flicker of movement drew Xavier's attention upward, Aelriva, descending slowly from the beams. Her wings glowed with threads of elemental leylight, her expression unreadable. She hovered beside the long table, arms folded, voice calm but laced with undercurrent. Her gaze deepened, voice low and laced with ancient weight. "Three lines stir beneath yer feet, Ard'Maelor, Earth, Life, an' Death. A root structure, aye, firm an' breathin'. But ye've left one thread still dreamin'... one that remembers the fire. The forge-heart slumbers yet."

She turned, motioning toward the stone beneath them. "The other five lines o' ley, the rest of the eight that bind to the Syr'Vailen, lie deeper still, hidden in the Deeps beneath this very place. Each with a core, sealed an' silent, waitin' to be found. When ye rouse them, one by one, the Grand Nexus shall awaken in full. And with it... the reckonin' the gods sought to bury."

Ella's brow furrowed, a faint realization of the thread left dreaming, blooming behind her eyes. "The forge."

Aelriva's gaze turned to her, just briefly, before returning to Xavier. "Mael'Anthir."

Xavier drew a slow breath. He had seen it before, early in his time here. On the third day, when the ruins still whispered their secrets and Aelriva first warned him to wait. Even then, the forge had called to something inside him. The great anvil that was cracked but humming with dormant power, the faded runes, the warmth that refused to die.

He reached beneath his coat and drew out the rune-sealed pouch. From within, he withdrew the Heart of Creation, an ember-crystal of impossible hue, beating faintly like a sleeping star.

"I found this during one of the first quests you gave me," he said, glancing at Aelriva. "You told me not to use it. Not then."

Aelriva gave no confirmation. But her silence carried the weight of memory.

Sihri leaned forward slightly, peering at the crystal. "So that's what's been giving off heat through your pack all this time."

Lianna tilted her head. "I thought that was just your sword misbehaving."

Liosan signed something brief, and Lianna translated with a smirk. "He says if it explodes, he gets your boots."

Aelriva finally spoke, softly this time. "It ain't a flame, Ard'Maelor. It's a legacy. That stone holds the soul of the mountain's breath. And the forge? She remembers what it meant to shape the world."

Lythara narrowed her eyes. "I've heard whispers... from wandering bladesmiths and demon-marked artisans. Forge fires that bound soul to steel. Myth, mostly. Nothing real."

Ella stepped forward, eyes locked on the crystal in Xavier's hand. "It's real. And if you wake it, you won't just be lighting a forge, you'll be declaring that Rynthavael is more than a haven. It will become a source of power, of influence."

Kaelar exhaled, slowly. "Ain't never seen one o' these 'legendary places' meself. But the ground around that forge? It hums like a beast waitin' to breathe."

Vaerin folded her arms. "The forge was stabilized by the builders months ago. Cleared, supported, but something about it, the heart of it... was always out of reach."

Xavier looked to the door. "It's time." He turned toward the path that led out of Hearthstead Hall and toward the northern rise, where chimneys broke through old stone, and the mountain's soul waited to be rekindled. "The Mael'Anthir has waited long enough."

#

The northern slope of Rynthavael held its breath. In the distance the Mael'Anthir stood nestled against the rise, just a short walk from Hearthstead Hall. It was a part of the village but it radiated gravity far older than the other structures around it. No guards stood watch here, no banners flew. Only stone, wind, and silence remained to mark the site where fire once ruled.

But it had changed from what Xavier remembered of it. Where once ruin had reigned, now restoration stood in its place. Builders had cleared debris, reinforced collapsed arches, and patched fractured walls. Pine rafters, hewn from the local woods, interlocked with remnants of Sylmyrian steel. New walkways had been laid with reclaimed slate and iron nails. Stone joints were filled with mortar, and chimneys reopened to the sky. It was well done but still, it was the work of mortal hands. It was not yet the work of or the soul of the forge.

Xavier stepped onto the outer threshold. The floor

resonated beneath his boots, as if the building itself stirred faintly in recognition. The others followed him inside in silence.

Ella's breath was steady. Lianna's eyes scanned each rebuilt wall. Lythara's gaze was narrow, calculating. Sihri ran her fingers along a nearby column, eyes wide. Liosan spun a half-circle, balancing briefly on the narrow railing before perching like a bird.

Ahead, at the forge's center, stood the Crucible Heart, still dormant. Warm to the touch but somehow lacking.

Aelriva floated overhead. Her wings shimmered with the colors of igniting ley, molten gold and deep stone-red. Her eyes glinted with ley-born light as she looked toward the heart of the stonework. "The shell stands, aye... but its soul lies still." Her voice softened, almost reverent. "Till the flame is kindled and the lines awakened, it remains but a shadow of what once was."

Xavier moved forward slowly. The core platform held ten workstations centered around smaller anvils, now cleared and stabilized. Around them rose braziers, smelters, and embedded pillars, all repaired with mundane materials, their surfaces bearing marks of hammer and chisel. The repairs had been functional, practical. Temporary.

He approached the central anvil, set upon a cracked dais of stone and metal. Even in its dormant state, it pulsed faintly as if it was waiting. From beneath his cloak, Xavier withdrew the Heart of Creation once again. The crystal within pulsed with emberlight slow, like a slumbering breath. Carefully he placed it into the socket beneath the anvil.

For a heartbeat, nothing stirred. Then....

A sudden resonance swept the chamber. The Heart

flared, casting molten light across the stone. A deep hum echoed through the walls. The floor veins ignited, casting threads of orange-gold ley energy outwards in a spiraled pattern. Glyphs surged to life across every beam and pillar.

Before the awestruck eyes of those gathered to watch the forge responded. The rebuilt sections began to change. Where wood had been used, it blackened, not with fire, but with transformation. The pine turned dark and dense, its grain hardening into ironbark-like strength. Nails vanished into the structure as Sylmyrian sigils rewrote the joinery, pulling foreign repairs into harmony with the original design.

Stonework shimmered, the mortar between blocks evaporating as the seams sealed themselves with a metallic sheen. Mortared cracks smoothed over with living stone, flexing as if awakened sinew beneath flesh. In moments, the entire structure reformed, no longer patched, but whole. The forge remade itself.

The mundane became mythic.

The cold tools on the walls vibrated, their edges sharpening with whispered song. A faint roar echoed through the reopened chimneys, not fire, but breath.

The Crucible Heart ignited.

A pillar of golden light shot upward from the center hearth, striking the highest arch. The heat was felt not on skin, but in soul.

Aelriva's voice rang out above them. "The Mael'Anthir is awakened. The Flame of the Mountain's Soul remembers its name."

Lythara took a step back, her crimson eyes wide with shock. "It's reforging the space itself... rewriting reality."

Sihri's voice was hushed. "The masons repaired it. But

the forge just... claimed it."

Lianna touched the reshaped railing. "It's not new. It's what it was always meant to be."

Ella stepped beside Xavier. "This is no longer a forge, Xavier. It's a beacon."

And Xavier stood at its heart, no longer in a ruin, no longer in the past. Now in a place reborn, both ancient and new.

A legendary forge once more.

Xavier's prompts exploded once again.

---

**Hidden Quest Completed:** The Flame Rekindled

Without prompt or prophecy, you have done what few could imagine—you have reawakened Mael'Anthir, the legendary forge of the Sylmyrians. The Crucible Heart burns once more, and with it, the breath of creation stirs in Rynthavael. This act was not given to you by system or seer... and yet it has been seen.

The world responds. The ley lines hum louder. The forge speaks.

**Completion Outcomes:**

- Mael'Anthir Restored: A Legendary Building has been brought back from ruin, unlocking ancient crafting potential and ley-bound infusion systems.
- Forge Resonance Stabilized: The Crucible Heart now radiates Earth-aligned mana, empowering nearby structures and projects.
- Sylmyrian Legacy Reclaimed: Echoes of forgotten craftsmanship stir, hinting at long-lost techniques soon to be rediscovered.

---

**Rewards:**

- +6000 Experience.
- New Crafting Interfaces Unlocked.

"Some quests are not given, they are earned. The Mael'Anthir remembers its master's hand. The world watches... and takes note."

**World Event Triggered – Mael'Anthir Reforged**

**Legendary Structure Reawakened:** Mael'Anthir: the Flame of the Mountain's Soul

The world stirs. It has been centuries since a Legendary Structure, true and whole,was built or reforged. Not since the closing days of the Magewar has the world borne witness to such a feat. Across Arath, whispers rise like wind through broken stone. Smiths fall silent at their anvils. Scholars frantically scour old texts. In the deepest halls and highest courts, one name is murmured: Xavier.

Through mortal will and forgotten rite, the forge of the forgotten smithlords has been reawakened. The Crucible Heart burns once more. A flame not of fire, but of soul and legacy. The reappearance of Mael'Anthir has sent ripples through ley-bound structures, divine observers, and even the black-market archives of the Reaver Clans.

You have gained: +4000 Reputation

Your reputation has increased from Level 3: "Somewhat Known, Still Forgettable - Ah, you've been spotted once or twice. Someone might remember you from a tavern brawl or for getting lost in the woods. But don't expect anyone to remember your name unless it's written on your cloak."

to

Level 4: "Getting There, Not Quite Famous - You're the talk

of a few villages, but the rest of the kingdom still thinks you're just another wanderer. Maybe you've fought off a dragon, but they're still debating whether it was truly you or just the wind."

**You have discovered:** The Mael'Anthir Awakened – Legendary Structure Recognized

**Designation:** Mael'Anthir – The Flame of the Mountain's Soul

**Type:** Legendary Crafting Forge

**Status:** Awakened

**Location:** Rynthavael – Northern Slope

**Bound Authority:** Ard'Maelor – Xavier Ardynvael

**Resonant Leylines:** 3 of 8

- Earth – Aligned
- Life – Present, Locked
- Death – Present, Locked
- Fire – Required to unlock full resonance

The forge remembers. Born in flame. Tempered in stone. Reclaimed by mortal will. Through the Heart of Creation, you have reawakened The Mael'Anthir, seat of the Sylmyrian smithlords, but its soul burns incomplete.

Mael'Anthir – Current State

**Crucible Heart:** Active - The ley-hearth now burns steadily, empowering all crafts performed within. Heat is soul-linked, not elemental, and will not falter.

**Structure Reforged:** Complete - All mundane reconstruction has been rewritten by Syr'Vailen ley-signature. The forge now exists as a fully awakened legendary structure.

**Residual Ley Resonance:** Detected

- Life and Death leylines are present but sealed.
- Full integration requires attunement to Fire.
- When Fire aligns, the Crucible will unlock its true memory and begin drawing on fourfold ley-weaving for mastercraft evolution.

**Environmental Stabilization:** Active - The forge resists overgrowth, decay, and magical tampering. The ley-thread itself maintains harmony within its domain.

## Unlocked Capabilities

- Legendary Crafting Tier Enabled
- Masterwork, Artifact, and Runebound item forging
- Access to forging rituals involving resonance tracking and spirit-binding
- Supports rare metal shaping and ley-reactive alloys
- Sylmyrian Inscriptions Reactivated
- Glyphwork along upper walls responds to Xavier's bloodline
- Additional crafting blueprints, enchantments, and relic reformation possible upon deeper attunement

## Vocations Unlocked at Forge

- Grandmaster Smith – Weapon and armor of immortal design
- Rune-Binder – Fusion of leyscript and steel
- War Engineer – Arcane siegecraft and ley-fortification artisan

## Forge Attunement Progression

- Leylines Resonating: 3 / 8

- Life (Present, Locked)
- Death (Present, Locked)
- Earth (Active)
- **FIRE LEY LINE REQUIRED TO UNLOCK TRUE FORGE MEMORY**
- Other ley lines (Water, Air, Light, Darkness) are currently dormant

**Next Step:** The forge lives, but it does not yet dream. Awaken the Fire ley line to unseal its memory.

Ard'Maelor - Choose how The Mael'Anthir shall serve the future of Rynthavael.

#

Xavier stood in the center of The Mael'Anthir, still framed in the soft golden glow of the leyfire, as arc after arc of runic light pulsed gently beneath his feet. The prompts temporarily overwhelmed him. Not one. Not two. A cascade of luminous glyph-screens unfolded before his eyes, layered with complex detail: forge resonance patterns, ley-alignment thresholds, structural memory overlays, crafting tier designations, and vocational awakenings. Each shimmered with words and descriptions he had no understanding to fully parse out currently. One prompt line caught his attention however, bold and blood-red: FIRE LEY LINE REQUIRED TO UNLOCK TRUE FORGE MEMORY

Xavier's breath stilled. This was not just a forge; it was a living memory waiting to be fully restored. He blinked once, deliberately, and waved the prompts away.

As his vision cleared, the forge's light settled into a steady pulse. He turned back toward the others. Ella stood steady beside him, calm and composed. Aelriva hovered just beyond the light's reach, a quiet sentinel of wings and drifting glow. Lianna crouched beside Frostclaw, her gaze sharp and focused. Liosan hung upside-down from a crossbeam, rocking back and forth with slow, playful motion, his tail flicking lazily in rhythm. Sihri stood slightly apart, arms folded, golden eyes narrowed in thoughtful awe, ears twitching as if listening to something only she could hear. Lythara remained by one of the support columns, arms crossed, and eyes narrowed. The crimson orbs were not hostile, but wary, her body language coiled like someone waiting for the truth to finish unfolding. Near Xavier's boots, Valkra paced in slow circles, tail low but ears perked, the young shadowmane's instincts stirred by something deep and old in the fire's resonance.

And then the stillness shattered. From beyond the forge doors came the sounds of rising commotion, calls from the nearby paths, feet pounding against stone and moss, breathless voices carried on wind. The pulse of power from the Crucible Heart had swept through the settlement like a heartbeat heard through the earth.

Aelriva's eyes flicked to the doorway. "They felt it."

Ella nodded. "Every soul in Rynthavael just learned something woke."

Xavier stepped from the platform, moving toward the open archway. Already the sound of commotion echoed up the path—startled voices, quickened footsteps, the village itself responding to the pulse of ancient flame. Braegor Voidiron arrived first, broad-shouldered and steady, his heavy boots grinding against stone with each step. The elder Gan Ceann blacksmith paused at the threshold, his one good eye narrowing as he scanned the forge with the scrutiny of a man who had seen too many false fires, and yet, even he looked reverent. At his side, came Rilsa the dwarven lass apprenticed to the elder smith, her soot-stained apron clutched in one hand, eyes wide and shining.

She didn't speak, but her posture trembled with awe. She had heard the forge hum before. Now it sang.

Behind them, villagers arrived in waves, Lila Fairbrook, still in her herbal apron, eyes wide. Orrik Deepstonee, his sleeves rolled and hands chalked with stone dust, slowed just shy of the threshold, slack-jawed in wonder. Ferran Greenfield, earth still clinging to his boots from the fields, came last among the first, gaze flicking to the glowing stonework and reformed walkways with the wary curiosity of a man who knew the difference between a field that was tilled... and one that had been changed.

No one spoke. They simply looked, at the newly alive forge, at the arcane warmth that drifted from its vents, at the figures standing within its heart.

Lila exhaled. "Is it...?"

Vaerin's voice answered from just behind the last group. "It is."

She stepped forward to stand beside Xavier. "And now that the forge is awake, so too must the village rise with it."

Xavier glanced at her then nodded. "Then let's begin."

An hour later, within Hearthstead Hall, everyone had gotten over the initial wonder of the newest structure of the settlement. The warmth of the Mael'Anthir still clung to Xavier's skin as he stood once more within the central circle of Rynthavael's great hall. Around him were those who had earned a place in shaping the village's path forward.

Vaerin stood by his side as Steward. Orrik crossed his arms with calm patience. Lila sat with a half-empty satchel at her feet. Ferran paced near one of the support beams, nervous energy barely contained. Several new faces lingered near the walls young, alert, curious.

Xavier raised his hand. "The village has grown. The Syr'Vailen is awakening. And now... the forge speaks." He turned to Vaerin. "We need to fill the roles that growth demands."

She nodded. "And we have those ready."

After several hours of discussion and advice from Vaerin, Coren, Aelriva and Braegor on who would best fill certain open roles Xavier smiled looking at his updated interface for the village.

**Steward/Mayor:** Vaerin Mossvale - Officially confirmed. Will oversee village planning, coordination, and internal law as Xavier focuses outward.

**Farmer/Grower:** Ferran Greenfield - Long handling crop rotation and foraging coordination informally, Ferran is now officially granted the village's outer fields to expand food production.

**Hunter/Tracker:** Amara Redgrove – The human ranger in name if not class she had taught Xavier early on and now she is tasked with mapping the lesser-used trails, eastern approaches, and locating anomalies in the wilds.

**Guards/Sentinels:** Mixed Trainees under Coren Halewood - Young Animari and settlers, human and otherwise, now train under the steady eye of the retired Arenvalis guard captain. They form the core of Rynthavael's defense force.

**Cook/Baker:** Frida Deepstone - Named as the chief cook of Rynthavael she fully embraces leading the small army of individuals that ensure everyone is well fed.

**Blacksmith/Armorer:** Braegor Voidiron – The Gan'Cean smith happily accepted the role of the village smith. With his apprentice Rilsa and the rest of the villagers skilled in this craft they are anxious to take advantage of the new legendary structure.

The list went on with several more roles filled and another handful open but with possibilities.

As the meeting wound down, Xavier stepped back and let the voices rise, collaboration forming in every corner. Amara spoke quietly with Lianna. Ferran debated irrigation routes with Lila. Orrik and Coren exchanged thoughts on reinforcing the gate.

And through it all, the nexus pulsed beneath their feet, alive, aware.

Now, Rynthavael had a forge, Rynthavael had a voice, and it even could claim it had a people shaping its future.

# CHAPTER THIRTY-FOUR

*Whispers in Flame*

Across the world everyone was blinking in astonishment as a new prompt revealed itself to them.

---

**[WORLD EVENT – LEGENDARY STRUCTURE AWAKENED]**

**Designation:** Mael'Anthir – The Flame of the Mountain's Soul

**Type:** Legendary Crafting Forge

A force long silent has stirred. A soul-forge of the old world now breathes anew.

**Location:** Undisclosed

**Bound Authority:** Unknown

**Status:** Awakened

**Impact:** Ongoing

The ley threads shiver. The balance tilts. The gods do not smile.

The world remembers.

---

Beyond the prompt the world reacted to the resurgence of a legendary structure. It began as a shudder in the stone.

In the high mountain city of Karveth, a dwarven runesinger froze mid-hammerstrike as the air in his forge turned heavy and still. The flame in his furnace flared azure, then sank into gold before vanishing entirely, leaving the coals cold but pulsing faintly, eerily like the heartbeat of something too vast to see. His anvil cracked down the center, not from heat or pressure, but from something deeper.

Far across the continent, in the jungle temples of A'kalan, a priestess of the Veiled Pantheon fell to her knees before a statue of Danu, her silver bowl of scrying waters boiling over with light that flickered through eight impossible hues. She gasped as a single word etched itself in steam upon the air: Return.

In the sun-scorched wastes of Sar'Faen, desert winds twisted unnaturally, lifting patterns of sand into spirals that held shape too long. One formed a sigil none had seen in over an age, etched only once into a sealed vault during the end of the Magewar. The symbol glowed, then crumbled into nothing.

Across Arath, the subtle and the sacred stirred. Blacksmiths dreamt of blazing mountains. Shamans woke screaming of stone cracked open by fire. Oracle bowls shattered. Earthquakes danced across leyline intersections, mild, but pointed. And finally, in the low places where divine eyes always watched, those eyes blinked, once, confused.

The world did not know who had awakened Mael'Anthir. Nor where it burned. Nor why the forge of legends had stirred at last but something ancient had drawn breath.

And all of Arath had heard the echo.

#

Deep beneath Thandor's Reach, the Sanctum of Vigilant Flame stirred for the first time in generations.

Twelve lanterns, each bound with divine iron and ritual wax, flared in unison—casting no warmth, only shadow twisted into false light. At the center of the room, the runic dais pulsed with a rhythm that did not match any divine cycle. Not celestial, not sanctioned, and not supposed to exist.

Inquisitor-Vigilant Coraz stood motionless as the system glyphs along the chamber's ceiling ignited one by one.

A scryer nearby dropped to her knees, her breath ragged. "This is not a leyline flare," she whispered. "It is... deeper. Structural. Mortal-coded."

Coraz's voice was quiet but cold. "What name?"

"Mael'Anthir."

Several priest-scholars froze.

One, wrapped in archival chains of sanctioned knowledge, stepped forward slowly. "That name... should not exist. It is not in any scripture. Not in divine records. Not even in the Magewar fragments."

Another, an oracle, blindfolded in black ash and waxed parchment, spoke from the inner alcove. "It was not erased. It was lost, before the gods formalized record, before the Edict, before the Magewar Reckoning. A name from the forgotten stone. From the age when mortals built things even the gods could not unmake."

Coraz's gaze did not shift. "If the structure is real... then what stirred it?"

The scryer pressed her scorched fingers to the basin

again. "We cannot locate it. The veil is perfect. Bound by a signature older than all current forms of divine architecture. Possibly a soulmark. Possibly an artifact."

Coraz turned to the flame, now dimmed but pulsing, and alive. "Dispatch the Redeemed, quietly. I want all known smith-guilds monitored. Archive any dreams, forge-flickers, or memory resurgences among gifted craftsmen. Not by divine trace. If this Mael'Anthir has returned..." He paused. "Then something walks Arath that should have died with the first cities."

The oracle answered softly, "Or never died at all."

Meanwhile, the wind shifted over Ironhaven.

Atop the broken ramparts of the Reavers' stronghold, blackened stone carved from the mountain's wounded flank, embers danced without a source. There was no fire, no forge, yet the air tasted of coal and blood. Beneath it, iron. Deeper still... memory.

Karn Vorrik, the Reavers' field captain and successor to Lythara's abandoned command, stood alone in the wind. His eyes glowed faintly, embers clinging to infernal blood. The moment the world prompt echoed across Arath, he felt the itch behind his teeth. Power, Old power, not divine, not structured, not sanctioned. He didn't need to understand it. He only needed to hunt it.

A shadow moved behind him. One of the warbrands, Zaleth, a scarred brute with sigils cut into his own flesh, bowed his head.

"We felt it in the weapons caches. Swords we have not used in months hummed. One cracked from spontaneous heat. There is no forge here, Captain."

Vorrik didn't respond. His gaze was still fixed westward, toward the unseen heart of the Silverwood where it was thought the fugitives had fled. "Mael'Anthir," he repeated quietly. "Heard that word once. Drunken mage said it in a death chant. Thought it was a curse, or a prayer." He tilted his head. "Now it's a target."

Zaleth grinned. "We gonna find it?"

"We do not need to. Not yet." Vorrik's grin mirrored the wind's cold bite. "Let the gods scramble. Let the Chainsworn chase ghosts."

He turned, walking back toward the keep's interior, where weapons were being sharpened and hounds already stirred. "When it breaks the surface... when whoever lit that flame comes up for air... We'll be waiting."

#

Back in Rynthavael, the Mael'Anthir stood in quiet dominion over the northern rise, a silent pillar of heatless presence. It needed no words, no ceremony, the forge's pulse had already joined the breath of Rynthavael, as if it had always been there just waiting to be remembered. Though it was a marvelous structure, it did not command attention. It merely existed and it was not idle.

Smoke curled from its tall vent, a thin ribbon against the canopy sky. Inside, the first crafting had begun. There was no ritual nor any magic, just labor steady, reverent, purposeful.

Braegor Voidiron, the village smith, worked at the forge's heart. A broad-shouldered Gan Ceann, he stood at the anvil while his detached head rested on a polished oak pedestal nearby, his eyes mostly remained fixed on his own hands with calm scrutiny. His hammer rose and fell in rhythm, the cadence of a man who did not question what he felt beneath his feet. The forge answered his skill, not with flame, but acceptance.

Around him, several other smiths from the village worked in synchronized quiet, junior blacksmiths, metalworkers, apprentices and the like, all adjusting their techniques as they felt the subtle responses of the forge beneath their tools. They did not understand it fully, but they knew better than to ignore it.

Among them was Rilsa Voidiron. Eighty-nine years old and still in the spring of her dwarven youth, Rilsa carried herself with squared shoulders and sharp eyes. Her long black braid was tied back in three loops, and her apron already bore fresh soot. Though she was adopted, her name had never been questioned, Braegor had raised her as kin, and she wore the Voidiron name like forged plate. She moved between stations quickly, double-checking heat levels, measuring quenches, adjusting grindstones. She didn't speak unless spoken to, not today. She had fallen back into her normal routine since her rescue with the other villagers from Bramblegate, and though she still kept a hammer close at hand she had finally shown signs of relaxing and returning to normal. Today, she kept glancing at Braegor, and once, when no one else was watching, his head gave a slight nod of approval. She smiled but didn't linger. Today wasn't about praise. It was about earning it.

The tools they shaped were simple, hinges, fastenings, nails, but even these bore something else. Metal cooled cleaner. Weight balanced sharper. The Mael'Anthir remembered how to craft before the world forgot how to ask. Ideas were forming in Braegor's head on how to better bring out qualities in weapons and armor that would outfit those who would see to the safety of the village.

Outside, the rest of Rynthavael moved under a sky that seemed to hold its breath. Beneath the soil, the Syr'Vailen ley nexus pulsed with three fully awakened threads: Earth, steady and anchoring; Life, vibrant and stirring growth where it passed; and Death, solemn and unshakable, like a silent watcher in the roots of the world. The village felt different now. Stone held its mortar better. Wood grain twisted subtly toward the wind providing better strength and shelter. Calming dreams came longer, quieter, and more vivid.

In the central clearing, the final preparations for departure came together in silence. Xavier moved with focused calm, assigning roles for the village, checking loadouts for his team, and reconfirming Vaerin's full stewardship and Coren Halewood's control of the watch. They had taken care of Rynthavael in his absence before and would likely do so many times in the future. He wanted them to know they had his support and trust.

Nearby, Ella stood beside him, arms folded, her presence steady as she reviewed march order and supply notes. She said little, but her attention missed nothing. Lianna moved methodically through weapons and gear checks, tightening bowstrings, inspecting blades, and adjusting Sihri's studded fist wraps without needing to be asked. Sihri ran her warmups in the gravel ring beyond the hall, her movements measured and economical, her body preparing in ways words couldn't. Liosan was already gone from sight. A coil of thin rope draped neatly over a rooftop beam was the only sign he had ever been there.

Lythara stood alone on the edge of the northern path, her back half-turned to the forge. She hadn't gone back inside, not since the awakening. It was not because it rejected her, it hadn't felt negative to her in any way as a matter of fact. It was just... there was something about the way it felt. Something buried under stone and silence that pulled at her, not with heat or power, but with memory she couldn't reach. It reminded her of something she couldn't place, and that, more than anything, unsettled her.

Her gloved fingers tapped once against the hilt of her dagger, then stilled. She rolled her shoulders, muttered something too low to hear, and returned to the others.

#

Dawn came quietly. The light over Rynthavael was pale and golden, filtering through the tall wood canopy like a breath held between moments. The village did not stir beyond its normal routine, no one came to see them off. The outside of the cooking fires the hearths burned low. Sentries watched from shadowed towers but did not speak. There were no overt farewells, no blessings. Only the dawn mist curling through the streets and the hush of parting footsteps.

The group assembled near the eastern path, just beyond the edge of the outer gardens. They passed the final structures of the village, homes and workshops now familiar as breath. A place they had helped shaped even in their absence, stone by stone, into something real. As they left those paths behind, each of them felt it. A subtle ache in the chest, a pull, like walking away from something warm into cold air.

Lianna looked back once, though she said nothing. Sihri, always restless, slowed her pace without meaning to. Even Liosan, silent and unseen, moved with an uncharacteristic stillness in the trees above.

Ella walked beside Xavier, her expression thoughtful, eyes soft with that quiet awareness she carried so easily. She wasn't grim, she rarely was, but there was a stillness to her this morning. As if she, too, felt something stirring. It was not fear, more the acceptance of the gravity of what came next. She nudged his shoulder once, gently, and gave him a smile that said more than words. Then they kept walking.

The trail carried them northeast, through wildwood paths that still bent around Rynthavael's area of influence. The land here still listened, roots shifted gently for their steps, birdsong paused when they passed. It was another ten miles before they reached the outer edge of the Syr'Vailen's influence. Xavier felt it the moment they crossed. The moment the subtle trace of familiar ley lines, Earth, Life, and Death, quieted to mere murmurs in the back of his mind. A subtle stilling, a silence behind the senses. It wasn't loss, it wasn't even danger. It was simply absence, the quiet of a heartbeat no longer felt.

He didn't say anything, but his step adjusted ever so slightly. A breath drawn deeper. A hand lowered toward the hilts at his sides, in readiness. They had fully left Rynthavael behind again.

Now they walked toward Bramblegate, roughly five days towards the northeast. Then on to the Wildlands border and through those unfriendly lands claimed by the Kingdom of Arenvalis. The road ahead held no welcome. It would be weeks before they reached Thandor's Reach and danger was likely to be along every step.

Lythara was the one to break the silence, voice low as the trees began to press in tighter around the trail. "Someone's going to notice this. If they haven't already."

Xavier gave a faint nod but didn't answer. The group moved forward without another word. Around them, the forest closed, a wild sanctuary and hopefully peaceful trek for a while at least.

# CHAPTER
# THIRTY-FIVE

*The Quiet Crown*

The roads still ran through the Silverwood, old hunting lanes, merchant trails, and paths carved by centuries of passing hooves and boots. But the group stayed off them. Not because they were guarded. But because they could be. And that was reason enough.

Lianna led, her Iskari features sharp in the dappled light. She wore the Warden armor of Verdantspire, muted greens and slate leathers fitted for silent movement. Frostclaw padded beside her, silent and alert. They didn't make any unnecessary noise, they knew each other too well to need to. Their bonded nature made them more extensions of each other than true individuals. They had walked these lands together too many times. Her eyes scanned high branches and low ferns, and when she paused, it wasn't hesitation. It was respectful, as with most wardens she knew the forest did not belong to them. It permitted their passage.

Liosan scouted ahead, childlike in motion but never careless. He spun off branches, slid across fallen logs, and vanished behind thick trunks. His body moved with fluid grace, an effortless dance honed through instinct and repetition. Every few turns, he left quiet signs for Lianna to read, a twist of moss, a snapped twig, a specific pebble turned the wrong way.

Though mute, he was a language of movement unto himself. His silence was not absence but presence, deep and deliberate. The forest accepted him, and he in turn read it like scripture, the twitch of a bird's wing, the distant rustle of disturbed leaves, the soft hush of a predator too slow to matter. In Liosan, the wilds saw no threat, only one of their own.

The canopy above thickened as they advanced, light breaking only in narrow shafts. The smells of loam, damp bark, and crushed fern rose with each step. Ferns brushed Xavier's knees as he moved near the middle of the formation, his pace measured and steady. Vaeltheris, in short sword form, rested on his left hip. At his right, the Emberstone short sword shimmered faintly with buried heat. He moved without hurry, one hand often grazing the hilt of either blade. Valkra moved beside him in wide arcs, sweeping through brush and returning often, her coat like a flowing shadow in the sun-dappled green. Where Frostclaw walked like a ghost, Valkra prowled like consequence.

Ella walked to Xavier's left. Her armor matched his style, light leather reinforced for agility, practical and silent. A matched pair of short swords hung mirrored at her hips; their hilts worn but well maintained. A compact bow sat across her back, its string waxed, and a quiver bound tight to the small of her back, its ingenious design allowing her to reach for and pull arrows free without them falling out of its hold. The collar at her neck bore the etched runes of an Arathian slave binding, but it was inert, the power held within it could not reach her through it due to her unique nature. She had donned it for Lianna's sake during

Ironhaven's infiltration. She wore it still, a quiet testament of solidarity.

She hummed now and then, a quiet, wordless note that drifted between breaths. It was not song, not truly. It was memory and wonder, wrapped in stillness. The tune was never the same, yet always familiar. The notes carried weight, and though no language shaped them, they resonated with something older than speech.

Sihri grumbled from her usual place near the rear. "Too many trees. Too many eyes. Not enough sky."

Her own collar still active, though free of commands, twitched faintly against her neck as she ducked under a crooked branch. She thumped the side of her shoulder against a trunk and growled, more irritated than injured. "One good tunnel would fix half this nonsense."

She adjusted the wrappings around her fists as she walked, glancing now and then at low dips in the trail, instinctively checking for signs of burrows, cave mouths, any opening into the deeper places she still trusted. Her homeland was sand, not leaf. A child of the desert, not the forest. Though she knew tunnels. She had bled and fought in them beneath the scorched southern plateaus, she did not trust the forest. Its silence was different. Its roots were too alive.

Ahead of her, Lythara stepped over a tangle of roots and turned her head slightly. "A tunnel would get you buried before you saw daylight again. These woods might be watching, but they don't collapse when the wind changes."

She moved with calm confidence, her booted steps light and deliberate. Her crimson eyes scanned the tree line with military precision. She wore no slave collar, she never had. Her chains had been infernal, carved into her flesh and soul through a pact with Ivarik Tharn long before the Edict.

Under him she had led the Redmaw Reavers on raids across the Wildlands and into Animari territory. Verdantspire had, in fact, known her name in fire and blood.

She had walked through blood and flame under Ivarik Tharn's contract, her will bound, her actions shaped. But now she chose. And it was that freedom offered by Xavier, not demanded that held her attention more than any order or leash ever could. He hadn't forced her to follow. He had given her the option, and to someone born of chaos, that mattered more than any oath.

Lianna hadn't forgotten the succubus' past, and she remained vigilant for possible betrayal. However, Lythara for her part, had not stopped earning the Iskari woman's trust since Ironhaven. She didn't linger in command, didn't push forward. She followed when needed and spoke only when her insight was necessary. She hadn't changed her nature, but she had changed her direction.

Liosan accepted her presence without question. He trusted who Lianna trusted, and now, who Xavier did too.

The small party traveled like this for days. The forest thickened in spring bloom, green and golden in the late season. Moss ran rampant across every stone. Vines hung like skeletal curtains. Somewhere above, a hawk called and was answered. Once, they passed an old hunting stand abandoned long ago, its wood silvered with age and the scent of rain. The further they went, the fewer signs of civilization remained. They crossed dry streambeds and bypassed an old Animari trail marker carved into stone, a warning glyph half-covered by ivy. None touched it.

On the fifth day, the ground sloped down into a shadowed grove. The earth there was soft, too soft. Xavier crouched beside a leaning pine and pressed his palm into the dirt. His eyes closed for a breath.

"The ley's still here," he said quietly. "Subtle like breath beneath the soil. Not gone. Just distant. I can feel the Syr'Vailen nexus still, faint and steady, but we've passed beyond its reach. The ley lines are still alive, they always are but they've grown faint here. Dim. Like a river running beneath layers of stone, still flowing but harder to feel."

Ella knelt beside him, fingers trailing a thin root. "Not broken. Just holding its breath. Like it remembers something heavy standing on it."

Lythara joined them, crouching low. Her fingers moved with the precision of someone used to tracing magical seams, brushing aside pine needles until she revealed a stone, flat, worn, shaped like a hinge or the base of something older.

Her crimson eyes narrowed as she extended her awareness, attuned not to the raw pull of mana but to its resonance, the way it layered through the world. She was an enchanter by training, her skills forged in layered bindings and subtle weaves, not the wild breath of ley lines. Yet even she could sense the sluggishness in the flow here. More than magic, though, it was instinct that drew her close, the same intuition that guided her through shadows, that made her a deadly shadowdancer.

"This isn't dead ground," Lythara murmured. "It's not empty either. Mana like this... it's resting. Like something coiled under the surface. Not like the deep power near Verdantspire where it hums with life. Rynthavael as well, there's something there too. Old, awake in its bones. But this? This feels more like the Shattered Expanse. Like those ruined reaches near the borders there, scarred and wary, as if something once shattered still echoes through the ley. Not wild, but hesitant. Tethered to memory instead of flow. It's not gone. It's remembering. Holding to something old and heavy, like it's waiting to be unburied. Not broken. Just bound in memory. Held still, until something changes."

The silence that followed was not awkward. It was acknowledgment.

Lianna raised her hand from a small rise ahead. "Left bend. Streambed cut. No recent tracks. Safer."

Sihri exhaled through her nose. "You all act like the dirt is whispering secrets."

Lianna didn't turn. "It does. You just do not listen."

Liosan flicked a quick hand signal from a branch above and vanished again, not even rustling the leaves.

That night, they camped beneath a ridge where the trees bent low and the air clung damp against the skin. No fire. Just cold rations, hard-packed ground, and long silences. The air smelled of leaf mold and slow decay, but it was clean, and for the moment safe.

Frostclaw curled against Lianna without a sound. Valkra lay close to Xavier, twin tails twitching gently.

Ella sat a few feet from him, cleaning her bow. The hum returned, softer now, as if it wasn't meant to be heard at all. It came and went in waves, like wind shifting through hollow stone.

Xavier listened, not to the melody, but to the meaning beneath it. It wasn't a song. It was memory made breath.

#

It was on the sixth day they noticed that the trees had thinned. Not all at once, but gradually, like the breath of the forest was being held a little longer with each step. The thick, whispering green of the Silverwood receded into sparser undergrowth, the canopy thinning enough that the pale sun filtered clearly through. Beyond a ridge of moss-crowned stone, the shape of a wall appeared: cracked timber, long-untended.

Bramblegate.

Lianna slowed as they came into view of it, ears flicking, tail lowering in stillness. The scent of ash had long since faded, but memory lingered in the soil. Frostclaw walked beside her in silence, pressing close without needing command.

What had once been a modest border town now lay in ruin. The wooden wall was mostly collapsed, but enough remained to hint at its former perimeter. Gateposts leaned at crooked angles. Vines had overtaken the beams, and thorns crept across the outer fence like nature trying to stitch the wound closed. On one beam, dark streaks marred the grain, blood, soaked deep into the wood and never scrubbed away. Dirt near the broken gate had turned dark and brittle, where blood had pooled long ago and baked into the soil. Where the path split into the town, a splash of deep rust stained the stone, as though something once bled out beneath the open sky and the earth refused to forget.

"They didn't even take the time to strip fully it," Sihri murmured behind them. Her voice had lost its usual sharpness. "Just hit it and moved on."

Ella said nothing. Her eyes traced the line of rooftops that were no longer whole, the burned shapes conjuring a memory etched into her bones. This had been one of the first trips she had taken with Xavier in Arath, just days after his arriving. The fire had still smoldered. The screams had still echoed enough to help them find those still being tormented and used. Chains had hung from overturned wagons and posts, the scent of blood still strong enough to sting the eyes. She remembered stepping into one of those buildings and finding a child curled beneath a table, barely breathing, her voice gone from screaming. They had saved her, but not all. Not nearly enough.

Xavier passed through the broken gateway, one hand brushing the wood as he stepped beneath the remnants of the arch. His jaw tightened, but his eyes swept the space like someone stepping back into a grave they'd once helped dig. "It hasn't changed," he murmured. "The bones are still here. Just... older."

There had been no effort to rebuild. No one had come back. Ferns pushed up through what remained of the street. The cobbles were split and shifting, many pulled aside by time or weather. Crates and carts once used for trade were now cracked husks, their metal fittings rusted or looted. A few still had faded paint on the sides, symbols of merchants that no longer passed this way.

Lianna moved slowly toward the town square. She stepped lightly, not from fear but reverence. Here, where stone met scorched wood, had been the center of Bramblegate. Now it was a shallow depression in the earth, with only the dry outline of the well and the warped base of the old noticeboard left behind.

Liosan crouched beside it, tilting his head at the foundation. He touched a stone that had clearly been cracked by heat, then turned it over to find an old glyph carved into the underside. Not a spell, just a sign of welcome. He set it gently back.

"Some of these made it to Rynthavael," Lianna said softly, as if to no one. "About fifty of the town's people made it out after the raid. Xavier and Ella brought them back. They were the first to settle the valley. The rest..." She didn't finish.

Frostclaw nosed at the broken doorway of a house, then backed away with a low growl. Just beyond the threshold, a long stain stretched across warped floorboards, soaked so deeply into the grain it had turned the wood black.

Scattered bones lay against the far wall, half buried beneath collapsed roofing. This had been one of the worst houses. Xavier had found three people here. He hadn't said much after dragging the bodies out for burial. Bones still lay inside now, gnawed and scattered. Not all of the raiders had been human, and not all of the victims had died cleanly.

"We passed through just after it happened," Xavier said. "The smoke hadn't even cleared. Chains were still warm from use. Some of the bodies hadn't been buried. We didn't have time for all of them. We buried the villagers where we could, marked the graves in what ground wasn't burned or scattered. The raiders, we left to the animals. No one mourned them."

Ella crouched beside him, brushing dust from a piece of broken blade. Her fingers lingered on it longer than they should have. "This was hers," she said quietly. "The little girl. She had this in her hand when I found her in the corner. Too small to fight. Too smart to scream. We found her before the raiders came back."

Valkra paced slowly at the edge of the square. She was silent, but the fur along her spine was bristling. She stopped near an overturned bench, sniffed once, and let out a soft exhale. Not a growl, not a warning, just a recognition. She too had been here with Xavier and Ella, though had remained outside the fighting. She had matured and leveled quickly in her time with the group.

Lythara stood apart from the others, near the breached edge of the outer wall. Her arms were crossed, eyes scanning the ridgeline beyond. Her posture was not tense, but alert. "No patrols," she said. "They don't bother with ruins."

Xavier rose. "They don't need to. They think no one would come back."

"They're not entirely wrong," Ella said, glancing at the others. "Most wouldn't."

Sihri kicked at a half-buried crate, her ears twitching in discomfort. "We shouldn't stay long. Feels like the place is holding its breath." Her voice was quieter now, the weight of it unfamiliar. She had seen death before, fought in blood-soaked pits where the air stank of iron and despair. But this was different. This was not a place where death had a crowd or rules. It was not a contest. This was a graveyard, and the ground remembered.

Lianna turned, her expression unreadable. "We camp outside the walls."

They moved with care back toward the forest's edge, settling beneath a thicket of dense-branched fir. The trees here were close-knit, the undergrowth sparse enough for clear vision but tangled enough to conceal them from casual view. There was no fire. Even Valkra curled close to Xavier without needing to be called. Frostclaw lay near Lianna, unmoving. Sihri rested against a low log, tightening the bindings of her steel-studded leather wraps with idle focus. She adjusted their fit around her knuckles, checking for loosened studs or frayed edges. There was nothing to sharpen, not really, but checking them gave her hands something to do and her thoughts something to anchor to. Liosan vanished partway up a tree, unseen but watching. Lythara sat with her back to a stone, not quite in the group's center, but not apart either. Her blade was unsheathed but idle in her hands. Ella rested with her bow laid across her lap, eyes closed but not asleep. The hum returned, almost imperceptible. Like a memory whispered through bark.

Eventually, it was Lianna who broke the silence. Her voice was low, the weight of command stripped away by remembrance of the devastation. "They'll expect us to follow the river east."

"We won't," Xavier replied. "We cut north. The ravine trail."

Ella opened her eyes. "No patrols there. Too unstable. No reason to watch it."

"No reason except someone with purpose might take it," Lythara said. Her tone was even, but something flickered behind her eyes.

Sihri grunted. "Perfect. Let's twist our ankles to stay one step ahead of fate."

"Better a twisted ankle than a blade in the ribs," Lianna muttered.

No one argued that point. Death hung like an unwelcome cloak on their thoughts.

The air was colder that night. Not from wind, but from memory. Bramblegate didn't cry out. It didn't accuse. It only lingered. Like smoke clinging to cloth long after the fire had gone out.

As the moon rose over the treetops, Xavier found himself awake, staring at the stars he couldn't name. He hadn't spoken much since entering the ruins. Ella stirred beside him, not speaking, but near enough that he felt that her hum almost returned. But it didn't.

Not here. Not this close to Bramblegate.

They would move in the morning. And the silence would remain behind them.

#

As the light broke the horizon in the morning, the forest was quieter. Not in sound, but in feeling. As if Bramblegate's silence had seeped outward into the roots of the Silverwood. Mist hung low along the underbrush, clinging to branches and draping across old game trails like tattered veils. It dampened the breath and dulled even the rustle of leaves. No birdsong stirred the canopy. No distant call from deer or low chitter of treefolk echoed back. The only movement came from the soft steps of the group as they broke camp in silence.

They left no trace, no ashes, no trampled ground, no scent marker if they could help it. Lianna moved with intent, her Ranger and Warden training at the forefront. She re-covered paths with light branchwork and layered false trails where necessary. Liosan had vanished early, already weaving through the perimeter like a wraith.

Lianna led with more tension than the day before. Her ears twitched at every shift in the breeze, and Frostclaw stayed closer than usual, body low, ears flicking toward unseen cues. They were no longer merely navigating the wilds. They were slipping through the edge of watchful land.

Xavier walked just behind the duo, his eyes distant but alert. The air felt heavier here, the faint pulse of ley energy more muted than near Rynthavael. He could still sense the distant thread of Syr'Vailen through the ley beneath his feet, but it had grown faint, more memory than song.

Ella moved beside him, her bow already strung with an arrow in hand. She hadn't spoken much since the night before. Her hum had returned briefly during the pre-dawn watch but had faded by the time they broke camp. There was a tightness to her expression, not pain, but focused intent. She matched Xavier's pace exactly, her movements economical, practiced.

Sihri trailed a few steps behind them, not quite grumbling, but certainly not at ease. Her foot caught on a root and she hissed softly, brushing the damp leaves away. "At least a tunnel has got the decency to stay level," she muttered, brushing dew from her legs.

"And collapse behind you," Lythara said, her voice neutral as she passed just beside the Rabbitkin.

Sihri scowled. "You say that like it is a bad thing."

"Only if you're planning to go back." Rejoined the succubus.

It had become something of a pattern between them. Whenever the terrain turned rough or the forest grew too thick, Sihri would grumble about tunnels, and Lythara would answer with the same dry retort. Neither admitted it, but the banter had begun to soften the space between them. A kind of rhythm had formed, sharp-edged but familiar.

Lythara scanned the trees, crimson eyes sweeping left and right. She walked near the flank but was never far from reach. Her hand rested lightly on the hilt of her blade, and the faint shimmer of mana around her wrists showed she was keeping at least one enchantment at the ready.

The terrain changed gradually. Slopes thickened with stone roots and uneven footing, the beginning of the ancient ground that bordered Arenvalis. Patches of moss-covered rock jutted from the forest floor, and narrow gullies cut through the brush like old scars.

Liosan reappeared near a twisted maple, giving a flick of his fingers and tapping twice against his thigh before pointing up the incline.

Lianna nodded without hesitation. "Higher ground. Better visibility."

They moved as one, climbing the narrow incline with care. The air changed with each step, cooler, drier, touched by a faint wind that smelled of pine smoke and old stone.

At the ridge, the trees broke just enough to offer a broad

western view. The sky was pale and stretched, and for a moment, all was still. Then they saw it.

Far on the horizon, dark tendrils of smoke rose in thick, steady columns. Not one. Not two. Many.

Ironhaven burned.

The smoke was not the lazy gray of campfires or village hearths. It was black. Roiling. Alive with motion and heat. It stretched upward in great towers, clawing at the sky.

No one spoke at first. Frostclaw growled low. Valkra stiffened, her ears flat, muscles tense. Even the wind felt sharper here, as if it carried the memory of something more than flame.

Xavier was the first to breathe. "Verdantspire," he said softly. "They moved."

Lianna crouched at the ridge, narrowing her eyes. Her hand shaded her brow. "More than one burn point. Multiple fires. Deliberate positioning. That's not wild. That's strategy."

Ella took a slow breath. "They're drawing eyes. Giving us room."

"And giving the gods something else to watch," Lythara added. "Divine focus is like a lantern in the dark. They just made another light."

Sihri folded her arms. "Yeah, and drew every moth in a mile to it. That much smoke brings more than attention. It brings response."

"It brings questions," Xavier said. "And noise. That may be all we need."

They watched the fire for a few minutes longer. The smoke didn't fade. If anything, it grew darker, thicker, whipped by rising air.

"There's risk in this," Lianna said finally. "They're burning a snake den to distract the hawks."

"It will work," Xavier said. "Because it has to."

Liosan tapped his thigh again and gestured northward. He did not point toward the smoke. He pointed to movement, not people, but dust shifting in the air. Patrols might be sweeping west already.

Lianna rose. "We move. Stay below the ridge line. East curve first, then hook north."

No one argued and they descended into shadow again, the firelight of the horizon behind them.

As they walked, the implications grew louder in silence. Verdantspire had risked open retaliation. Attacks like these weren't surgical; they were statements. Messages written in fire.

Lythara walked beside Xavier for a time. Her voice was soft, but steady. "That was bold, and reckless. They don't know who might answer. Chainsworn, the military, or something worse."

"They know the price," Xavier replied.

She gave a half-nod. "Then so do we."

Sihri glanced toward the smoke one last time. "They lit the fire. Hope someone's ready to carry the torch."

Behind them, the wind shifted bringing the smoke of the burning slaver town towards the ruins of one of its victims, and Bramblegate grew smaller with every step.

#

The lowlands near Arenvalis held a tension that could not be measured in miles or weather. It was in the air, in the shape of the land, in the way the birds were no longer singing and the insects fell quiet by dusk. Even without borders marked by stone or flag, they knew when they had crossed from wild soil into claimed ground. Land they had only recently fled and now willingly returned to.

The change was subtle. The underbrush grew thinner, yet more orderly. Trees stood straighter, less wild in posture. Paths once twisted by nature now curved with purpose, remnants of old trails woven into the shape of the land. The wild had not retreated, but it had been pushed, coaxed into alignment by ancient hands.

Lianna halted near a stone outcrop just past a dry creekbed. Her posture sharpened instantly; one hand raised in warning. The group gathered around her as she pointed to a boulder embedded in the hillside. On its surface, a rune pulsed faintly, a series of interwoven lines and spirals etched deep and glowing dim blue beneath the rising sun.

"Watching ward," she said quietly. "Divine signature. It is not triggered by movement, just records it."

Ella stepped beside her, crouching low. "Still active. Old, but reinforced recently. Tied to the Edict."

Xavier stepped forward, studying the rune. His brow furrowed as he knelt, examining its construction. It was layered, not a single glyph but a latticework of intent. He could feel the pulse of it beneath his skin, not strong, but persistent. The lines were not just decorative. They followed logic and pattern.

He reached toward it but did not touch it. "It is almost like a listening spell," he murmured. "Only passive. There is no alert. No trap. Just memory."

Ella nodded. "A divine observer. It records presence, sends that knowledge elsewhere. Somewhere that is still bound to the Edict most likely. Not immediately like an alarm, but it adds to a greater weight."

"Can I learn it?" Xavier asked.

She glanced at him. "You are starting to see how the language works. Study it. Trace the logic. Do not copy it, understand it."

He nodded and pulled out his journal, sketching the rune carefully. As he did, faint hints of its structure began to settle in his mind. Not just the shape, but the intention behind it: awareness, clarity, presence. He would not be able to recreate it, not yet, but he could learn from it.

Lythara stood watch, her stance stiff. "These are not Chainsworn markings. They are temple runes. Only priests or sanctioned wardens can place them."

"Same source," Lianna muttered. "The Edict does not care which hands it moves through, only that they obey."

Sihri scowled, stepping around the ward. "So they are watching. Not just people, gods."

From then on, they moved with greater care. They camped on stone when they could, soft ground when they must. Always cold, always hidden, but when the ground was stable and the air quiet, they began to train.

Each evening, after making camp and setting watches, the group would clear a space among the brush and stretch of earth. Wooden weapons were drawn from their packs, carved roughly but balanced well enough for practice. While they took turns amongst themselves, Sihri and Lianna sparred often, each testing the other in close strikes and fast movement, and Xavier often trained with Ella using paired short blades, his Vaeltheris shifting into a dulled training form each time they crossed weapons.

He began to notice something new. Each time he fought, each time he moved with the blade, patterns came more easily. Movements he had not drilled suddenly felt familiar.

Parries, footwork, angled strikes, skills he should have needed weeks to refine seemed to settle into his muscles as if remembered from a life he had never lived. The blade was teaching him. Or perhaps more accurately, the knowledge bound within Vaeltheris was seeping into him. Not in words or flashes of memory, but in instinct, in rhythm, in form.

Even Lythara joined the drills, moving with deceptive smoothness, her style marked by elegant, sharp arcs. She rotated between facing Xavier and Ella, offering quiet corrections or unexpected feints that forced them to adapt. Liosan never sparred long but slipped between mock duels to test reactions, darting like a shadow. Sihri grumbled about his habit of stealing hits, but her tone grew lighter with each match.

It was not about show. It was preparation. They knew what lay ahead would not be kind. So, they trained. They learned each other's rhythms and adjusted. Timing, reach, pressure, weight. Learning not only their own rhythm, skills and limits but each other's and how to complement them. The hours of silence between movement began to feel less hollow, filled now with breath and sweat and shared resolve.

Frostclaw and Valkra circled or watched from the perimeter, alert but calm. The animals understood what the group was doing. They too knew the smell of coming battle.

Each night, when the sparring was done, they returned to silence. But it no longer felt empty.

For three more days, they wound their way deeper into Arenvalis territory. Glyphs appeared with increasing frequency, carved into stone markers, set into trees, even painted in fading oils along old shrine walls. Some glowed with quiet energy, others were inert, but each one reminded them they were being observed.

Liosan marked every glyph in silence, altering their course subtly each time to avoid drawing direct attention. The group followed, their paths winding farther from the roads and deeper through forgotten paths.

On the seventh day, they came upon a field marked by a battle long past. Broken weapons jutted from the earth like rusted thorns. Grass grew in tangled patterns, avoiding places where shields and armor still rotted beneath the soil. In the center, divine sigils hovered faintly above the ground, rotating in slow, silent rhythm.

Lianna knelt, her voice low. "Do not step inside."

Even Liosan did not stray far. He crouched nearby, eyes narrowed, motionless.

Lythara circled the edge, gaze locked on the hovering symbols. "These are not common sanctifications. Too old. Too precise. It is not a remembrance site."

Ella nodded. "I see no connection to Solara or the Radiant gods. The edges are... wrong. They likewise are not tied to Danu or the Veiled gods. This feels of something from the Boundless pantheon"

Lianna rose slowly, dusting her fingers off. "This feels like a focus point. Not divine worship. A conduit, maybe. I have seen patterns like this in places Verdantspire avoids."

Xavier watched the sigils twist slowly above the ground, their motion too smooth, too quiet. "Could this be a preparation site?"

"Possibly," Lythara said, her voice quieter now. "Not a place of death, but something waiting beneath it. I have seen wards like this used to preserve a presence. Not rest or peace. It is more a form of maintenance."

Ella frowned, her expression hardening. "These runes

hum like binding glyphs, but they are not aligned to hold anything out. They are holding something in."

No one spoke for a moment.

Lianna finally stepped back. "It is a tether. Whatever battle happened here... someone, or something, claimed the ground afterward."

Xavier exhaled through his nose, thoughtful. "Then this is not a scar. It is a seed."

The group gave the field a wide berth. Whatever purpose the hovering sigils served, none of them wanted to see what waited underneath.

On the tenth day, the hills began to rise. Stone veins ran like scars beneath their feet. Shrines became more frequent, some whole, others half-buried or shattered. One bore a statue of a faceless figure with open hands. Another had been wrapped in vines so thick even Lianna's blade could not part them.

At twilight on the twelfth day, they crested a final ridge. The light stretched long across the land, painting the sky in muted gold. And there, rising from the earth like a buried crown, stood Thandor's Reach.

The capital of Arenvalis, pale stone towers, walls of etched granite. On high poles banners of faded authority hung fluttering in the high breeze. They did not move toward the gates. Instead, they headed towards the base of the rise. At the foot of the slope, hidden by roots and the bones of a long-collapsed hill road, they found what they were searching for. A narrow vent tucked behind overgrown bramble and broken masonry. It was not a sewer; it wasn't really a tunnel meant for normal people. Instead, it was a vent, a servant path. But most importantly it was supposed to be forgotten.

It was open. Just enough. Xavier knelt beside the stonework, fingers brushing along the broken rim. The seal was fractured, not shattered, but split with precision.

Liosan checked for traps and found none. He could feel that there had been magic, long dissolved. He signed it clearly.

Ella examined the edge, fingertips glowing faintly. "This was sealed by ritual. Divine-scribed. But someone broke it from the inside."

Lianna frowned. "Not our plan. Verdantspire did not open this."

Xavier stood slowly. "Then someone else is already inside."

The air that spilled from the vent was cold. It carried damp stone, iron, and something older. Something that had been waiting.

"Prepare yourselves," he said quietly. "We're going in blind." And without another word, they descended into the dark.

# CHAPTER THIRTY-SIX

*Beneath the Reach*

They entered the tunnel in silence. No torchlight, only breath and boots and the steady descent into old stone. The broken vent curved sharply downward, never meant for full-grown warriors, just the smoke and servants of a forgotten age. Dust clung to the walls and the air did not move.

Liosan led, his playful nature had vanished as he stepped into the tunnel. Now he moved like he belonged to the dark, silent, sure-footed, crouched low. His twin, Lianna, followed a few paces back, bow slung and hands light on her blade. She watched him more than the path. They moved in sync, as they always had, brother and sister, tracker and ghost.

Xavier came next, with one hand brushing the tunnel wall. Behind him padded Sihri, steps near silent, every sense attuned. Ella followed, her blades sheathed, and her demeanor calm but alert. Lythara brought up the rear, daggers loose in her grip, crimson eyes flicking constantly to walls and shadows.

Valkra and Frostclaw followed last. The tunnel was tight for them, but they pressed forward without hesitation.

Loyalty guided their steps, not fear. Valkra's ears twitched at every shift in air, and Frostclaw's low growl barely echoed, but neither beast faltered. They belonged to those ahead, and that bond outweighed instinct.

It was clear that the tunnel predated the Edict. Xavier could barely feel ley lines beneath his feet. The tunnel bore no etched runes. Just pressure and immense age. It was old stone shaped by mortal hands, perhaps escape tunnels, or servant paths long forgotten.

Xavier slowed and let his palm settle flat against the wall. The Earth whispered tension. "Hold," he said quietly. "Stress in the right flank. Too much weight. If we rush it, it folds."

Sihri crouched low and swept her hand along the dusty floor. "Pressure plate," she murmured. "Set shallow. Could snap the wall if it's nudged."

As she moved, nearing the trap the plate illuminated a deep red to Xavier. His trap awareness skill confirmed what she had found.

Liosan slipped ahead. Gone in an instant. He returned moments later and signed to Lianna, three paths, left sealed, center trapped, right passable.

Lianna nodded. "We go right."

They moved with grace they had earned in previous tunnels and dungeons, each step placed, each breath held where needed. This wasn't a march; this was an infiltration. An old chamber opened around them, collapsed crates and shattered wall hooks scattered across the floor. The tunnels were now illuminated by sparse torchlight. They were used just not often it seemed. A warped glyph still burned low on the far wall, Lythara identified Solara's sunburst marred by flame, its rays scorched into curling ridges like scales.

Ella studied it. "It is Solara like Lythara said, but the law was bent. Someone tried to change it."

"They failed," Lythara said coldly. "The Edict adapts. Even in ash."

They moved on in thought. Then it hit. It was not sound or light, instead it was sudden pressure.

Lythara staggered mid-step. Her shoulders jerked back, eyes flashing wide though it was not in fear, but in recognition. Threads of gold and void-black light twisted into being around her, pulling tight across her arms, chest, and throat. They formed symbols mid-air: scales, sunrays, and something colder, jagged, bone-like ridges etched in silence. They were chains without metal, law without voice. A divine snare.

She dropped to one knee, breath catching as the filaments pulsed, reacting to every heartbeat. They didn't just bind, they branded. The air around her thickened as sigils formed behind her: a spiral of law, arcing like a noose over the floor.

Xavier spun toward her and froze. He didn't reach for her, he didn't dare and risk being caught in the trap himself. Instead, his hand went to the stone, to the glyph's origin point, searching, reading, feeling.

---

**RUNE DECIPHERING - Triggered**

**Construct Identified:** Infernal Conscription Trap

**Type:** Divine Passive Snare

**Designation:** Seal-Linked Resonant Judgment

**Origin:** Triune Composite (Solara, Aran, Nekros)

**Trigger:** Legacy of Binding – Infernal Pact Signature

---

**Structure:** Soul recognition through divine imprint memory

**Function:** Suppress, Expose, Humiliate

**Secondary Layer:** Broadcast-capable to seal nexus anchors

**Risk:** Continued resistance may tether subject to seal as new anchor

Xavier's jaw clenched. "It's not just containment," he said. "It's designed to display her. To mark her as fallen and feed the lock more weight."

Lythara snarled through gritted teeth. The snare flexed again, and her body arched in reaction this time not from pain, but from resistance. Her skin smoked along the collarbone, where faint brand-scars tried to resurface. Echoes of the old infernal contract shimmered under the divine strain.

Sihri hissed from behind. "It's feeding on what she used to be?"

Xavier nodded grimly. "And if she doesn't break it now, it'll bind her again. Permanently."

Lythara didn't respond. Her daggers were already drawn, they had been from the moment they entered the tunnel. Not in defense but in purpose though bound as she was, they were near to useless.

She breathed in concentrating on one long, centered draw. The darkness at the edge of the corridor stretched to her fingertips. Not magic per se, at least not spellwork. It was more of a skill innate to her specialization. Just movement, refined in a hundred ambushes, a thousand kills. Shadow bent around her. In one smooth slip of motion, she stepped out of the center of the glyph, vanished, and reappeared behind the sigil's spiral ring. Her dagger snapped outward, slicing through the stabilizing rune hidden just behind the wall's fracture line.

The trap cracked like glass under pressure. The lingering filaments collapsed as the glyph disintegrated in pieces.

Lythara stood breathing hard, one hand pressed against the stone. "Even now," she muttered, "they try to leash me."

Xavier stepped forward but kept his voice low. "It is clear they rebuilt this place on obedience on that edict of order. You're proof that defiance survives."

She didn't look at him, instead she sheathed her blades without speaking again.

The small group continued on. The risks now even more defined, they didn't speak for a while. Liosan moved ahead in silence. Lianna kept pace beside Xavier, her eyes sharp for any mark from her brother. She said nothing at first, but when they passed beneath a bent arch carved with chipped prayer rings, she broke the stillness.

"You all right?" Her voice carried back to the succubus. It wasn't soft. But it wasn't cold either.

Lythara didn't shift her motion. "I am now."

"You froze." Lianna's tone wasn't angry, just sharp, like truth exposed.

"I remembered."

Lianna gave a short nod. Recognition of the reaction if not agreement.

Sihri muttered, "Trap like that? Damn near a second branding."

"They weren't just trying to bind her," Xavier added. "They wanted her seen. The rune would have marked her and reported its capture."

Ella glanced at him, her expression unreadable. "You think there'll be more?"

"There always are," he sighed.

They pressed forward again, deeper into the stone beneath the city.

Liosan halted near the next turn. Two fingers tapped against the wall, sharp, deliberate action in signal.

Lianna read the sign. "One ahead. Divine."

Xavier stepped quietly to the bend and peered ahead. In the flickering torchlight a man stood still as stone. Black and silver robes over plate-trimmed armor. His chest bore two marks interwoven: A sunburst and a pair of balanced scales.

Chainsworn. It had to be. He leaned back and murmured "Single man, sunburst and scales on his chest."

Lythara scowled a moment in thought. "Solara and Aran maybe?"

Ella nodded in agreement and Xavier peeked back around the corner.

The man raised a hand, and a glyph formed mid-air just beyond his fingertips, its form radiant and precise.

Xavier didn't reach for his weapons. He let *Insight* flare.

---

**INSIGHT – Apprentice Rank Activated**

Partial Profile Provided

**Name:** Unknown

**Race:** Human

**Class Archetype:** Warden

**Subclass:** Judicator – Divine suppression specialist

**Condition:** Healthy

**Role:** Anchor – Sanctum-linked enforcer, reactive to breach

**Magic State:** Channeling glyph resonance through divine oath

"He's not here to fight. He's here to hold."

Xavier marveled for a moment at the increase in information after the skill had improved to the next rank.

Lythara, however, moved before the Warden's glyph finished forming. She was there one moment then she was gone. The shadows folded over itself and she reappeared behind him in a blur of silence. One of her wicked daggers slid beneath his ribs. The other cut upward through the casting hand, shattering the forming glyph with the sound of cracking glass.

He crumpled like a marionette with its strings cut. She let him fall as she flicked the vestiges of blood from her knives.

Xavier knelt beside the body. One of the dead man's bracers still glowed faintly though its glyph thread fading rapidly. "He was part of it," Xavier said. "A living seal." This was confirmed by the minimize prompt he read marking the man's death.

**You have slain a Chainsworn Judicator**

You have slain a divine-tethered Warden acting as a living anchor for the Sanctum of Order. His death has unbalanced the triune seal and weakened the divine hold over the prison beneath Thandor's Reach. The gods will feel the breach.

**+2,400 Experience**

**+1 Divine Awareness Fragment** (Passive Tracking Increased. Update: All tracking and divination of Xavier is prevented by the Amulet of the Unknown)

+20 Reputation with Animari Resistance

-15 Reputation with Chainsworn Order

"Divine constructs remember what they lose."

Ella's voice was steady though there was a tinge of horror in her tone. "This lock, it isn't just stone. It's people. It's belief."

Lianna turned toward the corridor ahead. "And they're watching who breaks it."

No one disagreed as the realization gave voice to new threats. Instead, they moved on, and ahead, the air grew heavier.

#

The corridor narrowed, then widened again, sloping slightly downward until it opened into a chamber that felt colder than the air outside. It wasn't the chill that made them pause, instead it was the pressure. The air pressed in on them, not with temperature, but with presence. A spiritual gravity that settled against skin and bone, thick with divine intent. Xavier could feel the resonance before he saw the source, a tension in his bones, a buzz against his skull. The others felt it too, even Valkra and Frostclaw hesitated at the threshold, their ears pinned, muscles taut.

Stone pillars lined the edges, twelve in total, arranged in perfect symmetry, each spaced precisely apart in rigid measure. Their placement was intentional, uncompromising. This was not a chamber of worship, but enforcement. A hall of divine precision. Some pillars bore fractures from age or unseen strain, yet even damaged, they retained their alignment. Most of the glyphs had faded into silence, but three remained: one in gold, one in silver, one in black. They pulsed in measured cadence, like a heartbeat regulated by will, not life. The air carried a scent of old incense and ash, ritualistic remnants of a time when holy authority still echoed here.

Lythara stopped just inside the chamber. Her voice was low, but steady. "We've found the seal."

Xavier stepped forward. In the center of the far wall, framed by fluted supports and worn carvings, stood a massive stone door. It was not shaped to open. There were no hinges, no seam. Only a smooth slab of rock bearing an etched tri-fold sigil: a blazing sun, a pair of balanced scales, and a hollow-eyed skull, all interlocked. Radiance, Judgment, Death.

The symbols glowed faintly, but not evenly. The skull flickered briefly, the light within it stuttered.

Xavier stepped closer. Vaeltheris pulsed once at his side, then dimmed again, as if shrinking away.

Ella came up beside him, frowning. "That's why it won't speak. This isn't a ward. It's a lock."

Xavier examined the edges of the seal. Bladed runes circled the triune glyph, etched so finely they looked like veins across the stone. They were deep, too deep for mortal hands. Some flickered subtly, like threads unraveling in slow motion.

He reached toward them, but his hand stopped inches short. "I feel it," he muttered. "But I don't understand it."

"It's divine," Lythara said quietly. "Not just in purpose. In construction."

Lianna glanced between the three glowing glyphs. "That's Solara, Aran, and Nekros?"

Lythara nodded. "Radiant, Veiled, and Boundless. A triune edict." Her gaze lingered on the seal as she added, "Most believe such cooperation among the pantheons is rare, impossible even. But there are whispers, rumors that, during the founding years of the Edict, the lawful deities of all three pantheons united for a single purpose. Not to protect, not to destroy, but to suppress. To drive chaos out of the world and implement a perfect order. What they sealed here is more recent however, and its purpose remains unclear, only that it was important enough to bend their pride and place their marks together.

Sihri crossed her arms. "Three gods working together. That never ends well."

Ella walked the curve of the chamber, trailing her fingers just above the stone. "This entire structure is a divine prison. Not to hold something out, but to keep something in, and now one of its anchors is broken."

Xavier turned sharply. "The Judicator?"

She nodded. "He was tethered. A living conduit, but not for all three. He carried the mark of Solara and Aran. Not Nekros. Still, with him gone..."

The skull mark flickered again, its glow twitching like a dying ember. Though the fallen Chainsworn bore no connection to Nekros, the weakening of the seal's Radiant and Veiled conduits had unbalanced the triune symmetry. Triune Divine constructs relied on harmony, when one thread faltered, the entire weave strained. A subtle distortion ran through the air like a snapped harp string. The floor beneath their feet vibrated faintly, a tremor felt more than heard. Something behind the seal stirred, not in awareness, but in pressure. Not awakened, but shifting.

The seal had not failed, but it had begun to lean.

A ripple passed across the surface of the door, faint, a hairline defect. A seam that hadn't been visible before now caught Xavier's eye. It split vertically through the center of the skull and into the lower edge of the scales.

"An imperfection," he whispered.

Ella crouched and studied the edge of the glyph. "It's reacting. Not enough to open, not yet, but it's weakened."

Lythara stepped closer, her eyes narrowing. "The others will know. A death like his… it leaves a mark. They'll feel it."

Lianna shifted beside her brother. "Then we don't have long."

Xavier exhaled, stepping back from the door. "Thoughts?"

"Unseat one of the gods, or mimic their authority," Ella said. "Anything less is just scratching at stone."

Xavier frowned. "I can't defeat a god."

"No," Lythara said. "But you killed one of their anchors. That's enough to tilt the seal's balance."

They stood in silence, the pulsing glyphs marking each breath. The room felt tighter with every passing moment.

Finally, Xavier turned. "We make camp. Not here, pull back one corridor. Watch both ways. I need time to think."

There was no dissent as they turned away, quiet and deliberate, each step echoing in the stillness. Behind them, the triune seal pulsed once, softly, rhythmically, like a held breath through stone. It wasn't bright. It wasn't loud. But the presence behind it stirred with awareness, not just of their actions, but of who they were. The lock did not open and the door did not move.

#

They withdrew from the seal chamber without haste, but with every step measured. The silence clung to them as they retreated, not just a silence of sound, but of judgment withheld. The corridor one bend back offered a shallow alcove, a break in the wall where stone had once collapsed, then been cleared by deliberate hands. It wasn't secure, but it was defensible. The walls bore faint traces of old design, prayer-carved channels, and beveled motifs now chipped by time. It was likely they were deeper beneath one of the central temples above, though which god held sway over this region of the Reach remained unspoken. That would have to do.

They set no fire. The corridor itself held old signs of maintenance, iron brackets with torches, and here and there, narrow alcoves where oil lamps still hung. Some flickered weakly, tended perhaps by unseen hands or left burning for the Chainsworn who patrolled these depths. Faint traces of soot marked the ceiling in lines. It was clear this place, however ancient, had not been entirely forgotten. The dim, uneven light was enough to cast shifting shadows across the alcove. Vaeltheris gave a faint glow where it lay against Xavier's lap, a pulse of warmth rather than light.

Lianna took first watch, Liosan disappearing up the corridor to scout in the direction they hadn't come. Sihri and Ella unrolled bedrolls without speaking. Lythara sat near the far edge of the alcove, cross-legged, daggers laid across her knees. She had cleaned them but kept them drawn. Xavier noticed the tension in her shoulders, a tightness that hadn't eased since the snare. He sat near the succubus, not too close, but not far apart either. Like her he began to clean Vaeltheris.

"We were right to come," he said softly, to no one in

particular.

Lythara didn't look at him. "You should speak that certainty to the thing behind the door."

"I would," he replied, "if I thought it would listen."

Silence lingered heavy in the air. Ella eventually sat beside him. "That seal wasn't just meant to hold. It was meant to last. You don't etch a glyph that deep unless you intend it to outlive empires."

Sihri grunted from her bedroll. "Or outlast witnesses."

Lianna's voice came quietly from the edge of the watch. "There were no names on that door. Just symbols. No dedication, no script, that's not how Animari do it." She hesitated before adding, "That's how you bury a memory not a monster."

"No," Lythara murmured. "It's how gods do it. When they don't want you to know who they fear, or what they need, kept silent."

The quiet that followed was heavier than stone. A thread of suspicion wound silently between them, none of them dared voice the thought, but each felt its shape. A king, perhaps. Sealed not to protect the world, but to preserve the gods' rule. For the rest of that camp, no one raised their voice above a whisper. Even their dreams, when they came, spoke only in hushes.

#

They did not sleep well. The stone did not offer rest. It pressed back against breath and thought, carrying every exhale as if the earth itself listened. No nightmares came, but neither did peaceful dreams, only fragments, whispers that curled at the edge of thought. Voices that spoke in hushed tones, not words, but impressions: a throne half-buried in ash, the sound of chains dragged across marble, and a heartbeat that wasn't their own. They were dreams that did not wake them but lingered like fog long after eyes opened.

Lianna sat against the wall near the entrance, her bow laid across her knees. She had not moved in over an hour, lost in thought. Sihri tossed once, then settled back into her bedroll. Lythara did not sleep at all. She remained still, cross-legged, her blades resting across her lap. Her gaze focused on the far wall. Even the mostly implacable Ella, silent and calm, looked as though she was waiting rather than resting.

Vaeltheris pulsed lightly where Xavier rested. He sat too long in stillness, thoughts tangled in the seal and the flicker behind the skull glyph. Pressure built along the edges of thought. Purpose pressed into stone and something watched.

A whisper of movement down the hall. Lianna shifted. Her hand went up, open. Warning. Liosan appeared in the torchlight without a sound. His hair was damp with sweat, his fingers quick as he signed: Guards shifting. Two above. Armor. Uncertain route.

As Lianna translated, Ella frowned. "They know something is wrong."

"Then the Judicator's death is no longer a secret," Lythara said, rising without sound. "Or the seal has begun to resonate beyond this depth."

Xavier glanced toward the corridor, then to the walls. He stood and pressed one hand to the stone, his Earth-sense told him nothing of gods or their divine intentions, but it did not lie silent either. Something beneath the surface pulsed faintly, not like a ley line or lifeform, but like a command signal. Regular and intentionally restrained.

"It's not a warning. Too calm for that," he murmured.

"It's a check-in. Something making sure the seal is still whole."

One of the oil lamps hanging on the opposite wall flickered. The flame bent sideways for a moment, casting a crooked shadow against the alcove's entrance. For a heartbeat, it looked like the outline of a man, broad of shoulder, head bowed beneath invisible chains. The flicker passed and the shadow vanished. No one spoke for several seconds staring at the alcove.

"It is watching us," Sihri finally said. "Whatever is behind that seal, or what is holding it shut."

Frostclaw growled softly from her place at the wall's edge. Valkra crept nearer to Xavier, her body low, ears pinned. Both animals sensed it too.

"They will send more," Ella said quietly. "Chainsworn, guards, soldiers, priests, or worse."

"Then we do not wait," Lythara answered. "We act before they reinforce."

"We do not know enough," Lianna snapped. "What if the seal fails because we pushed too soon?"

Xavier didn't answer right away. He looked down at the faint glow of Vaeltheris, then toward the corridor. "No action yet," he said at last. "But the gods are listening. So, we plan for what we'll say when they ask us why we knocked."

#

The lamplight dimmed with the hours, until only a handful of flickering wicks remained, throwing distorted shapes across the corridor. Outside the alcove, the seal chamber waited, still closed, still pulsing, still watching. The weight of the triune glyphs lingered, pressing into their thoughts like a hand against the mind. The pressure was not pain or command. It was just presence, constant and silent.

Lianna finally broke the quiet. "If we act, we risk breaking it. If we do nothing, the gods or their agents will send more." Her voice was low but firm, laced with the kind of tension that came not from fear, but from readiness unmet.

Sihri sat up, rubbing sleep from her eyes. "They will send them either way. We have already gone too deep. They will not let that go unanswered." She looked toward the shadows with narrowed eyes. "It does not matter how quiet we were. This place knows we are here."

Ella ran a hand along the carvings on the alcove wall. "There is power in silence. They have kept this secret for a reason. If we speak the wrong truth too early, they will bury us with it."

No one laughed. Not even Sihri. Xavier sat with his back to the stone, Vaeltheris resting across his knees once again. The blade pulsed faintly with a slow, steady rhythm, like a second heartbeat. He had stopped looking at the others, instead he was watching the corridor that led back to the seal.

"They sealed someone," he said at last. "Not something. There's no threat beyond that door except what it reveals."

Lythara's eyes glinted crimson in the low light. "You think it is the king?"

"I think it's someone too important to erase, and too dangerous to leave walking." He replied.

Lianna frowned, arms folded tight. "If it is Rorik, and we free him, what does that make us?"

Xavier looked up at her. "That depends on what they made of him... And what he remembers."

Frostclaw stirred near Lianna's side, tail twitching against the stone. Valkra crept closer to the alcove entrance again, her low posture and rigid stillness showing the same unease that hung in the air.

Then came a rustle of movement. Liosan reappeared in the torchlight like a shadow returning to form. His movements were sharp and efficient. His hands flashed in a series of signs. Xavier read them instantly but said nothing. He already knew the message before a moment later, Lianna began to translate out of habit, signing back in return so Liosan could follow the rest of the conversation. "City waking. Priests stirring. Soldiers alert. Movement toward temple levels. Five, maybe six."

Ella exhaled. "That's not routine."

Lythara stood slowly, blades already in hand. "They are repositioning. Closing the path."

Time was running thin. Xavier stood as well, his motions steady despite the tension threading through his limbs. "We prepare. I'm not breaking that seal blind. But we need to know more and soon."

He turned to each of them in turn, voice low but resolute. "Ella, help me study the runes. Anything familiar, anything flawed. Lythara, keep watch with Lianna if they send Chainsworn again, I want warning. Sihri, rest while you can. If this turns violent, I need you ready. Lianna let Liosan know to mark every path back out, and have him check for alternate ascents in case they cut our entry route."

They nodded one by one, trusting in his judgement, there was no protest and there was no hesitation.

Xavier looked once more toward the sealed chamber. The pulse behind the stone had not changed, but it no longer felt distant.

"If they buried the truth behind a door," he said, "then our silence ends when we choose it, not when they command it."

# CHAPTER THIRTY-SEVEN

*The Fractured Brand*

They returned to the chamber that held the seal and what they could only assume was the king's prison without speaking. Each of their footsteps echoed with a faint, dissonant ring, sounding too sharp, too clear. Except it wasn't sound, not truly. It was the weight of magic, divine and ancient, humming beneath the stone. The deeper they moved into the sanctum, the more it felt like walking into the breath of something enormous. Not fully asleep, but dreaming and aware.

The corridor behind them narrowed into stillness as they crossed its threshold. Here, the world felt thinner. The air was neither warm nor cold, only dense, thick with meaning, thick with presence. Even their shadows stretched unnaturally long, as though they were cast by a light that didn't exist.

The triune glyph upon the sealed door, sun, scales, skull, remained etched in unmoving stone, yet something had changed. The change was not overt, it wasn't even really a physical change. But perceptibly it seemed that the glyphs no longer slept. Instead, they felt like they were watching the chamber now.

Ella moved first, brushing her fingers along the wall's smooth surface. Carved glyphs responded faintly to her touch, pulsing beneath her skin like the beat of a buried heart. "It's shifting," she whispered. "Not the glyphs. The pressure." Her voice didn't echo. It was devoured by the weight in the room.

Xavier dropped to one knee and laid his palm flat against the floor. The stone vibrated ever so slightly, not from the stone itself tremoring, but from purpose. Something beneath was stirring, slow and inevitable. Not just awakening but remembering. "It's aligning itself again," he said. "Slowly."

Vaeltheris, held in his other hand, rested against his thigh. It was warm and restless, and the blade's subtle pulses were uneven, like a creature sniffing the air for danger it couldn't yet see. Xavier frowned, turning it in his hand. The weapons faint glow hadn't shifted. Instead, he got the impression that it was watching, not outward but inward. As if it were being read.

The others slowly filed into the chamber as well. Distinctly aware of the shift in its atmosphere. Lythara entered last, her boots made no sound as she crossed the threshold. Her eyes swept the chamber once, then settled on the seal. She froze, and her breath caught just briefly, as her fingers curled into fists. "Something is watching again," she said.

Her voice was different, tight, coiled, like a blade waiting for release.

Sihri stepped up beside her, ears flicking. "Not someone?"

Lythara shook her head. "No. Not a person. A... presence. Old. Cold. Too big to name."

The others spread out slowly, weapons close, senses open. Even Frostclaw moved cautiously now, his massive paws silent on the stone. Then it started. A sudden lurch, like the chamber exhaled. The torches did not flicker. The glyphs did not move, but every living thing in the chamber felt it. Like stepping from shallow water into sudden depth.

Xavier flinched as a cold ripple passed over him. The mark over his ribs burned, not with pain or burning, but with memory. Cold fingers brushing across his soul. A whisper without words, curling through him like smoke. He grunted once, and held a hand pressed to his chest.

Ella turned sharply, her eyes wide as she looked at him. "The mark?"

He nodded once. "It's not reacting, I don't think. It's more like... it's being... evaluated."

At that moment, a shimmer passed over Lythara's skin, and thin light traced itself along the curve of her collarbone. Like Xavier's mark it was not heat, not command, just judgment. Old and sterile. The mark that had once bound her flickered into view for a breath and was gone in the next.

Ella's brows furrowed. She crossed toward Lythara and Xavier, glancing between them. "It's finding the gaps. Reassigning roles."

"The seal's trying to restore itself," Xavier muttered, rising slowly. "It's not dead. It's correcting."

Lythara scoffed bitterly. "It will not bind me again." The silver glow dimmed, but the echo of its presence lingered. She rubbed her arms as if she could still feel it.

Sihri crouched beside one of the chamber's anchor stones. Her fingertips hovered over the carvings there. "This place was built for symmetry," she murmured.

627

"Three parts, three roles, and now it is out of balance."

Ella studied the glyphs with a growing unease. "The Veiled anchor... whoever it was, they're not here."

Xavier nodded grimly. "And the Radiant one, the Judicator, fell yesterday."

Frostclaw paced near the center, ears flat, hackles raised. He didn't growl, his demeanor spoke volumes as he kept his tail swept low, and muscles bunched beneath his fur.

"It's reading us," Lianna said softly, her gaze locked on the door. "Figuring out which of us fit the roles it lost."

Vaeltheris vibrated once in Xavier's grip, as if it were affirming what the Iskari woman postulated, then settled.

Liosan emerged from the shadows near the entryway, his expression unreadable. He tapped his fingers against a column once, twice, then pointed at Xavier and Lythara without a word. Xavier nodded slowly.

"Not by name," Ella murmured, voice tight. "By fit."

A long silence stretched between them. It was not just absence of sound, but the presence of expectancy. The chamber itself had become an audience to the assessment.

Then, the triune seal pulsed. A single cycle through each of the represented colors. A flicker of white-gold, then silver, then black. Each flash aligned with the echo of a divine signature, Radiance, Judgment, Death, flaring in search of balance.

Then it repeated again. This time, however, it was deeper, slower. Behind the radiance of the seal, beyond stone and spell and time, the prison stirred with awareness.

A bound consciousness shifted in its chains, pulled toward an infliction of order it did not request.

The structure was reacting, recalibrating, desperate to maintain the triune lock that held the bound being in check, and at that moment, the prison noticed them not only as just the intruders but more so as the replacements.

#

The pressure in the chamber shifted again only this time they could feel it was with a focused intent.

Lythara stiffened. Her eyes darted to the seal, then upward toward the ceiling, then back to the floor. She didn't breathe. "He's coming," she said. "Folding space again just like before."

Xavier turned sharply, scanning the chamber. The pressure, dense and coiling, felt familiar, though it tugged at the edge of memory. His grip on Vaeltheris tightened.

"It's like... beneath Ironhaven," he muttered. "That moment before he appeared. The silence folding inward. Reality thinning." He looked at Lythara. "Is it the same?"

She gave a sharp nod. "Pressure. Stillness. Collapse. He's not arriving. He's already here. Just needs the moment to catch up."

The torches along the chamber walls dimmed, fading to mere embers as the light bent inward toward the seal.

Ella raised her blades in one smooth motion. "Get ready," she said quietly. Her voice was calm, but every muscle was taut. Near her ankles the ebon shape of Valkra crouched, her twin tails twitching in menace.

Sihri moved to the left flank, crouched behind a jagged slab of fallen stone. Lianna drew her bow, knocking an arrow in a single fluid movement. The hulking form of Frostclaw at her side, low and tense. Liosan vanished without a word.

The air of the chamber folded in on itself, not with

sound, but with vacuum an emptiness of space soon to be filled. A whisper of a scream, the sound too low for the ears, but felt deep in the bones, shuddered across the chamber as space buckled.

Then, with impossible smoothness, Ivarik Tharn was simply there. Simply appearing instead of stepping out of the void like beneath Ironhaven.

No flare hailed his arrival, no roar and no blast of heat. Just presence. He stood before the seal, tall and motionless, as if he'd always belonged there.

He stood resplendent in his blacksteel ceremonial plate that glistened under the half-light, etched with glyphs that pulsed in tandem with the seal behind him. At the center of his chestplate sat the grinning skull of Nekros, carved from obsidian and inlaid with veins of dark silver that bled downward like tears. His cloak was torn, but regal. His stance was neither aggressive nor defensive. He was not there to fight, instead he was there to finish something.

Ella's blades remained steady, but her eyes narrowed. Lythara didn't move. She just stared, teeth bared slightly in animus. Xavier stepped forward until he stood clear of the group, Vaeltheris in his left hand, Emberstone in his right.

"Ivarik," he said.

The man inclined his head, though it was not respectfully, not mockingly either. Just acknowledgment.

"I see the seal has begun responding," Ivarik said, his voice clear and resonant. "As I expected."

"You've lost your anchors," Xavier replied coldly.

Ivarik glanced past him, taking in the group with a glance. "Halestorm, the Veiled anchor," he said. "Slain nearly two weeks ago during the Verdantspire attack on Ironhaven. I assume that was your distraction. Clever though ultimately fruitless."

No one answered, it was clearly more statement than question.

He turned toward Lythara. "And the Radiant thread was cut yesterday. The Judicator fell beneath your blade I am guessing. It was to abrupt too be anything else." His eyes flicked towards the shadows that held Liosan. "Although…" he mused aloud.

Lythara said nothing, her expression stony and her crimson eyes flaring in hatred.

"So here we are," Ivarik said. "With two threads severed, and the seal unraveling. And yet… it adapts."

Three of the outer pillars shimmered faintly, black, gold, and silver. They were not lit flames, and it wasn't really light, it felt as though they were shifting in alignment.

"It always has." Ivarik continued. He stepped forward, boots making no sound against the stone. "The glyphs are already choosing," he said.

His eyes found Lythara first. "You, bound once by judgment, shaped in contract, and then loosed from the chains but never beyond reach truthfully. The Veiled mark still knows you. You have walked in shadow and light both. It remembers."

A shimmer of silver light flickered just above her chest. Not a brand this time, instead it was a pull. Lythara's fists clenched. Her lips curled, but she said nothing.

Then Ivarik turned to Xavier. "And you," he said, his voice changing, softening, almost reverent. "The Kael'Sharyn bearer. The soul that will not die. You are not merely part of the equation. You are its flaw. Its answer. Its paradox."

Xavier's mark flared cold beneath his shirt. The

Shardbrand pulsed once, just once, but enough that every soul in the chamber felt it.

"I do not think Solara knows your name yet," Ivarik said. "But she knows what you represent. Chaos within balance. Death within life. A thread she cannot braid, so she must bind."

Xavier raised his weapons. "You won't be binding anything."

"I won't need to," Ivarik replied. "The seal has already chosen. I merely bring it to conclusion."

The pillars pulsed again their aspects clear. Radiance. Judgment. Death. They were not balanced, but they were aligned.

Lythara dropped slightly as a shimmer of the glyph light coiled around her wrists. Not chains, threads, new bindings.

Xavier's feet shifted slightly. The mark tugged, not to restrain, but to position.

Ella stepped forward between them. "You're trying to force a reset," she said. "Rewrite the seal. Using us, using them." She gestured towards Xavier and Lythara.

"I am not forcing anything," Ivarik replied calmly. "The seal itself demands completion. Its will is older than this chamber. Older than any god. Balance is not law. It is necessity."

Behind him, the prison stirred again shifting not in power but once more in awareness. The seal's pillars pulsed once more, sun, scales, skull, and the choice was made.

#

The world shuddered with the weight of its choice.

Xavier moved first, blades drawn, eyes burning with

resolve. Vaeltheris sang like a storm in his grip, the emberstone short sword hissed with heat as he carved a path forward. His strikes came fast and measured, testing Ivarik's defenses.

Slash. Twist. Feint. Thrust.

Clang. Spark. Blood.

Vaeltheris slipped past the divine shroud guarding Ivarik's skin and bit deep into rune-etched muscle beneath. The emberstone blade flared as it struck the man in his thigh, blackening flesh with fire.

Ivarik grunted but stood unmoved. Moments later a gauntlet shot out. Xavier blocked, but the force still sent him stumbling. Ivarik advanced, hammering blow after blow. Xavier ducked one, rolled beneath another, then drove both blades into the gap under Ivarik's arm.

The shroud cracked.

Lythara slid in from the side, she was pure shadow in motion. Her daggers blurred, twin arcs of infernal steel flashing toward his throat. Ivarik twisted, catching one by the hilt, but the second sank deep into his hip and again blood spilled.

He bellowed and spun with savage force, backhanding her across the mouth. Lythara flew sideways and skidded, her shoulder slamming into a pillar. She groaned but rolled to her feet, blood trailing from her temple as she stood on unsteady feet.

"I'm not done," she snarled her eyes refocusing on the individual who held her captive for so many centuries.

Lianna loosed a barrage of arrows. One scraped his shoulder. One deflected mid-air. One struck deep into a wound Xavier had made. However, Ivarik made no reaction. Growling, she tossed the bow down and drew steel before charging in, flanking with Frostclaw. Her blade to his ribs, the huge snow leopard bounding to his chest. Frostclaw's claws raked his face, drawing thin lines of blood. Lianna shifted and stabbed low, but her blade struck the divine aura and bounced.

Ivarik moved in a blur, sweeping Lianna off her feet with a brutal kick. She hit the ground hard, winded, clutching her ribs. Frostclaw lunged again, only to be grabbed mid-air and slammed into the ground. The great cat whimpered, stunned.

Sihri appeared at his side, launching a fierce combo, a low jab, elbow to the gut, and a snapping hook to the temple. She moved like a storm, but her strikes landed with dull thuds against divine muscle. She snarled and drove her heel into his knee.

Ivarik moved. His palm crashed into her collarbone, sending her flying. She flipped in the air, landed hard, and slid across the smooth stone floor.

She staggered up to her knees slowly, gasping. "Okay," she spat blood. "That hurt."

Liosan struck from behind. He'd crept low during the chaos, using the pillars for cover. Now he leapt his blades flashing, aiming for joints and seams. One blade struck the back of Ivarik's knee, bounced. His momentum carried upwards as the second aimed for the back of the man's neck.

Ivarik turned, caught the strike mid-air, and slammed Liosan down hard. Once. Twice. Then he simply tossed the Iskari male aside like a rag.

Ella fired twice. The first arrow shattered. The second bent in mid-air from divine pressure. She growled, dropped her bow, and dove into melee, her twin swords seeking flesh. Her strikes were fast. One cut his side. The second raked across his vambrace. The third found a gap... and skidded away harmlessly.

He slammed his arm outward, striking her head-on. Ella spun from the impact, slammed into a column, and dropped to one knee. Blood stained her lips.

Xavier was back. He roared in defiance, his blades arcing in tandem. The emberstone one scorched Ivarik's shoulder. Vaeltheris stabbed through Ivarik's hip. Xavier dodged a retaliatory strike and slashed deep across the thigh of the devil.

That actually seemed to hurt. Just not enough.

Lythara rejoined, circling behind. She dropped low, swept his legs. One dagger stabbed upward. It sank into a gap between ribs and she twisted the blade. She grinned as blood poured down his armor.

"Still bleeding," she almost cooed in malicious delight.

Ivarik snarled and drove his elbow into her chest. The sound of bone crunching filled the air. She gasped, collapsing against the floor. She was still was conscious, still trying to rise despite the brutal injury.

It was then that Valkra leapt in. A blur of black fur and fury, the panther cub flew from the shadows, fangs sinking into Ivarik's forearm. He roared, not in pain, but surprised insult, and slammed her to the floor with enough force to shake the stones.

She yelped, tumbled, and lay still. Her limbs limp but body still shifting with her breathing.

"NO!" Xavier dove past Ivarik trying to protect the small shadowmane and catching a backhand with his shoulder. He spun with the force of the blow and buried Vaeltheris in Ivarik's ribs. The devil grunted.

Then...he struck decisively.

A hand to Xavier's chest. Over the Shardbrand. No sound, just rupture and reality bent. A wave of silent force hurled Xavier backward. He hit the ground, bounced, and crashed into a pillar nearly shattering it. As his emberstone blade flew from his grip, Vaeltheris clattered away, and he lay still.

Lythara screamed. It was not pain, it was a loss. She surged back, despite the pain tearing through her chest, her body trembling with fury. In quick succession her daggers found his chest, shoulder, side. One buried in flesh. She left it there. Ivarik bled.

The seal behind them cracked.

Xavier did not rise.

#

Silence fell within the chamber, not the kind that was born of absence, but the weighty, crushing silence of aftermath. The kind that settled when something fundamental had broken.

Ivarik stood at the edge of the seal, blood sliding down his armor in lazy trickles. His breath came slower now, more labored, though he fought not to show it. The dagger Lythara had left buried in his ribs glowed faintly, infernal steel hissing against his enchanted plate.

Still, he ignored it. His gaze was fixed not on the weapon, nor the others, but on the glyph. Sun. Scales. Skull. It pulsed once, erratic and unstable. "It realigns," he muttered, almost reverently. "The Kael'Sharyn cannot escape function even in death."

He raised his hand. Threads of glyph light extended from his palm to the seal, thin tendrils seeking to rebind what had unraveled, but the response was delayed and sluggish. Like a beast stirred too often from slumber.

Lythara staggered to her feet. Her ribs ached, her skin burned, but she moved with the tenacity of fury. "You think it will accept your guidance again? After this?"

"It does not need to accept," Ivarik replied, his voice dry. "It needs only balance."

Then came the twitch. Xavier's body, still crumpled at the base of the cracked pillar, moved. Just a flicker, his fingers curling inward.

Ella was beside him in an instant. She dropped to her knees, brushing aside fragments of the broken stone and unbinding his armor to expose his torso. His chest didn't rise at first, but then... A shallow breath.

Her lips parted. "Xavier?"

The Shardbrand lit like a stoked forge illumination illumination flooding the chamber in radiance. No flames. Just light, pure, brilliant, and terrible. Cracks spider webbed across his skin, jagged lines that glowed from within. The core shimmered like an opalescent storm, pulsing to a rhythm not of this world. It did not beat like a heart. It resonated.

Ivarik turned and for the first time, uncertainty touched his face.

Ella reached for Xavier's shoulder as he stirred again. He blinked slowly; his eyes unfocused. His voice was hoarse.

"What... was her name?" he rasped. "My sister. I... lost it. I can't remember her name..." There was an undertone of pain in his words.

Ella gripped his hand. "You're here. You're with us. That's what matters."

He looked down at his chest. The Shardbrand spread like shattered glass beneath his skin. His torso was a lattice of glowing fractures, the jagged paths racing from the wellspring over his heart down his ribs, up his throat, and across one shoulder.

A heartbeat passed. The seal pulsed, once, then buckled. The triune glyph flared violently. Silver light burst and dimmed. Gold flickered like dying embers. The skull fractured.

Ivarik reeled back as feedback surged along his bindings. The glyphs on his armor erupted in sparks. He screamed, not in pain, but in disbelief. "The system...!" he gasped. "It chose him... it was meant to choose him! How did he escape its grasp?"

His voice trembled, not with pain but with existential disbelief. The 'system' the triune seal forged through divine will, ritual, and centuries of encoded logic was meant to self-correct. Solara had nudged its logic subtly, aligning it to target the one force she feared most: the Kael'Sharyn. She had expected to trap chaos within order, to bind the storm before it could tear through her perfect lattice. But the seal hadn't bound Xavier.

It had selected him. Not as a prisoner, but as a pillar, and in doing so, it introduced the very flaw it was designed to resist. Xavier's very resurrection, his refusal to remain fixed, was not an anomaly. It was a paradox. The divine construct, structured to contain death and control judgment, had accepted the living contradiction. It had embraced the impossible, and it broke.

The triune structure shattered under the weight of paradox. It had bet on immortality. It had not understood what it meant to be Kael'Sharyn.

Xavier rose to his feet. Ella helped him only with her presence. His steps were slow, deliberate, inexorable. The glow of the Shardbrand lit the ruined chamber in a halo of defiance.

Glyph light ruptured in every direction. The seal collapsed inward. Judgment unraveled. Radiance fell. Even death paused. The collapse drew attention from deep beneath the seal, and something stirred, something that should never have known his name.

Ivarik's glyphs failed one by one. The skull of Nekros on his chestplate cracked, spiderwebbed, and shattered. The seal had tried to bind a being it could not define. A divine construct built on symmetry was now staring at chaos incarnate.

Ivarik screamed. He clawed at the bindings on his arms, trying to suppress the feedback, but the sigils turned against him. The backlash struck his spine, his core, his soul. With a final, desperate gesture, he drew power from the last remnant of Nekros' will and vanished in a spiral of black ether.

The chain of balance was broken. One pillar collapsed entirely, toppling over in a cascade of sacred stone and echoing force. The glyph at the center dimmed until only a faint shimmer of broken light remained. The chamber grew still.

The party stared at the aftermath. Valkra whimpered softly in Sihri's arms. Frostclaw groaned beside Lianna. Ella shifted slowly, her eyes fixed on Xavier.

Lythara wiped blood from her mouth, lips curling into a breathless grin. "Well. That was... inconveniently glorious."

In the center of the room, surrounded by the echoes of defiance, Xavier stood immobile. The Shardbrand on his chest still burned with its illumination. The seal was broken, and the world had shifted, and from the heavens, the stars witnessed a divine compact broken and the soul that had cracked it.

#

The renewed silence that followed Ivarik's retreat was deeper than the one before. Again, the chamber hung not with the stillness of hesitation, nor the lull between strikes. It was filled with the silence that accompanied the collapse of ancient rules undone.

Ella was the first to move. She stepped carefully across the fractured seal chamber, her boots crunching softly over flakes of divine crystal and broken glyph etched stone. Each step forward seemed louder than the last. The world had held its breath, but no one knew how, or whether, it should begin breathing again.

Xavier stood at the center of it all, bare-chested, broken, and barely upright. The Shardbrand pulsed gently now, its glow no longer searing but steady. A fractured constellation sprawled across his torso, each crack humming faintly with residual power. His eyes were distant, not lost, but turned inward, as if weighing something he couldn't quite grasp.

Ella reached him and touched his arm. "You're with us," she said, not as a question but as an anchor.

He nodded, once, but even that motion carried gravity.

Behind her, Lianna helped Frostclaw to his feet. The snow leopard limped heavily but growled at nothing, low and warning. Sihri still held Valkra close, one hand shielding the cub's ribs. Liosan reappeared near a broken arch, watching Xavier in quiet, unreadable stillness.

Lythara approached, favoring one leg, her crimson eyes catching what little light remained. "We need to leave," she said. "This chamber won't hold. The balance is gone."

Almost as if summoned by her words, a deep groan rumbled through the foundation. A fracture spiderwebbed across the chamber floor, racing through old channels of power. One of the remaining columns split down the middle with a sharp crack that echoed like thunder in the hollow space.

"The collapse has begun," Ella said, voice grave. "And the seal... the structure itself, it was part of the sanctum's foundation. The moment we broke it, we began tearing out the spine of this entire place."

Sihri looked around. "So we run?"

"No," Xavier said quietly, eyes fixed on the newly exposed dais. "We finish it."

He limped toward the rear platform of the seal chamber, where the triune energy once converged. What remained was jagged and broken, fractured lines of divine authority bleeding off into the stone.

The dais was circular, ringed by stairs cracked and crumbling. Fragments of shattered glyph etched steel lay scattered across its rim. Three conduits, now blackened and inert, once channeled the anchor forces of Radiance, Judgment, and Death. The remained as little more than brittle, hollow veins.

The center held a stone basin. It was not deep, not ornate. It was merely simple and carved. Within it, a figure lay still.

"He's here," Xavier said. "Rorik."

The others gathered in a semicircle around the basin. No one spoke as they gazed down on the form of the ruler. King Rorik Ironthorn looked like a fallen warrior buried beneath glass. A thin sheen of translucent glyph light encased him, pulsing faintly like a dying heartbeat. His body bore the wear of time, not battle, his face gaunt, cheeks hollow, but not skeletal. His beard had gone streaked with gray. His hair was long, tangled. His once-regal armor bore rust and ash, as if he'd been frozen in the moment of despair.

His crown had slipped to the dais floor beside the basin. Dust and divine residue clung to its edge.

"Stasis," Ella murmured. "A containment ritual. Bound to the seal."

"Not designed to preserve," Lythara added, peering at the glyphs. "Just to pause. He wasn't meant to survive forever, just long enough to never interfere."

"Can we break it?" Lianna asked. Her voice was low. She was kneeling beside Frostclaw, one hand on his side, the other ready to draw her blade.

Xavier moved forward, raising his hand to touch the glyph shell. The Shardbrand glowed brighter in response, and when he opened his palm, light spilled across the arcane sheath in soft pulses.

The chamber dimmed further as the energy reached down. Threads of light passed from Xavier's mark into the glyphs and found a sympathetic resonance between forces older than the crown and deeper than the gods. The shell began to crack.

Ella stepped beside him and placed her hand over his. "Together," she whispered as she lent her own essence, that of the souls inhabiting Vaeltheris, to his own.

Cracks spread in spiraling patterns. The glyph shell hissed once then shattered in silence, shards turning to motes of light. The moment the stasis broke, King Rorik inhaled sharply. His body seized. His eyes shot open, wild, unfocused. He reached for a weapon that wasn't there, half-rising in a desperate lunge.

"Where..." he rasped.

Xavier caught his shoulders, guiding him back down.

"Easy. You're safe."

Rorik's vision sharpened as his breath evened. He saw Ella. Then Lianna. Then the faces of the others, all strangers, and finally, he saw Xavier.

His brows furrowed. "You... are not of Arenvalis."

"No," Xavier said. "But I am the one who broke the seal."

"Ivarik," Rorik growled. His hand clenched air. "The glyphs. The... the court. What has happened?"

"It's done," Ella said gently. "The seal is broken. Ivarik fled. The grip of the shadow court, at least in this city, is shattered."

Rorik stared down at the basin's edge. At the place he'd lain for years.

"I failed them," he whispered. "I let him speak for me. Let him twist the law in my name."

"You weren't the only one deceived," Ella said.

"No," Rorik said, gripping the edge of the dais as he stood. "But I was the king."

Behind them, the sanctum rumbled louder. Dust and debris showered down in a wave from the outer chamber. One of the side corridors collapsed with a thunderous roar.

"We're out of time," Lianna said. "We need to go. Now."

They helped Rorik to his feet. Despite his time in stasis, his legs held. The strength of a warrior-king still lived beneath the rust.

They moved quickly, retracing their steps. But the path was not as it had been. The structure was buckling, divine architecture unraveling with every passing second. Light flickered across the walls like memories being erased.

They passed shattered watchposts, fallen guardians

once held by glyph, and relics that had once glowed now dim and dull. A statue of Solara cracked at the waist and fell into dust as they ran beneath it.

And then... a breeze touched them, cold and clean.

Lythara slowed just long enough to breathe it in. "Real air. Almost forgot what that felt like."

They reached the final stretch of tunnel, emerging from the claustrophobic sanctum depths into the broader vent passage they had once entered through. No torchlight guided them, only breath, boots, and the faint promise of sky ahead.

The passage curved sharply downward before ascending again, never meant for warriors or royalty, only smoke, servants, and the unseen hands of an age long passed. Dust clung to the walls. The air was dry and motionless. Here, the divine had never reached. It was stone born of labor, not blessing.

Liosan led them as he had before, silent and sure-footed, his presence ghostlike as he slipped between shadows. Lianna followed her brother closely, bow at her side, hand near her blade, eyes flicking more to him than the path ahead.

Xavier ran his fingers along the stone, the familiar cold reassuring despite the storm still echoing inside him. Behind him, Sihri moved in steady silence, Valkra tucked against her side. Ella followed, quiet, but her eyes were sharp. Lythara brought up the rear, favoring one leg, her daggers still loose in her hands.

Frostclaw padded beside Lianna now, low and limping but unyielding.

The path was narrow, but it widened slowly until the passage yawned out into a forgotten antechamber, one last seal between them and the open air.

The gates stood cracked. Stone, not sanctified as in the depths below. The gates hinges were still rusted, and dust choked the cracks. Xavier and Ella reached out together and pushed. The doors opened with a groan, not a hymn. Outside, dusk had begun to fall.

The sun dipped low behind the western ridge, casting a golden veil across the city. Even after all the time that had passed, smoke from Verdantspire's coordinated strike still hung in the far southern skies, curling high above the arid plains of the wildlands. Beneath them, the mountain moaned.

They turned in time to see it. One of the grand temples that towered above them, once a bastion of divine law, was collapsing in slow, juddering waves. Stone groaned under the weight of unmaking, ages of divine craftsmanship crumbling in reverent silence. Gold-leafed columns trembled as they bent inward, no longer supported by the divine lattice that once reinforced them.

One of the upper domes split down its center. A deep crack snaked from base to peak, and with a sharp report like splitting bone, the dome gave way. Shattered tiles and glyph-marked masonry rained down into the temple square below, throwing up a plume of dust and divine residue that shimmered in the amber light of dusk.

It wasn't the city falling, only the one temple, but to those who had lived under its shadow, under the laws written into its foundation, it would feel like the world had cracked.

The statues lining the rooftop, each one depicting a deity of order and dominion, fractured in slow succession. One split across the chest. Another lost its arms. Solara's likeness, tallest and most central, shattered from within.

Her outstretched hands, carved in blessing, broke at the wrists. The head, crowned in radiant stone, fell first. It struck the flagstones and shattered, sending the carved laurel scattering like broken promises. The temple's sanctum, its sealed heart, died as it had lived: slow, solemn, and absolute.

Around them, the city stirred, from alleys and upper windows, balconies and market lanes, the people of Thandor's Reach gathered. Drawn not by summons, but by instinct. By the impossible sight of collapse where there had once been only silence and reverence. Children were pulled back by parents. Elders whispered to one another. A few marked themselves with holy signs. Others knelt, thinking it was judgment come at last. However, most stared at the man who emerged from the ruin, King Rorik Ironthorn.

He stepped into the light of the square as if surfacing from a long-buried grave. His armor was cracked but still bore the insignia of the royal line. His crown, held in one hand, glinted with a mixture of ash and memory.

Xavier walked beside him, a silent shadow. Lythara and Ella flanked the other side. Sihri emerged behind them with Valkra in her arms, while Lianna supported Frostclaw's weight. Liosan, silent and unseen by the crowd, watched from the edges.

The crowd gasped but did not speak. Rorik looked out over them, not with the pride of a king returning, nor the desperation of one demanding recognition. He looked with the weariness of a man who had seen too much of what had been done in his name.

"The city doesn't know," he said quietly. His voice didn't carry far, but the others heard it clearly. "That I live."

Xavier stepped beside him, speaking low. "They will."

Rorik turned to him, truly turned, and for the first time, he looked at Xavier not as the man who broke his prison, but as something more. He nodded, slowly, not in gratitude instead in understanding.

"Then it begins." Rorik stated softly.

Ella's voice broke the moment like wind through broken glass. "What begins?"

Rorik turned his gaze back to the skyline, where the banners of the those who had made up the shadow court still flew, and the chains of law still clung to the city gates. His voice rang out then, louder. This time it was not for them; it was for the city. "Justice."

# CHAPTER THIRTY-EIGHT

*The King Returned*

Dawn broke over Thandor's Reach not with horns, but with silence.

Dust still lingered in the heights of the temple quarter, curling above shattered columns and broken sanctums like incense offered to gods who no longer listened. The statue of Solara remained where it had fallen during the night, her radiant crown shattered across the temple square, her head sundered at the base of the steps. The wind carried dust and fine flakes of divine crystal into the upper tiers of the city, blanketing stonework and silence alike, and into that silence, the king returned.

Rorik Ironthorn did not walk in any form of ceremony. His armor bore the weight of rust and years, etched with forgotten glyphs and dulled livery, but it did not sag. His stride was sure, measured. One hand rested on the hilt of a blade he no longer drew; the other held his crown, it was not worn, but carried, as if to remind the city that sovereignty could be reclaimed without flourish.

He walked flanked not by nobility or guards, but by strangers. Xavier moved beside him, cloak drawn over his chest, the Shardbrand pulsing faintly beneath the fabric.

Ella paced to the king's other side, her expression sharp, eyes constantly scanning. Lythara trailed a step behind, loose and watchful, her crimson gaze sweeping windows and archways with practiced suspicion. Sihri carried Valkra in one arm, the cub resting quietly but alert. Lianna walked ahead, bow slung over one shoulder, Frostclaw padding beside her with a limp and a low growl rumbling in his throat.

Liosan moved between them all. He wasn't trailing far behind anymore. Nor clinging solely to Lianna's shadow. Instead, he wove between awnings and second-story ledges, circling the group from above, then dropping down just long enough to walk behind Xavier's right flank, matching pace in ghost-quiet steps. He didn't make a sound, and he didn't linger long, but he stayed closer than he ever had before. At one point, Xavier glanced back and caught a glimpse of him crouched atop a nearby alcove. Lio's expression was unreadable, but he nodded once. It was a small, deliberate gesture, then he once again vanished from sight.

The city did not cheer, it did not celebrate. It was in too much shock as it watched. Balconies filled with silent witnesses. Doors cracked open. Merchants held their breath behind half-raised stalls. No one dared speak. Not yet. Because it was not clear whether this was a procession of triumph... or judgment.

The small procession passed beneath the Arch of Authority at the edge of the upper district. It was cracked now, one of the marble edict slabs hanging loose where divine magic had unraveled the seal. The inscriptions once read: Balance is Order. Obedience is Peace. Law is Light. Now only the word Obedience remained unbroken.

Rorik slowed. His eyes traced the break. "Let it stand," he said.

Xavier turned to him. "You don't want it torn down?"

"No." Rorik's voice was firm. "I want it remembered. Cracked, but visible. So they know exactly what we let rise in our silence."

The guards at the inner gate waited. Four of them stood dressed in ceremonial plate, gold-silver over black, Arenvalis colors, chests rigid, jaws tight. They'd heard the temple collapse hours before. They'd seen the smoke, seen the dust, heard of the collapsed temple. They'd whispered of rebellion. But they hadn't expected him.

One stepped forward. An officer. His voice barely held its edge. "Your Majesty... we were told you had taken a vow of seclusion. That Chancellor Tharn spoke with your voice."

Rorik stopped three paces from him. "Ivarik Tharn spoke in my name with no leave to do so. His word is no longer law."

The officer faltered. "We... we served under royal seal..."

"You served shadow," Rorik said coldly. "But if your loyalty remembers its roots, then open the gate."

A long pause stretched. The officer looked to his fellows. Then bowed, stiffly. "Yes, Your Majesty."

The gates opened. The creaking of stone and iron rang louder than any horn, and Thandor's Reach beheld the king. They entered the inner ward of the palace, its domes untouched by fire but shadowed now in truth. Statues of old kings lined the marble avenue, but none wore Rorik's face. His was never carved. Never allowed. The shadow court had claimed continuity by denying him image and monument alike.

Now he walked through their legacy, unyielding. Every footstep echoed against the polished stone.

One of the high ministers stood at the edge of the reflecting pool, dressed in silver-trimmed robes. He froze at the sight of them, Rorik at the head, Ella and Xavier just behind, the others fanning out like wolves cloaked in silence. Lythara bared her teeth slightly as he turned and fled. Sihri smirked.

Liosan, high above, walked along a narrow beam near the vaulted ceiling, pausing just long enough to drop a small stone into the fountain the fleeing minister had passed. He made no sound, but the flick of his ears said enough. He'd marked the man.

Lianna looked up, smiled faintly at her brother's signal, and kept walking.

Rorik didn't watch the man retreat. Instead, he climbed the shallow dais of the royal hall and pushed open the heavy doors himself. No one waited inside. The hall had been emptied in the night, its banners still bearing the gold sigil of divine law, one of the sigils burned into Ivarik's armor. The throne stood in solitude, framed by two high windows that bled morning light across its stone.

For a long moment, Rorik stood at the base of the dais. He looked not at the throne, but at the steps leading up to it, as though weighing more than just his own legs. Then he climbed. He did not sit right away. He turned first, facing the empty chamber as dust motes drifted through columns of light.

"I ruled in name," he said, his voice quiet. "They made sure I never ruled in truth." His gaze found Xavier. "But you broke the seal they used to bind me. So now I must break what they built."

He lowered the crown slowly, deliberately, onto his brow... and sat.

The throne of Arenvalis accepted its king, not with fanfare, nor applause, only silence. But the world had shifted, and the reckoning had begun.

#

The throne hall did not echo like it once had. The great chamber, once meant to amplify the will of kings, now held its breath. Dust clung to every ledge. The light through the high windows no longer glimmered, instead it hung dull and gray, as if the sun itself waited to see what would come next.

Xavier stood at the foot of the dais, arms crossed loosely, the Shardbrand mark now hidden beneath a half-drawn cloak. Behind him, Ella watched the chamber like a battlefield. Lythara leaned casually against a pillar, twirling a dagger between two fingers. Lianna and Sihri remained further back, near the entrance where Frostclaw lay resting and Valkra slept in Sihri's arms.

The rest of the room was not empty. Word had spread of the King's return had, and it had done so quickly. Nobles began to arrive in clusters, some in formal robes, others still dressed in half-rumpled tunics quickly donned during their rush to the chamber, their expressions ranging from confusion to barely contained dread. High functionaries entered next, followed by military liaisons, priests, and the members of the advisory circle who had long claimed to speak for the crown.

Now, they all looked up at the dais and saw Rorik seated, and none of them knew what to say.

For his part King Rorik waited for no announcement, no procession. He simply raised one hand and spoke. "I am Rorik Ironthorn, sovereign of Arenvalis. Not by decree, but by right. And by blood."

Silence met his words from the gathered onlookers.

"Many of you have claimed my name in my absence. You've enacted laws in my name, passed orders in my voice, ruled as if I had forgotten my crown." He let his gaze drift across the assembly. "That ends now."

Still, no one spoke, and a small, stifled cough was heard somewhere in the gathering.

"Ivarik Tharn is gone. Fled. His false court has dissolved. His glyph-seal that had locked me away has been shattered. The gods he served no longer hear him."

A ripple of tension passed through the room like a breeze before a storm. One of the elder advisors stepped forward, Chancellor Dareth, known for his silver tongue and colder heart. He bowed stiffly.

"Your Majesty, forgive us. We only acted in your stead as was necessary. The Divine Edict of Order demanded firm hands."

Rorik's eyes turned to him. "And what did your firm hands do, Chancellor? Did they shackle children in the name of law? Burn villages to preserve purity? Did they strip the Animari of dignity beneath a seal that I never signed?"

Dareth hesitated before blurting out a protest. "The Animari posed unrest…"

"The Animari," Rorik said sharply, "were hunted, enslaved, and sold like livestock. And in my name. You will speak no justification for it here."

He stood. It was not a gesture of fury, but of finality. The weight of kingship coalesced around him, not as divine mandate, but as living truth. For the first time in years, the throne of Arenvalis did not look like a monument. It looked like a burden someone chose to carry.

"My first decree," Rorik said, his voice steady, "is this: The Animari are no longer bound under separate law. Their rights are equal to any citizen of Arenvalis. Their chains, their brands, their collars all abolished."

Gasps spread through the assembly. One priest paled and sank into a seat. A general clenched his jaw and looked to his lieutenants. Two merchant-lords exchanged urgent glances.

Rorik didn't stop. "My second decree is this: The Divine Edict of Order is no longer law within Arenvalis. No prayer shall override justice. No holy seal shall override the crown. Let the gods debate their order elsewhere, we will build a future not upon supposed holy mandate, but upon truth."

That silence, the stunned, breathless kind, spread again. It wasn't reverence. It was fear.

Ella leaned toward Xavier, her voice low. "They'll either bend or burn."

Lythara chuckled softly. "Let them try to burn. I brought oil."

At the dais, Rorik let the tension build a heartbeat longer, then sat again. He looked to the open doors at the back of the hall, where common folk had begun to filter in, hesitantly, curiously. A girl in a simple dress. A baker with flour on his hands. A limping Animari with a healed brand across his neck.

"This hall belongs to the people of Arenvalis," Rorik said, louder now as he motioned for the common folk to enter. "And so does its future."

He turned to Chancellor Dareth. "You will submit your records for inspection. You will stand trial if they show complicity. As will every member of the court who supported Tharn's edicts."

Dareth opened his mouth, but the king's gaze silenced him. Rorik looked past him to the rest.

"Anyone who wishes to resign, do so now. Anyone who wishes to serve the true crown, be welcome. But know this, this kingdom will not serve gods before justice ever again."

The hall remained silent, but not still. Their world had cracked, and Arenvalis, for the first time in a decade, stood on its own feet.

#

The noble exodus began within the hour. No bells were rung. No alarms were raised, but messengers slipped out through side passages with sealed scrolls. Personal guards rearmed in silence. Doors once guarded by the royal crest were suddenly bolted from within, and the Shadow Court, for the first time since its rise, cast real shadows in retreat.

Liosan was already moving. He'd slipped from the throne hall's ledge the moment Rorik issued his first decree. Now, he moved like smoke between walls and stonework, skipping through rafters and abandoned balconies with the surety of someone who had never needed permission to be anywhere. His eyes tracked patterns. His hands tagged windows. He wasn't hunting. Not yet. He was cornering.

From a third-floor parapet above the east wing, he gestured once to those who had come out to stand below, three fingers tapped to his collarbone, then flicked outward in a spiral.

Lianna, watching from the garden approach, nodded. Her voice was calm but firm. "They're scattering."

Xavier stood beside her, watching the sprawl of the noble district as the sun climbed higher. "They know Rorik's free. And they know they're no longer protected."

Lythara emerged from the shade of a nearby colonnade,

adjusting her gloves, twin daggers already sheathed at her back. "Scattering is good. Easier to isolate. Panic makes mistakes."

From the hall's northern edge, a crash echoed, followed by shouting.

Sihri stepped into view, cracking her knuckles. "Found one. He ran into a storage hall and tripped over a statue. Shame really. Such a fine robe, too." She held up a gold-threaded sash. It was ripped and stained with what looked like wine.

Lianna raised an eyebrow. "Alive?"

"For now." The Leopari woman shrugged.

They regrouped in the inner cloister courtyard, the outer gardens now filling with city officials and commonfolk trying to understand what had just happened. Rorik had not emerged again, yet. He'd sent word that the guard was to stand down from martial enforcement until the purge of court corruption was complete.

He had given Xavier and his allies full authority to act, on his name, not divine mandate.

Liosan dropped down from the roof without a sound and held up a sealed scroll. It bore the sigil of High Minister Alreth, a known advisor to Tharn and one of the key voices in implementing Animari slave laws.

Ella took it with a nod. "This'll bury him."

Sihri gestured over her shoulder. "He's in the west wing. Thought locking a gilded door would stop me. Turns out solid kicks still work."

Lythara smirked. "Remind me never to argue with your feet."

Inside, under direct authority from Rorik, the Arbiter's Chamber was reopened. It had once been a place of royal inquiry, long shuttered by Tharn's orders. Now its high windows glowed with daylight and truth.

The nobles were brought in, one by one over the next few days.

Some came in quiet shame. Others ranted about "unlawful trials" and "heretical coups." A few invoked Solara's name.

Xavier stood in silence while they spoke. He didn't need to reply.

Ella read the scrolls. Lythara named the contracts. Lianna presented the marked records pulled from noble safes, proof of purchased lives, of traded Animari, of forged decrees.

When one merchant-lord claimed ignorance, Sihri simply dropped a bag of coins bearing the same sigil as his collar registry. "Found it in your steward's bedchamber," she said. "Would you like me to show you the ledger too? Or just the floorboards you had it buried under?"

None were executed, not yet. Documentation of their crimes was simply compiled and set aside. Rorik had ordered no blood, only reckoning. They were stripped of land, of coin, of title, and in the end, of the power they had stolen.

The Shadow Court, so long unseen, so long untouchable, collapsed not in flame, but in sunlight, symbol of Solara, one of the deities they were supposedly upholding with their dark dealings and Arenvalis saw it fall.

#

Several more days passed. The palace was quieter now. Not silent, such a place was never truly silent, but instead, it held the kind of quiet that settles over a place where the shouting had stopped, but the consequences remained.

Xavier stood alone in the high alcove above the outer garden, near an open-air balcony that overlooked the great road leading down from the noble tier. The wind was mild, dry and it smelled faintly of crumbled ash and worn stone, the remnants of divine collapse that had yet to be swept clean.

He leaned against the balustrade, one hand braced on the cool marble, the other pressed lightly against his chest. The Shardbrand mark was restless, more so than when he was first branded with it after his first death. It was not burning, not flaring, just unsettled. Like a tremor in the earth before the fault gives way. Its jagged threads pulsed beneath his skin, not just above his heart now but curling toward his shoulder, down his side, spreading like a map of pressure points drawn in fractured light.

He closed his eyes, and for a moment, just a moment, he remembered someone though he couldn't remember her name. It was not Danu, not Ella. Someone else important to him, he was sure of it. There was a woman's voice, laughing, earthly. Deep down he knew it was from before he came to Arath.

His sister. The memory was there one heartbeat, gone the next.

He exhaled sharply, not in pain, but in grief. It was a hollowing sensation, like something had been scooped out of him when he wasn't looking, and only now had he realized it was missing.

He heard footsteps behind him. He didn't bother to turn, there was no need for it. From the sounds and gait, he already knew who was there.

Ella came to stand beside him, not speaking right away.

Just being present. After a few breaths, she said softly, "You're dimmer today."

He glanced sideways. "Thanks."

She smirked faintly. "Not to me." She touched the mark behind her ear. "Your aura has diminished though. I felt it this morning. You're resonating less."

"It's not the ley lines," he murmured. "It's... me."

He lifted the edge of his tunic. The Shardbrand shimmered dully beneath, its opalescent well still at the center, but the lines that spidered out had changed. They were thinner, more threadbare in places, as though bits of him had faded from the inside out.

"I lost something," he said. "I don't even know what it was. It's just... gone, but I can feel the space it left."

Ella reached out, brushing her fingertips near the brand but not touching it. "You died again."

He nodded slowly. "That makes twice."

She didn't speak right away. Then, very quietly, she asked, "Do you remember all of us?"

His eyes met hers.

"Yes," he said, but it wasn't immediate, not instinctive. It was that hesitation that hurt more than the truth.

Her hand lingered near his for a moment before lacing her fingers through his. "This path you walk, it was never going to be without cost."

"I know that but I thought the cost would be pain," he muttered. "Not forgetting who I am. Not losing myself along the way."

From the archway behind them, another figure approached with light, careful steps. Lythara. She didn't speak as she stepped into the frame. Her expression unreadable, crimson eyes catching the filtered daylight through the balcony. She didn't interrupt. She just leaned against the column, arms folded.

Xavier glanced toward her. "You're quiet."

She tilted her head. "You're broken." It wasn't mockery. It was observation.

Ella frowned slightly and glared at the woman, but Xavier let out a quiet breath. "Yeah. I guess I am."

Lythara pushed off the pillar and walked closer, gaze fixed not on his face, but on the Shardbrand. She knelt in front of him, not submissive, but focused, and looked at the pattern with a narrowed eye.

"I saw something like this once," she said. "A long time ago. During the War of the Veins. A warrior marked by three gods, one blessing, one curse, and one claiming. He lived longer than any man should... but he couldn't remember what side he fought for by the end."

Xavier said nothing though his face looked grim.

"He died weeping," she added. "Couldn't remember his own daughter's name."

Ella stiffened, but Xavier didn't flinch. He just let the words settle.

Lythara stood again, brushing a bit of ash from her knee. "You've got a long road left," she said. "But if you forget us, me, Ella, Lianna..." She met his eyes. "We'll remind you. And if that fails... I'll write it in your skin."

That earned the faintest smirk from the troubled man.

Then she was gone, disappearing back through the archway like a shadow that had never quite belonged to the light.

Ella watched her go. "She was oddly comforting."

"Surprisingly, yeah," Xavier said, voice quieter now. He turned back toward the balcony.

Below them, in the courtyard, Rorik stood once more before his people, no longer giving decrees, just listening. A young Animari boy held a broken collar in his hand. One of the palace smiths melted it down into slag beside him. Change had begun.

But Xavier knew now, intimately, that change, even a good change, came with erosion. He remained on the balcony long after Ella left. Watching, waiting, one hand resting lightly over the mark that pulsed beneath his skin.

The price was being paid. He also knew, deep in his bones, that it wasn't over yet.

#

Dusk settled over Thandor's Reach like a breath the city had held for too long. The shattered temple district no longer smoked, but the scent of scorched and broken sanctum stone lingered in the air. The sun dipped low against the horizon, casting its last light across broken statues and fractured rooftops. The banners of the divine order, still raised in places, hung limp, unclaimed by wind, untouched by faith.

Xavier stood just inside the eastern archway of the palace, watching as the day retreated into shadow. He wasn't alone for long. King Rorik approached without ceremony, his armor traded for a simple cloak and courtly attire. He moved with the slow stiffness of a man reinhabiting his own bones, but there was strength still in his posture, and clarity in his eyes.

"I thought you'd already left," he said.

Xavier shook his head. "Soon, we need to get back home

and let everyone know what has transpired."

They stood in silence for a moment. Behind them, the palace guards were changing shifts. For the first time in years, they wore no divine sigils, just the crown of Arenvalis, embossed in burnished steel.

"You freed me," Rorik said quietly. "But more than that... you gave me back my voice."

"You always had it," Xavier replied. "They just locked it away and buried it."

The king gave a grim smile. "And I let them, Ivarik seemed trustworthy at first."

Xavier smirked slightly. "I've heard devils often do."

Rorik turned, glancing toward the spires where the statues of the gods had once stood. One still remained, a half-broken likeness of Solara, arms cracked at the wrists.

"She will not forgive what comes next," Rorik murmured.

"Then it's her turn to stay silent," Xavier said.

Rorik nodded. "Your name is not yet known to the world, but it will be."

Xavier's expression stayed neutral. "That's not why I'm here."

"No," Rorik said. "But it's why they will come for you."

He reached out and clasped Xavier's forearm in the old warrior's grip, short, strong, final. "Arenvalis owes you. Whatever path you walk now, you will not walk it alone."

"I never do," Xavier said, and turned toward the courtyard. "Thank you though, I have a feeling your strength will eventually be needed."

The others waited near the broken gate leading down

the slope toward the lower city. Ella was securing her bow to her back. Sihri adjusted the bindings around Valkra, now awake and curled against her chest. Lythara leaned against the stone frame of the gate, flipping a dagger over her knuckles. Lianna stood beside Frostclaw, helping him shift his weight as he walked. And Liosan, high above, perched on the curved arch of the gate, balanced with his arms outstretched like a cat walking wind. The moment Xavier approached, he dropped lightly to the ground, landing beside Lianna without a word. He didn't glance at Xavier, but he didn't step away either.

Ella looked up. "Ready?"

Xavier nodded. They slipped from the palace under cover of dusk, not escorted, not declared, just gone. Down quiet roads, through alleys still recovering from divine collapse, past stone sanctuaries where the gods no longer watched. The people didn't stop them, instead some stared, and some turned away. But many simply nodded, wordlessly acknowledging the end of something, and the start of something else.

They crossed the main bridge out of the city and onto the roads down the slopes just as night took the sky. Behind them, Thandor's Reach glowed faintly with new fires, none of them from temples. Ahead of them, the road southwest bent toward the trees, toward the Silverwood. Toward home.

Xavier walked at the front, cloak pulled tight, the Shardbrand dim beneath his skin. The others followed, step by step, shadow by shadow. A companionable silence had fallen over the group as they traveled. No collars were worn now, none were needed to protect against unjust laws. Instead, it was just a small group traveling on the road.

# CHAPTER
# THIRTY-NINE

*Echoes of Ash and Stone*

The Wildlands had begun to breathe again. It was not sudden, there was no thunderclap. No divine retraction felt in the bones. But day by day, step by step, the signs mounted, they were subtle as moss on stone, quiet as roots pushing through buried ash. Something had lifted from the land and took with it the strangling weight. The land had been held beneath law and death, bound by the Chainsworn, burdened by order, bled dry by Nekros's will. Now, it stirred with life once again.

The party traveled openly now. The roads that once demanded silence and evasion no longer carried patrols or eyes. The journey from Thandor's Reach to the edge of the Silverwood took nearly two weeks, and the farther they walked, the more the land remembered how to live.

On the third day, they saw birds. Finches. A hawk. A raven circling above an old chapel where the sunburst of Arenvalis had been scratched away. At the edge of a broken watchtower, a vine had wrapped around a rusted collar and burst into leaf.

Lianna brushed a sprig of green with her fingertips. "They're returning."

Xavier nodded. "Or maybe we've stopped whatever was driving them away."

By the fifth day, they passed a hillside camp. A Duskhari healer knelt beside a human boy with a wrapped arm. A Felvari woman sharpened tools beside a dwarf whose old noble tabard had been stripped to plain cloth. A Lynari child sat on a rock carving small animals from bark. One of them waved as the group passed.

Lianna smiled and lifted her hand in return. "They aren't afraid."

Lythara glanced back toward the camp. "Not yet rulers but no longer prey. They still have a long way to go."

On the seventh day, they reached the battlefield. The place hadn't changed in shape. The stumps were still there, blackened husks. Rusted blades still jutted from the dirt like dying teeth, but the air no longer held its breath. The stillness was no longer unnatural.

The quiet was honest now. Before, this place had waited. Glyphs hovered over the dead land, twisted sigils of divine preservation. They also had clung to stone and bone alike, unseen but unmistakable. They had held the dead in suspension, bound by Nekros's will. Not peace. Not rest. Just waiting.

Now, however, those glyphs, sigils, and runes were gone or lifeless themselves.

Ella stepped forward, knelt at the edge of the field, and pressed her hand into the dry, dark soil. "No resistance," she said softly. "No echo."

"They've let go," Xavier murmured behind her. "Or someone has."

Lythara moved slowly through the ashes, each step careful. Measured. "This place was claimed. Ivarik anchored it. Without him… the dead released themselves."

Sihri crouched beside a helmet, now split and filled with moss. She turned it over once, then let it fall. "And the land didn't fight them."

They stood in silence for a while. No cold weight. No voices from the edge of hearing. Only the wind, and the memory of blood.

By the eleventh day, deer wandered the hills. Wildflowers spread across old patrol paths. Liosan perched above a shaded brook, his gaze tracking a fox as it darted into brush. He didn't move to follow. He just watched.

Further on, a stone marker bore a new sigil: a spiral of clawmarks with soot still fresh in its grooves. "Order is dead. Balance breathes."

On the fourteenth day, they reached the treeline. The Silverwood waited for their return, tall, green, patient. Mist curled between its roots. Songbirds sang from high branches. The ground softened beneath their feet.

And nestled several days further, within the wood's protective reach, Verdantspire Haven came into view.

The obelisk rose like crystal grown from the earth. Its glow was faint but steady. Wooden scaffolds and vine-wrapped archways circled the heart of the settlement. Hearth smoke curled above roofs. Hammers struck stone. Voices carried across open space, they were not barking orders but calling names.

It had once been Animari alone, shielded against the reach of Arenvalis. But since the rise of Rynthavael, things had begun to change.

Now, among the Lupari, Leonari, Felvari, Cervari, Iskari, and others, walked humans, dwarves, halflings, even a few Marked Ones. The wounded and the cast out. The forgotten and the rebuilding.

But no elves still, it seemed that they remained apart, as ever.

At the edge of the workgrounds, a pair of Lupari secured heavy rope while a dwarf adjusted a pulley rig. A Cervari herbalist traded bundles of dried root with a human baker under a tarp of stitched hides. Near the scaffold, a boy with small horn-nubs lifted a wooden beam with a grunt, cheered on by a Leonari woman with arms like tree trunks and a smile as broad as the horizon.

No one bowed. No one begged. They simply worked.

Lianna breathed deep. "Home."

Sihri stretched her arms overhead. "Smells like bread. And no one's trying to kill us."

Lythara raised a brow. "I might stay longer this time."

Xavier looked at the obelisk, at the walls, at the trees beyond. Something in him settled, low and steady. No words. Just that silence that speaks louder than breath.

Ella touched his shoulder, and they stepped beneath the living arches. Verdantspire Haven opened its arms to them, and did not close them again.

#

While Verdantspire had never needed saving it had reached out for aid.

The settlement itself had endured. Sheltered in the shadowed cradle of the Silverwood, shielded by twisted paths and ancient trees, hidden from maps and memory. It had been the one place Arenvalis could never reach, not with gold, not with glyphs, not even with god-blessed chains. The same could not be said for its outlying posts and hamlets.

As Xavier and his companions crossed through one of the Haven's living gates, arched trees bound by woven vines and Animari sigils, they noticed that something had changed.

It was not the place. They could feel it in the air. They also noticed it in the people. The eyes watching them from woven balconies and moss-lined windows. The threat was gone, and in its place: a question. Not of survival, but of what now.

They passed beneath the open ring of the Haven's outer circle. A group of young Cervari and Felvari children sprinted across a high-rope bridge, calling warnings and laughter down to the crowd below. A dwarf bent over an anvil and repaired a snapped plowshare with an Iskari apprentice holding the tongs steady. Two Lupari Wardens leaned against a shaded post, one chewing barkroot while the other sharpened a long-handled axe.

Some stared. Most watched, but none turned away.

"They were always safe," Ella said softly beside Xavier. "But now they're wondering if they're... the threat to loved ones is truly gone"

He nodded once. "That's the difference."

The path opened to the Lir'Valis Nexus, the crystalline heart of Verdantspire. Pale green light shimmered from within its tall structure, faint, not blinding, but alive. The air around it vibrated gently, as if the stone itself knew change had come.

The platform had been cleared at its base. Woven forest banners hung behind the ceremonial dais, no symbols of kingdoms, only the spiral-knot emblem of the Haven itself: roots coiled inward, then reaching out.

Around the circle, a crowd had gathered. Animari from

every subrace: Leonari, Iskari, Duskhari, Lynari, Ursari, Cervari, Vulpiri, and more. But among them now stood others, humans with old scars, dwarves who had shed their family crests, halflings wrapped in trade cloaks, a Marked One child clinging to her adoptive guardian's sleeve.

It was not unity completely yet, but it was a start.

Then the Elders stepped forward. Seven in number. Each a voice of bloodline and history. At their center stood Kaelith Moonstride, the Lynari High Speaker. Her robes flowed like low mist, slate-toned and embroidered with thread that shimmered faintly with sky-blue runes. Her golden eyes held clarity and stillness, and when she raised her hand, the crowd fell quiet.

To her right, Thror Ironpaw stood with arms crossed, the Ursari's frame a wall of fur and muscle. His brow was low, his gaze heavy. He had seen war, and peace. And measured them both without favor.

Beside him, Veyara Frostwhisper, the Iskari, bore herself like a still blade, white-haired, ice-eyed, unblinking. She scanned Xavier's group with a hunter's silence.

To Kaelith's left stood Lyselle Silvermist, the Vulpiri, whose amber eyes danced with some inner amusement. Her red-streaked hair caught every shift in the breeze. If she was judging, she was also entertained.

Behind her stood Sylara Dawnshade, the Cervari, serene and unmoving, her hands folded with the grace of still water.

Further out, Khoran Dusksworn of the Duskhari lingered half in shadow, black-clad and watchful, like the whisper of movement that leaves no track.

And finally, at the edge of the dais, stood Arvyn Flamefeather, the Falconi, his gaze sharp as a hawk's, feathered braid fluttering with each shift in the clearing's breeze.

Together, they did not need words, their presence alone was enough.

Kaelith stepped forward. "Verdantspire remembers," she said. "We remember every name branded. Every collar blessed by a priest's hand. Every child marked in silence and forgotten by the law that called it peace."

Her voice never rose. And yet every Animari in the clearing leaned forward to hear.

She turned to Xavier. "You left us with a promise of change. What do you return with?"

Xavier stepped onto the Nexus platform. The crystal pulsed beneath him, not glowing, not dramatic, just acknowledging.

"The law is broken," he said. "The throne answers to itself again. The chains have no weight in Arenvalis. No pen may write them. No seal may bind them." He looked not just to the Elders, but to those beyond. "You were never broken. The law was, and now the world knows it."

Kaelith turned to the council, and the Elders, as one, spoke the words that had waited generations. "The chains of the throne are broken. Verdantspire is unbound."

A shimmer passed through the air around the Nexus, like a single breath held, then released. In the next moment Xavier's vision was obscured with new prompts.

**QUEST COMPLETE**D: Breaking the Chains of the Throne

The Animari in Arenvalis were not only enslaved by chains, but by the laws that made their bondage sacred, and the silence of a king imprisoned within his own throne. You crossed borders as a shadow, pierced the heart of Thandor's Reach, and unmasked the rot beneath its golden banners. Through subterfuge, steel, and truth, you freed King Rorik from the grip of the Shadow Court and shattered the decrees that branded the Animari as property. Now, with the court fallen and the crown restored, the laws lie in ruins. What rises in their place is still uncertain, but for the first time in generations, the Animari are no longer bound by ink, collar, or silence.

- The Shadow Court has fallen.
- King Rorik Ironthorn rules again.
- Animari within the borders of Arenvalis are no longer property by law.

**Base Rewards Gained:**

- +25,000 Experience
- +1,000 Reputation (Regional)
- Major Faction Standing Increase: Verdantspire Haven
- Title Earned: Breaker of the Court

**Bonus Rewards Gained (based on resolution method):**

- +5,000 XP – Decisive Victory (Ivarik Defeated)
- +3,000 XP – Court Infiltration Accomplished
- +2,000 XP – Diplomatic Accord with King Rorik

Total Experience Gained: 35,000 XP

**Congratulations Lord of Rynthavael!**

Settlement Relationship Level Increased

- Previous Status: Reliable Allies (+10,000)
- New Status: Close Bond (+50,000)

The threads between Rynthavael and Verdantspire Haven have grown into something deeper than alliance.

Trust has become kinship. Aid has become instinct. The two settlements now share more than defense, they share purpose. Traditions. Memory. Celebration. Grief.

Your people are no longer just neighbors. You are family.

**Unlocked:** Settlement Trait – Shared Resilience

- Automatic mutual aid during crises
- Shared seasonal celebrations and remembrance rituals
- Increased morale, trade stability, and cross-cultural growth

"The forest does not grow alone. Neither do we."
– High Speaker Kaelith Moonstride

When he had read that prompt, he noticed a new one minimized behind it.

**Lord Vael of Rynthavael you have done the unthinkable.**

Settlement Relationship Level Updated

- Previous Status: Open Hostility (–50,000)
- New Status: Mutual Respect (+1,000)

Where once there was a threat, now there is recognition.

The fall of the Shadow Court and the restoration of King Rorik's sovereignty have ended the blooded standoff between your people and Arenvalis. Though no treaty binds you, no sword is drawn either.

Your name carries weight in their halls, not as a threat, but as a force that shaped the kingdom's future. The grudges of lords may linger, but the crown remembers who broke the chains.

**New Diplomatic Stance:** Mutual Respect

- Non-aggression is the default stance.
- Limited cooperation may be offered during times of crisis.

SHADOWS OVER THE WILDLANDS

- Diplomatic requests have a chance to succeed where once they would have been denied.

"You did what no one else could. I do not forget that."
– King Rorik Ironthorn

Closing the second prompt he was about to return his attention to the present when a now familiar radiant symphony of chimes reverberated through his head, accompanied by a booming voice reading the notification:

**"Hark and Hear! You have ascended in power. You are now Level 22!**

The touch of the divine lingers upon you, granting **6 attribute points per level** to shape your destiny, an exceptional gift, elevated from the ordinary **4 points** by the **Blessings of the Gods (Danu).**
**Total attribute points remaining 12**.

Choose wisely, for these points will define your path. You **have 3 days** to assign them, or they will fall to the whims of fate.

Your growing prowess earns you a boon: **20% skill allocation** to distribute among your known skills.
**Total skill allocation remaining 40%**

This is your chance to sharpen the blade of a favored talent, forge new strength in an untapped domain, or balance your growth across disciplines. Let this moment be a cornerstone of your greatness.

**Rise, Seeker of Glory. The world awaits your will. Seek adventure, seek wisdom, seek love... and let your legend be forged in your choices. LIVE!"**

He blinked that prompt away and focused on his surroundings. The air didn't erupt in celebration. Instead, it deepened the weight of the bond between his people and those of Verdantspire filled the air with portent.

Lyselle tilted her head. "Well. That's one way to make an entrance."

Thror grunted. Whether it was approval or skepticism, no one could tell.

Veyara's gaze lingered on Lianna,cool, assessing. But after a moment, she inclined her head by a fraction. Just enough.

Kaelith stepped forward again and met Xavier's eyes. "You have not made us safe," she said. "We were always safe. However, you have ensured the safety of our people and families outside of the Haven."

"I know." Xavier dipped his head slightly and smiled to the elder Lynari.

She continued, "but you've made us seen. And for some... that will be more dangerous."

Xavier didn't flinch. "We'll face that too."

Kaelith studied him a moment longer. Then, before the entire Haven, the High Speaker of Verdantspire bowed. Not deeply, but truly.

As they stepped back, Lythara broke the silence with a quiet laugh. "No spears at our backs. No whispers in the dark. Almost makes me nervous."

Ella gave her a sidelong look. "Enjoy it while it lasts."

Lianna's hand brushed Frostclaw's fur. "It means we did something real."

Xavier turned to the trees, where the light filtered in over the path beyond. "Now we see what it grows into."

#

They left Verdantspire as the sun dipped lower in the sky, filtering through the forest canopy like scattered gold. They knew they would be welcome to shelter there for the night or longer, but the siren call of home quickened their feet. Behind them, the sounds of Verdantspire softened, laughter, tools, quiet voices, the hush of something earned.

No guards followed and no watchers trailed them. They were known and respected now free to move about as they wanted. Surrounding them were just the trees, and the path, and the knowledge that, for the first time in a long time, they weren't running or harried.

The trail carried them east, deeper into the Silverwood. The earth here was rich and dark, tangled with roots and spongy with moss. Birdsong drifted high above them. The canopy stretched in broad arches overhead, like a cathedral carved from living green. It was not long before they passed familiar ground, a spot where the remnants of a past battle lay hidden beneath growth and time.

The path took them along the high ridge east of the Haven, where they passed a shallow rise overlooking the fields beyond, the very place where, weeks ago, Xavier had performed a mission with the twins. They had fought a brutal skirmish against slavers and broken caravan guards, and Xavier had experienced his first death in this world.

This time, the land was different. The blackened soil had softened under moss and time. The crude camps and shattered banners were gone. There was no stench of rot, no wrongness in the air. Whatever blood had been spilled here had been buried by steady hands, the Animari Wardens, as they always did, swift to lay the fallen to rest and deny disease or dark claim.

Aware now of Nekros's corruption in Arenvalis they were happy that he had never touched the Silverwood. His reach had stretched far, but not here, not into the haven's roots and not into its guarded dead.

Lianna paused beside a broken spear haft, half-sunk in earth.

"It's clean," she said softly.

"No divine rot?" Xavier asked.

She shook her head. "None. It's just land now. Scarred, but breathing."

Liosan crouched nearby, tracing a finger through the ash-lined grass. He didn't speak, but the way his shoulders eased said enough.

They had passed through here once under pressure and desperate to find taken friends and family. Now, they passed through again as themselves.

They continued on, the quiet thickening as they climbed down into a grove of silverleaf and blackpine. A spring burbled through the roots at the base of the hill, its sound mingling with the rustle of the canopy above.

Sihri flopped onto a mossy stone beside the stream and exhaled. "Finally. Somewhere we're not being chased, stabbed, or glared at."

Valkra padded to her side and settled in a coil, her chin resting on her paws.

Ella knelt by the water and cupped it in her hands. "We've earned a pause."

"Too short," Lianna muttered, scanning the trees.

Lythara tilted her head skyward. "It's strange. Not planning the next cut. The next lie."

Xavier crouched by the stream and watched the ripples. "I thought it would feel like more," he said.

Ella glanced at him. "You thought peace would cheer."

"It doesn't," he murmured. "It rests."

They sat in companionable silence for a while, no voices, no rush. Only the weight of what had been done.

Then Xavier's eyes turned south. "The Hollow Depths," he said.

Lianna's tone turned sharp. "Back to that already? Is that not where we first found you?" She indicated to Lison and herself as she spoke.

"There's still something down there." He replied.

"You left it sealed for a reason," Ella said. "But doors don't stay quiet forever."

Xavier stood slowly. "We've bought ourselves time. That's all. The deeper dangers don't wait."

They rest of the group rose not with urgency, but with understanding. In Arenvalis the chain was broken. But not the world was not safe, and the work was not done... not yet at least.

# CHAPTER FORTY

*The Path to Fire*

It only took a couple days to reach the entrance to the Rynthavael mines, the front part of the Hollow Depths. The soft glow of moss light painted the tunnel walls in hues of green and blue as Xavier descended first, one hand trailing the smoothed edge of the rope ladder anchored near the shaft's mouth. The descent into the caverns and tunnels no longer felt like plunging into the unknown, it felt like returning to ground earned in pain and memory.

Above him, the sounds of his companions echoed softly: the rasp of armor, the rustle of packs, a faint growl from Valkra. Ella's footsteps were as light as ever, but he could always tell when she followed. She never let him go first without watching for the fall. Liosan came next, spinning once on the rope before he landed lightly beside Xavier with a soundless grin, his arms held out as if savoring a game. The moment his boots touched stone, though, his demeanor changed, childlike energy folded into focused silence. He crouched low and surveyed the chamber like a shadow scenting danger.

The shaft opened into the first chamber, where thick moss and clinging fungi once made every breath a choking risk. Now, bioluminescent lichen had been carefully cultivated across the ceiling, strung with alchemical pots to suppress the heavier spores. Stone markers and warning sigils were etched along the floor, placed there by miners who now labor under Xavier's banner.

Sihri dropped down beside him with a light thud, sniffing once. "Still damp," she muttered, wrinkling her nose. "Smells like a pit fight with no crowd."

"Would be without the bloodstains, too," Lythara added dryly as she followed, her sanguine eyes sweeping across the walls. "At least the air no longer tries to kill us."

Lianna came last, Frostclaw slinking down the slope behind her with practiced grace. The big snowcat paused, sniffed toward the far tunnels, and let out a low chuff. "It's quiet," Lianna said, narrowing her eyes, "but not dead."

The group passed through the fungus chamber, once a spore-choked deathtrap, now harvested and controlled. Xavier's footfalls slowed near the spot where he had once fumbled blindly through the dark, shirt tied over his mouth, praying he wouldn't collapse. The memory flickered, half-ghost and half-shadow. Liosan lingered at the edges of the path, eyes tracking every seam in the stone, his playful aura now vanished, replaced by the still alertness of a stalking cat.

They pressed on. At the first intersection, they came upon the stone cairn, a small, reverently placed monument of carefully stacked rock. At its base, barely visible unless one knelt close, was the etched symbol of Danu: a spiral of growth encircling a drop of falling flame. Xavier paused, drawing a hand across the top stone. Homage to the fallen dwarven explorer he had found during his first foray into these tunnels.

"She should've made it home," he murmured.

Ella stepped beside him, silent. She placed a fingertip just above the spiral mark, letting the warmth of her presence settle into the moment. "She did, in a way."

No one spoke for several steps after that. They passed miners who nodded in acknowledgement while continuing to swing their picks and hammers. Eventually they reached the ironbound doors, once rusted nearly shut, now reinforced with fresh steel braces and dwarven hinges, restored by Rynthavael's smiths. Two sentinels stood beside the door, one Felvari, one dwarf, both clad in reinforced leather stitched with Rynthavael's crest. They stood a respectful distance back, weapons sheathed but ready. At Xavier's approach, they saluted with a fist over the heart.

"No movement past the doors, Ard'Maelor," the dwarf said. "Mine crews work the upper shafts, but no one's gone beyond. The doors remain closed unless by yer leave."

Xavier nodded, laying a hand on the ironbound wood. The once-corroded rings were clean now, the hinges reset by skilled hands from the forge. He drew a slow breath, then he pulled.

The doors groaned open, revealing a dark corridor beyond, the air colder, the stone untouched. But it wasn't just the absence of miners that made it different. Here, the mines ended, and the rest of the Depths began again.

Just ahead, the stone ledge narrowed, opening to a vast chasm that yawned beneath the earth like a sleeping god's breath. The faint glimmer of blue water shimmered far below. The bridge waited, and beyond it, the last secrets of the Hollow Depths.

The moment the last foot crossed the boundary of Rynthavael's mines, the air shifted. The tunnel walls narrowed. Glowcaps and torch sconces ended. Stone dust thickened with each step, and then, the corridor opened. The world dropped away beyond the ledge.

Xavier halted at the brink. Below them, a vast

subterranean chasm stretched wide and deep. Faintly glowing blue water far beneath shimmered in slow, silent movement, the color too pale to be natural. The echoes of that quiet flow resonated with a strange, ghostly rhythm, one he remembered well.

The bridge had not changed. Thirty feet long, six feet wide, it stretched like a cracked tongue of stone over the void. Its edges were jagged and bare, no railings, no guide, just rock and memory. Along the surface, a dozen or more arrow shafts still jutted from between the stones, faded and weathered from time.

Xavier stepped forward slowly, his torch held low. "This is the bridge I crossed during my first descent. It's rigged, pressure plates across fourteen stones. If you step wrong, the whole thing collapses into the river."

Lianna's expression tightened. She moved to the edge but kept a careful distance. "Is that… your doing?" she asked, pointing to the shafts.

Xavier nodded. "Markers. Each one's beside a pressure plate. Back then, I crawled across. Didn't have much choice."

Sihri gave a low whistle. "Remind me not to complain about your paranoia, Xavier."

Lythara crouched low to examine one of the old arrows, brushing the surface around it. "It was a good plan," she said quietly. Then, after a beat, "Still feels like something is watching."

"Nothing down there's moved since," Xavier said. "But I won't take chances." He turned back to the group. "We cross single file. Slow. I'll lead."

Ella placed a hand gently on his shoulder. "You know the way."

Xavier stepped onto the stone bridge with the practiced confidence of repetition, a rhythm he'd painstakingly learned during his crawl the last time. One foot forward, half-step to the side, shift left for a quarter foot, lean forward, sidestep the trap near the crack. The stones groaned faintly underfoot but held.

One by one, the others followed. Ella was next, her stride light and unhurried, her balance unerring. Lythara after, every motion taut and focused. Sihri came behind her, whispering something about "no bottom and no wings." Lianna followed next, Frostclaw keeping perfectly to her heel. Liosan grinned briefly at Valkra, then flipped into a handstand to follow the same path of the others until he arrived in the darkness along the bridge's far edge, the childlike joy was gone in an instant as he dropped to all fours in silence, not a whisper of motion giving him away. Valkra brought up the rear, steps nearly silent despite her size.

The group made it safely across, no one stumbled, no stone gave way. And on the far side, Xavier turned toward the hidden alcove carved into the wall just beside the exit. "I left something here."

He dropped to one knee, pulling aside a flat stone panel. Inside, wrapped in cloth, was his old fallback cache: a single Potion of Fire Resistance, two small silver ingots, and a pouch of dwarven-marked gold.

Sihri raised a brow. "That your rainy day fund?"

"Emergency stash," Xavier replied, handing her the potion. "We're going deeper. I don't plan on needing it, but I didn't plan on giant spiders last time, either."

She gave a quiet grunt of agreement, and he tucked the items away.

Then they turned to look for the next challenge. Beyond the ledge rose a new corridor, carved and ancient, utterly distinct from the rough tunnels behind them. The walls were lined with faintly glowing engravings and stylized glyphs worn soft by time.

Liosan skipped ahead a few paces, his fingers tracing the grooves of the carvings with wide-eyed curiosity. His movements had a spring again, spinning lightly on the balls of his feet, though his eyes remained sharp. When Xavier motioned him back, he obeyed with a quick tumble backward, flashing a toothy grin before settling back into silence.

Lythara moved closer to the wall, frowning. Her eyes roved the engravings slowly, lips parting but no words coming out. "...Feels like I should know this," she whispered. "Like a dream from long ago. But when I reach for it, it's just fog."

Ella approached beside Lythara; her expression somber. "It's not your fault. What was taken... is not easily returned."

Xavier stepped past them, eyes on the walls. The memory was strong here, the weight of enchantment still humming low, faint enough to escape the untrained, but familiar to his senses, and Ella's.

"It's Sylmyrian," he said. "I couldn't be sure before. I am now."

Lianna and Sihri exchanged glances.

"You're certain?" Lianna asked.

Ella only nodded. "He is, as am I."

Valkra growled low at the threshold. The air here was colder than it should be.

Xavier turned back to the group, jaw set. "Beyond here is what the map labels the Echoing Hall. Follow my lead. There are… things… best left undisturbed."

The carved corridor swallowed them in silence. Xavier's boots touched the first length of engraved stone, and the sound echoed too sharply, distorted by enchantment rather than acoustics. Every footstep rang like a hammer on crystal, amplified by the hidden forces that still slept beneath the stone.

Unlike the rest of the Hollow Depths, this passage wasn't raw rock. Every surface had been shaped with purpose. The floor was smooth, engraved with spiraling grooves that shimmered faintly underfoot. The walls bore sweeping murals in bas-relief—figures carved into the stone with such precision they looked ready to step free. Blue and green ley-thread flickered faintly between them, dormant but not dead.

To most, it looked like faded art. To Xavier, it looked like memory came to life.

"The Echoing Hall…" he said softly, letting his torchlight dance across the first section of mural.

Miners were depicted on an exquisite scale, carving into a mountain's heart beneath crystalline spires. Above them, robed figures channeled ley energy between suspended gems, conducting forces like music. The scene pulsed faintly under Xavier's light, reacting to his presence.

He brushed his fingers near the wall, careful not to touch. "Don't be fooled. It's reactive. The whole hall is."

Ella stepped beside him. "I feel the hum," she said. "These veins once flowed freely."

Lythara paused by a depiction of three dwarves fleeing a collapsing tunnel. Behind them, spiderlike shadows slithered along the carved walls, not etched, but moving. She drew back, her pupils narrowing. "...They're moving. The shadows."

"They did for me too," Xavier confirmed. "Illusion, not threat. But it doesn't feel like one."

"Why build this?" Sihri asked. "To frighten workers?"

"To teach," Xavier answered. "Or warn."

Liosan had wandered a few steps ahead, tilting his head this way and that at the murals, his posture relaxed but alert. He traced the air with both hands as though mimicking the spellwork etched into the stone and then glanced back at Lianna and signed a quick pattern: danger ahead, patterns below.

Farther down, the murals grew darker, collapse, death, and then silence. The final stretch showed massive stone guardians flanking what looked like a seal. Their eyes were inset with glinting gemstones, and old dwarven runes looped around their feet.

"By stone we toil, by stone we are protected. Let no shadow disrupt the harmony of the depths." Xavier recited it from memory.

Frostclaw snarled low and turned in a circle. Even he didn't like the way the air moved here.

At the hallway's midpoint, Xavier held up a hand. The floor ahead became a grid of stone tiles, too precise to be natural.

"This is the trigger zone. Step wrong, and the floor sounds an alarm. And if that happens..."

"The spiders come," Ella finished, her tone grim.

"You didn't fight them all, then?" Lianna asked.

"I did," he said.

Lianna drew an arrow but kept it lowered. "You nearly didn't make it back, didn't you?"

He replied simply. "No, I nearly didn't walk out."

He pointed to the tile just ahead of him, third from the left in the first row. "Start here. The mural gives the rest of the pattern."

They studied it together. Each tile showed a faint rune corresponding to one of the murals along the hall. If matched properly to the leyline sequence shown earlier, Growth, Collapse, Ward, Harmony, it guided the correct path across.

"I'll walk it first," Xavier said. "One at a time. I'll call out each step as you follow."

Xavier crouched near the threshold, eyes scanning the first row of stone tiles. "Right," he said, voice low but steady, "start third from the left. That one's safe."

He stepped lightly onto the indicated square. The tile sank a fraction under his weight but held firm, no sound, no glow, no alarm. He glanced back. "Ella, follow me exactly."

She stepped forward, mirroring his placement.

Xavier turned back to the next row, recalling the mural sequence in his mind, the leyline flows, the runes, the subtle positioning of each phase. "Next row... fifth tile. Far right. One step over and forward."

His boot moved with care, heel first, testing the edge. Again, nothing.

"Row three, second tile. Just left of center. Easy now."

Behind him, he heard the faint shuffle of movement as Ella mirrored the step, then Lythara's quieter shift onto the stone after her.

"Row four," he muttered, eyeing the glyph just beneath the dust. "Fourth tile. Between those cracks, see it? Step there."

They did.

"Row five... first tile. Hug the left edge."

He exhaled once through his nose and moved. The rest of the path unfolded in his memory, imprinted from his first desperate run. Each tile a memory. Each rune a consequence. "One wrong step and this whole hall lights up," he reminded. "And we'll be elbow-deep in spiders."

"I would prefer not," Lianna said flatly, guiding Frostclaw with a gentle hand.

"Then don't improvise," Xavier called back, his tone dry. He stepped to the final tile, then across onto solid stone.

Behind him, one by one, the rest of the group followed in precise silence, Xavier calling each movement like a practiced drill. Ella followed, matching his stride exactly. Lythara was next, fluid and sure-footed, despite the tension. Sihri crossed slower, her nose twitching, muttering softly in her desert tongue. Lianna guided Frostclaw patiently. Valkra came last, eyes darting.

Liosan... danced. He followed the steps precisely, but did so in rhythm, arms wide like a tightrope walker, once twirling, once bending low to tap a tile before stepping. Despite it all, his balance was perfect, his grin impish.

By the time Valkra crossed, tail twitching, they had all passed the sequence clean. No alarms. No glowing runes. No spiders. Just the deep, humming quiet of magic that had waited centuries to be respected again. All of them made it safely, and then the hallway fell silent again. At the end of the corridor, the floor changed, no more traps. Just ancient stone and the lingering scent of still air and dust.

Xavier looked back once, eyes scanning the silent murals. They didn't move now. The danger was past, but something still watched. He could feel it.

"Keep your blades ready," he murmured. "The crystal cavern's next."

They stepped through the final archway into crystal-lit air, the entrance to the Essence Garden beyond. The hallway gave way to light. Not firelight, nor torch, but the strange, natural radiance of ley-touched crystal. The stone beneath their feet shifted subtly, becoming smoother, more polished. Xavier slowed as he approached the arch ahead, raising a hand to warn the others.

"Step carefully. The floor's sound, but the light can disorient you."

Then they passed through. The cavern opened like a jewel split in two, wide, arched, and filled with towering spires of glowing crystalline growth. Some rose from the floor in jagged arcs, others hung down from the ceiling like petrified thunderbolts. Each vibrated faintly with an underlying hum, inaudible to the ear but felt in the bones.

The walls shimmered in eight hues, faint and pulsing: emerald-green, warm golden yellow, cerulean-blue, shadowy violet, crimson, a soft golden green, black, and a pale sky silver. The crimson flickered irregularly, unsteady, but present.

Lythara's breath caught. "By all the shadows..." she whispered, eyes wide. "They're... untouched. Real. Gods, I haven't seen crystal beds like this since..." She broke off suddenly, blinking hard. "I don't know," she admitted. "But it feels... important."

Ella moved beside the succubus, her expression serene. "They're ley-bonded," she said. "Each one aligned to a different flow. Earth, Life, Death... and more."

Xavier moved toward the nearest cluster. "This is where I found the first resonance shard. There used to be a creature here, a crystalline ooze type thing, feeding off the ley energy. I killed it."

He knelt beside one of the spires, running his hand just above its surface. "It's safe now but be cautious with the harvesting. These crystals hum with power still... especially here."

Lythara didn't need further encouragement. She moved to a grouping of violet and crimson shards, retrieving a small hooked blade from her pouch. Her touch was delicate, reverent, like a jeweler working by memory more than sight.

"These are not just enchantment fuel," she murmured, crouching beside a cluster of softly glowing shards. "They're essence anchors... real ones. The cut, the harmonics... whoever shaped these knew magic like it was breath. I don't remember how I know that, but I do." She trailed a finger just above the crystal's surface, her expression caught somewhere between wonder and frustration. "It's like a tune I can hum but never heard."

"You can harvest them?" Lianna asked, eyeing a cluster of green shards with wariness.

"Only the outer points," Lythara replied, voice hushed. "Touch the core, you risk disrupting the flow."

Ella nodded. "The resonance is delicate. Best leave the deep roots."

Sihri crouched beside a red-orange vein. "This one's... warm." She looked up at Xavier. "That bad?"

He hesitated. "It wasn't warm before."

Ella reached toward it, eyes narrowing. "The Fire line is

beginning to stir," she said softly. "Not here, not fully. But the resonance has shifted since we first came."

"The Mael'Anthir's been humming," Xavier murmured. "And this cavern feels like it's listening."

Lianna, arms crossed, kept watch near the arch. "Let's not linger."

Still, it took time. The group collected several essence shards: emerald-green for Earth, midnight black for Death, cerulean-blue for Water, and a few faintly glowing crimson shards for Fire, though the Fire-aligned ones were unstable, warm to the touch, and barely safe to handle.

Xavier returned to the small fissure where he'd once claimed his first shard. Behind the cracked edge of the stone, half-buried in mineral dust, lay another faint glimmer. He reached in carefully and pulled it free. Another Shard of Resonance, dull on one side, sharp on the other, faintly glowing from within.

He held it up. "Same as before," he said. "Might be enough for another forging. Or something else."

Ella touched it briefly, then nodded. "It's not spent. It still sings."

Liosan danced in lazy arcs near the far edge of the cavern, pretending to chase the shifting lights between crystal shadows. He didn't touch anything, but he moved like he belonged to the place, his fingers sketching invisible lines through the air, his feet never quite still.

With pockets heavier and the cavern humming faintly behind them, the group turned to the far end of the chamber, where another arch waited. The stone there was older, darker. Dampness lingered in the air, and the sound of dripping water echoed softly from the next chamber.

Sihri rolled her shoulders and flexed her fingers. "That

feel in the air…"

Xavier nodded. "According to the map, the Sunken Reliquary is next."

#

The dripping sound continued from beyond the archway. It was slow, deliberate, like a clock counting heartbeats instead of time. Xavier stepped into the chamber first, torchlight casting long shadows across the water-slick floor. The air thickened immediately. It smelled of old stone, cold iron, and something brittle, like dried parchment soaked in forgotten magic.

Faint light shimmered on the water's surface, cast by the broken glow of a fractured ley-dais rising from the flooded center of the room. The structure stood half-submerged, its glyphs flickering in disordered pulses like a heartbeat struggling to remember its rhythm. Statues lined the chamber's edge, some toppled, others cracked through the waist. Their Sylmyrian armor was unmistakable to Xavier having seen similar in the crypt beneath Rynthavael. They stood with hands outstretched, warders of something long forgotten.

"Not a vault," Xavier said quietly. "A boundary."

Ella's eyes narrowed. "It is frayed. Something was anchored here once."

Sihri crouched near the water's edge, sniffed. "Still air. No rot. No movement."

Valkra growled once, and the water rippled.

A shimmer rose from the depths, slow and deliberate. A pale humanoid form emerged, taller than any of them, swathed in translucent spectral armor that gleamed faintly beneath the surface. Its body hovered rather than walked, and where its face should have been there was only the curve of a smooth helm, hollow-eyed and fixed forward. It said nothing, instead it merely turned.

Xavier immediately activated *Insight*.

| **Name:** Guardian Wraith | **Disposition:** Bound Vigilance |
| --- | --- |

The Guardian Wraith is a spectral sentinel created during the final years of the Sylmyrian Dominion. It has no soul of its own, only a fragment of directive will bound to the ruin it protects. Its form is humanoid but elongated and unnatural, wrapped in translucent echoes of Sylmyrian armor. It hovers inches above the surface of water or stone, phasing partially through solid matter as it moves. Its limbs trail with threads of radiant energy, remnants of ley line resonance leaking from its fractured core.

Though it does not speak, the Wraith reacts to magical disruption and intrusion with near-immediate hostility. It is not driven by hatred, but by purpose long severed from context. It exists only to defend the ley-dais it is anchored to, attacking anyone who approaches with spectral weaponry and ley-imbued force. When threatened, it will phase beneath water or stone, reemerging to strike unpredictably

Despite its haunting presence, the Guardian Wraith is not a being of evil or malice, it is a vigilant relic, locked in an endless loop of forgotten duty.

| **Health:** 145 / 145 | **Stamina:** ∞ (as a spectral construct) | **Mana:** 80 / 80 |
| --- | --- | --- |

Xavier's grip tightened on Vaeltheris. "It's not a ghost," he said. "It's a warden. Bound to the ruin."

The Guardian Wraith surged forward without warning, silent, impossibly fast, and Xavier met it head-on.

Vaeltheris clashed with the wraith's spectral blade in a flicker of blue-white sparks. His strike passed partly through the creature, slowed but not stopped. The second sword, Emberstone, struck lower and met a flicker of resistance, like steel carving through freezing mist.

"It phases!" Xavier shouted, stepping wide. "Strike it when it's solid!"

Lianna loosed an arrow from the flank. It passed through the wraith's shoulder without even slowing. She held back on her second shot.

Lythara flickered behind the creature, a coil of darkness snapping around its midsection as she reappeared near the dais. Her tether strained as the creature twisted against it, but it slowed.

From the upper alcoves, Liosan moved like a whisper. He had vanished the moment they entered the chamber, climbing silently along broken reliefs and collapsed stonework, high above the central dais. Now, as the wraith twisted against Lythara's tether, he dropped like a shadow, twin blades in hand. He struck low and fast, one blade carving along the creature's exposed flank, the other raking behind its knee with expert precision. Both strikes passed through partially, but his timing was perfect, disrupting its stability mid-phase.

The wraith recoiled, then retaliated. It sank into the water like vapor and reappeared behind the succubus. Its blade raked across her ribs before she could vanish again. The strike didn't cut so much as burn, light curling up across her skin in a searing arc. She hissed, her eyes flashing red.

"Should have expected that," she muttered, vanishing in shadow again.

Sihri was already moving. She darted across floating slabs of stone and launched herself bodily into the wraith's side. Her first punch passed through its chest. The second cracked into something deeper, disrupting its shimmer.

The cracks across the dais flared gold, veins of light threading outward like molten roots. Xavier felt the sudden shift in the air, a pulse building beneath the stone, drawing breath.

"Down!" he shouted, diving behind a broken statue.

The dais erupted in a burst of blinding golden light. Radiant force rippled outward in a wave that swept across the chamber, crashing into stone, water, and bone.

Xavier rolled clear, the heat skimming past him. Lythara twisted into a low crouch behind a broken pillar, cloak flaring around her. Valkra dropped flat with a growl, ears pressed back, the blast shearing just over her shadowed fur.

Sihri wasn't fast enough. The shockwave caught her in the chest, sending her stumbling back with a hiss. Her skin steamed faintly where the light had struck, and she clenched her fists with a snarl. Frostclaw yelped and recoiled, the blast raking across his flank, leaving singed fur and a seared line of skin.

Liosan, already high along the stone columns again, melted into shadow before the blast hit, his smaller frame vanishing into a crevice of safety like a wraith himself.

Ella stood her ground. She did not shield, did not brace. She simply moved with the pulse, letting it pass over her like wind over stone, her expression calm, unreadable.

The light faded, and in the space it left behind, the Guardian Wraith flickered forward once more.

Sihri skidded back across the wet stone, chest smoking faintly. "It's getting angry."

"Good," Xavier growled, stepping back in.

He struck again, Vaeltheris crackling as it pierced the wraith's chest. Emberstone followed, flaring in contact. The Guardian staggered, its form buckling under the strain of the twin impact. Its incorporeal shimmer faltered, and it began to solidify.

Lianna fired, the arrow wrapped in frost sap. This time it struck true, anchoring into the shoulder. The wraith recoiled.

"Now!" Xavier shouted.

Lythara struck from behind, her twin daggers slicing into the exposed gaps between spectral armor. The wraith shrieked, its cry was not rage, but strain.

Sihri surged forward again, her fists balled tight, pushing the steel embedded in the leather wraps outward. She spun, dropped low, and hammered a blow into its core.

The wraith staggered, partially suspended in the air, its limbs convulsing with dissonant light.

And then Liosan was there again, leaping from a stone ledge above the dais. His descent was silent, deadly. Both blades plunged forward, aimed for the creature's spine and base of the skull. The first strike phased, but the second hit a moment of flickering solidity, drawing a visible shudder through the wraith's form.

It tried to retreat.

But Ella stepped into its path, eyes cold, one hand raised. She did not attack, but her presence alone drew the thing's attention. She spoke only one word. "Enough."

The Guardian froze.

Xavier moved in and crossed his blades.

Ella spoke again, firmer. "Rest."

The strike was clean. One blade cut high, the other low, meeting in the center of the spectral chest.

The Guardian Wraith unraveled in a shimmer of radiant ash and light. Its scream echoed off the walls and then was gone.

Throughout the chamber, silence returned.

The dais dimmed, but its light was not extinguished. Its pulse evened, steady now, reclaimed by the Master of the Syr'Vailen.

---

**Quest Updated:** Whose House 1

**Type:** Settlement Quest

**Status:** In Progress

**Progress:** 1/4 Unique Locations Explored

Though you hold dominion over the lands surrounding Rynthavael, dominion does not mean knowledge, and knowledge brings safety. The Silverwood and the hidden warrens beneath it are vast, and not all who dwell within them are friendly, mortal, or even known.

You have begun the work of true stewardship. With the Hollow Depths explored and reclaimed, you have taken the first step in understanding the wild territory under your rule. But three more locations remain to be discovered and documented. Only then will Rynthavael truly be prepared to grow without fear of what sleeps nearby.

As this is a Settlement Quest, it cannot be refused.

**Objective:**

---

- Explore 4 unique, significant locations within the 20-mile territory surrounding Rynthavael
- Determine their nature, threats, or potential benefits
- Integrate this knowledge into Rynthavael's settlement ledger

**Current Progress:**

- Hollow Depths – Cleared and integrated into the settlement mining network
- Unknown Location
- Unknown Location
- Unknown Location

**Potential Rewards (Upon Completion):**

- +500 Experience
- Reduced local danger from monster nests and rogue elements
- Discovery of new resource nodes, ruins, or relics
- Opportunities for future settlement expansion or defensive upgrades
- Other unknown benefits tied to explored sites

Ella exhaled slowly. "Its bond is broken."

Xavier lowered his weapons. "The Depths are ours now."

They moved through the chamber with care. Beneath the dais, in a sealed recess, Xavier uncovered a soft-blue circlet, faintly pulsing with abjuration glyphs.

Nearby, wrapped in water-resistant oilcloths, lay several Sylmyrian scrolls, including texts on ley-crystal amplification, theories on sealed ley lines, and a cryptic mention of the Iron Thread beneath the mountain.

As they were examining the rest of the chamber, Liosan drifted to the far side, fingers trailing the edge of a cracked column. He paused mid-step, head tilted. "There," he signed, motioning toward the base of the far wall.

When Xavier looked where Liosan had indicated he noticed a small section of the far wall glowing a soft white, something he had come to recognize as a hidden location. Moving closer, Xavier pried loose a section of stone along the base of the wall, an alcove was exposed, half-swallowed by calcified sediment and warped time. The stone flaked away in layers, revealing the faint glimmer of something beneath, a cache, sealed and sunken, its interior still untouched by decay.

Inside, wrapped in ancient oilcloth and nestled beneath fragments of collapsed masonry, lay a forgotten trove of treasure.

The first glint was coin, not modern gold or silver, but the soft metallic shimmer of Sylmyrian-minted currency. He pulled out a handful carefully. They were oval coins of electrum, alloyed with faint traces of mythril, stamped with the spiral-flame crest of House Kael'Thiran. Each bore the inscription "Kael'Taris Ascendant – 12745", in glyphs no longer used. There were over two hundred in total.

Ella leaned in, eyes catching the shimmer. "These are from before the Skyfire Cataclysm" she said quietly.

Lythara's eyebrow rose at that. "They would predate even the mage wars if that were true. These aren't just currency, they're history."

Xavier nodded. The coins had no direct value under modern Arathian exchange, no Copper, Silver, or Platinum denominations etched anywhere, but in terms of collector worth or arcane trade? They'd be valued well above even platinum fingers in the right circles.

Beneath the coins, he found a sealed leather pouch. Inside were six cut gems: a deep garnet, pale aquamarine, cloudy smoky quartz, clear peridot, a bright citrine, and a slightly cracked but brilliant sapphire. Each gem bore asymmetrical faceting, carved not for aesthetics but to refract leyline light. Each one also pulsed faintly in Ella's presence.

"These are tuned," she said, lifting one with care. "Their shaping harmonizes with resonance flows. They could be set into enchantments... or structures."

Beneath those, wrapped in cloth and fitted into a tight groove in the cache's corner, was a soft leather tool roll, its contents gleaming even in the low light. Five copper-handled implements, finely wrought, engraved with near-microscopic runes.

Lythara traced a fingertip along one, nostrils flaring. "Craftsman's tools," she murmured. "Not for stone or war, but they'd etch runes like they were breathin'. That pattern? Still active."

Xavier passed a hand above the tools, and one glowed faintly in response to his touch.

"Alignment detection," Ella confirmed. "And maybe more. These are made to function within a ley-active structure."

Xavier nodded once and began repacking the coins wrapped in cloth, gems secured in their pouch, tools laid back with reverence.

"Not bad for a ruin buried in silence," he said.

Lythara smirked. "You learn to listen deep enough... even the stone starts talking back."

In a crystal casket tucked beneath a toppled statue, they found the last relic. A pair of crimson-threaded hand wraps, that were humming faintly with dormant heat.

Sihri held them up, brows raised. "Now this," she

murmured, "was worth the bruises."

"They are still warm," Ella noted.

"When we get them back to Rynthavael, Aelriva can identify them for us." Xavier said. He cast one last look over the chamber. There were no more guardians, no more illusions, just the waiting dark. As the prompt updating his quest stated, the ruin was theirs now, and with that it was time to return home once again.

#

They reached Rynthavael by dusk on the second day. The walk from the Hollow Depths had been quiet. The kind of silence earned through effort, not enforced by tension. They had crossed shaded forest trails, narrow stone passes, and the old hunter's ridge, all without trouble. There was no need to speak. The crucible of their shared experiences filled the space between them, and they traveled in companionable silence.

Xavier paused in thought for a moment and shifted his gaze to examine the party tab in his UI, something he hadn't looked at in quite some time. Ella and Lianna were there just as they had been since they had become his companions. Interestingly, however, he now had the option to accept the others as well. With a quick mental flex, he accepted Lythara, Sihri and Liosan as his companions as well. Closing the tab, he smiled as he saw all five of his companions' portraits and vital details now hovering in the edge of his vision.

By the time the valley opened, and the first watch posts came into view, the haze of travel had settled across their shoulders. Hearthstead's chimneys smoked in the distance. Lanterns flickered to life in the twilight. The village welcomed them not with cheers, but a quiet familiarity, a place that had learned to wait for its people to return.

At the village edge, the group paused.

Sihri stretched her arms with a groan. "Not fighting anything for at least a day."

Lianna rolled her shoulders, nodding once. "We'll scout west after rest."

Liosan was already balancing on the edge of a wooden fence, spinning once with a flourish before dropping into a crouch and miming a dramatic bow to no one in particular. He offered Lianna a silent flourish of his hand, an offer to join her on the scouting run, and she answered with a small, knowing nod. He beamed and tumbled backward into a roll before hopping back up, spinning in place.

Lythara said nothing. She only gave Xavier a long look before slipping away on her own tasks.

Ella placed a gentle hand on his back. "You're not finished, are you?"

"No," Xavier said. "Not yet."

He turned from the street and walked alone. Down past the quiet alleys of the forge quarter. Past the ivy-draped façade of Hearthstead Hall, and lower still, into the warrens below, where stone remembered a time before the village had walls, before the forge had a name.

The door to the Nexus chamber opened quietly. The village crafters had designed the door to provide more security for the chamber. Inside, the Syr'Vailen mosaic spread across the floor like the eye of creation itself. Xavier took a moment to stop and just study the design once again.

Spanning the center of the circular chamber, the mosaic was crafted from countless shards of glass, polished stone, and gemstones, each sliver set by hands that understood power in color and shape. The floor was a radiant mandala of elemental energy, arranged in eight perfect arcs.

Each arc represented an element: Light, Fire, Earth, Death, Dark, Water, Air, and Life, arrayed in that order around the circle, radiating outward like the spokes of an eternal wheel. Their colors dominated each slice, white-gold brilliance for Light, crimson and molten orange for Fire, lush emerald and soil-brown for Earth, slate gray and ghost-pale blue for Death, deep indigo and violet-black for Dark, seafoam and cerulean for Water, sky silver and soft gray for Air, and vibrant greens and pinks for Life.

At the heart of the pattern, all colors converged. The center was a whorl of motion and stillness, no one hue prevailed. It was a hypnotic blend where each thread touched the others, a true Nexus. Beneath it, power stirred, soft but undeniable.

Each element was marked by a symbol, inlaid in the an ancient style: a sunburst, a flame, a mountain, a feather, a wave, a crescent moon, a flower, and a skeletal hand. The symbols gleamed faintly even when dormant.

Only three of the eight arcs pulsed with life now, Earth, Life, and Death. The rest lay quiet but not cold. The mosaic was a map and a heartbeat.

Xavier stepped inside and placed the two relics on the mosaic's edge: the ley-attuned circlet and the crimson-threaded wraps taken from the Reliquary. They had not yet been studied in full, but their resonance lingered in his mind.

Light stirred from the upper recesses of the chamber. Aelriva drifted down like mist, wings fluttering once before she touched down with bare feet on the edge of the mosaic. The pixie's gown, woven of moss-veined threads and dew-kissed ivy, trailed behind her like a fragment of the forest given breath. Her gaze, though barely the height of Xavier's shin, held the weight of centuries.

Aelriva hovered close, her eyes glinting with old memory as she looked upon the circlet. "This one," she murmured, her tone low and sure, "was woven for wards, abjurations, bindin's... shields. It strengthens what resists. Aye, it defends."

| You have discovered: Leybound Circlet | **Item Class:** Rare |
|---|---|
| | **Item Quality:** Exquisite |
| | **Weight:** 0.3 kg |
| | **Durability:** 90/100 |
| | **Description:** A finely wrought circlet of silversteel alloyed with trace earth ley-crystal dust, this headpiece bears softly glowing glyphs etched around its inner band. It pulses faintly in rhythm with ley-line resonance, providing subtle, reactive magical protection. The circlet is said to have been crafted near an active ley nexus, granting it latent defensive enchantments tied to the Earth Ley Line. |
| | **Traits:** |
| | • Reactive Barrier: Grants a passive +1 defense bonus against ranged attacks. |
| | • Ley Pulse Shielding: Once per long rest, |

| | when the wearer is struck by a spell, the circlet activates to absorb up to 15 points of magical damage. |
| | • Ley Attunement: If the wearer is standing on or near a ley line, the circlet grants an increased resistance to magical effects for one minute. |

Then she drifted over the wraps, her wings giving a gentle hum. "An' these," she said with more interest, "are well-forged. Fire-threaded, aye, but whole in their own right. They don't need a line to burn... only a bearer wi' fists to match."

| **You have discovered:** Emberfang Wraps | **Item Class:** Rare |
| | **Item Quality:** Exquisite |
| | **Type:** Wondrous Item (Unarmed Combat – Handwraps) |
| | **Material:** Reinforced syl-thread cloth interwoven with copper-glass filament and ember-cored stitching |
| | **Weight:** 0.4 kg |
| | **Durability:** 100/100 |
| | **Description:** These crimson-threaded wraps glimmer faintly with ember-glow embroidery. Though heatless to the touch, they carry a |

persistent inner warmth, subtly felt through the skin. They were recovered from a sealed crystal casket deep within the Sunken Reliquary, untouched since the collapse of the Sylmyrian Dominion. The threads resonate softly near sources of fire or Fire-aspected ley energy, and their runes stir in the presence of awakened flame.

**Properties & Effects:**

- +5 Bonus to unarmed attack and damage.
- Blazing Strikes (1/day)
- The wearer may ignite the wraps for 3 minutes.
- During this time, unarmed strikes deal an additional 4-8 fire damage on hit.
- Shattering Pulse (vs Constructs or Undead)
- When hitting a Construct or Undead with an unarmed strike, there is a chance of the target becoming

more vulnerable to fire damage until the end of the wearer's next turn.
- Usable once per target per combat.

**Passive Effect:**

- The wraps stay subtly warm at all times ensuring the wearer remains comfortable at all temperatures.
- In proximity to a fully awakened Fire ley line, the effects may strengthen or evolve based on local resonance.

She hovered in place for a moment longer, thoughtful. "They'll wake deeper once the mountain stirs, but they already sing wi' flame. That's no ember, Ard'Maelor, it's a brand waitin' for battle."

Xavier crouched beside the Fire rune embedded in the mosaic's outer ring. Its sigil, sharp, angular, and rimmed in deep crimson, remained dormant, but beneath the stone, he felt it.

Heat, but it was not like the forge. It was like pressure, like breath.

"The forge is humming," he said softly.

Aelriva's voice lowered with it. "Aye. Because the heart below heard ye. An' it knows what comes next."

She didn't vanish this time. She simply turned and

walked the edge of the mosaic, her tiny steps tracing a careful arc across the dormant threads: Fire, Air, Water, Light, Dark. Her wings gave a single slow beat before she slipped upward into shadow, her form dispersing like pollen caught in the breeze.

Xavier remained kneeling, hand resting on the cold stone. The Forge may have been stirring. But the mountain, the mountain was listening, and the ember beneath it had only just begun to breathe.

That night, Xavier dreamed.

He walked not through fields or memories, but a corridor of molten stone and ash. The floor beneath his feet shimmered with veins of half-cooled lava. Ancient dwarven glyphs pulsed faintly beneath layers of soot, their meanings half-lost to time, half-carved into memory. Vaulted ceilings loomed overhead, and shattered ironworks jutted from broken platforms and collapsed walls, ruins of forges long extinguished.

Heat curled in waves through the air, but it did not burn. It pressed against him like a question unanswered.

Then a voice spoke. Danu's voice, not gentle, and not distant. But low and present as if resonating from the stone itself.

"The Ironspire holds the thread ye seek. Fire sealed, not extinguished. An' somethin' else stirs wi' it, forgotten, but nae dead."

Xavier turned, searching the corridor. No figure stood there. Only the echo of her presence.

He stepped forward once, then again, drawn toward a distant glow. A forge-heart, long buried, pulsed in time with his breath. Sparks drifted upward like falling stars reversed. The world folded around it, and for a moment, he saw an image…

…a dwarven vault, sealed behind runic iron.

A slumbering guardian, encased in obsidian chains. A single flame, flickering without fuel. And then he woke.

His breath caught in the quiet of morning. Hearthstead had not yet stirred. Pale light brushed the window frame. He sat up slowly, eyes narrowing. Across his chest, just above the Shardbrand, was a faint smear of soot.

#

Later that morning, sunlight spilled through the windows of Hearthstead Hall's central chamber, casting long shadows across the table where maps and parchment lay scattered. The hall had become a war room of sorts, its wooden beams now adorned with carved tokens, pinned reports, and crude route sketches of the western passes.

Xavier stood at the table's edge, one hand resting on a parchment showing the range of the Ironspire Mountains. His other hand traced the path they would take, northwest, beyond the edge of Silverwoods. As he did so he finished recounting the dream, Danu's words, the soot across his chest, and the sealed forge.

"I don't think the Fire ley line is dead," he said. "It's beneath the Syr'Vailen like the others. But something in the Ironspire is blocking it, like it is dammed or diverted. Until that flow is freed, we can't awaken it here."

Ella, seated beside him, nodded slowly. "The forge hums even now. But it's incomplete. It's reacting, not to the ruin, but to the pressure. Like something waiting for its current."

Lythara had her feet propped on the table's edge, a crystalline shard held between thumb and forefinger. "I hear it too," she murmured. "Mael'Anthir's tone changed last night. It's… calling for flame."

"Not just flame," Ella said. "Balance. Completion. It wants its kin."

Lianna leaned over the edge of the map, eyes narrowed as she studied the topography. "We'll take a path through the elder pine trails and cross the stonefold valley. Not the fastest, but steady."

Liosan was upside down in one of the rafters above, arms dangling lazily. He pointed at a curl in the map with one foot, then swung down in a single, silent flip to crouch beside his sister.

He tapped twice beside the marked pass.

Lianna translated. "Two days west to that point. Maybe three if the weather shifts."

Xavier nodded. "And from there, we'll have weeks before we reach the Ironspire proper, weeks more before we find the right passes or settlements."

"It's a journey," Ella agreed.

Sihri wandered in, chewing on a strip of dried apple. "So we're just... marching into a mountain to poke at forgotten fire?"

"We're not poking," Xavier replied. "We're reclaiming what was sealed. It's time."

Sihri smirked. "Sounds like poking with extra steps."

Ella rolled a map scroll closed and rose to her feet. "We'll leave soon, but there is work to finish here first."

Xavier looked at the gear they'd laid aside, relics, supplies, and fragments of an older world brought back into the light. Among them, Aelriva had returned the wraps identified from the Sunken Reliquary. Their crimson threads gleamed faintly, wrapped in flame-patterned silk, their surface still radiating a subtle warmth.

He lifted them and turned toward Sihri. "Catch."

She snatched the bundle from the air one-handed, arching a brow as she unwrapped it. The moment her fingers brushed the wraps, a soft pulse shimmered across the threadwork, heat without flame, waiting to be called.

Sihri gave a low whistle. "Now these... these I like."

"They're yours," Xavier said. "They suit you better than anyone else here."

"Damn right they do," she muttered, already testing the weight of them. Her smile was sharp and satisfied. "Gonna have fun breaking these in."

He nodded once, then turned back to the others. "The Ironspire is next. And whatever waits beneath it."

Lianna and Liosan exchanged a glance. She gave a short nod, and he vanished into the rafters with a silent spin of approval.

They would not leave immediately. Rynthavael still needed their presence, structures to complete, routes to secure, new settlers to accommodate. It would be weeks, perhaps a full month, before the expedition to the Ironspire could begin in earnest.

Preparations had begun, but the road would wait until the land, and they were ready.

#

Far from the quiet of Rynthavael, light spilled through towering stained-glass arches in a cathedral of impossible geometry, Solara's sanctum in the Celestial Dominion of Aurithal, a radiant edifice woven from solar flame and divine will. Mirrors of golden aether turned in slow orbits overhead, casting shafts of concentrated brilliance down onto the alabaster floor. The great hall was silent but for the hiss of light as it struck reality.

Solara stood at the center of the sanctum, clad in a mantle of burning gold and light-forged steel, her luminous eyes fixed on the shifting web of fate unraveling in the vast disc before her. Threads of law and divine order twisted and frayed in the wake of a mortal's interference.

Her fingers curled around the edge of the sun-forged table. "This was meant to stabilize," she murmured, her voice like the ringing of bells at dawn. "A countermeasure, not a crucible."

She reached again for the threads of fate, only to find void. Something stirred in the heart of the Silverwood, a region where her divine perception faded to gray. She could see the roads around it, the edges of the forest where her followers walked, even the outer ridges near Bramblegate, but the central reaches resisted. She sensed only absence, no details, no locations, no names. She did not yet know what was hidden in the Silverwood, only that it was not visible through the lattice of her dominion. The mystery vexed her more for its shape than its substance. The shrouded region was neither warded nor corrupted, it was simply... missing.

Then darkness in the wildlands, though fading, Nekros's influence like rot beneath a gleaming wound.

Her jaw tightened. "You overreached, fool. You and your corpse-walkers have broken the silence."

With a single gesture, she swept the vision aside and turned her focus to her most trusted, a circle of high-priestesses and divine heralds who knelt in solemn readiness, their forms glowing with filtered grace. Though on another plane, her will passed through them like fire in the bloodstream, divine communion threading their thoughts with purpose.

"Find the source," she communed, her voice rippling through the minds of her chosen. "There is disruption in the balance, something buried deep in the earth, veiled even from my sight. It distorts the leyflows beneath the mountain. Seek it. Report all anomalies. Speak to every flame."

One of the high-priests lifted his head slightly. "Lady of Order, we cannot trace it. The veiling is complete. Not even your fire penetrates."

Solara's expression did not change, but the air around her shimmered with heat. "Then look elsewhere. The fault line is not in the heavens, but the earth."

Behind her, the disc shimmered once more, but showed nothing. No image. No trace. The veiling was absolute. Where threads should have been, there was only absence, a perfect void where Xavier's soul-sign should have flared brightest.

Her lips thinned, though the veil gave her no name, no object, no sign of what blocked her gaze. Whatever force masked the source, it was ancient, and complete.

"No matter," she said, turning from the light. "Even unseen, all flames cast shadow."

The saga continues in Book 3 – The Iron Oath.